THE COLLECTED STORIES OF
VERNOR VINGE

THE COLLECTED STORIES OF VERNOR VINGE

VERNOR VINGE

TOR®

A Tom Doherty Associates Book
New York

THE COLLECTED STORIES OF VERNOR VINGE

Copyright © 2001 by Vernor Vinge

Edited by James Frenkel.

This book is printed on acid-free paper.

Book Design by Jane Adele Regina

A Tor Book
Published by Tom Doherty Associates, LLC
175 Fifth Avenue
New York, NY 10010

www.tor.com

Tor® is a registered trademark of Tom Doherty Associates, LLC.

ISBN 0-312-87373-5

First Edition: November 2001

Printed in the United States of America

0 9 8 7 6 5 4 3 2 1

Copyright Acknowledgments

To all my editors
(including those who have rejected my stories)
for their help over the years

Acknowledgments

I would like to thank my editor for this book, Jim Frenkel. More people than I can name have helped me with these stories, but in particular I want to thank those who helped with the new story in this collection, *Fast Times at Fairmont High*: Sara Baase-Mayers, David Baxter, John Carroll, Bob Fleming, Jim Frenkel, Peter Flynn, Mike Gannis, Pat Hillmeyer, Cherie Kushner, Keith Mayers, Phil Pournelle, Bill Rupp, Mary Q. Smith, and Joan D. Vinge.

Contents

Foreword

The year 1965 is special for me: that's when I made my first science-fiction sale. In the next few years I sold a number of stories. My ideal length was around twelve thousand words. Shorter than that wasn't enough space to make the point of the story, and with longer stories, I had trouble coordinating characters and detail. Eventually, I became comfortable with novel-length stories. Most of my short fiction has been anthologized, stories scattered through many books: orphans moving from home to home. Publishers are reluctant to do one-author collections—with happy exceptions, such as the Baen collections in the 1980s and now this Tor collection in 2001.

The Collected Stories of Vernor Vinge contains almost all my published short fiction to date. For the record, the omissions are:

- *True Names,* which is included in *True Names and the Opening of the Cyberspace Frontier;*
- "Grimm's Story," which is the core of my novel, *Tatja Grimm's World.*

Finally, this Tor collection contains a first appearance, the novella *Fast Times at Fairmont High* (hot off the word processor).

—VERNOR VINGE
August 2001

"Bookworm, Run!"

I was a child in the 1950s, a little boy who could talk and write better than he could think, but who had a good imagination, and read everything he could by people much smarter than he. I wanted to know the future of science, to participate in revolutions to come.

Science fiction seemed a window on all this. I wanted interstellar empires (interplanetary ones at the least). I wanted supercomputers and artificial intelligence and effective immortality. All seemed possible. In fact, our technological success is ultimately based on intelligence. If we could use *technology* to increase (or create) intelligence . . .

The first story I ever wrote (that sold) was a look at this idea. Instead of Artificial Intelligence (AI), I used Intelligence Amplification (IA). The means seemed at hand: After all (I thought) what is memory but retrieval of information? Why couldn't human reason be augmented by hardware? (Perhaps it's fortunate that at the time I had no technical knowledge of computers. I might have become discouraged, ended up writing *really* hardcore science-fiction . . . about punch cards and batch processing.)

It was 1962. I was a senior in high school, and I wanted to write about the first man to have a direct mind-to-computer link. I even thought I might be the first person ever to write of such a thing. (In that, of course, I was wrong—but the theme was rare compared to nowadays.) I worked very hard on the story, applying everything I knew about SF writing. I put together a social background that I thought would make things interesting even where the story sagged: cheap fusion/electricity converters had been invented (that worked at room-temperature!), trashing the big power utilities and causing a short-term depression. (In a sense, this was a sequel to Randall Garrett's story, "Damned If You Don't." I admired that story very much; economic depressions were faraway, alien beasts to me.) And of course, there would be experiments with chimpanzees before the IQ amplifier was tried on my human hero.

Having thought things out, I described the plot to my little sister (a tenth-grader). She suffered through my endless recounting, then remarked, "Except for the part about the chimpanzee, it sounds pretty dull." What a comedown. Still . . . she had a point. The chimpanzee story had an obvious ending. After it made me famous, I could write the *important* story, the one with a human hero.

John W. Campbell liked the chimpanzee part, too. (And unlike my sister, he got a kick out of the Randall Garrett references.) Eventually, he bought the story for *Analog.*

So. It's 1984 (as seen by a teenager from the early 1960s), and we have a hero with a very serious problem:

*T*hey knew what he'd done.

Norman Simmons cringed, his calloused black fingers grasped *Tarzan of the Apes* so tightly that several pages ripped. Seeing what he had done, Norman shut the book and placed it gently on his desk. Then, almost shaking with fear, he tried to roll himself into a ball small enough to escape detection. Gradually he relaxed, panting; Kimball Kinnison would never refuse to face danger. There must be a way out. He knew several routes to the surface. If no one saw him . . .

They'd be hunting for him; and when they caught him, he would die.

He was suddenly anxious to leave the prefab green aluminum walls of his room and school—but what should he take? He pulled the sheet off his bed and spread it on the floor. Norman laid five or six of his favorite books on the sheet, scuttled across the room to his closet, pulled out an extra pair of red and orange Bermuda shorts, and tossed them on top of the books. He paused, then added a blanket, his portable typewriter, his notebook, and a pencil. Now he was equipped for any contingency.

Norman wrapped the sheet tightly about his belongings and dragged the makeshift sack to the door. He opened the door a crack, and peeked out. The passageway was empty. He cautiously opened the door wide and stepped down onto the bedrock floor of the tunnel. Then he dragged the sheet and its contents over the doorsill. The bag dropped the ten inches which separated the aluminum floor of his room from the tunnel. The typewriter landed with a muffled clank. Norman glanced anxiously around the corner of the room, up the tunnel. The lights were off in the Little School. It was Saturday and his teachers' day off. The Lab was closed, too, which was unforeseen good luck, since the aloof Dr. Dunbar was usually there at this time.

He warily circled about a nearby transport vehicle. *Model D-49 Ford Cargo Carrier, Army Transport Mark XIXe. Development Contract D-49f1086-1979. First deliveries, January, 1982 . . . RESTRICTED Unauthorized use of RESTRICTED materials is punishable by up to 10 years imprisonment, $10,000 fine, or both: Maintenance Manual: Chapter 1, Description . . . The Mark XIXe is a medium speed transport designed to carry loads of less than fifteen tons through constricted areas, such as mine tunnels or storage depots. The "e" modification of the Mark XIX indicates the substitution of a 500-hp Bender fusion power source for the Wankel engine originally intended for use with the XIX. As the Bender pack needs only the natural water vapor in the air for fuel, it is an immense improvement over any other power source. This economy combined with the tape programmed auto-pilot, make the XIXe one of . . .* Norman shook his head, trying to cut off the endless flow of irrelevant information that came to mind. With practice, he was sure that he would eventually be able to pick out just the data he needed to solve problems, but in the meantime the situation was often very confusing.

The passage he was looking for was between the 345th and 346th fluorescent tube—counting from his room; it was on the left side of the tunnel. Norman began running, at the same time pulling the sack behind him. This was an awkward position for him and he was soon forced to a walk. He concentrated on counting the lighting tubes that were hung from the roof of the tunnel. Each fluorescent cast harsh white light upon the walls of the tunnel, but between the tubes slight shadows lingered. The walls of the passage were streaky with whorls almost like wood or marble, but much darker and grayish-green. As he walked a slight draft of fresh air from faraway air regenerators ruffled the hair on his back.

NORMAN FINALLY TURNED TO FACE THE LEFT WALL OF THE PASSAGE AND stopped—343-344-345. The liquid streaks of pyrobole and feldspar appeared the same here as in any other section of the tunnel. Taking another step, Norman stood at the darkest point between the two lights. He carefully counted five hand-widths from the point where the wall blended into the floor. At this spot he cupped his hands and shouted into the wall: "Why does the goodwife like Dutch Elm disease for tea?"

The wall replied: "I don't know. I just work here."

Norman searched his memory, looking for one piece of information among the billions. "Well, find out before her husband does."

There was no reply. Instead, a massive section of bedrock swung noiselessly out of the wall, revealing another tunnel at right-angles to Norman's.

He hurried into it, then paused and glanced back. The huge door had already shut. As he continued up the new tunnel, Norman was careful to count the lights. When he came to number forty-eight, he again selected a place on the wall and shouted some opening commands. The new tunnel was slanted steeply upward as were the next three passages which Norman switched to. At last he reached the spot in the sixth tunnel which contained the opening to the surface. He paused, feeling both relief and fear: Relief because there weren't any secret codes and distances to remember after this; fear because he didn't know what or who might be waiting for him on the other side of this last door. What if they were just hiding there to shoot him?

Norman took a deep breath and shouted: "There are only 3,456,628 more shopping days till Christmas."

"So?" came the muffled reply.

Norman thought: *NSA (National Security Agency) cryptographic (code) analysis organization. Report Number 36390.201. MOST SECRET. (Unauthorized use of MOST SECRET materials is punishable by death.): "Mathematical Analysis of Voice and Electronic Pass Codes," by Melvin M. Rosseter, RAND contract 748970-1975. Paragraph 1: Consider L, an m by n matrix (rectangular array—arrangement) of (n times m) elements (items) formed by the Vrevik product* . . . Norman screamed shrilly. In his haste, he had accepted the wrong memories. The torrent of information, cross-references, and explanatory notes, was almost as overwhelming as his experience the time he foolishly decided to learn all about plasma physics.

With an effort he choked off the memories. But now he was getting desperate. He had to come up with the pass code, and fast.

Finally, "So avoid the mash. Shop December 263."

A LARGE SECTION OF THE CEILING SWUNG DOWN INTO THE TUNNEL. THROUGH the opening, Norman could see the sky. But it was gray, not blue like the other time! Norman had not realized that a cloudy day could be so dreary. A cold, humid mist oozed into the tunnel from the opening. He shuddered, but scrambled up the inclined plane which the lowered ceiling section formed. The massive trapdoor shut behind him.

The air seemed still, but so cold and wet. Norman looked around. He was standing atop a large stony bluff. Scrub trees and scraggly brush covered most of the ground, but here and there large sections of greenish, glacier-scoured bedrock were visible. Every surface glistened with a thin layer of water. Norman sneezed. It had been so nice and warm the last time. He peered out over the lower land and saw fog. It was just like the description in the "Adventures of the Two and the Three." The fog hung in the lower land like some tenuous sea, filling rocky fjords in the bluff. Trees and bushes and boulders seemed to lurk mysteriously within it.

This mysterious quality of the landscape gave Norman new spirit. He was a bold adventurer setting out to discover new lands.

He was also a hunted animal.

Norman found the small footpath he remembered, and set off across the bluff. The wet grass tickled his feet and his hair was already dripping. His books and typewriter were getting an awful beating as he dragged them over the rough ground.

He came to the edge of the bluff. The grass gave way to a bedrock shelf overlooking a drop of some fifty feet. Over the years, winter ice had done its work. Sections of the face of the cliff had broken off. Now the rubble reached halfway up the cliff, almost like a carelessly strewn avalanche of pebbles except that each rock weighed many tons. The fog worked in and out among the boulders and seemed to foam up the side of the cliff.

Norman crept to the edge of the cliff and peered over. Five feet below was a ledge about ten inches wide. The ledge slanted down. At its lower end it was only seven feet above the rocks. He went over, clinging to the cliff with one hand, and grasping the sack, which lay on the ground above him, with the other. Norman had not realized how slimy the rocks had become in the wet air. His hand slipped and he fell to the ledge below. The sack was jerked over the edge, but he kept his hold on it. The typewriter in the sack hit the side of the cliff with a loud clang.

He collected his wits and crawled to the lower part of the ledge. Here he again went over, but was very careful to keep a firm grip. He let go and landed feet first on a huge boulder directly below. The sack crashed down an instant later. Norman clambered over the rocks and soon had descended to level ground.

Nearby objects were obscured by the fog. It was even colder and damper than above. The fog seemed to enter his mouth and nose and draw away his warmth. He paused, then started in the direction that he remembered seeing the airplane hangar last time. Soon he was ankle deep in wet grass.

After about one hundred yards, Norman noticed a darkness to his left. He turned and approached it. Gradually the form of a light plane was defined. Soon he could clearly see the Piper Cub. *Four place, single-jet aircraft; maximum cargo weight, 1200 pounds; minimum runway for takeoff with full load, 90 yards; maximum speed, 250 miles per hour.* Its wings and fuselage shone dully in the weak light. Norman ran up to the Cub, clambered over the struts, and pulled himself into the cabin. He settled his sack in the copilot's seat and slammed the door. The key had been left in the ignition: Someone had been extremely careless.

Norman inspected the controls of the little aircraft. Somehow his fear had departed, and specific facts now came easily to mind. He saw that there was an autopilot on the right-hand dash, but it was of a simple-minded variety and could handle only cruising flight.

He reached down and felt the rudder pedals with his feet. By bracing his back against the seat he could touch the pedals and at the same time hold the steering wheel. Of course, he would not be able to see out very easily, but there really wasn't very much to see.

He had to get across the border fast and this airplane was probably the only way.

He turned the starter and heard the fuel pumps and turbines begin rotating. Norman looked at the dash. What was he supposed to do next? He pushed the button marked FLASH and was rewarded with a loud *ffumpf* as the jet engine above the wing ignited. He twisted the throttle. The Cub crawled across the field, picking up speed. It bounced and jolted over the turf.

. . . Throttle to full, keeping stick forward . . . until you are well over stall speed (35 miles per hour for a 1980 Cub) . . . pull back gently on the stick, being careful to remain over . . . (35 miles per hour) . . .

He craned his neck, trying to get a view ahead. The ride was becoming smooth. The Cub was airborne! Still nothing but fog ahead. For an instant the mist parted, revealing a thirty-foot Security fence barely fifty yards away. He had to have altitude!

. . . Under no circumstances should high angle-of-attack (climb) maneuvers be attempted without sufficient air speed . . .

Instructions are rarely the equal of actual experience, and now Norman was going to learn the hard way. He pushed at the throttle and pulled back hard on the stick. The little aircraft nosed sharply upward, its small jet engine screaming. The air speed fell and with it the lifting power of the wings. The Cub seemed to pause for an instant suspended in the air, then fell back. Jet still whining, the nose came down and the plane plunged earthwards.

IMAGINE A PLATE OF SPAGHETTI—NO SAUCE OR MEATBALLS. O.K., NOW PICture an entire room filled with such food. This wormy nightmare gives you some idea of the complexity of the First Security District, otherwise known as the Labyrinth. By analogy each strand of spaghetti is a tunnel segment carved through bedrock. The Labyrinth occupied four cubic miles under the cities of Ishpeming and Negaunee in the Upper Peninsula of Michigan. Without the power of controlled nuclear fusion such a maze could never have been made. Each tunnel was connected to several others by a random system of secret hatches, controlled by voice and electronic codes. Truly the First Security District was the most spyproof volume in the solar system. The Savannah plant, the CIA, Soviet IKB, and the entire system of GM factories could have co-existed in it without knowledge of one another. As a matter of fact, thirty-one different Security projects, laboratories, and military bases existed in the Labyrinth with their co-ordinates listed in a single filing computer—and there's the rub . . .

"Because he's been getting straight A's," Dr. William Dunbar finished.

Lieutenant General Alvin Pederson, Commander of the First Security District, looked up from the computer console with a harried expression on his face. The two men were alone in the chamber containing the memory bank of United States Government Files Central, usually referred to as Files Central or simply Files. Behind the console were racks of fiberglass, whose orderly columns and rows filled most of the room.

At the base of each rack, small lasers emitted modulated and coherent light; as the light passed through the fibers, it was altered and channeled by subtle impurities in the glass. Volume for volume, the computer was ten thousand times better than the best cryogenic models. Files Central contained all the information, secret and otherwise, possessed by the U.S.—including the contents of the Library of Congress, which managed to fill barely ten percent of Files' capacity. The fact that Pederson kept his office here rather than at Continental Air Defense Headquarters, which occupied another part of the Labyrinth, indicated just how important the functions of Files were.

Pederson frowned. He had better things to do than listen to every overwrought genius that wanted to talk to him, though Dunbar usually spoke out only when he had something important to say. "You'd better start at the beginning, Doctor."

The mathematician began nervously. "Look. Norman has never had any great interest in his schoolwork. We may have given the chimp high intelligence with this brain-computer combination, but he has the emotional maturity of a nine-year-old human. Norman is bright, curious—and *lazy*; he would rather read science fiction than study history. His schoolwork has always been poorly and incompletely done—until six weeks ago. Since then he has spent virtually no time on real studying. At the same time he has shown a complete mastery of the factual information in his courses. It's almost as if he had an eidetic memory of *facts that were never presented to him*. As if . . ."

Dunbar started on a different tack. "General, you know how much trouble we had co-ordinating the chimp's brain with his computer in the first place. On the one hand you have an African chimpanzee, and on the other an advanced optical computer which theoretically is superior even to Files here. We wanted the chimp's brain to co-operate with the computer as closely as the different parts of a human brain work together. This meant that the computer had to be programmed to operate the way the chimp's mind did. We also had to make time-lapse corrections, because the chimp and the computer are not physically together. All in all, it was a terrifically complicated job. It makes the Economic Planning Programs look like setting up Fox and Geese on a kid's Brain Truster kit." Seeing the other's look of impatience, Dunbar hurried on. "Anyway, you remember that we needed to use the Files computer, just to program *our* computer. And the two machines had to be electronically connected."

The scientist came abruptly to the point. "If by some accident or mechanical failure, the link between Files and Norman *were never cut, then* . . . then the chimp would have complete access to U.S. Files."

Pederson's preoccupation with other matters disappeared. "If that's so, we've got one hell of a problem. And it would explain a lot of other things. Look." He shoved a sheet of paper at Dunbar. "As a matter of routine, Files announces how much information it has supplied to queries during every twenty-four-hour period. Actually it's sort of a slick gimmick to impress visitors with how efficient and useful Files is, supplying information to twenty or thirty different agencies at once. Up until six weeks ago the daily reading hung around ten to the tenth bits per day. During the next ten days it climbed to over ten to the twelfth—then to ten to the fourteenth. We couldn't hunt down the source of the queries and most of the techs thought the high readings were due to mechanical error.

"Altogether, Files has supplied almost ten to the fifteenth bits to—someone. And that, Doctor, is equal to the total amount of information contained in Files. It looks as if your monkey has programmed himself with all the information the U.S. possesses."

PEDERSON TURNED TO THE QUERY PANEL, TYPED TWO QUESTIONS. A TAPE REEL by the desk spun briefly, stopped. Pederson pointed to it. "Those are the co-ordinates of your lab. I'm sending a couple men down to pick up your simian friend. Then I'm sending some more men to wherever his computer is."

Pederson looked at the tape reel expectantly, then noticed the words gleaming on a readout screen above the console:

The co-ordinates you request are not On File.

Pederson lunged forward and typed the question again, carefully. The message on the screen didn't even flicker:

The co-ordinates you request are not On File.

Dunbar leaned over the panel. "It's true, then," he said hoarsely, for the first time believing his fears. "Probably Norman thought we would punish him if we found out he was using Files."

"We would," Pederson interrupted harshly.

"And since Norman could use information On File, he could also *erase* information there. We hardly ever visit the tunnel where his computer was built, so we haven't noticed until now that he had erased its co-ordinates."

Now that he knew an emergency really existed, Dunbar seemed calm. He continued inexorably, "And if Norman was this fearful of discovery, then he probably had Files advise him when you tried to find the location of his computer. My lab is only a couple hundred feet below the surface—and he surely knows how to get out."

The general nodded grimly. "This chimp seems to be one step ahead of us all the way." He switched on a comm, and spoke into it. "Smith, send a couple men over to Dunbar's lab. . . . Yeah, I've got the co-ordinates right here." He pressed another switch and the reel of tape spun, transmitting its magnetic impressions to a similar reel at the other end of the hookup. "Have them grab the experimental chimp and bring him down here to Files Central. Don't hurt him, but be careful—you know how bright he is." He cut the circuit and turned back to Dunbar.

"If he's still there, we'll get him; but if he's already made a break for the surface, there's no way we can stop him now. This place is just too decentralized." He thought for a second, then turned back to the comm and gave more instructions to his aide.

"I've put in a call to Sawyer AFB to send some airborne infantry over here. Other than that, we can only watch."

A TV panel brightened, revealing a view from one of the hidden surface cameras. The scene was misty, and silent except for an occasional dripping sound.

Several minutes passed; then a superbly camouflaged and counter-balanced piece of bedrock in the center of their view swung down, and a black form in orange Bermuda shorts struggled out of the ground, dragging a large white sack. The chimp shivered, then moved off, dis-appearing over the crest of the bluff.

Pederson's hands were pale white, clenched in frustration about the arms of his chair. Although the First Security District was built under Ishpeming, its main entrances were fifteen miles away at Sawyer Armed Forces Base. There were only three small and barely accessible entrances in the area where Norman had escaped. Fortunately for the chimpanzee, his quarters had been located near one of them. The area which con-tained these entrances belonged to the Ore REclamation Service, a gov-ernment agency charged with finding more efficient methods of low-grade ore refining. (With the present economic situation, it was a rather superfluous job since the current problem was to get *rid* of the ore on hand rather than increase production.) All this indirection was designed to hide the location of the First Security District from the en-emy. But at the same time it made direct control of the surface difficult.

A shrill sound came from the speaker by the TV panel. Dunbar puz-zled, "Sounds almost like a light jet."

Pederson replied, "It probably is. The ORES people maintain a small office up there for appearances' sake, and they have a Piper Cub . . . *Could that chimp fly one?*"

"I doubt it, but I suppose if he were desperate enough he would try anything."

Smith's voice interrupted them, "General, our local infiltration radar has picked up an aircraft at an altitude of fifteen feet. Its present course will take it into the Security fence." The buzzing became louder. "The pilot is going to stall it out! It's in a steep climb . . . eighty feet, one hundred. It's stalled!"

The buzzing whine continued for a second and then abruptly ceased.

THE TYPEWRITER DEPARTED THROUGH THE FRONT WINDSHIELD AT GREAT speed. Norman Simmons came to in time to see his dog-eared copy of *Galactic Patrol* disappear into the murky water below. He made a wild grab for the book, missed it, and received a painful scratch from shards of broken windshield. All that remained of his belongings was the second volume of the Foundation series and the blanket, which somehow had been draped half in and half out of the shattered window. The bottom edge of the blanket swung gently back and forth just a couple of inches above the water. The books he could do without; they really had only sentimental value. Since he had learned the Trick, there was no need to physically possess any books. But in the cold weather he was sure to need the blanket; he carefully retrieved it.

Norman pushed open a door, and climbed onto the struts of the Cub for a look around. The plane had crashed nose first into a shallow pond. The jet had been silenced in the impact, and the loudest sound to be heard now was his own breathing. Norman peered into the fog. How far was he from "dry" land? A few yards away he could see swamp vegetation above the still surface of the water; beyond that, nothing but mist. A slight air current eased the gloom. There! For an instant he glimpsed dark trees and brush about thirty yards away.

Thirty yards, through cold and slimy water. Norman's lips curled back in revulsion as he stared at the oily liquid. Maybe there was an aerial route, like Tarzan used. He glanced anxiously up, looking for some overhanging tree branch or vine. No luck. He would have to go *through* the water. Norman almost cried in despair at the thought. Suffocating visions of death by drowning came to mind. He imagined all the creatures with pointy teeth and ferocious appetites that might be lurking in the seemingly placid water: piranhas to strip his bones and—no, they were tropical fish, but something equally deadly. If he could only pretend that it were clear, ankle-deep water.

Dal swam silently toward the moonlit palms and palely gleaming sands just five hundred yards away. Five hundred yards, he thought exultantly, to freedom, to his own kind. The enemy could never penetrate the atoll's camouflage. . . . He didn't notice a slight turbulence, the swift emergence of a leathery tentacle from the water. But he fought desperately as he felt it tighten about his leg. Dal's screams were bubbly gurglings inaudible above the faint drone of the surf, as he was hauled effortlessly into the depths and sharp, unseen teeth. . . .

For a second his control lapsed, and the fictional incident slipped in.

In the comfort of his room, the death of Dal had been no more than the pleasantly chilling end of a villain; here it was almost unbearable. Norman extended one foot gingerly into the water, and quickly drew it back. He tried again, this time with both feet. Nothing bit him and he cautiously lowered himself into the clammy water. The swamp weeds brushed gently against his legs. Soon he was holding the strut with one hand and was neck deep in water. The mass of weeds had slowly been compressed as he descended and now just barely supported his weight, even though he had not touched bottom. He released his grip on the strut and began moving toward shore. With one hand he attempted to keep his blanket out of the water while with the other he paddled. Norman glanced about for signs of some hideous tentacle or fin, saw nothing but weeds.

He could see the trees on the shore quite clearly now, and the weeds at his feet seemed backed by solid ground. Just a few more yards— Norman gasped with relief as he struggled out of the water. He noticed an itching on his legs and arms. There had been blood-drinkers in the water after all, but fortunately small ones. He paused to remove the slugs from his body.

Norman sneezed violently and inspected his blanket. Although the mists had made it quite damp, he wrapped it around himself. Only after he was more or less settled did he notice the intermittent thrumming sound coming through the trees on his left. It sounded like the transport vehicles back in the tunnels, or like the automobiles that he had heard and seen on film.

Norman scrambled through the underbrush in the direction of the noises. Soon he came to a dilapidated four-lane asphalt highway. Every minute or so, a car would appear out of the mist, travel through his narrow range of vision, and disappear into the mist again.

MOST SECRET (Unauthorized use of MOST SECRET materials is punishable by death.) He had to get to Canada or they would kill him for sure. He knew millions, *billions* of things labeled MOST SECRET. Nearly all were unintelligible. The rest were usually boring. A very small percentage were interesting, like something out of an adventure story. And some were horrifying bits of nightmare couched in cold, matter-of-fact words. But all were labeled MOST SECRET, and his access to them was certainly unauthorized. If only he had known beforehand the consequences of Memorizing It All. It had been so easy to do, and so useful, but it was also a deadly, clinging gift.

Now that the airplane had crashed, he had to find some other way to get to Canada. Maybe one of these cars could take him some place where he would have better luck in his attempt. For some reason, the idea didn't trigger warning memories. Blissfully unaware that a talking chimpanzee is not a common sight in the United States, Norman started down the embankment to the shoulder of the highway, and in the immortal tradition of the hitchhiker in *Two for the Road*, stuck out his thumb.

THREE MINUTES PASSED; HE CLUTCHED THE BLANKET MORE TIGHTLY TO HIMself as his teeth began to chatter. In the distance he heard the thrum of an approaching vehicle. He stared eagerly in the direction of the sound. Within fifteen seconds, a sixty-ton ore carrier emerged from the fog and lumbered toward him. Norman jumped up and down in a frenzy, waving and shouting. The blanket gave him the appearance of a little Amerind doing a particularly violent rain dance. The huge truck rolled by him at about thirty-five miles per hour. Then when it was some forty yards away, the driver slammed on the brakes and the doughy rollagon tires bit into asphalt.

Norman ran joyfully toward the cab, not noticing the uncared-for condition of the starboard ore cranes, the unpainted and dented appearance of the cab, or the wheezy putputting of the Wankel rotary engine—all signs of dilapidation which would have been unthinkable four years before.

He stopped in front of the cab door and was confronted by a pair of cynical, bloodshot eyes peering at him over a three-day growth of beard. "Who . . . Whash are you?" (The condition of the driver would have been unthinkable four years ago, too.)

"My name's Norman—Jones." Norman slyly selected an alias. He resolved to act dull, too, for he knew that most chimps were somewhat stupid, and couldn't speak clearly without the special operations he had had. (In spite of his memory and intelligence, Norman had an artificial block against ever completely realizing his uniqueness.) "I want to go to"—he searched his memory—"Marquette."

The driver squinted and moved his head from side to side as if to get a better view of Norman. "Say, you're a monkey."

"No," Norman stated proudly, forgetting his resolution, "I'm a chimpanzee."

"A talkin' monkey," the driver said almost to himself. "You could be worth plen . . . wherezhu say you wanna go . . . Marquette? Sure, hop in. That's where I'm takin' this ore."

Norman clambered up the entrance ladder into the warm cab. "Oh, thanks a lot."

The ore carrier began to pick up speed. The highway had been blasted through greenish bedrock, but it still made turns and had to climb over steep hills.

The driver was expansive, "Can't wait to finish this trip. This here is my las' run, ya know. No more drivin' ore fer the government an' its 'Public Works Projects.' I know where to get a couple black market fusion packs, see? Start my own trucking line. No one'll ever guess where I get my power." He swerved to avoid a natural abutment of greenish rock that appeared out of the mist, and decided that it was time to turn on his fog lights. His mind wandered back to prospects of future success, but along a different line. "Say, you like to talk, Monkey? You could make me a lot of money, ya know: 'Jim Traly an' His Talkin' Monkey.' Sounds good, eh?"

With a start, Norman realized that he was listening to a drunk. The driver's entire demeanor was almost identical to that of the fiend's henchman in "The Mores of the Morgue." Norman had no desire to be a "talkin' monkey" for the likes of Traly, whose picture he now remembered in Social Security Records. The man was listed as an unstable, low competence type who might become violent if frustrated.

As the ore carrier slowed for a particularly sharp turn, Norman decided that he could endure the cold of the outside for a few more minutes. He edged to the door and began to pull at its handle. "I think I better get off now, Mr. Traly."

The ore carrier slowed still more as the driver lunged across the seat and grabbed Norman by one of the purple suspenders that kept his orange Bermuda shorts up. A full grown chimpanzee is a match for most men, but the driver weighed nearly three hundred pounds and Norman was scared stiff. "You're staying right here, see?" Traly shouted into Norman's face, almost suffocating the chimpanzee in alcohol vapor. The driver transferred his grip to the scruff of Norman's neck as he accelerated the carrier back to cruising speed.

"Crashed in a shallow swamp just beyond the Security fence, sir." The young Army captain held a book up to the viewer. "This copy of Asimov was all that was left in the cabin, but we dredged up some other books and a typewriter from the water. It's only about five feet deep there."

"But where did the chim . . . the pilot go?" Pederson asked.

"The pilot, sir?" The captain knew what the quarry was but was following the general's line. "We have a man here from Special Forces who's a tracker, sir. He says that the pilot left the Cub and waded ashore. From there, he tracked him through the brush to the old Ishpeming-Marquette road. He's pretty sure that the . . . um . . . pilot hitched a ride in the direction of Marquette." The captain did not mention how surprised the lieutenant from Special Forces had been by the pilot's tracks. "He probably left the area about half an hour ago, sir."

"Very well, Captain. Set up a guard around the plane; if anyone gets nosy, tell them that ORES has asked you to salvage their crashed Cub. Fly everything you found in the cabin and swamp back to Sawyer and have it sent down here to Files Central."

"Yes, sir."

Pederson cut the connection and began issuing detailed instructions to his chief aide over another circuit. Finally he turned back to Dunbar. "That chimp is not going to remain one step ahead of us for very much longer. I've alerted all the armed forces in the Upper Peninsula to start a search, with special concentration on Marquette. It's lucky that we have permission to conduct limited maneuvers there or I might have an awful time just getting permission to station airbornes over the city.

"And now we can take a little time to consider ways of catching this Norman Simmons, rather than responding spastically to *his* initiative."

Dunbar said quickly, "In the first place, you can cut whatever connection there is between Files and Norman's computer."

Pederson grinned. "Good enough. That was mixed in with the rest of the instructions I've given Smith. If I remember right, the two computers were connected by a simple copper cable, part of the general cable net that was installed interweaving with the tunnel system. It should be a simple matter to cut the circuit where the cable enters the Files room."

The general thought for a moment. "The object now is to catch the chimp, discover the location of the chimp's computer, or both. Down here we can't do anything directly about the chimp. But the computer has to be in contact with Norman Simmons. Could we trace these emanations?"

Dunbar blinked. "You know that better than I, General. The Signal Corps used our experiment to try a *quote* entirely new concept in communications *unquote*. They supplied all the comm equipment, even the surgical imbeds for Norman. And they are playing it pretty cozy with the technique. Whatever it is, it goes through almost anything, does not travel faster than light, and can handle several billion bits per second. It might even be ESP, if what I've read about telepathy is true."

Pederson looked sheepish. "I do recognize the 'new concept' you mention. I just never connected the neutri . . . this technique with your project. But I should have known; we have only one way to broadcast through solid rock as if it were vacuum. Unfortunately, with the devices we have now, there's no way of getting a directional bearing on such transmissions. With enough time and as a last resort we might be able to jam them, though."

Now it was Dunbar's turn to make a foolish suggestion. "Maybe if a thorough search of the tunnels were made, we could find the—"

Pederson grimaced. "Bill, you've been here almost three years. Haven't you realized how complicated the Labyrinth is? The maze is composed of thousands of tunnel segments spread through several cubic miles of bedrock. It's simply too complex for a blind search—and there's only one set of blueprints," he jerked a thumb at the racks of fiberglass. "Even for routine trips, we have to make out tapes to plug into the transport cars down there. If we hadn't put his quarters close to ground level, so you could take him for walks on the surface, Norman would still be wandering around the Labyrinth, even though he knows what passages to take.

"About twice a day I ride over to Continental Air Defense Headquarters. It takes about half an hour and the trip is more tortuous then a swoopride at a carnival. CAD HQ could be just a hundred yards from where we're sitting, or it could be two miles—in any direction. For that matter, I don't really know where *we* are right now. But then," he added with a sly smile, "neither do the Russki or Han missilemen. I'm sorry, Doctor, but it would take years of random searching to find the computer."

And Dunbar realized that he was right. It was general policy in the First Security District to disperse experiments and other installations as far as possible through the tunnel maze. So it had been with Norman's computer. With its own power source the computer needed no outside assistance to function.

The scientist remembered its strange appearance, resting like a huge jewel in a vacant tunnel—where? It was a far different sight from the appearance of Files. Norman's computer had the facets of a cut gem, although this had been a functional rather than an aesthetic necessity. Dunbar remembered the multi-color glows that appeared near its surface; further in, the infinite reflections and subtle refractions of micro-component flaws in the glass blended into a mysterious flickering, hinting at the cheerful though immature intelligence that was Norman Simmons. This was the object which had to be found.

Dunbar broke out of his reverie. He started on a different tack. "Really, General, I don't quite see how this situation can be quite as desperate as you say. Norman isn't going to sell secrets to the Reds; he's as loyal as a human child could be—which is a good deal more than most adults, because he can't rationalize disloyalty so easily. Besides, you know that we were eventually going to provide him with large masses of data, anyway. The goal of this whole project is to test the possibility of giving humans an encyclopedic mental grasp. He just saw how much the information could help him, and how much easier it could be obtained than by study, and he pushed the experiment into its next phase. He shouldn't be punished or hurt because of that. This situation is really no one's fault."

Pederson snapped back, "Of course, it's no one's fault; that's just the hell of it. When no one is to blame for something, it means that the situation is fundamentally beyond human control. To me, your whole project is taking control away from people and giving it to *others*. Here an experimental animal, a chimpanzee, has taken the initiative away from the U.S. Government—don't laugh, or so help me—" The general made a warning gesture. "Your chimp is more than a co-ordinator of information; he's also *smarter* than he was before. *What're the humans we try this on going to be like?*"

Pederson calmed himself with a deliberate effort. "Never mind that now. The important thing is to find Simmons, since he appears to be the only one who," Pederson groaned, "knows where his brains are. So let's get practical. Just what can we expect from him? How easy is it for him to correlate information in his memory?"

Dunbar considered. "I guess the closest analogy between his mind and a normal one is to say that he has an eidetic memory—and a *very* large one. I imagine that when he first began using the information he was just swamped with data. Everything he saw stimulated a deluge of related memories. As his subconscious became practiced, he probably remembered only information that was pertinent to a problem. Say that he saw a car, and wondered what year and make it was. His subconscious would hunt through his copy of Files—at very high speed—and within a tenth of a second Norman would 'remember' the information he had just wondered about.

"However, if for some reason he suddenly wondered what differential equations were, it would be a different matter, because he couldn't *understand* the information presented, and so would have to wade through the same preliminary material that every child must in order to arrive at high-school math. But he could do it very much faster, because of the ease with which he could pick different explanations from different texts. I imagine he could get well into calculus from where he is now in algebra with a couple hours of study."

"In other words, the longer he has this information, the more dangerous he'll be."

"Uh, yes. However, there *are* a couple things on our side. First, it's mighty cold and damp on the surface, for Norman at least. He is likely to be very sick in a few hours. Second, if he travels far enough away from the First Security District, he will become mentally disoriented. Although Norman doesn't know it—unless he has specifically considered the question—he could never get much farther than fifteen miles

away and remain sane. Norman's mind is a very delicate balance between his organic brain and the hidden computer. The coordination is
just as subtle as that of different nerve paths in the human brain. The
information link between the two has to transmit more than a billion
bits of information per second. If Norman gets beyond a certain point,
the time lapse involved in transmission between him and the computer
will upset the coordination. It's something like talking by radio with a
spacecraft; beyond a certain distance it is difficult or impossible to maintain a meaningful conversation. When Norman goes beyond a certain
point it will be impossible for him to think coherently."

Dunbar was struck by an unrelated idea. He added, "Say, I can see
one reason why this could get sticky. What if Norman got picked up by
foreign agents? That would be the biggest espionage coup in the history
of man."

Pederson smiled briefly. "Ah, the light dawns. Yes, some of the information this Simmons has could mean the death of almost everyone
on Earth, if it were known to the wrong people. Other secrets would
merely destroy the United States.

"Fortunately, we're fairly sure that the Reds' domestic collapse has
reduced their overseas enterprises to about nil. As I remember it, there
are only one or two agents in all of Michigan. Thank God for small
favors."

BORIS KUCHENKO SCRATCHED AND WAS MISERABLE. A FEW MINUTES BEFORE,
he had been happily looking forward to receiving his weekly unem-
ployment check and then spending the afternoon clipping articles out
of the *NATO Armed Forces Digest* for transmission back to Moscow. And
now this old coot with his imperious manner was trying to upset everything. Kuchenko turned to his antagonist and tried to put on a brave
front. "I am sorry, Comrade, but I have my orders. As the ranking Soviet
agent in the Upper Peninsu—"

The other snapped back, "Ranking agent, nothing! You were never
supposed to know this, Kuchenko, but you are a cipher, a stupid dummy
used to convince U.S. Intelligence that the USSR has given up massive
espionage. If only I had some decent agents here in Marquette, I
wouldn't have to use idiots like you."

Ivan Sliv was an honest-to-God, effective Russian spy. Behind his
inconspicuous middle-aged face, lurked a subtle mind. Sliv spoke five
languages and had an excellent grasp of engineering, mathematics, ge-
ography, and history—*real* history, not State-sponsored fairy tales. He
could make brilliantly persuasive conversation at a cocktail party or
commit a political murder with equal facility. Sliv was the one really in
charge of espionage in the militarily sensitive U.P. area. He and other

equally talented agents concentrated on collecting information from Sawyer AFB and from the elusive First Security District.

The introduction of Bender's fusion pack had produced world-wide depression, and the bureaucracies of Russia had responded to this challenge with all the resiliency of a waterlogged pretzel. The Soviet economic collapse had been worse than that of any other major country. While the U.S. was virtually recovered from the economic depression caused by the availability of unlimited power, counter-revolutionary armies were approaching Moscow from the West *and* the East. Only five or ten ICBM bases remained in Party hands. But the Comrades had been smart in one respect. If you can't win by brute force, it is better to be subtle. Thus the planetary spy operations were stepped up, as was a very secret project housed in a system of caves under the Urals. Sliv's mind shied away from that project—he was one of the few to know of it, and that knowledge must never be hinted at.

Sliv glared at Kuchenko. "Listen, you fat slob: I'm going to explain things once more, if possible in words of one syllable. I just got news from Sawyer that some Amie superproject has backfired. An experimental animal has escaped from their tunnel network and half the soldiers in the U.P. are searching for it. They think it's here in Marquette."

Kuchenko paled, "A war virus test? Comrade, this could be—" the fat Soviet agent boggled at the possibilities.

Sliv swore. "No, no, no! The Army's orders are to *capture*, not destroy the thing. We are the only agents that are in Marquette now, or have a chance to get in past the cordon that's sure to be dropped around the city. We'll split up and—" He stopped and took conscious notice of the buzzing sound that had been building up over the last several minutes. He walked quickly across the small room and pushed open a badly cracked window. Cold air seemed to ooze into the room. Below, the lake waters splashed against the pilings of the huge automated pier which incidentally contained this apartment. Sliv pointed into the sky and snapped at the bedraggled Kuchenko. "See? The Amie airbornes have been over the city for the last five minutes, at least. We've got to get going, man!"

But Boris Kuchenko was a man who liked his security. He miserably inspected his dirty fingernails, and began, "I really don't know if this is the right thing, Comrade. We—"

THE FOG HAD DISAPPEARED, ONLY TO BE REPLACED BY A COLD DRIZZLE. JIM Traly guided the ore carrier through Marquette to the waterfront. Even though drunk, he maintained a firm grip on Norman's neck. The carrier turned onto another street, and Norman got his first look at Lake Superior. It was so gray and cold; beyond the breakwater the lake seemed to blend with the sullen hue of the sky. The carrier turned again. They were now moving parallel to the water along a row of loading piers. In spite of the rollagons, the carrier dipped and sagged as they drove over large potholes in the substandard paving material. The rain had collected in these depressions and splashed as they drove along. Traly apparently recognized his destination. He slowed the carrier and moved it to the side of the street.

Traly opened his door and stepped down, dragging Norman behind him. With difficulty the chimpanzee kept his balance and did not land on his head. The drunk driver was muttering to himself, "Las' time I drive this trash. They can pick up the inventories themselves. Good riddance." He kicked a rollagon. "Just wait till I get some Bender fusion packs. I'll show 'em. C'mon, you." He gave Norman a jerk, and began walking across the street.

The waterfront was almost deserted. Traly was heading for what appeared to be the only operating establishment in the area: a tavern. The bar had a rundown appearance. The "aluminum" trim around the door had long since begun to rust, and the memory cell for the bar's sky sign suffered from amnesia, so that it now projected into the air:

The D-unk PuT pavern

Traly entered the bar, pulling Norman in close behind. Once the fluorescents had probably lighted the place well, but now only two or three in a far corner were operating.

He pulled Norman around in front of him and seemed eager to announce his discovery of the "talkin' monkey." Then he noticed that the bar was almost empty. No one was sitting at any of the tables, although there were half empty glasses of beer left on a few of them. Four or five men and the barkeeper were engaged in an intense discussion at the far end of the room. "Where is everybody?" Traly was astonished.

The barkeeper looked up. "Jimmy! Right at lunch President Langley came on TV an' said that the government was going to let us buy as many Bender fusion boxes as we want. You could go out an' buy one right now for twenty-five bucks. When everybody heard that, why they just asked themselves what they were doin' sittin' around in a bar when they could have a job an' even be in business for themselves. Not much profit for me this afternoon, but I don't care. I know where I can get some junk copters. Fit 'em out with Bender packs and start a tourist service. You know: See the U.P. with Don Zalevsky." The bartender winked.

Traly's jaw dropped. He forgot Norman. "You really mean that there's no more black market where we can get fusion boxes?"

One of the customers, a short man with a protuberant beak and a bald pate, turned to Traly. "What do you need a black market for when you can go out an' buy a Pack for twenty-five dollars? Well, will you look at that: Traly's disappointed. Now you can do whatcher always bragging about, go out and dig up some fusion boxes and go into business." He turned back to the others.

"And we owe it all to President Langley's fizical and economic policies. Bender's Pack coulda destroyed our nation. Instead we only had a little depression, an' look at us now. Three years after the invention, the economy's on an even keel enough to let us buy as many power packs as we want."

Someone interrupted. "You got rocks in your head, buddy. The government closed down most of the mines so the oil corporations would have a market to make plastics for; we get to produce just enough ore up here so no one starves. Those 'economic measures' have kept us all hungry. If the government had only let us buy as many Packs as we wanted and not interfered with free competition, there wouldna been no depression or nothing."

From the derisive remarks of the other customers, this appeared to be a minority opinion. The Beak slammed his glass of beer down and turned to his opponent. "You know what woulda happened if there wasn't no 'interference'?" He didn't wait for an answer. "Everybody woulda gone out an bought Packs. All the businesses in the U.S. woulda gone bankrupt, 'cause anyone with a Bender and some electric motors would hardly need to buy any regular goods, except food. It wouldn't have been a depression, it woulda been just like a jungle. As it is, we only had a short period of adjustment," he almost seemed to be quoting, "an' now we're back on our feet. We got power to burn; those ore buckets out in the bay can fly through the air and space, and we can take the salt out of the water and—"

"Aw, you're jus' repeating what Langley said in his speech."

"Sure I am, but it's true." Another thought occurred to him. "And *now* we don't even need Public Works Projects."

"Yeah, no more Public Works Projects," Traly put in, disappointed.

"There wouldn't have been no need for PWP if it wasn't for Langley and his loony ideas. My old man said the same thing about Roosevelt." The dissenter was outnumbered but voluble.

NORMAN HAD BECOME ENGROSSED IN THE ARGUMENT. IN FACT HE WAS SO interested that he had forgotten his danger. Back in the District he had been made to learn some economics as part of his regular course of study—and, of course, he could remember considerably more about the subject. Now he decided to make his contribution. Traly had loosened his grip; the chimpanzee easily broke the hold and jumped to the top of the counter. "This man," he pointed to the Beak, "is right, you know. The Administration's automatic stabilizers and discretionary measures prevented total catastro—"

"What is *this*, Jimmy?" The bartender broke the amazed silence that greeted Norman's sudden action.

"That's what I've been trying to tell you guys. I picked up this monkey back in Ishpeming. He's like a parrot, only better. Jus' listen to him. I figure he could be worth a lot of money."

"Thought you were going into the trucking business, Jimmy."

Traly shrugged. "This could be a lot greener."

"That's no parrot-talk," the Beak opined. "The monkey's *really* talking. He's smart like you and me."

Norman decided that he had to trust someone. "Yes I am, yes I am! And I need to get into Canada. Otherwise—"

The door to the Drunk Pup Tavern squeaked as a young man in brown working clothes pushed it halfway open. "Hey, Ed, all of you guys. There's a bunch of big Army copters circling the bay, and GI's all over. It doesn't look like any practice maneuver." The man was panting as if he had run several blocks.

"Say, let's see that," moved the Beak. He was informally seconded. Even the bartender seemed ready to leave. Norman started. *They* were still after him, and they were close. He leaped off the counter and ran through the half-open door, right by the knees of the young man who had made the announcement. The man stared at the chimpanzee and made a reflex grab for him. Norman evaded the snatch and scuttled down the street. Behind him, he heard Traly arguing with the man about, "Letting my talking monkey escape."

He had dropped his blanket when he jumped onto the counter. Now the chill drizzle made him regret the loss. Soon he was damp to the skin again, and the water splashed his forearms and legs as he ran through spots where water had collected in the tilted and cracked sections of sidewalk. All the shops and dives along the street were closed and boarded up. Some owners had left in such disgust and discouragement that they had not bothered even to pull in their awnings. He stopped under one such to catch his breath and get out of the rain.

Norman glanced about for some sign of airborne infantrymen, but as far as he could see, the sky was empty of men and aircraft. He examined the awning above him. For several years the once green plastic fabric had been subjected alternately to baking sun and rotting rain. It was cheap plastic and now it hung limp, the gray sky visible through the large holes in the material. Norman looked up, got an idea. He backed away from the awning and then ran toward it. He leaped and caught its rusting metal frame. The shade sagged even more, but held. He eased himself over the frame and rested for an instant on the top; then pulled himself onto the windowsill of a second-story apartment.

Norman looked in, saw nothing but an old bed and a closet with one lonely hanger. He caught the casing above the window and swung up. It was almost like being Tarzan. (Usually, Norman tended to identify himself with Tarzan rather than with the Lord-of-the-Jungle's chimpanzee flunkies.) He caught the casing with his toes, pushed himself upwards until he could grasp the edge of the flat roof. One last heave and he was lying on that tar-and-gravel roofing material. In places where the tar had been worn away, someone had sprayed plastite, but more time had passed and that "miracle construction material" had deteriorated, too.

The roofs provided scant cover from observation. Fifty feet away; Norman saw the spidery black framework of a radio tower mounted on the roof of another building. It was in good repair; probably it was a government navigation beacon. Norman sneezed several times, violently. He crawled warily across the roof toward the tower. The buildings were separated by a two-foot alley which Norman easily swung across.

He arrived at the base of the tower. Its black plastic members gleamed waxily in the dull light. As with many structures built after 1980, Hydrocarbon Products Administration regulations dictated that it be constructed with materials deriving from the crippled petroleum and coal industries, Norman remembered. In any case, the intricate framework provided good camouflage. Norman settled himself among the girders and peered out across Marquette.

THERE WERE HUNDREDS OF THEM! IN THE DISTANCE, TINY FIGURES IN Allservice green were walking through the streets, inspecting each building. Troop carriers and airtanks hung above them. Other airtanks patrolled some arbitrary perimeter about the city and bay. Norman recognized the setup as one of the standard formations for encirclement and detection of hostile forces. With confident foreknowledge he looked up and examined the sky above him. Every few seconds a buckrogers fell out of the apparently empty grayness. After a free fall of five thousand feet, the airborne infantrymen hit their jets just two or three hundred feet above the city. Already, more than twenty of them were posted over the various intersections.

The chimpanzee squinted, trying to get a clearer view of the nearest buckrogers. Images seen through the air behind and below the soldier seemed to waver. This and a faint screaming sound was the only indication of the superheated air shot from the Bender powered thermal element in the soldier's backpack. The infantryman's shoulders seemed lopsided. On more careful inspection Norman recognized that this was due to a GE fifty-thousand line reconnaissance camera strapped to the soldier's upper arm and shoulder. The camera's eight-inch lens gaped blackly as the soldier turned (rotated?) in the chimp's direction.

Norman froze. He knew that every hyper-resolution picture was being transmitted back to Sawyer AFB where computers and photo-interp teams analyzed them. Under certain conditions just a clear footprint or the beady glint of Norman's eyes within the maze of girders would be enough to bring a most decisive—though somewhat delayed—reaction.

As the buckrogers turned away, Norman sighed with relief. But he knew that he wouldn't remain safe for long. Sooner or later—most likely sooner—they would be able to trace him. And then . . . With horror he remembered once again some of the terrible bits of information that hid in the vast pile he knew, remembered the punishments for unauthorized knowledge. *He had to escape them!* Norman considered the means, both fictional and otherwise, that had been used in the past to elude pursuers. In the first place, he recognized that some outside help was needed, or he could never escape from the country. Erik Satanssen, he remembered, always played the double agent, gaining advantages from both sides right up to the denouement. Or take Slippery Jim DiGriz . . . the point was there are always some loopholes even in the most mechanized of traps. What organization would have a secret means of getting across Lake Superior into Canada? The Reds, of course!

Norman stopped fiddling with his soaked suspenders, and looked up. That was the pat answer, in some stories: Pretend to side up with the baddies just long enough to get out of danger and expose them at the same time. Turning around, he gazed at the massive automated pier jutting out into the bay. At its root were several fourth-class apartments—and in one of them was the only Soviet agent in the Upper Peninsula! Norman remembered more about Boris Kuchenko. What sort of government would employ a slob like that as a spy? He racked his memory but could find no other evidence of espionage in the U.P. area.

Many tiny details seemed to crystallize into an idea. It was just like in some stories where the hero appears to pull his hunches out of the thin air. Norman *knew* without any specific reason, that the Soviets were not as incapacitated as they seemed. Stark, Borovsky, Ivanov were smart boys, much smarter than the so-called Bumpkinov incompetents they had replaced. If Stark had been in power in the first place, the Soviet Union might have survived Bender's invention without losing more than a few outlying SSR's. As it was the Party bosses controlled only the area immediately around Moscow and some "hardened" bases in the Urals. Somehow Norman felt that, if all the mental and physical resources of the rulers had been used against the counterrevolutionaries, the Reds' position would have to be better. Borovsky and Ivanov especially, were noted for devious, backdoor victories. Something smelled about this spy business.

If Kuchenko was more than he seemed, there might be a way out even yet. If he could trick the Reds into thinking he was a stupe or a traitor, they might take him to some hideout in Canada. He knew they would be interested in him and his knowledge; that was his passport and his peril. They must never know the things *he* knew. And then later, in Canada, maybe he could expose the Russian spies and gain forgiveness.

THE NEAREST BUCKROGERS WAS NOW FACING DIRECTLY AWAY FROM NORman's tower. The chimpanzee moved away from the tower, hurried to the edge of the roof, and swung himself over. Now he was out of the line of sight of the infantryman. He reached the ground and scampered across the empty street. Soon he was padding along the base of the huge auto pier. Finally he reached the point where the street was swallowed by the enclosed portion of the pier. Norman ran into the dimness, at least he was out of the rain now. Along the side of the inner wall was a metal grid stairway. The chimp clambered up the stairs, found himself in the narrow corridor serving the cheap apartments which occupied what otherwise would have been dead space in the warehouse pier. He paused before turning the doorknob.

". . . . Move fast!" The knob was snatched from his fingers, as someone on the other side pulled the door open. Norman all but fell into the room. "What the hell!" The speaker slammed the door shut behind the chimpanzee. Norman glanced about the room, saw Boris Kuchenko frozen in the act of wringing his hands. The other man spun Norman around, and the chimpanzee recognized him as one Ian Sloane, civilian employee No. 36902u at Sawyer AFB; so the hunch had been right! The Reds *were* operating on a larger scale than the government suspected.

Norman assumed his best conspiratorial air. "Good morning, gentlemen . . . or should I say Comrades?"

The older man, Sloane, kept a tight grip on his arm. A look of surprise and triumph and oddly—fear, was on his face. Norman decided to go all the way with the double-agent line. "I'm here to offer my services, uh, Comrades. Perhaps you don't know quite what and who I am . . ." He looked around expectantly for some sign of curiosity. Sloane—that was the only name Norman could remember, but it couldn't be his real one—gazed at him attentively, but kept a tight grip on his arm. Seeing that he was going to get no response, Norman continued less confidently. "I . . . I know who you are. Get me out of the country and you'll never regret it. You must have some way of escaping—at the very least some hiding place." He noticed Boris Kuchenko glance involuntarily at a spot in the ceiling near one of the walls. There was an ill-concealed trap hacked raggedly out of the ceiling. It hardly seemed the work of a master spy.

At last Sloane spoke. "I think we can arrange your escape. And I am sure that we will not regret it."

His tone made Norman realize how naïve his plan had been. These agents would get the information and secrets from him or they would destroy him, and there was no real possibility that he would have any opportunity to create a third, more acceptable alternative. The fire was much hotter than the frying pan, and fiction was vaporized by reality. He was in trouble.

Pfft.

The tiny sound came simultaneously with a pinprick in his leg. The curtains drawn before the window jerked slightly. A faint greenish haze seemed to hang in the air for an instant, then disappeared. He scratched his leg with his free hand and dislodged a black pellet. Then he knew that the photo-interpretation group at Sawyer had finally found his trail. They knew exactly where he was, and now they were acting. They had just fired at least two PAX cartridges into the room, one of which had failed to go off. The little black object was a cartridge of that famous nerve gas.

During the Pittsburgh Bread Riots back in '81, screaming mobs, the type that dismember riot police, had been transformed into the most docile groups by a few spoken commands and a couple of grams of PAX diffused over the riot area. The stuff wasn't perfect, of course; in about half a percent of the population there were undesirable side effects such as pseudo-epilepsy and permanent nerve damage; another half percent weren't affected by normal dosages at all. But the great majority of people immediately lost all power to resist outside suggestion. He felt Sloane's grip loosening.

Norman pulled away and spoke to both men. "Give me a boost through that trapdoor."

"Yes, sir." The two men agreeably formed a stirrup and raised the chimpanzee toward the ceiling. As they did, Norman suddenly wondered why the gas had not affected him. *Because I'm not all here!* He answered himself with an almost hysterical chuckle. The gas could only affect the part of him that was physically present. And, though that was a very important part, he still retained some of his own initiative.

As Norman pushed open the trap, there was a splintering crash from the window as a buckrogers in full battle gear came hurtling feet first into the room. With a spastic heave, the chimp drew himself into the darkness above. From below he heard an almost plaintive, "Halt!" then Sloane's formerly menacing voice; "We'll go quietly, Officer."

NORMAN PICKED HIMSELF UP AND BEGAN RUNNING. THE WAY WAS DIMLY LIT from windows mounted far above. Now that his eyes were adjusted, he could see bulky crates around him and above him. He looked down, and gasped, for he could see crates below him, too. He seemed suspended. Then Norman remembered. In the dim light it wasn't too evident, but the floor and ceiling of this level were composed of heavy wire mesh. From a control board somewhere in the depths of the building, roller segments in the mesh could be turned on, and the bulkiest crates could be shuttled about the auto pier like toys. When in operation the pier could handle one million tons of merchandise a day; receiving products from trucks, storing them for a short time, and then sliding them into the holds of superfreighters. This single pier had been expected to bring the steel industry to Marquette, thus telescoping the mining and manufacturing complexes into one. Perhaps after the Recovery it would fulfill its promise, but at the moment it was dead and dark.

Norman zigzagged around several crates, scampered up an incline. Behind him he could hear the infantrymen, shed of their flying gear, scrambling through the trap door.

They would never believe his honesty now that he had been seen consorting with the communists. Things did indeed look dark—he complimented himself on this pun delivered in the midst of danger—but he still had some slim chance of escaping capture and the terrible punishment that would be sure to follow. He had one undetonated PAX cartridge. Apparently its relatively gentle impact with his flesh had kept it from popping. Perhaps not all the soldiers were wearing the antiPAX nose filters—in which case he might be able to commandeer a helicopter. It was a wild idea, but the time for cautious plans was past.

The pier seemed to extend forever. Norman kept moving. He had to get away; and he was beginning to feel very sick. Maybe it was some effect of the gas. He ran faster, but even so he felt a growing terror. His mind seemed to be dissolving, disintegrating. Could *this* be the effect of PAX? He groped mentally for some explanation, but somehow he was having trouble remembering the most obvious things, while at the same time extraneous memories were swamping him more completely than they had for weeks. He should know what the source of the danger was, but somehow . . . *I'm not all here!* That was the answer! But he couldn't understand what its significance was anymore. He no longer could form rational plans. Only one goal remained—to get away from the things that were stalking him. The dim gray glow far ahead now seemed to offer some kind of safety. If he could only reach it. Intelligence was deserting him, and chaos was creeping in.

Faster!

3,456,628 more shopping days until Christmas . . . Latitude 40.9234°N, Longitude 121.3018°W: Semi-hardened Isis missile warehouse; 102 megatons total . . . Latitude 59.00160°N, Longitude 87.4763°W: Cluster of three Vega class Submarine Launched Ballistic Missiles; 35 megatons total . . . depth 105.4 fathoms . . . All-serv IFF codes as follows: I. 398547 . . . 436344 . . . 51 . . . "Hey, let me out!" *. . . Master of jungle poised, knife ready as . . . the nature of this rock formation was not realized until the plutonist theory of Bender's . . . New Zealand Harbor Defense of Wellington follows: Three antisubmarine detection rings at 10.98 miles from . . . REO factory depot Boise, Idaho contains 242,925 million-hp consumer fusion packs; inventory follows.* Cold gray light shining in the eyes. And I must escape or . . . *"die with a stake driven through his heart," the professor laughed.* STOP or you'll fall; MOVE or you'll die; escape escape escape seascape orescape 3scape5scape2pecape4ea 1a00p30 6891 35010112131010001010110000101010100001111010101—

The chimpanzee crouched frozen and glared madly at the soft gray light coming through the window.

THE TINY BLACK FACE LOOKED UP FROM THE STARCHED WHITE OF THE PILLOW and stared dazedly at the ceiling. Around the bed hung the glittering instruments of the SOmatic Support unit. Short of brain tissue damage, the SOS could sustain life in the most terribly mangled bodies. At the moment it was fighting pneumonia, TB, and polio in the patient on the bed.

Dunbar sniffed. The medical ward of the Labyrinth used all the latest procedures—gone was the antiseptic stink of earlier years. The germicidals used were a very subtle sort—and only a shade different from antipersonnel gases developed in the '60's and '70's. William Dunbar turned to Pederson, the only other human in the room. "According to the doctors, he'll make it." Dunbar gestured to the unconscious chimp. "And his reactions to those questions you asked him under truth drug indicate that no great damage has been done to his 'amplified personality.' "

"Yeah," Pederson replied, "but we won't know whether he responded truthfully until I have these coordinates for his computer checked out." He tapped the sheet of paper on which he had scrawled the numbers Norman had called off. "For all we know, he may be immune to truth drug in the same way he is to PAX."

"No, I think he probably told the truth, General. He is, after all, in a very confused state.

"Now that we know the location of his computer, it should be an easy matter to remove the critical information from it. When we try the invention on a man we can be much more careful with the information initially presented."

Pederson stared at him for a long moment. "I suppose you know that I've always opposed your project."

"Uh, yes," said Dunbar, startled, "though I can't understand why you do."

Pederson continued, apparently without noticing the other's answer, "I've never quite been able to convince my superiors of the dangers inherent in the things you want to do. I think I can convince them now and I intend to do everything in my power to see that your techniques are never tried on a human, or for that matter, on any creature."

Dunbar's jaw dropped. "But why? We *need* this invention! Nowadays there is so much knowledge in so many different areas that it is impossible for a man to become skilled in more than two or three of them. If we don't use this invention, most of that knowledge will sit in electronic warehouses waiting for insights and correlations that will never occur. The human-computer symbiosis can give man the jump on evolution and nature. Man's intellect can be ex—"

Pederson swore. "You and Bender make a pair, Dunbar; both of you see the effects of your inventions with narrow utopian blinders. But yours is by far the more dangerous of the two. Look what this one chimpanzee has done in under six hours—escaped from the most secure post in America, eluded a large armed force, and deduced the existence of an espionage net that we had completely overlooked. Catching him was more an *accident* than anything else. If he had had time to think about it, he probably would have deduced that distance limit and found some way to escape us that really would have worked. And this is what happens with an experimental *animal*! His intelligence has increased steadily as he developed a firmer command of his information banks. We captured him more or less by chance, and unless we act fast while he's drugged, we won't be able to hold him.

"And you want to try this thing on a man!

"Tell me, Doctor, who are you going to give godhood to first, hm-m-m? If your choice is wrong, the product will be more satanic than divine. It will be a devil that we cannot possibly beat except with the aid of some fortuitous accident, for we can't outthink that which, by definition, is smarter than we. The slightest instability on the part of the person you choose would mean the death or *domestication* of the entire human race."

Pederson relaxed, his voice becoming calmer. "There's an old saw,

Doctor, that the only truly dangerous weapon is a man. By that standard, you have made the only advance in weaponry in the last one hundred thousand years!" He smiled tightly. "It may seem strange to you, but I oppose arms races and I intend to see that you don't start one."

William Dunbar stared, pale-faced, entertaining a dream and a nightmare at the same time. Pederson noted the scientist's expression with some satisfaction.

This tableau was interrupted by the buzzing of the comm. Pederson accepted the call. "Yes," he said, recognizing Smith's features on the screen.

"Sir, we just finished with those two fellows we picked up on the auto pier," the aide spoke somewhat nervously. "One is Boris Kuchenko, the yuk we've had spotted all along. The other is Ivan Sliv, who's been working for the last nine months as a code man at Sawyer under the name of Ian Sloane. We didn't suspect him at all before. Anyway, we gave both of them a deep-probe treatment, and then erased their memories of what's happened today, so we could release them and use them as tracers."

"Fine," replied Pederson.

"They've been doing the darndest things, those spies." Smith swallowed. "But that isn't what this call is about."

"Oh?"

"Can I talk? Are you alone?"

"Spit it out, Smith."

"Sir, this Sliv is really a top man. Some of his memories are under blocks that I'm sure the Russkies' never thought we could break. Sir—he knows of a project the Sovs are running in an artificial cave system under the Urals. They've taken a dog and wired it—wired it into a computer. Sliv has heard the dog talk, just like Dunbar's chimp. Apparently this is the big project they're pouring their resources into to the exclusion of all others. In fact, one of Sliv's main duties was to detect and obstruct any similar project here. When all the bugs have been worked out, Stark, or one of the other Red chiefs is going to use it on himself and—"

Pederson turned away from the screen, stopped listening. He half noticed Dunbar's face, even paler than before. He felt the same sinking, empty sensation he had four years before when he had heard of Bender's fusion pack. Always it was the same pattern. The invention, the analysis of the dangers, the attempt at suppression, and then the crushing knowledge that no invention can really be suppressed and that the present case is no exception. Invention came after invention, each

with greater changes. Bender's pack would ultimately mean the dissolution of central collections of power, of cities—but Dunbar's invention
meant an increased *capability* for invention.

Somewhere under the Urals slept a very smart son of a bitch indeed . . .

And so he must choose between the certain disaster of having a Russian dictator with superhuman intelligence, and the probable disaster
involved in beating the enemy to the punch.

He knew what the decision must be; as a practical man he must adapt
to changes beyond his control, must plan for the safest possible handling
of the unavoidable.

. . . For better or worse, the world would soon be unimaginably different.

Of course, I never wrote the "important" story, the sequel about the first amplified
human. Once I tried something similar. John Campbell's letter of rejection began:
"Sorry—you can't write this story. Neither can anyone else." The moral: Keep
your supermen offstage, or deal with them when they are children (Wilmar Shiras's
Children of the Atom), or when they are in disguise (Campbell's own story "The
Idealists"). (There is another possibility, one that John never mentioned to me:
You can deal with the superman when s/he's senile. This option was used to
very amusing effect in one episode of the *Quark* television series.)

"Bookworm, Run!" and its lesson were important to me. Here I had tried a
straightforward extrapolation of technology, and found myself precipitated over an
abyss. It's a problem writers face every time we consider the creation of intelligences greater than our own. When this happens, human history will have reached
a kind of singularity—a place where extrapolation breaks down and new models
must be applied—and the world will pass beyond our understanding. In one
form or another, this Technological Singularity haunts many science-fiction writers: A bright fellow like Mark Twain could predict television, but such extrapolation is forever beyond, say, a dog. The best we writers can do is creep up on
the Singularity, and hang ten at its edge.

(My extended song-and-dance about this idea is at *http://www.rohan.sdsu.edu/
faculty/vinge/misc/singularity.html*. In that 1993 essay, I try to track the history
of this idea in the twentieth century. Since then I have come to realize even more
how my 1960s orientation was simply a product of ideas that others—such as
Licklider, Ashby, and Good—had put into the air.)

THE ACCOMPLICE

Warning: There are spoilers in this introduction.

Fred Pohl published my short story "The Accomplice" in the April 1967 issue of *If.* It was only my third story to appear in print. Wolgang Jeschke included a German translation of the story in his collection, *Science Fiction Story-Reader 16.* Its only other appearances were in two program books. So "The Accomplice" is among my least-reprinted stories. Why is that?

The quality of the writing is about average for what I could manage in the 1960s. The hero's background is probably more intriguing than in my earlier stories. And the ideas? Ah, there's the problem. To date, "The Accomplice" is the most irritating combination of embarrassing gaffes and neat insights that I have ever created. More than once, I have held it back from reprint collections.

Darrell Schweitzer wrote a marvelously kind and generous piece about the things I got right in "The Accomplice" (*The New York Review of Science Fiction*, April 1996, pp. 14–15). As with a lot of SF stories, if you are allowed to pick the good calls, it can look deeply prophetic. "The Accomplice" takes place in 1993. I wrote the story in mid-1966. Either I'm smarter than I think, or I must have been exposed to Moore's Law. (In 1965, Gordon Moore observed that certain aspects of computer power appeared to be doubling every year or two. In fact, this progress has continued into the early twenty-first century.) In any case, it looks like I have estimated the power of a 1993-era supercomputer fairly well. A major point of the story was that in just a few more years this computer power would be available on the consumer market. And yet . . . and yet, damn it, I still missed the impact that home computers would have on our world.

My central inspiration for writing the story was a computer application that has turned out to be spectacularly important: I had always been in love with Disney's *Fantasia.* In 1963, just out of high school, during my first visit to Disneyland, it occurred to me that computers could be used to automate cartoon creation, putting—I thought—large-scale dramatic productions within the reach of individual artists. (Most of this has come to pass, though our largest projects still involve enormous teams of bright people.) The idea of computer animation was probably an independent insight, though I know now that people like Ivan Sutherland were already hard at work with real implementations! Years would pass before computers would be powerful enough to do high-quality motion imagery. *That* I got right!

And this illustrates a subtle deficiency in the vision of this story (well, it's subtle compared to the other deficiencies!). For years before the first computer-animated short features, people were talking about the possibilities. Before *Fantasia*-class computer-animated features were possible, computer animation had become an industry. And yet, in my story, computer animation comes as a big surprise, suddenly emerging when computers are powerful enough to do significant figure animation in a major movie release. The generic form of this problem is widespread in SF, and very hard to avoid. With rare exceptions, if a story gimmick is something that could plausibly grow out of the present, then it and its consequences can't reasonably be presented as a surprise in the story.

Some of the story's failures don't bother me: the aircars and the extremely successful space program of my 1993 era. Maybe that's because such misforecasts have been so common in SF. (Besides, aircars may finally turn up now that they have become a joke. :-)

So what are the truly wretched things about "The Accomplice"? They're mainly things like missing personal computers, failing to draw the inevitable conclusions from the things that I did get right. There's the apparent sexism. There's the "TV tape cartridge" that must be manually threaded into the video tape recorder. There's . . . arghh, it's too embarrassing to go on. But you can read the story and see for yourself.

And yet, I have a soft spot in my heart for "The Accomplice." Nineteen-sixty-six seems a strange and alien time to me now; I can see myself peering out of it and wondering. I am very pleased the story has a chance to see daylight again.

(I did a little searching about the history of computer animation. Here is what I came up with in June 2001. I would be interested to learn of other references.
http://www.sun.com/960710/feature3/alice.html graphics
http://www.sun.com/960710/feature3/cg.html)

There was a thief on my staff. Hell. It was someone I trusted, too; it had to be.

Arnold Su grinned enthusiastically as he laid the proof on my desk. "Computer time is expensive, Mr. Royce," he pontificated. Now *that* was a discovery. "And someone has embezzled more than seventy hours on our 4D5 during the last year."

I raised my eyes prayerfully to the mural that covered three walls of my office. The holograph gave the three-dimensional illusion that we were perched among tall conifers somewhere in the Canadian Rockies. You'd never guess that my office is buried under the Royce building in Greater San Diego.

"God preserve me from your efficiency, Arnold. Seventy hours on the 4D5 computer is worth four million dollars. You're an extraordinary security officer; it only took you a year to discover that someone is robbing us blind."

Su was pained by my unjustified criticism. "It's someone with a private computer readout."

"You're pretty good at the obvious." Most computers, especially the really big ones like our 4D5, can be programmed by remote consoles in the offices of favored company researchers. Such use is automatically recorded for later review.

"So it must be someone highly placed in the company. Someone smart. Chief, he actually programmed the computer to cover up for him. The 4D5 has been keeping two sets of books to conceal the embezzlement from our weekly checks."

Of course there have been cases of computer-camouflaged embezzlement (usually of money) in the past—that's one reason why CPA's are computer technicians. However it takes a real expert to thoroughly cover his tracks. Evidently we were up against an expert. "How did you discover the theft, then, Arnie?"

Arnold's grin spread even further across his face. This was the question he had been waiting for. "Boss, you really don't appreciate me. I've been expecting something like this for a long time. My section has an agreement with Control Data Corporation. Every year we audit their computer complex with ours, and vice versa. That way the problem is reduced to a battle of the computers, and we can detect this sort of automated deception. But the crook started embezzling sometime after the 1992 audit, so he wasn't discovered until yesterday."

I picked up Arnold's report. "Any idea who the culprit is?" Four million dollars, I thought. If I ever got my hands on the crook who—no wonder our general efficiency had fallen off in the last year.

"Not the vaguest," Su replied, "except that he's a company VIP with computer privileges. Now if you had just let me bug the executive offices and washrooms . . ."

"You know, Arnie," I said slowly, "sometimes I think you would have been just as comfortable on Herr Himmler's staff as you are here."

Arnold turned red. "Sorry, Boss, I didn't mean—"

"Never mind." Su is a good man, the graduate of one of this country's best schools of business administration. It's just that he's an incurable snoop, which makes him, properly supervised, an excellent security officer.

Su continued, subdued, "We can't even reconstruct what sort of problems the computer was doing during those seventy hours. The thief did a magnificent job on that computer."

I looked down the valley in the mural. Someone I trusted had sold me out. I'd worked twenty years to make the name Royce synonymous with computers and to make Royce Technology, Inc., competitive with IBM and CDC. In that time, I've collected a lot of good men under one corporate roof. They are the backbone of Royce, more than I, with my high school diploma, ever was. And one of them was rotten. Who?

There was one individual who might be able to find that answer. I got up and started for the door. "We're going to see Howard."

"Prentice?" asked Su. He grabbed his report off my desk and followed me. "You don't think that he's responsible?" Arnold was genuinely shocked.

"Of course not," I said, locking the door to my office.

When we were out of earshot of my secretaries and their recording equipment I continued. "Whoever we're up against obviously knows computers inside and out. We can't catch him with old-fashioned automation techniques. We're going to have to get him by exploiting the human angle. Howard Prentice has been kicking around longer than both of us put together. He knows human nature, and he knows more ways to skin a sucker than we'll ever imagine. He makes the perfect investigator." I noticed the hurt look on Arnold's face and added quickly: "On a unique case like this."

It's only five minutes by aircar from Chula Vista to the Royce Research Labs at Oceanside. In fifteen minutes we were standing in the hall outside Prentice's lab. I prefer to see people in person rather than by phone—I get more out of them. But this time it backfired: Prentice wasn't in his lab, which was locked. I was starting back to the parking lot when Su stopped me.

"Just a minute, Boss." He produced a flat, metal plate and inserted it in the lock. "Master key," he explained confidentially. "Now we can wait for him in here."

I was too surprised to bawl him out for this latest invasion of privacy. Besides, he'll never grow up.

The room lighted up as we entered. Packed against one wall were the usual programming typers and TV screens. I also recognized a high-resolution video tape recorder and a picture reader. Stacked in orderly rows along the work benches were hundreds of Prentice's oil paintings. Sometimes I wondered whether he considered himself an artist or a scientist—though I didn't care what he did with his time as long as he completed assigned projects. Su was already rummaging among the paintings—admiring them I think.

Prentice couldn't be out for long. As a section chief he was in charge of thirty different computer labs. And right then his section was busy designing the optical and communications system for that probe NASA wanted to boost out toward Alpha Centauri A next year.

I sat down in the chair before the computer console and tried to relax.

The holograph on his desk caught my eye. It was a color pic of Howard and Moira taken on their diamond wedding anniversary. Moira must be more than ninety years old. Only one woman in a billion could look even faintly attractive after a haul like that—but tall and slim, somehow Moira managed it. She was holding Howard's arm like a fifteen-year-old who'd just discovered boys. Quite a gal; quite a man she had, too. Howard must be pushing ninety-five. You know, he personally worked for Thomas Edison? Fact. The man's like history. When the 1929 Depression came he was a top executive for some oil company out East. The Depression apparently soured him on industry. He spent the next forty years—an ordinary adult lifetime—in Greenwich Village as an artist-bum, a beatnik. Then, some time around 1970, he changed careers again. *He entered college.* If you're old enough, maybe you remember the headlines: **75-YR-OLD FROSH VOWS HE'LL GET PH.D.**—in math, no less. And he did it. Howard's been with me for fifteen years.

One of my best men. I tapped an impatient tattoo on the arms of the chair. But where the devil was he now? "Boss, this stuff is tremendous!" I stood up to see what Arnold was talking about. He was pointing at several paintings he had pulled out from the bottom of the pile. Su is quite an art and film fan. He has a tape collection of all films made since 1980, as well as a very large collection of paintings from all periods.

He had reason to admire Howard's paintings, though. Prentice is an excellent, maybe a great, painter. Though he's done many traditional abstractionist pieces, Howard has been a neo-realist ever since I've known him. Take the paintings in the lab; they were all clear and unambiguous as far as execution went. There were landscapes, portraits, interiors. But the landscapes were from no area in the real world. And the portraits were expressionless mugshots: face on, quarter face, profile. Not all of the subjects were even human. Every canvas was the same size. Over the years I often asked Howard about this, but he always answered with some line about artistic profundity. I don't think he even let us see everything he did.

Arnold had called me over to see three landscapes he had discovered. When he placed them side by side it was like a composite photo—a panoramic view. It was one of the most spectacular things I'd seen by Prentice.

When I looked at it, the lights in the room seemed to dim a little. In the picture it was night. A sickle moon lit a deep valley or mountain pass. Our viewpoint was halfway up the side of the valley. Scrubby brush and volcanic slag were visible nearby. Far away, down in the center of the valley, was a castle or fortress, its immense black structure outlined by the moonlight. Though vast and strong, somehow it was also decayed and diseased—a skull rotting in the earth. Around the castle were fields of purple flowers glimmering faintly with their own light (fluorescing paint?). But the flowers weren't beautiful—even at this distance they were fungi growing on death's decay.

I pulled my attention away from the landscape. It was the most hostile I'd seen by Prentice. And somehow it was familiar. I often got that "seen-before" feeling with Howard's stuff—though usually his landscapes provoked awe rather than fear. The picture would have been even more impressive if it had been painted on a single canvas rather than split up on separate ones.

Then I noticed the picture reader at the end of the bench. We use pic readers to program images directly into the logic of a computer. This is an expensive procedure since it preempts a lot of the computer's circuits. It's usually simpler to keep pictorial information on tape, but sometimes we want the computer to operate directly and continuously on information in a picture—to alter a perspective, say—and we have to use the reader.

A horrible suspicion was forming in my mind. I picked up one of the paintings and laid it on the flat glass plate at the top of the reader. It fit perfectly. Now I knew why all the paintings were the same size.

Forgetting Su, I reached up and pulled a heavy notebook off the shelf above the bench. I had to snoop. I had to find some legitimate excuse for the man I now suspected.

The notebook was a motion study. We use them when we have to program the computer on changing spatial rotations—as with complicated machinery; the computer has to know the position of every part of the machine at every instant in order to predict performance and detect bugs. The interior page was titled: *Vol. XIX—Hand Technik*. I riffled through the pages. There were thousands of rough sketches showing the human hand in every position. Beside each sketch was a numerical description of the motion from that position to the next. *Volume XIX?* Why, Prentice must have a separate notebook for facial expressions, a notebook for every class of motion! And it was all set for programming. His project—whatever it was—was huge. He must have been planning this for years. From the evidence in the lab it was certainly big enough to cost seventy hours of 4D5 time. Prentice was the rat all right. But why had he embezzled the time? And what had he done with it?

There was a noise from the doorway. Arnold looked up from the picture he had been admiring and said cheerfully, "Hi, Howard!"

"Hello." Prentice set his briefcase on the bench and hung up his jacket. Then he turned to look at me. "This is my private office, Bob," he said mildly.

I didn't bite. I was too mad for subtlety. "Prentice, you've got some explaining to do." I gestured at the paintings and the picture reader.

"Someone's been stealing 4D5 time, and I think it's you."

Prentice glanced at Su. "So you finally ran a cross-audit, eh, Arnold? Well, I knew I wouldn't have more than a year. I got what I gambled for."

Su looked even more surprised than I felt. Prentice had spent a whole year concealing the fraud, and now he was calmly confessing.

"Just what was worth four million dollars of Royce's time?" I snapped.

"Would you like to see?" He did not wait for an answer. "I've got one of the last tapes right here." He reached into his briefcase and pulled out a TV tape cartridge.

"Moira and I have always been appalled by the fact that so many art forms are beyond the means of a single artist. Take the film industry: most movies cost many millions of dollars and require the services of hundreds of artists—actors, directors, photographers." Prentice threaded the tape through the multiple heads of the videotape recorder. You'd think he had invited us over for home movies. The gall of the man. I didn't stop him though. I suppose I was curious. What could be worth a ruined career to Prentice?

"Anyway," he continued, "back around 1957, I saw a way to give filmmaking to the individual artist. Since then, everything Moira and I have done has been directed toward this goal. At first we didn't realize how complicated the job was and how far computers had to go before they could help us with what we wanted. But I got my degree, and we kept at it." He hooked the tape into the reception cartridge and snapped the cover into place. "With the aid of the 4D5 we've animated one of the great novels of the twentieth century."

"You've used the 4D5 to make a cartoon!" Arnold was obviously fascinated by the concept. He had completely forgotten that Prentice was talking about a crime.

For the first time since he had entered the lab, Prentice seemed annoyed. "Yes, I guess it is a cartoon—like da Vinci's Mona Lisa is a doodle. Cut the lights, will you, Arnold?"

The lights went out, and Prentice turned on the recorder. The TV screen on the wall came alive. I gasped. *Night. The landscape with the purple flowers.* But what a difference. This was a window on another world. If I had felt uneasy looking at the paintings, I felt terror now. Three tiny figures struggled up the side of the valley. Suddenly I knew why this scene was familiar. Prentice had animated Tolkien's *Lord of the Rings*! If you've ever taken high school English (and if you haven't, I'll hire you—my ego needs someone in this outfit with less education than I have), I'm sure you've read Tolkien's book. We were watching the scene where Frodo, Samwise, and Gollum come up the stairs to Kirth Ungol past the fortress Minas Morgul—the skull thing in the valley. Prentice's version was much more realistic and fearsome than anything I had ever imagined.

I realized Prentice was still talking. "Moira and I worked thirty years on the paintings, the motion studies, the script, the sound track; but without the 4D5 to integrate what we had created, we'd be left with a warehouse full of paintings and notebooks."

The three figures stopped to rest. Our viewpoint moved in for a close-up. The three were arguing in low, frightened tones. Now I knew why Prentice's portraits were expressionless; they were the patterns on which Prentice, through the 4D5, imposed emotion and movement.

This was no cartoon. The figures were fine portraits, come alive to argue in whispers. I could see Frodo's blank resignation, the fear in Samwise, the glittery green of Gollum's eyes as he fought with the other two. Yet it was all a synthesis of oil paintings and motion studies—the product of Howard's genius and the 4D5's analysis. Without a break in continuity, the "camera" dollied back to reveal the ancient stone stair that stretched high into the mountains. The three stood up and continued their long climb toward Shelob's Lair.

Click. The tape ended. Prentice turned on the lights. I sat dazed for a second, trying to bring myself back to the real world.

"That tape is just five minutes long," said Prentice. "The whole animation is more than four hours."

Su recovered first. "My God, Howard. That's tremendous. It's the greatest advance in art technique in fifty years."

"At least," agreed Prentice. "Now, anything a writer or painter can imagine can be staged."

"Sure," I said sarcastically, "as long as the painter is willing to steal four million dollars of computer time."

Prentice turned to me. "Not really, Bob. Computer time is only expensive because of the scarcity of 4D5-class computers and the number of problems that can't be solved except by the 4D5. On the basis of past progress, I'll wager that in five years you'll be selling computers as good as the 4D5 for less than ten thousand dollars. Anybody who really wants an animator will be able to have one."

"And you just couldn't wait."

He smiled, "That's right. I've waited thirty years. I don't know if I'll be around for another five."

"Well, I'm going to make you wish you'd taken the chance. When I get done with you, there'll be nothing left for the Tolkien estate to pick over."

Arnold broke in, "Just a second, Boss."

I turned on him angrily, "Look Su, can't you understand? Prentice has *stolen* four million dollars of *my money*!" My voice rose half an octave.

"It's your money I'm talking about, Chief. Did you ever see *Fantasia* or *Magica*?"

"Disney's feature-length animation? Yes."

"Do you have any idea what they cost?"

"Don't play games, Arnold. I know you're an expert. How much?"

"*Fantasia* was made way back in 1940. It cost Disney more than two million dollars. But when they got around to *Magica* thirty-five years later, the price tag had risen to twenty-seven million dollars, even though *Magica* is a much poorer job. Nowadays, almost any mainline picture—whether animation or with real actors—costs more than ten million dollars. Howard's actually discovered a *cheap* way of making films."

"Why didn't you just ask for the time then?" I asked Prentice.

Howard looked stubborn. He has his own peculiar brand of integrity. "Bob, do you honestly believe you would've said yes? I'm an artist. I may be a good researcher, but that was a means to an end. Moira and I had to do this, even though I knew it'd hurt Royce in the short run."

"Chief, it doesn't matter whether Howard planned this to help you or not. The point is, he's dropped a fortune in your lap."

When Arnold put it that way . . . Four million dollars wasn't too bad for a topnotch movie, and if Howard had had organized help, besides his wife, it might have cost a lot less. It would be at least eight years before we miniaturized computers like the 4D5 for the consumer market. Until then, filmmaking would remain the prerogative of the large organization. It had taken Howard years to perfect this technique, so we were way ahead of potential competition. Figuratively speaking, we were standing on the ground floor of a whole new industry.

Su saw that I was swayed. "Well?"

"Well," I said grudgingly, "I guess we're in the movie business." I didn't realize how true I spoke till we got that first Oscar.

THE PEDDLER'S APPRENTICE

For years, I have been fascinated by Fredric Brown's short story, "Letter to a Phoenix." What if a lone human survived beyond his civilization, and the next, and the next? Brown's protagonist was nearly immortal. A similar effect could be achieved by an ordinary human, using some kind of suspended animation. What motive could such a traveler have—beyond crazed curiosity? Perhaps I could have a merchant who traded across time intead of space. But my merchant could move in only one direction . . . and the problem of estimating "consumer demand" at the next port would be truly enormous.

I worked off and on with the idea in the late 1960s; I had part of the story written, but I couldn't push it through to an ending. I put the story aside, and this turned out to be the most clever thing I could have done.

From 1972 to 1979 I was married to Joan D. Vinge. Of course, we talked about our various projects all the time; it was a great pleasure to scheme with such a good writer. Yet for all our plot discussions, only once did we collaborate on a story: I showed Joan my "merchant out of time" fragment and told her my plans for how the story might end. We chatted it up, decided that a story "frame" was needed to hold the loose parts together. (I think this is one of the few times either of us has used that device.) Joan wrote the frame and the latter part of "The Peddler's Apprentice," then rewrote my draft. The result appears below. Keep in mind that up to a certain point I was writing (with some later revision by Joan), and after that it is Joan's writing. Can you spot the break?

Lord Buckry I of Fyffe lounged on his throne, watching his two youngest sons engaged in mock battle in the empty Audience Hall. The daggers were wooden but the rivalry was real, and the smaller boy was at a disadvantage. Lord Buckry tugged on a heavy gold earring; thin, brown-haired Hanaban was his private favorite. The boy took after his father both in appearance and turn of mind.

The lord of the Flatlands was a tall man, his own unkempt brown hair graying now at the temples. The blue eyes in his lean, foxlike face still perceived with disconcerting sharpness, though years of experience kept his own thoughts hidden. More than twenty years had passed since he had won control of his lands; he had not kept his precarious place as lord so long without good reason.

Now his eyes flashed rare approval as Hanaban cried. "Trace, look there!" and, as his brother turned, distracted, whacked him soundly on the chest.

"Gotcha!" Hanaban shrieked delightedly. Trace grimaced with disgust.

Their father chuckled, but his face changed suddenly as the sound of a commotion outside the chamber reached him. The heavy, windowed doors at the far end of the room burst open; the Flatlander courier shook off guards, crossed the high-ceilinged, echoing chamber and flung himself into a bow, his rifle clattering on the floor. "Your lordship!"

Lord Buckry snapped his fingers; his gaping children silently fled the room. "Get up," he said impatiently. "What in tarnation is this?"

"Your lordship." The courier raised a dusty face, wincing mentally at his lord's Highland drawl. "There's word the sea kingdoms have raised another army. They're crossing the coast mountains, and—"

"That ain't possible. We cleaned them out not half a year since."

"They've a lot of folk along the coast, your lordship." The horseman stood apologetically. "And Jayley Sharkstooth's made a pact this time with the Southlands."

Lord Buckry stiffened. "They've been at each other's throats long as I can remember." He frowned, pulling at his earring. "Only thing they've got in common is—me. Damn!"

He listened distractedly to the rider's report, then stood abruptly, dismissing the man as an afterthought. As the heavy doors of the hall slid shut he was already striding toward the elevator, past the shaft of the ballistic vehicle exit, unused for more than thirty years. His soft-soled Highlander boots made no sound on the cold polished floor.

From the parapet of his castle he could survey a wide stretch of his domain, the rich, utterly flat farmlands of the hundred-mile-wide valley—the lands the South and West were hungry for. The fields were dark now with turned earth, ready for the spring planting; it was no time to be calling up an army. He was sure his enemies were aware of that. The day was exceptionally clear, and at the eastern reaches of his sight he could make out the grayed purple wall of the mountains: the Highlands, that held his birthplace—and something more important to him now.

The dry wind ruffled his hair as he looked back across thirty years; his sunburned hands tightened on the seamless, ancient green-blackness of the parapet. "Damn you, Mr. Jagged," he said to the wind. "Where's your magic when I *need* it?"

THE PEDDLER CAME TO DARKWOOD CORNERS FROM THE EAST, ON WIM Buckry's seventeenth birthday. It was early summer, and Wim could still see sun flashing on snow up on the pine-wooded hill that towered above the Corners; the snowpack in the higher hills was melting at last, sluicing down gullies that stood dry through most of the year, changing Littlebig Creek into a cold, singing torrent tearing at the earth below the cabins on the north side of the road. Even a week ago the East Pass had lain under more than thirty feet of snow.

Something like silence came over the townspeople as they saw the peddler dragging his cart down the east road toward the Corners. His wagon was nearly ten feet tall and fifteen long, with carved, bright-painted wooden sides that bent sharply out over the wheels to meet a gabled roof. Wim gaped in wonder as he saw those wheels, spindly as willow wood yet over five feet across. Under the cart's weight they sank half a foot and more into the mud of the road, but cut through the mud without resistance, without leaving a rut.

Even so, the peddler was bent nearly double with the effort of pulling his load. The fellow was short and heavy, with skin a good deal darker than Wim had ever seen. His pointed black beard jutted at a determined angle as he staggered along the rutted track, up to his ankles in mud. Above his calves the tooled leather of his leggings gleamed black and clean. Several scrofulous dogs nosed warily around him as he plodded down the center of the road; he ignored them as he ignored the staring townsfolk.

Wim shoved his empty mug back at Ounze Rumpster, sitting nearest the tavern door. "More," he said. Ounze swore, got up from the steps, and disappeared into the tavern.

Wim's attention never left the peddler for an instant. As the dark man reached the widening in the road at the center of town, he pulled his wagon into the muddy morass where the Widow Henley's house had stood until the Littlebig Creek dragged it to destruction. The stranger had everyone's attention now. Even the town's smith had left his fire, and stood in his doorway gazing down the street at the peddler.

The peddler turned his back on them as he kicked an arresting gear down from the rear of the painted wagon and let it settle into the mud. He returned to the front of the cart and moved a small wheel set in the wood paneling: a narrow blue pennant sprouted from the peak of the gable and fluttered briskly; crisp and metallic, a pinging melody came from the wagon. That sound emptied the tavern and brought the re-mainder of the Corners' population onto the street. Ounze Rumpster nearly fell down the wooden steps in his haste to see the source of the music; he sat down heavily, handing the refilled mug to Wim. Wim ignored him.

As the peddler turned back to the crowd the eerie music stopped, and the creek sounded loud in the silence. Then the little man's surprising bass voice rumbled out at them, "Jagit Katchetooriantz is my name, and fine wrought goods is my trade. Needles, adze-heads, blades—you need 'em?" He pulled a latch on the wagon's wall and a panel swung out from its side, revealing rows of shining knifeblades and needles so fine Wim could see only glitter where they caught the sunlight. "Step right on up, folks. Take a look, take a feel. Tell me what they might be worth to you." There was no need to repeat the invitation—in seconds he was surrounded. As the townspeople closed around him, he mounted a small step set in the side of the wagon, so that he could still be seen over the crowd.

Wim's boys were on their feet; but he sat motionless, his sharp face intent. "Set down," he said, just loudly enough. "Your eyes is near busting out of your heads. They'd skin us right fast if we try anything here. There's too many. Set!" He gave the nearest of them, Bathecar Henley, a sideways kick in the shin; they all sat. "Gimme that big ring of yours, Sothead."

Ounze Rumpster's younger brother glared at him, then extended his jeweled fist from a filthy woolen cuff. "How come you're so feisty of a sudden, Wim?" He dropped the ring peevishly into the other's hand. Wim turned away without comment, passing the massive chunk of gold to Bathecar's plump, fair girlfriend.

"All right, Emmy, you just take yourself over to that wagon and see about buying us some knifeblades—not too long, say about so." He stretched his fingers. "And find out how they're fastened on the rack."

"Sure, Wim." She rose from the steps and minced away across the muddy road toward the crowd at the peddler's wagon. Wim grimaced, reflecting that the red knit dress Bathecar had bought her was perhaps too small.

The peddler's spiel continued, all but drowning out the sound of Littlebig Creek: "Just try your blades 'gin mine, friends. Go ahead. Nary a scratch you've made on mine, see? Now how much is it worth, friends? I'll take gold, silver. Or craft items. And I need a horse—lost my own, coming down those blamed trails." He waved toward the East Pass. The townspeople were packed tightly together now as each of them tried for a chance to test the gleaming metal, and to make some bid that would catch the peddler's fancy. Emmy wriggled expertly into the mass; in seconds Wim could see her red dress right at the front of the crowd. She was happily fondling the merchandise, competing with the rest for the stranger's attention.

Hanaban Kroy shifted his bulk on the hard wooden step. "Three gold pigs says that outlander is from down west. He just come in from the east to set us all to talking. Nobody makes knives like them east of the pass."

Wim nodded slightly. "Could be." He watched the peddler and fingered the thick gold earring half-hidden in his shaggy brown hair.

Across the road, the merchant was engaged in a four-way bidding session. Many of the townsfolk wanted to trade furs, or crossbows, but Jagit Katchetooriantz wasn't interested. This narrowed his potential clientele considerably. Even as he argued avidly with those below him, his quick dark eyes flickered up and down the street, took in the gang by the tavern, impaled Wim for a long, cold instant.

The peddler lifted several blades off the rack and handed them down, apparently receiving metal in return. Emmy got at least two. Then he raised his arms for quiet. "Folks, I'm really sorry for dropping in so sudden, when you all wasn't ready for me. Let's us quit now and try again tomorrow, when you can bring what you have to trade. I might even take on some furs. And bring horses, too, if you want to. Seein' as how I'm in need of one, I'll give two, maybe three adze-heads for a good horse or mule. All right?"

It wasn't. Several frustrated townsfolk tried to pry merchandise off the rack. Wim noticed that they were unsuccessful. The merchant pulled the lanyard at the front of the cart and the rack turned inward, returning carved wood paneling to the outside. As the crowd thinned, Wim saw Emmy, clutching two knives and a piece of print cloth, still talking earnestly to the peddler.

The peddler took a silvery chain from around his waist, passed it through the wheels of his cart and then around a nearby tree. Then he followed Emmy back across the road.

Ounze Rumpster snorted. "That sure is a teensy ketter. Betcha we would bust it right easy."

"Could be . . ." Wim nodded again, not listening. Anger turned his eyes to blue ice as Emmy led the peddler right to the tavern steps.

"Oh, Bathecar, just lookit the fine needles Mr. Ketchatoor sold me."

Sothead struggled to his feet. "You stupid little—little— We told you to buy knives. Knives! And you used my ring to buy needles!" He grabbed the cloth from Emmy's hands and began ripping it up.

"Hey—!" Emmy began to pound him in useless fury, clawing after her prize. "Bathecar, make him stop!" Bathecar and Ounze pulled Sothead down, retrieved needles and cloth. Emmy pouted, "Big lout."

Wim frowned and drank, his attention fixed on the peddler. The dark man stood looking from one gang member to another, hands loosely at his sides, smiling faintly; the calm black eyes missed nothing. Eyes like that didn't belong in the face of a fat peddler. Wim shifted uncomfortably, gnawed by sudden uncertainty. He shook it off. How many chances did you get up here, to try a contest where the outcome wasn't sure— He stood and thrust out his hand. "Wim Buckry's the name, Mr. Ketchatoor. Sorry about Sothead; he's drunk all the time, 'truth."

The peddler had to reach up slightly to shake his hand. "Folks mostly call me Jagit. Pleased to meet you. Miss Emmy here tells me you and your men sometimes hire out to protect folks such as me."

Behind him, Bathecar Henley was open-mouthed. Emmy simpered; every so often, she proved that she was not as stupid as she looked. Wim nodded judiciously. "We do, and it's surely worth it to have our service. There's a sight of thieves in these hills, but most of them will back down from six good bows." He glanced at Sothead. "Five good bows."

"Well then." The pudgy little man smiled blandly, and for a moment Wim wondered how he could ever have seen anything deadly in that face. "I'd like to give you some of my business."

AND SO THEY CAME DOWN OUT OF THE HIGH HILLS. IT WAS EARLY SUMMER, but in the Highlands more like a boisterous spring: Under the brilliant blue sky, green spread everywhere over the ground, nudging the dingy hummocks of melting snow and outcropping shelves of ancient granite. Full leaping streams sang down the alpine valleys, plunged over falls and rapids that smashed the water to white foam and spread it in glinting veils scarcely an inch deep over bedrock. The ragged peaks skirted with glacier fell farther and farther behind, yet the day grew no warmer; everywhere the chill water kept the air cool.

The peddler and his six "protectors" followed a winding course through deep soughing pine forest, broken by alpine meadows where bright star-like flowers bloomed and the short hummocky grass made their ankles ache with fatigue. They passed by marshes that even in the coolness swarmed with eager mosquitoes, and Wim's high moccasins squelched on the soft dank earth.

But by late afternoon the party had reached Witch Hollow Trail, and the way grew easier for the horse pulling the merchant's wagon. Somewhere ahead of them Ounze Rumpster kept the point position; off to the side were fat Hanaban, Bathecar, and Shorty, while Sothead Rumpster, now nearly sober, brought up the rear. In the Highlands even the robbers—particularly the robbers—journeyed with caution.

For most of the day Wim traveled silently, listening to the streaming water, the wind, the twittering birds among the pines—listening for sounds of human treachery. But it seemed they were alone. He had seen one farmer about four miles outside of Darkwood Corners and since then, no one.

Yesterday the peddler had questioned him about the area, and how many folk were in the vicinity of the Corners, what they did for a living. He'd seemed disappointed when he'd heard they were mostly poor, scattered farmers and trappers, saying his goods were more the kind to interest rich city folk. Wim had promptly allowed as how he was one of the few Highlanders who had ever been down into the Great Valley, all the way to the grand city of Fyffe; and that they'd be more than glad to guide him down into the Flatlands—for a price. If a little greed would conceal their real intentions, so much the better. And the peddler's partial payment, of strange, jewel-studded silver balls, had only added to the sincerity of their interest in his future plans.

Wim glanced over at the peddler, walking beside him near the dappled cart horse. Up close, the stranger seemed even more peculiar than at a distance. His straight black hair was cut with unbelievable precision at the base of his neck; Wim wondered if he'd set a bowl on his head and cut around it. And he smelled odd; not unpleasant, but more like old pine-needles than man. The silver thread stitched into the peddler's soft leather shirt was finer than Wim had ever seen. That would be a nice shirt to have—Wim tugged absently at the loops of bead and polished metal hanging against his own worn linen shirt.

Though short and heavy, the stranger walked briskly and didn't seem to tire; in fact, became friendlier and more talkative as the afternoon passed. But when they reached Witch Hollow he fell silent again, looking first at the unusual smoothness of the path, then up at the naked bedrock wall that jutted up at the side of the narrow trail.

They had walked for about half a mile when Wim volunteered, "This here's called Witch Hollow. There's a story, how once folk had magic to fly through the air in strange contraptions. One of them lost his magic hereabouts—up till twenty years ago, there was still a place you could see the bones, and pieces of steel, they say, all rusted up. Some say this trail through the holler ain't natural, either."

Jagit made no reply, but walked with his head down, his pointy black beard tucked into his chest. For the first time since they had begun the journey he seemed to lose interest in the scenery. At last he said, "How long you figure it's been since this flying contraption crashed here?"

Wim shrugged. "My granther heard the story from his own granther."

"Hmm. And that's all the . . . magic you've heard tell of?"

Wim decided not to tell the peddler what he knew about Fyffe. That might scare the little man into turning back, and force a premature confrontation. "Well, we have witches in these hills, like Widow Henley's cousin, but they're most of them fakes—least the ones I seen. Outside of them and the bad luck that folks claim follows sin"—a grin twitched his mouth—"well, I don't know of no magic. What was you expecting?"

Jagit shook his head. "Something more than a piddling failed witch, that's sure. The more I see of this country, the more I know it ain't the place I started out for."

They walked the next mile in silence. The trail pierced a granite ridge;

Wim glimpsed Hanaban high up on their left, paralleling the wagon. Red-faced with exertion, he waved briefly down at them, indicating no problems. Wim returned the signal, and returned to his thoughts about the peculiar little man who walked at his side. Somehow he kept remembering yesterday, Hanaban whining, "Wim, that there little man smells rotten to me. I say we should drop him," and the unease that had crept back into his own mind. Angry at himself as much as anything, he'd snapped, "You going yellow, Han? Just because a feller's strange don't mean he's got an evil eye." And known it hadn't convinced either of them . . .

Perhaps sensing the drift of his silence, or perhaps for some other reason, the peddler began to talk again. This time it was not of where he was going, however, but rather about himself, and where he had come from—a place called Sharn, a land of such incredible wonders that if Wim had heard the tale from someone else he would have laughed.

For Sharn was a land where true magicians ruled, where a flying contraption of steel would be remarkable only for its commonness. Sharn was an immense land—but a city also, a city without streets, a single gleaming sentient crystal that challenged the sky with spears of light. And the people of Sharn by their magic had become like gods; they wore clothing like gossamer, threw themselves across the sky in lightning while thunder followed, spoke to one another over miles. They settled beneath the warm seas of their borders, the weather obeyed them, and they remained young as long as they lived. And their magic made them dreadful warriors and mighty conquerors, for they could kill with scarcely more than a thought and a nod. If a mountain offended them they could destroy it in an instant. Wim thought of his Highlands, and shuddered, touching the bone hilt of the knife strapped to his leg.

Jagit had come to Sharn from a land still farther east, and much more primitive. He had stayed and learned what he could of Sharn's magic. The goods he brought to Sharn were popular and had brought high prices; during the time he had spent in the enchanted land he had acquired a small collection of the weaker Sharnish spells. Then he left, to seek a market for these acquisitions—some land where magic was known, but not so deeply as in Sharn.

As the peddler finished his tale, Wim saw that the sun had nearly reached the ridge of the hills to the west before them. He walked on for several minutes, squinting into the sunset for traces of lost Sharn.

The trail curved through ninety degrees, headed down across a small valley. Half hidden in the deepening shadow that now spread over the land, a precarious wooden bridge crossed a stream. Beyond the bridge the pines climbed the darkened hillside into sudden sunlight. Along the far ridgeline, not more than a mile away, ten or twelve immense, solitary trees caught the light, towering over the forest.

"Mr. Jagged, you're the best liar I ever met." Stubbornly Wim swallowed his awe, felt the peddler's unnerving eyes on his face as he pointed across the valley. "Just beyond that ridgeline's where we figure on putting up tonight. A place called Grandfather Grove. Could be you never seen trees that big even in Sharn!"

The peddler peered into the leveling sunlight. "Could be," he said. "I'd surely like to see such trees, anyhow."

They descended from the sunlight into rising darkness. Wim glimpsed Ounze's high felt hat as he walked out of the shadow on the other side of the valley, but none of the other gang members were visible. Wim and the peddler were forced to leave Witch Hollow Trail, and the going became more difficult for horse and wagon; but they reached the edge of the Grandfather Grove in less than half an hour, passing one of the soaring trees, and then two, and three. The dwarfed, spindly pines thinned and finally were gone. Ahead of them were only the grandfather trees, their shaggy striated trunks russet and gold in the dying light. The breeze that had crossed the valley with them, the roaring of the stream behind them, all sounds faded into cathedral silence, leaving only the cool, still air and the golden trees. Wim stopped and bent his head back to catch even a glimpse of the lowest branches, needled with pungent golden-green. This was their land, and he knew more than one tale that told of how the trees guarded it, kept pestiferous creatures away, kept the air cool and the soil fragrant and faintly moist throughout the summer.

"Over here." Hanaban's voice came muted from their left. They rounded the twenty-foot base of a tree, and found Hanaban and Bathecar, setting a small fire with kindling they had carried into the grove— Wim knew the bark of the grandfather trees was almost unburnable. The struggling blaze illuminated an immense pit of darkness behind them: the gutted trunk of an ancient grandfather tree, that formed a living cave-shelter for the night's camp.

By the time they had eaten and rotated lookouts, the sun had set. Wim smothered the fire, and the only light was from the sickle moon following the sun down into the west.

The peddler made no move to bed down, Wim noticed with growing irritation. He sat with legs crossed under him in the shadow of his wagon; motionless and wearing a dark coat against the chill, he was all but invisible, but Wim thought the little man was looking up into the sky. His silence stretched on, until Wim thought he would have to pretend to sleep himself before the peddler would. Finally Jagit stood and walked to the rear of his wagon. He opened a tiny hatch and removed two objects.

"What's them?" Wim asked, both curious and suspicious.

"Just a bit of harmless magic." He set one of the contraptions down on the ground, what seemed to be a long rod with a grip at one end. Wim came up to him, as he put the second object against his eye. The second contraption looked much more complex. It glinted, almost sparkled in the dim moonlight, and Wim thought he saw mirrors and strange rulings on its side. A tiny bubble floated along the side in the tube. The peddler stared through the gadget at the scattering of pale stars visible between the trees. At last he set the device back inside the wagon, and picked up the rod. Wim watched him cautiously as the other walked toward the cave tree; the rod looked too much like a weapon.

Jagit fiddled at the grip of the rod, and an eerie whine spread through the grove. The screaming faded into silence again, but Wim was sure that now the front of the rod was spinning. Jagit set it against the moon-silvered bark of the cave tree, and the tip of the rod began to bore effortlessly into the massive trunk.

Wim's voice quavered faintly. "That . . . that there some of your Sharnish magic, Mr. Jagged?"

The peddler chuckled softly, finishing his experiment. "It ain't hardly that. A Sharnish enchantment is a lot craftier, a lot simpler *looking*. This here's just a simple spell for reading the Signs."

"Um." Wim wavered almost visibly, his curiosity doing battle with his fear. There was a deep, precise hole in the cave tree. *Just because a fellow's strange, Han, don't mean he's got an evil eye. . . .* instinctively Wim's fingers crossed. Because it looked like the peddler might not be the world's biggest liar; and that meant— "Maybe I better check how the boys is settled."

When the peddler didn't answer, Wim turned and walked briskly away. At least he hoped that was how it looked; he felt like running. He passed Ounze, half-hidden behind a gigantic stump; Wim said nothing, but motioned for him to continue his surveillance of the peddler and his wagon. The rest stood waiting at a medium-sized grandfather tree nearly a hundred yards from the cave tree, the spot they had agreed on last night in Darkwood Corners. Wim moved silently across the springy ground, rounding the ruins of what must once have been one of the largest trees in the grove: a four-hundred-foot giant that disease and the years had brought crashing down. The great disc of its shattered root system rose more than thirty feet into the air, dwarfing him as he dropped down heavily beside Hanaban.

Bathecar Henley whispered. "Ounze and Sothead I left out as guards."

Wim nodded. "It don't hardly matter. We're not going to touch that peddler."

"What!" Bathecar's exclamation was loud with surprise. He lowered his voice only slightly as he continued. "One man? You're ascared of one man?"

Wim motioned threateningly for silence. "You heard me. Hanaban here was right—that Jagged is just too damn dangerous. He's a warlock, he's got an evil eye. And he's got some kind of knife back there that can cut clean through a grandfather tree! And the way he talks, that's just the least . . ."

The others' muttered curses cut him off. Only Hanaban Kroy kept silent.

"You're crazy, Wim," the hulking shadow of Shorty said. "We've walked fifteen miles today. And you're telling us it was for nothing! It'd be easier to farm for a living."

"We'll still get something, but it looks like we'll have to go honest for a while. I figure on guiding him down, say to where the leaf forests start, and then asking pretty please for half of what he promised us back at the Corners."

"I sure as hell ain't going to follow nobody that far down toward the Valley." Bathecar frowned.

"Well, then, you can just turn around and head back. I'm running this here gang, Bathecar, don't you forget it. We already got something out of this deal, them silver balls he give us as first payment—"

Something went *hisss* and then *thuk*: Hanaban sprawled forward, collapsed on the moonlit ground beyond the tree's shadow. A crossbow bolt protruded from his throat.

As Wim and Bathecar scrabbled for the cover of the rotting root system, Shorty rose and snarled, "That damn peddler!" It cost him his life; three arrows smashed into him where he stood, and he collapsed across Hanaban.

Wim heard their attackers closing in on them, noisily confident. From what he could see, he realized they were all armed with crossbows; his boys didn't stand a chance against odds like that. He burrowed his way deeper into the clawing roots, felt a string of beads snap and shower over his hand. Behind him Bathecar unslung his own crossbow and cocked it.

Wim looked over his shoulder, and then, for the length of a heartbeat, he saw the silvery white of the moon-painted landscape blaze with harshly shadowed blue brilliance. He shook his head, dazzled and wondering; until amazement was driven from his mind by sudden screams. He began to curse and pray at the same time.

But then their assailants had reached the fallen tree. Wim heard them thrusting into the roots, shrank back farther out of reach of their knives. Another scream echoed close and a voice remarked, "Hey, Rufe, I got the bastard as shot Rocker last fall."

A different voice answered, "That makes five then. Everybody excepting the peddler and Wim Buckry."

Wim held his breath, sweating. He recognized the second voice—Axl Bork, the oldest of the Bork brothers. For the last two years Wim's gang had cut into the Bork clan's habitual thievery, and up until tonight his quick-wittedness had kept them safe from the Borks' revenge. But tonight—how had he gone so wrong tonight? Damn that peddler!

He heard hands thrusting again among the roots, closer now. Then abruptly fingers caught in his hair. He pulled away, but another pair of hands joined the first, catching him by the hair and then the collar of his leather jerkin. He was hauled roughly from the tangle of roots and thrown down. He scrambled to his feet, was kicked in the stomach before he could run off. He fell gasping back onto the ground, felt his knife jerked from the sheath; three shadowy figures loomed over him. The nearest placed a heavy foot on his middle and said, "Well, Wim Buckry. You just lie still, boy. It's been a good night, even if we don't catch that peddler. You just got a little crazy with greed, boy. My cousins done killed every last one of your gang." Their laughter raked him. "Fifteen minutes and we done what we couldn't do the last two years.

"Lew, you take Wim here over to that cave tree. Once we find that peddler we're going to have us a little fun with the both of them."

Wim was pulled to his feet and then kicked, sprawling over the bodies of Hanaban and Shorty. He struggled to his feet and ran, only to be tripped and booted by another Bork. By the time he reached the cave tree his right arm hung useless at his side, and one eye was blind with warm sticky blood.

The Borks had tried to rekindle the campfire. Three of them stood around him in the wavering light; he listened to the rest searching among the trees. He wondered dismally why they couldn't find one wagon on open ground, when they'd found every one of his boys.

One of the younger cousins—scarcely more than fifteen—amused himself half-heartedly by thrusting glowing twigs at Wim's face. Wim slapped at him, missed, and at last one of the other Borks knocked the burning wood from the boy's hand; Wim remembered that Axl Bork claimed first rights against anyone who ran afoul of the gang. He squirmed back away from the fire and propped himself against the dry resilient trunk of the cave tree, stunned with pain and despair. Through one eye he could see the other Borks returning empty-handed from their search. He counted six Borks altogether, but by the feeble flame-cast light he couldn't make out their features. The only one he could have recognized for sure was Axl Bork, and his runty silhouette was missing. Two of the clansmen moved past him into the blackness of the cave tree's heart, he heard them get down on their hands and knees to crawl around the bend at the end of the passage. The peddler could have hidden back there, but his wagon would have filled the cave's entrance. Wim wondered again why the Borks couldn't find that wagon; and wished again that he'd never seen it at all.

The two men emerged from the tree just as Axl limped into the shrinking circle of firelight. The stubby bandit was at least forty years old, but through those forty years he had lost his share of fights, and walked slightly bent-over; Wim knew that his drooping hat covered a hairless skull marred with scars and even one dent. The eldest Bork cut close by the fire, heedlessly sending dust and unburnable bark into the guttering flames. "Awright, where in the mother-devil blazes you toad-gets been keeping your eyes? You was standing ever' whichway from this tree, you skewered every one of that damn Buckry gang excepting Wim here. Why ain't you found that peddler?"

"He's gone, Ax, gone." The boy who had been playing with Wim seemed to think that was a revelation. But Axl was not impressed, his backhand sent the boy up against the side of the tree.

One of the other silhouetted figures spoke hesitantly. "Don't go mis-believing me when I tell you this, Axl . . . but I was looking straight at this here cave tree when you went after them others. I could see that peddler clear as I see you now, standing right beside his wagon and his horse. Then all of a sudden there was this blue flash—I tell you. Ax, it was *bright*—and for a minute I couldn't see nothing, and then when I could again, why there wasn't hide nor hair of that outlander."

"Hmm." The elder Bork took this story without apparent anger. He scratched under his left armpit and began to shuffle around the dying fire toward where Wim lay. "Gone, eh? Just like that. He sounds like a right good prize. . . ." He reached suddenly and caught Wim by the collar, dragged him toward the fire. Stopping just inside the ring of light, he pulled Wim up close to his face. The wide, sagging brim of his hat threw his face into a hollow blackness that was somehow more terrible than any reality.

Seeing Wim's expression, he laughed raspingly, and did not turn his face toward the fire. "It's been a long time, Wim, that I been wanting to learn you a lesson. But now I can mix business and pleasure. We're just gonna burn you an inch at a time until you tell us where your friend lit out to."

WIM BARELY STIFLED THE WHIMPER HE FELT GROWING IN HIS THROAT; AXL Bork began to force his good hand inch by inch into the fire. All he wanted to do was to scream the truth, to tell them the peddler had never made him party to his magic. But he knew the truth would no more be accepted than his cries for mercy; the only way out was to lie— to lie better than he ever had before. The tales the peddler had told him during the day rose from his mind to shape his words, "Just go ahead. Ax! Get your fun. I know I'm good as dead. But so's all of you—" The grip stayed firm on his shoulders and neck, but the knotted hand stopped forcing him toward the fire. He felt his own hand scorching in the super-heated air above the embers. Desperately he forced the pain into the same place with his fear and ignored it. "Why d'you think me and my boys didn't lay a hand on that peddler all day long? Just so's we could get ambushed by you?" His laughter was slightly hysterical. "The truth is we was scared clean out of our wits! That foreigner's a warlock, he's too dangerous to go after. He can reach straight into your head, cloud your mind, make you see what just plain isn't. He can kill you, just by looking at you kinda mean-like. Why"—and true inspiration struck him—"why, he could even have killed one of your perty cousins, and be standing here right now pretending to be a Bork, and you'd never know it till he struck *you* dead. . . ."

Axl swore and ground Wim's hand into the embers. Even expecting it, Wim couldn't help himself; his scream was loud and shrill. After an instant as long as forever Axl pulled his hand from the heat. The motion stirred the embers, sending a final spurt of evil reddish flame up from the coals before the fire guttered out, leaving only dim ruby points to compete with the moonlight. For a long moment no one spoke; Wim bit his tongue to keep from moaning. The only sounds were a faint rustling breeze, hundreds of feet up among the leafy crowns of the grandfather trees—and the snort of a horse somewhere close by.

"Hey, we ain't got no horses," someone said uneasily.

Seven human figures stood in the immense spreading shadow of the cave tree, lined in faint silver by the setting moon. The Borks stood very still, watching one another—and then Wim realized what they must just have noticed themselves: there should have been eight Bork kinsmen. Somehow the peddler had eliminated one of the Borks during the attack, so silently, so quickly, that his loss had gone unnoticed. Wim shuddered, suddenly remembering a flare of unreal blue-white light, and the claims he had just made for the peddler. If one Bork could be killed so easily, why not two? In which case—

"He's here, pretending to be one of you!" Wim cried, his voice cracking.

And he could almost feel their terror echoing back and forth, from one to another, growing—until one of the shortest of the silhouettes broke and ran out into the moonlight. He got only about twenty feet, before he was brought down by a crossbow quarrel in the back. Even as the fugitive crumpled onto the soft, silver dirt a second crossbow thunked and another of the brothers fell dead across Wim's feet.

"That was Clyne, you . . . warlock!" More bows lowered around the circle.

"Hold on now!" shouted Axl. There were five Borks left standing; two bodies sprawled unmoving on the ground. "The peddler got us in his spell. We got to keep our sense and figure out which of us he's pretendin' to be."

"But Ax, he ain't just in disguise, we woulda seen which one he is . . . he—he can trick us into believing he's anybody!"

Trapped beneath the corpse, all Wim could see were five shadows against the night. Their faces were hidden from the light, and bulky clothing disguised any differences. He bit his lips against the least sound of pain; now was no time to remind the remaining Borks of Wim Buckry— But the agony of his hand pulsed up his arm until he felt a terrible dizziness wrench the blurring world away and his head drooped . . .

He opened his eyes again and saw that only three men stood now in the glade. Two more had died; the newest corpse still twitched on the ground.

Axl's voice was shrill with rage. "You . . . monster! You done tricked all of us into killing each other!"

"No, Ax, I had to shoot him. It was the peddler, I swear. Turn him over. Look! He shot Jan after you told us to hold off—"

"Warlock!" a third voice cried. "All of them dead—!" Two crossbows came down and fired simultaneously. Two men fell.

Axl stood silent and alone among the dead for a long moment. The moon had set at last, and the starlight was rare and faint through the shifting branches of the grandfather tree far overhead. Wim lay still as death, aware of the smell of blood and sweat and burned flesh. And the sound of footsteps, approaching. Sick with fear he looked up at the dark stubby form of Axl Bork.

"Still here? Good." A black-booted foot rolled the dead body from his legs. "Well, boy, you better leave me look at that hand." The voice belonged to Jagit Katchetooriantz.

"Uh." Wim began to tremble. "Uh. Mr. Jagged . . . is that . . . you?"

A light appeared in the hand of the peddler who had come from Sharn.

Wim fainted.

EARLY MORNING FILLED THE GRANDFATHER GROVE WITH DUSTY SHAFTS OF light. Wim Buckry sat propped against the cave tree's entrance, sipping awkwardly at a cup of something hot and bitter held in a bandaged hand. His other hand was tucked through his belt, to protect a sprained right shoulder. Silently he watched the peddler grooming the dappled cart horse; glanced for the tenth time around the sunlit grove, where no sign of the last night's events marred the quiet tranquility of the day. Like a bad dream the memory of his terror seemed unreal to him now, and he wondered if that was more witchery, like the drink that had eased the pains of his body. He looked down, where dried blood stained his pants. *I'll take care of the remains*, the peddler had said. It was real, all right—all of the Borks. And all of his boys. He thought wistfully for a moment of the jewelry that had gone into the ground with them; shied away from a deeper sense of loss beneath it.

The peddler returned to the campfire, kicked dirt over the blaze. He had had no trouble in getting a fire to burn. Wim drew his feet up; the dark eyes looked questioningly at his sullen face.

"Mr. Jagged"—there was no trace of mockery in that title now—"just what do you want from me?"

Jagit dusted off his leather shirt. "Well, Wim—I was thinking if you was up to it, maybe you'd want to go on with our agreement."

Wim raised his bandaged hand. "Wouldn't be much pertection, one cripple."

"But I don't know the way down through that there Valley, which you do."

Wim laughed incredulously. "I reckon you could fly over the moon on a broomstick and you wouldn't need no map. And you sure as hell don't need pertecting! Why'd you ever take us on, Mr. Jagged?" Grief sobered him suddenly, and realization— "You knew all along, didn't you? What we were fixing to do. You took us along so's you could watch us, and maybe scare us off. Well, you needn't be watching me no more. I—we already changed our minds, even before what happened with them Borks. We was fixing to take you on down like we said, all honest."

"I know that." The peddler nodded. "You ever hear an old saying, Wim: 'Two heads are better than one'? You can't never tell; you might just come in handy."

Wim shrugged ruefully, and wondered where the peddler ever heard that "old saying." "Well . . . ain't heard no better offers this morning."

THEY LEFT THE GRANDFATHER TREES AND CONTINUED THE DESCENT TOWARD the Great Valley. Throughout the early morning the pine woods continued to surround them, but as the morning wore on Wim noticed that the evergreens had given way to oak and sycamore, as the air lost its chill and much of its moisture. By late in the day he could catch glimpses between the trees of the green and amber vastness that was the valley floor, and pointed it out to the peddler. Jagit nodded, seeming pleased, and returned to the aimless humming that Wim suspected covered diabolical thoughts. He glanced again at the round, stubby merchant, the last man in the world a body'd suspect of magical powers. Which was perhaps what made them so convincing. . . . "Mr. Jagged? How'd you do it? Hex them Borks, I mean."

Jagit smiled and shook his head. "A good magician never tells how. What, maybe, but never how. You have to watch, and figure how for yourself. That's how you get to *be* a good magician."

Wim sighed, shifted his hand under his belt. "Reckon I don't want to know, then."

The peddler chuckled. "Fair enough."

Surreptitiously, Wim watched his every move for the rest of the day. After the evening meal the peddler again spent time at his wagon in the dark. Wim, sprawled exhausted by the campfire, saw the gleam of a warlock's wand but this time made no move to investigate, only crossing his fingers as a precautionary gesture. Inactivity had left him with too much else to consider. He stared fixedly into the flames, his hand smarting.

"Reckon we should be down to the valley floor in about an hour's travel, tomorrow. Then you say we head northwest, till we come to Fyffe?"

Wim started at the sound of the peddler's voice. "Oh . . . yeah, I reckon. Cut north and any road'll get you there; they all go to Fyffe."

" 'All roads lead to Fyffe'?" The peddler laughed unexpectedly, squatted by the fire.

Wim wondered what was funny. "Anybody can tell you the way from here, Mr. Jagged. I think come morning I'll be heading back; I . . . we never figured to come this far. Us hill folk don't much like going down into the Flatlands."

"Hm. I'm sorry to hear that, Wim." Jagit pushed another branch into the fire. "But somehow I'd figured it you'd really been to Fyffe?"

"Well, yeah. I was . . . almost." He looked up, surprised. "Three, four years ago, when I was hardly more'n a young'un, with my pa and some other men. See, my granther was the smith at Darkwood Corners, and he got hold of a gun—" And he found himself telling a peddler-man things everyone knew, and things he'd never told to anyone: How his grandfather had discovered gunpowder, how the Highlanders had plotted to overthrow the lords at Fyffe and take the rich valley farmlands for themselves. And how horsemen had come out from the city to meet them, with guns and magic, how the amber fields were torn and reddened and his pa had died when his homemade gun blew up in his face. How a bloody, tight-lipped boy returning alone to Darkwood Corners had filled its citizens with the fear of the Lord, and of the lords of Fyffe. . . . He sat twisting painfully at a golden earring. "And—I heard tell as how they got dark magics down there that we never even saw, so's to keep all the Flatlanders under a spell. . . . Maybe you oughta think again 'bout going down there too, Mr. Jagged."

"I thank you for the warning, Wim." Jagit nodded. "But I'll tell you— I'm a merchant by trade, and by inclination. If I can't sell my wares, I got no point in being, and I can't sell my wares in these hills."

"You ain't afraid they'll try to stop you?"

He smiled. "Well, now, I didn't say that. Their magic ain't up to Sharn, I'm pretty sure. But it is an unknown. . . . Who knows—they may turn out to be my best customers; lords are like to be free with their money." He looked at Wim with something like respect. "But like I say, two heads are better than one. I'm right sorry you won't be along. Mayhap in the morning we can settle accounts—"

In the morning the peddler hitched up his wagon and started down toward the Great Valley. And not really understanding why, Wim Buckry went with him.

EARLY IN THE DAY THEY LEFT THE WELCOME SHELTER OF THE LAST OAK FOREST, started across the open rolling hills of ripening wild grasses, until they struck a rutted track heading north. Wim stripped off his jerkin and loosened his shirt, his pale Highland skin turning red under the climbing sun of the Valley. The dark-skinned peddler in his leather shirt smiled at him, and Wim figured, annoyed, that he must enjoy the heat. By noon they reached the endless green corduroy fringe of the cultivated Flatlands, and with a jolt they found themselves on paved road. Jagit knelt and prodded the resilient surface before they continued on their way. Wim vaguely remembered the soft pavement, a bizarre luxury to Highland feet, stretching all the way to Fyffe; this time he noticed that in places the pavement was eaten away by time, and neatly patched with smooth-cut stone.

The peddler spoke little to him, only humming, apparently intent on searching out signs of Flatlander magic. *A good magician watches* . . . Wim forced himself to study the half-remembered landscape. The ripening fields and pasturelands blanketed the Valley to the limit of his sight, like an immense, living crazy-quilt in greens and gold, spread over the rich dark earth. In the distance he could see pale mist hovering over the fields, wondered if it was a trick of witchery or only the heat of the day. And he saw the Flatlanders at work in the fields by the road, well-fed and roughly dressed; tanned, placid faces that regarded their passage with the resigned disinterest that he would have expected of a plow-mule. Wim frowned.

"A rather curious lack of curiosity, I'd say, wouldn't you?" The peddler glanced at him. "They're going to make bad customers."

"Look at 'em!" Wim burst out angrily. "How could they do all of this? They ain't no better farmers 'n Highlanders; in the hills you work your hands to the bone to farm, and you get nothing, stones— And look at them, they're fat. How, Mr. Jagged?"

"How do *you* think they do it, Wim?"

"I—" He stopped. *Good magicians figure it out* . . . "Well—they got better land."

"True."

"And . . . there's magic."

"Is there now?"

"You saw it—them smooth-bedded streams, this here road; it ain't natural. But . . . they all look as how they're bewitched, themselves, just like I heard. Mayhap it's only the lords of Fyffe as have all the magic—it's them we got to watch for?" He crossed his fingers.

"Maybe so. It looks like they may be the only customers I'll have, too, if this doesn't change." The peddler's face was devoid of expression. "Quit crossing your fingers, Wim; the only thing that'll ever save you from is the respect of educated men."

Wim uncrossed his fingers. He walked on for several minutes before he realized the peddler spoke like a Flatlander now, as perfectly as he'd spoken the Highland talk before.

Late in the afternoon they came to a well, at one of the farm villages that centered like a hub in a great wheel of fields. The peddler dipped a cup into the dripping container, and then Wim took a gulp straight from the bucket. A taste of bitter metal filled his mouth, and he spat in dismay, looking back at the merchant. Jagit was passing his hand over— no, dropping something *into* the cup—and as Wim watched the water began to foam, and suddenly turned bright red. The peddler's black brows rose with interest, and he poured the water slowly out onto the ground. Wim blanched and wiped his mouth hard on his sleeve. "It *tastes* like poison!"

Jagit shook his head. "That's not poison you taste; I'd say farming's just polluted the water table some. But it is drugged." He watched the villagers standing with desultory murmurs around his wagon.

"Sheep." Wim's face twisted with disgust.

The peddler shrugged. "But all of them healthy, wealthy, and wise . . . well, healthy and wise, anyway . . . healthy—?" He moved away to offer his wares. There were few takers. As Wim returned to the wagon, taking a drink of stale mountainwater from the barrel on the back, he heard the little man muttering again, like an incantation, "Fyffe . . .Fyffe . . . Dyston-Fyffe, they call it here. . . . *District Town Five*? . . . Couldn't be." He frowned, oblivious. "But then again, why couldn't it—?"

For the rest of that day the peddler kept his thoughts to himself, looking strangely grim, only pronouncing an occasional curse in some incomprehensible language. And that night, as they camped, as Wim's weary mind unwillingly relived the loss of the only friends he had, he wondered if the dark silent stranger across the fire shared his loneliness; a peddler was always a stranger, even if he was a magician. "Mr. Jagged, you ever feel like going home?"

"Home?" Jagit glanced up. "Sometimes. Tonight, maybe. But I've come so far, I guess that would be impossible. When I got back, it'd all be gone." Suddenly through the flames his face looked very old. "What made it home was gone before I left. . . . But maybe I'll find it again, somewhere else, as I go."

"Yeah . . ." Wim nodded, understanding both more and less than he realized. He curled down into his blanket, oddly comforted, and went soundly to sleep.

MINOR WONDERS CONTINUED TO ASSAIL HIM ON THEIR JOURNEY, AND ALSO the question, "Why?"; until gradually Jagit's prodding transformed his superstitious awe into a cocky curiosity that sometimes made the peddler frown, though he made no comment.

Until the third morning, when Wim finally declared, "Everything's a trick, if'n you can see behind it, just like with them witches in the hills. Everything's got a—reason. I think there ain't no such thing as magic!"

Jagit fixed him with a long mild look, and the specter of the night in the Grandfather Grove seemed to flicker in the dark eyes. "You think not, eh?"

Wim looked down nervously.

"There's magic, all right, Wim; all around you here. Only now you're seeing it with a magician's eyes. Because there's a reason behind everything that happens; you may not know what it is, but it's there. And knowing that doesn't make the thing less magic, or strange, or terrible— it just makes it easier to deal with. That's something to keep in mind, wherever you are. . . . Also keep in mind that a *little* knowledge is a dangerous thing."

Wim nodded, chastened, felt his ears grow red as the peddler muttered, "So's a little ignorance . . ."

The afternoon of the third day showed them Fyffe, still a vague blot wavering against the horizon. Wim looked back over endless green toward the mountains, but they were hidden from him now by the yellow

Flatland haze. Peering ahead again toward the city, he was aware that the fear that had come with him into the Great Valley had grown less instead of greater as they followed the familiar-strange road to Fyffe. The dappled cart horse snorted loudly in the hot, dusty silence, and he realized it was the peddler with his wagon full of magics that gave him his newfound courage.

He smiled, flexing his burned hand. Jagit had never made any apology for what he'd done, but Wim was not such a hypocrite that he really expected one, under the circumstances. And the peddler had treated his wounds with potions, so that bruises began to fade and skin to heal almost while he watched. It was almost—

Wim's thoughts were interrupted as he stumbled on a rough patch in the road. The city, much closer now, lay stolidly among the fields in the lengthening shadows of the hot afternoon. He wondered in which field his father—abruptly turned his thoughts ahead again, noticing that the city was without walls or other visible signs of defense. *Why?* Mayhap because they had nothing to fear— He felt his body tighten with old terrors. But Jagit's former grim mood had seemingly dropped away as his goal drew near, as though he had reached some resolution. If the peddler was confident, then Wim would be, too. He looked on the city with magician's eyes; and it struck him that a more outlandish challenge had most likely never visited the lords of Fyffe.

They entered Fyffe, and though the peddler seemed almost disappointed, Wim tried to conceal his gaping with little success. The heavy stone and timber buildings crowded the cobble-patched street, rising up two and three stories to cut off his view of the fields. The street's edge was lined with shop fronts; windows of bull's-eyed glass and peeling painted signs advertised their trade. The levels above the shops, he supposed, were where the people lived. The weathered stone of the curbs had been worn to hollows from the tread of countless feet, and the idea of so many people—5,000, the peddler had guessed—in so little area made him shudder.

They made their way past dully-dressed, well-fed townsfolk and farmers finishing the day's commerce in the cooling afternoon. Wim caught snatches of sometimes heated bargaining, but he noticed that the town showed little more interest in the bizarre spectacle of himself and the peddler than had the folk they dealt with on their journey. Children at least ought to follow the bright wagon—he was vaguely disturbed to realize he'd scarcely seen any, here or anywhere, and those he saw were kept close by parents. It seemed the peddler's business would be no better here than in the hills after all. *Like hogs in a pen . . .* He glanced down the street, back over his shoulder. "Where's all the hogs?"

"What?" The peddler looked at him.

"It's clean. All them folk living here and there ain't any garbage. How can that be, less'n they keep hogs to eat it? But I don't see any hogs. Nor—hardly any young'uns."

"Hmm." The peddler shrugged, smiling. "Good questions. Maybe we should ask the lords of Fyffe."

Wim shook his head. Yet he had to admit that the city so far, for all its strangeness, had shown him no signs of any magic more powerful or grim than that he'd seen in the fields. Perhaps the lords of Fyffe weren't so fearsome as the tales claimed; their warriors weren't bewitched, but only better armed.

The street curved sharply, and ahead the clustered buildings gave way on an open square, filled with the covered stalls of a public marketplace. And beyond it— Wim stopped, staring. Beyond it, he knew, stood the dwelling of the lords of Fyffe. Twice as massive as any building he had seen, its pilastered green-black walls reflected the square like a dark, malevolent mirror. The building had the solidity of a thing that had grown from the earth, a permanence that made the town itself seem ephemeral. Now, he knew, he looked on the house for magic that might match the peddler and Sharn.

Beside him, Jagit's smile was genuine and unreadable. "Pardon me, ma'am," the peddler stopped a passing woman and child, "but we're strangers. What's that building there called?"

"Why, that's Government House." The woman looked only mildly surprised. Wim admired her stocking-covered ankles.

"I see. And what do they do there?"

She pulled her little girl absently back from the wagon. "That's where the governors are. Folks go there with petitions and such. They—govern, I suppose. Lissy, keep away from that dusty beast."

"Thank you, ma'am. And could I show you—"

"Not today. Come on, child, we'll be late."

The peddler bowed in congenial exasperation as she moved on. Wim sighed, and he shook his head. "Hardly a market for Sharnish wonders here, either, I begin to think. I may have outfoxed myself for once. Looks like my only choice is to pay a call on your lords of Fyffe over there; I might still have a thing or two to interest them." His eyes narrowed in appraisal as he looked across the square.

At a grunt of disapproval from Wim, Jagit glanced back, gestured at the lengthening shadows. "Too late to start selling now, anyway. What do you say we just take a look—" Suddenly he fell silent.

Wim turned. A group of half a dozen dour-faced men were approaching them; the leader bore a crest on his stiff brimmed hat that Wim remembered. They were unslinging guns from their shoulders. Wim's question choked off as they quietly circled the wagon, cut him off from the peddler. The militiaman addressed Jagit, faintly disdainful. "The Governors—"

Wim seized the barrel of the nearest rifle, slinging its owner into the man standing next to him. He wrenched the gun free and brought it down on the head of a third gaping guard.

"Wim!" He froze at the sound of the peddler's voice, turned back. "Drop the gun." The peddler stood unresisting beside his wagon. And the three remaining guns were pointing at Wim Buckry. Face filled with angry betrayal, he threw down the rifle.

"Tie the hillbilly up. . . . The Governors require a few words with you two, peddler, as I was saying. You'll come with us." The militia leader stood back, unperturbed, as his townsman guards got to their feet.

Wim winced as his hands were bound roughly before him, but there was no vindictiveness on the guard's bruised face. Pushed forward to walk with the peddler, he muttered bitterly, "Whyn't you use your magic!"

Jagit shook his head. "Would've been bad for business. After all, the lords of Fyffe have come to *me*."

Wim crossed his fingers, deliberately, as they climbed the green-black steps of Government House.

The hours stretched interminably in the windowless, featureless room where they were left to wait, and Wim soon tired of staring at the evenness of the walls and the smokeless lamps. The peddler sat fiddling with small items left in his pockets; but Wim had begun to doze in spite of himself by the time guards returned at last, to take them to their long-delayed audience with the lords of Fyffe.

The guards left them to the lone man who rose, smiling, from behind a tawny expanse of desk as they entered the green-walled room. "Well, at last!" He was in his late fifties and plainly dressed like the townsmen, about Wim's height but heavier, with graying hair. Wim saw that the smiling face held none of the dullness of their captors' faces. "I'm Charl Aydricks, representative of the World Government. My apologies for keeping you waiting, but I was—out of town. We've been following your progress with some interest."

Wim wondered what in tarnation this poor-man governor took himself for, claiming the Flatlands was the whole world. He glanced past Aydricks into the unimpressive, lamp-lit room. On the governor's desk he noticed the only sign of a lord's riches he'd yet seen—a curious ball of inlaid metals, mostly blue but blotched with brown and green, fixed on a golden stand. He wondered with more interest where the other

lords of Fyffe might be; Aydricks was alone, without even guards . . .
Wim suddenly remembered that whatever this man wasn't, he was a
magician, no less than the peddler.

Jagit made a polite bow. "Jagit Katchetooriantz, at your service. Merchant by trade, and flattered by the interest. This is my apprentice—"

"—Wim Buckry." The governor's appraising glance moved unexpectedly to Wim. "Yes, we remember you, Wim. I must say I'm surprised to
see you here again. But pleased—we've been wanting to get ahold of
you." A look of too much interest crossed Aydricks' face.

Wim eyed the closed door with longing.

"Please be seated." The governor returned to his desk. "We rarely get
such . . . intriguing visitors—"

Jagit took a seat calmly, and Wim dropped into the second chair,
knees suddenly weak. As he settled into the softness he felt a sourceless
pressure bearing down on him, lunged upward like a frightened colt
only to be forced back into the seat. Panting, he felt the pressure ease
as he collapsed in defeat.

Jagit looked at him with sympathy before glancing back at the governor; Wim saw the peddler's fingers twitch impotently on the chair-
arm. "Surely you don't consider us a threat?" His voice was faintly
mocking.

The governor's congeniality stopped short of his eyes. "We know
about the forces you were using in the Grandfather Grove."

"Do you now! That's what I'd hoped." Jagit met the gaze and held it.
"Then I'm obviously in the presence of some technological sophistication, at last. I have some items of trade that might interest you. . . ."

"You may be sure they'll receive our attention. But let's just be honest
with each other, shall we? You're no more a peddler than I am; not
with what we've seen you do. And if you'd really come from the east—
from anywhere—I'd know about it; our communications network is
excellent. You simply appeared from nowhere, in the Highlands Preserve. And it really was nowhere on this earth, wasn't it?"

Jagit said nothing, looking expectant. Wim stared fixedly at the tex-
tured green of the wall, trying to forget that he was witness to a debate
of warlocks.

Aydricks stirred impatiently. "From nowhere on this earth. Our moon
colony is long gone; that means no planet in this system. Which leaves
the Lost Colonies—you've come from one of the empire's colony
worlds, from another star system, Jagit; and if you expected that to
surprise us after all this time, you're mistaken."

Jagit attempted a shrug. "No—I didn't expect that, frankly. But I
didn't expect any of the rest of this, either; things haven't turned out
as I'd planned at all. . . ."

Wim listened in spite of himself, in silent wonder. Were there worlds beyond his own, that were no more than sparks in the black vastness of earth's night? Was that where Sharn was, then, with its wonders; beyond the sky, where folks said was heaven—?

". . . Obviously," the governor was saying, "you're a precedent-shattering threat to the World Government. Because this is a *world* government, and it has maintained peace and stability over millennia. Our space defense system sees to it that—outsiders don't upset that peace. At least it always has until now; you're the first person to penetrate our system, and we don't even know how you did it. That's what we want to know—*must* know, Jagit, not who you represent, or where, or even why, so much as *how*. We can't allow anything to disrupt our stability." Aydricks leaned forward across his desk; his hand tightened protectively over the stand of the strange metal globe. His affability had disappeared entirely, and Wim felt his own hopes sink, realizing the governor somehow knew the peddler's every secret. Jagit wasn't infallible, and this time he had let himself be trapped.

But Jagit seemed undismayed. "If you value your stability that much, then I'd say it's time somebody did disturb it."

"That's to be expected." Aydricks sat back, his expression relaxing into contempt. "But you won't be the one. We've had ten thousand years to perfect our system, and in that time no one else has succeeded in upsetting it. We've put an end at last to all the millennia of destructive waste on this world. . . ."

Ten thousand years—? As Aydricks spoke, Wim groped to understand a second truth that tore at the very roots of his comprehension:

For the history of mankind stretched back wonder on wonder for unimaginable thousands of years, through tremendous cycles filled with lesser cycles. Civilization reached highs where every dream was made a reality and humanity sent offshoots to the stars, only to fall back, through its own folly, into abysses of loss when men forgot their humanity and reality became a nightmare. Then slowly the cycle would change again, and in time mankind would reach new heights, that paradoxically it could never maintain. Always men seemed unable in the midst of their creation to resist the urge to destroy, and always they found the means to destroy utterly.

Until the end of the last great cyclical empire, when a group among the ruling class saw that a new decline was imminent, and acted to prevent it. They had forced the world into a new order, one of patternless stability at a low level, and had stopped it there. ". . . And because of us that state, free from strife and suffering, has continued for ten thousand years, unchanged. Literally unchanged. I am one of the original founders of the World Government."

WIM LOOKED UNBELIEVINGLY INTO THE SMILING, UNREMARKABLE FACE; found the eyes of a fanatic and incredible age.

"You're well preserved," Jagit said.

The governor burst into honest laughter. "This isn't my original body. By using our computer network we're able to transfer our memories intact into the body of an 'heir': someone from the general population, young and full of potential. As long as the individual's personality is compatible, it's absorbed into the greater whole, and he becomes a re-vitalizing part of us. That's why I've been keeping track of Wim, here; he has traits that should make him an excellent governor." The too-interested smile showed on the governor's face again.

Wim's bound hands tightened into fists—the invisible pressure forced him back down into the seat, his face stricken.

Aydricks watched him, amused. "Technological initiative and personal aggressiveness are key factors that lead to an unstable society. Since, to keep stability, we have to suppress those factors in the population, we keep control groups free from interference—like the hill folk, the High-landers—to give us a dependable source of the personality types we need ourselves.

"But the system as a whole really is very well designed. Our computer network provides us with our continuity, with the technology, com-munications, and—sources of power we need to maintain stability. We in turn ensure the computer's continuity, since we preserve the knowl-edge to keep it functioning. There's no reason why the system can't go on forever."

Wim looked toward the peddler for some sign of reassurance; but found a grimness that made him look away again as Jagit said, "And you think that's a feat I should appreciate: that you've manipulated the fate of every being on this planet for ten thousand years, to your own ends, and that you plan to go on doing it indefinitely?"

"But it's for their own good, can't you see that? We ask nothing from this, no profit for ourselves, no reward other than knowing that hu-manity will never be able to throw itself into barbarism again, that the cycle of destructive waste, of rise and fall, has finally been stopped on earth. The people are secure, their world is stable, they know it will be safe for future generations. Could your own world claim as much? Think of the years that must have passed on your journey here—would you even have a civilization to return to by now?"

Wim saw Jagit forcibly relax; the peddler's smile reappeared, full of irony. "But the fact remains that a cycle of rise and fall is the natural order of things—life and death, if you want to call it that. It gives hu-manity a chance to reach new heights, and gives an old order a clean death. Stasis is a coma—no lows, but no highs either, no *choice*. Some-how I think that Sharn would have preferred a clean death to this—"

"Sharn? What do you know about the old empire?" The governor leaned forward, complaisance lost.

"Sharn—?" Wim's bewilderment was lost on the air.

"They knew everything about Sharn, where I come from. The crystal city with rot at its heart, the Games of Three. They were even seeing the trends that would lead to this, though they had no idea it would prove so eminently successful."

"Well, this gets more and more interesting." The governor's voice hardened. "Considering that there should be no way someone from out-side could have known of the last years of the empire. But I suspect we'll only continue to raise more questions this way. I think it's time we got some answers."

Wim slumped in his seat, visions of torture leaping into his mind. But the governor only left his desk, passing Wim with a glance that sug-gested hunger, and placed a shining band of filigreed metal on Jagit's head.

"You may be surprised at what you get." Jagit's expression remained calm, but Wim thought strain tightened his voice.

The governor returned to his chair. "Oh, I don't think so. I've just linked you into our computer net—"

Abruptly Jagit went rigid with surprise, settled back into a half-smile; but not before Aydricks had seen the change. "Once it gets into your mind you'll have considerable difficulty concealing anything at all. It's quick and always effective; though unfortunately I can't guarantee that it won't drive you crazy."

The peddler's smile faded. "How civilized," he said quietly. He met Wim's questioning eyes. "Well, Wim, you remember what I showed you. And crossing your fingers didn't help, did it?"

Wim shook his head. "Whatever you say, Mr. Jagged. . . ." He sus-pected he'd never have an opportunity to remember anything.

Suddenly the peddler gasped, and his eyes closed, his body went limp in the seat. "Mr. Jagged—?" But there was no response. Alone, Wim wondered numbly what sort of terrible enchantment the metal crown held, and whether it would hurt when the computer—whatever that was—swallowed his own soul.

"Are you monitoring? All districts? Direct hookup, yes." The governor seemed to be speaking to his desk. He hesitated as though listening, then stared into space.

Wim sagged fatalistically against his chair, past horror now, ignoring—and ignored by—the two entranced men. Silence stretched in the green room. Then the light in the room flickered and dimmed momentarily.

Wim's eyes widened as he felt the unseen pressure that held him down weaken slightly, then return with the lighting. The governor frowned at nothing, still staring into space. Wim began ineffectually to twist at his bound hands. However the magic worked in this room, it had just stopped working; if it stopped again he'd be ready. . . . He glanced at Jagit. Was there a smile—?"

"District Eighteen here. Aydricks, what is this?"

Wim shuddered. The live disembodied head of a red-haired youth had just appeared in a patch of sudden brightness by the wall. The governor turned blinking toward the ghost.

"Our reception's getting garbled. This data can't be right, it says he's . . ." The ghostly face wavered and the voice was drowned in a sound like water rushing. ". . . it, what's wrong with the transmission? Is he linked up directly? We aren't getting anything now—"

Two more faces—one old, with skin even darker than the peddler's, and one a middle-aged woman—appeared in the wall, protesting. And Wim realized then that he saw the other lords of Fyffe—and truly of the world—here and yet not here, transported by their magic from the far ends of the earth. The red-haired ghost peered at Wim, who shrank away from the angry, young-old eyes, then looked past to Jagit. The frown grew fixed and then puzzled, was transformed into incredulity. "No, that's impossible!"

"What is it?" Aydricks looked harassed.

"I know that man."

The black-haired woman turned as though she could see him. "What do you mean you—"

"I know that man too!" Another dark face appeared. "From Sharn, from the empire. But . . . after ten thousand years, how can he be the *same* . . . Aydricks! Remember the Primitive Arts man, he was famous, he spent . . ." the voice blurred, ". . . got to get him out of the comm system! He knows the comm-sat codes, he can—" The ghostly face dematerialized entirely.

Aydricks looked wildly at the unmoving peddler, back at the remaining governors.

Wim saw more faces appear, and another face flicker out; *the same man* . . .

"Stop him, Aydricks!" The woman's voice rose. "He'll ruin us. He's altering the comm codes, killing the tie-up!"

"I can't cut him off!"

"He's into my link now, I'm losing con—" The red-haired ghost disappeared.

"Stop him, Aydricks, or we'll burn out Fyffe!"

"Jagged! Look out!" Wim struggled against his invisible bonds as he saw the governor reach with grim resolution for the colored metal globe on his desk. He knew Aydricks meant to bash in the peddler's skull, and the helpless body in the chair couldn't stop him. "Mr. Jagged, wake up!" Desperately Wim stuck out his feet as Aydricks passed; the governor stumbled. Another face disappeared from the wall, and the lights went out. Wim slid from the chair, free and groping awkwardly for a knife he no longer had. Under the faltering gaze of the ghosts in the wall, Aydricks fumbled toward Jagit.

Wim grabbed at Aydricks's feet just as the light returned, catching an ankle. The governor turned back, cursing, to kick at him, but Wim was already up, leaping away from a blow with the heavy statue.

"Aydricks, stop the peddler!"

Full of sudden fury, Wim gasped, "Damn you, you won't stop it this time!" As the governor turned away Wim flung himself against the other's back, staggering him, and hooked his bound hands over Aydricks's head. Aydricks fought to pull him loose, dropping the globe as he threw himself backward to slam his attacker against the desk. Wim groaned as his backbone grated against the desk edge, and lost his balance. He brought his knee up as he fell; there was a sharp *crack* as the governor landed beside him, and lay still. Wim got to his knees; the ancient eyes stabbed him with accusation and fear, "No. Oh, *no*." The eyes glazed.

A week after his seventeenth birthday, Wim Buckry had killed a ten-thousand-year-old man. And, unknowingly, helped to destroy an empire. The room was quiet; the last of the governors had faded from the wall. Wim got slowly to his feet, his mouth pulled back in a grin of revulsion. All the magic in the world hadn't done this warlock any good. He moved to where Jagit still sat entranced, lifted his hands to pull the metal crown off and break the spell. And hesitated, suddenly unsure of himself. Would breaking the spell wake the peddler, or kill him? They had to get out of here; but Jagit was somehow fighting the bewitchment, that much he understood, and if he stopped him now—His hands dropped, he stood irresolutely, waiting. And waiting.

His hands reached again for the metal band, twitching with indecision; jerked back as Jagit suddenly smiled at him. The dark eyes opened and the peddler sat forward, taking the metal band gently from his own head with a sigh. "I'm glad you waited. You'll probably never know how glad." Wim's grin became real, and relieved.

Jagit got unsteadily to his feet, glanced at Aydricks's body and shook his head; his face was haggard. "Said you might be a help, didn't I?" Wim stood phlegmatically while the peddler who was as old as Sharn itself unfastened the cords on his raw wrists. "I'd say our business is finished. You ready to get out of here? We don't have much time."

Wim started for the door in response, opened it, and came face-to-face with the unsummoned guard standing in the hall. His fist connected with the gaping jaw; the guard's knees buckled and he dropped to the floor, unconscious. Wim picked up the guard's rifle as Jagit appeared beside him, motioning him down the dim hallway.

"Where is everybody?"

"Let's hope they're home in bed; it's four-thirty in the morning. There shouldn't be any alarms."

Wim laughed giddily. "This's a sight easier than getting away from the Borks!"

"We're not away yet; we may be too late already. Those faces on the wall were trying to drop a—piece of sun on Fyffe. I think I stopped them, but I don't know for sure. If it wasn't a total success, I don't want to find out the hard way." He led Wim back down the wide stairway, into the empty hall where petitioners had gathered during the day. Wim started across the echoing floor but Jagit called him back, peering at something on the wall; they went down another flight into a well of darkness, guided by the peddler's magic light. At the foot of the stairs the way was blocked by a door, solidly shut. Jagit looked chagrined, then suddenly the beam of his light shone blue; he flashed it against a metal plate set in the door. The door slid back and he went through it.

Wim followed him, into a cramped, softly glowing cubicle nearly filled by three heavily padded seats around a peculiar table. Wim noticed they seemed to be bolted to the floor, and suddenly felt claustrophobic.

"Get into a seat, Wim. Thank God I was right about this tower being a ballistic exit. Strap in, because we're about to use it." He began to push lighted buttons on the table before him.

Wim fumbled with the restraining straps, afraid to wonder what the peddler thought they were doing, as a heavy inner door shut the room off from the outside. Why weren't they out of the building, running? How could this— Something pressed him down into the seat cushions like a gentle, insistent hand. His first thought was of another trap; but as the pressure continued, he realized this was something new. And then, glancing up past Jagit's intent face, he saw that instead of blank walls, they were now surrounded by the starry sky of night. He leaned forward—and below his feet was the town of Fyffe, shrinking away with every heartbeat, disappearing into the greater darkness. He saw what the eagle saw . . . he was flying. He sat back again, feeling for the re-assuring hardness of the invisible floor, only to discover suddenly that his feet no longer touched it. There was no pressure bearing him down now, there was nothing at all. His body drifted against the restraining straps, lighter than a bird. A small sound of incredulous wonder escaped him as he stared out at the unexpected stars.

And saw a brightness begin to grow at the opaque line of the horizon, spreading and creeping upward second by second, blotting out the stars with the fragile hues of dawn. The sun's flaming face thrust itself up past the edge of the world, making him squint, rising with arcane speed and uncanny brilliance into a sky that remained stubbornly black with night. At last the whole sphere of the sun was revealed, and continued to climb in the midnight sky while now Wim could see a thin streak of sky-blue stretched along the horizon, left behind with the citron glow of dawn still lighting its center. Above the line in darkness the sun wore the pointed crown of a star that dimmed all others, and below it he could see the world at the horizon's edge moving into day. And the horizon did not lie absolutely flat, but was bowing gently downward now at the sides. . . . Below his feet was still the utter darkness that had swallowed Fyffe. He sighed.

"Quite a view." Jagit sat back from the glowing table, drifting slightly above his seat, a tired smile on his face.

"You see it too?" Wim said hoarsely.

The peddler nodded. "I felt the same way, the first time. I guess everyone always has. Every time civilization has gained space flight, it's been rewarded again by that sight."

Wim said nothing, unable to find the words. His view of the bowed horizon had changed subtly, and now as he watched there came a further change—the sun began, slowly but perceptibly, to move backward down its track, sinking once more toward the point of dawn that had given it birth. Or, he suddenly saw, it was they who were slipping, back down from the heights of glory into his world's darkness once more. Wim waited while the sun sank from the black and alien sky, setting where it had risen, its afterglow reabsorbed into night as the edge of the world blocked his vision again. He dropped to the seat of his chair, as though the world had reclaimed him, and the stars reappeared. A heavy lurch, like a blow, shook the cubicle, and then all motion stopped.

He sat still, not understanding, as the door slid back in darkness and a breath of cold, sharp air filled the tiny room. Beyond the doorway was darkness again, but he knew it was not the night of a building hallway.

Jagit fumbled wearily with the restraining straps on his seat. "Home the same day . . ."

Wim didn't wait, but driven by instinct freed himself and went to the doorway. And jerked to a stop as he discovered they were no longer at ground level. His feet found the ladder, and as he stepped down from its bottom rung he heard and felt the gritty shifting of gravel. The only other sounds were the sigh of the icy wind, and water lapping. As his eyes adjusted they told him what his other senses already knew—that he was home. Not Darkwood Corners, but somewhere in his own cruelly beautiful Highlands. Fanged shadow peaks rose up on either hand, blotting out the stars, but more stars shone in the smooth waters of the lake; they shivered slightly, as he shivered in the cold breeze, clammy with sweat under his thin shirt. He stood on the rubble of a mountain pass somewhere above the treeline, and in the east the gash between the peaks showed pinkish-gray with returning day.

Behind him he heard Jagit, and turned to see the peddler climbing slowly down the few steps to the ground. From outside, the magician's chamber was the shape of a truncated rifle bullet. Jagit carried the guard's stolen rifle, leaning on it now like a walking stick. "Well, my navigation hasn't failed me yet." He rubbed his eyes, stretched.

Wim recalled making a certain comment about flying over the moon on a broomstick, too long ago, and looked again at the dawn, this time progressing formally and peacefully up a lightening sky. "We flew here. Didn't we, Mr. Jagged?" His teeth chattered. "Like a bird. Only . . . we f-flew right off the world." He stopped, awed by his own revelation. For a moment a lifetime of superstitious dread cried that he had no right to know of the things he had seen, or to believe— The words burst out in a defiant rush. "That's it. Right off the world. And . . . and it's all true: I heard how the world's round like a stone. It must be true, how there's other worlds, that's what you said back there, with people just like here; I seen it, the sun's like all them other stars, only it's bigger. . . ." He frowned. "It's—closer? I—"

Jagit was grinning, his teeth showed white in his beard. "Magician, first-class."

Wim looked back up into the sky. "If that don't beat all—" he said softly. Then, struck by more practical matters, he said. "What about them ghosts? Are they going to come after us?"

Jagit shook his head. "No. I think I laid those ghosts to rest pretty permanently. I changed the code words in their communications system. A good part of it is totally unusable now. Their computer net is broken up, and their space defense system must be out for good, because they didn't destroy Fyffe. I'd say the World Government is finished; they don't know it yet, and they may not go for a few hundred years, but they'll go in the end. Their grand 'stability' machine has a monkey wrench in its works at last. . . . They won't be around to use their magic in these parts anymore, I expect."

Wim considered, and then looked hopeful. "You going to take over back there, Mr. Jagged? Use your magic on them Flatlanders? We could—"

But the peddler shook his head. "No, I'm afraid that just doesn't interest me, Wim. All I really wanted was to break the hold those other magician sorts had on this world; and I've done that already."

"Then . . . you mean you really did all that, you risked our necks, for nothing? Like you said, because it just wasn't right, for them to use their magic on folks who couldn't stop them? You did it for us—and you didn't want *any*thing? You must be crazy."

Jagit laughed. "Well, I wouldn't say that. I told you before: All I want is to be able to see new sights, and sell my wares. And the World Government was bad for my business."

Wim met the peddler's gaze, glanced away undecided. "Where you going to go now?" He half expected the answer to be, Back beyond the sky.

"Back to bed." Jagit left the ballistic vehicle, and began to climb the rubbly slope up from the lake; he gestured for Wim to follow.

Wim followed, breathing hard in the thin air, until they reached a large fall of boulders before a sheer granite wall. Only when he was directly before it did he realize they had come on the entrance to a cave hidden by the rocks. He noticed that the opening was oddly symmetrical; and there seemed to be a rainbow shimmering across the darkness like mist. He stared at it uncomprehendingly, rubbing his chilled hands.

"This is where I came from, Wim. Not from the East, as you figured, or from space as the governor thought." The peddler nodded toward the dark entrance. "You see, the World Government had me entirely misplaced—they assumed I could only have come from somewhere outside their control. But actually I've been here on earth all the time; this cave has been my home for fifty-seven thousand years. There's a kind of magic in there that puts me into an 'enchanted' sleep for five or ten thousand years at a time here. And meanwhile the world changes. When it's changed enough, I wake up again and go out to see it. That's what I was doing in Sharn, ten thousand years ago: I brought artworks from an earlier, primitive era; they were popular, and I got to be something of a celebrity. That way I got access to my new items of trade— my Sharnish magics—to take somewhere else, when things changed again.

"That was the problem with the World Government—they interrupted the natural cycles of history that I depend on, and it threw me out of synch. They'd made stability such a science they might have kept things static for fifty or a hundred thousand years. Ten or fifteen thousand, and I could have come back here and outwaited them, but fifty thousand was just too long. I had to get things moving again, or I'd have been out of business."

Wim's imagination faltered at the prospect of the centuries that separated him from the peddler, that separated the peddler from everything that had ever been a part of the man, or ever could be. What kind of belief did it take, what sort of a man, to face that alone? And what losses or rewards to drive him to it? There must be something, that made it all worthwhile—

"There have been more things *done*, Wim, than the descendants of Sharn have *dreamed*. I am surprised at each new peak I attend. . . . I'll be leaving you now. You were a better guide than I expected; I thank you for it. I'd say Darkwood Corners is two or three days journey northwest from here."

Wim hesitated, half afraid, half longing. "Let me go with you—?"

Jagit shook his head. "There's only room for one, from here on. But you've seen a few more wonders than most people already; and I think you've learned a few things, too. There are going to be a lot of opportunities for putting it all to use right here, I'd say. You helped change your world, Wim—what are you going to do for an encore?"

Wim stood silent with indecision; Jagit lifted the rifle, tossed it to him.

Wim caught the gun, and a slow smile, filled with possibilities, grew on his face.

"Good-bye, Wim."

"Good-bye, Mr. Jagged." Wim watched the peddler move away toward his cave.

As he reached the entrance, Jagit hesitated, looking back. "And Wim—there are more wonders in this cave than you've ever dreamed of. I haven't been around this long because I'm an easy mark. Don't be tempted to grave-rob." He was outlined momentarily by rainbow as he passed into the darkness.

Wim lingered at the entrance, until at last the cold forced him to move and he picked his way back down the sterile gray detritus of the slope. He stopped again by the mirror lake, peering back past the magician's bullet-shaped vehicle at the cliff face. The rising sun washed it in golden light, but now somehow he really wasn't even sure where the cave had been.

He sighed, slinging his rifle over his shoulder, and began the long walk home.

LORD BUCKRY SIGHED AS MEMORIES RECEDED, AND WITH THEM THE GNAWING desire to seek out the peddler's cave again; the desire that had been with him for thirty years. There lay the solutions to every problem he had ever faced, but he had never tested Jagged's warning. It wasn't simply the risk, though the risk was both deadly and sufficient—it was the knowledge that however much he gained in this life, it was ephemeral, less than nothing, held up to a man whose life spanned half that of humanity itself. Within the peddler's cave lay the impossible, and that was why he would never try to take it for his own.

Instead he had turned to the possible and made it fact, depending on himself, and on the strangely clear view of things the peddler had left him. He had solved every problem alone, because he had had to, and now he would just have to solve this one alone too.

He stared down with sudden possessive pride over the townsfolk in the square, his city of Fyffe now ringed by a sturdy wall. . . . So the West and the South were together, for one reason, and one alone. It balanced the scales precariously against plenty of old hatreds, and if something were to tip them back again— A few rumors, well-placed, and they'd be at each other's throats. Perhaps he wouldn't even need to raise an army. They'd solve that problem for him. And afterward—

Lord Buckry began to smile. He'd always had a hankering to visit the sea.

I confess I don't know Jagit's real motives. I can imagine the character, what he said and did, but as for motive . . . Jagit's explanation for destroying the current civilization is certainly reasonable: the World Government was frustrating whatever reason Jagit had for traveling down time. Maybe he was just a merchant with a desire to see new things, but I think he had an additional agenda: Perhaps he wondered why the Singularity never occurred, and was searching for a civilization that would finally break free from the wheel of fate. Perhaps all the previous civilizations *had* ended in Singularities, leaving Jagit to make sure that it could happen again. Rereading the story, I feel very much like Wim at the end, awed . . . and a little afraid to learn the truth.

Did you guess where I stopped writing and Joan began? The last thing I did was the rescue from Axl Bork's gang. I wrote my part of the story over a summer, one page per day (for me, a strange way to write—but fun). Beyond the rescue scene I had only general ideas, and things stagnated; finishing the story was a fortunate and interesting collaboration.

THE UNGOVERNED

At least four of the stories in this collection take place in the aftermath of a catastrophic war. A couple of them use the setting as a stage for admonishment. But there is another reason for some post-catastrophe stories: such a war could postpone the Technological Singularity and leave the world intelligible to us mere humans. Lots of writers have earned their fortunes "in the aftermath" when high tech and medievalism can be jumbled in many different ways.

It's hard to know the long-range consequences of a general war. Conceivably it could mean the end of the human race. The war and the years immediately after would be as terrible as advertised. But the race would probably survive. Such a war would be a great detour into darkness, but as the years passed and the survivors grew old, and their children's children became adults . . . the bad times would be remembered as a distant misfortune. There could be happiness and bright times for those descendants; the war might be the end of *our* world, but not of theirs. Most of our informational heritage exists in a million libraries, even more robust than humanity. And I don't buy the arguments that technology couldn't restart because our civilization has consumed all the easily accessible resources. With the exception of petroleum, post-debacle civilizations might well find Earth's resources *more* accessible than before. (Non-poisoned urban ruins make great open pit mines.)

In some scenarios, the post-war civilization might have high levels of education and a clear vision of the past. This is the sort of background I have in the next story: I suppose that luck finally runs out for our current civilization, that we have a general war and worse times than I can describe (or want to imagine). Yet at the far end of it all there is another opportunity for prosperity and progress. I especially wanted to investigate two questions in this story: What sort of government might exist in such an era? How would the new civilization deal with nuclear weapons, and the possibility that everything gained could be lost again? The story's title reveals my answer to the first question. My answer to the second is equally radical.

Al's Protection Racket operated out of Manhattan, Kansas. Despite the name, it was a small, insurance-oriented police service with about 20,000 customers, all within 100 kilometers of the main shop. But apparently "Al" was some kind of humorist: His ads had a gangster motif, with his cops dressed like twentieth-century hoodlums. Wil Brierson guessed that it was all part of the nostalgia thing. Even the Michigan

State Police—Wil's outfit—capitalized on the public's feeling of trust in old names, old traditions.

Even so, there's something more dignified about a company with a name like "Michigan State Police," thought Brierson as he brought his flier down on the pad next to Al's HQ. He stepped out of the cockpit into an eerie morning silence: It was close to sunrise, yet the sky remained dark, the air humid. Thunderheads marched around half the horizon. A constant flicker of lightning chased back and forth within those clouds, yet there was not the faintest sound of thunder. He had seen a tornado killer on his way in, a lone eagle in the far sky. The weather was almost as ominous as the plea East Lansing HQ had received from Al's just four hours earlier.

A spindly figure came bouncing out of the shadows. "Am I glad to see you! The name's Alvin Swensen. I'm the proprietor." He shook Wil's hand enthusiastically. "I was afraid you might wait till the front passed through." Swensen was dressed in baggy pants and a padded jacket that would have made Frank Nitti proud. The local police chief urged the other officer up the steps. No one else was outside; the place seemed just as deserted as one might expect a rural police station to be early on a weekday morning. Where was the emergency?

Inside, a clerk (cop?) dressed very much like Al sat before a comm console. Swensen grinned at the other. "It's the MSP, all right. They're really coming, Jim. They're really coming! Just come down the hall, Lieutenant. I got my office back there. We should clear out real soon, but for the moment, I think it's safe."

Wil nodded, more puzzled than informed. At the far end of the hall, light spilled from a half-open door. The frosted glass surface was stenciled with the words "Big Al." A faint smell of mildew hung over the aging carpet and the wood floor beneath settled perceptibly under Wil's 90-kilo tread. Brierson almost smiled: maybe Al wasn't so crazy. The gangster motif excused absolutely slovenly maintenance. Few customers would trust a normal police organization that kept its buildings like this.

Big Al urged Brierson into the light and waved him to an overstuffed chair. Though tall and angular, Swensen looked more like a schoolteacher than a cop—or a gangster. His reddish-blond hair stood out raggedly from his head, as though he had been pulling at it, or had just been wakened. From the man's fidgety pacing about the room, Wil guessed the first possibility more likely. Swensen seemed about at the end of his rope, and Wil's arrival was some kind of reprieve. He glanced at Wil's nameplate and his grin spread even further. "W. W. Brierson. I've heard of you. I knew the Michigan State Police wouldn't let me down; they've sent their best."

Wil smiled in return, hoping his embarrassment didn't show. Part of his present fame was a company hype that he had come to loathe. "Thank you, uh, Big Al. We feel a special obligation to small police companies that serve no-right-to-bear-arms customers. But you're going to have to tell me more. Why so secretive?"

Al waved his hands. "I'm afraid of blabbermouths. I couldn't take a chance on the enemy learning I was bringing you into it until you were on the scene and in action."

Strange that he says "enemy," and not "crooks" or "bastards" or "hustlers." "But even a large gang might be scared off knowing—"

"Look, I'm not talking about some punk gang. I'm talking about the Republic of New Mexico. Invading us." He dropped into his chair and continued more calmly. It was almost as if passing the information on had taken the burden off him. "You're shocked?"

Brierson nodded dumbly.

"Me, too. Or I would have been up till a month ago. The Republic has always had plenty of internal troubles. And even though they claim all lands south of the Arkansas River, they have no settlements within hundreds of kilometers of here. Even now I think this is a bit of adventurism that can be squelched by an application of point force." He glanced at his watch. "Look, no matter how important speed is, we've got to do some coordinating. How many attack patrols are coming in after you?"

He saw the look on Brierson's face. "What? Only one? Damn. Well, I suppose it's my fault, being secret-like, but—"

Wil cleared his throat. "Big Al, there's only me. I'm the only agent MSP sent."

The other's face seemed to collapse, the relief changing to despair, then to a weak rage. "G-God d-damn you to hell, Brierson. I may lose everything I've built here, and the people who trusted me may lose everything they own. But I swear I'm going to sue your Michigan State Police into oblivion. Fifteen years I've paid you guys premiums and never a claim. And now when I need max firepower, they send me one asshole with a ten-millimeter popgun."

Brierson stood, his nearly two-meter bulk towering over the other. He reached out a bearlike hand to Al's shoulder. The gesture was a strange cross between reassurance and intimidation. Wil's voice was soft but steady. "The Michigan State Police hasn't let you down, Mr. Swensen. You paid for protection against wholesale violence—and we intend to provide that protection. MSP has *never* defaulted on a contract." His grip on Alvin Swensen's shoulder tightened with these last words. The two eyed each other for a moment. Then Big Al nodded weakly, and the other sat down.

"You're right. I'm sorry. I'm paying for the results, not the methods. But I know what we're up against, and I'm damned scared."

"And that's one reason why I'm here, Al: to find out exactly what we're up against before we jump in with our guns blazing and our pants down. What are you expecting?"

Al leaned back in the softly creaking chair. He looked out through the window into the dark silence of the morning, and for a moment seemed to relax. However improbably, someone else was going to take on his problems. "They started about three years ago. It seemed innocent enough, and it was certainly legal." Though the Republic of New Mexico claimed the lands from the Colorado on the west to the Mississippi on the east, and north to the Arkansas, in fact, most of their settlements were along the Gulf Coast and Rio Grande. For most of a century, Oklahoma and northern Texas had been uninhabited. The "border" along the Arkansas River had been of no real concern to the Republic, which had plenty of problems with its Water Wars on the Colorado, and of even less concern to the farmers at the southern edge of the ungoverned lands. During the last ten years, immigration from the Republic toward the more prosperous north had been steadily increasing. Few of the southerners stayed in the Manhattan area: most jobs were farther north. But during these last three years, wealthy New Mexicans had moved into the area, men willing to pay almost any price for farmland.

"IT'S CLEAR NOW THAT THESE PEOPLE WERE STOOGES FOR THE REPUBLIC government. They paid more money than they could reasonably recoup from farming, and the purchases started right after the election of their latest president. You know—Hastings Whatever-his-name-is. Anyway, it made a pleasant boom time for a lot of us. If some wealthy New Mexicans wanted isolated estates in the ungoverned lands, that was certainly their business. All the wealth in New Mexico couldn't buy onetenth of Kansas, anyway." At first, the settlers had been model neighbors. They even signed up with Al's Protection Racket and Midwest Jurisprudence. But as the months passed, it became obvious that they were neither farmers nor leisured rich. As near as the locals could figure out, they were some kind of labor contractors. An unending stream of trucks brought raggedly dressed men and women from the cities of the south: Galveston, Corpus Christi, even from the capital, Albuquerque. These folk were housed in barracks the owners had built on the farms. Anyone could see, looking in from above, that the newcomers spent long hours working in the fields.

Those farms produced on a scale that surprised the locals, and though it was still not clear that it was a profitable operation, there was a ripple of interest in the Grange journals; might manual labor hold an economic edge over the automatic-equipment rentals? Soon the workers were hiring out to local farmers. "Those people work harder than any reasonable person, and they work dirt cheap. Every night, their contract bosses would truck 'em back to the barracks, so our farmers had scarcely more overhead than they would with automatics. Overall, the NMs underbid the equipment-rental people by five percent or so."

Wil began to see where all this was leading. Someone in the Republic seemed to understand Midwest Jurisprudence. "Hmm, you know, Al, if I were one of those laborers, I wouldn't hang around in farm country. There are labor services up north that can get an apprentice butler more money than some rookie cops make. Rich people will always want servants, and nowadays the pay is tremendous."

Big Al nodded. "We've got rich folks, too. When they saw what these newcomers would work for, they started drooling. And that's when things began to get sticky." At first, the NM laborers could scarcely understand what they were being offered. They insisted that they were required to work when and where they were told. A few, a very few at first, took the job offers. "They were really scared, those first ones. Over and over, they wanted assurances that they would be allowed to return to their families at the end of the workday. They seemed to think the deal was some kidnap plot rather than an offer of employment. Then it was like an explosion: They couldn't wait to drop the farm jobs. They wanted to bring their families with them."

"And that's when your new neighbors closed up the camps?"

"You got it, pal. They won't let the families out. And we know they are confiscating the money the workers bring in."

"Did they claim their people were on long-term contracts?"

"Hell, no. It may be legal under Justice, Inc., but indentured servitude isn't under Midwest—and that's who they signed with. I see now that even that was deliberate.

"It finally hit the fan yesterday. The Red Cross flew a guy out from Topeka with a writ from a Midwest judge: He was to enter each of the settlements and explain to those poor folks how they stood with the law. I went along with a couple of my boys. They refused to let us in and punched out the Red Cross fellow when he got insistent. Their chief thug—fellow named Strong—gave me a signed policy cancellation, and told me that from now on they would handle all their own police and justice needs. We were then escorted off the property—at gunpoint."

"So they've gone armadillo. That's no problem. But the workers are still presumptively customers of yours?"

"Not just presumptively. Before this blew up, a lot of them had signed individual contracts with me and Midwest. The whole thing is a setup, but I'm *stuck*."

Wil nodded. "Right. Your only choice was to call in someone with firepower, namely my company."

Big Al leaned forward, his indignation retreating before fear. "Of course. But there's more, Lieutenant. Those workers—those slaves—were part of the trap that was set for us. But most of them are brave, honest people. They know what's happening, and they aren't any happier about it than I am. Last night, after we got our butts kicked, three of them escaped. They walked fifteen kilometers into Manhattan to see me, to beg me *not* to intervene. To beg me not to honor the contract.

"And they told me why: For a hundred kilometer stretch of their truck ride up here, they weren't allowed to see the country they were going through. But they heard plenty. And one of them managed to work a peephole in the side of the truck. He saw armored vehicles and attack aircraft under heavy camouflage just south of the Arkansas. The damn New Mexicans have taken part of their Texas garrison force and holed it up less than ten minutes flying time from Manhattan. And they're ready to move."

It was possible. The Water Wars with Aztlán had been winding down these last few years. The New Mexicans should have equipment reserves, even counting what they needed to keep the Gulf Coast cities in line. Wil got up and walked to the window. Dawn was lighting the sky above the far cloud banks. There was green in the rolling land that stretched away from the police post. Suddenly he felt very exposed here: Death could come out of that sky with precious little warning. W. W. Brierson was no student of history, but he was an old-time movie freak, and he had seen plenty of war stories. Assuming the aggressor had to satisfy some kind of public or world opinion, there had to be a provocation, an excuse for the massive violence that would masquerade as self-defense. The New Mexicans had cleverly created a situation in which Wil Brierson—or someone like him—would be contractually obligated to use force against their settlements.

"So. If we hold off on enforcement, how long do you think the invasion would be postponed?" It hurt to suggest bending a contract like that, but there was precedent: In hostage cases, you often used time as a weapon.

"It wouldn't slow 'em up a second. One way or another they're moving on us. I figure if we don't do anything, they'll use my 'raid' yesterday as their excuse. The only thing I can see is for MSP to put everything it can spare on the line when those bastards come across. That sort of massive resistance might be enough to scare 'em back."

Brierson turned from the window to look at Big Al. He understood now the shaking fear in the other. It had taken guts for the other to wait here through the night. But now it was W. W. Brierson's baby. "Okay, Big Al. With your permission, I'll take charge."

"You got it, Lieutenant!" Al was out of his chair, a smile splitting his face.

Wil was already starting for the door. "The first thing to do is get away from this particular ground zero. How many in the building?"

"Just two besides me."

"Round 'em up and bring them to the front room. If you have any firearms, bring them, too."

WIL WAS PULLING HIS COMM EQUIPMENT OUT OF THE GUNSHIP WHEN THE other three came out the front door of Al's HQ and started toward him. He waved them back. "If they play as rough as you think, they'll grab for air superiority first thing. What kind of ground vehicles do you have?"

"Couple of cars. A dozen motorbikes. Jim, open up the garage." The zoot-suited trooper hustled off. Wil looked with some curiosity at the person remaining with Al. This individual couldn't be more than fourteen years old. She (?) was weighted down with five boxes, some with makeshift carrying straps, others even less portable. Most looked like communications gear. The kid was grinning from ear to ear. Al said, "Kiki van Steen, Lieutenant. She's a war-game fanatic—for once, it may be worth something."

"Hi, Kiki."

"Pleased to meetcha, Lieutenant." She half-lifted one of the suitcase-size boxes, as though to wave. Even with all the gear, she seemed to vibrate with excitement.

"We have to decide where to go, and how to get there. The bikes might be best, Al. They're small enough to—"

"Nah." It was Kiki. "Really, Lieutenant, they're almost as easy to spot as a farm wagon. And we don't have to go far. I checked a couple minutes ago, and no enemy aircraft are up. We've got at least five minutes."

He glanced at Al, who nodded. "Okay, the car it is."

The girl's grin widened and she waddled off at high speed toward the garage. "She's really a good kid, Lieutenant. Divorced though. She spends most of what I pay her on that war-game equipment. Six months ago she started talking about strange things down south. When no one would listen, she shut up. Thank God she's here now. All night she's been watching the south. We'll know the second they jump off."

"You have some hidey-hole already set, Al?"

"Yeah. The farms southwest of here are riddled with tunnels and caves. The old Fort Riley complex. Friend of mine owns a lot of it. I sent most of my men out there last night. It's not much, but at least they won't be picking us up for free."

Around them insects were beginning to chitter, and in the trees west of the HQ there was a dove. Sunlight lined the cloud tops. The air was still cool, humid. And the darkness at the horizon remained. Twister weather. *Now who will benefit from that?*

The relative silence was broken by the sharp coughing of a piston engine. Seconds later, an incredible antique nosed out of the garage onto the driveway. Wil saw the long black lines of a pre-1950 Lincoln. Brierson and Big Al dumped their guns and comm gear into the back seat and piled in.

This nostalgia thing can be carried too far, Wil thought. A restored Lincoln would cost as much as all the rest of Al's operation. The vehicle pulled smoothly out onto the ag road that paralleled the HQ property, and Wil realized he was in an inexpensive reproduction. He should have known Big Al would keep costs down.

Behind him the police station dwindled, was soon lost in the rolling Kansas landscape. "Kiki. Can you get a line-of-sight on the station's mast?"

The girl nodded.

"Okay. I want a link to East Lansing that looks like it's coming from your stationhouse."

"Sure." She phased an antenna ball on the mast, then gave Wil her command mike. In seconds he had spoken the destination codes and was talking first to the duty desk in East Lansing—and then to Colonel Potts and several of the directors.

When he had finished, Big Al looked at him in awe. "One hundred assault aircraft! Four thousand troopers! My God. I had no idea you could call in that sort of force."

Brierson didn't answer immediately. He pushed the mike into Kiki's hands and said, "Get on the loudmouth channels, Kiki. Start screaming bloody murder to all North America." Finally he looked back at Al, embarrassed. "We don't, Al. MSP has maybe thirty assault aircraft, twenty of them helicopters. Most of the fixed-wing jobs are in the Yukon. We could put guns on our search-and-rescue ships—we do have hundreds of those—but it will take weeks."

Al paled, but the anger he had shown earlier was gone. "So it was a bluff?"

Wil nodded. "But we'll get everything MSP has, as fast as they can bring it in. If the New Mexican investment isn't too big, this may be enough to scare 'em back." Big Al seemed to shrink in on himself. He gazed listlessly over Jim's shoulder at the road ahead. In the front seat, Kiki was shrilly proclaiming the details of the enemy's movements, the imminence of their attack. She was transmitting call letters and insignia that could leave no doubt that her broadcast came from a legitimate police service.

The wind whipped through the open windows, brought the lush smells of dew and things dark green. In the distance gleamed the silver dome of a farm's fresh produce bobble. They passed a tiny Methodist church, sparkling white amidst flowers and lawn. In back, someone was working in the pastor's garden.

The road was just good enough to support the big tires of farm vehicles. Jim couldn't do much over 50 kph. Every so often, a wagon or tractor would pass them going the other way—going off to work in the fields. The drivers waved cheerfully at the Lincoln. It was a typical farm country morning in the ungoverned lands. How soon it would change. The news networks should have picked up on Kiki by now. They would have their own investigative people on the scene in hours with live holo coverage of whatever the enemy chose to do. Their programming, some of it directed into the Republic, might be enough to turn the enemy's public opinion against its government. *Wishful thinking.*

More likely the air above them would soon be filled with screaming metal—the end of a generation of peace.

Big Al gave a short laugh. When Wil looked at him questioningly, the small-town cop shrugged. "I was just thinking. This whole police business is something like a lending bank. Instead of gold, MSP backs its promises with force. This invasion is like a run on your 'bank of violence.' You got enough backing to handle normal demands, but when it all comes due at once . . ."

. . . *you wind up dead or enslaved.* Wil's mind shied away from the analogy. "Maybe so, but like a lot of banks, we have agreements with others. I'll bet Portland Security and the Mormons will loan us some aircraft. In any case, the Republic can never hold this land. You run a no-right-to-bear-arms service; but a lot of people around here are armed to the teeth."

"Sure. My biggest competitor is Justice, Inc. They encourage their customers to invest in handguns and heavy home security. Sure. The Republic will get their asses kicked eventually. But we'll be dead and bankrupt by then—and so will a few thousand other innocents."

Al's driver glanced back at them. "Hey, Lieutenant, why doesn't MSP pay one of the big power companies to retaliate—bobble places way inside the Republic?"

Wil shook his head. "The New Mexico government is sure to have all its important sites protected by Wáchendon suppressors."

Suddenly Kiki broke off her broadcast monologue and let out a whoop. "Bandits! Bandits!" She handed a display flat over the seat to Al. The format was familiar, but the bouncing, jostling ride made it hard to read. The picture was based on a sidelooking radar view from orbit, with a lot of data added. Green denoted vegetation and pastel overlays showed cloud cover. It was a jumble till he noticed that Manhattan and the Kansas River were labeled. Kiki zoomed up the magnification. Three red dots were visibly accelerating from a growing pockwork of red dots to the south. The three brightened, still accelerating. "They just broke cloud cover," she explained. Beside each of the dots a moving legend gave what must be altitude and speed.

"Is this going out over your loudmouth channel?"

She grinned happily. "Sure is! But not for long." She reached back to point at the display. "We got about two minutes before Al's stationhouse goes boom. I don't want to risk a direct satellite link from the car, and anything else would be even more dangerous."

Point certain, thought Wil.

"Geez, this is incredible, just incredible. For two years the Warmongers—that's my club, you know—been watching the Water Wars. We got software, hardware, cryptics—everything to follow what's going on. We could predict, and bet other clubs, but we could never actually participate. And now we have a real *war*, right *here*!" She lapsed into awed silence, and Wil wondered fleetingly if she might be psychopathic, and not merely young and naive.

"Do you have outside cameras at the police station?" He was asking Kiki as much as Al. "We should broadcast the actual attack."

The girl nodded. "I grabbed two channels. I got the camera on the comm mast pointing southwest. We'll have public opinion completely nailed on this."

"Let's see it."

She made a moue. "Okay. Not much content to it, though." she flopped back onto the front seat. Over her shoulder, Wil could see she had an out-sized display flat on her lap. It was another composite picture, but this one was overlaid with cryptic legends. They looked vaguely familiar. Then he recognized them from the movies: They were the old, old shorthand for describing military units and capabilities. The Warmongers Club must have software for translating multispec satellite observations into such displays. Hell, they might even be able to listen in on military communications. And what the girl had said about public opinion—the club seemed to play war in a very universal way. They *were* crazy, but they might also be damned useful.

Kiki mumbled something into her command mike, and the flat Al was holding split down the middle: On the left they could follow the enemy's approach with the map; on the right they saw blue sky and farmland and the parking lot by the stationhouse. Wil saw his gunship gleaming in the morning sunlight, just a few meters below the camera's viewpoint.

"Fifteen seconds. They might be visible if you look south."

The car swerved toward the shoulder as Jim pointed out the window. "I see 'em!"

Then Wil did, too. A triple of black insects, silent because of distance and speed. They drifted westward, disappeared behind trees. But to the camera on the comm mast, they did not drift: They seemed to hang in the sky above the parking lot, death seen straight on. Smoke puffed from just beneath them and things small and black detached from the bodies of the attack craft, which now pulled up. The planes were so close that Wil could see shape to them, could see sun glint from canopies. Then the bombs hit.

Strangely, the camera scarcely jolted, but started slowly to pan downward. Fire and debris roiled up around the viewpoint. A rotor section from his flier flashed past, and then the display went gray. He realized that the panning had not been deliberate: The high comm mast had been severed and was toppling.

Seconds passed and sharp thunder swept over the car, followed by the fast-dying scream of the bombers climbing back into the sky.

"So much for the loudmouth channels," said Kiki. "I'm for keeping quiet till we get underground."

Jim was driving faster now. He hadn't seen the display, but the sounds of the explosions were enough to make all but the least imaginative run like hell. The road had been bumpy, but now seemed like washboard. Wil gripped the seat ahead of him. If the enemy connected them with the broadcasts . . .

"How far, Al?"

"Nearest entrance is about four kilometers as the crow flies, but we gotta go all around the Schwartz farm to get to it." He waved at the high, barbed-wire fence along the right side of the road. Cornfields stretched away north of it. In the distance, Wil saw something—a harvester?—amidst the green. "It'll take us fifteen minutes—"

"Ten!" claimed Jim emphatically, and the ride became still wilder.

"—to make it around the farm."

They crested a low hill. Not more than 300 meters distant, Wil could see a side road going directly north. "But we could take that."

"Not a chance. That's on Schwartz land." Big Al glanced at the state trooper. "And I ain't just being law-abiding, Lieutenant. We'd be as good as dead to do that. Jake Schwartz went armadillo about three years ago. See that hulk out there in the field?" He tried to point, but his arm waved wildly.

"The harvester?"

"That's no harvester. It's armor. Robot, I think. If you look careful you may see the gun tracking us." Wil looked again. What he had thought was a chaff exhaust now looked more like a high-velocity catapult.

Their car zipped past the T-intersection with the Schwartz road; Wil had a glimpse of a gate and keep-out signs surmounted by what looked like human skulls. The farm west of the side road seemed undeveloped. A copse at the top of a near hill might have hid farm buildings.

"The expense. Even if it's mostly bluff—"

"It's no bluff. Poor Jake. He always was self-righteous and a bit of a bully. His police contract was with Justice, Inc., and he claimed even they were too bleedin' heart for him. Then one night his kid—who's even stupider than Jake—got pig drunk and killed another idiot. Unfortunately for Jake's boy, the victim was one of my customers. There are no amelioration clauses in the Midwest/Justice, Inc. agreements. Reparations aside, the kid will be locked up for a long time. Jake swore he'd never contract his rights to a court again. He has a rich farm, and since then he's spent every gAu from it on more guns, more traps, more detectors. I hate to think how they live in there. There are rumors he's brought in deathdust from the Hanford ruins, just in case anybody succeeds in getting past everything else."

Oh boy. Even the armadillos up north rarely went that far.

The last few minutes Kiki had ignored them, all her attention on the strategy flat on her lap. She wore a tiny headset and was mumbling constantly into her command mike. Suddenly she spoke up. "Oops. We're not going to make it, Big Al." She began folding the displays, stuffing them back into her equipment boxes. "I monitored. They just told their chopper crews to pick us up. They got us spotted easy. Two, three minutes is all we have."

Jim slowed, shouted over his shoulder. "How about if I drop you and keep going? I might be kilometers gone before they stop me." Brierson had never noticed any lack of guts among the unarmed police services.

"Good idea! Bye!" Kiki flung open her door and rolled off into the deep and apparently soft vegetation that edged the road.

"Kiki!" screamed Big Al, turning to look back down the road. They had a brief glimpse of comm and processor boxes bouncing wildly through the brush. Then Kiki's blond form appeared for an instant as she dragged the equipment deeper into the green.

From the trees behind them they could hear the *thup thupthup* of rotors. Two minutes had been an overstatement. Wil leaned forward. "No, Jim. Drive like hell. And remember: There were only three of us."

The other nodded. The car squealed out toward the center of the road, and accelerated up past 80. The roar and thump of their progress momentarily drowned out the sound of pursuit. Thirty seconds passed, and three helicopters appeared over the tree line behind them. *Do we get what they gave the stationhouse?* An instant later white flashed from their belly guns. The road ahead erupted in a geyser of dirt and rock. Jim stepped on the brakes and the car swerved to a halt, dipping and bobbing among the craters left by the shells. The car's engine died and the thumping of rotors was a loud, almost physical pressure around them. The largest craft settled to earth amidst its own dust devil. The other two circled, their autocannons locked on Big Al's Lincoln.

The passenger hatch on the grounded chopper slid back and two men in body armor hopped out. One waved his submachine gun at them, motioning them out of the car. Brierson and the others were hustled across the road, while the second soldier went to pick up the equipment they had in the car. Wil looked back at the scene, feeling the dust in his mouth and on his sweating face—the ashes of humiliation.

His pistol was pulled from its holster. "All aboard, gentlemen." The words were spoken with a clipped, Down West accent.

Wil was turning when it happened. A flash of fire and a muffled thud came from one of the hovering choppers. Its tail rotor disappeared in a shower of debris. The craft spun uncontrollably on its main rotor and fell onto the roadway behind them. Pale flame spread along fuel lines, sputtering in small explosions. Wil could see injured crew trying to crawl out.

"I said *get aboard*." The gunman had stepped back from them, his attention and the muzzle of his gun still on his captives. Wil guessed the man was a veteran of the Water Wars—that institutionalized gangsterism that New Mexico and Aztlán called "warfare between nations." Once given a mission, he would not be distracted by incidental catastrophes.

The three "prisoners of war" stumbled into the relative darkness of the helicopter's interior. Wil saw the soldier—still standing outside— look back toward the wreck, and speak emphatically into his helmet mike. Then he hopped on and pulled the hatch to. The helicopter slid into the air, hanging close to the ground as it gradually picked up speed. They were moving westward from the wreck, and there was no way they could look back through the tiny windows.

An accident? Who could have been equipped to shoot down an armored warcraft in the middle of Kansas fields? Then Wil remembered: Just before it lost its tail, the chopper had drifted north of the roadway, past the high fence that marked Armadillo Schwartz's land. He looked at Big Al, who nodded slightly. Brierson sat back in the canvas webbing and suppressed a smile. It was a small thing on the scale of the invasion, but he thanked God for armadillos. Now it was up to organizations like the Michigan State Police to convince the enemy that this was just the beginning, that every kilometer into the ungoverned lands would cost them similarly.

ONE HUNDRED AND EIGHTY KILOMETERS IN SIX HOURS. REPUBLICAN CASU-alties: one motorcycle/truck collision, and one helicopter crash—that probably a mechanical failure. Edward Strong, Special Advisor to the President, felt a satisfied smile come to his lips every time he glanced at the situation board. He had seen more casualties on a Freedom Day parade through downtown Albuquerque. His own analysis for the Pres-ident—as well as the larger, less imaginative analysis from JCS—had predicted that extending the Republic through Kansas to the Mississippi would be almost trivial. Nevertheless, after having fought meter by bloody meter with the fanatics of Aztlán, it was a strange feeling to be advancing hundreds of kilometers each day.

Strong paced down the narrow aisle of the Command and Control van, past the analysts and clerks. He stood for a moment by the rear door, feeling the air-conditioning billow chill around his head. Cam-ouflage netting had been laid over the van, but he could see through it without difficulty: Green leaves played tag with shadows across pale yellow limestone. They were parked in a wooded creek bed on the land Intelligence had bought several years earlier. Somewhere to the north were the barracks that now confined the people Intelligence had im-ported allegedly to work the farms. Those laborers had provided what-ever legal justification was needed for this move into the ungoverned lands. Strong wondered if any of them realized their role—and realized that in a few months they would be free of poverty, realized that they would own farms in a land that could be made infinitely more hospi-table than the deserts of the Southwest.

Sixteen kilometers to the northeast lay Manhattan. It was a minor goal, but the Republic's forces were cautious. It would be an impor-tant—though small—test of their analysis. There were Tinkers in that town and in the countryside beyond. The precision electronics and re-lated weapons that came out of the Tinkers' shops were worthy of re-spect and caution. Privately, Strong considered them to be the only real threat to the success of the invasion he had proposed to the President three years earlier. (Three years of planning, of cajoling resources from other departments, of trying to inject imagination into minds that had been closed for decades. By far, the easiest part had been the operations here in Kansas.)

The results of the move on Manhattan would be relayed from here to General Crick at the head of the armor driving east along Old70. Later in the afternoon, Crick's tank carriers should reach the outskirts of Topeka. The Old U.S. highway provided a mode of armored operations previously unknown to warfare. If the investiture of Manhattan went as planned, then Crick might have Topeka by nightfall and be moving the remainder of his forces on to the Mississippi.

Strong looked down the van at the time posted on the situation board. The President would be calling in 20 minutes to witness the move against Manhattan. Till then, a lull gapped in Strong's schedule. Perhaps there was time for one last bit of caution. He turned to the bird colonel who was his military liaison. "Bill, those three locals you picked up— you know, the protection-racket people—I'd like to talk to them before the Chief calls in."

"Here?"

"If possible."

"Okay." There was faint disapproval in the officer's voice. Strong imagined that Bill Alvarez couldn't quite see bringing enemy agents into the C&C van. But what the hell, they were clean—and there was no way that they could report what they saw here. Besides, he had to stay in the van in case the Old Man showed up early.

Minutes later, the three shuffled into the conference area at the front of the van. Restraints glinted at their hands and ankles. They stood in momentary blindness in the darkness of the van, and Strong had a chance to look them over; three rather ordinary human beings, dressed in relatively extraordinary ways. The big black wore a recognizable uniform, complete with badges, sidearm holster, and what appeared to be riding boots. He looked the model fascist. Strong recognized the Michigan State "Police" insignia on his sleeve. MSP was one of the most powerful gangster combines in the ungoverned lands. Intelligence reported they had some modern weapons—enough to keep their "clients" in line, anyway.

"Sit down, gentlemen." Amidst a clanking of shackles, the three sat, sullen. Behind them an armed guard remained standing. Strong glanced at the intelligence summary he had punched up. "Mr., uh, Lieutenant Brierson, you may be interested to know that the troops and aircraft you asked your bosses for this morning have not materialized. Our intelligence people have not changed their estimate that you were making a rather weak bluff."

The northerner just shrugged, but the blond fellow in the outrageously striped shirt—Alvin Swensen, the report named him—leaned forward and almost hissed. "Maybe, maybe not, asshole! But it doesn't matter. You're going to kill a lot of people, but in the end you'll be dragging your bloody tail back south."

Figuratively speaking, Strong's ears perked up. "How is that, Mr. Swensen?"

"Read your history. You're stealing from a free people now—not a bunch of Aztlán serfs. Every single farm, every single family is against you, and these are educated people, many with weapons. It may take a while. It may destroy a lot of things we value. But every day you stay here, you'll bleed. And when you've bled enough to see this, then you'll go home."

Strong glanced at the casualty report on the situation board, and felt laughter stealing up. "You poor fool. What free people? We get your video, your propaganda, but what does it amount to? There hasn't been a government in this part of the continent for more than eighty years. You petty gangsters have the guns and have divided up the territory. Most of you don't even allow your 'clients' firearms. I'll wager that the majority of your victims will welcome a government where there is a franchise to be exercised, where ballots, and not MSP bullets, decide issues.

"No, Mr. Swensen, the little people in the ungoverned lands have no stake in your *status quo*. And as for the armed groups fighting some kind of guerrilla war against us—Well, you've had it easier than you know for a long time. You haven't lived in a land as poor as old New Mexico. Since the Bobble War, we've had to fight for every liter of water, against an enemy far more determined and bloodthirsty than you may imagine. We have prevailed, we have revived and maintained democratic government, and we have remained free men."

"*Sure.* Free like the poor slobs you got locked up over there." Swensen waved in the direction of the workers' barracks.

Strong leaned across the narrow conference table to pin Swensen with his glare. "Mister, I grew up as one of those 'slobs.' In New Mexico, even people that poor have a chance to get something better. This land you claim is practically empty—you don't know how to farm it, you don't have a government to manage large dam and irrigation projects, you don't even know how to use government agriculture policy to encourage its proper use by individuals.

"Sure, those workers couldn't be told why they were brought here. But when this is over, they will be heroes, with homesteads they had never imagined being able to own."

Swensen rocked back before the attack, but was plainly unconvinced.

Which makes sense, thought Strong. *How can a wolf imagine anyone sincerely wishing good for sheep?*

An alert light glowed on Strong's display and one of the clerks announced, "Presidential transmission under way, Mr. Strong." He swore behind his teeth. The Old Man was early. He'd hoped to get some information out of these three, not just argue politics.

A glowing haze appeared at the head of the conference table and quickly solidified into the image of the fourth President of the Republic. Hastings Martinez was good-looking with bio-age around fifty years— old enough to inspire respect, young enough to appear decisive. In Strong's opinion, he was not the best president the Republic had seen, but he had the advisor's respect and loyalty nevertheless. There was something in the very responsibility of the office of the Presidency that made its holder larger than life.

"Mr. President," Strong said respectfully.

"Ed," Martinez's image nodded. The projection was nearly as substantial as the forms of those truly present; Strong didn't know whether this was because of the relative darkness within the van, or because Martinez was transmitting via fiber from his estate in Alva, just 300 kilometers away.

Strong waved at the prisoners. "Three locals, sir. I was hoping to—"

Martinez leaned forward. "Why, I think I've seen you before." He spoke to the MSP officer. "The ads Michigan State Police uses; our intelligence people have shown me some. You protect MSP's client mobs from outside gangs."

Brierson nodded, smiled wryly. Strong recognized him now and kicked himself for not noticing earlier. If those ads were correct, then Brierson was one of the top men in the MSP.

"They make you out to be some sort of superman. Do you honestly think your people can stop a modern, disciplined army?"

"Sooner or later, Mr. Martinez. Sooner or later."

The President smiled, but Strong wasn't sure whether he was piqued or truly amused. "Our armor is approaching Manhattan on schedule, sir. As you know, we regard this action as something of a benchmark. Manhattan is almost as big as Topeka, and has a substantial cottage electronics industry. It's about the closest thing to a city you'll find in the ungoverned lands." Strong motioned for the guard to remove the three prisoners, but the President held up his hand.

"Let 'em stay, Ed. The MSP man should see this firsthand. These people may be lawless, but I can't believe they are crazy. The sooner they realize that we have overwhelming force—and that we use it fairly— the sooner they'll accept the situation."

"Yes, sir." Strong signaled his analysts, and displays came to life on the situation board. Simultaneously, the conference table was overhung with a holographic relief map of central Kansas. The northerners looked at the map and Strong almost smiled. They obviously had no idea of the size of the New Mexican operation. For months the Republic had been building reserves along the Arkansas. It couldn't be entirely disguised; these three had known something about the forces. But until the whole military machine was in motion, its true size had escaped them. Strong was honest with himself. It was not New Mexican cleverness that had outwitted northern electronics. The plan could never have worked without advanced countermeasures equipment—some of it bought from the northerners themselves.

Computer-selected radio traffic became a background noise. He had rehearsed all this with the technicians earlier; there was not a single aspect of the operation that the President would miss. He pointed at the map. "Colonel Alvarez has one armored force coming north from Old70. It should enter Manhattan from the east. The other force left here a few minutes ago, and is approaching town along this secondary road." Tiny silver lights crept along the map where he pointed. A few centimeters above the display, other lights represented helicopter and fixed-wing cover. These coasted gracefully back and forth, occasionally swooping close to the surface.

A voice spoke against a background of turbine noise, to announce no resistance along the eastern salient. "Haven't really seen anyone. People are staying indoors, or else bobbled up before we came in range. We're avoiding houses and farm buildings, sticking to open fields and roads."

Strong expanded one of the views from the western salient. The situation board showed a picture taken from the air: A dozen tanks moved along a dirt road, trails of dust rising behind them. The camera chopper must have been carrying a mike, for the rumbling and clanking of treads replaced the radio traffic for a moment. Those tanks were the pride of New Mexico. Unlike the aircraft, their hulls and engines were 100 percent Product of the Republic. New Mexico was poor in most resources, but like Japan in the twentieth century, and Great Britain before that, she was great in people and ingenuity. Someday soon, she would be great in electronics. For now, though, all the best reconnaissance and communication gear came from Tinkers, many in the ungoverned lands. That was an Achilles' heel, long recognized by Strong and others. It was the reason for using equipment from different manufacturers all over the world, and for settling for second-class gear in some of the most critical applications. How could they know, *for certain*, that the equipment they bought was not booby-trapped or bugged? There was historical precedent: The outcome of the Bobble War had been due in large part to Tinker meddling with the old Peace Authority's reconnaissance system.

Strong recognized the stretch of road they were coming up on: A few hundred meters beyond the lead tank lay an irregular blackened area and the twisted metal that had once been a helicopter.

A puff of smoke appeared by the lead tank, followed by the faint crack of an explosion. Bill Alvarez's voice came on an instant after that. "Under fire. Light mortar." The tank was moving again, but in a large circle, toward the ditch. Guns and sensors on the other armor swung north. "The enemy was lucky, or that was a smart round. We've got radar backtrack. The round came from beyond the other side of the farm we're passing. Looks like a tunnel entrance to the old Fort Riley— Wait, we got enemy radio traffic just before it happened."

His voice was replaced by the crackling of high amplification. The new voice was female, but barely understandable. "General van Steen to forces [unintelligible]. You may fire when ready." There was a screaking sound and other voices.

Strong saw Swensen's jaw sag in surprise, or horror. *"General van Steen?"*

Colonel Alvarez's voice came back. "There were replies from several points farther north. The original launch site has fired two more rounds." As he spoke, black smoke appeared near the treads of two more tanks. Neither was destroyed, but neither could continue.

"Mr. President, Mr. Strong, all rounds are coming from the same location. These are barely more than fireworks—except that they're smart. I'll wager 'General van Steen' is some local gangster putting up a brave front. We'll see in a minute." On the holomap, two blips drew away from the other support aircraft and began a low-level dash across the miniature Kansas landscape.

The President nodded, but addressed another unseen observer. "General Crick?"

"I concur, sir." Crick's voice was as loud and clear as Alvarez's, though the general was 50 kilometers to the east, at the head of the column en route to Topeka. "But we've seen an armored vehicle in the intermediate farmland, haven't we, Bill?"

"Yes," said Alvarez. "It's been there for months. Looks like a hulk. We'll take it out, too."

Strong noticed the northerners tense. Swensen seemed on the verge of screaming something. *What do they know?*

The attack planes, twin engine green-and-gray jobs, were on the main view now. They were only 20 or 30 meters up, well below the camera viewpoint, and probably not visible from the enemy launch site. The lead craft angled slightly to the east, and spewed rockets at an unmoving silhouette that was almost hidden by the hills and the corn. A second later, the target disappeared in a satisfying geyser of flame and dirt.

And a second after *that*, hell on earth erupted from the peaceful fields: Beams of pale light flashed from unseen projectors, and the assault aircraft became falling, swelling balls of fire. As automatic fire control brought the tanks' guns to bear on the source of the destruction, rocket and laser fire came from other locations immediately north of the roadway. Four of the tanks exploded immediately, and most of the rest were on fire. Tiny figures struggled from their machines, and ran from the flames.

North of the farm, Strong thought he saw explosions at the source of the original mortar attack. Something was firing in that direction, too!

Then the camera chopper took a hit, and the picture swung round and round, descending into the firestorm that stretched along the roadway. The view went dark. Strong's carefully planned presentation was rapidly degenerating into chaos. Alvarez was shouting over other voices, demanding the reserves that still hung along Old70 directly south of Manhattan, and he could hear Crick working to divert portions of his air cover to the fight that was developing.

It wasn't till much later that Strong made sense of the conversation that passed between the northerners just then:

"Kiki, how could you!" Swensen slumped over the holomap, shaking his head in despair (shame?).

Brierson eyed the displays with no visible emotion. "What she did is certainly legal, Al."

"Sure it is. And immoral as hell. Poor Jake Schwartz. Poor Jake."

The view of the battle scene reappeared. The picture was almost the same perspective as before but grainier and faintly wavering—probably from a camera aboard some recon craft far south of the fighting. The holomap flickered as major updates came in. The locals had been thorough and successful. There were no effective New Mexican forces within five kilometers of the original flareup. The force dug in to the farmland was firing rockets southward, taking an increasing toll of the armored reinforcements that were moving north from Old70.

"Crick here, Mr. President." The general's voice was brisk, professional. Any recriminations with Intelligence would come later. "The enemy is localized, but incredibly well dug in. If he's isolated, we *might* be able to bypass him, but neither Alvarez nor I want something like that left on our flank. We're going to soften him up, then move our armor right in on top."

Strong nodded to himself. In any case, they had to take this strong point just to find out what the enemy really had. In the air over the holomap, dozens of lights moved toward the enemy fortress. Some flew free ballistic arcs, while others struck close to the ground, out of the enemy's direct fire. Across the table, the holo lit the northerners' faces: Swensen's seemingly more pale than before, Brierson's dark and stolid. There was a faint stench of sweat in the air now, barely perceptible against the stronger smells of metal and fresh plastic.

Damn. Those three had been surprised by the ambush, but Strong was sure that they understood what was behind the attack, and whence the next such would come. Given time and Special Service drugs, he could have the answers. He leaned across the table and addressed the MSP officer. "So. You aren't entirely bluff. But unless you have many more such traps, you won't do more than slow us up, and kill a lot of people on both sides."

Swensen was about to answer, then looked at Brierson and was silent. The black seemed to be deliberating just what or how much to say; finally, he shrugged. "I won't lie to you. The attack had nothing to do with MSP forces."

"Some other gang then?"

"No. You just happened to run into a farmer who defends his property."

"Bull." Ed Strong had spent his time in the military in combat along the Colorado. He knew how to read the intelligence displays and manage tactics. But he also knew what it was like to be on the ground where the reality was bullets and shrapnel. He knew what it took to set up a defense like the one they had just seen. "Mr. Brierson, you're telling me one man could afford to buy the sort of equipment we saw and to dig it in so deep that even now we don't have a clear picture of his setup? You're telling me that one man could afford an MHD source for those lasers?"

"Sure. That family has probably been working at this for years, spending every spare gAu on the project, building the system up little by little. Even so," he sighed. "they should be out of rockets and juice soon. You could lay off."

The rain of rocket-borne and artillery high explosives was beginning to fall upon the target. Flashes and color sparkled across the screen, more an abstract pattern than a landscape now. There was no human life, no equipment visible. The bombers were standing off and lobbing their cargo in. Until the enemy's defenses were broken, any other course was needless waste. After a couple minutes, the airborne debris obscured all but the largest detonations. Napalm flared within, and the whole cloud glowed beautiful yellow. For a few seconds, the enemy lasers still flashed, spectacular and ineffective in all the dirt. Even after the lasers died, the holomap showed isolated missiles emerging from the target area to hunt for the bombers. Then even those stopped coming.

Still the barrage continued, raising the darkness and light high over the Kansas fields. There was no sound from this display, but the *thud-thudding* of the attack came barely muffled through the hull of the C&C van. They were, after all, less than 7,000 meters from the scene. It was mildly surprising that the enemy had not tried to take them out. Perhaps Brierson was more important, and more knowledgeable, than he admitted.

Minutes passed, and they all—President and gangsters alike—watched the barrage end and the wind push the haze away from the devastation that modern war can make. North and east, fires spread through the fields. The tanks—and final, physical possession of the disputed territory—were only minutes away.

The destruction was not uniform. New Mexican fire had focused on the projectors and rocket launchers, and there the ground was pulverized, ripped first by proximity-fused high explosives, then by digger bombs and napalm. As they watched, recon craft swooped low over the landscape, their multiscanners searching for any enemy weapons that might be held in reserve. When the tanks and personnel carriers arrived, a more thorough search would be made on foot.

Finally, Strong returned to Brierson's fantastic claim. "And you say it's just coincidence that this one farmer who spends all his money on weapons happens to be on our line of march."

"Coincidence and a little help from General van Steen."

President Martinez raised his eyes from the displays at his end. His voice was level, but Strong recognized the tension there. "Mr., uh, Brierson. Just how many of these miniforts are there?"

The other sat back. His words might have seemed insolent, but there was no sarcasm in his voice. "I have no idea, Mr. Martinez. As long as they don't bother our customers, they are of no interest to MSP. Many aren't as well hidden as Schwartz's, but you can't count on that. As long as you stay off their property, most of them won't touch you."

"You're saying that if we detect and avoid them, they are no threat to our plans?"

"Yes."

The main screen showed the tank forces now. They were a few hundred meters from the burning fields. The viewpoint rotated and Strong saw that Crick had not stinted: at least 100 tanks—most of the reserve force—were advancing on a 5,000-meter front. Following were even more personnel carriers. Tactical air support was heavy. Any fire from the ground ahead would be met by immediate destruction. The camera rotated back to show the desolation they were moving into. Strong doubted that anything living, much less anything hostile, still existed in that moonscape.

The President didn't seem interested in the display. All his attention was on the northerner. "So we can avoid these stationary gunmen till we find it convenient to deal with them. You are a great puzzle, Mr. Brierson. You claim strengths and weaknesses for your people that are equally incredible. And I get the feeling you don't really expect us to believe you, but that somehow *you* believe everything you're saying."

"You're very perceptive. I've thought of trying to bluff you. In fact, I did try earlier today. From the looks of your equipment"—he waved his hand at the Command and Control consoles, a faintly mocking smile on his face—"we might even be able to bluff you back where you belong. *This once.* But when you saw what we had done, you'd be back again—next year, next decade—and we'd have to do it all over again without the bluffs. So, Mr. Martinez, I think it best you learn what you're up against the first time out. People like Schwartz are just the beginning. Even if you can rub out them and services like MSP, you'll end up with a guerrilla war like you've never fought—one that can actually turn your own people against you. You do practice conscription, don't you?"

The President's face hardened, and Strong knew that the northerner had gone too far. "We do, as has every free nation in history—or at least every nation that was determined to stay free. If you're implying that our people would desert under fire or because of propaganda, you are contradicting my personal experience." He turned away, dismissing Brierson from his attention.

"They've arrived, sir." As the tanks rolled into position on the smoking hillsides, the personnel carriers began disgorging infantry. The tiny figures moved quickly, dragging gear toward the open tears in the earth. Strong could hear an occasional popping sound: Misfiring engines? Remnant ammo?

Tactical aircraft swept back and forth overhead, their rockets and guns ready to support the troopers on the ground. The techs' reports trickled in.

"Three video hard points detected," small arms fire chattered. "Two destroyed, one recovered. Sonoprobes show lots of tunnels. Electrical activity at—" The men in the picture looked up, at something out of view.

Nothing else changed on the picture, but the radars saw the intrusion, and the holomap showed the composite analysis: a mote of light rose leisurely out of the map—500 meters, 600. It moved straight up, slowed. The support aircraft swooped down upon it and—

A purple flash, bright yet soundless, seemed to go off *inside* Strong's head. The holomap and the displays winked down to nothing, then came back. The President's image reappeared, but there was no sound, and it was clear he was not receiving.

Along the length of the van, clerks and analysts came out of that stunned moment to work frantically with their equipment. Acrid smoke drifted into the conference area. The safe, crisp displays had been replaced by immediate, deadly reality.

"High flux nuke." The voice was calm, almost mechanical.

High flux nuke. Radiation bomb. Strong came to his feet, rage and horror burning inside him. Except for bombs in lapsed bobbles, no nuclear weapon had exploded in North America in nearly a century. Even during the bitterest years of the Water Wars, both Aztlán and New Mexico had seen the suicide implicit in nuclear solutions. But here, in a rich land, without warning and for no real reason—

"You *animals!*" he spat down upon the seated northerners.

Swensen lunged forward. "God damn it! Schwartz isn't one of my customers!"

Then the shock wave hit. Strong was thrown across the map, his face buried in the glowing terrain. Just as suddenly he was thrown back. The prisoners' guard had been knocked into the far wall; now he stumbled forward through Martinez's unseeing image, his stun gun flying from his hand.

From the moment of the detonation, Brierson had sat hunched, his arms extended under the table. Now he moved, lunging across the table to sweep up the gun between his manacled hands. The muzzle sparkled and Strong's face went numb. He watched in horror as the other twisted and raked the length of the van with stunfire. The men back there had themselves been knocked about. Several were just coming up off their knees. Most didn't know what hit them when they collapsed back to the floor. At the far end of the van, one man had kept his head. One man had been as ready as Brierson.

Bill Alvarez popped up from behind an array processor, a five millimeter slug-gun in his hand, flashing fire as he moved.

Then the numbness seemed to squeeze in on Strong's mind, and everything went gray.

WIL LOOKED DOWN THE DIM CORRIDOR THAT RAN THE LENGTH OF THE COMmand van. No one was moving, though a couple of men were snoring. The officer with the handgun had collapsed, his hands hanging limp, just a few centimeters from his pistol. Blue sky showing through the wall above Wil's head was evidence of the fellow's determination. If the other had been a hair faster . . .

Wil handed the stun gun to Big Al. "Let Jim go down and pick up the slug gun. Give an extra dose to anyone who looks suspicious."

Al nodded, but there was still a dazed look in his eyes. In the last hour, his world had been turned upside down. How many of his customers—the people who paid for his protection—had been killed? Wil tried not to think about that; indirectly, those same people had been depending on MSP. Almost tripping on his fetters, he stepped over the fallen guard and sat down on the nearest technician's saddle. For all New Mexico being a foreign land, the controls were familiar. It wasn't too surprising. The New Mexicans used a lot of Tinker electronics, though they didn't seem to trust it: much of the equipment's performance was downgraded where they had replaced suspicious components with their own devices. Ah, the price of paranoia.

Brierson picked up a command mike, made a simple request, and watched the answer parade across the console. "Hey, Al, we stopped transmitting right at the detonation!" Brierson quickly entered commands that cleared Martinez's image and blocked any future transmissions. Then he asked for status.

The air conditioning was down, but internal power could keep the gear going for a time. The van's intelligence unit estimated the nuke had been a three kiloton equivalent with a 70 percent radiance. Brierson felt his stomach flip-flop. He knew about nukes—perhaps more than the New Mexicans. There was no legal service that allowed them and it was open season on armadillos who advertised having them, but every so often MSP got a case involving such weapons. Everyone within 2,000 meters of that blast would already be dead. Schwartz's private war had wiped out a significant part of the invading forces.

The people in the van had received a sizable dose from the Schwartz nuke, though it wouldn't be life-threatening if they got medical treatment soon. In the division command area immediately around the van, the exposure was somewhat higher. How long would it be before those troops came nosing around the silent command vehicle? If he could get a phone call out—

But then there was Fate's personal vendetta against W. W. Brierson: Loud pounding sounded at the forward door. Wil waved Jim and Al to be quiet. Awkwardly, he got off the saddle and moved to look through the old-fashioned viewplate mounted next to the door. In the distance he could see men carrying stretchers from an ambulance; some of the burn cases would be really bad. Five troopers were standing right at the doorway, close enough that he could see blistered skin and burned clothing. But their weapons looked fine, and the wiry noncom pounding on the door was alert and energetic. "Hey, open up in there!"

Wil thought fast. What was the name of that VIP civilian? Then he shouted back (doing his best to imitate the clipped New Mexican accent), "Sorry, Mr. Strong doesn't want to breach internal atmosphere." *Pray they don't see the bullet holes just around the corner.*

He saw the sergeant turn away from the door. Wil lip-read the word *shit*. He could almost read the noncom's mind: The men outside had come near to being french-fried, and here some silkshirt supervisor was worried about so-far-nonexistent fallout.

The noncom turned back to the van and shouted, "How about casualties?"

"Outside of rad exposure, just some bloody noses and loose teeth. Main power is down and we can't transmit," Wil replied.

"Yes, sir. Your node has been dropped from the network. We've patched backward to Oklahoma Leader and forward to div mobile. Oklahoma Leader wants to talk to Mr. Strong. Div mobile wants to talk to Colonel Alvarez. How long will it be till you're back on the air?"

How long can I ask for? How long do I need "Give us fifteen minutes," he shouted, after a moment.

"Yes, sir. We'll get back to you." Having innocently delivered this threat, the sergeant and his troopers moved off.

Brierson hopped back to the console. "Keep your eyes on the sleepers, Al. If I'm lucky, fifteen minutes should be enough time."

"To do what? Call MSP?"

"Something better. Something I should have done this morning." He searched through the command menus for satellite pickups. The New Mexican military was apparently leery of using subscription services, but there should be some facility for it. Ah, there it was. Brierson phased the transmitter for the synchronous satellite the Hainan commune had hung over Brazil. With narrow beam, he might be able to talk through it without the New Mexicans realizing he was transmitting. He tapped in a credit number, then a destination code.

The display showed the call had reached Whidbey Island. Seconds passed. Outside, he could hear choppers moving into the camp. More ambulances? *Damn you, Rober. Be home.*

The conference area filled with bluish haze, then became a sunlit porch overlooking a wooded bay. Sounds of laughter and splashing came faintly from the water. Old Roberto Richardson never used less than full holo. But the scene was pale, almost ghostly—the best the van's internal power supply could do. A heavyset man with apparent age around thirty came up the steps onto the porch and sat down; it was Richardson. He peered out at them. "Wil? Is that you?"

If it weren't for the stale air and the dimness of the vision, Wil could almost believe he'd been transported halfway across the continent. Richardson lived on an estate that covered the whole of Whidbey Island. In the Pacific time zone it was still morning, and shadows swept across lawn-like spaces that stretched away to his manicured forests. Not for the first time, Wil was reminded of the faerie landscapes of Maxfield Parrish. Roberto Richardson was one of the richest men in the world; he sold a line of products that many people cannot resist. He was rich enough to live in whatever fantasy world he chose.

Brierson turned on the pickup that watched the conference table.

"*Dios*. It *is* you, Wil! I thought you were dead or captured."

"Neither, just yet. You're following this ruckus?"

"*Por cierto*. And most news services are covering it. I wager they're spending more money than your blessed Michigan State Police on this war. Unless that nuke was one of yours? Wili, my boy, that was spectacular. You took out twenty percent of their armor."

"It wasn't one of ours, Rober."

"Ah. Just as well. Midwest Jurisprudence would withdraw service for something like that."

Time was short, but Wil couldn't resist asking, "What is MSP up to?"

Richardson sighed. "About what I'd expect. They've finally brought some aircraft in. They're buzzing around the tip of Dave Crick's salient. The Springfield Cyborg Club has gone after the New Mexican supply lines. They were causing some damage. A cyborg is a bit hard to kill, and Norcross Security is supplying them with transports and weapons. The New Mexicans have Wáchendon suppressors down to battalion level, so there's no bobbling. The fighting looks quite twentieth century.

"You've got a lot of public opinion behind you—even in the Republic, I think—but not much firepower.

"You know, Wil, you fellows should have bought more from me. You saved a few million, maybe, passing up those aerial torpedoes and assault craft, and the tanks. But look where you are now. If—"

"Jesus, that's Robber Richardson!" It was Big Al; he had been watching the holo with growing wonder.

Richardson squinted at his display. "I can hardly see anything on this, Wil. Where in perdition are you calling from? And to you, Unseen Sir, it's *Roberto* Richardson."

Big Al walked toward the sunlit porch. He got within an apparent two meters of Richardson before he banged into the conference table. "You're the sort of scum who's responsible for this! You sold the New Mexicans everything they couldn't build themselves: the high-performance aircraft, the military electronics." Al waved at the cabinets in the darkened van. What he claimed was largely true. Wil had noticed the equipment stenciled with Richardson's logo, "USAF Inc—Sellers of Fine Weapon Systems for More than Twenty Years"; the New Mexicans hadn't even bothered to paint it out. Roberto had started out as a minor Aztlán nobleman. He'd been in just the right place at the time of the

Bobble War, and had ended up controlling the huge munition dumps left by the old Peace Authority. That had been the beginning of his fortune. Since then, he had moved into the ungoverned lands, and begun manufacturing much of his own equipment. The heavy industry he had brought to Bellevue was almost on the scale of the twentieth century—or of modern New Mexico.

Richardson came half out of his chair and chopped at the air in front of him. "See here. I have to take enough such insults from my niece and her grandchildren. I don't have to take them from a stranger." He stood, tossed his display flat on the chair, and walked to the steps that led down to his shaded river.

"Wait, Rober!" shouted Brierson. He waved Big Al back to the depths of the van. "I didn't call to pass on insults. You wondered where I'm calling from. Well, let me tell you—"

By the time he finished, the old gunrunner had returned to his seat. He started to laugh. "I should have guessed you'd end up talking right out of the lion's mouth." His laughter halted abruptly. "But you're trapped, aren't you? No last minute Brierson tricks to get out of this one? I'm sorry, Wil, I really am. If there were anything I could do, I would. I don't forget my debts."

Those were the words Wil had been hoping to hear. "There's nothing you can do for me, Rober. Our bluff in this van is good for just a few minutes, but we could all use a little charity just now."

The other looked nonplussed.

"Look, I'll bet you have plenty of aircraft and armor going through final checkout at the Bellevue plant. And I know you have ammunition stocks. Between MSP and Justice, Inc. and a few other police services, we have enough war buffs to man them. At least we have enough to make these New Mexicans think twice."

But Richardson was shaking his head. "I'm a charitable man, Wil. If I had such things to loan, MSP could have some for the asking. But you see, we've all been a bit outsmarted here. The New Mexicans—and people I now think are fronting for them—have options on the next four months of my production. You see what I mean? It's one thing to help people I like and another to break a contract—especially when reliability has always been one of my most important selling points."

Wil nodded. So much for that brilliant idea.

"And it may turn out for the best, Wil," Richardson continued quietly. "I know your loudmouth friend won't believe this, coming from me, but I think the Midwest might now be best off not to fight. We both know the invasion can't stick, not in the long run. It's just a question of how many lives and how much property is going to be destroyed in the meantime, and how much ill feeling is going to be stored up for the future. Those New Mexicans deserve to get nuked and all the rest, but that could steel them for a holy war, like they've been fighting along the Colorado for so long. On the other hand, if you let them come in and take a whack at 'governing'—why, in twenty years, you'll have them converted into happy anarchists."

Wil smiled in spite of himself. Richardson was certainly the prime example of what he was talking about. Wil knew the old autocrat had originally been an agent of Aztlán, sent to prepare the Northwest for invasion. "Okay, Rober. I'll think about it. Thanks for talking."

Richardson seemed to have guessed Wil's phantom position on his porch. His dark eyes stared intensely into Wil's. "Take care of yourself, Wili."

The cool, northern playground wavered for a second, like a dream of paradise, then vanished, replaced by the hard reality of dark plastic, glimmering displays, and unconscious New Mexicans. *What now, Lieutenant?* Calling Rober had been his only real idea. He could call MSP, but he had nothing helpful to tell them. He leaned on the console, his hands sliding slickly across his sweating face. Why not just do as Rober suggested? Give up and let the force of history take care of things.

No.

First of all, there's no such thing as "the force of history," except as it existed in the determination and imagination of individuals. Government had been a human institution for thousands of years; there was no reason to believe the New Mexicans would fall apart without some application of physical force. Their actions had to be shown to be impractically expensive.

And there was another, more personal reason. Richardson talked as though this invasion were something special, something that transcended commerce and courts and contracts. That was wrong. Except for their power and their self-righteousness, the New Mexicans were no different from some chopper gang marauding MSP customers. And if he and MSP let them take over, it would be just as much a default. As with Rober, reliability was one of MSP's strongest selling points.

So MSP had to keep fighting. The only question was, what could he and Al and Jim do now?

Wil twisted around to look at the exterior view mounted by the hatch. It was a typically crass design flaw that the view was independent of the van's computers and couldn't be displayed except at the doorway.

There wasn't much to see. The division HQ was dispersed, and the van itself sat in the bottom of a ravine. The predominant impression was of smoking foliage and yellow limestone. He heard the keening of light turbines. *Oh boy*. Three overland cars were coming their way. He recognized the sergeant he had talked to a few minutes earlier. If there was anything left to do, he'd better do it now.

He glanced around the van. Strong was a high presidential advisor. Was that worth anything? Wil tried to remember. In Aztlán, with its feudal setup, such a man might be very important. The safety of just a few leaders was the whole purpose of that government. The New Mexicans were different. Their rulers were elected; there were reasonable laws of succession, and people like Strong were probably expendable. Still, there was an idea here: Such a state was something like an enormous corporation, with the citizens as stockholders. The analogy wasn't perfect—no corporation could use the coercion these people practiced on their own. And there were other differences. But still. If the top people in such an enormous organization were threatened, it would be enormously more effective than if, say, the board of directors of MSP were hassled. There were at least ten police services as powerful as MSP in the ungoverned lands, and many of them subcontracted to smaller firms.

The question, then, was how to get their hands on someone like Hastings Martinez or this General Crick. He punched up an aerial view from somewhere south of the combat area. A train of clouds had spread southeast from the Schwartz farm. Otherwise, the air was faintly hazy. Thunderheads hung at the northern horizon. The sky had that familiar feel to it. Topeka Met Service confirmed the feeling: This was tornado weather.

Brierson grimaced. He had known that all day. And somewhere in the back of his mind, there had been the wild hope that the tornados would pick the right people to land on. Which was absurd: Modern science could kill tornadoes, but no one could direct them. *Modern science can kill tornadoes*. He swallowed. There *was* something he could do—if there was time. One call to headquarters was all he needed.

Outside, there was pounding on the door and shouting. More ominous, he heard a scrabbling noise, and the van swayed slightly on its suspension: Someone was climbing onto the roof. Wil ignored the footsteps above him, and asked the satellite link for a connection to MSP. The black and gold Michigan State logo had just appeared when the screen went dead. Wil tapped futilely at emergency codes, then looked at the exterior view again. A hard-faced major was standing next to the van.

Wil turned on the audio and interrupted the other. "We just got sound working here, Major. What's up?"

This stopped the New Mexican, who had been halfway through shouting his message at them. The officer stepped back from the van and continued in more moderate tones. "I was saying there's no fallout problem." Behind him, one of the troopers was quietly barfing into the bushes. There might be no fallout, but unless the major and his men got medical treatment soon, they would be very sick soldiers. "There's no need for you to stay buttoned up."

"Major, we're just about ready to go back on the air. I don't want to take any chances."

"Who am I speaking to?"

"Ed Strong. Special Advisor to the President." Wil spoke the words with the same ponderous importance the real Ed Strong might have used.

"Yes, sir. May I speak with Colonel Alvarez?"

"Alvarez?" Now that was a man the major must know. "Sorry, he got the corner of an equipment cabinet in the head. He hasn't come to yet."

The officer turned and gave the sergeant a sidelong look. The noncom shook his head slightly. "I see." And Wil was afraid that he really did. The major's mouth settled into a thin line. He said something to the noncom, then walked back to the cars.

Wil turned back to the other displays. It was a matter of seconds now. That major was more than suspicious. And without the satellite transmitter, Brierson didn't have a chance of reaching East Lansing or even using the loudmouth channels. The only comm links he had that didn't go through enemy nodes were the local phone bands. He could just reach Topeka Met. They would understand what he was talking about. Even if they wouldn't cooperate, they would surely pass the message back to headquarters. He ran the local directory. A second passed and he was looking at a narrowband black-and-white image. A young, good-looking male sat behind an executive-sized desk. He smiled dazzlingly and said, "Topeka Meteorological Service, Customer Relations. May I help you?"

"I sure hope so. My name's Brierson, Michigan State Police." Wil found the words tumbling out, as if he had been rehearsing this little speech for hours. The idea was simple, but there were some details. When he finished, he noticed the major coming back toward the van. One of his men carried comm gear.

The receptionist at Topeka Met frowned delicately. "Are you one of our customers, sir?"

"No, damn it. Don't you watch the news? You got four hundred tanks coming down Old70 toward Topeka. You're being invaded, man—as in *going out of business*!"

The young man shrugged in a way that indicated he never bothered with the news. "A gang invading Topeka? Sir, we are a *city*, not some farm community. In any case, what you want us to do with our tornado killers is clearly improper. It would be—"

"Listen," Wil interrupted, his voice placating, almost frightened. "At least send this message on to the Michigan State Police. Okay?"

The other smiled the same dazzling, friendly smile that had opened the conversation. "Certainly, sir." And Wil realized he had lost. He was talking to a moron or a low-grade personality simulator; it didn't matter much which. Topeka Met was like a lot of companies—it operated with just enough efficiency to stay in business. Damn the luck.

The voices from the exterior pickup were faint but clear, "—whoever they are, they're transmitting over the local phone bands, sir." It was an enlisted man talking to the New Mexican major. The major nodded and stepped toward the van.

This was it. No time left to think. Wil stabbed blindly at the directory. The Topeka Met Customer Relations "expert" disappeared and the screen began blinking a ring pattern.

"All right, Mr. Strong," the major was shouting again, loudly enough so that he could be heard through the hull of the van as well as over the pickup. The officer held a communications headset. "The President is on this line, sir. He wishes to speak with you—right now." There was a grim smile on the New Mexican's face.

Wil's fingers flicked across the control board; the van's exterior mike gave a loud squawk and was silent. With one part of his mind, he heard the enlisted man say, "They're still transmitting, Major."

And then the ring pattern vanished from the phone display. Last chance. Even an auto answerer might be enough. The screen lit up, and Wil found himself staring at a five-year-old girl.

"Trask residence." She looked a little intimidated by Wil's hulking, scowling image. But she spoke clearly, as one who has been coached in the proper response to strangers. Those serious brown eyes reminded Brierson of his own sister. Bounded by what she knew and what she understood, she would try to do what was right.

It took a great effort to relax his face and smile at the girl. "Hello. Do you know how to record my call, Miss?"

She nodded.

"Would you do that and show it to your parents, please?"

"Okay." She reached offscreen. The recording telltale gleamed at the corner of the flat, and Wil began talking. Fast.

The major's voice came over the external pickup: "Open it up, Sergeant." There were quick footsteps and something slapped against the hatch.

"Wil!" Big Al grabbed his shoulder. "Get down. Away from the hatch. Those are slug-guns they have out there!"

But Brierson couldn't stop now. He pushed Al away, waved for him to get down among the fallen New Mexicans.

The explosion was a sharp cracking sound that rocked the van sideways. The phone connection held, and Wil kept talking. Then the door fell, or was pulled outward, and daylight splashed across him.

"Get away from that phone!"

On the display, the little girl seemed to look past Wil. Her eyes widened. She was the last thing W. W. Brierson saw.

THERE WERE DREAMS. IN SOME HE COULD ONLY SEE. IN OTHERS, HE WAS blind, yet hearing and smell were present, all mixed together. And some were pure pain, winding up and up while all around him torturers twisted screws and needles to squeeze the last bit of hurt from his shredded flesh. But he also sensed his parents and sister Beth, quiet and near. And sometimes when he could see and the pain was gone, there were flowers—almost a jungle of them—dipping near his eyes, smelling of violin music.

Snow. Smooth, pristine, as far as his eyes could see. Trees glazed in ice that sparkled against cloudless blue sky. Wil raised his hand to rub his eyes and felt faint surprise to see the hand obey, to feel hand touch face as he willed it.

"Wili, Wili! You're really back!" Someone warm and dark rushed in from the side. Tiny arms laced around his neck. "We knew you'd come back. But it's been so *long*." His five-year-old sister snuggled her face against him.

As he lowered his arm to pat her head, a technician came around from behind him. "Wait a minute, honey. Just because his eyes are open doesn't mean he's back. We've gotten that far before." Then he saw the grin on Wil's face, and *his* eyes widened a bit. "L-Lieutenant Brierson! Can you understand me?" Wil nodded, and the tech glanced over his head—probably at some diagnostic display. Then he smiled, too. "You do understand me! Just a minute, I'm going to get my supervisor. Don't touch anything." He rushed out of the room, his last words more an unbelieving mumbling to himself than anything else: "I was beginning to wonder if we'd ever get past protocol rejection."

Beth Brierson looked up at her brother. "Are you okay, now, Wili?"

Wil wiggled his toes, and *felt* them wiggle. He certainly felt okay. He nodded. Beth stepped back from the bed. "I want to go get Mom and Dad."

Wil smiled again. "I'll be right here waiting."

Then she was gone, too. Brierson glanced around the room and recognized the locale of several of his nightmares. But it was an ordinary hospital room, perhaps a little heavy on electronics, and still, he was not alone in it. Alvin Swensen, dressed as offensively as ever, sat in the shadows next to the window. Now he stood up and crossed the room to shake hands.

Wil grunted. "My own parents aren't here to greet me, yet Big Al *is*."

"Your bad luck. If you'd had the courtesy to come around the first time they tried to bring you back, you would have had your family and half MSP waiting for you. You were a hero."

"Were?"

"Oh, you still are, Wil. But it's been a while, you know." There was a crooked smile on his face.

Brierson looked through the window at the bright winter's day. The land was familiar. He was back in Michigan, probably at Okemos Central Medical. But Beth didn't look much older. "Around six months, I'd guess."

Big Al nodded. "And, no, I haven't been sitting here every day watching your face for some sign of life. I happened to be in East Lansing today. My Protection Racket still has some insurance claims against your company. MSP paid off all the big items quick, but some of the little things—bullet holes in outbuildings, stuff like that—they're dragging their heels on. Anyway, I thought I'd drop by and see how you're doing."

"Hmm. So you're not saluting the New Mexican flag down there in Manhattan?"

"What? Hell no, we're not!" Then Al seemed to remember who he was talking to. "Look, Wil, in a few minutes you're gonna have the medical staff in here patting themselves on the back for pulling off another medical miracle, and your family will be right on top of that. And after *that*, your Colonel Potts will fill you in again on everything that's happened. Do you really want Al Swensen's Three-Minute History of the Great Plains War?"

Wil nodded.

"Okay." Big Al moved his chair close to the bed. "The New Mexicans pulled back from the ungoverned lands less than three days after they grabbed you and me and Jim Turner. The official Republic view was that the Great Plains Action was a victory for the decisive and restrained use of military force. The 'roving gangster bands' of the ungoverned wastes had been punished for their abuse of New Mexican settlers, and one W. W. Brierson, the ringleader of the northern criminals, had been killed."

"I'm dead?" said Wil.

"Dead enough for their purposes." Big Al seemed momentarily uneasy. "I don't know whether I should tell a sick man how much sicker he once was, but you got hit in the back of the head with a five-millimeter exploder. The Newmex didn't hurt me or Jim, so I don't think it was vengeance. But when they blew in the door, there you were, doing something with their command equipment. They were already hurting, and they didn't have any stun guns, I guess."

A five-millimeter exploder. Will knew what they could do. He *should* be dead. If it hit near the neck, there might be some forebrain tissue left, but the front of his face would have been blown out. He touched his nose wonderingly.

Al saw the motion. "Don't worry. You're as beautiful as ever. But at the time, you looked *very* dead—even to their best medics. They popped you into stasis. The three of us spent nearly a month in detention in Oklahoma. When we were 'repatriated,' the people at Okemos Central didn't have any trouble growing back the front of your face. Maybe even the New Mexicans could do that. The problem is, you're missing a big chunk of brain. He patted the back of his head. "*That* they couldn't grow back. So they replaced it with processing equipment, and tried to interface that with what was left."

Wil experienced a sudden, chilling moment of introspection. He really should be dead. Could this all be in the imagination of some damned prosthesis program?

Al saw his face, and looked stricken. "Honest, Wil, it wasn't *that* large a piece. Just big enough to fool those dumbass New Mexicans."

The moment passed and Brierson almost chuckled. If self-awareness were suspect, there could scarcely be certainty of anything. And in fact, it was years before that particular terror resurfaced.

"Okay. So the New Mexican incursion was a great success. Now tell me why they *really* left. Was it simply the Schwartz bomb?"

"I think that was part of it." Even with the nuke, the casualties had not been high. Only the troops and tankers within three or four thousand meters of the blast were killed—perhaps 2,000 men. This was enormous by the standards Wil was used to, but not by the measure of the Water Wars. Overall, the New Mexicans could claim that it had been an "inexpensive" action.

But the evidence of casual acceptance of nuclear warfare, all the way down to the level of an ordinary farmer, was terrifying to the New Mexican brass. Annexing the Midwest would be like running a grade school where the kids carried slug guns. They probably didn't realize that Schwartz would have been lynched the first time he stepped off his property if his neighbors had realized beforehand that he was nuke-armed.

"But I think your little phone call was just as important."

"About using the tornado killers?"

"Yeah. It's one thing to step on a rattlesnake, and another to suddenly realize you're up to your ankles in 'em. I bet the weather services have equipped hundreds of farms with killers—all the way from Okemos to Greeley." And, as Wil had realized on that summer day when last he was truly conscious, a tornado killer is essentially an aerial torpedo. Their use was coordinated by the meteorological companies, which paid individual farmers to house them. During severe weather alerts, coordinating processors at a met-service headquarters monitored remote sensors, and launched killers from appropriate points in the countryside. Normally, they would be airborne for minutes, but they could loiter for hours. When remote sensing found a twister, the killers came in at the top of the funnel, generated a 50-meter bobble, and destabilized the vortex.

Take that loiter capability, make trivial changes in the flight software, and you have a weapon capable of flying hundreds of kilometers and delivering a one tonne payload with pinpoint accuracy. "Even without nukes they're pretty fearsome. Especially if used like you suggested."

Wil shrugged. Actually, the target he had suggested was the usual one when dealing with marauding gangs. Only the scale was different.

"You know the Trasks—that family you called right at the end? Bill Trask's brother rents space for three killers to Topeka Met. They stole one of them and did just like you said. The news services had spotted Martinez's location; the Trasks flew the killer right into the roof of the mansion he and his staff were using down in Oklahoma. We got satellite pics of what happened. Those New Mexican big shots came storming out of there like ants in a meth fire." Even now, months later, the memory made Big Al laugh. "Bill Trask told me he painted something like 'Hey, hey Hastings, the *next* one is for real!' on the fuselage. I bet even yet, their top people are living under concrete, wondering whether to keep their bobble suppressors up or down.

"But they got the message. Inside of twelve hours, their troops were moving back south and they were starting to talk about their statesmanship and the lesson they had taught us."

Wil started to laugh, too. The room shimmered colorfully in time with his laughter. It was not painful, but it was disconcerting enough to make him stop. "Good. So we didn't need those bums from Topeka Met."

"Right. Fact is, they had me arrest the Trasks for theft. But when they finally got their corporate head out of the dirt, they dropped charges and tried to pretend it had been their idea all along. Now they're modifying their killers and selling the emergency-control rights."

Far away (he remembered the long hallways at Okemos Central), he heard voices. And none familiar. *Damn.* The medics were going to get to him before his family. Big Al heard the commotion, too. He stuck his head out the door, then said to Wil, "Well, Lieutenant, this is where I desert. You know the short version, anyway." He walked across the room to pick up his data set.

Wil followed him with his eyes. "So it all ended for the best, except—"

Except for all those poor New Mexican souls caught under a light brighter than any Kansas sun, except for—"Kiki and Schwartz. I wish they could know how things turned out."

Big Al stopped halfway to the door, a surprised look on his face. "Kiki and Jake? One is too smart to die and the other is too mean! She knew Jake would thump her for bringing the New Mexicans across his land. She and my boys were way underground long before he wiped off. And Jake was dug in even deeper.

"Hell, Wil, they're even bigger celebrities than you are! Old Jake has become the Midwest's pop armadillo. None of us ever guessed, least of all him: He *enjoys* being a public person. He and Kiki have buried the hatchet. Now they're talking about a worldwide club for armadillos. They figure if one can stop an entire nation state, what can a bunch of them do? You know: 'Make the world safe for the ungoverned.' "

Then he was gone. Wil had just a moment to chew on the problems van Steen and Schwartz would cause the Michigan State Police before the triumphant med techs crowded into his room.

How serious am I about the anarcho-capitalism in "The Ungoverned"? It is something I think could really work. In fact, it's the endpoint of many good trends of the last five hundred years. I don't think it could work without a high degree of individual understanding (awareness of where one's long-term self-interest lies), and a generally tranquil atmosphere; events such as those in this story had better be the *exception.* If you are interested in a detailed nonfiction analysis of such ideas, I strongly recommend David Friedman's *The Machinery of Freedom.* If you'd like to see my future history before and after the time of "The Ungoverned," there is a prequel novel, *The Peace War,* and a sequel, *Marooned in Realtime.*

The point I make about nuclear weapons in "The Ungoverned" is more controversial (and hopefully irrelevant). In the twentieth century we lived in fear of proliferation and put what trust we had in nuclear monopolies. The trouble with nuclear monopolies is that while they may prevent worldwide nuclear war, if one *does* happen it could involve the use of *thousands* of weapons. Heaven forbid that there be such a catastrophe, but the most likely post-war scenario is one in which nukes are occasionally used, but never in large numbers—basically because large power blocs are not tolerated by their smaller neighbors. Such a world would be a moderately dangerous place (especially for bullies), but it might be safer than our world. (Henry Kuttner made some of these points in his novel, *Mutant.* Of all the pre-Hiroshima nuclear SF, his story may be the least remembered—and the most prophetic.) In the long run, of course, even individuals will have enormous destructive power—just another reason why one planet is too small a place for a race to live safely.

LONG SHOT

By itself, it seems unlikely that war could destroy the human race, or even bring a permanent halt to our slide into the Singularity. Yet the universe itself can be a rough place; we have plenty of evidence of mass extinctions. If we had a technology-smashing war *plus* an extended natural catastrophe, we could join the dinosaurs.

And of course, there are natural cataclysms that can destroy not just life but entire planets. Fortunately, the most extreme stellar catastrophes—such as supernovas—are impossible for a star like our sun. What about smaller events, burps in the life of otherwise placid stars? We have no guarantee that our sun is safe from these. What would we do if, in the next fifteen years, we discovered that our sun was about to enter an extended period of increased luminance, frying the surfaces of the inner planets? Given a decade, could we establish a self-sustaining colony in the outer solar system? If not, could we find Earth-like planets elsewhere? At present, sending even the smallest probe to the nearest stars is just beyond our ability. Not a single living person could be saved. Whatever we tried would indeed be a . . .

LONG SHOT

They named her Ilse, and of all Earth's creatures, she was to be the longest lived—and perhaps the last. A prudent tortoise might survive three hundred years and a bristle-cone pine six thousand, but Ilse's designed span exceeded one hundred centuries. And though her brain was iron and germanium doped with arsenic, and her heart was a tiny cloud of hydrogen plasma, Ilse *was*—in the beginning—one of Earth's creatures: she could feel, she could question, and—as she discovered during the dark centuries before her fiery end—she could also forget.

Ilse's earliest memory was a fragment, amounting to less than fifteen seconds. Someone, perhaps inadvertently, brought her to consciousness as she sat atop her S-5N booster. It was night, but their launch was imminent and the booster stood white and silver in the light of a dozen spotlights. Ilse's sharp eye scanned rapidly around the horizon, untroubled by the glare from below. Stretching away from her to the north was a line of thirty launch pads. Several had their own boosters, though none were lit up as Ilse's was. Three thousand meters to the west were more lights, and the occasional sparkle of an automatic rifle. To the east, surf marched in phosphorescent ranks against the Merritt Island shore.

There the fragment ended: she was not conscious during the launch. But that scene remained forever her most vivid and incomprehensible memory.

When next she woke, Ilse was in low Earth orbit. Her single eye had been fitted to a one hundred and fifty centimeter reflecting telescope so that now she could distinguish stars set less than a tenth of a second apart, or, if she looked straight down, count the birds in a flock of geese two hundred kilometers below. For more than a year Ilse remained in this same orbit. She was not idle. Her makers had allotted this period for testing. A small manned station orbited with her, and from it came an endless sequence of radioed instructions and exercises.

Most of the problems were ballistic: hyperbolic encounters, transfer ellipses, and the like. But it was often required that Ilse use her own telescope and spectrometer to discover the parameters of the problems. A typical exercise: determine the orbits of Venus and Mercury; compute a minimum energy flyby of both planets. Another: determine the orbit of Mars; analyze its atmosphere; plan a hyperbolic entry subject to constraints. Many observational problems dealt with Earth: determine atmospheric pressure and composition; perform multispectrum analysis of vegetation. Usually she was required to solve organic analysis problems in less than thirty seconds. And in these last problems, the rules were often changed even while the game was played. Her orientation jets would be caused to malfunction. Critical portions of her mind and senses would be degraded.

One of the first things Ilse learned was that in addition to her private memories, she had a programmed memory, a "library" of procedures and facts. As with most libraries, the programmed memory was not as accessible as Ilse's own recollections, but the information contained there was much more complete and precise. The solution program for almost any ballistic, or chemical, problem could be lifted from this "library," used for seconds, or hours, as an integral part of Ilse's mind, and then returned to the "library." The real trick was to select the proper program on the basis of incomplete information, and then to modify that program to meet various combinations of power and equipment failure. Though she did poorly at first, Ilse eventually surpassed her design specifications. At this point her training stopped and for the first—but not the last—time, Ilse was left to her own devices.

Though she had yet to wonder on her ultimate purpose, still she wanted to see as much of her world as possible. She spent most of each daylight pass looking straight down, trying to see some order in the jumble of blue and green and white. She could easily follow the supply rockets as they climbed up from Merritt Island and Baikonur to rendezvous with her. In the end, more than a hundred of the rockets were floating about her. As the weeks passed, the squat white cylinders were fitted together on a spidery frame.

Now her ten-meter-long body was lost in the webwork of cylinders and girders that stretched out two hundred meters behind her. Her programmed memory told her that the entire assembly massed 22,563.901 tons—more than most ocean-going ships—and a little experimenting with her attitude control jets convinced her that this figure was correct.

Soon her makers connected Ilse's senses to the mammoth's control mechanisms. It was as if she had been given a new body, for she could feel, and see, and use each of the hundred propellant tanks and each of the fifteen fusion reactors that made up the assembly. She realized that now she had the power to perform some of the maneuvers she had planned during her training.

FINALLY THE GREAT MOMENT ARRIVED. COURSE DIRECTIONS CAME OVER THE maser link with the manned satellite. Ilse quickly computed the trajectory that would result from these directions. The answer she obtained was correct, but it revealed only the smallest part of what was in store for her.

In her orbit two hundred kilometers up, Ilse coasted smoothly toward high noon over the Pacific. Her eye was pointed forward, so that on the fuzzy blue horizon she could see the edge of the North American continent. Nearer, the granulated cloud cover obscured the ocean itself. The command to begin the burn came from the manned satellite, but Ilse was following the clock herself, and she had determined to take over the launch if any mistakes were made. Two hundred meters behind her, deep in the maze of tanks and beryllium girders, Ilse felt magnetic fields establish themselves, felt hydrogen plasma form, felt fusion commence. Another signal from the station, and propellant flowed around each of ten reactors.

Ilse and her twenty-thousand-ton booster were on their way.

Acceleration rose smoothly to one gravity. Behind her, vidicons on the booster's superstructure showed the Earth shrinking. For half an hour the burn continued, monitored by Ilse, and the manned station now fallen far behind. Then Ilse was alone with her booster, coasting away from Earth and her creators at better than twenty kilometers a second.

So Ilse began her fall toward the sun. For eleven weeks she fell. During this time, there was little to do: monitor the propellants, keep the booster's sun-shade properly oriented, relay data to Earth. Compared to much of her later life, however, it was a time of hectic activity.

A fall of eleven weeks toward a body as massive as the sun can result in only one thing: speed. In those last hours, Ilse hurtled downwards at better than two hundred and fifty kilometers per second—an Earth to Moon distance every half hour. Forty-five minutes before her closest approach to the sun—perihelion—Ilse jettisoned the empty first stage and its sunshade. Now she was left with the two-thousand-ton second stage, whose insulation consisted of a bright coat of white paint. She felt the pressure in the propellant tanks begin to rise.

Though her telescope was pointed directly away from the sun, the vidicons on the second stage gave her an awesome view of the solar fireball. She was moving so fast now that the sun's incandescent prominences changed perspective even as she watched.

Seventeen minutes to perihelion. From somewhere beyond the flames, Ilse got the expected maser communication. She pitched herself and her booster over so that she looked along the line of her trajectory. Now her own body was exposed to the direct glare of the sun. Through her telescope she could see luminous tracery within the solar corona. The booster's fuel tanks were perilously close to bursting, and Ilse was having trouble keeping her own body at its proper temperature.

Fifteen minutes to perihelion. The command came from Earth to begin the burn. Ilse considered her own trajectory data, and concluded that the command was thirteen seconds premature. Consultation with Earth would cost at least sixteen minutes, and her decision must be made in the next four seconds. Any of Man's earlier, less sophisticated creations would have accepted the error and taken the mission on to catastrophe, but independence was the essence of Ilse's nature: she overrode the maser command, and delayed ignition till the instant she thought correct.

THE SUN'S NORTHERN HEMISPHERE PASSED BELOW HER, LESS THAN THREE solar diameters away.

Ignition, and Ilse was accelerated at nearly two gravities. As she swung toward what was to have been perihelion, her booster lifted her out of elliptic orbit and into a hyperbolic one. Half an hour later she shot out from the sun into the spaces south of the ecliptic at three hundred and twenty kilometers per second—about one solar diameter every hour. The booster's now empty propellant tanks were between her and the sun, and her body slowly cooled.

Shortly after burnout, Earth off-handedly acknowledged the navigation error. This is not to say that Ilse's makers were without contrition for their mistake, or without praise for Ilse. In fact, several men lost what little there remained to confiscate for jeopardizing this mission, and Man's last hope. It was simply that Ilse's makers did not believe that she could appreciate apologies or praise.

Now Ilse fled up out of the solar gravity well. It had taken her eleven weeks to fall from Earth to Sol, but in less than two weeks she had regained this altitude, and still she plunged outwards at more than one hundred kilometers per second. That velocity remained her inheritance from the sun. Without the gravity-well maneuver, her booster would have had to be five hundred times as large, or her voyage three times as long. It had been the very best that men could do for her, considering the time remaining to them.

So began the voyage of one hundred centuries. Ilse parted with the empty booster and floated on alone: a squat cylinder, twelve meters wide, five meters long, with a large telescope sticking from one end. Four light-years below her in the well of the night she saw Alpha Centauri, her destination. To the naked human eye, it appears a single bright star, but with her telescope Ilse could clearly see two stars, one slightly fainter and redder than the other. She carefully measured their position and her own, and concluded that her aim had been so perfect that a midcourse correction would not be necessary for a thousand years.

For many months, Earth maintained maser contact—to pose problems and ask after her health. It was almost pathetic, for if anything went wrong now, or in the centuries to follow, there was very little Earth could do to help. The problems were interesting, though. Ilse was asked to chart the nonluminous bodies in the Solar System. She became quite skilled at this and eventually discovered all nine planets, most of their moons, and several asteroids and comets.

In less than two years, Ilse was farther from the sun than any known planet, than any previous terrestrial probe. The sun itself was no more than a very bright star behind her, and Ilse had no trouble keeping her frigid innards at their proper temperature. But now it took sixteen hours to ask a question of Earth and obtain an answer.

A strange thing happened. Over a period of three weeks, the sun became steadily brighter until it gleamed ten times as luminously as before. The change was not really a great one. It was far short of what Earth's astronomers would have called a nova. Nevertheless, Ilse puzzled over the event, in her own way, for many months, since it was at this time that she lost maser contact with Earth. That contact was never regained.

Now Ilse changed herself to meet the empty centuries. As her designers had planned, she split her mind into three coequal entities. Theoretically each of these minds could handle the entire mission alone, but for any important decision, Ilse required the agreement of at least two of the minds. In this fractionated state, Ilse was neither as bright nor as quick-thinking as she had been at launch. But scarcely anything happened in interstellar space, the chief danger being senile decay. Her three minds spent as much time checking one another as they did over-seeing the various subsystems.

The one thing they did not regularly check was the programmed memory, since Ilse's designers had—mistakenly—judged that such checks were a greater danger to the memories than the passage of time.

Even with her mentality diminished, and in spite of the caretaker tasks assigned her, Ilse spent much of her time contemplating the universe that spread out forever around her. She discovered binary star systems, then watched the tiny lights swing back and forth around each other as the decades and centuries passed. To her the universe became a moving, almost a living, thing. Several of the nearer stars drifted almost a degree every century, while the great galaxy in Andromeda shifted less than a second of arc in a thousand years.

Occasionally, she turned about to look at Sol. Even ten centuries out she could still distinguish Jupiter and Saturn. These were auspicious observations.

Finally it was time for the mid-course correction. She had spent the preceding century refining her alignment and her navigational observations. The burn was to be only one hundred meters per second, so accurate had been her perihelion impulse. Nevertheless, without that correction she would miss the Centauran system entirely. When the second arrived and her alignment was perfect, Ilse lit her tiny rocket—and discovered that she could obtain at most only three quarters of the rated thrust. She had to make two burns before she was satisfied with the new course.

For the next fifty years, Ilse studied the problem. She tested the rocket's electrical system hundreds of times, and even fired the rocket in microsecond bursts. She never discovered how the centuries had robbed her, but extrapolating from her observations, Ilse realized that by the time she entered the Centauran system, she would have only a thousand meters per second left in her rocket—less than half its designed capability. Even so it was possible that, without further complications, she would be able to survey the planets of both stars in the system.

But before she finished her study of the propulsion problem, Ilse discovered another breakdown—the most serious she was to face:

She had forgotten her mission. Over the centuries the pattern of magnetic fields on her programmed memory had slowly disappeared—the least used programs going first. When Ilse recalled those programs to discover how her reduced maneuverability affected the mission, she discovered that she no longer had any record of her ultimate purpose. The memories ended with badly faded programs for biochemical reconnaissance and planetary entry, and Ilse guessed that there was something crucial left to do after a successful landing on a suitable planet.

Ilse was a patient sort—especially in her cruise configuration—and she didn't worry about her ultimate purpose, so far away in the future. But she did do her best to preserve what programs were left. She played each program into her own memory and then back to the programmed memory. If the process were repeated every seventy years, she found that she could keep the programmed memories from fading. On the other hand, she had no way of knowing how many errors this endless repetition was introducing. For this reason she had each of her subminds perform the process separately, and she frequently checked the ballistic and astronomical programs by doing problems with them.

Ilse went further: she studied her own body for clues as to its purpose. Much of her body was filled with a substance she must keep within a few degrees of absolute zero. Several leads disappeared into this mass. Except for her thermometers, however, she had no feeling in this part of her body. Now she raised the temperature in this section a few thousandths of a degree, a change well within design specifications, but large enough for her to sense. Comparing her observations and the section's mass with her chemical analysis programs, Ilse concluded that the mysterious area was a relatively homogeneous body of frozen water, doped with various impurities. It was interesting information, but no matter how she compared it with her memories she could not see any significance to it.

Ilse floated on—and on. The period of time between the midcourse maneuver and the next important event on her schedule was longer than Man's experience with agriculture had been on Earth.

As the centuries passed, the two closely set stars that were her destination became brighter until, a thousand years from Alpha Centauri, she decided to begin her search for planets in the system. Ilse turned her telescope on the brighter of the two stars . . . call it Able. She was still thirty-five thousand times as far from Able—and the smaller star . . . call it Baker—as Earth is from Sol. Even to her sharp eye, Able didn't show as a disk but rather as a diffraction pattern: a round blob of light—many times larger than the star's true disk—surrounded by a ring of light. The faint gleam of any planets would be lost in that diffraction pattern. For five years Ilse watched the pattern, analyzed it with one of her most subtle programs. Occasionally she slid occulting plates into the telescope and studied the resulting, distorted, pattern. After five years she had found suggestive anomalies in the diffraction pattern, but no definite signs of planets.

No matter. Patient Ilse turned her telescope a tiny fraction of a degree, and during the next five years she watched Baker. Then she switched back to Able. Fifteen times Ilse repeated this cycle. While she watched, Baker completed two revolutions about Able, and the stars' maximum mutual separation increased to nearly a tenth of a degree. Finally Ilse was certain: she had discovered a planet orbiting Baker, and perhaps another orbiting Able. Most likely they were both gas giants. No matter: she knew that any small, inner planets would still be lost in the glare of Able and Baker.

There remained less than nine hundred years before she coasted through the Centauran system.

Ilse persisted in her observations. Eventually she could see the gas giants as tiny spots of light—not merely as statistical correlations in her carefully collected diffraction data. Four hundred years out, she decided that the remaining anomalies in Able's diffraction pattern must be another planet, this one at about the same distance from Able as Earth is from Sol. Fifteen years later she made a similar discovery for Baker.

If she were to investigate both of these planets she would have to plan very carefully. According to her design specifications, she had scarcely the maneuvering capability left to investigate one system. But Ilse's navigation system had survived the centuries better than expected, and she estimated that a survey of both planets might still be possible.

Three hundred and fifty years out, Ilse made a relatively large course correction, better than two hundred meters per second. This change was essentially a matter of pacing: It would delay her arrival by four months. Thus she would pass near the planet she wished to investigate and, if no landing were attempted, her path would be precisely bent by Able's gravitational field and she would be cast into Baker's planetary system.

Now Ilse had less than eight hundred meters per second left in her rocket—less than one percent of her velocity relative to Able and Baker. If she could be at the right place at the right time, that would be enough, but otherwise . . .

ILSE PLOTTED THE ORBITS OF THE BODIES SHE HAD DETECTED MORE AND MORE accurately. Eventually she discovered several more planets: a total of three for Able, and four for Baker. But only her two prime candidates—call them Able II and Baker II—were at the proper distance from their suns.

Eighteen months out, Ilse sighted moons around Able II. This was good news. Now she could accurately determine the planet's mass, and so refine her course even more. Ilse was now less than fifty astronomical units from Able, and eighty from Baker. She had no trouble making spectroscopic observations of the planets. Her prime candidates had plenty of oxygen in their atmospheres—though the farther one,

Baker II, seemed deficient in water vapor. On the other hand, Able II had complex carbon compounds in its atmosphere, and its net color was blue green. According to Ilse's damaged memory, these last were desirable features.

The centuries had shrunk to decades, then to years, and finally to days. Ilse was within the orbit of Able's gas giant. Ten million kilometers ahead her target swept along a nearly circular path about its sun, Able. Twenty-seven astronomical units beyond Able gleamed Baker.

But Ilse kept her attention on that target, Able II. Now she could make out its gross continental outlines. She selected a landing site, and performed a two hundred meter per second burn. If she chose to land, she would come down in a greenish, beclouded area.

Twelve hours to contact. Ilse checked each of her subminds one last time. She deleted all malfunctioning circuits, and reassembled herself as a single mind out of what remained. Over the centuries, one third of all her electrical components had failed, so that besides her lost memories, she was not nearly as bright as she had been when launched. Nevertheless, with her subminds combined she was much cleverer than she had been during the cruise. She needed this greater alertness, because in the hours and minutes preceding her encounter with Able II, she would do more analysis and make more decisions than ever before.

One hour to contact. Ilse was within the orbit of her target's outer moon. Ahead loomed the tentative destination, a blue and white crescent two degrees across. Her landing area was around the planet's horizon. No matter. The important task for these last moments was a biochemical survey—at least that's what her surviving programs told her. She scanned the crescent, looking for traces of green through the clouds. She found a large island in a Pacific-sized ocean, and began the exquisitely complex analysis necessary to determine the orientation of amino acids. Every fifth second, she took one second to re-estimate the atmospheric densities. The problems seemed even more complicated than her training exercises back in Earth orbit.

Five minutes to contact. She was less than forty thousand kilometers out, and the planet's hazy limb filled her sky. In the next ten seconds she must decide whether or not to land on Able II. Her ten-thousand-year mission was at stake here. For once Ilse landed, she knew that she would never fly again. Without the immense booster that had pushed her out along this journey, she was nothing but a brain and an entry shield and a chunk of frozen water. If she decided to bypass Able II, she must now use a large portion of her remaining propellants to accelerate at right angles to her trajectory. This would cause her to miss the upper edge of the planet's atmosphere, and she would go hurtling out of Able's planetary system. Thirteen months later she would arrive in the vicinity of Baker, perhaps with enough left in her rocket to guide herself into Baker II's atmosphere. But, if that planet should be inhospitable, there would be no turning back: she would have to land there, or else coast on into interstellar darkness.

Ilse weighed the matter for three seconds and concluded that Able II satisfied every criterion she could recall, while Baker II seemed a bit too yellow, a bit too dry.

Ilse turned ninety degrees and jettisoned the small rocket that had given her so much trouble. At the same time she ejected the telescope which had served her so well. She floated indivisible, a white biconvex disk, twelve meters in diameter, fifteen tons in mass.

She turned ninety degrees more to look directly back along her trajectory. There was not much to see now that she had lost her scope, but she recognized the point of light that was Earth's sun and wondered again what had been on all those programs that she had forgotten.

Five seconds. Ilse closed her eye and waited.

Contact began as a barely perceptible acceleration. In less than two seconds that acceleration built to two hundred and fifty gravities. This was beyond Ilse's experience, but she was built to take it: her body contained no moving parts and—except for her fusion reactor—no empty spaces. The really difficult thing was to keep her body from turning edgewise and burning up. Though she didn't know it, Ilse was repeating—on a grand scale—the landing technique that men had used so long ago. But Ilse had to dissipate more than eight hundred times the kinetic energy of any returning Apollo capsule. Her maneuver was correspondingly more dangerous, but since her designers could not equip her with a rocket powerful enough to decelerate her, it was the only option.

Now Ilse used her wits and every dyne in her tiny electric thrusters to arc herself about Able II at the proper attitude and altitude. The acceleration rose steadily toward five hundred gravities, or almost five kilometers per second in velocity lost every second. Beyond that Ilse knew that she would lose consciousness. Just centimeters away from her body the air glowed at fifty thousand degrees. The fireball that surrounded her lit the ocean seventy kilometers below as with daylight.

Four hundred and fifty gravities. She felt a cryostat shatter, and one branch of her brain short through. Still Ilse worked patiently and blindly to keep her body properly oriented. If she had calculated correctly, there were less than five seconds to go now.

She came within sixty kilometers of the surface, then rose steadily back into space. But now her velocity was only seven kilometers per second. The acceleration fell to a mere fifteen gravities, then to zero.

She coasted back through a long ellipse to plunge, almost gently, into the depths of Able II's atmosphere.

At twenty thousand meters altitude, Ilse opened her eye and scanned the world below. Her lens had been cracked, and several of her gestalt programs damaged, but she saw green and knew her navigation hadn't been too bad.

It would have been a triumphant moment if only she could have remembered what she was supposed to do *after* she landed.

At ten thousand meters, Ilse popped her paraglider from the hull behind her eye. The tough plastic blossomed out above her, and her fall became a shallow glide. Ilse saw that she was flying over a prairie spotted here and there by forest. It was near sunset and the long shadows cast by trees and hills made it easy for her to gauge the topography.

Two thousand meters. With a glide ratio of one to four, she couldn't expect to fly more than another eight kilometers. Ilse looked ahead, saw a tiny forest, and a stream glinting through the trees. Then she saw a glade just inside the forest, and some vagrant memory told her this was an appropriate spot. She pulled in the paraglider's forward lines and slid more steeply downwards. As she passed three or four meters over the trees surrounding the glade, Ilse pulled in the rear lines, stalled her glider, and fell into the deep, moist grass. Her dun and green paraglider collapsed over her charred body so that she might be mistaken for a large black boulder covered with vegetation.

The voyage that had crossed one hundred centuries and four light-years was ended.

ILSE SAT IN THE GATHERING TWILIGHT AND LISTENED. SOUND WAS AN UN-dreamed of dimension to her: tiny things burrowing in their holes, the stream gurgling nearby, a faint chirping in the distance. Twilight ended and a shallow fog rose in the dark glade. Ilse knew her voyaging was over. She would never more again. No matter. That had been planned, she was sure. She knew that much of her computing machinery—her mind—had been destroyed in the landing. She would not survive as a conscious being for more than another century or two. No matter.

What did matter was that she knew that her mission was not completed, and that the most important part remained, else the immense gamble her makers had undertaken would finally come to nothing. That possibility was the only thing which could frighten Ilse. It was part of her design.

She reviewed all the programmed memories that had survived the centuries and the planetary entry, but discovered nothing new. She investigated the rest of her body, testing her parts in a thorough, almost destructive, way she never would have dared while still centuries from her destination. She discovered nothing new. Finally she came to that load of ice she had carried so far. With one of her cryostats broken, she couldn't keep it at its proper temperature for more than a few years. She recalled the apparently useless leads that disappeared into that mass. There was only one thing left to try.

Ilse turned down her cryostats, and waited as the temperature within her climbed. The ice near her small fusion reactor warmed first. Somewhere in the frozen mass a tiny piece of metal expanded just far enough to complete a circuit, and Ilse discovered that her makers had taken one last precaution to insure her reliability. At the base of the icy hulk, next to the reactor, they had placed an auxiliary memory unit, and now Ilse had access to it. Her designers had realized that no matter what dangers they imagined, there would be others, and so they had decided to leave this back-up cold and inactive till the very end. And the new memory unit was quite different from her old ones, Ilse vaguely realized. It used optical rather than magnetic storage.

Now Ilse knew what she must do. She warmed a cylindrical tank filled with frozen amniotic fluid to thirty-seven degrees centigrade. From the store next to the cylinder, she injected a single microorganism into the tank. In a few minutes she would begin to suffuse blood through the tank.

It was early morning now and the darkness was moist and cool. Ilse tried to probe her new memory further, but was balked. Apparently the instructions were delivered according to some schedule to avoid unnecessary use of the memory. Ilse reviewed what she had learned, and decided that she would know more in another nine months.

"Long Shot" was many things to me. I wanted the apotheosis of all the planetary missions that dominated space exploration in the twentieth century. I wanted to describe the smallest colony mission that could ever be attempted. (In fact, my only authorly reason for "blowing up" the sun was to justify such a screwball attempt.)

The part of the adventure that I show is certainly a "long shot," but it's not the most desperate part of the mission. At the end of the story, we know that Ilse is bearing human zygotes. Consider her size: She could contain many zygotes, but nowhere near the mass to bring them all to term. And what will she do with the babies? How to feed them, how to teach them? Surely, humanity did not expect that there was an alien civilization at the target. (Hmm, maybe they did! We only know what Ilse remembers. An alien race would be a cop-out, but it would make writing a sequel more fun.) Hey, I really do have some ideas about Ilse's future (and that is the true "long shot" behind the title). The unwritten sequel would probably take place about ten years later, and a good title might be "Firstborn Son."

Of course, Ilse is far from being the smallest possible interstellar probe. Early in the twentieth century, Svante Arrhenius suggested that micro-organisms might survive interstellar voyages, spreading some forms of life throughout the universe. Even if done deliberately, such "probes" would be slow and limited things. Since writing "Long Shot," I've seen discussions of directed, *useful* probes much smaller than Ilse: Robert L. Forward has described an interstellar probe massing just a few grams ("Starwisp," Hughes Research Labs Research Report 555, June 1983). Mark Zimmermann has combined that idea with AI to suggest sentient probes in the same mass range. Look around you! Similar travelers may be snugged away in that pebble on the driveway, in the odd thistledown floating across the yard.

APARTNESS

Michael Moorcock bought "Apartness" for *New Worlds SF*. It was my first sale (though "Bookworm, Run!" was written earlier). "Apartness" was later anthologized by Don Wollheim and Terry Carr in one of their best-of-the-year collections. Such success was a dream come true for this beginning writer. But I wonder if the story's success had much connection with the question that originally brought me to write it: Why are there no "Eskimos"—no long-established human societies—in Antarctica? Is it too remote from potential colonists, or is the place that much less hospitable than the arctic? I did some reading, concluded that both reasons had some virtue. There might be a few places on the continent that could support pretechnical human settlers, but those colonists would need real motivation. So the question was to find such motivation. Given the context of 1964, there was a terrible possibility—and the story came close to writing itself.

B ut he saw a light! *On the coast.* Can't you understand what that means?" Diego Ribera y Rodrigues leaned across the tiny wooden desk to emphasize his point. His adversary sat in the shadows and avoided the weak glow of the whale oil lamp hung from the cabin's ceiling. During the momentary pause in the argument, Diego could hear the wind keening through the masts and rigging above them. He was suddenly, painfully conscious of the regular rolling of the deck and slow oscillations of the swinging lamp. But he continued to glare at the man opposite him, and waited for an answer. Finally Capitán Manuel Delgado tilted his head out of the shadows. He smiled unpleasantly. His narrow face and sharp black moustache made him look like what he was: a master of power—political, military, and personal.

"It means," Delgado answered, "people. So what?"

"That's right. People. On the Palmer Peninsula. The Antarctic Continent is inhabited. Why, finding humans in Europe couldn't be any more fantastic—"

"*Mire*, Señor Profesor. I'm vaguely aware of the importance of what you say." There was that smile again. "But the *Vigilancia*—"

Diego tried again. "We simply have to land and investigate the light. Just consider the scientific importance of it all—" The anthropologist had said the wrong thing.

Delgado's cynical indifference dropped away and his young, experienced face became fierce. "Scientific import! If those slimy Australian friends of yours wanted to, they could give us all the scientific knowledge ever known. Instead they have their sympathizers"—he jabbed a finger at Ribera—"run all about the South World doing 'research' that's been done ten times as well more than two centuries ago. The pigs don't even use the knowledge for their own gain." This last was the greatest condemnation Delgado could offer.

Ribera had difficulty restraining a bitter reply, but one mistake this evening was more than enough. He could understand though not approve Delgado's bitterness against a nation which had been wise (or lucky) enough not to burn its libraries during the riots following the North World War. *The Australians have the knowledge, all right,* thought Ribera, *but they also have the wisdom to know that some fundamental changes must be made in human society before this knowledge can be reintroduced, or else we'll wind up with a South World War and no more human race.* This was a point Delgado and many others refused to accept. "But really, Señor Capitán, we *are* doing original research. Ocean currents and populations change over the years. Our data are often quite different from those we know were gathered before. This light Juarez saw tonight is the strongest evidence of all that things are different." And for Diego Ribera, it was especially important. As an anthropologist he had had nothing to do during the voyage except be seasick. A thousand times during the trip he had asked himself why he had been the one to organize the ecologists and oceanographers and get them on the ship; now he knew. If he could just convince this bigoted sailor . . .

Delgado appeared relaxed again. "And too, Señor Profesor, you must remember that you 'scientists' are really superfluous on this expedition. You were lucky to get aboard at all."

That was true. El Presidente Imperial was even more hostile to scientists of the Melbourne School than Delgado was. Ribera didn't like to think of all the boot-licking and chicanery that had been necessary to get his people on the expedition. The anthropologist's reply to the other's last comment started out respectfully, almost humbly. "Yes, I know you are doing something truly important here." He paused. *To hell with it,* he thought, suddenly sick of his own ingratiating manner. *This fool won't listen to logic or flattery.* Ribera's tone changed. "Yeah, I know you are doing something *truly* important here. Somewhere up in Buenos Aires the Chief Astrologer to el Presidente Imperial looked at his crystal ball or whatever and said to Alfredo IV in sepulchral tones: 'Señor Presidente, the stars have spoken. All the secrets of joy and wealth lie on the floating Isle of Coney. Send your men southward to find it.' And so you, the *Vigilancia NdP,* and half the mental cripples in Sudamérica are wandering around the coast of Antarctica looking for

Coney Island." Ribera ran out of breath and satire at the same time. He knew his long-caged temper had just ruined all his plans and perhaps put his life in danger.

Delgado's face seemed frozen. His eyes flickered over Ribera's shoulder and looked at a mirror strategically placed in the space between the door frame and the top of the cabin's door. Then he looked back at the anthropologist. "If I weren't such a reasonable man you would be orca meat before morning." Then he smiled, a sincere friendly grin. "Besides, you're right. Those fools in Buenos Aires aren't fit to rule a pigsty, much less the Sudamérican Empire. Alfredo I was a man, a superman. Before the war-diseases had died out, he had united an entire continent under one fist, a continent that no one had been able to unite with jet planes and automatic weapons. But his heirs, especially the one that's in now, are superstitious tramps. . . . Frankly, that's why I can't land on the coast. The Imperial Astrologer, that fellow Jones y Urrutia, would claim when we returned to Buenos Aires that I had catered to you Australian sympathizers and el Presidente would believe him and I would probably end up with a one-way ticket to the Northern Hemisphere."

Ribera was silent for a second, trying to accept Delgado's sudden friendliness. Finally he ventured, "I would've thought you'd like the astrologers; you seem to dislike us scientists enough."

"You're using labels, Ribera. I feel nothing toward labels. It is success that wins my affection, and failure my hate. There may have been some time in the past when a group calling themselves astrologers could produce results. I don't know, and the matter doesn't interest me, *for I live in the present.* In our time the men working in the name of astrology are incapable of producing results, are conscious frauds. But don't be smug; your own people have produced damn few results. And if it should ever come that the astrologers are successful, I will take up their arts without hesitation and denounce you and your Scientific Method as superstition—for that is what it would be in the face of a more successful method."

The ultimate pragmatist, thought Ribera. *At least there is one form of persuasion that will work.* "I see what you mean, Señor Capitán. And as to success: there is one way that you could land with impunity. A lot can happen over the centuries." He continued half-slyly, "What was once a floating island might become grounded on the shore of the continent. If the astrologers could be convinced of the idea . . ." He let the sentence hang.

Delgado considered, but not for long. "Say! That is an idea. And I personally would like to find out what kind of creature would prefer this icebox over the rest of the South World.

"Very well. I'll try it. Now get out. I'm going to have to make this look like it's all the astrologers' idea, and you are likely to puncture the illusion if you're around when I talk to them."

Ribera lurched from his chair, caught off balance by the swaying of the deck and the abruptness of his dismissal. Without a doubt, Delgado was the most unusual Sudamérican officer Ribera had ever met.

"*Muchísimas gracias*, Señor Capitán." He turned and walked unsteadily out the door, past the storm light by the entrance, and into the wind-filled darkness of the short Antarctic night.

THE ASTROLOGERS DID INDEED LIKE THE IDEA. AT TWO-THIRTY IN THE MORN-ing (just after sunrise) the *Vigilancia, Nave del Presidente*, changed course and tacked toward the area of coast where the light had been. Before the sun had been up six hours, the landing boats were over the side and heading for the coast.

In his eagerness, Diego Ribera y Rodrigues had scrambled aboard the first boat to be launched, not noticing that the Imperial Astrologers had used their favored status on the expedition to commandeer the lead craft. It was a clear day, but the wind made the water choppy and frigid saltwater was splattered over the men in the boat. The tiny vessel rose and fell, rose and fell, with a monotony that promised to make Ribera sick.

"Ah, so you are finally taking an interest in our Quest," a reedy voice interrupted his thoughts. Ribera turned to face the speaker, and recognized one Juan Jones y Urrutia, Subassistant to the Chief Astrologer to el Presidente Imperial. No doubt the vapid young mystic actually believed the tales of Coney Island, or else he would have managed to stay up in Buenos Aires with the rest of the hedonists in Alfredo's court. Beside the astrologer sat Capitán Delgado. The good captain must have done some tremendous persuading, for Jones seemed to regard the whole idea of visiting the coast as his own conception.

Ribera endeavored to smile. "Why yes, uh—"

Jones pressed on. "Tell me; would you have ever suspected life here, you who don't bother to consult the True Fundamentals?"

Ribera groaned. He noticed Delgado smiling at his discomfort. If the boat went through one more rise-fall, Ribera thought he'd scream; it did and he didn't.

"I guess we couldn't have guessed it, no." Ribera edged to the side of the boat, cursing himself for having been so eager to get on the first boat.

His eyes roamed the horizon—anything to get away from the vacu-ous, smug expression on Jones' face. The coast was gray, bleak, covered with large boulders. The breakers smashing into it seemed faintly yellow or red where they weren't white foam—probably coloring from the algae and diatoms in the water; the ecology boys would know.

"Smoke ahead!" The shout came thinly through the air from the second boat. Ribera squinted and examined the coast minutely. There! Barely recognizable as smoke, the wind-distorted haze rose from some point hidden by the low coastal hills. What if it turned out to be some sluggishly active volcano? That depressing thought had not occurred to him before. The geologists would have fun, but it would be a bust as far as he was concerned. . . . In any case, they would know which it was in a few minutes.

Capitán Delgado appraised the situation, then spoke several curt commands to the oarsmen. The crew's cadence shifted, and the boat turned ninety degrees to move parallel to the shore and breakers five hundred meters off. The trailing boats imitated the lead craft's maneuver.

Soon the coast bent sharply inward, revealing a long, narrow inlet. The night before, the *Vigilancia* must have been directly in line with the channel in order for Juarez to see the light. The three boats moved up the narrow channel. Soon the wind died. All that could be heard of it was a chill whistle as it tore at the hills which bordered the channel. The waves were much gentler now and the icy water no longer splashed into the boats, though the men's parkas were already caked with salt. Earlier the water had seemed faintly yellow; now it appeared orange and even red, especially farther up the inlet. The brilliant bacterial contamination contrasted sharply with the dull hills, hills that bore no trace of vegetation. In the place of plant life, uniformly gray boulders of all sizes covered the landscape. Nowhere was there snow; that would come with the winter, still five months in the future. But to Ribera this "summer" landscape was many times harsher than the bleakest winter scene in Sudamérica. Red water, gray hills. The only things that seemed even faintly normal were the brilliant blue sky, and the sun, which cast long shadows into the drowned valley; a sun that seemed always at the point of setting even though it had barely risen.

Ribera's attention wandered up the channel. He forgot the sea sickness, the bloody water, the dead land. He could see *them*; not an ambiguous glow in the night, but people! He could see their huts, apparently made of stone and hides, and partly dug into the ground. He could see what appeared to be leather-hulled boats or kayaks along with a larger, white boat (now what could that be?), lying on the ground before the little village. He could see people! Not the expressions on their faces nor the exact manner of their clothing, but he could see them and that was enough for the instant. Here was something truly new; something the long dead scholars of Oxford, Cambridge, and UCLA had never learned, could never have learned. Here was something that mankind was seeing for the first and not the second or third or fourth time around!

What brought these people here? Ribera asked himself. From the few books on polar cultures that he had read at the University of Melbourne, he knew that generally populations are forced into the polar regions by competing peoples. What were the forces behind this migration? Who were these people?

The boats swept swiftly forward on the quiet water. Soon Ribera felt the hull of his craft scrape bottom. He and Delgado jumped into the red water and helped the oarsmen drag the boat onto the beach. Ribera waited impatiently for the two other boats, which carried the scientists, to arrive. In the meantime, he concentrated his attention on the natives, trying to understand every detail of their lives at once.

None of the aborigines moved; none ran; none attacked. They stood where they had been when he had first seen them. They did not scowl or wave weapons, but Ribera was distinctly aware that they were not friendly. No smiles, no welcome grimness. They seemed a proud people. The adults were tall, their faces so grimy, tanned, and withered that the anthropologist could only guess at their race. From the set of their lips, he knew that most of them lacked teeth. The natives' children peeped around the legs of their mothers, women who seemed old enough to be great-grandmothers. If they had been Sudaméricans, he would have estimated their average age as sixty or seventy, but he knew that it couldn't be more than twenty or twenty-five.

From the pattern of fatty tissues in their faces, Ribera thought he could detect evidence of cold adaptation; maybe they were Eskimos, though it would have been physically impossible for that race to migrate from one pole to the other while the North World War raged. Both their parkas and the kayaks appeared to be made of seal hide. But the parkas were ill-designed and much bulkier than the Eskimo outfits he had seen in pictures. And the harpoons they held were much less ingenious than the designs he remembered. If these people were of the supposedly extinct Eskimo race, they were an extraordinarily primitive branch of it. Besides, they were much too hairy to be full-blooded Indians or Eskimos.

With half his mind, he noticed the astrologers glance at the village and dismiss it. They were after the Isle of Coney, not some smelly aborigines. Ribera smiled bitterly; he wondered what Jones' reaction would be if the astrologer ever learned that Coney had been an amusement park. Many legends had grown up after the North World War and the one about Coney Island was one of the weirdest. Jones led his men up one of the nearer hills, evidently to get a better view of the area. Capitán Delgado hastily dispatched twelve crewmen to accompany the mystics. The good sailor obviously recognized what a position he would be in if any of the astrologers were lost.

Ribera's mind returned to the puzzle: Where were these people from? How had they gotten here? Perhaps that was the best angle on the problem: People don't just sprout from the ground. The pitiful kayaks— they weren't true kayaks; they didn't enclose the lower body of the user—could hardly transport a person ten kilometers over open water. What about that large white craft, farther up the beach? It seemed a much sturdier vessel than the hide and bone "kayaks." He looked at it more closely—the white craft might even be made of fiberglass, a pre-War construction material. Maybe he should get a closer look at it.

A shout attracted Ribera's attention; he turned. The second landing craft, bearing the majority of the scientists, had grounded on the rocky beach. He ran down the beach to the men piling out of the boat, and gave them the gist of his conclusions. Having explained the situation, Ribera selected Enrique Cardona and Ari Juarez, both ecologists, to accompany him in a parley with the natives. The three men approached the largest group of natives, who watched them stonily. The Sudamér- icans stopped several paces before the silent tribesmen. Ribera raised his hands in a gesture of peace. "My friends, may we look at your beautiful boat yonder? We will not harm it." There was no response, though Ribera thought he sensed a greater tenseness among the natives. He tried again, making the request in Portuguese, then in English. Cardona attempted the question in Zulunder, as did Juarez in broken French. Still no acknowledgment, but the harpoons seemed to quiver, and there was an all but imperceptible motion of hands toward bone knives.

"Well, to hell with them," Cardona snapped finally. "C'mon, Diego, let's have a look at it." The short-tempered ecologist turned and began walking toward the mysterious white boat. This time there was no mis- taken hostility. The harpoons were raised and the knives drawn.

"Wait, Enrique," Ribera said urgently. Cardona stopped. Ribera was sure that if the ecologist had taken one more step he would have been spitted. "Wait," Diego Ribera y Rodrigues continued. "We have plenty of time. Besides, it would be madness to push the issue." He indicated the natives' weapons.

Cardona noticed the weapons. "All right. We'll humor them for now." He seemed to regard the harpoons as an embarrassment rather than a threat. The three men retreated from the confrontation. Ribera noticed that Delgado's men had their pistols half drawn. The expedition had narrowly avoided a bloodbath.

The scientists would have to content themselves with a peripheral inspection of the village. In one way this was more pleasant than direct examination, for the ground about the huts was littered with filth. In a century or so this area would have the beginnings of a soil. After ten minutes or so the adult males of the tribe resumed their work mending the kayaks. Apparently they were preparing for a seal-hunting expedition; the area around the village had been hunted free of the seals and seabirds that populated most other parts of the coast.

If only we could communicate with them, thought Ribera. The aborigines themselves probably knew (at least by legend) what their origins were. As it was, Ribera had to investigate by the most indirect means. In his mind he summed up the facts he knew: The natives were of an indeterminate race; they were hairy, and yet they seemed to have some of the physiological cold-weather adaptations of the extinct Eskimos. The natives were primitive in every physical sense. Their equipment and techniques were far inferior to the ingenious inventions of the Eskimos. And the natives spoke no currently popular language. One other thing: the fire they kept alive at the center of the village was an impractical affair, and probably served a religious purpose only. Those were the facts; now, who the hell were these people? The problem was so puzzling that for the moment he forgot the dreamlike madness of the gray landscape and the "setting" noonday sun.

A half hour and more passed. The geologists were mildly ecstatic about the area, but for Ribera the situation was becoming increasingly exasperating. He didn't dare approach the villagers or the white boat, yet these were the things he most wanted to do. Perhaps this impatience made him especially sensitive, for he was the first of the scientists to hear the clatter of rolling stones and the sound of voices over the shrill wind.

He turned and saw Jones and company descending a nearby hill at all but breakneck speed. One misstep and the entire group would have descended the hill on their backs rather than their feet. The rolling stones cast loose by their rush preceded them into the valley. The astrologers reached the bottom of the hill, far outdistancing the sailors delegated to protect them, and continued running.

"Wonder what's trying to eat them?" Ribera asked Juarez half-seriously.

As he plunged past Delgado, Jones shouted, "—think we may have found it, Capitán—something man-made rising from the sea." He pointed wildly toward the hill they had just descended.

The astrologers piled into a boat. Seeing that the mystics really intended to leave, Delgado dispatched fifteen men to help them with the craft, and an equal number to go along in another boat. In a couple of minutes, the two boats were well into the channel and rowing fast toward open water.

"What the hell was that about?" Ribera shouted to Capitán Delgado.

"You know as much as I, Señor Profesor. Let's take a look. If we go for a little walk"—he nodded to the hill—"we can probably get within sight of the 'discovery' before Jones and the rest reach it by boat. You men stay here." Delgado turned his attention to the remaining crewmen. "If these primitives try to confiscate our boat, demonstrate your firearms to them—on them.

"The same goes for you scientists. As many men as possible are going to have to stay here to see that we don't lose that boat; it's a long, wet walk back to the *Vigilancia*. Let's go, Ribera. You can take a couple of your people if you want."

Ribera and Juarez set out with Delgado and three ship's officers. The men moved slowly up the slope, which was made treacherous by its loose covering of boulders. As they reached the crest of the hill the wind beat into them, tearing at their parkas. The terrain was less hilly but in the far distance they could see the mountains that formed the backbone of the peninsula.

Delgado pointed. "If they saw something in the ocean, it must be in that direction. We saw the rest of the coast on our way in."

The six men started off in the indicated direction. The wind was against them and their progress was slow. Fifteen minutes later they crossed the top of a gentle hill, and reached the coast. Here the water was a clean bluish-green and the breakers smashing over the rocky beach could almost have been mistaken for Pacific waters sweeping into some bleak shore in the Province of Chile. Ribera looked over the waves. Two stark, black objects broke the smooth, silver line of the horizon. Their uncompromising angularity showed them to be artificial.

Delgado drew a pair of binoculars from his parka. Ribera noted with surprise that the binoculars bore the mark of the finest optical instruments extant: U.S. Naval war surplus. On some markets, the object would have brought a price comparable to that of the entire ship *Vigilancia*. Capitán Delgado raised the binoculars to his eyes and inspected the black forms of the ocean. Thirty seconds passed. "*¡Madre del Presidente!*" he swore softly but with feeling. He handed the binocs to Ribera. "Take a look, Señor Profesor."

The anthropologist scanned the horizon, spotted the black shapes. Though winter sea ice had smashed their hulls and scuttled them in the shallow water, they were obviously ships—atomic or petroleum powered, pre-War ships. At the edge of his field of vision, he noticed two white objects bobbing in the water; they were the two landing boats from the *Vigilancia*. The boats disappeared every few seconds in the trough of a wave. They moved a little closer to the two half-sunken ships, then began to pull away. Ribera could imagine what had happened: Jones had seen that the hulks were no different from the relics of the Argentine navy sunk off Buenos Aires. The astrologer was probably fit to be tied.

Ribera inspected the wrecks minutely. One was half capsized and hidden behind the other. His gaze roamed along the bow of the nearer vessel. There were letters on that bow, letters almost worn away by the action of ice and water upon the plastic hull of the ship.

"My God!" whispered Ribera. The letters spelled: *S—Hen—k—V—woe—d*. He didn't need to look at the other vessel to know that it had once been called *Nation*. Ribera dumbly handed the binoculars to Juarez.

The mystery was solved. He knew the pressures that had driven the natives here. "If the Zulunders ever hear about this . . ." Ribera's voice trailed off into silence.

"Yeah," Delgado replied. He understood what he had seen, and for the first time seemed somewhat subdued. "Well, let's get back. This land isn't fit for . . . it isn't fit."

The six men turned and started back. Though the ship's officers had had an opportunity to use the binoculars, they didn't seem to understand exactly what they had seen. And probably the astrologers didn't realize the significance of the discovery, either. That left three, Juarez, Ribera, and Delgado, who knew the secret of the natives' origin. If the news spread much further, disaster would result, Ribera was sure.

The wind was at their backs but it did not speed their progress. It took them almost a quarter-hour to reach the crest of the hill overlooking the village and the red water.

Below them, Ribera could see the adult male natives clustered in a tight group. Not ten feet away stood all the scientists, and the crewmen. Between the two groups was one of the Sudaméricans. Ribera squinted and saw that the man was Enrique Cardona. The ecologist was gesturing wildly, angrily.

"Oh, no!" Ribera sprinted down the hill, closely followed by Delgado and the rest. The anthropologist moved even faster then the astrologers had an hour before, and almost twice as fast as he would have thought humanly possible. The tiny avalanches started by his footfalls were slow compared to his speed. Even as he flew down the slope, Ribera felt himself detached, analytically examining the scene before him.

Cardona was shouting, as if to make the natives understand by sheer volume. Behind him the ecologists and biologists stood, impatient to inspect the village and the natives' boat. Before him stood a tall, withered native, who must have been all of forty years old. Even from a distance the native's bearing revealed intense, suppressed anger. The native's parka was the most impractical of all those Ribera had seen; he could have sworn that it was a crude, sealskin imitation of a double-breasted suit.

Almost screaming, Cardona cried, "God damn it, why can't we look at your boat?" Ribera put forth one last burst of speed, and shouted at Cardona to stop his provocation. It was too late. Just as the anthropologist arrived at the scene of the confrontation, the native in the strange parka drew himself to his full height, pointed to all the Sudaméricans, and screeched (as nearly as Ribera's Spanish-thinking mind could record), "—*in di nam niutrantsfals mos yulisterf*—"

The half-raised harpoons were thrown. Cardona went down instantly, transfixed by three of the weapons. Several other men were hit and felled. The natives drew their knives and ran forward, taking advantage of the confusion that the harpoons had created. A painfully loud *BAM* erupted beside Ribera's ear as Delgado fired his pistol, picking off the leader of the natives. The crewmen recovered from their shock, began firing at the aborigines. Ribera whipped his pistol from a pouch at his side and blasted into the swarm of primitives. Their single-shot pistols emptied, the scientists and crew were reduced to knives. The next few seconds were total chaos. The knives rose and fell, gleaming more redly than the water in the cove. The anthropologist half stumbled over squirming bodies. The air was filled with hoarse shouts and sounds of straining men.

The groups were evenly matched and they were cutting each other to pieces. In some still calm part of his mind Ribera noticed the returning boats of the astrologers. He glimpsed the crewmen aiming their muskets, waiting for a clear shot at the primitives.

The turbulence of the fray whirled him about, out of the densest part of the fight. They had to disengage; another few minutes and there wouldn't be one in ten left standing on the beach. Ribera screamed this to Delgado. Miraculously the man heard him and agreed; retreat was the only sane thing to do. The Sudaméricans ran raggedly toward their boat, with the natives close behind. Sharp cracking sounds came from over the water. The crewmen in the other boats were taking advantage of the dispersion between pursuers and pursued. The Sudaméricans reached their boat and began pushing it into the water. Ribera and several others turned to face the natives. Musket fire had forced most of the primitives back, but a few still ran toward the shore, knives drawn. Ribera reached down and snatched a small stone from the ground. Using an almost forgotten skill of his "gentle" childhood, he cocked his arm and snapped the rock forward in a flat trajectory. It caught one of the natives dead between the eyes with a sharp *smack*. The man plunged forward, fell on his face, and lay still.

Ribera turned and ran into the shallow water after the boat. He was followed by the rest of the rearguard. Eager hands reached out from the boat to pull him aboard. A couple more feet and he would be safe.

The blow sent him spinning forward. As he fell, he saw with dumb horror the crimson harpoon which had emerged from his parka just below the right side pocket.

Why? Must we forever commit the same blunders over and over, and over again? Ribera didn't have time to wonder at this fleeting incongruous thought, before the redness closed about him.

A GENTLE BREEZE, CARRYING THE HAPPY SOUNDS OF DISTANT PARTIES, ENtered the large windows of the bungalow and caressed its interior. It was a cool night, late in summer. The first mild airs of fall made the darkness pleasant, inviting. The house was situated on the slight ridge which marked the old shoreline of La Plata; the lawns and hedges outside fell gently away toward the general plain of the city. The faint though delicate light from the oil lamps of that city defined its rectangular array of streets, and showed its buildings uniformly one or two stories high. Farther out, the city lights came to an abrupt end at the waterfront. But even beyond that there were the moving, yellow lights of boats and ships navigating La Plata. Off to the extreme left burned the bright fires surrounding the Naval Enclosure, where the government labored on some secret weapon, possibly a steam-powered warship.

It was a peaceful scene, and a happy evening; preparations were almost complete. His desk was littered with the encouraging replies to his proposals. It had been hard work but a lot of fun at the same time. And Buenos Aires had been the ideal base of operations. Alfredo IV was touring the western provinces. To be more precise, el Presidente Imperial and his court were visiting the pleasure spots in Santiago (as if Alfredo had not built up enough talent in Buenos Aires itself). The Imperial Guard and the Secret Police clustered close by the monarch (Alfredo was more afraid of a court coup than anything else), so Buenos Aires was more relaxed then it had been in many years.

Yes, two months of hard work. Many important people had to be informed, and confidentially. But the replies had been almost uniformly enthusiastic, and it appeared that the project wasn't known to those who would destroy its goal; though of course the simple fact that so many people had to know increased the chances of disclosure. But that was a risk that had to be taken.

And, thought Diego Ribera, *it's been two months since the Battle of Bloody Cove.* (The name of the inlet had arisen almost spontaneously.) He hoped that the tribe hadn't been scared away from that spot, or, infinitely worse, driven to the starvation point by the massacre. If that fool Enrique Cardona had only kept his mouth shut, both sides could have parted peacefully (if not amicably) and some good men would still be alive.

Ribera scratched his side thoughtfully. Another inch and he wouldn't have made it himself. If that harpoon had hit just a little further up . . . Someone's quick thinking had added to his initial good luck. That someone had slashed the thick cord tied to the harpoon which had hit Ribera. If the separation had not been made, the cord would most likely have been pulled back and the harpoon's barb engaged. Even as miraculous was the fact that he had survived the impalement and the poor medical conditions on board the *Vigilancia*. Physically, all the damage that remained was a pair of neat, circular scars. The whole affair was enough to give you religion, or, conversely, scare the hell out of you. . . .

And come next January he would be headed back, along with the secret expedition that he had been so energetically organizing. Nine months was a long time to wait, but they definitely couldn't make the trip this fall or winter, and they really did need time to gather just the right equipment.

Diego was taken from these thoughts by several dull thuds from the door. He got up and went to the entrance of the bungalow. (This small house in the plushiest section of the city was evidence of the encouragement he had already received from some very important people.) Ribera had no idea who the visitor could be, but he had every expectation that the news brought would be good. He reached the door, and pulled it open.

"Mkambwe Lunama!"

The Zulunder stood framed in the doorway, his black face all but invisible against the night sky. The visitor was over two meters tall and weighed nearly one hundred kilos; he was the picture of a superman. But then, the Zulunder government made a special point of using the super-race type in its dealings with other nations. The procedure undoubtedly lost them some fine talent, but in Sudamérica the myth held strong that one Zulunder was worth three warriors of any other nationality.

After his first outburst, Ribera stood for a moment in horrified confusion. He knew Lunama vaguely as the Highman of Trueness—propaganda—at the Zulunder embassy in Buenos Aires. The Highman had made numerous attempts to ingratiate himself with the academic community of la Universidad de Buenos Aires. The efforts were probably aimed at recruiting sympathizers against that time when the disagreements between the Sudamérican Empire and the Reaches of Zulund erupted into open conflict.

Wildly hoping that the visit was merely an unlucky coincidence, Ribera recovered himself. He attempted a disarming smile, and said, "Come on in, Mkambwe. Haven't seen you in a long time."

The Zulunder smiled, his white teeth making a dazzling contrast with the rest of his face. He stepped lightly into the room. His robes were woven of brilliant red, blue, and green fibers, in defiance of the more somber hues of Sudamérican business suits. On his hip rested a Mavimbelamake 20-millimeter revolver. The Zulunders had their own peculiar ideas about diplomatic protocol.

Mkambwe moved lithely across the room and settled in a chair. Ribera hurried over and sat down by his desk, trying unobtrusively to hide the letters that lay on it from the Zulunder's view. If the visitor saw and understood even one of those letters, the game would be over.

Ribera tried to appear relaxed. "Sorry I can't offer you a drink, Mkambwe, but the house is as dry as a desert." If the anthropologist got up, the Zulunder would almost certainly see the correspondence. Diego continued jovially, desperately trying to dredge up reminiscences. ("Remember that time your boys whited their faces and went down to la Casa Rosada Nueva and raised hell with the—")

Lunama grinned. "Frankly, old man, this visit is business." The Zulunder spoke with a dandyish, pseudo-Castilian accent, which he no doubt thought aristocratic.

"Oh," Ribera answered.

"I hear that you were on a little expedition to Palmer Peninsula this January."

"Yes," Ribera replied stonily. Perhaps there was still a chance; perhaps Lunama didn't know the whole truth. "And it was supposed to be a secret. If el Presidente Imperial found out that your government knew about it—"

"Come, come, Diego. That isn't the secret you are thinking of. I know that you found what happened to the *Hendrik Verwoerd* and the *Nation*."

"Oh," Ribera replied again. "How did you find out?" he asked dully.

"You talked to many people, Diego," he waved vaguely. "Surely you didn't think that every one of them would keep your secret. And surely you didn't think you could keep something this important from us." He looked beyond the anthropologist and his tone changed. "For three hundred years we lived under the heels of those white devils. Then came the Retribution in the North and—"

What a quaint term the Zulunders use for the North World War, thought Ribera. It had been a war in which every trick of destruction—nuclear, biological, and chemical—had been used. The mere residues from the immolation of China had obliterated Indonesia and India. Mexico and América Central had disappeared with the United States and Canada. And North Africa had gone with Europe. The gentlest wisps from that biological and nuclear hell had caressed the Southern Hemisphere and nearly poisoned it. A few more megatons and a few more disease strains and the war would have gone unnamed, for there would have been no one to chronicle it. This was the Retribution in the North which Lunama so easily referred to.

"—and the devils no longer had the protection of their friends there. Then came the Sixty-Day Struggle for Freedom."

There were both black devils and white devils in those sixty days—and saints of all colors, brave men struggling desperately to avert genocide. But the years of slavery were too many and the saints lost, not for the first time.

"At the beginning of the Rising we fought machine guns and jet fighters with rifles and knives," Lunama continued, almost self-hypnotized. "We died by the tens of thousands. But as the days passed *their* numbers were reduced, too. By the fiftieth day *we* had the machine guns, and *they* had the knives and rifles. We boxed the last of them up at Kapa and Durb," (he used the Zulunder terms for Capetown and Durban) "and drove them into the sea."

Literally, added Ribera to himself. *The last remnants of White Africa were physically pushed from the wharves and sunny beaches into the ocean.* The Zulunders had succeeded in exterminating the Whites, and thought they succeeded in obliterating the Afrikaner culture from the continent. Of course they had been wrong. The Afrikaners had left a lasting mark, obvious to any unbiased observer; the very name Zulunder, which the present Africans cherished fanatically, was in part a corruption of English.

"By the sixtieth day, we could say that not a single White lived on the continent. As far as we know, only one small group evaded vengeance. Some of the highest-ranking Afrikaner officials, maybe even the Prime Minister, commandeered two luxury vessels, the *SR Hendrik Verwoerd* and the *Nation*. They left many hours before the final freedom drive on Kapa."

Five thousand desperate men, women, and children crammed into two luxury ships. The vessels had raced across the South Atlantic, seeking refuge in Argentina. But the government of Argentina was having troubles of its own. Two light Argentine patrol boats badly damaged the *Nation* before the Afrikaners were convinced that Sudamérica didn't offer shelter.

The two ships had turned south, possibly in an attempt to round Tierra del Fuego and reach Australia. That was the last anyone had heard of them for more than two hundred years—till the *Vigilancia's* exploration of the Palmer Peninsula.

Ribera knew that an appeal to sympathy wouldn't dissuade the Zulunder from ordering the destruction of the pitiful colony. He tried a different tack. "What you say is so true, Mkambwe. But please, please don't destroy these descendants of your enemies. The tribe on the Palmer Peninsula is the only polar culture left on Earth." Even as Ribera said the words, he realized how weak the argument was; it could only appeal to an anthropologist like himself.

The Zulunder seemed surprised, and with a visible effort shelved the terrible history of his continent. "Destroy them? My dear fellow, whyever would we do that? I just came here to ask if we might send several observers from the Ministry of Trueness along on your expedition. To report the matter more fully, you know. I think that Alfredo can probably be convinced, if the question is put persuasively enough to him.

"Destroy them?" He repeated the question. "Don't be silly! They are *proof* of destruction. So they call their piece of ice and rock Nieutransvaal, do they?" He laughed. "And they even have a Prime Minister, a toothless old man who waves his harpoon at Sudaméricans." Apparently Lunama's informant had actually been on the spot. "And they are even more primitive than Eskimos. In short, they are savages living on seal blubber."

He no longer spoke with foppish joviality. His eyes flashed with an old, old hate, a hate that was pushing Zulund to greatness, and which might eventually push the world into another hemispheric war (unless the Australian social scientists came through with some desperately needed answers). The breeze in the room no longer seemed cool, gentle. It was cold and the wind was coming from the emptiness of death piled upon megadeath through the centuries of human misery.

"It will be a pleasure for us to see them enjoy their superiority." Lunama leaned forward even more intensely. "They finally have the apartness their kind always wanted. *Let them rot in it—*"

CONQUEST BY DEFAULT

For several years after this first sale, one editor rejected my every story with praise for how much he had liked "Apartness." I think he was referring to the parts of the story that had a moral for the times. I didn't have any bright ideas along those lines—but I did think that other stories might be possible in the same future.

I had enjoyed Chad Oliver's stories and I thought it would be fun to imagine what social science might look like coming out of an entirely different milieu. Modern anthropologists seem full of cultural relativism and self-conscious tolerance. Would it be possible to have a story set in some wider context, with an anthropology based on alien motives? I wanted a culture that was technologically superior to ours, workable, and yet so painfully different that accepting it would be hard even for open-minded people with our outlook.

So what would be sufficiently alien? Ever since high school, I've been fascinated with the notion of anarchy. Every anarchical scheme has some set of assumptions for why the participants will cooperate. (You can usually spot the assumption in the names: anarcho-communism, anarcho-capitalism . . .) There's a fundamental problem all such plans must face: how to prevent the formation of power groups large enough to in fact *be* the government. In the following story, "Conquest by Default," I attempted a frontal assault on this question.

An aside: I've always had a weakness for unpronounceable names and oddball orthographies. The names in this story were a problem from the beginning. I had just taken a descriptive linguistics course, and I was enthusiastic: my aliens can close their noses—*true* nasal stops and fricatives were possible for them! In the version John W. Campbell bought around 1967, I represented a voiceless nasal stop by the letter "p" with tilde and a voiced nasal fricative by the letter "v" with tilde. John told me he didn't think it would get past the typesetters. He was right. And even now, such oddball symbols can be hard to print. One editor, Jim Baen, kindly offered to accept photoready copy from me—so that *I* could set the type exactly as it should be. In this printing, I have chosen to represent the voiceless nasal stop as "%" and the voiced nasal fricative as "#".

This all happened a long time ago, and almost twenty light-years from where we're standing now. You honor me here tonight as a humanitarian, as a man who has done something to bring a temporary light to the eternal darkness that is our universe. But you deceive yourselves. I made the situation just civilized enough so that its true brutality, shed of bloody drapery, can be seen.

I see you don't believe what I say. In this whole audience I suspect that only a Melmwn truly understands—and she better than I. Not one of you has ever been kicked in the teeth by these particular facts of life. Perhaps if I told you the story as it happened to me—I could make you *feel* the horror you hear me describe.

Two centuries ago, the %wrlyg Spice & Trading Company completed the first interstellar flight. They were thirty years ahead of their nearest competitors. They had a whole planet at their disposal, except for one minor complication. . . .

The natives were restless.

My attention was unevenly divided between the beautiful girl who had just introduced herself, and the ancient city that shimmered in the hot air behind her.

Mary Dahlmann. That was a hard name to pronounce, but I had studied Australian for almost two years, and I was damned if I couldn't say a name. I clumsily worked my way through a response. "Yes, ah, Miss, ah, Dahlmann. I am Ron Melmwn, and I am the new Company anthropologist. But I thought the vice president for Aboriginal Affairs was going to meet me."

Ngagn Che# dug me in the ribs. "Say, you really can speak that gabble, can't you, Melmwn?" he whispered in Mikin. Che# was Vice President for Violence—an OK guy, but an incurable bigot.

Mary Dahlmann smiled uncertainly at this exchange. Then she answered my question. "Mr. Horlig will be right along. He asked me to meet you. My father is Chief Representative for Her Majesty's Government." I later learned that Her Majesty was two centuries dead. "Here, let me show you off the field." She grasped my wrist for a second—an instant. I guess I jerked back. Her hand fell away and her eagerness vanished. "This way," she said icily, pointing to a gate in the force fence surrounding the %wrlyg landing field. I wished very much I had not pulled away from her touch. Even though she was so blond and pale, she was a woman, and in a weird way, pretty. Besides, *she* had overcome whatever feelings she had against *us*.

There was an embarrassed silence, as the five of us cleared the landing craft and walked toward the gate.

The sun was bright—brighter than ours ever shines over Miki. It was also very dry. There were no clouds in the sky. Twenty or thirty people worked in the field. Most were Mikin, but here and there were clusters of Terrans. Several were standing around a device in the corner of the field where the fence made a joint to angle out toward the beach. The Terrans knelt by the device.

Orange fire flickered from the end of the machine, followed by a loud *guda-bam-bam-bam*. Even as my conscious mind concluded that we were under fire, I threw myself on the ground and flattened into the lowest profile possible. You've heard the bromide about combat making life more real. I don't know about that, but it's certainly true that when you are flat against the ground with your face in the dirt, the whole universe looks different. That red-tan sand was *hot*. Sharp little stones bit into my face. Two inches before my face a clump of sage had assumed the dimensions of a #ola tree.

I cocked my head microscopically to see how the others were doing. They were all down, too. Correction: That idiot Earthgirl was still standing. More than a second after the attack she was still working toward the idea that someone was trying to kill her. Only a dement or a Little Sister brought up in a convent could be so dense. I reached out, grabbed her slim ankle, and jerked. She came down hard. Once down, she didn't move.

Ngagn Che# and some accountant, whose name I didn't remember, were advancing toward the slug-thrower. That accountant had the fastest low-crawl I have ever seen. The Terrans frantically tried to lower the barrels of their gun—but it was really primitive and couldn't search more than five degrees. The little accountant zipped up to within twenty meters of the gun, reached into his weapons pouch, and tossed a grenade toward the Earthmen and their weapon. I dug my face into the dirt and waited for the explosion. There was only a muffled thud. It was a gas bomb—not frag. A green mist hung for an instant over the gun and the Terrans.

When I got to them, Che# was already complimenting the accountant on his throw.

"A private quarrel?" I asked Che#.

The security chief looked faintly surprised. "Why no. These fellows"— he pointed at the unconscious Terrans—"belong to some conspiracy to drive us off the planet. They're really a pitiful collection." He pointed to the weapon. It was composed of twenty barrels welded to three metal hoops. By turning a crank, the barrels could be rotated past a belt cartridge feeder. "That gun is hardly more accurate than a shrapnel bomb. This is nothing very dangerous, but I'm going to catch chaos for letting them get within the perimeter. And I can tell you, I am going to scorch those agents of mine that let these abos sneak in. Anyway, we got the pests alive. They'll be able to answer some questions." He nudged one of the bodies over with his boot. "Sometimes I think it would be best to exterminate the race. They don't occupy much territory but they sure are a nuisance.

"See," he picked up a card from the ground and handed it to me. It was lettered in neat Mikin: MERLYN SENDS YOU DEATH. "Merlyn is the name of the 'terrorist' organization—it's nonprofit. I think. Terrans are a queer lot."

Several Company armsmen showed up then and Che# proceeded to bawl them out in a very thorough way. It was interesting, but a little embarrassing, too. I turned and started toward the main gate. I still had to meet my new boss—Horlig, the Vice President for Abo Affairs.

Where was the Terran girl? In the fuss I had completely forgotten her. But now she was gone. I ran back to where we stood when the first shots were fired. I felt cold and a little sick as I looked at the ground where she had fallen. Maybe it had been a superficial wound. Maybe the medics had carried her off. But whatever the explanation, a pool of blood almost thirty centimeters wide lay on the sand. As I watched, it soaked into the sand and became a dark brown grease spot, barely visible against the reddish-tan soil. As far as appearances go, it could have been human blood.

HORLIG WAS A GLOYN. I SHOULD HAVE KNOWN FROM HIS NAME. AS IT WAS, I got quite a surprise when I met him. With his pale gray skin and hair, Herul Horlig could easily be mistaken for an Earthman. The Vice President for Aboriginal Affairs was either an Ostentatious Simplist or very proud of his neolithic grandparents. He wore wooden shin plates and a black breech-clout. His only weapon was a machine dartgun strapped to his wrist.

It quickly became clear that the man was unhappy with me as an addition to his staff. I could understand that. As a professional, my opinions might carry more weight with the Board of Directors and the President than his. Horlig did his best to hide his displeasure, though. He seemed a hard-headed, sincere fellow who could be ruthless, but nevertheless believed whatever he did was right. He unbent considerably during our meal at Supply Central. When I mentioned I wanted to interview some abos, he surprised me by suggesting we fly over to the native city that evening.

When we left Central, it was already dark. We walked to the parking lot, and got into Horlig's car. Three minutes later we were ghosting over the suburbs of Adelaide-west. Horlig cast a practiced eye upon the queer rectangular street pattern below, and brought us down on the lawn of a two-story wood house. I started to get out.

"Just a minute, Melmwn," said Horlig. He grabbed a pair of earphones and set the TV on pan. I didn't say anything as he scanned the quiet neighborhood for signs of hostile activity. I was interested: Usually a Simplist will avoid using advanced defense techniques. Horlig explained as he set the car's computer on SENTRY and threw open the hatch:

"Our illustrious Board of Directors dictates that we employ 'all security precautions at our disposal.' Bunk. Even when these Earth creatures attack us, they are less violent than good-natured street brawlers back home. I don't think there have been more than thirty murders in this city since %wrlyg landed twenty years ago."

I jumped to the soft grass and looked around. Things really were quiet. Gas lamps lit the cobblestone street and dimly outlined the wood buildings up and down the lane. Weak yellow light emerged from windows. From down the street came faint laughter of some party. Our landing had gone unnoticed.

Demoneyes. I stepped back sharply. The twin yellow disks glittered maniacally, as the cat turned to face us, and the lamps' light came back from its eyes. The little animal turned slowly and walked disdainfully across the lawn. This was a bad omen indeed. I would have to watch the Signs very carefully tonight. Horlig was not disturbed at all. I don't think he knew I was brought up a witch-fearer. We started up the walk toward the nearest house.

"You know, Melmwn, this isn't just any old native we're visiting. He's an anthropologist, Earth style. Of course, he's just as insipid as the rest of the bunch, but our staff is forced to do quite a bit of liaison work with him."

An anthropologist! This was going to be interesting, both as an exchange of information and of research procedures.

"In addition, he's the primary representative chosen by the Australian *gowernmen'* . . . a *gowernmen'* is sort of a huge corporation, as far as I can tell."

"Uh-huh." As a matter of fact, I knew a lot more about the mysterious *government* concept than Horlig. My Scholarate thesis was a theoretical study of macro organizations. The paper was almost rejected because my instructors claimed it was an analysis of a patent impossibility. Then came word that three macro organizations existed on Earth.

WE CLIMBED THE FRONT PORCH STEPS. HORLIG POUNDED ON THE DOOR. "THE fellow's name is Nalman."

I translated his poor pronunciation back to the probable Australian original: Dahlmann! Perhaps I could find out what happened to the Earthgirl.

There were shuffling steps from within. Whoever it was did not even bother to look us over through a spy hole. Earthmen were nothing if not trusting. We were confronted by a tall, middle-aged man with thin, silvery hair. His hand quavered slightly as he removed the pipe from his mouth. Either he was in an extremity of fear or he had terrible coordination.

But when he spoke, I knew there was no fear. "Mr. Horlig. Won't you come in?" The words and tone were mild, but in that mildness rested an immense confidence. In the past I had heard that tone only from Umpires. It implied that neither storm, nor struggle, nor crumbling physical prowess could upset the mind behind the voice. That's a lot to get out of six quiet words—but it was all there.

When we were settled in Scholar Dahlmann's den, Horlig made the introductions. Horlig understood Australian fairly well, but his accent was atrocious.

"As you must surely know, Scholar Dahlmann, the objective voyage time to our home planet, Epsilon Eridani II, is almost twelve years. Three days ago the third %wrlyg Support Fleet arrived and assumed a parking orbit around the Earth. At this instant, they soar omnipotent over the lands of your people." Dahlmann just smiled. "In any case, the first passengers have been unfrozen and brought down to the %wrlyg Ground Base. This is Scholar Ron Melmwn, the anthropologist that the Company has brought in with the Fleet."

From behind his thick glasses, Dahlmann inspected me with new interest. "Well, I certainly am happy to meet a Mikin anthropologist. Our meeting is something of a first I believe."

"I think so, too. Your institutions are ill-reported to us on Miki. This is natural since %wrlyg is primarily interested in the commercial and immigration prospects of your Northern Hemisphere. I want to correct the situation. During my stay I hope to use you and the other Terrans for source material in my study of your history and, uh, government. It's especially good luck that I meet a professional like yourself."

Dahlmann seemed happy to discuss his people and soon we were immersed in Terran history and cultures. Much of what he told me I knew from reports received, but I let him tell the whole story.

It seems that two hundred years before, there was a high-technology culture in the Northern Hemisphere. The way Dahlmann spoke, it was very nearly Mikin caliber—the North People even had some primitive form of space flight. Then there was a war. A war is something like a fight, only much bigger, bigger even than an antitrust action. They exploded more than 12,500 megatons of bombs on their own cities. In addition, germ cultures were released to kill anybody who survived the fusion bombs. Without radiation screens and panphagic viruses, it was a slaughter. Virtually all the mammals in the Northern Hemisphere were destroyed, and according to Dahlmann, there was, for a while, the fear that the radiation poisons and disease strains would wipe out life in the South World, too.

It is very difficult to imagine how anything like that could get started in the first place—the cause of "war" was one of the objects of my research. Of course the gross explanation was that the Terrans never developed the Umpire System or the Concept of Chaos. Instead they used the gargantuan organizations called "governments." But the underlying question was why they chose this weird governmental path at all. Were the Terrans essentially subhuman—or is it just luck that we Mikins discovered the True Way?

The war didn't discourage the Terrans from their fundamental errors. Three governments rose from the ashes of the war. The Australian, the Sudamérican, and the Zulunder. Even the smallest nation, Australia, had one thousand times as many people as the %wrlyg Spice & Trading Company. And remember that %wrlyg is already as big as a group can get without being slapped with an antitrust ruling by the Umpires.

I forgot my surroundings as Dahlmann went on to explain the present power structure, the struggle of the two stronger nations to secure colonies in portions of the Northern Hemisphere where the war poisons had dissipated. This was a very dangerous situation, according to the Terran anthropologist, since there were many disease types dormant in the Northern Hemisphere. That could start hellish plagues in the South World, for the Terrans were still more than a century behind the technology they had achieved before the blowup.

Through all this discussion, Horlig maintained an almost contemptuous silence, not listening to what we were saying so much as observing us as specimens. Finally he interrupted. "Well, I'm glad to see you both hit it off so well. It's getting too late for me though. I'll have to take my leave. No, you don't have to come back just yet, Melmwn. I'll send the car back here on auto after I get to Base."

"You don't have to bother with that, Horlig. Things look pretty tame around here. I can walk back."

"No," Horlig said definitely. "We have regulations. And there is always this Merlyn, you know."

THE MERLYN BUNGLERS DIDN'T FRIGHTEN ME, BUT I REMEMBERED THAT CAT'S Demoneyes. Suddenly I was happy to fly back. After Horlig had left, we returned to the den and its dim gas mantle lamps. I could understand why Dahlmann's eyesight was so bad—you try reading at night without electric lights for a couple decades and you'll go blind, too. He rummaged around in his desk and drew out a pouch of "tobacco." He fumbled the ground leaves into the bowl of his pipe and tamped them down with a clumsy forefinger. I thought he was going to burn his face when he lit the mixture. Back home, anyone with coordination that poor would be dead in less than two days, unless he secluded himself in a pacific enclave. This Terran culture was truly alien. It was different along a dimension we had never imagined, except in a few mathematical theories of doubtful validity.

The Terran sat back and regarded me for a long moment. Behind those thick lenses his eyes loomed large and wise. Now I was the one who seemed helpless. Finally he pulled back the curtains and inspected the lawn and the place where the car had rested. "I believe, Scholar Melmwn, that you are a reasonable and intelligent individual. I hope that you are even more than that. Do you realize that you are attending the execution of a race?"

This took me completely by surprise. "What! What do you mean?"

He appeared to ignore my question. "I knew when you people first landed and we saw your machines: Our culture is doomed. I had hoped that we could escape with our lives—though in our own history, few have been so lucky. I hoped that your social sciences would be as advanced as your physical. But I was wrong.

"Your Vice President for Aboriginal Affairs arrived with the Second %wrlyg Fleet. Is genocide the %wrlyg policy or is it Horlig's private scheme?"

This was too much. "I find your questions insulting, Terran! The %wrlyg Company intends you no harm. Our interests are confined to reclaiming and colonizing areas of your planet that you admit are too hot for you to handle."

Now Dahlmann was on the defensive. "I apologize, Scholar Melmwn, for my discourtesy. I dived into the subject too hastily. I don't mean to offend you. Let me describe my fears and the reasons for them. I believe that Herul Horlig is not content with the cultural destruction of Earth. He would like to see all Terrans dead. Officially his job is to promote cooperation between our races and to eliminate possible frictions. In fact, he has played the opposite role. Since he arrived, his every act has increased our mutual antagonism. Take for instance, the 'courtesy call' he made to the Zulunder capital. He and that armed forces chief of yours, Noggin Chem—is that how you pronounce the name?"

"Ngagn Che#," I corrected.

"They breezed into Pret armed to the teeth—fifteen air tanks and a military air-space craft. The Zulunder government requested that Horlig return the spaceship to orbit before they initiated talks. In response, the Mikins destroyed half the city. At the time I hoped that it was just the act of some demented gunner, but Horlig staged practically the same performance at Buenos Aires, the capital of Sudamérica. And this time he had no pretext whatsoever, since the Américans bent over backwards trying to avoid a clash. Every chance he gets, the man tries to prove how vicious Mikins can be."

I MADE A NOTE TO CHECK ON THESE EVENTS WHEN I RETURNED TO BASE. Aloud I said: "Then you believe that Horlig is trying to provoke terrorist movements like this Merlyn thing, so he'll have an excuse to kill all Terrans?"

Dahlmann didn't answer immediately. He carefully pulled back the curtain again and looked into the yard. The aircar had not yet returned. I think he realized that the mikes aboard the car could easily record what we were saying. "That's not quite what I mean, Scholar Melmwn. I believe that Horlig *is* Merlyn."

I snorted disbelief.

"I know it sounds ridiculous—but everything fits. Just take the word 'Merlyn.' In Australian this refers to a magician who lived ages ago in England—that was one of the great pre-war nations in the Northern Hemisphere. At the same time it is a word that easily comes to the lips of a Mikin since it is entirely pronounceable within your phoneme system—it contains no front oral stops. With its magical connotations, it is designed to set fear in Mikins. The word Merlyn is a convenient handle for the fear and hatred that Mikins will come to associate with Terran activities. But note—we Terrans are a very unsuperstitious lot, especially the Australians and the Zulunders. And very few Terrans realize how superstitious many Mikins—the witch-fearers and the demon-mongers—are. The Merlyn concept is the invention of a Mikin mind."

Dahlmann rushed on to keep me from interrupting. "Consider also: When terrorist attacks are thwarted and the Terrans captured, they turn out to be ill-equipped rumdums—not the skilled agents of some world-wide plot. But whenever great damage is done—say the detonation of the Company ammo stores last year—no one is caught. In fact, it is almost impossible to imagine how the job could be pulled off without Mikin technology. At first I discounted this theory, because so many Mikins were killed in the ammo blast, but I have since learned that you people do not regard such violence as improper business procedure."

"It depends on who you are working for. There are plenty of Violent Nihilists on Miki, and occasionally they have their own companies. If %wrlyg is one such, he's been keeping the fact a secret."

"What it adds up to is that Horlig is creating an artificial threat which he believes will eventually justify genocide. One last element of proof. You came in on a Fleet landing craft this afternoon, did you not? Horlig was supposed to greet you. He invited me out to meet you on the field, as the Chief Representative of Her Majesty's Government in Australia. This is the first friendly gesture the man has made in three years. As it happened I couldn't go. I sent my daughter, Mary. But when you actually landed, Horlig got a sliver from his shin board, or something equally idiotic, and so couldn't go onto the field—where just five minutes later a group of 'Merlyn's Men' tried to shoot the lot of you."

Mary Dahlmann. I stuttered over the next question. "How . . . how is your daughter, Scholar Dahlmann?"

Dahlmann was nonplussed for a moment. "She's fine. Apparently someone pulled her out of the line of fire. A bloody nose was the sum total of her injuries."

For some reason I felt great relief at this news. I looked at my watch; it was thirty minutes to midnight, the witching hour. Tonight especially I wanted to get back to Base before Demonsloose. And I hadn't known that Merlyn was the name of a wizard. I stood up. "You've certainly given me something to think about, Dahlmann. Of course you know where my sympathies ultimately lie, but I'll be alert for signs of the plot you speak of, and I won't tell anyone what you've told me."

The Terran rose. "That's all I ask." He led me out of the den, and into the darkened mainroom. The wood floor creaked comfortingly beneath the thick carpet. Crystal goblets on wood shelving were outlined in faint glistening reflection from the den light. To the right a stairway led to the second floor. Was *she* up there sleeping, or out with some male? I wondered.

As we approached the door, something much more pertinent occurred to me. I touched Dahlmann's elbow; he stopped, ready to open the door. "A moment, Scholar Dahlmann. All the facts you present fit another theory; namely, that some Terran, expert in Mikin ways, yourself perhaps, has manufactured Merlyn and the rumor that members of the %wrlyg Company are responsible for the conspiracy."

I couldn't tell for sure, but I think he smiled. "Your counter-proposal does indeed fit the facts. However, I am aware of the power that you Mikins have at your disposal, and how futile resistance would be." He opened the door. I stepped out onto the porch. "Good night," he said.

"Good night." I stood there for several seconds, listening to his retreating footsteps, and puzzling over our last exchange.

I TURNED AND WAS HALFWAY ACROSS THE PORCH WHEN A SOFT VOICE BEHIND me asked, "And how did you like Daddy?" I jumped a good fifteen centimeters, spun around with my wrist gun extended. Mary Dahlmann sat on a wooden swing hung from the ceiling of the porch. She pushed the swing gently back and forth. I walked over and sat down beside her.

"He's an impressive and intelligent man," I answered.

"I want to thank you for pulling me down this afternoon." Her mind seemed to jump randomly from one topic to another.

"Uh, that's OK. There really wasn't too much danger. The gun was so primitive that I imagine it's almost as unpleasant to be behind it as in front. I would've thought you'd be the first to recognize it as an attack. You must be familiar with Australian weapons."

"Are you kidding? The biggest gun I've ever seen was a twenty-millimeter rifle in a shooting exhibition."

"You mean you've never been under fire until today?" I saw that she hadn't. "I didn't mean to be insulting, Miss Dahlmann. I haven't really had much firsthand information about Terrans. That's one reason why I'm here."

She laughed. "If you're puzzled about us, then the feeling is mutual. Since my father became Chief Representative, he's been doing everything he can to interview Mikins and figure out the structure of your culture. I'll bet he spent half the night pumping you. As an anthropologist, you should be the best source he can find."

Apparently she wasn't aware of her father's true concerns.

"In the last three years we've managed to interview more than fifteen of you Mikins. It's crazy. You're all so different from one another. You claim you are all from the same continent, and yet each individual appears to have an entirely different cultural background. Some of you don't wear clothes at all, while others go around with every inch of their skin covered. Some, like Horlig, make a fetish of primitiveness. But we had one fellow here who had so many gadgets with him that he had to wear powered body armor. He was so heavy, he busted my father's favorite chair. We can't find any common denominator. Mikins believe in one god, or in many, or in none. At the same time, many of you are dreadfully superstitious. We've always wondered what aliens might be like, but we never guessed that—What's the matter?"

I pointed shakily at the creature in the street. She placed a reassuring hand on my arm. "Why, that's just a cat. Don't you have catlike creatures on Miki?"

"Certainly."

"Why the shock then? Are your cats poisonous or something?"

"Of course not. Many people keep them as pets. It's just that it's a bad sign to see one at night—an especially bad sign if it looks at you and its eyes glow." I was sorry when she withdrew her hand.

She looked at me closely. "I hope you won't be angry, Mr. Melmwn, but this is exactly what I mean. How can a race that travels between the stars believe in ill or good omens? Or have you developed magic as a science?"

"No, that's not it. Many Mikins don't believe in signs at all, and depending on whether you are a demon-monger or a witch-fearer, you recognize different signs. As for how I personally can believe in nonempirical, nonscientific signs—that's easy. There are many more causal relations in this universe than Mikin science will ever discover. I believe that witch-fearers have divined a few of these. And though I am quite a mild witch-fearer, I don't take any chances."

"But you are an anthropologist. I should think in your studies you would see so many different attitudes and superstitions that you would disregard your own."

I watched carefully as the cat went round the corner of the house.

Then I turned to look at Mary Dahlmann. "Is that how it is with Terran anthropologists? Perhaps then I should not translate my occupation as 'anthropology.' Before %wrlyg, I was employed by the Ana#og Pacific Enclave & Motor Corporation. A fine group. As anthropologist, my job was to screen the background attitudes of perspective employees. For instance, it just wouldn't do to have a Cannibal and a Militant Vegetarian work next to each other on the production line—they'd kill each other inside of three hours, and the corporation would lose money."

She pushed the swing back with an agitated kick. "But now we're back where we started. How can a single culture produce both cannibals and 'militant' vegetarians?"

I thought about it. Her question really seemed to go beyond cultures entirely—right to the core of reality. I had practiced my specialty within the Mikin framework—where such questions never came up. Maybe I should start with something basic.

"OUR SYSTEM IS FOUNDED ON THE CONCEPT OF CHAOS. THE UNIVERSE IS basically a dark and unhappy place—a place where evil and injustice and randomness rule. The ironic thing is that the very act of organization creates the potential for even greater ruin. Social organizations have a natural tendency to become monopolistic and inflexible. When they finally break down, it is a catastrophic debacle. So, we must accept a great deal of disorder and violence in our lives if we are to avoid a complete blowup later.

"Every Mikin is free to *try* anything. Naturally, in order to survive, groups of people cooperate—and from this you get the tens of thousands of organizations, corporations, and convents that make our civilization. But no group may become monopolistic. This is why we have Umpires. I don't think you have anything comparable. Umpires see that excessively large organizations are never formed. They keep our society from becoming rigid and unresponsive to the natural world. Our system has lasted a very long time." *Much longer than yours*, I added to myself.

She frowned. "I don't understand. Umpires? Is this some sort of police force? How do they keep governments from forming? What's to keep the Umpires from becoming a government themselves?"

If I didn't watch out, I was going to learn more about Miki than I did about Earth. Mary's questions opened doors I never knew existed. My answer was almost as novel to me as it was to her. "I suppose it's because the Umpire tradition is very old with us. With one minor exception, all Mikins have had this tradition for almost four thousand years. The Umpires probably originated as a priest class serving a number of different nomad tribes. There never were many Umps. They go unarmed. They have bred for intelligence and flexibility. There's quite a bit of, uh, mys-

tery—which we take for granted—surrounding them. I believe that they
live under the influence of some rather strange drugs. You might say
that they are brainwashed. In all history, there is no period in which
they have sought power. Though they spend most of their lives in the
abstract study of behavior science, their real task is to watch society for
signs of bigness.

"There's one watching %wrlyg right now. If he decides that %wrlyg
is too big—and that's a distinct possibility, since there are almost twelve
thousand %wrlyg employees altogether—the Ump will issue an, uh,
antitrust ruling, describing the situation and ordering certain changes.
There is no appeal. Defiance of an antitrust ruling is the only deed that
is recognized by all Mikins as a sin. When there is such defiance, all
Mikins are bound to take antitrust action—that is, to destroy the crim-
inal. Some antitrust actions have involved fusion bombs and armies—
they're the closest thing we have to wars."

She didn't look convinced. "Frankly, I can't imagine how such a system could avoid becoming a dictatorship of 'Umpires.' "

"I feel the same incredulity about your civilization."

"How big are your 'organizations'?"

"It might be a single person. More than half the groups on Miki are
just families or family groups. Anything goes unless it threatens stability—or becomes too large. The largest groups allowed are some of the
innocuous religious types—the Little Brother Association, for instance.
They preach approximately the principles I read of in your Christianity.
But they don't proselytize, and so manage to avoid antitrust rulings. The
largest 'hardware' organizations have about fifteen thousand employees."

"And how can a company support interstellar operations?"

"Yes, that's a very tricky point. %wrlyg had to cooperate with several
hundred industrial groups to do it. They came mighty close to antitrust."

She sat silently, thinking all this over. Then she asked, "When can
we expect an antitrust ruling against the Australian government?"

I laughed. "You don't have to worry about that. No offense, but antitrust can only apply to human groupings."

She didn't like that at all, but she didn't argue it either. Instead she
came back with, "Then that means we also don't have Umpire protection if %wrlyg commits genocide upon us."

That was a nasty conclusion but it fitted the letter of custom. Killing
millions of humans would warrant antitrust, but Terrans weren't human.

For an instant I thought she was laughing, low and bitter. Then her
face seemed to collapse and I knew she was crying. This was an unpleasant turn of events. Awkwardly, I put my arm around her shoulders
and tried to comfort her. She no longer seemed to me an abo, but simply
a person in pain. "Please, Mary Dahlmann. My people aren't monsters.

We only want to use places on your planet that are uninhabited, that are too dangerous for you. Our presence will actually make Earth safer. When we colonize the North World, we'll null the radiation poisons and kill the war viruses."

That didn't stop the tears, but she did move closer into my arms. Several seconds passed and she mumbled something like, "History repeats." We sat like that for almost half an hour.

It wasn't until I got back to Base that I remembered that I had been out between Demonsloose and Dawn without so much as a Hexagram.

I GOT MY EQUIPMENT INSTALLED THE NEXT DAY. I WAS ASSIGNED AN OFFICE only fifty-four hundred meters from the central supply area. This was all right with me since the site was also quite near the outskirts of Adelaide-west. Though the office was made entirely of local materials, the style was old #*imw*#. The basement contained my sleeping and security quarters, and the first floor was my office and business machines. The surface construction was all hand-polished hardwood. The roof was tiled with rose marble and furnished with night chairs and a drink mixer. At the center of the roof was a recoilless rifle and a live map of the minefield around the building. It was all just like home—which is what I had specified when I had signed the contract back on Miki. I had expected some chiseling on the specifications once we got out in the boondocks, but %wrlyg's integrity was a pleasant surprise.

After I checked out the equipment, I called Horlig and got a copy of his mission log. I wanted to check on Dahlmann's charges. Horlig was suspiciously unhappy about parting with the information, but when I pointed out that I was without a job until I got background info, he agreed to squirt me a copy. The incidents were more or less as Dahlmann had described them. At Pret, though, the Zulunders attacked the air tanks with some jury-rigged anti-aircraft weapon—so the retaliation seemed justified. There was also one incident that Dahlmann hadn't mentioned. Just five days before, Che#—on Horlig's orders—burned the food supplies of the Sudamérican colony at Panamá, thus forcing the Terran explorers to return to the inhabited portions of their continent. I decided to keep a close watch on these developments. There could be something here quite as sinister as Dahlmann claimed.

Later that day, Horlig briefed me on my first assignment. He wanted me to record and index the Canberra Central Library. The job didn't appeal at all. It was designed to keep me out of his hair. I spent the next couple weeks getting equipment together. I found Robert Dahlmann especially helpful. He telegraphed his superiors in Canberra and they agreed to let us use Terran clerical help in the recording operation. (I imagine part of the reason was that they were eager to study our equipment.) I never actually flew to Canberra. Horlig had some deputy take the gear out and instruct the natives on how to use it. It turned out Canberra library was huge—almost as big as the Information Services library at home. Just supervising the indexing computers was a full-time job. It was a lot more interesting than I thought it would be. When the job was done I would have many times the source material I could have collected personally.

A strange thing: As the weeks went by, I saw more and more of Mary Dahlmann. Even at this point I was still telling myself that it was all field work for my study of Terran customs. One day we had a picnic in the badlands north of Adelaide. The next she took me on a tour of the business district of the city—it was amazing how so many people could live so close together day after day. Once we even went on a train ride all the way to Murray Bridge. Railroads are stinking, noisy, and dirty, but they're fun—and they transport freight almost as cheaply as a floater does. Mary had that spark of intelligence and good humor that made it all the more interesting. Still I claimed it was all in the cause of objective research.

About six weeks after my landing I invited her to visit the %wrlyg Base. Though Central Supply is only four or five kilometers from Adelaide-west, I took her in by air, so she could see the whole Base at once. I think it was the first time she had ever flown.

THE %WRLYG PRIMARY TERRITORY IS A RECTANGULAR AREA FIFTEEN BY THIRTY kilometers. It was ceded by the Australian government to the Company in gratitude for our intercession in the Battle of Hawaii, seventeen years before. You might wonder why we didn't just put all our bases in the Northern Hemisphere, and ignore the Terrans entirely. The most important reason was that the First and Second Fleets hadn't had the equipment for a large-scale decontamination job. Also, every kilogram of cargo from Miki requires nearly 100,000 megatons of energy for the voyage to Earth: this is expensive by any reckoning. We needed all the labor and materials the locals could provide. Since the Terrans inhabited the Southern Hemisphere only, that's where our first base had to be.

By native standards %wrlyg paid extremely good wages. So good that almost thirty thousand Terrans were employed at the Ground Base. Many of these individuals lived in an area just off the Base, which Mary referred to as Clowntown. Its inhabitants were understandably enamored with the advantages of Mikin technology. Though their admiration was commendable, the results were a little ludicrous. Clowntowners tried to imitate the various aspects of Mikin life. They dressed eccentrically—by Terran standards—and adopted a variety of social behaviors. But their city was just as crowded as regular Australian urban areas.

And though they had more scraps of our technology than many places in Australia, their city was filthy. Anarchy just isn't practical in such close quarters. They had absorbed the superficial aspects of our society without ever getting down to the critical matters of Umpires and anti-trust. Mary had refused to go with me into Clowntown. Her reason was that police protection ceased to exist in that area. I don't think that was her real reason.

Below us, the blue sea and white breakers met the orange and gray-green bluffs of the shore. The great Central Desert extended right up to the ocean. It was difficult to believe that this land had once supported grass and trees. Scattered randomly across the sand and sage were the individual office and workshops of Company employees. Each of these had its own unique appearance. Some were oases set in the desert. Others were squat gray forts. Some even looked like Terran houses. And, of course, a good number were entirely hidden from sight, the property of Obscurantist employees who kept their location secret even from %wrlyg. Taken as a whole, the Base looked like a comfortable Metropolitan area on the A1 W1 peninsula. But, if the Company had originally based in the Northern Hemisphere, none of the amenities would have been possible. We would have had to live in prefab domes.

I swung the car in a wide arc and headed for the central area. Here was the robot factory that provided us with things like air tanks and drink mixers—things that native labor couldn't construct. Now we could see the general landing area, and the airy columns of Supply Central. Nearby was housing for groups that believed in living together: the sex club, the Little Brothers. A low annex jutted off from the Little Brothers building—the creche for children born of Non-Affective parents. They even had some half-breed Terran-Human children there. The biologists had been amazed to find that the two species could interbreed—some claimed that this proved the existence of a prehistoric interstellar empire.

I PARKED THE CAR AND WE TOOK THE LIFT TO THE OPEN EATING AREA AT THE top of Supply Central. The utilitarian cafeteria served the Extroverts on the Company staff. The position afforded an excellent view of the sailing boats and surfers as well as three or four office houses out in the sea.

We were barely seated when two Terran waiter-servants came over to take our order. One of them favored Mary with a long, cold look, but they took my order courteously enough.

Mary watched them go, then remarked, "They hate my guts, do you know that?"

"Huh? Why should they hate you?"

"I'm, uh, 'consorting' with the Greenies. That's you. I knew one of those two in college. A real nice guy. He wanted to study low-energy nuclear reactions: prewar scientists never studied that area thoroughly. His life ended when he discovered that you people know more than he'll ever discover, unless he starts over from the beginning on your terms. Now he's practically a slave, waiting on tables."

"A slave he's not, girl. %wrlyg just isn't that type of organization. That fellow is a trusted and well cared for servant—an employee, if you will. He can pack up and leave anytime. With the wages we pay, we have Terrans begging for jobs."

"That's exactly what I mean," Mary said opaquely. Then she turned the question around. "Don't you feel any hostility from your friends, for running around with an 'Earthie' girl?"

I laughed. "In the first place, I'm not running around. I'm using you in my studies. In the second place, I don't know any of these people well enough yet to have friends. Even the people I came out with were all in deep freeze, remember.

"Some Mikins actually support fraternization with the natives—the Little Brothers for instance. Every chance they get, they tell us to go out and make love—or is that verb just plain 'love'?—to the natives. I think there are some Company people who are definitely hostile toward you people—Horlig and Che#, for example. But I didn't ask their permission, and, if they want to stop me, they'll have to contend with this." I tapped the dart gun on my wrist.

"Oh?" I think she was going to say something more when the servants came out and placed the food on our table. It was good, and we didn't say anything for several minutes. When we were done we sat and watched the surfers. A couple on a powered board were racing a dolphin across the bay. Their olive skins glistened pleasantly against the blue water.

Finally she spoke. "I've always been puzzled by that Horlig. He's odd even for a Mikin—no offense. He seems to regard Terrans as foolish and ignorant cowards. Yet as a person, he looks a lot more like a Terran than a Mikin."

"Actually, he's a different subspecies from the rest of us. It's like the difference between you and Zulunders. His bone structure is a little different and his skin is pale gray instead of olive green. His ancestors lived on a different continent than mine. They never developed beyond a neolithic culture there. About four hundred years ago, my race colonized his continent. We already had firearms then. Horlig's people just shriveled away. Whenever they fought us, we killed them; and whenever they didn't, we set them away in preserves. The last preserve Gloyn died about fifty years ago, I think. The rest interbred with the mainstream. Horlig is the nearest thing to a full-blooded Gloyn I've seen. Maybe that's why he affects primitiveness."

Mary said, "If he weren't out to get us Terrans, I think I could feel sorry for him."

I couldn't understand that comment. Horlig's race may have been mistreated in the past, but he was a lot better off than his ancestors ever were.

THREE TABLES AWAY, ANOTHER COUPLE WAS ENGAGED IN AN INTENSE CONversation. Gradually it assumed the proportions of an argument. The man snapped an insult and the woman returned it with interest. Without warning, a knife appeared in her hand, flashed at the other's chest. But the man jumped backward, knocking over his chair. Mary gasped, as the man brought his knife in a grazing slash across the woman's middle. Red instantly appeared on green. They danced around the tables, feinting and slashing.

"Ron, do something! He's going to kill her."

They were fighting in a meal area, which is against Company regs, but on the other hand, neither was using power weapons. "I'm not going to do anything Mary. This is a lovers' quarrel."

Mary's jaw dropped. "A lovers' quarrel? What—"

"Yeah," I said, "they both want the same woman." Mary looked sick. As soon as the fight began, a Little Brother at the other end of the roof got up and sprinted toward the combatants. Now he stood to one side, pleading with them to respect the holiness of life, and to settle their differences peacefully. But the two weren't much for religion. The man hissed at the Little Brother to get lost before he got spitted. The woman took advantage of her opponent's momentary inattention to pink his arm. Just then a Company officer arrived on the roof and informed the two just how big a fine they would be subject to if they continued to fight in a restricted area. That stopped them. They backed away from each other, cursing. The Little Brother followed them to the lift as he tried to work out some sort of reconciliation.

Mary seemed upset. "You people lead sex lives that make free love look like monogamy."

"No, you're wrong, Mary. It's just that every person has a different outlook. It's as if all Earth's sex customs coexisted. Most people subscribe to some one type." I decided not to try explaining the sex club.

"Don't you have marriage?"

"That's just what I'm saying. A large proportion of us do. We even have a word analogous to your *missus*—a. For instance, Mrs. Smith is aSmith. I would say that nearly fifteen percent of all Mikins are monogamous in the sense you mean it. And a far greater percentage never engage in the activities you regard as perversions."

She shook her head. "Do you know—if your group had appeared without a superior technology, you would have been locked up in an insane asylum? I like you personally, but most Mikins are so awfully weird."

I was beginning to get irritated. "You're the one that's nuts. The %wrlyg employees here on Earth were deliberately chosen for their intelligence and compatibility. Even the mildly exotic types were left at home."

Mary's voice wavered slightly as she answered. "I . . . I guess I know that. You're all just so terribly different. And soon all the ways I know will be destroyed, and my people will all be dead or like you—more probably dead. No, don't deny it. More than once in our history we've had episodes like the colonization of Gloyn. Six hundred years ago, the Europeans took over North America from the stone-age Indians. One group of Indians—a tribe called the Cherokee—saw that they could never overcome the invaders. They reasoned that the only way to survive was to adopt European ways—no matter how offensive those ways appeared. The Cherokee built schools and towns; they even printed newspapers in their own language. But this did not satisfy the Europeans. They coveted the Cherokee lands. Eventually they evicted the Indians and forced-marched the tribe halfway across the continent into a desert preserve. For all their willingness to adapt, the Cherokee suffered the same fate that your Gloyn did.

"Ron, are you any different from the Europeans—or from your Mikin ancestors? Will my people be massacred? Will the rare survivor be just another Mikin with all your aw . . . all your alien customs? Isn't there any way you can save us from yourselves?" She reached out and grasped my hand. I could see she was fighting back tears.

There was no rationalizing it: I had fallen for her. I silently cursed my moralistic Little Brother upbringing. At that moment, if she had asked it, I would have run right down to the beach and started swimming for Antarctica. The feel of her hand against mine and the look in her eyes would have admitted to no other response. For a moment, I wondered if she was aware of the awful power she had. Then I said, "I'll do everything I can, Mary. I don't think you have to worry. We've advanced a long way since Gloyn. Only a few of us wish you harm. But I'll do anything to protect your people from massacre and exploitation. Is that enough of a commitment?"

She squeezed my hand. "Yes. It's a greater commitment than has been made in all the past."

"Fine," I said, standing up. I wanted to get off this painful subject as fast as possible. "Let me show you some of our equipment."

I took her over the Abo Affairs Office. The AAO wasn't a private residence-office, but it did bear Horlig's stamp. Even close up, it looked like a Gloyn rock-nest—a huge pile of boulders set in a marshy—and artificial—jungle. It was difficult, even for me, to spot the location of the recoilless rifles and machine guns. Inside, the neolithic motif was maintained. The computing equipment and TV screens were hidden behind woven curtains, and lighting came indirectly through chinks in the boulders. Horlig refused to employ Terrans, and his Mikin clerks and techs hadn't returned from lunch.

At the far end of the "room" a tiny waterfall gushed tinkling into a pool. Beyond the pool was Horlig's office, blocked from direct view by a rock partition. I noticed that the pool gave us an odd, ripply view into his office. That's the trouble with these "open" architectural forms: they have no real rooms, or privacy. In the water I could see the upside-down images of Horlig and Che#. I motioned Mary to be quiet, and knelt down to watch. Their voices were barely audible above the sound of falling water.

Che# was saying—in Mikin, of course: "You've been sensible enough in the past, Horlig. My suggestion is just a logical extension of previous policy. Once he's committed I'm sure that %wrlyg won't have any objections. The Terrans have provided us with almost all the materials we needed from them. Their usefulness is over. They're vermin. It's costing the Company two thousand man-hours a month to provide security against their attacks and general insolence." He waved a sheaf of papers at Horlig. "My plan is simple. Retreat from Ground Base for a couple weeks and send orbital radiation bombs over the three inhabited areas. Then drop some lethal viruses to knock off the survivors. I figure it would cost one hundred thousand man-hours total, but we'd be permanently rid of this nuisance. And our ground installations would be undamaged. All you have to do is camouflage some of our initial moves so that the Company officers on the Orbital Base don't catch—"

"Enough!" Horlig exploded. He grabbed Che# by the scruff of his cape and pulled him up from his chair. "You putrid bag of schemings. I'm reporting you to Orbit. And if you ever even *think* of that plan again, I personally will kill you—if %wrlyg doesn't do it first!" He shoved the Vice President for Violence to the floor. Che# got up, ready to draw and fire, but Horlig's wrist gun pointed directly at the other's middle. Che# spat on the floor and backed out of the room.

"What was that all about?" Mary whispered. I shook my head. This was one conversation I wasn't going to translate. Horlig's reaction amazed and pleased me. I almost liked the man after the way he had handled Che#. And unless the incident had been staged for my benefit, it shattered Robert Dahlmann's theory about Merlyn and Horlig. Could Che# be the one masquerading as a Terran rebel?

He had just used Terran sabotage as an excuse for genocide.

Or was Merlyn simply what it appeared to be: a terrorist group created and managed by deranged Terrans? Things were all mixed up.

Ngagn Che# stalked out of the passage that led to Horlig's office. He glared murderously at Mary and me as he swept past us toward the door hole.

I looked back into the pool, and saw the reflection of Horlig's face looking back out at me. Perhaps it was the ripple distortion from the waterfall, but he seemed just as furious with my eavesdropping as he had been with Che#. If it had been a direct confrontation, I would've expected a fight. Then Horlig remembered his privacy field and turned it on, blanking out my view.

MY LIBRARY PROJECT PROCEEDED RAPIDLY TO A CONCLUSION. EVERYTHING was taped, and I had 2e7 subjects cross-indexed. The computerized library became my most powerful research tool. Dahlmann hadn't been kidding when he said that the pre-war civilization was high class. If the North Americans and Asians had managed to avoid war, they probably would have sent an expedition to Miki while we were still developing the fission bomb. Wouldn't that have been a switch—the Terrans colonizing our lands!

In the two hundred years since the North World War, the Australians had spent a great deal of effort in developing social science. They hadn't given up their government mania, but they had modified the concept so that it was much less malevolent than in the past. Australia now supported almost eleven million people, at a fairly high standard of living. In fact, I think there was probably less suffering in Australia than there is in most parts of Miki. Too bad their way of life was doomed. The Terrans were people—they were human. (And that simple conclusion was the answer to the whole problem, though I did not see it then.) In all my readings, I kept in mind the solution I was looking for: some way to save the Terrans from physical destruction, even if it was impossible to save their entire culture.

As the weeks passed, this problem came to overshadow my official tasks. I even looked up the history of the Cherokee and read about Elias Boudinot and Chief Sequoyah. The story was chillingly similar to the situation that was being played out now by the Mikins and the Terrans. The only way that the Terrans could hope for physical safety was to adopt Mikin institutions. But even then, wouldn't we eventually wipe them out the same way President Andrew Jackson did the Cherokee? Wouldn't we eventually covet all the lands of Earth?

While I tried to come up with a long-term solution, I also kept track of Che#'s activities. Some of his men were pretty straight guys, and I got to know one platoon leader well. Late one evening about ten weeks after my landing, my armsman friend tipped me off that Che# was planning a massacre the next day in Perth.

I went over to see Horlig that night. From his reaction to Che#'s genocide scheme, I figured he'd squash the massacre plan. The Gloyn was working late. I found him seated behind his stone desk in the center of the AAO rock-nest. He looked up warily as I entered. "What is it, Melmwn?"

"You've got to do something, Horlig. Che# is flying three platoons to Perth. I don't know exactly what type of mayhem he's planning, but—"

"Rockingham."

"Huh?"

"Che# is flying to Rockingham, not Perth." Horlig watched me carefully.

"You knew? What's he going to do—"

"I know because he's doing the job at my suggestion. I've identified the abos who blew up our ammo warehouse last year. Some of the ringleaders are Rockingham city officials. I'm going to make an example of them." He paused, then continued grimly, as if daring me to object. "By tomorrow at this time, every tenth inhabitant of Rockingham will be dead."

I didn't say anything for a second. I couldn't. When I finally got my mouth working again, I said with great originality, "You just can't do this, Horlig. We've had a lot more trouble from the Sudaméricans and the Zulunders than we've ever had from the Australians. Killing a bunch of Aussies will just prove to everyone that Mikins don't want peace. You'll be encouraging belligerence. If you really have proof that these Rockingham officials are Merlyn's Men, you should send Che# out to arrest just those men and bring them back here for some sort of Company trial. Your present action is entirely arbitrary."

Horlig sat back in his chair. There was a new frankness and a new harshness in his face. "Perhaps I just made it all up. I'll fabricate some proof too, when necessary."

I hadn't expected this admission. I answered, "%wrlyg's Second Son himself is coming down from Orbit tomorrow morning. Perhaps you thought he wouldn't know of your plans until they were executed. I don't know why you are doing this, but I can tell you that the Second Son is going to hear about it the minute he gets off the landing craft."

Horlig smiled pleasantly. "Get out."

I TURNED AND STARTED FOR THE DOOR. I ADMIT IT: I WAS GOING SOFT IN THE brain. My only excuse is that I had been associating with the natives too long. They generally say what they think because they have the protection of an impartial and all-powerful police force. This thought occurred to me an instant before I heard the characteristic sound of wrist gun smacking into palm. I dived madly for the floor as the first 0.07 mm dart hit the right boulder of the door hole. The next thing I knew I was lying in the cubbyhole formed by two or three large boulders knocked loose by the blast. My left arm was numb; a rock splinter had cut through it to the bone.

In the next couple seconds, Horlig fired about twenty darts wildly. The lights went out. Rocks weighing many tons flew about. The rock nest had been designed for stability, but this demolition upset the balance and the whole pile was shifting into a new configuration. It was a miracle I wasn't crushed. Horlig screamed. The shooting stopped. Was he dead? The man was nuts to fire more than a single dart indoors. He must have wanted me pretty bad.

As the horrendous echoes faded away, I could hear Horlig swearing. The pile was unrecognizable now. I could see the sky directly between gaps in the rocks. Moonlight came down in silvery shafts through suspended rock dust. Half-human shapes seemed to hurk in the rubble. I realized now that the nest was much bigger than I had thought. To my left an avalanche of boulders had collapsed into some subterranean space. The surface portion of the nest was only a fraction of the total volume. Right now Horlig could be right on the other side of a nearby rock or one hundred meters away—the pile shift had been that violent.

"You still kicking, Melmwn, old man?" Horlig's voice came clearly. The sound was from my right, but not too close. Perhaps if I moved quietly enough I could sneak out of the pile to my aircar. Or I could play dead and wait for morning when Horlig's employees came out. But some of those might be partners in Horlig's scheme—whatever it was. I decided to try the first plan. I crawled over a nearby boulder, made a detour around an expanse of moonlit rock. My progress was definitely audible—there was too much loose stuff. Behind me, I could hear Horlig following. I stopped. This was no good. Even if I managed to make it out, I would then be visible from the pile, and Horlig could shoot me down. I would have to get rid of my opponent before I could escape. Besides, if he got away safely, Horlig could have Che#'s sentries bar me from the landing field the next day. I stopped and lay quietly in the darkness. My arm really hurt now, and I could feel from the wetness on the ground that I had left a trail of blood.

"Come, Melmwn, speak up. I know you're still alive." I smiled. If Horlig thought I was going to give my position away by talking, he was even crazier than I thought. Every time he spoke, I got a better idea of his position.

"I'll trade information for the sound of your voice, Melmwn." Maybe he was not quite so nuts after all. He knew my greatest failing: curiosity. If Horlig should die this night, I might never know what his motives were. And I was just as well armed as he. If I could keep him talking I stood to gain just as much as he.

"All right, Horlig. I'll trade." I had said more than I wanted to. The shorter my responses the better. I listened for the sound of movement. But all I heard was Horlig's voice.

"You see, Melmwn, I am Merlyn." I heard a slithering sound as he moved to a new position. He was revealing everything to keep me talking. Now it was my turn to say something.

"Say on, O Horlig."

"I should have killed you before. When you overheard my conversation with Che#. I thought you might have guessed the truth."

I had received a lot of surprises so far, and this was another. Horlig's treatment of Che#'s genocide scheme had seemed proof that Horlig couldn't be Merlyn. "But why, Horlig? What do you gain? What do you want?"

My opponent laughed. "I'm an altruist, Melmwn. And I'm a Gloyn; maybe the last full-blooded Gloyn. The Terrans are not going to be taken over by you the way you took over my people. The Terrans are people; they are human—and they must be treated as such."

I GUESS THE IDEA MUST HAVE BEEN FLOATING AROUND IN MY MIND FOR weeks. The Terrans were human, and should be treated as such. Horlig's statement triggered the whole solution in my mind. I saw the essential error of the Cherokee and of all my previous plans to save the Terrans. Horlig's motive was a complete surprise, but I could understand it. In a way he seemed to be after the same thing as I—though his methods couldn't possibly work. Maybe we wouldn't have to shoot it out.

"Listen Horlig. There's a way I can get what you want without bloodshed. The Terrans can be saved." I outlined my plan. I talked for almost two minutes.

As I finished, a dart smashed into a boulder thirty meters from my position. Then Horlig spoke. "I will not accept your plan. It is just what I'm fighting against." He seemed to be talking to himself, repeating a cycle that played endlessly, fanatically in his own brain. "Your plan would make the Terrans carbon-copy Mikins. Their culture would be destroyed as thoroughly as mine was. It is far better to die fighting you monsters than to lie down and let you take over. That's why I became Merlyn. I give the rebellious Terran elements a backbone, secret information, supplies. In my capacity as a Mikin official, I provoke incidents to convince the spineless ones of the physical threat to their existence. The Australians are the most cowardly of the lot. Apparently their government will accept any indignity. That's why I must be especially brutal at Rockingham tomorrow."

"Your plan's insane," I blurted without thinking. "%wrlyg could destroy every living thing on Earth without descending from orbit."

"Then that is better than the cultural assassination you intend! We will die fighting." I think he was crying. "I grew up on the last preserve. I heard the last stories. The stories of the lands and the hunting my people once had, before you came and killed us, drove us away, talked us out of everything of value. If we had stood and fought then, I at least would never have been born into the nightmare that is your world." There was silence for a second.

I crept slowly toward the sound of his voice. I tucked my left arm in my shirt to keep it from dragging on the ground. I guessed that Horlig was wounded too, from the slithery sound he made when he moved.

The man was so involved in his own world that he kept on talking. It's strange, but now that I had discovered a way to save the Terrans, I felt doubly desperate to get out of the rock-nest alive. "And don't, Melmwn, be so sure that we will lose to you this time. I intend to provoke no immediate insurrection. I am gathering my forces. A second robot factory was brought in with the Third Fleet. %wrlyg's Second Son is coming down with it tomorrow. With Che#'s forces on the West Coast it will be an easy matter for Merlyn's Men to hijack the factory and its floater. I already have a hidden place, in the midst of all the appropriate orefields, to set it up. Over the years, that factory will provide us with all the weapons and vehicles we need. And someday, someday we will rise and kill all the Mikins."

Horlig sounded delirious now. He was confusing Gloyn and Terran. But that robofactory scheme was not the invention of a delirious mind— only an insane one. I continued across the boulders—under and around them. The moon was directly overhead and its light illuminated isolated patches of rock. I knew I was quite near him now. I stopped and inspected the area ahead of me. Just five meters away a slender beam of moonlight came down through a chink in the rock overhead.

"Tomorrow, yes, tomorrow will be Merlyn's greatest coup."

As Horlig spoke I thought I detected a faint agitation in the rock dust that hung in that moonbeam. Of course it might be a thermal effect from a broken utility line, but it could also be Horlig's breath stirring the tiny particles.

I scrambled over the last boulder to get a clear shot that would not start an avalanche. My guess was right. Horlig sprang to his feet, and for an instant was outlined by the moonlight. His eyes were wide and staring. He was a Gloyn warrior in shin boards and breech-clout, standing in the middle of his wrecked home and determined to protect his way of life from the alien monsters. He was only four hundred years too late. He fired an instant before I did. Horlig missed. I did not. The last Gloyn disappeared in an incandescent flash.

I was in bad shape by the time I got out to my car and called a medic. The next couple hours seem like someone else's memories. I woke the Ump at 0230. He wasn't disturbed by the hour; Umpires can take anything in stride. I gave him the whole story and my solution. I don't think I was very eloquent, so either the plan was sharp or the Ump was especially good. He accepted the whole plan, even the ruling against %wrlyg. To be frank, I think it was a solution that he would have come to on his own, given time—but he had come down from the Orbital Base the week before, and had just begun his study of the natives. He told me he'd reach an official decision later in the day and tell me about it.

I flew back to my office, set all the protection devices on auto, and blacked out. I didn't wake until fifteen hours later, when Ghuri Kym— the Ump—called and asked me to come with him to Adelaide.

Just twenty-four hours after my encounter with Horlig, we were standing in Robert Dahlmann's den. I made the introductions. "Umpire Kym can read Australian but he hasn't had any practice with speaking, so he's asked me to interpret. Scholar Dahlmann, you were right about Herul Horlig—but for the wrong reasons." I explained Horlig's true motives. I could see Dahlmann was surprised. "And Che#'s punitive expedition to the West Coast has been called off, so you don't have to worry about Rockingham." I paused, then plunged into the more important topic. "I think I've come up with a way to save your species from extinction. Ghuri Kym agrees."

Kym laid the document on Dahlmann's desk and spoke the ritual words. "What's this?" asked Dahlmann, pointing at the Mikin printing.

"The English is on the other side. As the representative of the Australian government, you have just been served with an antitrust ruling. Among other things, it directs your people to split into no fewer than one hundred thousand autonomous organizations. Ngagn Che# is delivering similar documents to the Sudamérican and Zulunder governments. You have one year to effect the change. You may be interested to know that %wrlyg has also been served and must split into at least four competitive groups."

%wrlyg had been served with the antitrust ruling that morning. My employers were very unhappy with my plan. Kym told me that the Second Son had threatened to have me shot if I ever showed up on Company property again. I was going to have to lay low for a while, but I knew that %wrlyg needed all the men they could get. Ultimately,

I would be forgiven. I wasn't worried: the risk-taking was worth while if it saved the Terrans from exploitation.

I had expected an enthusiastic endorsement from Dahlmann, but he took the plan glumly. Kym and I spent the next hour explaining the details of the ruling to him. I felt distinctly deflated when we left. From the Terran's reaction you'd think I had ordered the execution of his race.

Mary was sitting on the porch swing. As we left the house, I asked Kym to return to the Base without me. If her father hadn't been appreciative, I thought that at least Mary would be. She was, after all, the one who had given me the problem. In a way I had done it all for her.

I sat down on the swing beside her.

"Your arm! What happened?" She passed her hand gently over the plastic web dressing. I told her about Horlig. It was just like the end of a melodrama. There was admiration in her eyes, and her arms were around me—boy gets girl, et cetera.

"And," I continued, "I found a way to save all of you from the fate of the Cherokee."

"That's wonderful, Ron. I knew you would." She kissed me.

"The fatal flaw in the Cherokee's plan was that they segregated themselves from the white community, while they occupied lands that the whites wanted. If they had been citizens of the United States of America, it would not have been legal to confiscate their lands and kill them. Of course we Mikins don't even have a word for 'citizen,' but Umpire law extends to all humans. I got the Umpire to declare that Terrans are a human species. I know it sounds obvious, but it just never occurred to us before.

"Genocide is now specifically barred, because it would be monopolistic. An antitrust ruling has already been served on Australia and the other Earth governments."

Mary's enthusiasm seemed to evaporate somewhat. "Then our governments will be abolished?"

"Why, yes, Mary."

"And in a few decades, we will be the same as you with all your . . . perversions and violence and death?"

"Don't say it that way, Mary. You'll have Mikin cultures, with some Terran enclaves. Nothing could have stopped this. But at least you won't be killed. I've saved—"

For an instant I thought I'd been shot in the face. My mind did three lazy loops, before I realized that Mary had just delivered a roundhouse slap. "You green-faced thing," she hissed. "You've saved us nothing. Look at this street. Look! It's quiet. No one's killing anyone. Most people are tolerably happy. This suburb is not old, but its way of life is—almost five hundred years old. We've tried very hard in that time to make it better, and we've succeeded in many ways. Now, just as we're on the verge of discovering how all people can live in peace, you monsters breeze in. You'll rip up our cities. 'They are too big' you say. You'll destroy our police forces. 'Monopolistic enterprise' you call them. And in a few years we'll have a planet-wide Clowntown. We'll have to treat each other as animals in order to survive on these oh-so-generous terms you offer us!" She paused, out of breath, but not out of anger.

And for the first time I saw the real fear she had tried to express from the first. She was afraid of dying—of her race dying; everybody had those fears. But what was just as important to her was her home, her family, her friends. The shopping center, the games, the theaters, the whole concept of courtesy. My people weren't going to kill her body, that was true, but we were destroying all the things that give meaning to life. I hadn't found a solution—I'd just invented murder without bloodshed. Somehow I had to make it right.

I tried to reach my arm around her. "I love you, Mary." The words came out garbled, incomprehensible. "I love you, Mary," more clearly this time.

I don't think she even heard. She pushed away hysterically. "Horlig was the one who was right. Not you. It is better to fight and die than—" She didn't finish. She hit frantically and inexpertly at my face and chest. She'd never had any training, but those were hard, determined blows and they were doing damage. I knew I couldn't stop her, short of injuring her. I stood up under that rain of blows and made for the steps. She followed, fighting, crying.

I stumbled off the steps. She stayed on the porch, crying in a low gurgle. I limped past the street lamp and into the darkness.

So there you have it: anarchy stabilized by *antitrust* laws! I certainly wouldn't suggest that in our real world, where such laws are chiefly used to maintain monopolies of power. With my alien invaders, the "laws" were more a matter of religious custom. Still, I suspect that the scheme's success must be the most *alien* thing about these aliens.

THE WHIRLIGIG OF TIME

As history extends past a Great War, the horror may be gone but there might be a feeling of sadness for the lost "golden age," for the mistakes that were made. I think that theme is clear in "Apartness" and "Conquest by Default." These two stories have little editorializing about the cause of the Great War or the nature of the aggressors; such issues are irrelevant to my protagonists. I did write one story, though, where one side *won* with a nuclear attack.

Back around 1970, I noticed a comment in *Aviation Week* that the (then) planned Sprint anti-ballistic missile could go from launch to 60,000 feet in four seconds. Scale that up just a little bit and there is an interesting side effect. The idea went onto a three-by-five card and into the little wooden box where I kept inspirations deferred. Eventually, it became "The Whirligig of Time." It was published in 1974, long before SDI.

The defense station high in the Laguna Mountains had been on alert since dawn. The clear fall day had passed without event, and now the dark was closing in over the pine-covered hills. A cool, dry wind blew among the trees, nudged at the deep layers of pine needles and slid around the defense station's armored cupolas. Overhead, between the dark silhouettes of the pines, the stars were out, brighter and more numerous than they could ever seem in a city's sky.

To the west, limning the dark Pacific, a narrow band of greenish yellow was all that was left of day, and the city was a fine dusting of light spread inward from the ocean. From the Laguna Mountains, eighty kilometers inland, the city seemed a surrealistic carpet of tiny glowing gems—the most precious of the treasures this station had been constructed to protect.

This was the last moment of comfortable tranquility that this land would know for many, many centuries.

The life in the forest—the birds asleep in the trees, the squirrels in their holes—heard and felt nothing; but deep within the station men looked out into space with microwave eyes, saw the tiny specks rising beyond the polar horizon, plotted their trajectories and predicted that hell would burn in heaven and on earth this night.

On the surface, concrete and steel cowlings whirred open to reveal the lasers and ABMs now tracking the enemies falling out of space. The birds fluttered nervously about their trees now, disturbed by the noises below, and a faint red light shone up from the holes in the ground. Yet from the next ridgeline over, the night would still have seemed silent, and the starlit pine forest undisturbed.

Halfway up in the northern sky, three new stars lit, so bright that a blue-white day shone on the forest, still silent. Their glare faded swiftly through orange to red and guttered out, leaving a play of pale green and gold to spread through the sky. Those pastel colors were the only visible sign of the immense fog of charged particles the explosions had set between ground radars and the missiles that were yet to come. The men in the station held their fire. The explosions had not completely blinded them—they still had a proxy view of part of the battle space from a synchronous satellite—but the distance to their targets was far too great.

In the skies to the north and east more miniature stars were visible— mostly defensive fires. The unnatural aurora spread from horizon to horizon, yet in the west the lights of the city glowed as placidly, as beautifully, as before the end began.

Now the defenders' radars could pick up the enemy warheads falling out of the ionospheric fog that had concealed them. But not one of the incoming missiles was targeted on the city to the west—all were falling in toward the defense station and the ICBM bases in the desert to the east. The defenders noticed this but had no time to puzzle over it. Their own destruction was seconds away unless they acted. The station's main laser fired, and the pines and the hills flashed red by its reflected light. The ten-centimeter beam was a hundred-kilometer-tall thread of fire, disappearing only at the top of the sensible atmosphere where there was no more air to be ionized. Its sound, the sound of whole tons of air being turned into plasma, was a bone-shattering crack that echoed off the distant hills to sweep back and forth across the land.

Now there was nothing left asleep in the forest.

And when the beam itself was gone, there—high in the sky—hung a pale blue thread, with a nob of faintly glowing yellow and gold at one end. The first target, at least, had been destroyed; the beam was so energetic it created its own miniature aurora as it passed through the ionosphere, and the knob at the end of it marked a vaporized target.

Then the other lasers began firing, and the sky was crisscrossed by strange red lightning. The ABMs streaking from the hillside contributed their own peculiar roar to this local armageddon. The tiny rockets were like flecks of molten metal spewed up on rays of fire and smoke. Their success or failure was determined in the scant five seconds of their powered flight—five seconds in which they climbed more than thirty kilometers into the sky. The spaces above the hills were filled with bright new stars, and the more frequent—yet less impressive—glows that marked successful laser interceptions.

For seventy-five seconds the battle in the spaces over the defense station continued. During that time the men could do little but sit and watch their machines—the defense demanded microsecond reflexes, and only the machines could provide that. In those seventy-five million microseconds, the station destroyed dozens of enemy missiles. Only ten of the attacking bombs got through; bright blue flashes on the eastern horizon marked the end of the ICBM bases there. Yet even those ten might have been intercepted, if only the station had not held back its reserve, waiting for the attack that must sooner or later come upon the great city to the west.

Seventy-five seconds—and the city they waited to protect still lay glowing beneath the yellow-green sky.

And then, from the middle of the gleaming carpet that was the city, one more new star was born. In an astronomical sense, it was a very small star; but to itself and to what lay nearby, it was an expanding, gaseous hell of fission-fusion products, neutrons, and X rays.

In seconds the city ceased to be, and the defenders in the mountains realized why all the enemy missiles had been targeted on military installations, realized what must be happening to the larger cities all across the land, realized how much easier it had been for the enemy to smuggle his bombs into the nation's cities than to drop them in along ballistic trajectories.

From where the yacht floated, a million kilometers above the ecliptic and six million behind the Earth in its orbit, the home planet was a marbled bluish ball, nearly as bright as a full moon yet only a quarter the size. The moon itself, a couple of degrees farther out from the sun, shone twice as bright as Venus. The rest of heaven seemed infinitely far away, misty sweeps of stars at the bottom of an endless well.

By the blue-white sunlight, the yacht was a three-hundred-meter silver crescent, devoid of fins and aerials and ports. In fact, the only visible marking was the Imperial escutcheon—a scarlet wreath and a five-pointed star—just short of the nose.

But from within, a large part of that hull was not opaque. Arching over the main deck it was as clear, as transparent, as the air of a desert night; and the lords and ladies attending the Prince's birthday party could see the Earth-Moon system hanging just above the artificial horizon created by the intersection of deck and hull. The scene was lost on most of them. Only a few ever bothered to look up into the strange sky. They were the fifteenth generation of an aristocracy that regarded the entire universe as its just due. They would have been just as bored—or just as amused—at Luna or back on the Avstralijan Riviera on Earth.

In all the two-million-ton bulk of the yacht, perhaps only four or five people were really aware of the surrounding emptiness:

Vanja Biladze floated near the center of the yacht's tiny control cabin—he liked to keep it at zero gee—steadying himself with one hand draped negligently around a wall strap. His three-man crew sat belted down to control saddles before the computer inputs and the holoscreens. Biladze gestured at the gray-white cone that tumbled slowly across the central screen. "Do you have any idea what it is, Boblanson?" he asked the fifth man in the control cabin.

The little man called Boblanson had just entered the cabin from the kennels belowdecks, and he still looked a bit green about the gills. His rickets-bent hands held tightly to the wall straps as his balding head bobbed about in an attempt to focus on the screen. The three crewmen seemed as intrigued by this twisted dwarf as by what the long-range scope was throwing on their screen. The men were new to the Imperial yacht, and Biladze guessed they had never before seen a non-Citizen in person. Outside of the Preserves, about the only place one could be found was in the Emperor's menageries.

Boblanson's nearsighted eyes squinted for a long moment at the screen. The ship's computer had superimposed a reticle on the image, indicating the cone was about a meter wide and perhaps three meters long. Ranging figures printed below the reticle showed the object was more than two hundred kilometers away. Even at that range the synthetic aperture scope resolved a lot of detail. The cone was not a smooth, uniform gray but was scored with hundreds of fine lines drawn parallel to its axis. There were no aerials or solar panels protruding from the cone. Every fifteen seconds the base of the object rotated into view, a dark uninformative hole.

The little man licked his lips nervously. If it had been possible to grovel in zero gee, Biladze was sure that Boblanson would have done so. "It is marvelous, Your Eminence. An artifact, to be sure."

One of the crewmen rolled his eyes. "We know that, you idiot. The question is, would the Prince be interested in it? We were told you are his expert on pre-Imperial spacecraft."

Boblanson bobbed his head emphatically, and the rest of his body bobbed in sympathy. "Yes, Eminence. I was born in the Prince's Kalifornija Preserve. For all these centuries, my tribes have passed from father to son the lore of the Great Enemy. Many times the Prince has sent me to explore the glowing ruins within the Preserves. I have learned all I can of the past."

The crewman opened his mouth—no doubt to give his acid opinion of illiterate savages who pose as archeologists—but Biladze broke in before the other could speak. The crewman was new to the Court, but not so new that he could get away with insulting the Prince's judgment. Biladze knew that every word spoken in the control cabin was monitored by Safety Committee agents hidden elsewhere in the ship, and every maneuver the crew undertook was analyzed by the Safety Committee's computers. Citizens of the Empire were used to surveillance, but few realized just how pervasive any eavesdropping could be until they entered the Imperial Service. "Let me rephrase Kolja's question," said Biladze. "As you know, we're tracking back along Earth's orbit. Eventually—in another fifteen hours, if we hadn't stopped for this thing—we will be far enough back to encounter objects in trojan orbits. Now there is some reason to believe that at least a few of the probes launched into Earthlike orbits eventually wound up near Earth's trojan points—"

"Yes, Eminence, I suggested the idea," said Boblanson. *So there is spirit in you after all*, thought Biladze with surprise; perhaps the little man knew that the Prince's pets sometimes counted for more than an Imperial Citizen. And the fellow's education obviously went beyond the folktales his tribe passed from generation to generation. The idea of looking for artifacts near the trojan points was clever, though Biladze guessed that careful analysis would show it to be impractical for at least two different reasons. But the Prince rarely bothered with careful analysis.

"In any case," continued Vanja Biladze, "we've found something, but it's nowhere near our destination. Perhaps the Prince will not be interested. After all, the chief reason for this excursion is to celebrate his birthday. We are not sure if the Emperor and the Prince and all the gentle people attending will really be too happy if we interrupt them with this matter. But we know that you have the special confidence of the Prince when it comes to his collection of pre-Imperial space probes. We hoped—"

We hoped you'd take us off the hook, fellow, thought Biladze. His predecessor at this job had been executed by the teen-age prince. His crime: interrupting the boy at dinner. For the thousandth time, Biladze wished he were back in the old-time Navy—where research had been disguised as maneuvers—or even back on Earth in some Gruzijan lab. The closer a Citizen came to the centers of power, the more of a madhouse the universe became.

"I understand, Eminence," said Boblanson, sounding as if he really did. He glanced once more at the screen, then back at Biladze. "And I assure you that the Prince would hate to pass this up. His collection is immense, you know. Of course it contains all the moon landers ever launched. They are rather easy to find, given your Navy's maps. He even has a couple of Martian probes—one Republican and one launched by the Great Enemy. And the surviving near-Earth satellites are generally quite easy to find, too. But the solar and outer planet probes—those are extremely difficult to recover, since they are no longer associated with any celestial body but roam through an immense volume of space. He has only two solar probes in his entire collection, and both were launched by the Republic. I've never seen anything like this," he motioned jerkily at the tumbling white cone on the screen. "Even if it were launched by your ancestors in the days of the Republic, it would still be a find. But if it belonged to the Great Enemy, it would be one of the Prince's favorite acquisitions, without doubt." Boblanson lowered his voice. "And frankly, I think it's conceivable that this spacecraft was not launched by either the Republic or the Great Enemy."

"What!" The exclamation came simultaneously from four throats.

The little man still seemed nervous and half-nauseated, but for the first time Biladze saw an almost hypnotic quality about him. The fellow was diseased, half-crippled. After all, he had been raised in a poisoned and desolate land, and since coming to the Imperial Service he had apparently been used to explore the radioactive ruins of the Great Enemy's cities. Yet with all that physical abuse, the mind within was still powerful, persuasive. Biladze wondered whether the Emperor realized that his son's pet was five times the man the Prince was.

"Yes, it would be fantastic," said Boblanson. "Mankind has found no evidence of life—much less intelligent life—anywhere else in the universe. But I know . . . I know the Navy once listened for signals from interstellar space. The possibility is still alive. And this object is so strange. For example, there is no communication equipment sticking through its hull. I know that you of the Empire don't use exterior aerials—but in the time of the Republic, all spacecraft did. And, too, there are no solar panels, though perhaps the craft had an isotopic power source. But the pattern of rays along its hull is the strangest thing of all. Those grooves are what you might expect on a meteorite or space probe—after it had come down through a planetary atmosphere. But there is simply no explanation for finding such an ablated hull out in interplanetary space."

That certainly decides the question, thought Biladze. Everything the non-Citizen had said was on tape somewhere, and if it ever came out that Vanja Biladze had passed up an opportunity to obtain an extraterrestrial artifact for the Prince's collection, there would be need for a new pilot on the Imperial yacht. "Kolja, get on the printer, and tell the Lord Chamberlain what Boblanson has discovered here." Perhaps that phras-

ing would protect him and the crew if the whirling gray cone did not
interest the Prince.

Kolja began typing the message on the intraship printer. Theoretically,
a Citizen could talk directly to the Lord Chamberlain, since that officer
was a bridge of sorts between the Imperial Court and its servants. In
fact, however, the protocol for speaking with any member of the aristocracy was so complex that it was safest to deal with such men in
writing. And occasionally, the written record could be used to cover
your behind later on—if the nobleman you dealt with was in a rational
mood. Biladze carefully read the message as it appeared on the readout
above the printer, then signaled Kolja to send it. The word ACKNOWL-
EDGED flashed on the screen. Now the message was stored in the Chamberlain's commbox on the main deck. When its priority number came
up, the message would appear on the screen there, and if the Lord
Chamberlain were not too busy supervising the entertainment, there
might be a reply.

Vanja Biladze tried to relax. Even without Boblanson's harangue he
would have given an arm and a leg to close with the object. But he was
far too experienced, far too cautious, to let such feelings show. Biladze
had spent three decades in the Navy—whole years at a time in deep
space so far from Earth-Luna and the pervasive influence of the Safety
Committee that the home world might as well not have existed. Then
the Emperor began his crackdown on the Navy, drawing them back into
near-Earth space, subjecting them to the scrutiny accorded his other
Citizens and outlawing what research they had been able to get away
with before. And with the new space drive, no point in the solar system
was more than hours from Earth, so such close supervision was practical. For many officers, the change had been a fatal one. They had
grown up in space, away from the Empire, and they had forgotten—or
else never learned—how to mask their feelings and behave with appropriate humility. But Biladze remembered well. He had been born at
Suhumi in Gruzija, a favorite resort of the nobility. For all the perfection
of Suhumi's blindingly white beaches and palm-dotted parks, death had
been waiting every moment for the disrespectful Citizen. And when he
had moved east to Tiflis, to the technical schools, life was no less precarious. For in Tiflis there were occasional cases of systematically dis-
loyal thoughts, thoughts which upset the Safety Committee far more
than accidental disrespect.

If that had been the sum of his experience on Earth, Biladze, like his
comrades, might have forgotten how to live with the Safety Committee.
But in Tiflis, in the spring of his last year at the Hydromechanical In-
stitute, he met Klaša. Brilliant, beautiful Klaša. She was majoring in

heroic architecture, one of the few engineering research fields the Emperors had ever tolerated on Earth. (After all, statues like the one astride Gibraltar would have been impossible without the techniques discovered by Klaša's predecessors.) So while his fellow officers managed to stay in space for whole decades at a time, Vanja Biladze had returned to Tiflis, to Klaša, again and again.

And he never forgot how to survive within the Imperial system.

Abruptly, Biladze's attention returned to the white-walled control room. Boblanson was eyeing him with a calculating stare, as if making some careful judgment. For a long moment, Biladze returned the gaze. He had seen only four or five non-Citizens in the flesh, though he had been piloting the Imperial yacht for more than a year. The creatures were always stunted, most often mindless—simple freaks kept for the amusement of noblemen with access to the vast Amerikan Preserves. This Boblanson was the only clever one Biladze had ever seen. Still, he found it hard to believe that the frail man's ancestors had been the Great Enemy, had struggled with the Republic for control of Earth. Very little was known about those times, and Biladze had never been encouraged to study the era, but he did know that the Enemy had been intelligent and resourceful, that it had never been totally defeated until it finally launched a sneak attack upon the Republic. The enraged Republic beat back the attack, then razed the Enemy's cities, burned its forests and left its entire continent a radioactive wasteland. Even after five centuries, the only people living in that ruin were the pitiful non-Citizens, the final victims of their own ancestors' treachery.

And the victorious Republic had gone on to become the world Empire.

That was the story, anyway. Biladze could doubt or disbelieve parts of it, but he knew that Boblanson was the ultimate descendant of a people who had opposed the establishment of the Empire. Vanja briefly wondered what version of history had been passed down the years to Boblanson.

Still no answer on the printer readout. Apparently the Lord Chamberlain was too busy to be bothered.

He said to Boblanson, "You are from the Kalifornija Preserve?"

The other bobbed his head. "Yes, Eminence."

"Of course I've never been there, but I've seen most of the Preserves from low orbit. Kalifornija is the most terrible wasteland of them all, isn't it?" Biladze was breaking one of the first principles of survival within the Empire: he was displaying curiosity. That had always been his most dangerous failing, though he rationalized things by telling himself that he knew how to ask safe questions. There was nothing really secret about the non-Citizens—they were simply a small minority living in areas too desolate to be settled. The Emperor was fond of parading the poor creatures on the holo, as if to say to his Citizens: "See what becomes of my opponents." Certainly it would do no harm to talk to this fellow, as long as he sounded appropriately impressed by the Enemy's great defeat and yet greater treachery.

Boblanson gave another of his frenetic nods. "Yes, Eminence. I regret that some of my people's greatest and most infamous fortresses were in the southern part of Kalifornija. It is even more to my regret that my particular tribe is descended from the subhumans who directed the attack on the Republic. Many nights around our campfires—when we could find enough wood to make a fire—the Oldest Ones would tell us the legends. I see now that they were talking of reaction-drive missiles and pumped lasers. Those are primitive weapons by the Empire's present standards, but they were probably the best that either side possessed in those days. I can only thank your ancestors' courage that the Republic and justice prevailed.

"But I still feel the shame, and my dress is a penance for my ancestry—it is a replica of the uniform worn by the damned creatures who inspired the Final Conflict." He pulled fretfully at the blue material, and for the first time Biladze really noticed the other's clothing. It wasn't that Boblanson's dress was inconspicuous. As a matter of fact, the blue uniform—with its twin silver bars on each shoulder—was ludicrous. In the zero gee of the control cabin, the pants were continually floating up, revealing Boblanson's bent, thin legs. Before, Biladze had thought it was just another of the crazy costumes the Imperial family decreed for the creatures in the menagerie, but now he saw that the sadism went deeper. It must have amused the Prince greatly to take this scarecrow and dress him as one of the Enemy, then have him grovel and scuttle about. The Imperial family never forgot its opponents, no matter how far removed they were in time or space.

Then he looked back into the little man's eyes and realized with a chill that he had seen only half the picture. No doubt the Prince had ordered Boblanson to wear the uniform, but in fact the non-Citizen was the one who was amused—if there was any room for humor behind those pale blue eyes. It was even possible, Biladze guessed, that the man had maneuvered the Prince into ordering that he be dressed in this way. So now Boblanson, descendant of the Great Enemy, wore that people's full uniform at the Court of the Emperor. Biladze shivered within himself, and for the first time put some real credit in the myths about the Enemy's subtlety, their ability to deceive and to betray. This man still remembered whatever had happened in those ancient times—and with greater feeling than any member of the Imperial family.

The word ACKNOWLEDGED vanished from the screen over the printer and was replaced by the Lord Chamberlain's jowly face. The crew bowed their heads briefly, tried to appear self-composed. The Chamberlain was unusually content to communicate by printer, so apparently their message—when it finally got his attention—was of interest.

"Pilot Biladze, your deviation from the flight plan is excused, as is your use of the Prince's pet." He spoke ponderously, the wattles swaying beneath his chin. Biladze hoped that old Rostov's implied criticism was *pro forma*. The Lord Chamberlain couldn't afford to be as fickle as most nobles, but he was a hard man, willing to execute his patrons' smallest whim. "You will send the creature Boblanson up here. You will maintain your present position relative to the unidentified object. I am keeping this circuit open so that you will respond directly to the Emperor's wishes." He stepped out of pickup range, ending the conversation as abruptly as if he had been talking to a computer. At least Biladze and his crew had been spared the trouble of framing a properly respectful response.

Biladze punched HATCH OPEN, and Boblanson's keepers entered the cabin. "He's supposed to go to the main deck," Biladze said. Boblanson glanced briefly at the main screen, at the enigma that was still slowly turning there, then let his keepers bind him with an ornamental leg chain and take him into the hallway beyond. The hatch slid shut behind the trio, and the crew turned back to the holographic image above the printer.

The camera sending that picture hadn't moved, but Rostov's obese hulk was no longer blocking the view and there was a lot to see. The yacht had been given to the Prince by the Emperor on the boy's tenth birthday. As with any Imperial gift, the thing was huge. The main deck—with its crystal ceilingwall open to all heaven—could hold nearly two thousand people. At least that many were up there now, for this party—the whole twenty-hour outing—celebrating the Prince's eighteenth birthday.

Many of the lords and ladies wore scarlet, though some had costumes of translucent and transparent pastels. The lights on the main deck had been dimmed, and the star clouds, crowned by Earth-Luna, hung bright above the revelers—an incongruous backdrop to the festivities. That these people should be the ones to rule those worlds . . .

Scattered through the crowd, he caught patches of gray and brown—the uniforms of the traybearers, doing work any sensible culture would reserve to machines. The servants scuttled about, forever alert to their betters' wishes, forever abjectly respectful. That respect must have been mainly for the benefit of Safety Committee observers, since most of the partygoers were so high on thorn-apple or even more exotic drugs that they wouldn't have known it if someone spit in their eye. The proceedings were about three-quarters of the way to being a full-blown orgy. Biladze shrugged to himself. It was nothing new—this orgy would simply be bigger than usual.

Then the tiny figures of Boblanson and his keepers came in from the right side of the holoscreen. The two Citizens walked carefully, their shoulders down, their eyes on the floor. Boblanson seemed to carry himself much the same, but after a moment Bilazde noticed that the little man shot glances out to the right and left, watching everything that went on. It was amazing. No Citizen could have gotten away with such brazen arrogance. But Boblanson was not a Citizen. He was an animal, a favored pet. You kill an animal if it displeases you, but you don't put the same social constraints on it that you would upon a human. No doubt even the Safety Committee passed over the fellow with only the most cursory inspection.

As the figures walked off to the left, Biladze leaned to the right to follow them in the holo and saw the Emperor and his son. Paša III was seated on his mobile throne, his costume a cascade of scarlet and jewels. Paša's face was narrow, ascetic, harsh. In another time such a man might have created an empire rather than inherited one. As it was, Paša had consolidated the autocracy, taking control of all state functions—even and especially research—and turning them to the crackpot search for reincarnators.

On only one issue could Paša be considered soft: his son was just eighteen today, yet the boy had already consumed the resources and the pleasures of a thousand adolescences. Saša X, dressed in skintight red breeches and diamond-encrusted belt, stood next to his father's throne. The brunette leaning against him had a figure that was incredibly smooth and full, yet the Prince's hand slid along her body as negligently as if he were stroking a baluster.

The keepers prostrated themselves before the throne and were recognized by the Emperor. Biladze bit back a curse. The damn microphone wasn't picking up their conversation! How would he know what Paša or his son wanted if he couldn't hear what was going on? All he was getting were music and laughter—plus a couple of indecent conversations close by the mike. This was the type of bungle that made the position of Chief Yacht Pilot a short-lived one, no matter how careful a man was.

One of his crew fiddled with the screen controls, but nothing could really be done at this end. They would see and hear only what the Lord Chamberlain was kind enough to let them see and hear. Biladze leaned toward the screen and tried to pick out from the general party noises the conversation passing between Boblanson and the Prince.

The two keepers were still prostrate at Paša's feet. They had not been given permission to rise. Boblanson remained standing, though his posture was cringing and timid. Servants insinuated themselves through the larger crowd to distribute drinks and candies to the Imperial party.

The Emperor and his son seemed totally unaware of this bustle of cringing figures about them. It was strange to see two men set so far above the common herd. And it all brought back a very old memory. It had been the summer of his last year at Tiflis, when he had found both Klaša and the freedom of the Navy. Many times during that summer, he and Klaša had flown into the Kavkaz to spend the afternoon alone in the alpine meadows. There they could speak their own minds, however timidly, without fear of being overheard. (Or so they thought. In later years, Biladze realized how terribly mistaken they had been. It was blind luck they were not discovered.) On those secret picnics, Klaša told him things that were never intended to go beyond her classes. The architecture students were taught the old forms and the meaning of the inscriptions to be found upon them. So Klaša was one of the few people in all the Empire with any knowledge of history and archaic languages, however indirect and fragmentary. It was dangerous knowledge, yet in many ways fascinating: In the days of the Republic, Klaša asserted, the word "Emperor" had meant something like "Primary Secretary," that is, an elected official—just as on some isolated Navy posts, the men elect a secretary to handle unit funds. It was an amazing evolution—to go from elected equal to near godling. Biladze often wondered what other meanings and truths had been twisted by time and by the kind of men he was watching on the holoscreen.

"—Father. I think it could be exactly what my creature says." The audio came loud and abrupt as the picture turned to center on the Prince and his father. Apparently Rostov had realized his mistake. The Chamberlain had almost as much to lose as Biladze if the Emperor's wishes were not instantly gratified.

Biladze breathed a sigh of relief as he picked up the thread of the conversation. Saša's high-pitched voice was animated: "Didn't I tell you this would be a worthwhile outing, Father? Here we've already run across something entirely new, perhaps from beyond the Solar System. It will be the greatest find in my collection. Oh, Father, we must pick it up." His voice rose fractionally.

Paša grimaced, and said something about Saša's "worthless hobbies." Then he gave in—as he almost always did—to the wishes of his son. "Oh very well, pick the damned thing up. I only hope it's half as interesting as your creature here," he waved a gem-filthy arm at Boblanson, "says it is."

The non-Citizen shivered within his blue uniform, and his voice became a supplicating whine. "Oh, dear Great Majesty, this trembling animal promises you with all his heart that the artifact is perfectly fit to all the greatness of your Empire."

Even before Boblanson got the tongue-twisting promise out of his mouth, Biladze had turned from the holo and was talking to his men. "Okay. Close with the object." As one of the crew tapped the control board, Biladze turned to Kolja and continued, "We'll pick it up with the third-bay waldoes. Once we get it inside, I want to check the thing over. I remember reading somewhere that the Ancients used reaction jets for attitude control and thrust—they never did catch on to inertial drive. There just might be some propellant left in the object's tanks after all these years. I don't want that thing blowing up in anybody's face."

"Right," said Kolja, turning to his own board.

Biladze kept an ear on the talk coming from the main deck—just in case somebody up there changed his mind. But the conversation had retreated from the specifics of this discovery to a general discussion of the boy's satellite collection. Boblanson's blue figure was still standing before the throne, and every now and then the little man interjected something in support of Saša's descriptions.

Vanja pushed himself off the wall to inspect the approach program his crewman had written. The yacht was equipped with the new drive and could easily attain objective accelerations of a thousand gravities. But their target was only a couple hundred kilometers away and a more delicate approach was in order: Biladze pressed the PROGRAM INITIATE, and the ship's display showed that they were moving toward the artifact at a leisurely two gravities. It should take nearly two hundred seconds to arrive, but that was probably within Saša's span of attention.

One hundred twenty seconds to contact. For the first time since he had called Boblanson into the control cabin ten minutes earlier, Biladze had a moment to ponder the object for himself. The cone was an artifact; it was much too regular to be anything else. Yet he doubted that it was of extraterrestrial origin, no matter what Boblanson thought. Its orbit had the same period and eccentricity as Earth's, and right now it wasn't much over seven million kilometers from Earth-Luna. Orbits like that just aren't stable over long periods of time. Eventually such an object must be captured by Earth-Luna or be perturbed into an eccentric orbit. The cone couldn't be much older than man's exploration of space. Biladze wondered briefly how much could be learned by tracing the orbit back through some kind of dynamical analysis. Probably not much.

Right now the only difference between its orbit and Earth's was the inclination: about three degrees. That might mean it had been launched from Earth at barely more than escape velocity, along a departure asymptote pointing due north. Now what conceivable use could there be for such a trajectory?

Ninety seconds to contact. The image of the slowly tumbling cone was much sharper now. Besides the faint scoring along its hull, he could see that the dull white surface was glazed. It really did look as if it had passed through a planet's atmosphere. He had seen such effects only once or twice before, since with any inertial drive it was a simple matter to decelerate before entering an atmosphere. But Biladze could imagine that the Ancients, having to depend on rockets for propulsion, might have used aerodynamic braking to save fuel. Perhaps this was a returning space probe that had entered Earth's atmosphere at too shallow an angle and skipped back into space, lost forever to the Ancients' primitive technology. But that still didn't explain its narrow, pointed shape. A good aerodynamic brake would be a blunt body. This thing looked as if it had been designed expressly to minimize drag.

Sixty seconds to contact. He could see now that the black hole at its base was actually the pinched nozzle of a reaction jet—added proof that this was an Earth-launched probe from before the Final Conflict. Biladze glanced at the holoscreen above the printer. The Emperor and his son seemed really taken with what they were seeing on the screen set before the throne. Behind them stood Boblanson, his poor nearsighted eyes squinting at the screen. The man seemed even stranger than before. His jaws were clenched and a periodic tic cut across his face. Biladze looked back at the main screen; the little man knew more than he had revealed about that mysterious cone. If he had not been beneath their notice, the Safety Committee would have long since noticed this, too.

Thirty seconds. What was Boblanson's secret? Biladze tried to connect the centuries-deep hatred he had seen in Boblanson with what they knew about the tumbling white cone: It had been launched around the time of the Final Conflict on a trajectory that might have pointed northwards. But the object hadn't been intended as a space probe since it had evidently acquired most of its speed while still within Earth's atmosphere. No sensible vehicle would move so fast within the atmosphere . . .

. . . *unless it was a weapon.*

The thought brought a sudden numbness to the pit of Biladze's stomach. The Final Conflict had been fought with rocket bombs fired back and forth over the North Pole. One possible defense against such weapons would be high-acceleration antimissile missiles. If one such missed its target, it might very well escape Earth-Luna—to orbit the sun, forever armed, forever waiting.

Then why hadn't his instruments detected a null bomb within it? The question almost made him reject his whole theory, until he remembered that quite powerful explosions could be produced with nuclear fission and fusion. Only physicists knew such quaint facts, since null bombs were much easier to construct once you had the trick of them. But had the Ancients known that trick?

Biladze casually folded his arms, kept his position by hooking one foot through a wall strap. Somewhere inside himself a voice was screaming: *Abort the approach, abort the approach!* Yet if he were right and if the bomb in that cone were still operable, then the Emperor and the three highest tiers of the nobility would be wiped from the face of the universe.

It was an opportunity no man or group of men had had since the Final Conflict.

But it's not worth dying for! screamed the tiny, frightened voice.

Biladze looked into the holoscreen at the hedonistic drones whose only talent lay in managing the security apparatus that had suppressed men and men's ideas for so long. With the Emperor and the top people in the Safety Committee gone, political power would fall to the technicians—ordinary Citizens from Tiflis, Luna City, Eastguard. Biladze had no illusions: ordinary people have their own share of villains. There would be strife, perhaps even civil war. But in the end, men would be free to go to the stars, from where no earthly tyranny could ever recall them.

Behind the Emperor and the nobles, Boblanson cringed no more. A look of triumph and hatred had come into his face, and Biladze remembered that he had said this would be a gift fit for the Empire.

And so your people will be revenged after all these centuries, thought Biladze. As vengeance it was certainly appropriate, but that had nothing to do with why he, Vanja Biladze, floated motionless in the control cabin and made no effort to slow their approach on the tumbling cone. He was scared as hell. Mere vengeance was not worth this price. Perhaps the future would be.

They were within a couple thousand meters of the object now. It filled the screen, as if it whirled just beyond the yacht's hull. Biladze's instruments registered some mild radioactivity in the object's direction.

Good-bye, Klaša.

SIX MILLION KILOMETERS FROM EARTH, A NEW STAR WAS BORN. IN AN AStronomical sense, it was a very small star, but to itself and what lay nearby it was an expanding plasmatic hell of fission-fusion products, neutrons, and gamma rays.

BOMB SCARE

Robert Heinlein once proposed five rules for success in selling fiction ("On the Writing of Speculative Fiction" in Lloyd Arthur Eshbach's *Of Worlds Beyond: The Science of Science-Fiction Writing*, Advent Publishers, 1964). The rules are simple, but following them *all* is difficult. Heinlein's fifth rule was essentially "keep your story on the market until it sells." The history of "Bomb Scare" certainly illustrates this principle, but with a little twist. I wrote the story in 1963 and got rejections from everywhere. Even I knew that it was a weak story, and so I never sent it to my favorite editor, John W. Campbell, Jr.; John was a person I didn't want to disappoint. By 1970, there was no choice. I either had to send it to *Analog*, or consider breaking Heinlein's fifth rule. . . .

John Campbell bought the story straightaway. So besides the importance of following Heinlein's rule, there may be another moral here: It doesn't pay to second-guess editors!

P rince Lal e'Dorvik dilated his mouth hole, and casually picked at pointy fangs. With great deliberation he inspected the sky: the Maelstrom glittered across fifty degrees, a spiral of silver mist. It's brilliance was dimmed by the gibbous blue planet that hung near the zenith. That blue light flooded through the transparent hull section onto the formal gardens of the Imperial Dorvik flagwagon. The soft brown sand dunes of the gardens were transformed into rolling blue carpets. An occasional ornamental lizard scurried across the sands. Within his vision, Prince Lal could see no less than five shrub-cacti: the excess vegetation made the scene almost sickeningly lush. Except for the bluish tinge of the landscape, Lal could almost imagine that he was back at Home in his winter palace.

With feigned nonchalance he turned to look at his companion, Grand General Harl e'Kraft. Prince Lal was thought harsh, in a civilization where the execution of ten thousand soldiers was considered morale-building discipline. Now he moved obliquely toward the subject at hand—with his reputation, he could afford to speak softly. "Is it always night?"

"Yes, Puissance, we keep the wagon oriented with the sun beneath the gardens' horizon. Of course, I could make a 'sunrise.' It would take less than fifteen minutes to turn the wagon . . ."

"Oh, don't bother," Lal responded smoothly. "I was just wondering what the 'super-sun' looks like." He glanced at the blue-green planet high in the sky. "Isn't it theoretically impossible for a giant star to have a planetary system?"

The young general sniffed warily at the bait. "Well, yes. Stars this size never develop solar systems by condensation. This one was probably formed by the accidental capture of three planets from some other system. Such things must be very rare, but we're bound to run across them eventually."

"Ah yes, there shouldn't be planets here, yet there are. And these planets are inhabited by an intelligent, technologically developed race. And we must have these 'improbable' planets as the industrial base for our expansion in this volume; yet we don't have them."

Lal paused, then struck with reptilian ferocity. *"Why not?"*

For a moment Harl sat frozen by the other's ophidian glare. With a visible effort he twitched his mouth hole open in a disarming smile. "Care for a milvak, Puissance?" He motioned to a shallow dish of hors d'oeuvres.

Lal had to admit that the general was a cool one. Though e'Kraft faced the Long Dying for his failure, he offered his superior candied meat rather than explanations. This was going to be interesting. He carefully speared one of the squirming milvaks with a wrist talon, and sank his fangs into the little mammal's hairless skin. With a sucking sound, he drained the animal of its vital fluids.

Harl e'Kraft waited politely until Lal had finished, then handed him a pack of color photographs.

"The Mush-faces are every bit as developed as you say. Their two outer worlds could supply us for any further expansion we might desire in Volume 095. They—"

Prince Lal slithered into a more comfortable position on the resting rack, and glanced at the top photograph. Mush-faces: that was an appropriate name for them. The olive-skinned monster that looked out of the photo seemed bloated, diseased.

". . . Have not invented mass-energy converters, but they do use a very efficient form of hydrogen fusion for their spacecraft. Their biggest spacewagons mass more than thirty thousand tons."

Not bad for hydrogen fusion drive, thought Lal. He glanced at the next picture. It was a schematic of a Mush-face battlewagon. There was the typical cigar shape of a fusion-powered craft, the magnetic venturis taking up much of the rear volume of the wagon. Ten rocket bombs were housed forward, with more snuggling under the craft's nose on outside racks.

"In one respect they are ahead of us technologically." Harl paused, then said slowly, "The Mush-faces can shield against our mass-energy converters."

This remark would have been greeted by a look of stupefied amazement if Lal's spies had not briefed him beforehand.

LAL'S THIRTY TIMES GREAT-GRANDFATHER, GHRISHNAK I, HAD CONQUERED three oases on Home by edge of sword. His twenty-one times great-grandfather, Elbrek IV, united all Home with gunpowder and steam-powered sandwagons. His twelve times great-grandfather launched the first rockets into orbit, and perfected the hydrogen bomb for use against a group of heretics in the South Polar Sands. But the sword, gunpowder, steam, even the hydrogen bomb, all these were as nothing before the mass-energy converter. It was a simple weapon in practice: place the converter at the proper distance from the target, turn it on, and any desired fraction of the target was changed directly into energy. If such a weapon could be shielded against, the Dorvik had lost one of their trump dice.

E'Kraft continued, "This effect is probably incidental. Since the Mush-faces don't have converters, it seems unlikely that they could intentionally design a defense against them. In any case, the only way we can destroy their craft is to convert a substantial amount of mass to energy just *outside* their screens. In other words we are reduced to using rocket bombs.

"They have an anatomical advantage, too, Puissance. A Mush-face can survive more than five times the acceleration that a Dorvik can. This mobility combined with their thousand gravity rocket bombs makes their space force more than a nuisance.

"Puissance, we have done as much damage as we dare to their industrial centers. It has not broken their will. Until we gain absolute control of local space, there will be no conquest." The general's statement was blunt, almost defiant.

Lal could imagine the tiny enemy craft flashing through the Dorvik fighter screen and firing rocket bombs at the Dorvik battlewagons. From the general's own account as well as Lal's spies, it was obvious that e'Kraft had made the best of a terrible situation. Supreme tactical skill was necessary to survive an enemy with longer legs and better defenses than one's own. He riffled through the rest of the photographs. They showed proposed modifications in the Dorvik reconnaissance skimmers, for use as self-propelled bombs. Lal's race hadn't used rocket bombs in three centuries, so now that they needed them, such weapons were unavailable.

When Lal finally spoke, his face and tone contained nothing complimentary. "So these pus-filled creatures are too stubborn for you? Your view is just too narrow, General." He pulled an ornamented slate from his waist pouch. "That sickeningly blue planet," Lal waved at the brilliant object directly overhead, "has twenty percent of the population and only three percent of the industry in this solar system. Its destruction would hardly impair the system's usefulness to us. This"—he gestured with the triangular slate—"is an order, signed by my father. It directs you to detonate this planet."

E'Kraft's tympanic membranes paled.

Prince Lal hissed gently. "You find this overly violent?"

"Y-yes." The general was still blunt.

"Perhaps, but that is the point. You will convert one trillionth of one percent of the planet's mass. The explosion will be so vast that it will gently scorch portions of the other two planets. The deed's very essence is violence and brutality; it will show this race that further resistance would be worse than any surrender." Lal recited several stanzas from the liturgy of Dominance, finishing with:

"Ours is all that is and we rule
    all those who be,
For we are the Dorvik, the sons
    of the Sands.
And to those who deny our rule
    we say:
Bow down—or be not.

"It is immaterial whether you believe this doggerel garbage. The point is, that by divine authority or not, our race must stay on top. The day we take second place in the universe will be the beginning of the end for the Dorvik. If through some weakness of spirit we fail to conquer this system, then we will be consigning ourselves to the museums of the future just as surely as if we were destroyed in battle."

In a single fluid motion, Lal reached out from his resting rack and handed his subordinate the order. "Implement this at once. And be sure you don't annihilate more than the mass fraction specified, else this whole solar system might be destroyed."

"I'm quite acquain—" e'Kraft was prevented from digging himself a grave by the appearance of one of his aides. The man's three-dimensional image flickered, then steadied.

"Puissance, General." The aide bowed to Lal and then to e'Kraft. "Thirteen seconds ago we detected a gravitic disturbance near the sun. Someone has entered the system."

"So!" Lal fumed. When he got his talons into the insubordinate wretch that dared enter the combat zone without prior announcement—

The aide continued excitedly, "Puissance, it doesn't respond to our IFF. It's not one of ours."

Prince Lal turned sharply to Harl. "Could the Mush-faces be experimenting with interstellar drive?"

"Unlikely, Puissance. The largest mass they've ever assembled in free fall was less than one hundred thousand tons. The smallest drive unit we have masses more than a billion."

That was the Dorvik's other trump. Without mass-energy converters, it was essentially impossible to hoist a drive unit into orbit, where it could operate.

The aide turned to look at someone outside of pickup range, and his excitement changed to pale and groveling terror. "The intruder is exactly one kill-radius from . . . from the sun!"

To convert a star—Lal gasped. While he had been ordering the destruction of a single inhabited planet, someone—*something*—absolutely evil had fused a bomb to murder a galaxy.

IT *WAS*, WHERE AN INSTANT BEFORE NOTHING HAD BEEN.

At one kill-radius from the primary, harsh white sunlight reflected blindingly off the little ovoid, all but blotting out the intricate gamma-colored designs that covered its surface.

Two creatures sat within the apparition. Considering the variety possible in this universe, they looked much like the Dorvik. A closer examination by someone trained and clever might have revealed a trimness and efficiency in the intruders' structure that was missing from the Dorvik—that is missing from any natural race. For the intruders' race had supervised its own evolution for more than 100,000 years. The result might not be remarkable in appearance, but the brains housed in those bodies were far quicker, far more subtle than anything unaided natural selection could produce. And though their grosser emotions were perhaps intelligible, any conversation presented here verges on falsehood in its incompleteness.

One of the creatures—identifiable by the two bristly spikes that grew tangentially from its head—turned to the other and said, in effect, "I still want S Doradus."

"Gyrd, this star is almost as big. And quite a bit easier to reach, too." The creature paused, adjusted the controls somehow. "Figuring the jump back is going to take all my concentration, so you'll have to cancel the relative velocity on the converter when we drop it."

The first replied. "No one tells me what to do, Arn."

An air of hostility just short of physical violence filled the tiny cabin. Then Gyrd submitted with a nod.

"That's better." Arn relaxed. "Just imagine all the maggots that will fry in the fire we're going to set."

LAL BROKE THE AWFUL SILENCE. "HOW FAR AWAY IS THIS OBJECT?"

"Twelve billion kilometers, Puissance. We won't be able to detect it by electromagnetic means for another ten hours."

"How long would it take to compute a jump to its location?"

The aide did some fast figuring. "If we use everything, including our tactical computers, about ten minutes."

"Very well, put everything you have on the problem. We'll jump one of our battlewagons."

"Yes, Puissance—"

"But, Puissance, what about the Mush-faces? If we don't use the tactical computers for minimal defense, they'll tear our fleet apart."

Lal scarcely hesitated. "We'll have to take those losses. If we can't stop that . . . thing . . . near the sun, we'll all be dead anyway, and the Dorvik empire will be destroyed in less than ten centuries." He noticed that the aide was still waiting nervously. Lal turned to the man's image and shrilled, "Move!" The aide bowed spastically and the image vanished.

The prince struggled to bring his voice back into control. "General, evacuate one of your battlewagons. We'll annihilate its entire mass right next to the Enemy." His emphasis capitalized the word; the Mush-faces were merely an enemy.

"Yes, Puissance."

"Ten minutes."

Harl nodded, began giving orders on his private comm. In the presence of a member of the Imperial Family he was reduced to the status of messenger boy.

Lal had given his orders, and now had to endure a small eternity as they were executed. Somewhere he knew mountainous computers were ticking away at the calculations involved in even the shortest jump. Somewhere else, ten thousand men were trying to abandon their battlewagon before the deadline he had set. And somewhere, twelve billion kilometers away, was an object that had to be destroyed else the galaxy would die.

A brilliant red star appeared just above the gardens' pseudo horizon. The dot expanded, becoming fainter as it grew, the mad red eye of a monster. Almost simultaneously, three closely spaced red "stars" shone just two degrees away from the first. Lal recognized the characteristic glow of fusion bombs. The Mush-faces must have discovered that the Dorvik defense patterns were no longer adaptive. Without tactical computers, the Dorvik were squatting milvaks before the attack. Those bombs couldn't have been closer than 100,000 kilometers, but the enemy was moving in.

"Enemy rocket bomb at fifty thousand kilometers and closing," said a disembodied voice.

Lal strained for some glimpse of the enemy. He noticed the silvery crescent of another Dorvik battlewagon some two hundred kilometers away, but that was all.

Both men sat in the flagwagon's imperial gardens and counted their last seconds.

A white glare lit the gardens. Lal looked up, startled. The battlewagon he had noticed before had fired its rockets and now moved slowly across the sky. The brilliance of its jets brought temporary daylight to the gardens.

"It won't work," Harl whispered.

But somehow it did. The feebleminded rocket bomb accepted the other battlewagon as its target of opportunity, and the gardens' curving crystal walls turned opaque as the wagon's screens powered up. When the walls cleared, the other wagon was gone: ten thousand men and the gross annual product of an entire continent had been vaporized in less than a millisecond.

General e'Kraft's fangs clattered together with suppressed emotion. To lose men in war was expected, but to sit defenselessly and let an enemy destroy you with inferior weapons was nightmare. Abruptly he looked up, as if listening to some private voice. "Puissance, the crew of the *Vengeance* have removed to the *Sword of Alkra*."

Several more red dots appeared near the zenith, but Lal ignored them. The fleet would have to hold together just a little longer. . . .

The aide reappeared. "Computations complete, Puissance. Just tell us which bat—"

"The *Vengeance*. As soon as the jump is made and you are sure the Enemy is nearby, annihilate the entire mass of the wagon."

Lal's urgency was conveyed to the other man, who vanished without even bowing.

Harl said something on his private circuit, and a flat image appeared before them. "That's from a camera aboard the *Vengeance*. It's transmitting by gravitic means, so we'll be able to see everything up to the detonation."

The picture showed the Maelstrom with the Mush-faces' planet off to one side. Abruptly the blue planet vanished. Startled, Lal glanced up and saw that the planet was still in his sky. He realized ashamedly that the *Vengeance* had made its jump. Since the wagon's orientation in space was still the same, the stars had not moved.

Then the camera turned and the constellations slid across the screen. The camera hunted—and found. At the center of the screen Lal saw a tiny white dot that drifted slowly across the field of stars. That was the Enemy. It couldn't be closer than ten thousand kilometers. The detonation of the *Vengeance* would be quite effective at that range, but the jump should have been more accurate.

Apparently the same thought had occurred to e'Kraft, who said, "Navigation, how far is the *Vengeance* from target?"

"Ten kilometers. The enemy craft is less than nine meters long."

Less than nine meters long. The smallest interstellar craft the Dorvik ever made was more than a kilometer wide. The Enemy was superior to anything Lal had imagined. If only there were some way to capture the Enemy craft, to learn its secrets. Possibly even more important, to learn what manner of monster would annihilate a sun.

"Detonate the *Vengeance*."

And the screen turned gray.

E'Kraft spoke. "The entire mass of the wagon has been converted to energy, Puissance."

Lal stared stupidly: it was so anticlimactic. They had just created more energy in a second than the average G-class star produces in an hour, yet this explosion was observable only as a blank image screen, or the motion of a tiny hand on the dial of a gravitic surge detector. It would take ten hours for the light from that explosion to reach them. Even then it would set houses afire on the blue planet.

How close it had been . . . another few seconds and the Enemy might have completed its obscene mission, and so doomed the Dorvik race. For the moment at least, all was saved. He turned to e'Kraft and saw relief mirrored in his eyes.

"General, I—"

He was interrupted by the reappearance of the general's aide. "Puissance, we detected a grave disturbance after the detonation."

"After?"

"Yes, Puissance. Somehow the intruder survived the detonation."

"That's impossible!" shrieked Lal, even as he accepted the awful truth. Nothing made by men could withstand the vast fireball that the *Vengeance* had become. *What were they fighting?*

The game might already be over. Lal's eyes looked across the imperial gardens, but his mind saw a wave of hell creeping out ever so slowly from an annihilated star. The energy from such a detonation would vaporize planets a hundred parsecs away; and the destruction would creep on, confined to the speed of light but pushing inexorably across the galaxy. His race would know of the explosion, and would retreat before the swelling sphere of oblivion, but little by little the galaxy would be taken away from them, until every planet was lifeless and his race . . .

"SEE! THE MAGGOTS HAVE GUESSED WHAT WE'RE GOING TO DO. THAT WAS a nasty jolt they just gave us, don't you think, Gyrd?

"The maggots are trying to avoid the big fry, but they can't save themselves." He paused, overcome by anticipations of delight.

"We'll watch the fire spread from nest to nest—for ten thousand years we'll watch them burn."

The other creature agreed enthusiastically, its earlier anger almost forgotten. Neither of them noticed a slight wavering in the air behind them. The distortion was in the far infrared and near microwave. The changing refractive indices moved through the visible, the ultraviolet, the gamma. Still Gyrd and Arn were too engrossed to notice.

"The converter is set to go when we jump, Arn. What's keeping you?"

"The navigation, of course. This is a galactic jump we're making. Give me a few more seconds."

"Idiot."

The shimmer took form. Gyrd turned from Arn and saw what had materialized behind them.

"Mother!"

But for her physical perfection she looked much like her remote ancestors, who tamed fire in Africa and—scant millennia later—played with fission under a stadium in Chicago. There was fear on her face, the fear of a parent who has discovered anew that untrained children are essentially monsters—and that if those children are godlings, then their evil can be satanic. She stared at her daughter, Gyrd, for a long moment, then said slowly, "Why are you here?"

My old friend Ken Winters suggested the gimmick in the preceding story. Nowadays (2001), the possibility of natural disasters so vast that they could cause damage thousands of light-years away is fairly well accepted. Ken's suggestion came from around 1960—maybe even earlier, when we were in elementary school.

THE SCIENCE FAIR

"The Science Fair" is one of the shortest stories I have ever written: a little one-idea story, that has some nice color. The original version that I submitted to Damon Knight (for his *Orbit* series) is almost what you see here. Damon rejected that with the comment that I had built up an ingenious background and then brought it down to the banal with the last few lines—and was there anything I could do to fix it?

That was a challenge. The solution was to break viewpoint discipline a little and look ahead at consequences. (I think this is entirely in the final two lines of the story.) Damon bought the revision, which you see here:

M y offices are under the tidal-wave breaker wall. I know, that's an unsavory and unsafe part of Newton. I was trapped there once for three tides after a really large earthquake smashed the wall and laid several tons of rubble over the walkdown to my rooms. On the other hand, having my offices there gives prospective clients the deliciously naughty feeling that they are dealing with the underworld. Then, when they see how solidly luxurious my offices are, they think that besides being a sinister figure, I am also a successful one.

When the girl knocked on my door, I was deep asleep on the pallet behind my desk—considering how much money I spend on those rooms, I can't afford to sleep anywhere else. I staggered up and walked to the door, swearing at myself for having let my receptionist go three tides earlier: for obvious reasons, there isn't much market for industrial spies during the Science Fair.

Even the city police corporation relaxes during the Fair, so I couldn't guess who my visitor might be. I opened the door.

Vision of visions! Large, soft eyes looked at me over a pertly turned nose and full moist lips. Her satiny skin glowed a deep, even infra, marking out firm, ripe curves. There was a lot to see, since her only clothing was a brief pair of rear leggings.

She was young and nervous. "You are Leandru Ngiarxis bvo-Ngiarxis?"

I smiled. "To the wide world, yes—but you may call me Ndruska."

She stepped inside. "Why do you keep it so dark in here?"

I wasn't about to tell her that she'd caught the master industrial spy asleep. So I lowered my head and ogled up at her. "The maiden glow of your skin is more than sufficient light for me."

She blushed bright infra from her shoulders up and tried to sound tough when she said, "See here, Ngiarxis, it's unpleasant enough to do business with someone of your sort. Please don't make it any worse by, by starting immoral advances."

"Just as you say, milady." I turned on the lights and crossed to the other side of the desk.

"Now, how may I . . . serve you?"

She lowered herself delicately onto a visitor's pallet. "My name is Yelén Dragnor bvo-Science-Fair-Committee." She produced the appropriate identification badge.

"Hmm. Are you any relation to the chief scientist of the House of Graun?"

She nodded. "Beoling Dragnor bvo-Graun is my father."

"Indeed, I am honored. I understand he is to give the popular lecture at the Fair, next-tide. You must be very proud."

She came to her knees, her brittle mask of sophistication cracking. "I am proud—very. But s-scared, too. We—the Science Fair Committee, that is—know the princes of Graun will m-murder Father rather than let him speak at the Fair."

I tried not to seem incredulous. I have never heard of any polity willing to risk its own dissolution merely to eliminate one scientist. "What does your father know that could be so distressing to the House of Graun?"

"I don't know. I-I don't know. Father won't tell the Committee. Of course, that's only proper, since his research is Graun property until the Fair actually begins. But he won't give us even a *hint*. The princes have tried to kill him once already, and we just have to find *someone* to protect him."

"And so you came to me."

"Y-yes. The Fair Committee knows your reputation. They're willing to pay you well—up to two hundred fifty-six acres of prime farmland. All, all you have to do is guard Father till next-tide. The Committee can protect him after that, when he gives his talk. . . . Will you do that?"

The Fair Committee must have known a lot about my reputation, considering the nubile creature they had sent with their proposition. I reached across the table and gently brushed the tears from her neck. "Don't worry, Lenska, I'll do what I can. It's really not terribly difficult to outsmart the princes of Graun." Besides, I still didn't believe they'd try something so stupid as assassinating a scientist on the eve of the Science Fair.

She perked up considerably at this and provided me with the particular information I would need to do the job. By the time she left she was almost cheerful. She had met the big, bad spy and found that while he was big, he wasn't so awfully bad.

At the top of the ramp she turned and looked down at me, her face a pale infra smudge against the sky. I promised to be at her father's apartment in less than half an hour.

She wagged her rear and was gone.

I'VE LIVED IN MORE THAN A FEW CITIES, BUT NEWTON-BY-THE-SEA WILL ALways be my favorite. I know, Benobles and Is-Hafn have their points: they're old, they're rich, and the ground underlying them is so stable that their buildings rise six, seven, even eight stories. But the snow in Benobles is more than three stories deep. It's so cold there that the city would be pitch-dark without its streetlamps. And Is-Hafn may have some great gamboling houses, but it's a two-hour steam sledge ride from the present ice harbor to the old city. Personally I'd rather live where I can keep my hooves warm.

That's easy to do in Newton. Just north of the city, Mt. Hefty pours a sixty-four-foot wide stream of incandescent red lava into the sea. At high tide, the water meets the molten rock just beyond the north sea wall, and a veil of steam rises far up over the city, casting an infra glow down upon it. Along the coast, south of the lava flow, the water is delightfully warm, and the beaches are smooth and sandy.

At the moment I couldn't see any of this. It was low tide and the lava met the sea several miles out. The steam generated was a faint gleam over my left shoulder, too far away to light my surroundings. If it hadn't been for the streetlamps, the only light would have been the bright splinters of red from half-shuttered windows, and the deep infra glow of occasional passersby. From my hiding place behind an ornamental deeproot tree, I inspected my surroundings. This was a luxurious section of town, not far from the Fairgrounds. The electric streetlamps cast long shadows up the sides of the apartment buildings that faced both sides of the street. Some of those buildings were three and even four stories tall, constructed pyramid fashion so that the top floor had only a quarter the area of the first. Silk-petal vines gleamed dark and glossy against their carven walls, the pollen making the air heavy and sweet.

Except for the faraway hiss of lava changing water into steam, all was quiet. The party in the building across the street had ended more than an hour ago, and by now the revelers were departed. No one had come down the street past my hiding place for nearly eight minutes. That's another nice thing about Newton: its citizens are generally asleep during the low tides, when things are darkest out. That makes things a lot easier for people like me.

I rose up off my rear and tried to get the cramps out of my legs. Even here in Newton, stakeouts are an uncomfortable bore. After about four hours on a job like this, even my hand torch and automatic pistol begin to feel awfully heavy. As usual I was wearing a body mask that covered everything but my eyes and nose. The mask is heavy and hot, but my skin glow is virtually invisible when I have it on.

For the umpteenth time I scanned up and down the street: no activity. And that fourth-floor window, the window to Beoling Dragnor's apartment, was still dark. This whole job was just a false alarm, I complained to myself. The Science Fair Committee had let itself be taken in by the paranoid ravings of a senile scientist. I had been employed against the princes of Graun before, and I knew they were brutal, but their brutality was not irrational or self-destructive. There was only one Science Fair in each generation. In the time between Fairs, a Graun researcher was practically Graun property, and his research results were as secret as Graun counterespionage could keep them. What prince would risk such a cozy situation just to prevent one scientist from talking at the Fair?

Just then the streetlamps went dim, slowly cooled to the point of invisibility.

So much for my theories.

Even the few lights left in the apartments went out. The bvo-Graun must have struck a power substation at least.

We have a simile in Newton: "Dark as the sky at low tide." Believe me, there are few things darker. And now, without streetlamps, the sky's darkness was everywhere. I couldn't see the pistol I held in my hand.

I stood very still and strained my ears. If this job were properly orchestrated, the bvo-Graun should be moving in now. I did hear something, a faint creaking. It seemed to come from the direction of Dragnor's apartment. I couldn't be sure, though. Even at low tide, the hiss of boiling seawater is loud enough to blur sharp hearing.

I looked into the sky. Nothing. What in Ge's name was going on? The only thing that could hover in the air so quietly was a balloon. But a balloon's air heater would have been too bright to look at. Even if they managed to shield the heater, there's no way they could stop the gas bag from glowing without making the whole contraption too heavy to fly. And I couldn't see even a shimmer.

I reached over my back and slid my hand torch out of its pocket. Using it would be a last resort, since it would make me a much better target than anyone else.

Several minutes passed. The creaking was unmistakable now, and I could hear body movements too. If the bvo-Graun were trying to involve Dragnor in a simulated accident, they would have to act fast, and

I'd have to be faster to stop them. Ge, I was going to have to use my torch after all.

Then, as it has so often in the past, the Ngiarxis family luck came through for me. The skies parted momentarily and the *stars* shone down on Newton! If you're from Benobles, maybe this doesn't seem so unusual. But here on the coast we're lucky if the sky clears once in a borning.

There must have been sixty-fours of stars: harsh, uncompromising points of light that burned in infra, red, and orange. Even at high tide, the sky above Newton is rarely so bright as it was during those few seconds.

The assassins *were* using a balloon. Its starlit hulk floated two hundred fifty-six feet above the street. Three men hung on slings beneath it. They were less than sixty-four feet up now and were closing in on Dragnor's window. They must have had guts to try something like that.

Aiming through a clear spot in the branches above me, I fired at the balloon. But I fired wide. I guess I'm just naturally big-hearted. Sixty-four feet is a long way to fall.

I shouldn't have bothered. The bvo-Graun recovered from their starstruck surprise and rained fire down on me and my little tree. Splinters of wood flew in all directions as their rockets exploded. They had the high ground with a vengeance.

So much for charity. My second shot was aimed for the balloon. The target was just too high up, though. My rocket missed it by at least eight feet. But he who flies hydrogen-filled balloons must be prepared to pay the price: the bottom of the gas bag exploded as my rocket passed under it, and in seconds the entire aircraft was engulfed by fire and thunder.

The ropes to two of the assassins were severed instantly and they fell to the street. Splash. The third fellow rappelled madly downward. He almost made it, being only sixteen feet above the street when his ropes burned through.

As I ran out from what was left of my concealment, flaming debris was still falling out of the sky. I stopped briefly by the corpse of the one who had fallen from sixteen feet. The man was a bvo-Graun all right. His body mask had all insignia removed, but the cut of the cloth was familiar.

What did this Dragnor have on the House of Graun, anyway?

THE FAIRGROUNDS ARE NEAR THE WESTERN EDGE OF NEWTON, ON A GENTLY sloping terrace facing the sea. For fifteen out of sixteen bornings, the grounds are unused except for occasional commercial shows or wandering amusement theaters that contract with the city for the use of the land. But once in every generation, tents cover the grounds and even sprawl into adjacent properties. A bonfire is set on the crestline west of the grounds, and by its glow the tents reflect every color you can imagine, no matter what the time of tide. And so the Science Fair is begun. In one tent you can see the most recent improvements in steam turbines, while in the next the latest techniques in podiatry are demonstrated, or a lecture in antibody reactions is in progress. The variety is nigh endless.

The crowd trying to squeeze into the main lecture tent was unbelievably large, and it took all my powers of infiltration to get to the tent's entrance. There the Fair Official badge I had been given was put to good use. I was searched and then admitted.

They were virtually sitting on each others' backs inside. I knew the Fair's popular lecture usually lives up to its name, but this was incredible. Even the name Beoling Dragnor wouldn't ordinarily draw like this. Apparently the people of Newton knew the scientist would report on something spectacular. What could it be? Telegraphy without wires? Perhaps a method of predicting earthquakes? Dragnor had never been pinned down to a single field so it was hard to guess. Doubly so for those who knew that Graun had tried to silence him.

I used my badge to reach the reserved pallets set right before the stage. Yelén Dragnor had already arrived. I squeezed in beside her, slipped my arm across her shoulders.

"Surprise, dear Lenska! Despite immense and perilous difficulties I have delivered your father safe and sound to the Speakers Subcommittee."

She wiggled delightedly, then remembered that she was the daughter of a researcher and I was a poor freeman. She said, "We are most grateful, sir Leandru." Her eyes said much more.

I glanced down the row of pallets. The pavilion was brightly lit and the costumes of the various personages in our special section gleamed and glittered in eight colors. At the end of the row sat the three official representatives of the House of Graun. They were dressed in ruffled pants and overcapes checkered bright orange and medium infra—the Graun colors. The one in the middle was Thorc Graun bvo-Graun, reputed to be the master of the House of Graun. At the moment, that individual had the look of a frustrated creditor. His pale eyes swept back and forth across the stage, occasionally rested on me. It was notice I could do without.

The stage was empty except for a small console set to one side. This increased the mystery, since what is science without gadgetry? I didn't have a chance to wonder on the question further, for just then attention sounded and the speaker walked on the stage.

Beoling Dragnor was an old man. He had lost much of his hair and his splotchily colored skin revealed poor circulation. He reached center stage, turned, and looked down upon us. For a long moment, the loudest sound was the sea three miles away.

"Good tide." The voice was cracked and squeaking but not weak, not timorous. "My name is now Beoling Dragnor bvo-Science-Fair-Committee. Before this Fair I served the House of Graun in Benobles." He nodded stiffly to the princes of Graun in the first row below him. "In at least one respect, Benobles is a superior city: the skies are clear there more often than any other city of my acquaintance. On the average, the stars are visible more than one hour in every sixty-four. I have observed and studied them for more than a generation."

A ripple of disappointment spread through the audience. Except for the discovery of the moon and its connection with the tides, astronomy had always seemed a singularly useless field.

But Dragnor continued his slow discourse. "We know very little about the stars. Many generations ago, Xlomenes Onasiu proposed that they are worlds similar to our own but much hotter—so hot that their surfaces are covered with glowing magma. Even now this is the best theory we have, though modern physics still can't justify all the details.

"Over the generations, a number of people have studied the stars from Benobles. I have used their observations to arrange the lamps which light this lecture pavilion. If you are sitting near the center of the pavilion, the relative positions and luminosities of these lamps will appear very much as did the sixteen brightest stars in the sky's fifth octant, sixty-four generations ago."

Dragnor nodded to a technician who sat by the console at the side of the stage. "The stars are probably the most stable features in our universe. In this case, a simple change of one rheostat will demonstrate how the stars appeared thirty-two generations ago."

The technician fiddled and one of the lamps shone several times brighter. I squinted over my shoulder at the light. All the other "stars" were ordinary heat lamps, but this variable one was actually an electric arc stopped down to low power.

"And finally the sky as it appears at present." The same star became yet brighter, till it was the brightest of all the stars in the display. The effect was not lost on the audience. An unhappy murmuring rose behind us.

Old Dragnor seemed unperturbed. After all, he presumably knew what was coming. "You have noticed that one particular star has waxed. In a technical lecture, to be given later, I will offer evidence that this increased brightness is not intrinsic but is due entirely to the motion of the star." He paused, let the audience guess where the talk was going.

When he spoke again it was with seeming irrelevance. "The city of Benobles is connected to the rest of the world by its steam sledge traffic. When it is not too cold I enjoy going to one of the outer sledge terminals to watch the express approach town. At first, all you can see of the sledge is its tiny headlight glowing in the far away. The light grows brighter and brighter, but it does not move left or right, up or down. At the last moment, when the light is brightest, it slides to one side as the express whips past the siding and goes on into the center of town.

"Until fifteen bornings ago, the Waxing Star represented above had no measurable proper motion. Then, shortly after the last Science Fair, I succeeded in measuring its motion. The drift is small: less than a minute of arc during all the time I have observed it, but more than large enough for me to predict the future position of the Star."

The murmuring around us was louder, more anxious. Thorc Graun clenched and unclenched his hands, all the while glaring at Dragnor.

The scientist continued, "I'll reserve the details of my calculations for a technical lecture. At this time, I will content myself with showing you our sky as it will appear only a few generations from now."

The Science Fair technician must have turned that arc light up to full. I shut my eyes but the glare seemed to go right through the eyelids. Every inch of exposed skin felt as though it were being flayed. Old Dragnor's calm voice went on. "The Waxing Star's closest approach to Ge will occur just eight generations from now. At that time, the Star will be many times brighter than the representation hung above us here. For two hundred fifty-six tides it will glow so brightly and then slowly fade, as it passes on by us."

The arc lamp was turned down, till it was merely a very bright light. I opened my eyes and looked around. Lenska Dragnor sagged against my side, her face hidden behind her hands. The audience seemed wilted, almost hypnotized. At the far end of our row, Thorc Graun looked as though he were gathering himself up to pounce onto the stage.

"My lords, do you know what this close passage will do to our world? I do not. Our ignorance is immense. Our instruments are crude. Within the range of error of my estimates, the Waxing Star might burn away our oceans. Failing that, it could easily melt the glaciers and drown us all.

"Our only hope for certain survival is the development of a science and a technology to meet the challenge. To achieve this, we must abolish all proprietary rights to inventions and discoveries. This Science Fair must be declared permanent!"

The crowd's dazed silence lasted only a moment. Then there was pandemonium. Half the noblemen and corporate chairmen in the pavilion were on their hooves, shouting. It was hard to blame them. They sank much of their resources into research, and now someone was suggesting that they give away the fruits of those endeavors. For that matter, where did Dragnor's suggestion put *me*? If all research were public knowledge, what use would there be for an industrial spy?

I had to pull Lenska back down onto her pallet as Thorc Graun bvo-Graun scrambled onstage and pushed Dragnor to one side. If the old man were not safe with his secret told, he would never be. The prince of Graun raced back and forth along the edge of the platform, shouting at the top of his lungs. I couldn't hear a word.

Behind us the city folk and the scientists pushed and jostled one another as various factions tried to approach the stage. For them, Dragnor's revelation far outshone the question of extending the Fair, and their shouted questions and speculations drowned out everything else.

Still, I doubt if a single one of them guessed that the Waxing Star was not nearly so important as what was *near* it.

The inspiration for "The Science Fair" came from wondering what the tail of the mass/frequency distribution would look like in the galaxy: smaller objects seem to be more common. But when objects get too small we often can't detect them anymore. Could there be gas giant planets wandering the galaxy? How about rocky, earth-sized planets? How about "globular clusters" of asteroids? Nowadays (2001), we know that there *are* things like wandering gas giants, though there are different theories about their formation. As far as I know, present theory does not foresee small, "rocky" objects wandering free—except as may be ejected from solar systems. Still, the idea of a sunless solar system, or a solar system centered on a brown dwarf, is intriguing.

Thanks, Damon, for making "The Science Fair" good enough to see the light of day!

GEMSTONE

It is a cliché that writers put their own experiences into their stories (a cliché that is not always true, fortunately). Personal unhappiness can have a writerly payoff. (This notion was beautifully treated in George R. R. Martin's "Portraits of His Children." I am convinced that story won a Nebula but not a Hugo because the authors—who are the Nebula voters—felt special kinship with the protagonist of the story.) In my case, an unhappy vacation as a child—and a happy vacation many years later in New Zealand—came together with a random idea from the ol' idea box. The result is a story that turns and turns, surely the most unbalanced thing I have ever written. Stan Schmidt initially rejected it, then wrote me three months later, asking to see it again. I'm very grateful that he bought it. Even if "Gemstone" never quite decides what it wants to be, it means something to me.

The summer of 1957 should have been Sanda's most wonderful vacation. She had known about her parents' plans since March, and all through the La Jolla springtime, all through the tedious spring semester of her seventh grade, she had that summer to dream about.

Nothing ever seemed so fair at first, and turned out so vile:

Sanda sat on the bedroom balcony of her grandmother's house and looked out into the gloom and the rain. The pine trees along the street were great dark shadows, swaying and talking in the dusk. A hundred yards away, toward downtown Eureka, the light of a single streetlamp found its way through pines to make tiny glittering reflections off the slick street. As every night these last four weeks, the wind seemed stronger when the daylight departed. She hunched down in her oversized jacket and let the driven mist wash at the tears that trickled down her face. Tonight had been the end, just the end. Daddy and Mom would be here in six days, and two or three days after that the three of them would drive back home. Six days. Sanda unclenched her jaws and tried to relax her face. How could she last? She would have to see Grandma at least for meals, at least to help around the house. And every time she saw Grandma she would feel the shame and know that she had ruined things.

And it isn't all my fault! Grandmother had her secrets, her smugness, her ignorance—flaws Sanda had never imagined during those short visits of years passed.

In the hallway beyond the bedroom, the Gemstone was at it again.

Sanda felt a wave of cold wash over her. For a moment the dark around her and the balcony beneath her knees were not merely chill and wet, but glacially frozen, the center of a lifeless and friendless waste. It was funny that now that she *knew* the house was haunted and *knew* precisely the thing that caused these moods, it was not nearly as frightening as before. In fact, it was scarcely more than an inconvenience compared to the *people* problems she had.

It had not always been this way. Sanda thought back to the beginning of the summer, trying to imagine blue skies and warm sun. Those first few days had been like the other times she remembered in Eureka. Grandmother's house sat near the end of its street, surrounded by pines. The only other trees were a pair of small palms right before the front steps. (These needed constant attention. Grandma liked to say that she kept them here just so her visitors from San Diego would never feel homesick.) The house had two storeys, with turrets and dormers coming out of the attic. Against the blue, cloudless sky it looked like a fairy-tale castle. The Victorian gingerbread had been carefully maintained through the years, and in its present incarnation gleamed green and gold.

Her parents had left for San Francisco after a one-day stay. The summer conference at USF was starting that week, and they weren't yet sure they had an apartment. Sanda's first night alone with Grandma had been everything she imagined. Even though the evening beyond the porch was turning chill, the living room still held its warmth. Grandma set her old electric heater in the middle of the carpeted floor so that it shone on the sofa side of the room. Then she walked around the book-lined walls pretending to search for the thing she so liked to show her grandchild.

"Not here, not here. Oh my, I hardly ever look at it nowadays. I forget where . . ." Sanda tagged along, noticing titles where her earlier, younger self had been impressed only by color and size. Grandma had a complete collection of *National Geographic*s. Where most families put such magazines in boxes and forget them, Grandmother had every issue there, as though they were some grand encyclopedia. And for Sanda, they were. On her last visit she had spent many an afternoon looking through the pictures. It was the only item she remembered for sure from this library. Now she saw dozens of books on polar exploration, meteorology, biology. Grandfather Beauchamp had been a great man, and Grandmother kept the library and its books, plaques, and certificates in honor of his memory.

"Ah, here it is!" She pulled the huge notebook down from its central position. She led Sanda back to the sofa. "Too big to sit in my lap, now, aren't you?" They grinned at each other and she opened the book across their laps, then put her arm across Sanda's shoulders.

The book was precisely organized. Every newspaper clipping, photo, article, was framed and had a short legend. Some of the pictures existed nowhere else in the world. Others could be found in articles in magazines like the *National Geographic* from the '20s and '30s. Rex Beauchamp had been on the "Terra Nova" expedition in 1910. If it hadn't been for a knee injury he would actually have been on Scott's tragic journey to the South Pole. Sanda sucked in her breath and asked the same question she had asked once before, "And so if his knee had been okay, why, he would have died with the others—and would never have met you, and you would never have had Dad, and—"

GRANDMA SLAPPED THE NOTEBOOK. "NO. I KNOW REX. HE WOULD HAVE made the difference. If they had just waited for him to get well, they could have made it back to the coast."

IT WAS AN ANSWER SHE HAD HEARD BEFORE, BUT ONE SHE WANTED TO HEAR again. Sanda sat back and waited for the rest of the story. After World War I, the Beauchamps had emigrated from Great Britain, and Grandfather participated in several American expeditions. There were dozens of pictures of him on shipboard and in the brave little camps the explorers had established along the Antarctic coast. Rex Beauchamp had been very handsome and boyish even in middle age, and it made Sanda proud to see him in those pictures—though he was rarely the center of attention. He always seemed to be in the background, or in the third row of the group portraits. Grandma said he was a doer and not a talker. He never had a college degree and so had to serve in technician and support jobs. But they depended on him nevertheless.

NOT ALL THE PICTURES WERE OF ICE AND SNOW. MANY OF THE EXPEDITIONS had worked out of Christchurch, New Zealand. On one occasion, Grandmother had gone along that far. It had been a wonderful vacation for her. She had pictures of the city and its wide, circular harbor, and others of her visiting the North Island and Maori country with Grandfather.

Sanda raised her eyes from the picture collection as her grandmother spoke. There were things in this room that illustrated her story more spectacularly than any photographs. The area around the sofa was brightly lit by one of the beautiful stained-glass lamps that Grandma had in every room. But at the limits of its light, the room glowed in mysterious blue and red and yellow from the higher panes in the glass. Dark polished wood edged the carpet and the moldings of every doorway. Beyond the electric heater she could see the Maori statues the Beauchamps had brought back from their stay at Rotorua. In normal light those figures carved in wooden relief seemed faintly comical, their pointed tongues stuck out like weapons, their hands held claw-like. But in the colored dimness the mother-of-pearl in their eyes shone almost knowingly, and the extended tongues were no childish aggression. Sanda wriggled with a moment of delicious fright. The Maori were all civilized now, Grandmother said, but they had been more hideously ferocious than any savages on Earth.

"Do you still have the *meri*, Grandma?"

"Yes indeed." She reached into the embroidered sewing stand that sat next to her end of the sofa and withdrew a graceful, eight-inch piece of stone. One end fit the hand, while the other spread out in a smooth, blunt-edged oval. It was beautiful, and no one but someone like Grandma—or a Maori—could know its true purpose. "This is what they fought with, not like American Indians with spears and arrows." She handed it to Sanda, who ran her fingers over the smoothness. "It's so short you have to come right up to your enemy and *whack*! right across the forehead." Sanda tried to imagine but couldn't. Grandma had so many beautiful things. Sanda had once overheard her mother complain to Daddy that these were thefts from an ancient heritage. Sanda couldn't see why; she was sure that Grandpa had paid for these things. And if he hadn't brought them back to Eureka, so many fewer people could have admired them.

Grandma talked on, well past Sanda's La Jolla bedtime. The girl found herself half hypnotized by the multicolored shadows of the lamp and the pale red from the heater. That heater sat on newspapers.

Sanda felt herself come wide awake. "That heater, Grandma. Isn't it dangerous?"

The woman stopped in mid-reminiscence. "What? No, I've had it for years. And I'm careful not to set it on the carpet where it might stain."

"But those newspapers. They're brown, almost burned."

Grandma looked at the heater. "My, you're a big girl now, to worry about such things. I don't know . . . Anyway, we can turn it off now. You should be going to bed, don't you think?"

Sanda was to sleep in the same room her father had used when he was little. It was on the second floor. As they walked down the hall to the bedroom, Grandma stopped by the heavy terrarium she kept there. Dad and Mother hadn't known quite what to make of it: the glass box was something new. Grandma had placed it so the wide skylight gave it sun through most of the day. Now moonlight washed over the glass and the stones. Pale reflections came off some of the smaller rocks. Grandma switched on the hall light and turned everything mundane. The terrarium was empty of life. There was nothing there but rocks of odd sizes mixed with river-washed gravel. It was like the box Sanda kept her pet lizards in. But there were not even lizards in this one. The only concessions to life were little plastic flowers, "planted" here and there in the landscape.

Grandma smiled wanly. "I think your Dad believes I'm crazy to put something like this here."

Sanda looked at the strange display for a moment and then suggested, "Maybe if you used real flowers?"

The old woman shook her head. "I like artificial ones. You don't have to water them. They never fade or die. They are always beautiful." She paused and Sanda remained diplomatically silent. "Anyway, it's the rocks that are the important thing here. I showed you pictures of those valleys your grandfather helped discover: the ones that don't have any snow in them, even though they're hundreds of miles inside Antarctica. These rocks are from one of those valleys. They must have been sitting there for thousands of years with nothing but the wind to upset them. Rex kept his collection in boxes down in the basement, but I think they are so much nicer up here. This is a little like what they had before."

Sanda looked into the cabinet with new interest. Some of the stones were strange. A couple looked like the meteorites she had seen in the Natural History Museum back home. And there was another, about the size of her head, that had a vaguely regular pattern in the gray and black minerals that were its substance.

Minutes later, Sanda was tucked into her father's old bed, the lights were out, and Grandmother was descending the stairs. Moonlight spread silver on the window sills, and the pines beyond were soft, pale, bright. Sanda sighed and smiled. So far, things were just as she dreamed and just as she remembered.

The last she wondered as she drifted off to sleep was why Grandmother put flowers in the terrarium if she really wanted to imitate the bleak antarctic valleys.

THAT FIRST DAY WAS REALLY THE LAST WHEN EVERYTHING WENT TOTALLY well. And looking back on it, Sanda could see symptoms of many of the things that were later to make the summer so unpleasant.

Physically everything was just as she remembered. The stair railings were a rich, deeply polished wood that she hardly ever saw in La Jolla. Everywhere was carpeting, even on the stairs. The basement was cool and damp and filled with all the mysterious things that Grandfather had worked with. But there were so many things that Grandma did and believed that were *wrong*. Some—like the flowers—were differences of opinion that Sanda could keep her mouth shut about. Others—like Grandma's use of the old electric heater—were really dangerous. When she spoke about those, Grandmother didn't seem to believe or understand her. The older woman would smile and tell her what a big girl

she was getting to be, but it was clear she was a little hurt by the sug-
gestions, no matter how diplomatically put. Finally Sanda had taken a
plastic mat off the back porch and slipped it under the heater in place
of the newspapers. But Grandma noticed, and furthermore pointed out
that the dirty mat had stained the beautiful carpet—just the thing the
nice clean newspapers had been there to prevent. Sanda had been
crushed: she'd been harmful when she wanted to be helpful. Grandmother was very good about it; in the end—after she cleaned the
carpet—she suggested putting the mat between the newspapers and the
heater. So the incident ended happily, after all.

But this sort of thing seemed to happen all the time: Sanda trying to
do something different, some hurt being caused to property or Grandma,
and then sincere apology and reconciliation. Sanda began to feel a little
haggard, and to watch the calendar for a different reason than before.
Just being with Grandma had been one of the big attractions of this
summer. Both she and Grandma were *trying*, but it wasn't working.
Sometimes Sanda thought that—no matter how often Grandma said
Sanda was a young grown-up now—she still thought Sanda was five
years old. She had seriously wanted Sanda to take afternoon naps. Only
when the girl assured her that her parents no longer required naps did
she relent. And Grandma never told her to do anything. She always
asked Sanda "wouldn't you like to" do whatever she wanted. It was
awfully hard to smile and say "oh yes, that would be fun" when in fact
it was a chore she would rather pass up. At home it was so much easier:
Sanda did as she was told, and did not have to claim to love it.

A week later the fair weather broke. It rained. And rained. And
rained. And when it wasn't raining it was cloudy; not cloudy as in La
Jolla, but a dripping, misty cloudiness that just promised more rain.
Grandma said it was often this way; Sanda had just been lucky on the
previous visits.

And it was about this time she began to be afraid of the upstairs.
Grandmother slept downstairs, though she stayed up very late at night,
reading or sewing. She would be easy to call if anything . . . bad happened. That did not help. At first it was like an ordinary fear of darkness.
Some nights a person is just more fidgety than others. And after the
weather turned bad it was easy to feel scared, lying in bed with the
wind and the rattle of rain against the windows. But this was different.
The feeling increased from night to night. It wasn't quite a feeling that
something was sneaking up on her. More it was a sense of utter desolation and despair. Sometimes it seemed as if the room, the whole
house, were gone and she was in just the antarctic wilderness that
Grandfather had explored. She had no direct visions of this—just the
feeling of cold and lifelessness extending forever. *Grandfather's ghost?*

Late one night Sanda had to go to the bathroom, which was down on the first floor next to Grandmother's bedroom. It was almost painful to move—so afraid was she of making a sound, of provoking whatever caused the mood that filled her room. When she passed the terrarium in the hallway, the feeling of cold grew stronger and her legs tensed for a sprint down the stairs. Instead she forced herself to stand still, then to walk slowly around the glass cage. Something in there was causing it. The terror was insidious, growing as she stood there—almost as if what caused this now knew it had a "listener." Sanda slept at the foot of the stairs that night.

After that, when night came and Grandmother had tucked her in, Sanda would creep out of bed, unwrap her sleeping bag, and quietly carry it onto the balcony that opened off her room. The extra distance and the extra wall reduced the psychic cold to a tolerable level. Many nights it was rainy, and it was always chill and a bit windy, but she had bought a really good sleeping bag for the Scouts, and she had always liked to camp out. Nevertheless, it wore her down to sleep like that night after night, and made it harder to be diplomatic and cheerful during the days.

In the daytime there was far less feeling of dread upstairs. Sanda didn't know whether this was because the second floor was basically a sunny, cheerful place or whether the ghost "slept" during the day. Whenever she walked past the terrarium she looked carefully into it. After a while, she thought she had the effect narrowed down to one particular rock—the skull-sized one with the strangely regular patterns of gray and black. As the days passed, the position of some of the rocks changed. There had been five plastic flowers in the terrarium when Sanda first saw it; now there were three.

There was one other mystery—which under other circumstances would have been very sinister, but which seemed scarcely more than an intriguing puzzle now. Several times, usually on stormy nights, a car parked in the grass just off the other side of the street, about forty yards north of the house. That was all; Sanda had noticed it only by accident. It looked like a '54 Ford. Once a match flared within the cab, and she saw two occupants. She smiled smugly, wistfully to herself; she could imagine what they were up to. But she was wrong. One night, when the rain had stopped yet clouds kept out the stars, the driver got out and walked across the street toward the house. He moved silently, quickly. Sanda had to lean out from the balcony to see him crouch in the bushes next to the wall where the electric power meter was mounted. He spent only half a minute there. She saw a tiny point of light moving over the power meter and the utility cables that came down from the telephone pole at the street. Then the phantom meter reader stood and ran back across the street, quietly relatching the door of his Ford. The car sat for several more minutes—as if they were watching the house for some sign of alarm—and then drove away.

She should have told Grandma. But then, if she were being as open as a good girl should be with a grandmother, she would have also confessed her fear of the upstairs and the terrarium. Those fears were shameful, though. Even if *real*, they were the type of childish thing that could only make her situation with Grandma worse. Grandmother was a clever person. Sanda knew that if she told her about the mysterious car, the older woman would either dismiss the story—or question her in sufficient detail to discover that Sanda was sleeping on the balcony.

So she dithered—and in the end told someone else.

FINDING THAT SOMEONE ELSE HAD BEEN A SURPRISE; SHE HADN'T REALLY known she was looking. Whenever the weather dried a little, Sanda tried to get outdoors. The city library was about three miles away, an easy ride on her father's old bicycle. Of course Grandmother had been uneasy about Sanda carrying library books in the saddle baskets of the bike. There was always the risk of splashing water or a sudden rainstorm. It was just another of the polite little conflicts they had. One or the other of them could always see some objection to a given activity. In the end—as usual—they compromised, with Sanda taking grocery bags and a little waxed paper for the books.

Today wasn't wet, though. The big blocks of cloud left plenty of space for the blue. To the northwest, the plume from the paper mill was purest white across the sky. The sun was warm, and the gusty breeze dry. It was the sort of day she once thought was every day in Eureka.

Sanda took a detour, biking back along the street away from town. The asphalt ended about thirty yards past Grandmother's lot. There were supposed to be more houses up here, but Grandma didn't think much of them. She passed one. It looked like a trailer used as a permanent home. A couple old cars, one looking very dead, were in front. The trees came in close to the road here, blocking out the sun. It felt a little like those great forests they'd driven through to get to Eureka. Even after a half day of sun, there was still a slow dripping from the needles. Everything was so green it might as well be dipped in paint. Once she had liked that.

She went a lot farther south than she had before. The road stopped at a dead end. A one-storey, red-shingled house was the last thing on the street. It was a real house, but it reminded Sanda of the trailer. It was such a different thing from Grandmother's house. There were a lot of small houses in La Jolla, but the weather back home was so dry and mild that buildings didn't seem to wear out. Here Sanda had the feeling that the damp, the cold, and the mildew were forever warring on the houses. This place had been losing the fight for some time.

She circled around the end of the road—and almost ran into a second bicyclist.

Sanda stopped abruptly and awkwardly. (The center bar on the bike was a little high for her.) "Where did you come from?" she asked a bit angrily.

The boy was taller than Sanda, and looked very strong. He must be at least fifteen years old. But his face was soft, almost stupid-looking. He waved at the red-shingled house. "We live here. Who are you?"

"Sanda Beauchamp."

"Oh, yeah. You're the girl staying with the old English lady."

"She is not an old lady. She's my grandmother."

He was silent for a moment, the baby-face expressionless. "I'm Larry O'Malley. Your grandmother is okay. Last summer I did her lawn."

Sanda untangled herself from the bicycle and they walked their bikes back the way she had come. "She has regular gardeners now."

"I know. She's very rich. Even more than last year."

Grandma wasn't rich. It was on the tip of her tongue to contradict him, but his second statement made her pause, puzzled. *Even more than last year?*

They had walked all the way back to Grandmother's before Sanda knew it. Larry wasn't really sullen. She wasn't sure yet if he was smart or stupid; she knew he wasn't as old as he looked. His father was a real lumberjack, which was neat. Most of Sanda's parents' friends were geologists and things like that.

They parked their bikes at the steps, and Sanda took him in to see Grandmother. As she had expected, the elder Beauchamp was not thrilled with Sanda's plans for the afternoon.

She looked uncertainly at the boy. "But, Larry, isn't that a long ride?"

Sanda was not about to let Larry blow it. "Oh no, Grandma, it's not much farther than the library. Besides, I haven't been to a movie in so long," which was true, though Grandmother's television did a great job of dragging in old movies from the only available station.

"What's the film? It's such a nice day to waste inside a theater."

"Oh, they're playing movies from the early fifties." That sounded safe. Grandma had complained more than once about the immorality of today's shows. Besides, if she heard the title, she would be sure to refuse.

Grandmother seemed almost distraught. Then she agreed, and walked out to the screened porch with them. "Come back before four."

"We will. We will." And they were off. She didn't know if it was the weather, or meeting Larry, or the prospect of the movie, but suddenly she felt wonderful.

THE THING FROM OUTER SPACE. THAT'S WHAT IT SAID ON THE MARQUEE. SHE felt a little guilty deceiving Grandma about the title. It wasn't really the sort of show her parents would want her to see. But just seeing a movie was going to be fun. It was like home. This theater reminded her a lot of the Cove in La Jolla. After they got their tickets they drifted down to the movie posters.

And Sanda began to feel a chill that was not in the air and that was not the vicarious thrill of watching a scary show. This *Thing* was supposed to be from outer space, yet the posters showed arctic wastes. . . .

She found herself walking more slowly, for the first time letting the boy do most of the talking. Then they were inside, and the movie had begun.

It was a terrible thing, almost as if God had created a personal warning, a personal explanation for Sanda Rachel Beauchamp. *The Thing* was what had been after her all these weeks. Oh, a lot of the details were different. The movie took place in the arctic; the alien monster—the Thing—was crudely man-shaped. Sanda sat, her face slack, all but hypnotized by these innocently filmed revelations. About halfway through the movie, Larry nudged her and asked if she were okay. Sanda just nodded.

The Thing had been stranded. In the polar wastes the temperature and lack of predators allowed it to survive a very long time. The dry antarctic valleys Grandpa discovered might be even better; Things from long, long ago would be right at the surface, not hidden beneath hundreds of feet of ice. The creature would be like a time bomb waiting to be discovered. When exposed to light and warmth—as Grandma had done by putting it in the sunny terrarium—it would come to life. The movie Thing looked for blood. Sanda's Thing seemed after something more subtle, more terrible.

Sanda was scarcely aware when the movie ended, so perfectly did its story merge with the greater terror she now felt. It was still middle afternoon, but the berglike clouds had melded together, thick and deep and dark. The wind was picking up, driving through her sweater and carrying occasional drops of wet. They recovered their bikes, Sanda dazed, Larry O'Malley silently observant.

It was uphill most of the way back, but now the wind was behind them. The forests beyond the town were blackish green, sometimes turned gray by passing mist. The scene didn't register with her. All she could think of was the cold and the ice and the thing waiting for her up ahead.

Larry reached out to grab her handlebars as the bike angled toward the ditch. "Really. What's the matter?"

And Sanda told him. About the strangely mottled antarctic rock and the terrarium. About its movement and the desolation it broadcast.

The boy didn't say anything when she finished. They worked laboriously up a hill past neat houses, some of them Victorian, none as beautiful as Grandmother's. As usual, traffic was light—nonexistent by the standards of home. They rode side by side with the entire road to themselves. Finally they reached the top and started down a gentle slope. Still Larry hadn't said anything. Sanda's haze of terror was broken by sudden anger. She pedaled just ahead of him and waved her hand in his face. *"Hey!* I was talking to you. Don't you believe me?"

Larry blinked, his wide face expressionless. He didn't seem to take offense. He spoke, but didn't directly answer her question. "I think your Grandma is a smart person. And I always thought she had some strange things in that house. She put the rock up there; she must know something about it. You should ask her straight out. Or do you think *she* wants to hurt you, too?"

Sanda lagged back even with Larry and felt a little bit ashamed. She should have brought this up with Grandma weeks ago. She knew why she had not. After all the little conflicts and misunderstandings, she had been afraid that a fearful story like this would have weakened her position even further, would have reinforced Grandma's view of her as a child. Saying these things out loud seemed to make them smaller. But having said them, she could also see that there was something *real* here, something to fear, or at least to be concerned about. She looked at Larry and smiled with some respect. Perhaps he wasn't very imaginative—after all, nothing seemed to disturb him—but being with him was like suddenly finding the ground in the surf, or waking up from a bad dream.

BLOCKS OF MIST CHASED BACK AND FORTH AROUND THEM, BUT THEY WERE still dry when they got home. They stood for a moment on the grassy shoulder of the road.

"If you want to go to the sand dunes tomorrow, we should start early. It's a long ride from here." She couldn't tell if he had already forgotten her story, or if he was trying to reassure her.

"I'll have to ask Grandmother," *about that and certain other things.* "I'll see you tomorrow, anyway."

Larry pedaled off toward his house, and Sanda walked the bike around to the toolshed. Grandma came out to the back porch, and worried over the damp on Sanda's sweater. She seemed nervous, and relieved to see Sanda back.

"My, you've been gone so long. I've got some sandwiches made up in the kitchen." As they walked into the house, Grandma asked her about the movie and about Larry. "You know, Sanda, I think the O'Malley boy is nice enough. But I'm not sure your mum and dad would want you spending so much time with him. Your interests are so different, don't you think?"

Sanda was not really listening. She took the other's hand. It was a childlike gesture that stopped the older woman short. "Grandma, there's something I've *got* to talk to you about. Please."

"Of course, Sanda."

They sat down, and the girl told her of the terror that soaked the upstairs every night so strongly that she must sleep on the balcony.

Grandma smiled tentatively and patted Sanda's hand. "I'll wager it's those Maori statues. They would scare anyone, especially in the dark. I shouldn't have told you all those stories about them. They're just wood and—"

"It's not them, Grandmother." Sanda tried to keep the frustration out of her voice. She looked out of the kitchen, down the hall into the living room. She could see one of the statues there, sticking its tongue at her. It was lovely, and frightening in a fun sort of way, but that was all. "It's the terrarium, and especially one rock there. When I'm near it, I can feel the cold get stronger."

"Oh, dear." Grandmother looked down at her hands and avoided Sanda's eyes. For a moment she seemed to be talking only to herself. "You must be very sensitive."

Sanda's eyes widened. Even after all this time, she hadn't really expected anyone to believe. And now she saw that Grandma had known something about this all along.

"Oh, Sanda, I'm so sorry. If I thought you could sense it, I would never have put you up there." She reached out to touch Sanda, and smiled. "There really is nothing to fear. That's my, uh, Gemstone." She stumbled on the name, looked faintly worried. "It has always been a little secret of your grandfather's and mine. If I tell you about it, will you keep the secret, too?"

The girl nodded.

"Let's go up there, and I'll show you. You're right that the stone can make you feel things. . . ."

As Grandma had told her before, Rex Beauchamp had found the Gemstone on one of the first expeditions into the dry valleys. He probably should have turned his discovery over to the expedition's collection. But in those early days there was a more casual attitude about individual finds, and besides, Grandfather was continually shunted aside from the credit he deserved. He was simply the fellow who fixed all the little things that went wrong. After retirement he hoped to set up his own small lab here, to look into this and several other mysteries he had come across over the years.

Grandfather had kept the Gemstone in a special locker down in the lab/basement. He hoped to imitate its original environment. At first Grandpa thought the rock was some special crystal that stored and reflected back the emotions of those around it. When he held it in his hand, he could feel the winds and desolation of the antarctic. If he touched it an hour later, he felt vague reflections of his mood *at the time of the previous encounter.*

When he cut it with a lapidary saw, the mental shriek of pain showed both of them the Gemstone was not psychic mineral, but a living thing.

"We never told anyone what we had discovered. Not even your father. Rex kept it in the basement, and as cold as possible. He was so afraid that it would die." They had reached the second floor and were walking down the short hallway toward the terrarium. The skylight was pale gray, and rain was beginning to splatter off it. The cold and loneliness were not quite as sharp as after dark, but it took an effort for Sanda to approach the rock.

"I looked at it differently. It seemed to me that if the Gemstone could survive all those centuries of no food, no water—well then, maybe it was tough. Maybe even it would like light and warmth. After your grandfather died, I took the stone and put it in this nice aquarium box up here where there is light. I know it is alive; I think it likes it up here."

Sanda looked down at the black and grey whorls that marked its rough exterior. The shape was not symmetrical, but it was regular. Even without the chill beating against her mind she should have known it was alive. "What . . . what does it eat?"

"Um." Grandma paused for just a second. "Some of the rocks. Even those flowers. I have to replace them now and again. But it's mindless. It's never done much more than what Rex originally noticed. It's just that now—up here in the light—it does them a bit more often." She saw the pain on Sanda's face. "You can feel the stone even that far away?" she asked wonderingly.

Grandma reached down and touched the top of the Gemstone with the palm of her hand. She winced. "Ah, it is projecting that old cold-and-desolate pattern. I can see why that bothers you. But it's not intended to be hurtful. I think it's just the creature's memory of the cold. Now just wait. It takes a minute or so for it to change. In some ways it's more like a plant than an animal."

The psychic chill faded. What remained was not threatening, but—with her present sensitivity—was unsettling. Grandma motioned her closer. "Here. Now you put your hand on it, and you'll see what I mean."

Sanda advanced slowly, her eyes on her grandmother's face. Above them, the rain droned against the skylight. *What if it's all a lie?* thought Sanda. Could the creature take people over and make them go after others?

But now that the mental pressure was gone, it seemed just a little bit unbelievable. She touched the Gemstone first with her fingertips and then with the flat of her hand. Grandmother's hand was still on the rock, though not quite touching hers. Nothing happened. It was cold as any rock might be in this room. The surface was rough, though regular. The seconds passed and slowly she felt it: It was Grandma! Her smile, a wave of affection—and behind that, disappointment and an emptiness more muted than the stone usually broadcast. Still, there was a warmth where before there had been only cold.

"Oh, Grandmother!" The older woman put her arm across Sanda's shoulders, and for the first time in weeks, the girl thought there might be a lasting reconciliation. Sanda's hand strayed from the Gemstone and brushed through the pebbles that were its bed. They were ordinary. The Gemstone was the only strange thing in the terrarium. Wait. She picked up a smallish pebble and held it in the light, scarcely noticing the sudden tension in Grandma's arm. The tiny rock might have been glassy except for the milky haze on its surface. It felt almost greasy. "This isn't a real rock, is it, Grandma?"

"No. It's plastic. Like the flowers. I just think it's pretty."

"Oh." She dropped it back into the terrarium. Another time, she might have been more curious. For now, everything was swamped by her relief in discovering that what had terrorized her for so long was not a threat but something very wonderful. "Thank you. I was so afraid." She laughed a little ruefully. "I really made a fool of myself this afternoon, telling Larry I thought the Gemstone was some kind of monster."

Grandmother's arm slipped away from her shoulder. "Sanda, you mustn't—" she began sharply. "Really, Sanda, you mustn't be going out with the O'Malley boy. He's simply too old for you."

Sanda's reply was casually argumentative; she was still immersed in a rosy feeling of relief. "Oh, Gran. He's going into ninth grade this fall. He's just big for his age."

"No. I'm sure your mother and dad would be very upset with me if I let you be off alone with him."

The sharpness of her tone finally came through to Sanda. Grandma had on her determined look. And suddenly the girl felt just as determined. There was no valid reason for her not to see Larry O'Malley. Grandma had hinted around at this before: she thought her neighbors up the road were lower class, both in background and present accomplishment. If there was one thing really wrong with Grandmother it was that she looked down on some people. Sanda even suspected that she was racially prejudiced. For instance, she called Negroes "colored people."

The double injustice of Grandma's demand was too much. Sanda thrust out her quivering jaw. "Grandmother, I'll go out with him if I want. You just don't want me to see him because he's poor . . . because he's Irish."

"*Sanda!*" The older woman seemed to shrink in upon herself. Her voice was choked, hard to understand. "I had so looked forward to this summer with you. B-but you're not the nice little girl you once were." She stepped around Sanda and hurried down the stairs.

Sanda looked after her, open-mouthed. Then she felt tears turning into sobs, and rushed into her bedroom.

SHE SAT ON THE BEDROOM BALCONY AND LOOKED OUT INTO THE GLOOM AND the rain. The pine trees along the street were great dark shadows, swaying and talking in the dusk. From a hundred yards away, the light of a single streetlamp found its way through the pines to make tiny glittering reflections off the slick street. She hunched down in her oversized jacket and let the driven mist wash at the tears that trickled down her face. Daddy and Mom would be here in six days. Six days. Sanda unclenched her jaws and tried to relax her face. How could she last?

She had sat here for hours, going around and around with these questions, never quite getting the pain rationalized, never quite finding a course of action that would not be still more painful. She wondered what Grandma was doing now. There had been no call to supper, or to help with supper. But there had been no sounds of cooking either. She was probably in her room, going through the same thing Sanda was. Grandma's last words . . . they almost described her own grief all these weeks.

Grandmother had looked so small, so frail. Sanda was almost as tall as she, but rarely thought about it. It must have been hard for Grandma to have a guest she thought of as a child, a guest to whom she must always show the most cheerful face, a guest with whom every disagreement was a tiny failure.

And even this vacation had not been all bad. There had been the evenings when the weather was nice and they had stayed out on the screened porch to play caroms or Scrabble. Those had been just as good as before—better in some ways, now that she could understand Grandma's little jokes and appreciate her impish grin when she made some clever countermove.

The girl sighed. She had been through these thoughts several times in the last hours. Each time she returned to them, they seemed to gain strength over the recriminations. She knew that in the end she would go downstairs, and try to make up. And maybe . . . maybe this time it could really work. This break had gone so deep and hurt so much that maybe they could start out in a new way.

She stood up and breathed the clean, cold, wet air. The keening of the Gemstone in the back of her mind was a prod now. There was more than cold in the Gemstone's call; there was a loneliness she knew came in part from those around it.

As Sanda turned to enter the bedroom, a flash of headlights made her look back. A car was driving slowly by. . . . It looked like a '54 Ford. She stayed very still until it was out of sight, then dropped to her knees so that just her head was above the balcony. If this were like the other visitations . . .

Sure enough, a couple minutes passed and the Ford was back—this time without its lights. It stopped on the other side of the road. The rain was heavy, and the wind came in gusts now. Sanda wasn't sure, but it looked like *two* people got out of the car. Yes. There were two. They ran toward the house, one for the power meter, the other heading out of sight to her left.

This was more than the mysterious intruders had ever done before. And somehow there was a purposefulness in it tonight. As if this were no rehearsal. Sanda leaned out from the balcony. Her curiosity was fast giving way to fear. Not the psychic, moody fear the Gemstone broadcast, but a sharp, call-to-action type of fear. *What is that guy doing?* The dark figure maneuvered a small light, and something else. There was a snapping noise that came faintly to her over the rain.

And then she knew. It wasn't just the power cable that came down to that side of the house; the phone line did, too.

Sanda whirled and dived back into her bedroom, shedding the jacket as she ran. She sprinted by the terrarium, barely conscious of the mood emerging from the Gemstone.

Grandmother stood at the bottom of the stairs, looking as if she were about to come up. She appeared tired, but there was a wan smile on her face. "Sanda, dear, I—"

"Grandma! Somebody's trying to break in. *Somebody's trying to break in!*" Sanda came down the stairs in two crashing leaps. There was a shadow on the porch where no shadow should have been. Sanda slammed the bolt to just as the doorknob began to turn. Behind her,

Grandmother stared in shocked silence. Sanda spun and ran toward the kitchen. Once they had the intruders locked out, what could she and Gran do without a phone?

She nearly ran into him in the kitchen. Sanda sucked in a breath so hard she squeaked. He was big and hooded. He also had a knife. Strange to see such a man in the middle of the glistening white kitchen—the homey, comforting, *safe* kitchen.

From the living room came the sound of splintering wood and Grandmother screamed. Running footsteps. Something metal being kicked over. Grandmother screamed again. "Shut your mouth, lady. I said, *shut it.*" The voice—though not the tone—was vaguely familiar. "Now where is that prissy little wimp?"

"I got her in here," called the man in the kitchen. He caught Sanda's upper arm in a grip as painful as any physical punishment she had ever received and marched her into the living room.

Grandma looked okay, just scared and very small next to the fellow holding her. Even with the hooded mask, Sanda thought she recognized him. It was the clerk from the little grocery store they shopped at. Behind them, the electric heater lay facedown, its cherry coils buried in the carpet.

The clerk shook Grandma at every syllable he spoke. "All right, lady. There's just one thing we want. Show us where they are and we'll go." This was the sense of what he said, though not the precise words. Many of those words were ones Sanda knew but had previously heard only from the rougher girls in gym class, where there was much smirking and giggling over their meaning. Here, said in deadly anger, those words were themselves an assault.

"I've a couple rings—"

"Lady, you're rich and we know how you got it."

Grandma's voice was quaking. "No, just my husband's investments." That was true: Sanda had overheard Grandma telling Sanda's surprised father the size of Rex Beauchamp's estate.

The clerk slapped her. "Liar. Two or three times a year you bring a diamond into Arcata Gems. A rough diamond. Your husband was the big-time explorer." There was sarcasm in the words. "Somewhere he musta found quite a pile of 'em. Either that or you got a diamond machine in your basement." He laughed at his joke, and suddenly the girl saw through several mysteries. *Not in the basement—upstairs.*

"We know you got 'em. We want 'em. We want 'em. We want 'em. We—" As he spoke, he slapped her rhythmically across the face. Someone was screaming; it was Sanda. She barely knew what she did then. From the corner of her eye she saw Grandma's *meri* lying on the sewing table. She swept it up with her free hand and pivoted swiftly around her captor, swinging the flattened stone club into the clerk's chest just below the ribs.

The man went down, dragging Grandmother to her knees. He sat on the floor for several seconds, his mouth opening and closing soundlessly. Finally he could take great, gasping breaths. "I'll. Kill. Her." He came to his feet, one hand still on Grandma's shoulder, the other weaving a knife back and forth in front of Sanda.

The other fellow grabbed the *meri* from Sanda's hand and pulled the girl back from the clerk. "No. Remember."

The clerk pressed his knife hand gently against his chest, and winced. "Yeah." He pushed Grandmother down onto the sofa and approached Sanda.

"Lady, I'm gonna cut on your kid till you start talking." He barely touched the knife to Sanda's forearm. It was so sharp that a thin line of red oozed, yet the girl scarcely felt it.

Grandma came off the sofa. "Stop! Don't touch her!"

He looked around at her. "Why?"

"I-I'll show you where the diamonds are."

The clerk was genuinely disappointed. "Yeah?"

"You won't hurt us afterwards?"

The one holding Sanda touched his mask. "All we want are the diamonds, lady."

Pause. "Very well. They're in the kitchen."

Seconds later, Mrs. Beauchamp showed them where. She opened the cabinet where she kept flour and sugar and withdrew a half-empty bag of rock salt. The clerk grabbed it from her, then swept the salt and pepper and sugar bowl off the kitchen table. He carefully upended the bag of rock salt and spread it so that no piece sat on another. "Do you see anything?" he said.

The other man spent several minutes examining the table. "One," he said, and moved a tiny stone to the edge of Grandmother's china rack. It looked glassy except for a milky haze on its surface. "Two." He looked some more.

No one spoke. The only sounds were the clerk's harsh breathing and the steady throbbing of rain against the windows. The night beyond the windows was black. The nearest neighbors were hidden beyond trees.

"That's all. Just the two."

The clerk's obscenities would have been screamed if his chest had been up to it. In a way, his quiet intensity was more frightening. "You sold ten of these the last three years. You claim you're down to *two*?"

Grandma nodded, her chin beginning to quiver.

"Do you believe her?"

"I don't know. But maybe it doesn't matter. We've got all night, and

I want to cut on that girl. Either way, I'll get what's due me." He motioned with his knife. "C'mere you."

"Just as well. I think they recognize you." The vise on Sanda's upper arm tightened and she found herself pushed toward the point of the knife.

"Smell something burning?" her captor said abruptly.

The clerk's eyes widened, and he stepped out of the kitchen to look down the hall. "Jesus, yes! The carpet and some newspapers. It's that heater."

"Unplug the heater. Roll the carpet over it. This place burns, we got nothing to search!"

"I'm trying." There were awkward shuffling sounds. "Need help."

The man holding Sanda looked at the two women. She saw his hand tighten on his knife. "I know where the rest of them are," Grandma suddenly said.

He grabbed her, too, and hustled them to the basement door. Sanda was shoved roughly through. She crashed backwards against the rack of brooms and fell down the steps, into the darkness. A second later Grandma's frail body fell on top of hers. The door slammed, and they heard the key turn in the lock.

The two of them lay dazed for a second. Next to her face, Sanda could smell the moldy damp of the stairs. Part of a mop seemed to be strung across her neck. "Are you okay, Grandmother?"

Her answer was immediate. "Yes. Are you?"

"Yes."

Grandma gave an almost girlish laugh. "You make rather a good pillow to land on, dear." She got up carefully and switched on the stairs light. There was that impish smile on her face. "I think they may have outsmarted themselves."

She led Sanda farther down the steps and switched on another light. The girl looked around the small basement, made even smaller by the old sample crates and Grandma's laundry area. There was no way out of here, no windows set at ground level. What was Grandmother thinking of?

The older woman turned and slammed shut the interior hatch that Grandfather had mounted in the stairwell. Sanda began to see what she had in mind: The top of the stairs could be locked from the kitchen side, but this heavy door was now locked from their side!

Grandmother walked across the floor toward a stack of cases that sat under the living room. "Rex wanted this to be his laboratory. He was going to refrigerate—actually try to imitate polar conditions. That turned out to be much too expensive, but the heavy doors he installed can be useful. . . . Help me with these crates, please, Sanda."

They were heavy, but Grandma didn't care if they went crashing to the floor. In minutes Sanda saw that they were uncovering another stairway, one that must open into the living room. "If they can put the fire out as easily as they should, then we'll simply wait them out. Even a small fire can be seen from the street and I'll wager the Fire Department will be here straight away. But if the fire wins free and the whole house goes . . ." There were new tears streaking her face. She swayed slightly on her feet, and Sanda realized that the older woman had been limping.

Sanda put her arm about her grandmother's waist. "Are you sure you're okay?"

Grandma looked at her and smiled. Her face was a little bit puffy, swelling from the blows to it. "Yes, dear." She bowed her head and touched her front teeth. "But my dentist will be overjoyed by all this, I fear."

Grandmother turned back to the door and wiped at a quartz port set in the metal. "I still don't know why Rex wanted this stair up to the living room. P'raps he just felt obligated to use both the surplus hatches he bought."

Sanda looked through the tiny window. It was a viewpoint on the living room she had never imagined. They were looking through the decorative drapes that covered the wall behind the sofa.

The robbers had pulled off their masks and were madly dragging furniture—including the sofa—away from the blaze. They had rolled the carpet over the fire, but it was still spreading, leaking out toward the TV and the Maori statues on the far wall.

The floor itself was starting to burn.

The men in the living room saw this, too. The clerk shouted something that came only faintly through the insulated walls. Then they ran out of view. The fire spread up the legs of the TV and onto a Maori statue. For a moment, the figure blazed in a halo of light. Flames played from the twisted hands, from the thrusting tongue.

The lights in the basement went out, but the red glow through the quartz window still lit Grandma's face. "They couldn't save it. They couldn't save it." Her voice was barely audible.

Heavy banging at the other hatch, the one to the kitchen. Sanda knew that was no rescue, but murder denied. The banging ceased almost immediately; these two witnesses would live to tell their story.

She looked back through the quartz. The fire was spreading along the far wall. Their side of the living room was untouched. Even the drapes seemed undamaged.

"I've got to go out there, Sanda."

"No! . . . I-I'm sorry, Gran. If they couldn't save it, we can't."

"Not the house, Sanda. I'm going to save the Gemstone." There was the strain of physical exertion in her voice, but the girl couldn't see what she was doing. Only Grandma's face was lit by the rose and yellow light. She was not pushing on the door; Sanda could see that much.

"You can't risk your life for diamonds, Grandma. Dad and Mom have money. You can stay—"

The older woman grunted as though pushing at something. "You don't understand. The diamonds have been wonderful. I could never have lived so free with just the money Rex left me. Poor Rex. The Gemstone was his greatest find. He knew that. But he kept it in a freezer down here, and never saw the miracle it really is.

"Sanda, the Gemstone is not just a thing that eats plastic flowers and passes diamonds. It is not just a thing that sends out feelings of cold and emptiness—those are simply its memories of Antarctica.

"Next to you and your dad—and your mum—I value the Gemstone more than anything. When I put my hand on it, it glows back at me—you felt that, too. It is friendly, though it scarce seems to know me. But when I touch it long enough, I feel Rex there, I feel the times he must have touched the stone . . . and almost I feel that he is touching me."

She grunted; Sanda heard something spinning on oiled bearings. There was a popping noise from the hatch and Sanda guessed it could be pushed open now.

"The fire is along the outer wall. I have room to get to the stairs. I can pick up the Gemstone and get out down the backstairs—on the other side of the house from the fire. You'll be safe staying here. Rex was very thorough. The basement is an insulated hull, even over the ceiling. The house could burn right down and you'd not be harmed."

"No, I'm going with you."

Grandmother took a breath. There was the look on her face of someone who must do something very difficult. "Sanda. *If you ever loved me*, you will obey me now; stay here."

Sanda's arms hung numb at her sides. If you *ever* loved me . . . It was many years before she could live with her inaction of the next few seconds.

Grandma pushed the door back. The drapes parted and there was a wave of heat, like standing near a bonfire. The air was full of popping and cracking, but the drapes that swung into the opening were not yet singed. Gran pulled the cloth away and pushed the door shut. Through the quartz window Sanda saw her moving quickly toward the stairs. She started up them—was almost out of sight—when she looked down, puzzlement on her face.

Sanda saw the fire burning out of the wall beneath her an instant before the stairs collapsed and Grandmother disappeared. The house groaned and died above her.

"Grand*ma*!" Sanda crashed against the metal door, but it would not open now; ceiling timbers had fallen across it. The scene beyond the quartz was no longer recognizably a home. The fire must have burned behind the walls and up under the stairwell. Now much of the second floor had collapsed onto the first. Everything she could see was a glowing jumble. The heat on her face was like looking through a kiln window. Nothing out there could live.

And still the heat increased. The fallen center of the upstairs left a natural flue through the skylight. For a few moments the heat and rushing winds lived in equilibrium, and the flames steadied to uniform brilliance. Brief stillness in hell.

She would have felt it sooner if she had been waiting for it, or if its mood hadn't been so different from all that went on about her: a chime of happiness, clear and warm. The feeling of sudden freedom and escape from cold.

Then she saw it: Its surface was no longer black and gray. It glowed like the ends of the burning timbers, but with overtones of violet that seemed to penetrate its body. And now that it moved, she could see the complete regularity of its shape. The Gemstone was a cross between a four-legged starfish and a very small pillow. It moved nimbly, gracefully through the red jumble beyond the quartz window, and Sanda could feel its exuberance.

Grandfather had been wrong. Grandmother had been wrong. The cold and desolation it had broadcast were not memories of antarctic centuries, but a wordless cry against what *still* was cold and dark to it. How could she have missed it before? Daddy's dog, Tyrann, did the same thing: locked out on a misty winter night he keened and keened his misery for hours.

Gemstone had been alone and cold much, much longer.

And now—like a dog—it frisked through the brightness, eager and curious. It stopped and Sanda felt its puzzlement. It pushed down into the chaos that had been the stairs. The puzzlement deepened, shaded into hurt. Gemstone climbed back out of the rubble.

It had no head, no eyes, but what she saw in its mind now was clear; it felt her and was trying to find where she was hiding. When it "saw" her it was like a searchlight suddenly fixing on a target; all its attention was on her.

Gemstone scuttled down from its perch and swiftly crossed the ruins. It climbed the wood that jammed shut the door and—from inches away—seemed to peer at her. It scampered back and forth along the timber, trying to find some way in to her. Its mood was a mix of abject friendliness, enthusiasm, and curiosity that shifted almost as fast as the glowing colors of its body. Before tonight it had taken minutes to change from one mood to another; before, it had been frozen to near unconsciousness. All those centuries before, it had been barely alive.

Sanda saw that it was scarcely more intelligent than she imagined dogs to be. It wanted to touch her and didn't realize the death that would bring. Gemstone climbed back to the little window and touched a paw to the quartz. The quartz grew cloudy, began to star. Sanda felt fear, and Gemstone immediately pulled back.

It didn't touch the quartz again, but rubbed back and forth across the surface of the door. Then it settled against the door and let Sanda "pet" it with her mind. This was a little like touching it had been before. But now the memories and emotions were deeper and changed quickly at her wish:

There was Grandmother, alive again. She felt Grandma's hand resting on her (its) back. Wistful sometimes, happy sometimes, lonely often. Before that there was another, a man. Grandpa. Bluff, inquisitive, stubborn. Before that . . . Colder than cold, not really conscious, Gemstone sensed light all around the horizon and then dark. Light and darkness. Light and darkness. Antarctic summer and antarctic winter. In its deadened state, the seasons were a flickering that went on for time the little mind in the starfish body could not comprehend.

And before that . . .

Wonderful warmth, even nicer than now. Being cuddled flesh against flesh. Being valued. There were many friends, personalities strange to Sanda but not unknowable. They all lived in a house that moved, that visited many places—some warm and pleasant, some not. It remembered the coldest. In its curiosity, Gemstone wandered away from the house, got so very cold that when the friends came out to search, they could not find. Gemstone was lost.

And so the long time of light-and-dark, light-and-dark had begun.

THE PURE, EVEN HELL OF THE FIRE LASTED ONLY A FEW MINUTES. GEMSTONE whimpered in her mind as the walls began to fall, and the wind-driven cycle of flame faltered. The hottest places were in the center of what had been the living room, but Gemstone remained propped against Sanda's door, either for her company or in hopes she could bring back the warm.

Rain was winning against fire. Steam and haze obscured the glowing ruins. There might have been sirens.

She felt Gemstone chill and slowly daze. Its tone was now the nearly mindless dirge of all the weeks before. Sanda slid to the floor. And cried.

"Gemstone" takes place in 1957. I've wondered what became of Sanda and her wonderful pet. I suppose there is some room for sequels. One idea sticks in my mind: Sanda ends up an artist, living in Arizona. She specializes in pottery. She is admired for the brushwork she does while the glaze is hot. She has the most marvelous collection of kilns, all connected by narrow tunnels to a large one that is always fired. . . .

JUST PEACE

I've had only two stories that were collaborations. Ordinarily, collaboration is a good way to work just as hard as ever—but only get paid half as much. (Keith Laumer summed up the problems in the title of his essay for the SFWA *Bulletin*: "How to Collaborate without Getting Your Head Shaved.") There were these two times though. Once was with my then-wife, Joan D. Vinge: in "The Peddler's Apprentice," I wrote the first part, got bogged down, and Joan finished it. The circumstances of the other collaboration were quite different: my friend Bill Rupp and I simply wanted to write an adventure story. We plotted the thing together, using various ideas we had been collecting. For instance, we both admired Poul Anderson's approach to conflict adventures, the way he acknowledges the right that adheres in some wise to almost any cause. Bill wrote the first draft, and I revised it. John W. Campbell bought it for *Analog*. (Sadly, this was the last sale I ever made to John; he died just a few months later.)

In its orbit about Jupiter, an artificial star flickered briefly, its essence oscillating between matter and energy. The complex disturbance generated by those pulsations spread out from the Solar System—in violation of several classical theories of simultaneity—at many times the speed of light.

Nineteen light-years away, a receiver on the second planet of the star delta Pavonis picked the signal out from the universal static of ultrawave radiation and . . .

Chente felt a slight, though abrupt, lurch as gravity fell to New Canadian normal. That was the only sign that the transmission had been accomplished. The cage's lights didn't even flicker.

("We can't know, of course, the exact conditions which faced your predecessor. His report is eighteen months overdue, however, so that we must expect the worst.")

Chente took a deep breath and stood, feeling for the moment exaltation: three times before he had sat in the transmission cage, and each time he had been disappointed.

(". . . believe you are ready, Chente. What can I say to a man about to travel nineteen light-years in an instant? For that matter, what will I say to the man who remains behind?")

The exit was behind his chair. Chente hit the control plate, and the hatch slid silently into the wall. Beyond was the control cubby of a ramscoop starship. Chente scrambled through the opening and stood in the small space behind the control saddle. The displays were all computer driven, and rather quaint. Neat lettering above one of the consoles read: INTERNATIONAL BUSINESS MACHINES OF CANADA—the original Canada back on Earth. Chente had spent hundreds of hours working out in a mock-up of this famous control room, but the real thing was subtly different. Here the air felt completely dead, sterile. The mock-up on Earth had been occupied by occasional technicians, whereas no one but Chente's predecessor had been in this room for more than a century. And it had been more than three centuries since the robot craft had sailed out of the Solar System.

A monument to empires passed, Chente thought as he slipped onto the saddle.

"Who goes there?" a voice asked in English.

Chente looked at the computer's video pickup. He had had plenty of practice with a similar think-box on Earth: the mech was barely sentient, but the best mankind could produce in the old days. Chente's superiors had theorized that after three hundred twenty years such a brain would be more than a little irrational. The human responded carefully, "Vicente Quintero y Jualeiro, agent of the Canadian Hegemony." He placed his ID before the pickup. Of course it was a fake—the Canadian Hegemony had ceased to exist one hundred years earlier. But the computer probably wouldn't accept any more recent authority.

"I have already received Vicente Quintero y Jualeiro."

It really is senile, thought Chente. "That is so. But another copy of Quintero remains on Earth, and was used for this latest transmission."

A long pause. "Very well, sir, I am at your disposal. I so rarely receive visitors, I— You require a situation report, of course." The vocoder's pleasant baritone assumed a sing-song tone, as if repeating some long-considered excuse. "After my successful landing on delta Pavonis II, I sent Earth a favorable report on the planet— Sir, most pertinent criteria *were* favorable. I see now my mistake . . . but it would have taken a new program to avoid making it. Shortly thereafter I received an initial transmission of fifteen hundred colonists together with enough ova and sperm to breed a colony. By 2220, the New Canada colony had a population of 8,250,000.

"Then . . . then the great planetary disturbance occurred."

Chente held up his hand. "Please. The Hegemony received your reports through 2240. We've reestablished contact to find out what's happened since then."

"Yes, sir. But I must report all the truth first. I wish no one to say that I have failed. I warned of the core collapse several weeks before it occurred. Yet still, most of the colony was destroyed. The disruption was so great, in fact, that the very continental outlines were changed.

"Sir, I have done my best to help the survivors, but their descendants have regressed terribly, have even formed warring nation-states. These groups covet every fragment of surviving technology. They stole my communication bombs so that I could no longer report to Earth. They have even attacked my own person, and attempted to cannibalize me. Fortunately my defenses are—" The computer broke off, and remained silent.

"What's the matter?"

"A small party is now climbing the hill I stand upon."

"Do they look hostile?"

"They are always hostile toward me, but this group is not armed. I suspect they saw the coronal discharge that accompanied your arrival. They probably drove here from Freetown."

"A city?" said Chente.

"Yes, a city-state which has remained neutral in the current warfare. It's built over the ruins of First-landing, the settlement I helped to found. Would you like to see our visitors?"

Chente leaned forward. "Of course!"

A large screen lit up to show a grass-covered slope. Coming up the hill toward the ship were twelve men and a woman. Beyond them, beyond the hill, the ocean stretched away unbroken to the horizon.

"¡Madre de Dios!" Chente gasped. On the old maps this hilltop was 3,500 kilometers inland. The continental outlines certainly had been changed by the catastrophe.

"Say again, sir?" said the computer.

"Never mind." Chente ignored the view and concentrated on the people who would soon be questioning him.

They made an interesting study in contrasts. To the left, a man and woman walked almost in lock step, though they remained discreetly apart. The man was dressed in simple black trousers and a short coat. His hat was stiff and wide-brimmed. The woman wore a long black dress that revealed nothing of her from below the neck. Her reddish hair was drawn back and tied with a black ribbon, and her grim face showed no sign of makeup. The two short men in the center wore jumpsuits, apparently modeled after the original colonists' dress. To the right, eight nearly naked men bent beneath an elaborate litter carrying a young male. As the group stopped, the litter was lowered, and he stepped jauntily to earth. The fellow's upper body was heavily oiled. He wore skin-tight breeches with an enormous codpiece. The grimly dressed couple on the left looked straight ahead, trying to avoid the sight of their companion on the far right.

"You see the cultural fragmentation that has occurred here on New Canada," the computer remarked.

"How far are they now?"

"Twenty meters."

"I may as well meet them. Off load the equipment that came through with me."

"Yes, sir." A hatch slid open and he entered the air lock beyond. Seconds later he was standing ankle-deep in turquoise grass, beneath a pale, pale blue sky. A slow breeze pushed with remarkable force against his jumpsuit: sea level air pressure on New Canada was almost twice Earth's. He was about to greet his visitors when the somber woman spoke, her voice tense with surprise.

"Chente!"

Chente bowed. "You have the advantage of me, ma'am. I take it you know my predecessor."

"The past tense would be more appropriate, Freeman Quintero. Your twin was murdered more than a year ago," the fellow in the skin-tight pants said, and smiled at the woman. Chente saw that in spite of his athletic build and flamboyant dress, the man was in his forties. The woman, on the other hand, seemed much younger than she had at a distance. Now she kept silent, but her companion said, "It was one of *your* ships he died on, you slave-holding animal." The shirtless dandy just shrugged.

"Please, gentlemen." The fat man in the center spoke up. "Recall that the condition of your presence here requires a certain mutual cordiality"—glares flickered back and forth between Shirtless and the puritans—"or at least courtesy. Mr. Quintero, I am Bretaign Flaggon, mayor of Freetown and governor of Wundlich Island. Welcome.

"The lady is Citizeness Martha Blount, ambassadress to Wundlich from the Commonwealth of New Providence, and," he rushed on as if trying to make both the introductions at once, "this gentleman is Bossman Pier Balquirth, Ambassador to Wundlich from the Ontarian Confederacy."

The woman seemed to have recovered from her initial surprise. Now she spoke with solemn formality. "New Providence regards you as our honored guest and citizen. Our nation awaits your—"

"Not so fast, Mistress Blount," Bossman Pier interrupted. "You aren't the only people brimming over with hospitality. I believe Freeman Quintero would be much more comfortable in a society which does not condemn dancing and music as a crime against nature."

"Please!" Flaggon repeated, "let's not have propaganda spoil the arrival of a visitor from the Mother World. As mayor, I wish to offer you any assistance you require, Mr. Quintero. I, uh . . . *Ah*! I will hold a banquet in your honor tonight. Of course, we will invite guests from both New Providence and Ontario." He sighed unhappily, recognizing the inevitable. "You can settle things then."

A faint hissing announced the opening of the freight port in the ship's hull. A lift slid down the ancient metal surface with Chente's "luggage."

"Mr. Quintero y Jualeiro," the computer's vocoder boomed from a hidden speaker, "have you further orders at this time?"

"No. I will keep in touch."

"Beyond this hill I cannot protect you, sir."

"I'll survive."

"Yes, sir," doubtfully.

"Damned machine," Bossman Pier said softly. His perpetual grin had vanished. "It should be helping us. Instead it shoots at anyone trying to make entrance. We had to leave most of our boys at the base of the hill or we couldn't have got this close. Can I help you with that equipment?"

Chente stepped between Balquirth's servants and the freight lift.

"No thanks. I can carry it myself."

The Ontarian smiled knowingly. "Perhaps you will survive, after all."

As they walked down the hillside, Vicente kept silent. *So I died here,* he thought. Well, that was no great surprise. But that he had been killed by the very colonists he had been sent to help made his mission seem doubly difficult. What had happened on New Canada these last one hundred thirty years?

The lush grass on the hilltop thrived everywhere. He was no botanist, but it looked like some terrestrial type brought by the first colonists. Other vegetation was less familiar. Large ferns and broad-leafed plants stood in scattered clumps. The trees looked like giant flowers: their trunks rose straight and tall, with purple foliage sprouting from the top. Except for the grass, the land had a strong Jurassic aspect. Chente half expected a large reptile to pop out of the bushes.

They had reached the base of the hill when his expectation materialized. A meter-wide *something* flew low over their heads, then circled above a nearby ridge.

"A gretch," Bretaign Flaggon said. "They're really quite common around here. That poor little fellow must have lost his mother."

The "poor little fellow" looked like a cross between a reptile and a buzzard. Chente grimaced. A nice place for a lifelong vacation. He'd never cared for paleontology.

At the base of the hill they stopped by a large three-wheeled vehicle and a group of armed men with bicycles. The powered tricycle was driven from a bench above and behind the passenger compartment. A brass tank and a piston cylinder sat below the driver's seat.

"Steamer?" Vicente asked, as he climbed into the cab.

"Quite right," Balquirth said. He swung up onto his slave-powered litter and looked down at Quintero. "If you're wise, you'll use something time-tested." He patted the satin pillows.

Flaggon and his driver climbed onto the upper bench, while Martha Blount and her aide got in with Chente. The armed bicyclists started down the road, and the auto got off with a jerk and a jump. The deep cushions could not disguise the absence of an adequate suspension, and acrid black smoke drifted from the fire box into the passenger compartment. Behind them, Bossman Pier's bearers were having no trouble keeping pace.

Minutes later the auto was puffing down a long slope that gave an overview of Freetown. The city was built around a crescent-shaped bay protected on the north by a huge granitic outcropping. Except for that headland, the bay was open to the sea.

"Have many storms?" he said to Martha.

"Dreadful ones," the woman answered, unsmiling. "But the tsunamis are worse—that's why the ships you see are anchored so far out. They come in to port only for loading."

The city rested on a sequence of terraces that climbed steeply up from the water's edge. Each terrace was split down the middle by a narrow, copper-paved street, while steps and coppered ramps provided communication between one level and the next.

Chente noticed that on the first three tiers the buildings were mostly warehouses and sheds. Nearly all these structures were made of wood and had a brand-new look. But above the third tier, the buildings were of massive stone construction, eroded and weather beaten. The most peculiar thing about the stone buildings was their long, narrow shape, their sharp, pointed ends. The prows of those stone arcs pointed uniformly out to sea.

Martha Blount followed his gaze. "The Freetowners use those wooden buildings for temporary storage of sea freight. They can count on everything in the first three terraces being leveled every two years or so. Beyond the third level, the tsunamis attenuate and the water breaks over the bows of the buildings."

The auto turned onto the fourth tier's main street, and slowed even further to get through the swarm of Freetowners moving to and from the stone-encased bazaars.

Chente shook his head in wonder. "You people certainly have managed to adapt."

"Adapt!" The New Providencian ambassador turned toward him, for the first time showing an emotion: rage. "We were nearly wiped out in the Cataclysm. That computer-driven monster up there on the hill gave us a real prize. With an advanced technology a colony on this planet could get along, but with that technology lost the place is a Hell. Adapt? Look—" She pointed out of the cab. They were passing near the edge of the terrace now, by blocks of gray rubble, stumpy walls. "Life on New Canada is a constant struggle simply to maintain ourselves. And all the while we're weighed down by those sybarites." She waved her hand back toward Bossman Pier's litter, some fifteen meters away. "They drain our resources. They fight us at every turn . . ." Her voice trailed off and she sat looking at Chente. For a moment some new emotion flickered across her face, but then she became impassive. Chente suddenly realized the reason for her silence: it was the second time around for Martha. No doubt she had sat in this same vehicle eighteen months earlier, and had had the same conversation with his predecessor.

Martha's hand moved toward him, then retreated. She said softly, "You really are Chente . . . alive again." Her tone became businesslike. "Be more careful, this time, will you please? Your knowledge, your equipment . . . many people would kill to get them." She was silent the rest of the way into town.

At sunset the heavy layers of dust in New Canada's atmosphere transformed the pale-blue sky into orange, red, and greenish brown. From where Chente sat within the Freetown banquet hall, the sky light shone through narrow, horizontal slits cut high up in the west wall to play gentle pastels of orange and green down upon the waiters and chattering guests. It was a most colorful tribute to volcanism.

The sky light faded slowly toward gray as the last unpleasant course of the meal was served. Above them, electric lamps mounted on large silver wheels were lit. Clusters of rubies and emeralds hung like clouds of colored stars around the glowing filaments. Occasionally the earth trembled faintly, causing the wheels to sway as if a slight breeze touched them.

The meal over, Bretaign Flaggon rose to deliver "a few words of welcome to our star-crossed [sic] visitor." Chente couldn't decide whether the phrase was a pun or a malaprop. The speech droned on and eventually the Earthman succeeded in ignoring it.

The hall's wide floor was covered from wall to wall with what could only be gold. The soft yellow metal behaved like some slow sea beneath the weight of the banquet tables and constant passage of human feet: tiny ripples barely a centimeter high stood frozen in its surface. New Canada had everything the Spanish Conquistadores had ever dreamed of. But this virtue was symtomatic of a serious vice. Heavy metals were plentiful near the planet's surface simply because New Canada's interior was much more poorly differentiated than Earth's. The starship's computer had reported this fact to its makers on first landing here, but had failed to notice that the process of core formation was ongoing. The cataclysm that hit the colony one hundred fifty years earlier was evidence of this continuing process. The abundance of metallic salts on the surface meant that less than one percent of New Canada's land area could be used for farming. And those same salts made the sea life uniformly poisonous. In contrast to the opulent banquet hall, the food served had been scarcely more than a spicy gruel.

"... Mr. Quintero." Applause sounded as Flaggon finished talking. The mayor motioned for Chente to rise and speak. The Earthman stood and bowed briefly. The applause was equally enthusiastic from the three groups seated at the horseshoe banquet table. On his right sat the Ontarian delegation, consisting of Bossman Pier, three associates, and a crowd of scantily dressed odalisques—all ensconced on piles of wide, deep pillows. Chente had been placed at the middle of the horseshoe with the Freetowners, while Martha Blount and her people sat along the left leg of the horseshoe. All through the meal, while the Ontarians caroused and the Freetowners chattered, the New Providencians had kept silent.

Finally the applause died, and people waited. From above them the tiny lights burned fiercely, but the stark shadows they cast held abysmal gloom. Chente saw a certain measure of fear in their attentive silence. No doubt many of them had sat right here less than two years before, and watched a man identical to the one they saw now. Intellectually they might accept the idea of duplicative transport, but historians had assured Chente that without a lifetime of experience no one could really accept such a thing. To his audience Chente was a man come back from the dead. Perhaps he could take advantage of this fear.

"I will be brief, as most of you will have heard this speech before." There was an uneasy movement and various exchanges of glances. Bossman Pier seemed the only one left with a smile on his face. "Your planet is undergoing a core collapse. A century ago a core tremor sank half a continent and virtually destroyed your civilization. Recently Earth has been able to reestablish communications with the starship on the hill behind Freetown. The link we have established is a tenuous one and you can't expect material aid. But Earth does have knowledge it can place at your disposal. Ultimately the core collapse will proceed to completion, and about ten million 'Cataclysms' worth of energy will be released. If this happens all at once, no life above the microbe level will be left on the planet. But, if it happens uniformly over a million year period, you would never even be aware of the change. From the frequency of earthquakes, you know that the latter possibility has already been ruled out. My mission is to discover where between these two extremes the truth lies. For it is entirely possible that a future Cataclysm will be powerful enough to wreck your civilization as it is now, yet mild enough so that with adequate forewarning and preparation you can survive."

Flaggon bobbed his head. "We understand, sir. And, as we did with your predecessor, we will cooperate to the limit of our resources."

Chente decided to pounce on the double meaning in Flaggon's inept phrasing. "Yes, I've heard about the splendid help you gave my predecessor. He is dead, I've been told." He waved down Flaggon's stammered clarification. "Ladies and gentlemen, someone among you killed me. That was an act that threatened all of New Canada. If I am killed again, there may be no more replacements, and you will face the core collapse in ignorance." Chente wondered briefly if he hadn't just invited his assassination with that last threat, but it was too late to retract it.

The distressed Flaggon again pledged his help. Both Balquirth and Martha Blount chorused similar promises.

"Very well, I'll need transportation for an initial survey. From my discussion with the ship's computer before this banquet, I've decided that the best place to start is the islands that were formerly the peaks of the Heavenraker Mountains."

Martha Blount came to her feet. "Citizen Quintero, one of our Navy's finest dirigibles is tied down here at Freetown. We could be ready to go in twenty-two hours, and it won't take more than another day to reach the Heavenraker Islands." On the other side of the horseshoe, Balquirth cleared his throat noisily and stood up. Martha Blount rushed on. "Don't . . . don't make the same mistake the first Quintero did. He accepted Ontarian hospitality rather than ours, only to die on an Ontarian ship."

Chente looked at the Bossman.

"Her story is true, but misleading," Balquirth said easily. He had the air of someone telling a lie that he expected no one to believe—or else a self-evident truth that needed no earnest protestations to support itself. "The first Quintero had the good judgment to use Ontarian transportation. But his death occurred when the ship we assigned him was attacked by the forces of some other state." He looked across the table at Martha Blount.

The Earthman didn't respond directly. "Mayor Flaggon, what's the weather like along the Heavenraker chain this time of year?"

The mayor looked to an aide, who said, "In late spring? Well, there are no hurricanes likely. Matter of fact, the Heavenrakers rarely get any bad storms. But the underground 'weather' is something else again. Freetown alone loses three or four ships a year out there—smashed by tsunamis as they sail close to shore."

"In that case I'd prefer to go by aircraft."

Balquirth shrugged amiably. "Then I must leave you to the clutches of Mistress Blount. I don't have a single flier in port, and Mayor Flaggon doesn't have a single flier in his state."

"Your concern is appreciated in any case, Bossman. Citizen Blount, I'd like to discuss my plans in more detail with your people."

"Tomorrow?" She seemed close to a triumphant smile.

"Fine." Vicente began to sit down, then straightened. "One more thing. According to the starship's computer, all nine communications bombs are missing from their storage racks up on the hill."

In order to generate ultrawave distortions matter must needs be annihilated. Chente referred to the specially constructed nuclear bombs whose detonation could be modulated to carry information at superlight speeds. Such devices lacked the "band width" to transmit the pattern of a human being—Earth's government used the tiny star that orbited where Callisto had once been for that job. Nevertheless, each of the communication bombs could be set to generate the equivalent of ten megatons of TNT, so they could do considerable damage if they were not hoisted into space prior to use.

The silence lengthened. Finally Chente said coldly, "I see. Your nation-states are playing strategic deterrence. That's a dangerous game, you recall. It cost Earth more than three hundred million lives a few centuries back. Your colony is in enough trouble without it."

His listeners nodded their agreement, but Chente saw—with a sick feeling—that his words were no more than platitudes to them.

THE NEW PROVIDENCIAN AIRSHIP *DILIGENCE* FLEW SOUTH FOR A DAY AND A half before it reached the first of the Heavenrakers. Chente saw a small village and a few farms in a sheltered bay near the coast, but the rest of the island was naked black rock. This was the first stop on a tour that would take them over 2,700 kilometers to the East Fragge, the Greenland-sized island that had once been the eastern end of the largest New Canadian continent. Chente had chosen this course since he wanted a baseline of observations along the planet's equator, and the Heavenrakers were the most convenient landmasses stretching along such a path. The survey went quickly, thanks to the help of the islanders, though they seemed happy only when the *Diligence* and its guns were preparing to depart.

Three days later the dirigible hung in the clear blue sky over the west coast of the Fragge. All around them thunder sounded. For hundreds of kilometers along the coast they could see tiny rivulets of cheery-colored molten rock dribbling off into the surf, converting the water into a low-lying fog beneath them. Looking inland at the extent of the frozen lava, Chente could see that the land-forming process had added thousands of square kilometers to the area.

Quintero turned to his companion at the railing. Martha Blount hadn't really changed in these last four days, but she had been revealed in a new aspect. For one thing, she had traded her full-length dress for a gray jumpsuit that covered her but hinted at a lot more than the dress had. From their discussions on the journey out he had found her to have a quick and lively mind that belied her outward reserve and con-vinced him that she had earned her high position. At times he found her interest in his equipment and plans somewhat too intense, and her political views too rigid, but he knew better than to expect anything else under the circumstances. And the more he knew of her, the more certain he was that her presence here was not motivated strictly by political interest: there had been something between Martha and the first Chente.

He gestured at the red and black landscape shimmering in the su-perheated air below them. "Are you sure you still want to come down with my landing party?"

She nodded. "I certainly do. It's not as dangerous as it looks. We'll be going many kilometers inland before we set down. I'm—doing a little reconnaissance here myself. I've never been in this part of the world."

FURTHER CONVERSATION BECAME IMPOSSIBLE AS THE NUCLEAR JETS LIT UP TO angle the *Diligence* down toward the black ridges that thrust up between the rivulets of fire. The jets were just one of many anachronisms in the New Providencian military machine. Apparently they had been salvaged from one of the colony's original helicopters. With them, the dirigible could make nearly fifty kilometers per hour in level flight.

The *Diligence* flew inland until the ground below was solid and cold. The airship descended rapidly, then leveled off just before its nose skid rasped across the jagged volcanic slag. Heavy grapnels were thrown out and the ship was drawn to Earth.

Vicente called to Ship's Captain Oswald, "Who'll be in charge of my ground party?"

"Flight corporal Nord," the officer said, pointing to a tall, muscular man, who together with three others was dragging explosives and equipment out of the *Diligence*'s cramped hold. "We'll stay on the ground just long enough to drop you off, Citizen Quintero. We're at the mercy of every breeze down here. We'll come back for you in twenty-two hours, unless you signal us earlier." He glanced at Martha. "Citizen Blount, I suggest you forego this landing. The country is pretty rough."

Martha looked back at him, and seemed faintly annoyed. "No, I insist."

Oswald frowned, but did not press the matter. "Very well. See you in a day or so."

Nord and two of the riflemen were the first to hit ground. Martha followed them. Then came Vicente, loaded down with his own special equipment. Two more riflemen with the explosives brought up the rear.

The landing site was a flat area at the top of a narrow ridge. The seven of them clambered down the hillside as the huge aircraft's engines throttled up. By the time they reached the bottom of the ravine that followed the ridge, the *Diligence* was already floating five hundred meters over their heads.

"Let's follow this gorge inland a bit," said Quintero. "From what I could see before we landed, it should widen out to where we can do some blasting without risking an avalanche."

"Anything you say," Nord replied indifferently. Chente watched the man silently as the other moved on ahead. One way or another, this would not be a routine exploration.

THE NEW PROVIDENCIANS SPENT MOST OF THE AFTERNOON SETTING OFF EXplosives in the slag. Their firecrackers were bulky and heavy, and the work went slowly. The bombs didn't amount to more than half a ton of TNT, a microscopically small charge to obtain any information about conditions within the planet. Fortunately Chente's instruments didn't measure mechanical vibrations as such, but considerably more subtle effects. Even so he had to rely on coincidence counters and considerable statistical analysis to derive a picture of what went on hundreds of kilometers below.

Toward evening the sky became overcast and it began to drizzle. Chente called off their work. In fact, his survey was now complete, and his grim conclusions were beyond doubt. A stiff breeze kept anyone from suggesting that they call down the *Diligence*. Even with perfect visibility, Oswald probably couldn't have brought the airship in against that wind.

By the time they set up camp in a deep hollow—almost a cave— beneath the cliff face, they were all thoroughly soaked. Nord put two of his men on watch at the entrance to the hollow, and the rest of the party took to their sleeping bags.

As the hours passed, the rain fell more heavily, and from the west the steady hissing of the lava masked nearly all other sounds. Abruptly, the cylinder that rested in Chente's hand vibrated against his palm: someone was tampering with his equipment. Chente raised his head and looked about the cavelet. The darkness was complete. He couldn't even see the sleeping bag he lay in. But now the years of training paid off: Chente relaxed, suppressed all background noise and listened for nearby sounds. There! At least one person was standing in his immediate vicinity. The fellow's breathing was shallow, excited. Farther away, toward the equipment cache, he could now hear even fainter sounds.

Quintero slipped quietly out of the sleeping bag which he had prudently left unbuttoned and moved toward the cavelet entrance, lifting and lowering his feet precisely to avoid the irregularities he remembered in the rocky ground. He probably would have got clear anyway, as the distant hissing and the sound of rain covered whatever sounds he made. He didn't dare pick up any equipment, however; he was forced to settle on what he'd kept with him.

Twenty meters out into the rain, he turned and lay down behind a small, sharp hummock of lava. He drew his tiny pistol. Several minutes passed. These were the most cautious assassins he had ever seen. As if to rebut the thought, two of the guards' hand torches lit. Their yellow beams shone down upon his and Martha's sleeping bags. The two other guards held their rifles trained on the bags, ready to fusillade.

Before the riflemen could utter more than gasps of astonishment, Chente shouted, "Out here!" All but one of the men turned toward his voice. Chente raised his pistol and shot the one who still had his rifle pointed at the sleeping bags. There was no report or flash, but his target virtually exploded.

The hand torches were doused as everyone scrambled for cover. "Martha!" he shouted. "Get out. Run off to the side!"

He couldn't tell whether she had, but he kept up a steady covering fire, sending stone chips flying in all directions off the cavelet's entrance.

Then someone stuck one of the torches on a pole and hoisted it up. The others moved briefly into the open to fire all at once down upon his exposed position. But the Earthman got off one last shot—into the explosives.

The concussion smashed the ground up into his face, and he never heard the cliffside fall across the cavelet, entombing his enemies.

SOMEONE WAS SHAKING HIM, AND HE FELT A NOSE AND A FOREHEAD NESTLED against the back of his neck. "Chente, please don't die again, please," came Martha's voice.

Chente stirred and looked into the wet darkness. His ears were buzzing, and the left side of his head was one vast ache.

"You all right?" he asked Martha.

"Yes," she said. Her hands tightened momentarily against him, but her voice was much calmer. Now that he was conscious she retreated again into a shell of relative formality. "The others must be dead though. The whole overhang came down on them. I followed the edge of the landfall trying to find you. You were not more than a couple of meters beyond it."

"You knew about this plan beforehand?" Chente's soft question was almost a statement.

"Yes—I mean, *no*. There were rumors that our Special Weapons Group killed the first Chente in an unsuccessful attempt to take his communications bomb. I believed those rumors. We used one of our bombs in the Nuclear Exchange of Year 317. The Special Weapons people have devised new uses, new delivery systems for our two remaining bombs, but what they really need are more nukes. In the last few months, I've had reports that the Weapons people are more eager than ever to get another bomb, that they have some special need for it. When you arrived, I was sure that between the Ontarians and our Weapons Group someone would try to kill you."

Chente shook his head, trying to end the buzzing pain. The motion only made him want to be sick. Finally he said, "Their assassination attempt seems incredibly clumsy. Why didn't they just do away with me once we were airborne?"

Now the Providencian ambassador seemed completely in control of herself. She said quietly, "That was partly my doing. I knew the Weapons people were waiting for another agent to be sent from Earth. When you came through, I made sure you were assigned to an airship crewed by regular Navy men. I was sure it was safe. For years Oswald has been part of the Navy faction opposed to the Special Weapons Group. But somehow they must have got through to him, and at least a few of his crewmen. Their murder attempt was clumsy, but it was a lot more than I had expected, under the circumstances."

Chente sat up and propped his head against his hands. This morass of New Providencian intrigue was not completely unexpected, but it was ludicrous. Even if the conspirators could dig his bomb out of the avalanche, it could not be fused without a voice-code spoken by Chente himself. He saw now his mistake in not revealing that fact upon landing. He had thought that all his dire warnings about the colonists' common peril would be enough to get cooperation. The situation was all the more ludicrous since he had seen how real the danger of core collapse was.

"Martha, do you know what I discovered during my survey?"

"No." She sounded faintly puzzled by this sudden change in topic.

"In one hundred fifty years or so there will be another core tremor, about as serious as the one you call the Cataclysm. You people simply don't have time to fight among yourselves. Your only option is to co-operate, to develop a technology advanced enough to ensure your survival."

"I see . . . Then the Special Weapons Group are fools as well as murderers. We should be working together to win the Ontarian war, so we can put all our resources into preparing for the next Cataclysm."

Chente wondered briefly if he were hallucinating. He tried again to explain. "I mean the war itself must be ended; not through victory, but simply through an end of hostilities. You need the Ontarians as much as they need you."

She shook her head stubbornly. "Chente, you don't realize what a ruthless, hedonistic crew the Ontarian rulers are. Until they're eliminated, New Providence will go on bleeding, so that no steps can be taken to protect us from the next Cataclysm."

Chente sighed, realizing that further argument would get him nowhere: he knew his own planet's history too well. He changed the subject. "Are there any settlements on the Fragge?"

"No cities, but there is at least one village about five hundred kilometers southeast of here. It's in the single pocket of arable land that's been discovered on the Fragge."

"That doesn't sound too bad. If we start out before dawn, we may be able to avoid Oswald's—"

"Chente, between here and wherever that village is, there's not a single plant or animal we can eat without poisoning ourselves."

"You'd rather take your chance with Oswald?"

"Certainly. It's obvious that not everyone aboard the *Diligence* was in on this."

"Martha, I think we can make it through to that village." He felt too dizzy to explain how. "Will you come along?"

Even in the darkness, he thought he felt a certain amount of amusement in her answer. "Very well . . . I could hardly return to the *Diligence* alone, anyway. It would give away the fact that you're out here somewhere." Her hand brushed briefly across his shoulder.

They started inland at the morning's first light, following along the bottom of one of the innumerable tiny ravines cut through the black rock. A temporary but good-sized stream ran down the middle so that they had to walk along the steep, rough ground near the side of the ravine. The buzzing was gone from Chente's head, but some of the dizziness remained. He was beginning to think that his inner ear had been "tumbled" by the explosion, giving him a permanent, though mild, case of motion sickness.

Martha appeared to be in much better condition. Quintero noticed that since she had made up her mind to come along, she seemed to be doing her best to ignore the fact that they were without food, or a reliable means of navigation.

Toward noon they drank rain water from a shallow puddle in the rocks. Twice during the afternoon Chente thought he heard the engines of the *Diligence*, nearly masked by the volcanic thunder to the west. By late afternoon, he estimated they were twenty kilometers inland—excellent progress, considering the ground they were crossing. The ravine became steadily shallower, until finally they left the lava fields and crossed into a much older countryside. The cloud cover swept away and the westering sun shone down from an orange-red sky upon the savannah-like plain ahead of them. That plain was not covered by grass, but by low, multiple-rooted plants that rose like thick green spiders from the ground.

Chente glanced at the sun, and then at the girl who trudged doggedly on beside him. Her initial reserves of energy were gone now and her face was set in lines of fatigue. "Rest break," he said, as they entered the greenery. They dropped down onto plants which, despite their disquieting appearance, felt soft and resilient—something like iceplant back on Earth. The abrupt movement made the world spin giddily around Chente's head. He waited grimly until the wave of dizziness passed, then pulled an oblong case from a pocket and began fiddling. Finally Martha spoke, her tired voice devoid of sarcasm, "Some Earthside magic? You're going to materialize some food?"

"Something like that." A small screen flashed to life on the wide side of the oblong. He sharpened the image, but it was still no more than abstract art to the uninitiated: a mixed jumble of blue and green and brown. He didn't look up as he said, "Martha, did you know that the starship left several satellites in orbit before it landed on New Canada?"

She leaned closer to him, looked down at the screen. "Yes. If you know where to look you can often see them at night."

"They were put up for your colony's use, and though you no longer have receiving equipment, they are still in working order."

"And this thing—"

". . . Is reading from a synchronous satellite some 40,000 kilometers up. This picture shows most of the Fragge."

Martha's fatigue was forgotten. "We never dreamed the satellites could still work. I feel like God looking down on things this way. Now we can find that village easily."

"Yes—" Using the controls at the side of the display he began to follow the Fragge's coastline at medium resolution.

Martha spoke up again. "I think we're seeing the north coast now.

At least, the part that isn't under cloud looks like the last map I saw. The village is to the southeast of us, so you're not going to find much of anything—"

Chente frowned, looked more closely at the screen, then increased the magnification. It was as if the camera had been dropped straight toward the ground. The tiny bay at the center of the screen swelled to fill the entire display. Now they were looking down through late afternoon haze at a large natural harbor. Chente identified thirty or forty piers and a number of ships. All along the waterfront buildings cast long, incriminating shadows. He pushed a button and five tiny red lights glowed over the image of one of those buildings.

Martha was silent for a long moment. She looked more closely at the picture, and finally she said, "Those ships, they're Ontarian. They have an entire naval base hidden away there. The scum! I can imagine what they're planning: to build up a large secret reserve, and then tempt us into a major battle. Why, Chente, this changes our entire naval situation. It—" Suddenly she seemed to realize that she was not sitting in some intelligence briefing, but was instead stranded thousands of kilometers from the people who could use this discovery.

Chente made no comment, but returned the magnification to its previous level. He followed the coastline all the way around to the south and eventually found two other settlements, both small villages.

"Now let's try to find some food," he said. "If I'm oriented properly, I've got the picture centered on our location." He stepped up the magnification. On the enlarged scale they could see individual hillocks and identify the small stream they had crossed half a kilometer back. Toward the top of the picture, a collection of spikelike shadows stretched several millimeters. He magnified the image still further.

"Animals," Chente said. "They look better than two meters long."

"Then they're buzzards."

"Buzzards?"

"Yes, herbivores. The next largest thing we know about on the Fragge is a predator not much more than a meter long."

Chente grinned at her. "I think I've materialized that food for you."

She looked dubious. "Only if I can acquire a taste for copper salts in my meat."

"Perhaps we can do something about that." He looked at the scale key that flickered near the bottom of the picture. "That herd isn't more than five thousand meters away. I hadn't expected luck this good. How long till sunset? Two hours?"

Martha glanced at the sun, which hung some thirty degrees off the stony ridges behind them. "More like ninety minutes."

"We'll have buzzard soup yet. Come on."

THE PACE HE SET WAS A SLOW ONE, BUT IN THEIR PRESENT STATE IT WAS about the best they could do. The spidery vegetation caught at their feet and the ground was not nearly as level as it looked. An hour and three quarters passed. Behind them the sun had set, and only the reddish sky-glow lighted their way. Chente touched Martha's elbow, motioned her to bend low. If they spooked the herd now, they would have a hungry night. They crawled over a broad hill crest, then lay down to scan the plain beyond. They had not been too cautious: the herd was some five hundred meters down the slope, near a waterhole. Chente almost laughed; buzzards, indeed! They certainly hadn't been named by the first-generation colonists. In this light the creatures might almost have been mistaken for tall men stooped over low against the ground. Their thin wings were clasped behind their backs as they walked slowly about.

Chente chose a medium-sized animal that was browsing away from the main group. He silently took his pistol from his coverall and aimed. The beast screamed once, then ran fifteen meters, right into the water-hole, where it collapsed. The others didn't need two warnings. The herd stampeded off to Chente's right. The creatures didn't run or fly—they bounded, in long, wing-assisted leaps. The motion reminded Chente of the impalas he had seen in the San Joaquin valley. In fact, their eco-logical niche was probably similar. *In which case*, he thought, *we'd better watch out for whatever passes for lions around here.*

The humans picked themselves up, and walked slowly down toward the abandoned waterhole. Vicente waded cautiously into the shallow, acrid-smelling water. The top of the buzzard's head was blown off. It was probably dead, but he didn't take any chances with it. By the time he got the hundred-kilo carcass out of the pool the short twilight was nearly ended. Martha took over the butchering—though she remarked that buzzards didn't have much in common with the farm animals she was used to. Apparently she had not spent her whole life administrating. He watched her work in the gathering darkness, glad for her help and gladder for her presence.

When the beast was cut into small enough pieces, Chente took a short cylinder from his coveralls and fed some of the meat into it. There was a soft buzzing sound, and then he pressed a cup into Martha's hand. "Buzzard soup. Minus the heavy metal salts."

He could just make out her silhouette as she slowly raised the cup to her lips and drank. She gagged several times but got it all down. When Chente had his first taste he understood her reaction. The sludge didn't *taste* edible.

"This will keep us alive?" Martha asked hoarsely.

"For a number of weeks, anyway. Over a longer time we'd need dietary supplements." He continued feeding the buzzard to the processor, and bagging the resulting slop.

"Why hasn't Earth given us the secret of this device, Vicente? Only one percent of New Providence has soil free from metallic poisons, and Ontario is only three or four times better off. With your processor we could conquer this planet."

He shook his head. "I doubt it. The machine is a good deal more complicated than it looks. On Earth, the technology to build one has existed for less than thirty years. It's not enough to remove the heavy metals from the meat. The result would still be poisonous—or at least nonnutritious. This thing actually reassembles the protein molecules it rips apart. For the technique to be of any use to you, we'd have to ship a factory whole. You just—"

Chente heard a faint hiss above and behind him. Martha screamed. As he whirled and drew his pistol he was bowled over by something that had glided in on them in virtual silence. Chente and the birdlike carnivore spun over in the spider-weed, the thing's beak searching for his face and throat but finding Chente's upthrust forearm instead. The claws and beak were like knives thrust into his chest and arm. He fired his pistol and the explosion sent the attacker into pieces all over him.

Chente rolled to a sitting position and played fire around the unseen landscape in case there were others waiting. But all he heard was vegetation and earth exploding as the water within them was brought violently to a boil.

The whole thing hadn't lasted more than ten seconds. Now the night was silent again. Chente had the impression that his attacker had been built more like a leopard than a bird. New Canada's dense atmosphere and low gravity made some peculiar things possible.

"Are you all right, Chente?"

The question made him aware of the slick flow of blood down his forearm, of the gashes across his ribs. He swore softly. "No bones broken, but I got slashed up. Are these creatures venomous?"

"No." He heard her move close.

"Good. The first-aid equipment I've got should be enough to keep me going, then. Let's get our stuff away from this waterhole or we'll be entertaining visitors all night long." He got stiffly to his feet.

They collected the bags of processed meat and then walked three hundred meters or so from the waterhole, where they settled down in the soft spider-weed. Chente took a pain killer, and for a while everything seemed hazy and pleasant. The night was mild, even warm. The humidity had dropped steadily during the afternoon, so that the ground felt dry. A heavy breeze pushed around them, but there were no identifiable animal sounds: New Canada had yet to invent insects, or their equivalent. The sky seemed clear, but the stars were not so numerous as in an earthly sky. Chente guessed that the upper-atmosphere haze cut out everything dimmer than magnitude three or four. He looked for Sol near the head of the Great Bear but he wasn't even sure he had spotted that constellation. More than anything else, this sky made him feel far from home.

He lay back, going over in his mind what he had discovered since his arrival. When his predecessor had failed to report, they had tried to prepare him more thoroughly for his return to New Canada. But none of the historians, none of the psychologists had guessed what an extreme social system had developed here. It must have begun as an attempt by the shattered colony to reform society after the Cataclysm, forging a fragile unity from zealous allegiance. But now it bled the warring nations dry, while blinding the people to the possibility of peace, and what was worse, to the absolute necessity of working together. By rights he should now be a hero among the New Canadians. By rights they should be taking the technical advice he could give to increase what small chances there might be to survive the next core tremor. Instead, he was marooned on this forlorn continent, and the only person who had any real desire to help him was just as much an hysterical nationalist as everyone else.

But his mission still remained, even if he couldn't get the locals to cooperate in saving themselves. In spite of its terrible problems, New Canada was a more viable colony than most. After four centuries of space flight, Earth knew how rare are habitable planets. Man's colonies were few. If those failed, there would be no hope for mankind ever to expand itself beyond the Solar System, and eventually the entire race would die of its own stagnation.

Somehow, he had to end this internecine fighting, or at least eliminate the possibility of nuclear war. Somehow he had to force the colonists to fight for survival. At the moment he could see only one possibility. It was a long shot and deception was its essence. How much deception, and of whom, he tried not to consider.

"Martha?"

"Yes?" She huddled tentatively against him, all reserve finally gone.

"We're going to make for that Ontarian base rather than the village south of here."

She stiffened. "What? No! In spite of what some of my people tried to do to you, the Ontarians are still worse. Why—"

"Two reasons. First, that naval base is only two hundred fifty kilometers away, not five hundred. Second, I mean to stop this warfare between your two states. There must be peace."

"A just peace? One where we won't have our mines expropriated by the Ontarians? One where we get our fair share of the farmland? One where feudalism is outlawed?"

Chente sighed. "Yes." *Something like that.*

"Then I'll do anything to help you. But how can going to the Ontarians bring peace?"

"You remember those red blips on my display? Those were signals from the transponders that are on each of the communications bombs. If I've been keeping count properly, this means that the Ontarians have all their nuclear weapons stored at this base. If I tell them of New Providence's treachery, and offer my services, I may eventually get a crack at those bombs."

"It might work. Certainly, the world isn't safe as long as those fanatics have the bomb, so perhaps it's worth the risk."

Quintero didn't answer. He gave one quick glance around, saw no "leopards" in the pale starlight. Then he drew Martha into his arms and kissed her, and wondered how many times he had kissed her before.

TWO HUNDRED AND FIFTY KILOMETERS IN FIVE DAYS WOULD HAVE BEEN NO burden for Chente if he had started fresh and uninjured. As it was, however, his dizziness and wounds slowed him down to the point where Martha could move as fast as he. Fortunately it didn't rain again and the nights remained warm. Waterholes were easily detected from orbit, and when they ran out of food after three days they had no trouble getting more meat—this time without having to fight for it.

But by the morning of the fifth day, they were both near the limit of their resources. Through the haze of pain-killer drugs and motion-sickness pills, the landscape gradually became unreal to Chente. He knew that soon he would stop walking, and no effort of will would get him moving again.

Beside him, Martha occasionally staggered. She walked flat-footedly now, no longer trying to favor her blisters. He could imagine the state of her feet after five days of steady walking.

Ahead stretched a long hill, its crest some five thousand meters away. Chente stopped and studied his display. "Just over that hill and we're home—"

Martha nodded, tried to smile. The news seemed to give them new strength and they reached the crest in less than ninety minutes. Below them lay the harbor they had discovered five days earlier on Chente's display. It was separated from the sea by overlapping headlands some ten kilometers further north. South of the green and brown buildings were the unpoisoned farmlands which apparently supported the base.

They looked down on the base only briefly, then silently started toward it. The possibility that they might be shot out of hand had occurred to them, but now they were too tired to worry much about it.

They were picked up by a patrol before they reached the tilled fields. The soldiers didn't shoot, but it was obvious that the visitors were unwelcome. Chente was relieved of his hardware and he and Martha were hustled into an olive-drab car that performed much more efficiently than the huffer Mayor Flaggon drove. Apparently the Ontarians could make fairly good machinery, when ostentation didn't require otherwise. Their captors made no attempt to prevent them from looking about as they drove through the base toward the water's edge, and Chente forced his tired mind to take in all he could. They tooled over the brick-paved road past row after row of warehouses—a testament to Ontarian perseverance. To bring so much equipment and material must have taken many carefully planned voyages. And to avoid Providencian detection, the supply convoys would have had to be small and inconspicuous.

They turned parallel to the long stone quay and drove between huge earthen reservoirs—presumably filled with vegetable oils—and piles of kindling. Further along the quay they passed several cruisers and a battleship. New Canadian ships were noticeably smaller than their counterparts in the old-time navies of Earth. A battleship here might run eight thousand tons and mount six 25-centimeter guns. A fleet of airships sat on the mudflats across the bay. No wonder Balquirth had had no fliers to spare on Wundlich.

Finally they stopped before a long three-story building that looked a good deal more permanent than the wooden warehouses. The driver unlocked the door to the passenger compartment and said, "Out." Two soldiers covered them with what looked like four-barreled shotguns as they followed the driver up the steps to the building's wide doorway.

THE INSIDE OF THE BUILDING WAS QUITE A CONTRAST TO THE CAMOUFLAGED exterior: deep-blue carpets covered the floor while paintings and tapestries were hung from the polished silver walls. Filament lamps glittered along the windowless hallway. They were led stumbling up two flights to a massive wooden door. One of the guards tapped lightly, and a muffled, though familiar, voice from beyond the door said, "Enter."

They did so and found Pier Balquirth surrounded by aides and a pair of curvaceous secretaries. "Freeman Quintero! I should have guessed it was you. And the lovely, though girdle-bound, Miss Blount. Indeed, no longer girdle-bound—?" He raised his eyebrows. "Sit down, please. I have the feeling you may fall down if you don't. I apologize that I don't give you a chance to rest before talking, but a decent regard for Machiavelli demands that I ask some questions while your defenses are down. Whatever happened to Captain Oswald and his gallant crew?"

Chente brought the Ontarian up to date. As he spoke, Balquirth removed a cigar from his desk and lit up. He drew in several puffs and exhaled green smoke. Finally he waved his hand in amusement. "That's pretty sloppy work for the Special Weapons Group, but I suppose they were trying to make your death seem an accident. I hope this opens your eyes, Freeman. Though the Special Weapons Group is the most ruthless bureaucracy within the tight little totalitarian state that calls itself New Providence, the other Groups aren't much better. New Providence may be slightly ahead of the Ontarian Confederation technologically, but they use their advantage simply to make life unbearable for their 'Citizens', and to spread misery to other folks as well."

Martha glared dully at Balquirth but kept silent. Chente recalled Balquirth's casual, almost reckless attitude back in Freetown. He came close to smiling. A dandy and a fool are not necessarily the same thing. "You know, I think you drove me into the arms of New Providence just to create this situation."

Balquirth looked faintly embarrassed. "That's close to the truth. I stuck my neck way out to get your predecessor on one of my vessels. The first Quintero completed his survey, and told me his discoveries— I'm sure you've made these same discoveries by now—but he wouldn't believe that a loose confederation like Ontario could handle the preparations for this core tremor. He kept insisting that both New Providence and Ontario must somehow unite and work together. These are nice sentiments, but he just didn't realize how intolerant and uncompromising Miss Blount's friends can be. When the New Providencians killed him, my government—and myself in particular—were the goats.

"This time I thought I'd let you go with the Providencians. They'd try to kill you and steal your gadgets, but I knew that without your active cooperation they wouldn't get much use out of them. And I knew you were too stubborn to let them cajole you over to their side. If you were killed, then they would look bad. If by some quirk they didn't manage to kill you, I was pretty sure that you would realize what an unpleasant bunch they are.

"I am truly pleased that you survived, however. Can we depend on your help, or are you even more stubborn than I had guessed?"

Chente didn't answer immediately. "Are you in charge here?"

Pier chuckled. "As those things go in the Ontarian Confederacy—yes. We've got men and material from four major bossdoms here, and their chiefs are at each other's throat half the time. But the base was my idea, and the Bossmanic Council in Toronto has appointed me temporarily superior to the three other bossmen involved."

The answer gave Chente a moment to think. In his way, the Ontarian was just as likable and just as much the capable fanatic as Martha. The only difference was that by accident of birth, one was supporting a loose feudal confederation and the other a more industrialized, more centralized regime. And both were so in love with their systems that they put national survival before the survival of the entire colony. Finally he said, "Your plan has convinced me—hell, it practically killed me. If you'll bring in the things they confiscated, I may be able to show you something you can use." Beside him, Martha's expression became steadily darker, though she still maintained her silence.

The bossman turned to one of his secretaries: "Darlene, go out and have Gruzinsky bring in any equipment he's holding. The rest of you leave, too—except Maclen, Trudeau, and our guests," he gestured at Chente and Martha. Chente glanced at his companion, wondered why Balquirth had permitted her to remain. Then he realized that the Ontarian had guessed his involvement with Martha, and was gauging his truthfulness by the exhausted woman's reactions.

A SOLDIER BROUGHT IN THE VARIOUS ITEMS TAKEN FROM CHENTE AND MARtha, and placed them on the low table that sat before Balquirth's empillowed throne. The bossman picked up Chente's weapon. It looked vaguely like a large-caliber pistol, except that the bore was filled with a glassy substance.

"This does what I think it does?" Bossman Pier asked.

"Yes. It's an energy weapon—but the radiation is in the submillimeter range, so there isn't much ionization along the beam path, and your target can't see where your fire is coming from. But you'll find this more interesting." He pulled the satellite display toward himself and pushed the green button on its side. The tiny screen lit up to show a section of coast and ocean. Balquirth was silent for several seconds. "Very pretty," he said finally, but the banter was gone from his voice. "I never guessed the satellites were still working."

"The colonial planners built them to last. They didn't expect you would be able to go up and repair them."

"Hm-m-m. Too bad they didn't build our ground receivers the same way. What's that?" Balquirth interrupted himself to point at a tiny white "vee" set in the open ocean between two wide cumulous cloud banks.

"A ship of some kind. Let's have a closer took." Chente stepped up the magnification. The craft was clearly visible, its white wake streaming out far behind it.

"Why, that's the *Ram*!" one of the Ontarian officers exclaimed. "This is incredible! That ship left thirty-three hours ago. She must be hundreds of kilometers out, and yet we can see her as if we were flying over in an airship. When was this picture taken?"

"Less than a second ago. The coverage is live."

"What area can be observed with this gadget?"

"Everything except the poles, though high resolution pictures are available only up to latitude forty-five degrees."

"Hm-m-m, we could reconnoiter the entire Inner Ocean." Pier touched one of the knobs. Now that Chente had activated the device it responded to the Ontarian's direction. The *Ram*'s image dwindled, slid to one side, and they looked down on an expanse of cloud-stippled ocean. Chente started. Almost off the left side of the screen was a cluster of wake "vees." Balquirth increased the magnification until the formation filled the screen.

"Those aren't ours," one of the officers said finally.

"Clearly," said Balquirth. "It's equally clear that this is a New Providencian fleet, Colonel Maclen. And their wakes point our way."

"Looks like four Jacob class battleships, half a dozen cruisers, and twenty destroyers," said the second, older officer. "But what are those ships in the trailing squadron?" His eyes narrowed. "They're troop transports!"

"Now, I wonder what an invasion force would be doing in this innocent part of the world," said Pier.

The older officer didn't smile at the flippancy. "From their wake angles I estimate they're making thirty kilometers an hour, Bossman. If I read the key on the screen right, that means we have less than forty-four hours."

Chente glanced across at Martha, saw her eyes staring back at him. Now he knew why the Special Weapons people had wanted another bomb. Pier noticed their exchange of looks.

"Any idea why this invasion should coincide with your arrival, Freeman Quintero?"

"Yes. My guess is that certain Providencian groups discovered your base here some months ago, but deferred attack until they could get still another nuclear bomb—namely the one I brought—for their stockpile."

The bossman nodded, then seemed to put the matter aside. "Admiral Trudeau, I intend to meet them at sea. We have neither the shore batteries nor the garrison to take them on at the harbor entrance."

The officer nodded, looking unhappy. "But even with this much warning," he nodded at the screen, "they've still caught us with our pants down. I only have three cruisers, two battleships, and a handful of escort craft in port. We can't stop four Jacob class battlewagons and a half dozen cruisers with that, Bossman."

"We have the bombs, sir," Colonel Maclen broke in.

"You Army sorts are all alike, Colonel," Admiral Trudeau snapped. "The only time you ever used a bomb, it was smuggled into New Providencian territory and exploded on the ground. On the open sea we need at least twenty kilometers clearance between our fleet and the target. It's mighty hard to sneak a dirigible, or a torpedo boat, across a gap that wide."

Maclen had no answer to the criticism. Chente suddenly saw an opportunity to get at the Ontarian bombs and perhaps to destroy the Providencian nuclear capability in the bargain. He said, "But those comm bombs were mounted on drive units powerful enough to boost them out of the atmosphere. Why don't you alter the drive program and let them deliver themselves?" The three Ontarians looked at him open-mouthed. Beside him he heard Martha gasp.

Balquirth said, "You can make such alterations?"

Chente nodded. "As long as we know the target's position, I'll have no problem."

Martha gave an inarticulate cry of rage as she lunged across the table, picked up the recon display and flung it to the floor. Maclen and Trudeau grabbed her, forced her away from the table. Balquirth retrieved the display. The picture on the screen still glowed crisp and true. He shook his head sadly at Martha. "That's it, then. Trudeau, sound general alarm. I want some kind of fleet ready to sail in twenty-two hours."

The Navy man left without a word. Balquirth turned back to the Earthman. "You're wondering why I don't keep the fleet here, and lob the bomb out to sea when the enemy comes in range?"

Chente considered wearily. "That would be the prudent thing to do—if you trusted me."

"Right. Unfortunately, I don't trust you that far. I'll let you decide which bomb you want, and let you supervise the launch, but I'd rather not risk this base on the possibility of a change in your heart. We may not have many ships here yet, but the physical plant we've developed makes this one of the best naval bases in our confederation—whether it remains secret or not."

Chente nodded. Martha murmured something; Balquirth turned to her and bowed almost graciously. "You may come along, too, if you wish, Miss Blount."

THE *FEARSOME*, ADMIRAL TRUDEAU'S FLAGSHIP, DISPLACED SEVENTY-THREE hundred tons and could run at better than forty kilometers per hour. She was doing at least that now. Chente stood on the bridge and looked out over the foredeck. After being treated by Ontarian medics, he had slept most of the preceding day. He felt almost normal now, except for a stiffness in his arm and side, and occasional attacks of vertigo.

He had studied naval types of the Twentieth Century quite thoroughly back home, and in many ways the *Fearsome* was a familiar craft. But there were differences. The Ontarian construction had a faintly crude, misshapen appearance. Standardized production techniques were only beginning to appear in the Confederacy. And without petroleum resources or coal, the nations of New Canada were forced to use vegetable oils or wood to fire their boilers—the greasy black smoke that spouted from the *Fearsome*'s stacks was enough to cause a queasy stomach even if his inner ear and the rolling sea were not. The ship had a huge crew. Apparently its auxiliary devices were not connected to the central power plant. Even the big deck guns needed work squads to turn and angle them. In a sense the *Fearsome* was a cross between a Roman galley and a 1910 battleship.

So far Chente's jury-rigged plans had gone much more smoothly than he had dared to hope. At Balquirth's direction, Colonel Maclen had shown him the maximum security storage bunker where Ontario's five nuclear weapons were located. Only one was needed for this mission, but the Earthman had been allowed to check the missiles' drive units in making his selection. Apparently, neither Maclen or Balquirth realized that a simple adjustment of the drive unit could render the bomb itself permanently unusable. It had taken Chente only a moment to so adjust four of the five weapons.

Now the hastily formed Ontarian fleet was under full steam, with the bomb launch less than an hour away. In addition to the *Fearsome*, the fleet contained the battleship *Covenant* and two large cruisers—essentially as protection for that one bomb. When they were within missile range of the Providencians the Ontarian fleet would turn away, and Balquirth and Chente would take the bomb aboard the motorized boat which now sat near the *Fearsome*'s stern. Not until then would Chente be allowed to touch the bomb's trigger.

Chente looked down at Martha, who sat beside him on the bridge, gazing fixedly out at the ocean. Her wrists had been manacled, but when the sea got choppy, Admiral Trudeau had removed the cuffs so that she could more easily keep her balance. She had not spoken a single word for the last three hours, had seemed almost like a disinterested spectator. Chente touched her shoulder, but she continued to ignore him.

The starboard hatch opened and Balquirth, dressed now in utility coveralls and a slicker, stepped onto the bridge. He spoke briefly with Trudeau, then approached the Earthman. "We've got problems, Freeman. This storm has kicked up a bit faster than the weather people predicted. We can't spot our fleet on the display, and the New Providencian force will be under cloud cover in another fifteen minutes."

Chente shrugged, and the gesture brought a sharp pain to his side. "No matter. That satellite we're reading from was also intended for navigation. It's got radar powerful enough to scan the ocean. We'll be able to keep track of the other fleet almost as easily as if there were no storm at all."

"Ah, good. Let's go below and take a look at the display, then. You said we could launch the missile from twenty-five kilometers out?"

"That's the effective range. Actually the bomb's drive unit could push it much farther, but it wasn't designed as a weapon, so it would be terrifically inaccurate at greater ranges."

CHENTE AND BALQUIRTH LEFT THE BRIDGE AND WENT CAREFULLY DOWN THE steep ladderway to the charthouse. The sky was completely overcast now, and a gathering squall obscured the horizon. He could barely make out the forms of the escort craft, far off to the side. The hard cold wind that sleeted across the *Fearsome* presaged the storm's arrival.

The charthouse was hidden from the direct blast of the wind by several armored buttresses and a gun turret. Five armed seamen stood at the entrance; once they recognized Balquirth, there was no trouble getting inside. The charthouse itself was well insulated from the outside, as the instruments it housed required better care than men did. Balquirth had had all of Chente's equipment stowed here, along with the communications bomb, a two-meter-long cylinder of black plastic that rested in a case of native velvet near the cabin's interior bulkhead.

Maclen sat beside some bulky and primitive wireless equipment. The young colonel held a repeating slug gun at the ready position. He was the room's only occupant. Apparently Pier trusted only his top aides with this Pandora's box of Earthly artifacts.

"All secure, sir," Maclen said. "I let the navigator take some charts but no one else has been by."

"Very good, Colonel," said Balquirth. "All right, Freeman, it's all yours."

Chente approached the brass chart table and the satellite receiver. He fiddled briefly with the controls, and the screen turned gray. A tiny point of light moved slowly from left to right across the top of the screen, then returned to the left margin and started across again. "That's the scanning trace from the satellite. It's illuminating a square kilometer as it moves across the ocean. The satellite's maser isn't powerful enough to light up a larger area, so the picture must be built up from a sequence of scans." The tiny blip of light shifted down about a millimeter with each scan, but still nothing showed in its track. Finally, two golden blips appeared, and in the scan below that, another blip.

"The Providencians," Balquirth said, almost to himself.

Chente nodded. "At this resolution, it's difficult to see individual ships, but you get the idea of their formation."

"What's that red blip?" Bossman Pier pointed to the newest apparition.

"That must be a transponder on one of the Providencian bombs. All the communications bombs transmit a uhf signal in response to microwave from the satellite. I suppose that originally the gimmick was used to find dud bombs that fell back to the surface without detonating."

"So they really thought they were going to wipe us out," said Pier. "This is even better than I had hoped."

The scanning dot moved relentlessly across the screen, shifting down with each pass to reveal more and more of the Providencian fleet. Finally they could see the echelon structure of the enemy forces. For ten more scans, no new blips appeared. Then a single red blip showed up far south of the enemy fleet. Chente caught his breath.

Balquirth looked across the table at him. "How far is that bomb from us?" he said quietly.

Chente held up his hand, and watched the scanning dot continue across the screen. He remembered Martha's remarks about the Providencians having special delivery systems. Then the scanning dot showed the leading elements of the Ontarian fleet—just six lines below the red dot. "Less than ten kilometers, Bossman."

Balquirth didn't reply. He looked at the display's key, then rattled off some instructions into a speaking tube. General quarters sounded. Seconds later Chente heard the *Fearsome*'s big deck guns fire.

Finally Balquirth spoke to Chente. His voice was calm, almost as if their peril were someone else's. "How do you suppose they detected our fleet?"

"There are a number of ways. Martha said the Providencians were experimenting with a lot of gadgets of their own design. In fact they may not have detected us. That bomb is probably aboard a small, unmanned boat. They may just keep it thirty or forty kilometers ahead of their fleet. Then if it hears the sounds of propellers nearby it detonates."

"Ah, yes. Research and development—isn't it wonderful."

THEY STOOD WAITING IN SILENCE. TEN KILOMETERS AWAY, A BARRAGE OF heavy artillery was arcing down on the cause of that innocuous red blip. Any second now they would discover just how cleverly the New Providencians had designed their delivery system.

From outside the windowless charthouse came screams. No other sounds, just screams. Chente smelled fire, noticed the insulation around the closed hatch was beginning to smoke. He and Balquirth hit the deck, and Maclen was not far behind. The bomb's searing flash had crossed the ten kilometers separating them at the speed of light, but they would have to wait almost seven seconds for the water-borne shock wave to arrive.

Chente heard a monstrously loud ripping sound, felt the deck smash into his chest and head. He was not conscious when the airborne shock wave did its job, peeling back the charthouse bulkhead and part of the deck above them.

Chente woke with rain in his face, and the muffled sound of exploding ammunition and burning fuel all around. Behind all these sounds, and nearly as insistent, was a steady roar—the last direct evidence of the nuclear explosion.

The Earthman rolled over, cursing as he felt the stitches the Ontarian doctors had put in his side come apart. His head rang, his nose was bleeding, and his ears felt stuffed with cotton. But as he shook the rain out of his eyes he saw that the others in the charthouse had not fared so well. On the other side of the cabin, Maclen's body was sprawled, headless. Nearer, Balquirth lay unmoving, a pool of blood spreading from his mouth.

For a few moments Chente sat looking stupidly at the scene, wondering why he was alive. Then he began to think. His plans to destroy the Providencian bombs were ruined now that the Ontarian fleet had been destroyed. Or were they? Suddenly he realized that this turn of events might give him hope of completing his mission and still escaping both groups. Chente struggled to his feet, and noticed the deck was listing—or was it only his sense of balance gone awry again? He recovered the recon display and his pistol, then picked the communications bomb from its case. The bomb didn't mass more than fifteen kilograms, but it was an awkward burden.

Outside the charthouse the mutilated guards' bodies lay amid twisted metal. The ship's paint was scorched and curling even in the rain. The after part of the ship was swallowed by flame, and the few people he saw alive were too busy to notice him.

Martha. The thought brought him up short, and he reconsidered the possibilities. Then he turned and started toward the bridge. He could see the gaping holes where the glass had been blown out of the bridge's ports. Anybody standing by those ports would be dead now.

Then he saw her, crawling along the gangway above. The deck listed a full ten degrees as he pulled himself up a ladderway to reach her.

"Let's get off this thing!" he shouted over the explosions and the fire. He caught her arm and helped her to her feet.

"What—?" She shook her head. A trickle of blood ran from one ear down her neck. Her face was smeared with grime and blood.

He could barely hear her voice, and realized the explosion must have deafened them all. He held onto her and shouted again into her good ear. For a moment she relaxed against him, then pulled back, and he saw her lips mouth: "Not with . . . traitor!"

"But I was never going to use that bomb on your people. It was just a trick to get at the Ontarian bombs." It was the biggest lie he'd told her yet, but he knew she wanted to believe it.

He pointed toward the *Fearsome*'s stern, and shouted, "To the launch!" She nodded and they staggered across the tilting, twisted deck, toward the flames and the sound of explosions. Everyone they met was going in the opposite direction, and seemed in no mood to stop and talk.

NOW THERE WAS ONLY ONE NARROW PATH FREE OF FLAMES AND THE HEAT from either side was so intense it blistered their skin even as they ran through it. Then they were beyond the flames, on the relatively undamaged stern. Chente saw that the motor launch had been torn loose from its after mooring cable, and now its stern hung down, splashing crazily in the water. Several bodies lay unmoving on the scorched deck, but no one else was visible. They crawled down to where the bow of the launch stuck up over the railing. Chente had almost concluded they were alone on the stern, when Balquirth stepped from behind the wreckage next to the launch's moorings.

The Ontarian swayed drunkenly, one hand grasping the jagged and twisted metal for support. His other hand held a slug gun. The lower part of his face was covered with blood. Chente staggered toward him, and shouted, "Thought you were dead. We're going ahead with your plan."

Through the blood, Pier almost seemed to smile. He gestured at Martha. "No . . . Quintero," his voice came faintly over the sounds of rain and fire, ". . . think you've turned your coat . . ."

He raised the pistol, but Chente was close to him now. The Earthman lunged, knocking the gun aside with his bomb, and drove his fist hard into Pier's stomach. The other crumpled. Chente staggered back, clinging to the rail for support. It struck him that the fight must have looked like a contest between drunks.

He turned to Martha, and waved at the launch. "We'll have to jump for it, before that other cable breaks."

She nodded, her face pale with cold and fear. They were cut off from the rest of the ship by the spreading fire, and even as he spoke the *Fearsome* tilted another five or ten degrees. He climbed over the rail and jumped. The drop was only three meters, but his target was moving and he was holding the bomb. He hit hard on his bad side and rolled down the launch's steeply sloping deck.

Gasping for breath he dragged himself back up the deck and waved to Martha above him. She stood motionless, her fists tightly clenched about the railing. For a moment, Chente thought she would balk, but she slipped over the railing and jumped, her arms outstretched. He managed to break her fall and they both went sprawling. They crawled clumsily down the bobbing deck toward the craft's cockpit. Martha struggled through the tiny hatch, and Chente pushed the bomb after her. Then he turned and fired at the remaining mooring cable.

THE LAUNCH KNIFED INTO THE WATER AND FOR A MOMENT SUBMERGED COMpletely, but somehow Chente managed to keep from being washed away. The boat bobbed back to the surface, and he scrambled into the cockpit.

From his talks with Balquirth, Quintero knew the boat had a steam-electric power plant—it was ordinarily used for espionage work. Looking over the control panel, Chente decided that this was the most advanced Ontarian mechanism he had encountered—just the kind of luck they needed. He depressed the largest switch on the board and felt a faint humming beneath his feet. He eased the throttle forward. As the launch pulled slowly away from the foundering *Fearsome*, he thought he heard the whine and snick of small arms fire caroming off the boat's hull; apparently Balquirth was not easily put out of action. But now it was too late to stop their escape. The *Fearsome* was soon lost to sight amid the deep swells and pounding rain. The last Chente saw and heard of the Ontarian fleet was a pale orange glow through the storm, followed by a sound that might have been thunder. Then they were alone with the storm.

The storm was bad enough in itself. The tiny cabin spun like a compass needle, and several times Chente was afraid the boat would capsize. Somehow Martha managed to tie down the equipment and dig a couple of life jackets out of a storage cubby.

Chente fastened the recon screen to the control board, and inspected the radar display. On high resolution he could distinguish every vessel in the area. Even his motor launch showed—or at least the transponder on his communications bomb did. They would have no trouble navigating through this storm, if they didn't sink. He briefly thanked heaven that the comm bombs were about as clean as anything that energetic can be: nearly all the destruction was radiated as soft X rays. At least they didn't have to worry that the rain was drenching them in radio-active poisons.

"Now what?" Martha shouted finally. She had wedged herself in the corner, trying to keep her balance.

Chente hesitated. He had three choices. He could flee the scene immediately; he could use his bomb to destroy the Providencians and their remaining bomb—just as he and Balquirth had planned; or he could indulge in more treachery. The first option would leave the Providencians with a bomb, and an enormous advantage in the world. The second option would be difficult to execute; at this point Martha might be stronger than he was. He might have to kill her. Besides, if he exploded his bomb, he would have no way to make his report to Earth.

That left treachery. "We're going to try to get picked up by one of the ships in the Providencian fleet."

TWENTY MINUTES PASSED. AT THE TOP OF THE SCREEN THE LAUNCH'S BLIP moved closer and closer to the red dot that represented the last Providencian bomb. He kept the screen angled so that Martha didn't have a clear view of it.

They should be able to see the ship before much longer. He leaned his head close to Martha and said, "Do you know any signals that would keep them from shooting us out of hand?" He pointed at the electric arc lamp mounted in the windscreen.

Her voice came back faintly over the wind. "I know some diplomatic codes. We update them every fifteen days—they just might respect them."

"We'll have to chance it." Chente helped her light the arc lamp. But there was nothing to see except storm. Chente guided the launch so that its image on the screen approached the other. As they swung over the top of a swell, they saw a long gray shadow not more than two hundred meters ahead. It appeared to be an auxiliary craft, probably a converted cargo ship.

Chente reached across the panel and tapped new instructions into the display. Now the machine was reading the transponder's position from its internal direction finders. Beside him at the control panel, Martha awkwardly closed and opened the signaler's shutter. For nearly thirty seconds there was no reply. Chente held his breath. He expected that this particular ship would be manned by Special Weapons people, who might well be trigger-happy and extremely suspicious. On the other hand, depending on what they expected of the Ontarians, the weapons people might be cocksure and careless.

Finally a light high on one of the ship's masts blinked irregularly. "They acknowledge. They want us to move in closer."

Chente worked the electric boat closer and closer to the ship. Martha continued sending. They were about fifty meters out now, and they could make out the details of the other vessel. Quintero looked closely at his display, then scanned the ship's foredeck. He noticed a shrouded boat lashed down near the bow. Its position agreed with the location of the blip on his display. This was better than he had hoped. That was the twin of the robot boat that had nearly destroyed the Ontarian fleet.

He took one hand from the wheel, drew his pistol and fired a single low-power bolt. The thick windscreen shattered, throwing slivers of glass all around. He stepped the pistol's power to full and aimed at the other vessel's bow.

"No!" Martha screamed as she rammed him against the bulkhead. She was tall and strong and she fought desperately. They careened wildly about the cabin for several seconds before Chente got a solid, close-fisted blow to her solar plexus. She collapsed without a sound, and the Earthman whirled back to face the deadlier enemy.

The ship's main guns were turned toward him, but he was below them now. He sprayed fire all along the vessel, concentrating on the smaller deck guns and the shrouded boat. Clouds of steam quickly obscured the glowing craters his pistol gouged in the ship's hull, and then the fuel supply aboard the robot boat exploded in a ball of orange-red flame hot enough to melt the controls of the bomb within.

There was the sparkle of automatic fire from up in the ship's masts, and the cockpit seemed to shred around him. He fired upward blindly.

Chente grabbed the wheel and turned about. The seconds passed but there was no more Providencian gunfire. The sounds of the burning ship quickly faded behind them and they were alone.

THEY DROVE STEADILY WEST FOR THREE HOURS. THE SEAS FELL. JUST AS THE sun set, the cloud cover in the far west moved aside so that the sun shone red and gold through the narrow band between horizon and cloud.

His reconnaissance screen showed no sign of pursuit. More importantly, there was only one transponder blip glowing on Chente's display—his own.

The tiny launch was slowing, and finally Chente decided to try to fire its boiler. He eased the throttle back to null, and the boat sat bobbing almost gently in the sea the sun turned gold.

"Martha?" No response. "I had to do it."

"Had to?" Her tone showed despair and unbelieving indignation. She looked briefly up at him through her rain-plastered hair. "How many Providencians did you kill today?"

Chente didn't answer. The rationalizations that men use for killing other men stuck in his throat, at least for the moment. Finally he said, "I told you, I told the Ontarians: Unless you work together you will all be wiped out. But it didn't do any good just to say it. Now, Ontario and New Providence have a mutual enemy: me. I have the only nuclear weapon left, and I have means to deliver it. Soon I will control territory, too. Your nations will spend their energies to develop the technology to defeat me, and in the end you may be good enough to meet your real peril."

But Martha had resumed her study of the deck, and made no reply.

Chente sighed, and began to pull back the deck plates that should cover the boiler.

The sun set and the first stars of twilight shone through the gap between the clouds and the horizon. Nineteen light-years away, his likeness must still be awaiting his report. In a few weeks, Chente would make that report, using the Ontarian communications bomb. But the people of the New Canada would never know it, for that bomb was the lever he would use to take over some small Ontarian fiefdom. Already he must begin casting the net of schemes and the machinations that would stretch one hundred years into this miserable planet's future. It was small consolation to hope that his likeness would live to see other worlds.

There are a lot of things I like about "Just Peace." As a collaboration it went very smoothly. Bill and I had many small things in our idea boxes that found a nice home here: the Canadian background, the danger of colonizing a planet whose core was about to undergo a phase change.

We were vague about Chente's background on Earth. This was deliberate. I assumed Earth had already gone through the Technological Singularity. We see about as much of Earth as we could understand. One major aspect of Earth's technology leaks into this story: the duplicative transport used to bring Chente to New Canada. Not much is made of it here, but I find the idea immensely intriguing. If we could make exact copies of someone (not just clones, but exact down to quantum limits) what would this do to our concept of ego? The idea has been in SF for many years (at least back to Algis Budrys's *Rogue Moon* and Poul Anderson's *We Have Fed Our Sea*). There is plenty of mileage left in the gimmick. It is just one of the issues that I see looming in our future. Our most basic beliefs—including the concept of self itself—are in for rough times.

ORIGINAL SIN

Alien contact stories have always been a favorite of mine. I grew up with John Campbell's notion that the humans were short-lived, bright, and terribly aggressive compared to the wiser intellects of galactic civilization. *Why not turn that around?* Why not have a race even *more* short-lived, intelligent, and aggressive than humans? John's older/wiser races often tried to keep the human "superrace" confined to Earth. What would we do if confronted by aggressive primitives with the potential to run circles around us?

I hadn't seen any stories with this theme, but knowing science fiction I guessed that such had already been written. I needed something more. Many human personalities are piled deep with interacting layers of shame and loneliness and hatred. My fictional race would have even more inner turmoil. How to do it? A short lifespan would certainly intensify such problems, but I wanted something that would give individuals *real* reason to feel guilt. I remembered the extraordinary life cycle of the *hugl* (a nonsentient pest) in Silverberg and Garrett's *Shrouded Planet.* Maybe I could jazz that up, and apply it to an intelligent race. Thus was born . . .

ORIGINAL SIN

---

*F*irst twilight glowed diffusely from the fog. On the landscaped terraces that fell away from the hilltop, long rows of tiny crosses slowly materialized. Low trees dripped almost silently upon the sodden grass.

The officer in charge was young. This was his first assignment. And it was an assignment more important than most. He shifted his weight from one foot to the other. There must be something to do with his time—something to check, something to worry over; the machine guns. Yes. He could check those again. He moved rapidly up the narrow, concrete walk to where his gun crews manned their weapons. But the magazine feeds were all set, the muzzle chokes screwed down. Everything was just as proper as the last time he had checked, ten minutes earlier. The crews watched him silently, but resumed their whispered conversations as he walked away.

Nothing to do. Nothing to do. The officer stopped for a moment and stood trembling in the cool dampness. Christ, he was hungry.

Behind the troops, and even farther from the field of crosses, the morning twilight defined the silhouettes of the doctors and priests attendant. Their voices couldn't carry through the soggy air, but he could see their movements were *jerky, aimless. They had time on their hands, and that is always the greatest burden.*

The officer tapped his heavy boot on the concrete walk in a rapid tattoo of frustration. It was so quiet here.

The mists hid the city that spread across the lowlands. If he listened carefully he could hear auto traffic below. Occasionally, a ship in the river would sound its whistle, or a string of railway freight cars would faintly crash and rattle as it moved along the wharves. Except for these links with the everyday world, he might as well be at the end of time here on the hilltop with its grasses, its trees. Even the air seemed different here—it didn't burn into his eyes, and there was only a hint of creosote and kerosene in its smell.

It was brighter now. The ground became green, the fog a cherry brown. With a sigh of anguished relief, the officer glanced at his watch. It was time to inspect the cross-covered hillside. He nearly ran out onto the grass.

Low hedges curved back and forth between the white crosses to form an intricate topiary maze. He must check that pattern one last time. It was a dangerous job, but hardly a difficult one. There were less than a thousand critical points and he had memorized the scheme the evening before. Every so often he broke stride to cock a deadfall, or arm a claymore mine. Many of the crosses rose from freshly turned earth, and he gave these an especially wide berth. The air was even cleaner here above the grass than it had been back by the machine-guns, and the deep wet sod sucked at his feet. He gulped back saliva and tried to concentrate on his job. So hungry. Why must he be tempted so?

Time seemed to move faster, and the ground brightened steadily beneath his running feet. Twenty minutes passed. He was almost done. The ground was visible for nearly fifty meters through the brownish mists. The city sounds were louder, more numerous. He must hurry. The officer ran along the last row of crosses, back toward friendly lines—the cool sooty concrete, the machine-guns, the trappings of civilization. Then his boots were clicking on the walkway, and he paused for three seconds to catch his breath.

He looked at the cemetery. All was still peaceful. The preliminaries were completed. He turned to run to his gun crews.

Five more minutes. Five more minutes, and the sun would rise behind the fog bank to the east. Its light would seep down through the mists, and warm the grass on the hillside. Five more minutes and children would be born.

WHAT A GLORIOUS DUMP! THEY HAD ME HIDDEN IN ONE OF THE BETTER PARTS of town, on a slight rise about three kilometers east of the brackish river that split the downtown area in two. I stood at the tiny window of my "lab" and looked out across the city. The westering sun was a smudged reddish disk shining through the multiple layers of crap that city traffic pumped into the air. I could actually see bits of ash sift down from the high spaces above.

It was the rush hour. The seven-lane freeways that netted the city were a study in still life, with idling cars backed up thousands of meters at the interchanges. I could imagine the shark-faced drivers shaking their clawed fists at each other, frothing murderous threats. Even here on the rise, it was so hot and humid that the soot stuck to my sweating skin. Down in the city basin it must have been infernal.

Further across town was a cluster of skyscrapers, seventy and eighty stories high. Every fifteen seconds a five-prop airplane would cruise in from the east, make a one-eighty just above the rooftops, and attempt a landing at the airport between the skyscrapers and the river.

And beyond the river, misty in the depths of the smog, was the high ridgeline that blocked the ocean from view. The grayish-green expanse of the metropolitan cemetery ran across the whole northern end of the ridge.

Sounds like something out of a historical novel, doesn't it? I mean, I hadn't seen an aircraft in nearly seventy years. And as for cemeteries . . . This side of the millennium, such things just didn't exist—or so I had thought. But it was all here on Shima, and less than ten parsecs from mother Earth. It's not surprising if you don't recognize the name. Earthgov lists the planet's star + 56°2966. You can tell the Empire is trying to hide something when the only designation they have for a nearby K-star is a centuries-old catalog number. If you're old enough, though, you remember the name. Two centuries back, "Shima" was a household word. Not counting Earth, Shima was the second planet where man discovered intelligent life.

A lot has happened in two hundred years: the Not-Wars, the secession of the Free Human Worlds from Earthgov. Somewhere along the line, Earth casually rammed Shima under the rug. Why? Well, if nothing else, Earthgov is cautious (read: chicken). When humans first landed (remember spaceships?) on Shima, the native culture was paleolithic. Two centuries later, their technology resembled Earth's in the late Twentieth Century. Of course, that was no great shakes, but remember it took us thousands of years to get from stone ax to steam engine. It's really hard to imagine how the Shimans did it.

You can bet Earthgov didn't give 'em any help. Earth has always been scared witless by competition, while at the same time they don't have the stomach for genocide. So they pretend competition doesn't exist. The Free Worlds aren't like that. Over the last one hundred and fifty years, dozens of companies have tried to land entrepreneurs on the planet. The Earth Police managed to rub out every one of them.

Except for me (so far). But then, the people who hired me had had a lucky break. Earthgov occasionally imports Shimans to work as trouble-shooters. (The Empire would import a lot more—Shimans are incredibly quick at solving problems that don't require background work—except that Earthpol can't risk letting the aliens return with what they learn.) Somehow one such contacted the spy system that Samuelson Enterprises maintains throughout the Empire. Samuelson got in touch with me.

Together, S.E. and the Shimans bribed an Earthman to look the other way when I made my appearance on Shima. Yes, some Earthcops do have a price—in this case it was the annual gross product of an entire continent. But the bribe was worth it. I stood to gain one hundred times as much, and Samuelson Enterprises had—in a sense—been offered one of the biggest prizes of all time by the Shimans. But that, as they say, is another story. Right now I had to come across with what the Shimans wanted, or we'd all have empty pockets—or worse.

You see, the Shimans wanted immortality. S.E. had impaled many a hick world on that particular gaff, but never like this. The creatures were really desperate: no Shiman had ever lived longer than twenty-five Earth months.

I leaned out to look at the patterns of soot on the window sill, trying at the same time to ignore the laboratory behind me. It was filled with equipment the Shimans thought I might need: microtomes, ultracentrifuges, electron microscopes—a real antique shop. The screwy thing was that I did need some of those gadgets. For instance, if I had used my 'mam'ri at the prime integers, Earthpol would be there before I could count to three. I'd been on Shima four weeks, and considering the working conditions, I thought progress had been pretty good. But the Shimans were getting suspicious and very, very impatient. Samuelson had negotiated with them through third parties on Earth, and so hadn't been able to teach me the Shiman language. Sometime *you* try explaining biological chemistry with sign language and grunts. And these damn fidget brains seemed to think that a project was overdue if it hadn't been finished last week. I mean, the ol' Protestant Ethic stood like a naked invitation to hedonism next to what these underweight kangaroos practiced.

THREE DAYS EARLIER, THEY HAD POSTED ARMED GUARDS INSIDE MY LAB. As I stood glooming at the windowsill I could hear my three pals shuffling endlessly about the room, stopping every so often to poke into the equipment. Nothing short of physical violence could make them stay in one spot.

Sometimes I would look up from my bench to see one of them staring back at me. His gaze was not unfriendly—I've often looked at a steak just that way. When he saw me looking back, the Shiman would abruptly turn away, unsuccessfully trying to swallow slaver back from the multiple rows of inward curving teeth that covered his mouth. (Actually the creatures were omnivorous. In fact, they'd killed off virtually all animal life on the planet, and most of their vast population subsisted on cereal crops grown—in insufficient quantities—on well-defended collective farms.)

I could feel them staring at me right now. I had half a mind to turn around and show them a thing or three—Earthpol and its detection devices be damned.

This line of thought was interrupted as a sports car breezed up from the sentry gate three hundred meters away. I was housed in some sort of biological science complex. The place looked like a run-down Carnegie Library (if you remember what a library is), and was surrounded by hectares of blackened concrete. Beyond this were tank traps and a three-meter high barricade. Till now the only vehicles I had seen inside the compound were tracked military jobs.

The blue and orange sports car burned rubber as the driver skidded to a stop against the curb beneath my window. The driver bounded out of his seat, and double-timed up the walk. Typical. Shimans never slow down.

The passenger door opened, and a second figure appeared. Normal Shiman dress consists of a heavy jacket and a kilt which conceals their broad haunches and part of their huge feet. But this second fellow was wrapped from head to foot in black, a costume I had seen only once or twice before—some kind of penance outfit. And when he moved it wasn't with short rapid hops, but with longer slower strides, almost as if . . .

I turned back to my equipment. At most I had only seconds, not really enough time to set the devious traps I had prepared. The two were inside the building now. I could hear the rapid *thumpthumpthump* as the driver bounced up the stairs, and the softer sound of someone moving unseemly slow. But not slow enough. Through the door came the whistly buzz of Shiman talk. Perhaps those guards would do their job, and I would have a few extra seconds. No luck. The door opened. Driver and passenger stepped into my lab. With nearly Shiman haste, the veiled passenger whipped off the headpiece and dropped it to the floor. As expected, the face behind the veil was human. It was also female. The girl looked about the room expressionlessly. A sheen of sweat glistened on her skin. She brushed straight blond hair out of her face and turned to me.

"I wish to speak to Professor Doctor Hjalmar Kekkonen," she said. It was hard to believe that such a flat delivery could come from that sensuous mouth.

"That's one I'll grant," I said, wondering if she was going to read me my rights.

She didn't answer at once, and I could see the throb at her temple as she clenched her jaws. Her eyes, I noticed, were like her voice: pretty, but somehow dead and implacable. She pulled open her heavy black gown. Underneath she wore a frilly thing which wouldn't have been out of place in Tokyo—or with the Earth Police.

She stood at her full height and her gray eyes were level with mine. "It is hard for me to believe. Hjalmar Kekkonen holds the Chair of Biology at New London University. Hjalmar Kekkonen was the first commander of the Draeling Mercenary Division. Could anyone so brilliant act so stupidly?" Her flat sarcasm became honest anger. "I did my part, sir! Your appearance on Shima was undetected. But since you arrived you've been so 'noisy' that nothing could disguise your presence from my superiors in Earthpol."

Ah, so this was the cop Samuelson had bought. I should have guessed. She seemed typical of the egotistical squirts Earthpol uses. "Listen, Miss Whoever-you-are, I was thoroughly briefed. I've worn native textiles, I've eaten the stuff they call food here, I've even washed in gunk that makes me *smell* like a local. Look at this place—I don't have a single scrap of comfort."

"Well then, what is that?" She pointed at the coruscating pile of my *'mam'ri*.

"You know damn well what it is. I told you I've been briefed. I've only used it on a Hammel base. Without that much analysis, the job would take years."

"Professor Kekkonen, you have been briefed by fools. We in the Earth Police can detect such activity easily—even from the other side of Shima." She began refastening the black robe. "Come with us now." You can always spot Earthgov types; the imperative is their favorite mode.

I sat down, propped my heels on the edge of the lab bench. "Why?" I asked mildly. Earthgov people irritate easy, too. Her face turned even paler as I spoke.

"It may be that Miss Tsumo hasn't made things clear, sir." I did a double take. It was the cop's native driver speaking English. The gook's accent was perfect, though he spoke half again as fast as a human would. It was as if some malevolent Disney had put the voice of Donald Duck in the mouth of a shark.

"Professor, you are here working for a group of the greatest Shiman governments. Twenty minutes ago, Miss Tsumo's managers made discovery of this fact. At any minute the Earth Police will order our governments to give you up. Our people all want to help you, but they have knowledge of the power of Earth. They will attempt to do what they are ordered. For the next five minutes, I have authority to take you from here—but—after that it will probably be too late."

The gook made a hell of a lot more sense than the Tsumo character. The sooner we holed up someplace new, the better. I swung my feet off the bench and grabbed the heavy black robe Tsumo held out to me. She kept silent, her face expressionless. I've met Earthcops before. In their own way, some of them are imaginative—even likeable. But this creature had all the personality of a five-day-old corpse.

The native driver turned to my guards and began whistling. They called in some ranking officer who inspected a sheaf of papers the driver had with him. I had just finished with the robe and veil combination when the commanding officer waved us all toward the door. We piled down the stairs and through the exit. Outside, there was no activity beyond the usual sentries that patrolled the perimeter.

As the driver entered the blue and orange car, I crawled onto the narrow bench behind the front seat. The car sank under my weight. I mass nearly one hundred kilos and that's a lot more than the average Shiman. The driver turned the ignition, and the kerosene-eating engine turned over a couple of times, died. Tsumo got into the front seat and shut the door.

Still no alarms.

I wiped the sweat from my forehead and looked out the grimy window. Shima's sun had set behind the smog bank but here and there across the city lingered small patches of gold where the sun's rays fell directly on the ground. Something was moving through the sky from the south. A native aircraft? But Shiman fliers all had wings. The cigar-shaped flier moved rapidly toward the city. Its surface was studded with turrets—vaguely reminiscent of the gun blisters on a Mitchell bomber. God, this place brought back memories. The vehicle crossed a patch of sunlit ground. Its shadow was at least two thousand meters long.

I tapped Tsumo on the shoulder and pointed at the object that now hovered over the estuary beyond the city.

She glanced briefly into the sky, then turned to the native. "Sirbat," she said. "Hurry. Earthpol is already here." Sirbat—if that was the native's name—twisted the starter again and again. Finally the engine kicked over and stayed lit. Somehow all those whirling pieces of metal meshed and we were rolling toward the main gate. Sirbat leaned forward and punched a button on the dash. It was the car radio. The voice from the speaker was more resonant, more deliberate than is usual with Shimans.

Sirbat said, "The voice says, 'See the power of Earth over your city,' " The speaker paused as if to give everyone time to look up and see the airborne scrap heap over the estuary. Tsumo twisted about to face me. "That's the Earthpol 'flagship.' We tried to imagine what the Shimans

would view as the warcraft of an advanced technology, and that's what
we came up with. In a way, it's impressive."

I grunted. "Only a demented two-year-old could be impressed." Sirbat
hissed, his lips curling back from his fangs. He had no chance to speak
though, because we were rapidly coming up on the main gate. Sirbat
slammed on the brakes. I was leaning against the front dash when we
finally screeched to a stop beside the armored vehicle which guarded
the gateway's steel doors.

Sirbat waved his papers out the window, and screamed impatiently.
The turret man on the tank had aimed his machine gun at us, but I
noticed he was looking back over his shoulder at the Earthpol flagship.
The gunner's lips were peeled back in anger—or fear. Perhaps the floating mountain *was* somehow awesome to the Shiman psyche. I tried
briefly to remember how I had felt about aircraft, back before the turn
of the millennium.

Tsumo unobtrusively turned off the car radio, as a guard came over
and snatched the clearance papers from Sirbat. The two natives began
arguing over the authorization. From the tank, I could hear another
radio. It wasn't the voice from the flagship. This sounded agitated and
entirely Shiman. Apparently Earthpol was broadcasting on selected civilian frequencies. Score one against their side. If we could just get past
this checkpoint before Earthpol made its ultimatum.

The guard waved to the tank pilot, who disappeared inside his vehicle. Ahead of us electric motors whined and the massive steel door
swung back. Our sports car was already blasting forward as Sirbat
reached out of the window and plucked his authorization from the
guard's claws.

THE CITY'S STREETS WERE NARROW, CROWDED, BUT SIRBAT ZIPPED OUR CAR
from lane to lane like we were the only car around. Worst of all, Sirbat
was the most conservative driver in that madhouse. I haven't moved so
fast since the last time I was on skis. The buildings to right and left were
a dirty gray blur. Ahead of us, though, things stood still long enough to
get some sort of perspective. We were heading downtown—toward the
river. Over the roofs of the tenements, and through a maze of wires and
antennas, I could still see the bulk of the Earthpol flagship.

I grabbed wildly for support as the car screeched diagonally through
an intersection. Seconds later we crashed around another corner and I
could see all the way to the edge of the estuary.

Sirbat summarized the Earthpol announcement coming from the car
radio. "He says he's Admiral Ohara—"

"—that would be Sergeant Oharasan," said Tsumo.

"—and he orders Berelesk to turn over the person-eater and doer of crimes, Hjalmar Kekkonen. If not, destruction will come from the sky."

Several seconds passed. Then the entire sky flashed red. Straight ahead that color was eye-searingly bright as a threadlike ray of red-whiteness flickered from flagship to bay. A shockwave-driven cloud of steam exploded where the beam touched water. Sirbat applied the brakes and we ran up over the curb, finally came to a stop against a utility pole. The shock wave was visible as it whipped up the canyon of the street. It smashed over our car, shattering the front windshield.

Even before the car shuddered to a stop, Sirbat was out. And Tsumo wasn't far behind. The Shiman quickly ripped the identification tags from the rear windshield and replaced them with—counterfeits?

In those seconds the city was quiet, Earthpol's gentle persuasion still echoing through the minds of its inhabitants. Tsumo looked up and down the street. "I hope you see now why we had to run. By now the city and national armies are probably on the hunt for us. Once cowed, the Shimans are dedicated in their servility."

I pulled the black veil of my robe more tightly down over my head and swore. "So? What now? This place can't be more than four kilometers from the lab. We're still dead ducks."

Tsumo frowned. "Dead—ducks?" she said. "What dialect do you speak?"

"English, damn it!" Youngsters are always complaining about my language.

Sirbat hustled around the rear of the sports car to the sidewalk. "Go quick," he said and grasped my wrist with bone-crushing force. "I hear police coming." As we ran toward a narrow alley, I glanced up the street. The place was right out of the dark ages. I'd like to take some of these young romantics and stuff them into a real, old-fashioned slum like that one. The buildings were better than three stories high, and crushed up against each other. Windows and tiny balconies competed in endless complication for open air. Fresh-laundered rags hung from lines stretched between the buildings—to become filthy in the sooty air. The stench of garbage was the only detail the scene seemed to lack.

The moment of stunned shock passed. Some Shimans ran wildly around while others sat and gnawed at the curbing. This was panic, and it made their previous behavior look tame. The buildings were emptying, and the screams of the trampled went right through the walls. If we had been just ten meters farther away from that alley, we'd never have made it.

We huddled near the end of the hot cramped alley amid the crumbling remains of a couple of skeletons, and listened to the cries from beyond. Now I could hear the police sirens, too—at least that's what I assumed the bass *boohoohoo* to be. I turned my head and saw that it was just centimeters from the saurian immensity of Sirbat's fangs.

The Shiman spoke. "You may be all right. At one time I had good knowledge of this part of the city. There is a place we may use long enough for you to make good on your agreement with Shima." I opened my mouth to tell this nightmare he was an idiot if he thought I could make progress with nothing more than paper and pencil. But he was already running back the way we had come. I glanced at Tsumo. She sat motionless against the rotting wall of the alley. Her face wasn't visible behind the thick veil, but I could imagine the flat, hostile glare in her gray eyes. The look that sank a thousand ships.

I drew the sticker from my sleeve and tested its edge. There was no telling who would come back for us. I wouldn't have put anything past our toothy friend—and Earthpol was as bad.

What a screwed-up mess. Why had I ever let Samuelson persuade me to leave New London? A guy could get killed here.

SUNRISE. THE DISK BLAZED PALE ORANGE THROUGH THE FOG, AND MOMEN-tarily the world seemed clean, bright.

Silence. For those few seconds the muted sounds of the city died. The sun's warmth pressed upon the ground, penetrated the moist turf, and brought a call of life—and death—to those below.

The Shimans stood tense, and the silence stretched on: Ten seconds. Twenty. Thirty. Then:

A faint wail. The sound was joined by another, and another, till a hundred voices, all faint but together loud, climbed through the register and echoed off nearby hills.

The dying had discovered their mouths.

Near the middle of the green field, one cross among the thousands wavered and fell.

It was the first.

The fog blurred the exact form of the grayish creatures that spilled from the newly opened graves. As grave after grave burst open, the wailing screams died and a new sound grew—the low, buzzing hum of tiny jaws opening and closing, grinding and tearing. The writhing gray mass spread toward the edge of the field, and the ground it passed over was left brown, bare. A million mouths. They ate anything green, anything soft—each other. The horde reached the hedgework. There it split into a hundred feelers that searched back and forth through the intricate twisting of the maze. Where the hedge wall was narrow or low, the mouths began to eat their way through.

A command was given, and all along the crest of the hill the machine scat-

*terguns whirred, spraying a dozen streams of birdshot down on those points
where the horde was breaking out. The poisoned shot killed instantly, by the
thousands. And tens of thousands were attracted by the newly dead into the
field of fire.*

*Only the creatures which avoided the simplest branches of the maze escaped
death by nerve poison. And most of those survivors ran blindly into dead ends,
where claymore mines blasted their bodies apart.*

*Only the smartest, fastest thousand of the original million reached the upper
end of the maze. These had grown fat since they climbed from their fathers'
graves, yet they still moved forward faster than a man can walk. Not a blade
of grass survived their passage.*

I'LL SAY ONE THING ABOUT MY STAY ON SHIMA: IT CURED ME ONCE AND FOR
all of any nostalgia I had felt for pre-millennium Earth. Shima had the
whole bag: the slums, the smog, the overpopulation, the starvation—
and now this. I looked down from our hiding place at the congregation
standing below. The Shimans sang from hymnals, and their quacking
was at once alien and familiar.

On the dais near the front of the room was a podium—an altar, I
should say. The candelabra on the altar cast its weak light on the immense wooden cross that stood behind it.

It took me all the way back to Chicago, circa 1940—when a similar
scene had been weekly ritual. Funny, that was one bit of nostalgia I had
never wished to part with. But after seeing those shark-faced killers
mouthing the same chants, I knew the past would never seem the same.
The hymn ended but the congregation remained standing. Outside I
could hear the night traffic—and the occasional rumble of military vehicles. The city was not calm. A million tons of hostile metal still sat in
their sky.

Then the "minister" walked rapidly to the altar. The crowd moaned
softly. He was dressed all in black, and I swear he had a clerical collar
hung around the upper portion of his neckless body.

Tsumo shifted her weight, her thigh resting momentarily against mine.
Our friend Sirbat had hidden us in this cramped space above the hall. He
was supposedly negotiating with the reverends for better accommoda-
tions. The Earthpol girl peered through the smoked glass which shielded
us from the congregations's view, and whispered, "Christianity is popular
on Shima. A couple of Catholic Evangels introduced the cult here nearly
two centuries ago. I suppose any religion with a Paul would have sufficed,
but the Shimans never invented one of their own."

Below us, the parishioners settled back in their pews as the minister
began some sort of speech—and that sounded kind of familiar, too. I

glanced back at Tsumo's shadowed face. Her long blond hair glinted pale across her shoulders.

"Kekkonen," she continued, "do you know why Earthgov has quarantined Shima?"

An odd question. "Uh, they've made the usual 'cultural shock' noises but it's obvious they're just scared of the competition these gooks could provide, given a halfway decent technology. I'm not worried. Earthgov has never put enough store by human ingenuity and guts."

"Your problem, Professor Doctor, is that you can think of competition only on an economic level: a strange failing for one who considers himself so rough and tough. Look down there. Do you see those two at the end of the pew fight to hold the collection tray?"

The Shimans tugged the plate back and forth, snarling. Finally, the larger of the two raked his claws across the other's face, opening deep red cuts. Shorty squealed and released the plate. The victor ponderously drew a fat wallet from his blouse and dropped several silver slugs into the tray, then passed it down the row, away from his adversary. Those near the struggle gave it their undivided attention, while from the front of the hall the minister droned on.

"Are you familiar with the Shiman life cycle, Professor." It was a statement.

"Certainly." And a most economical system it was. From birth the creatures lived to eat—anything and everything. Growing from a baby smaller than your fist, in less than two years the average Shiman massed sixty kilograms. Twenty-one months after birth a thousand embryos would begin to develop in his combined womb/ovary—no sex was necessary for this to happen, though occasionally the Shimans did exchange genetic material through conjugation. For the next three months the embryos developed in something like the normal mammalian fashion, drawing nourishment from the parent's circulatory system. When the fetuses were almost at term the womb filled most of the adult's torso, absorbed most of the adult's food intake. Finally—and I still didn't understand the timing mechanism, since it seemed to depend on external factors—the thousand baby Shimans ate their way out of the parent, and began their own careers.

"Then you know that parricide and genocide are a way of life with these monsters. Earthgov is not the stupid giant you imagine, Professor. The challenge Shima presents us transcends economics. The Shimans are very much like locusts, yet their average intelligence is far greater than ours. In another century they will be our technological equal. You entrepreneurs will lose more than profits dealing with them—you'll be exterminated. The Shimans have only one natural disadvantage and that is their short life span. In twenty-four months, even *they* can't learn enough to coordinate their genius." Her whisper became soft, taut. "If you succeed, Professor, we will have lost the small chance we have for survival."

Miss Iceberg was blowing her cool. "Hell, Tsumo, I thought you were on our side. You're taking our money, anyway. If you're really so in love with Earthgov policy, why don't you blow the whistle on me?"

THE EARTHPOL AGENT WAS SILENT FOR NEARLY A MINUTE. AT FIRST I THOUGHT she was watching the services below, but then I noticed her eyes were closed. "Kekkonen, I had a husband once. He was an Evangel—a fool. Missionaries were allowed on Shima up to fifty years ago. That was probably the biggest mistake that Earthgov has ever made: Before the Christians came, the Shimans had never been able to cooperate with one another even to the extent of developing a language. The only thing they did together was to eat. Since they were faster and deadlier than anything else they would often come near to wiping out all life on a continent; at which point, they'd start eating each other and their own population would drop to near zero and stay there for decades. But then the Christians came and filled them with notions of sin and self-denial, and now the Shimans cooperate with each other enough so they can use their brains for something besides outsmarting their next meal.

"Anyway, Roger was one of the last missionaries. He really believed his own myths. I don't know if his philosophies conflicted with Shiman dogma, or if the monsters were just hungry one day: but my husband never came back."

I almost whistled. "OK, so you don't like Shimans—but hating them won't bring your husband back. That would take the skills of a million techs and the resources of . . ." My voice petered out as I remembered that that was about the size bribe Samuelson had offered her. "Hm-m-m, I guess I'm getting the picture. You want things both ways: to have your husband back, and to have a little vengeance, too."

"*Not vengeance*, Professor Doctor. You are just rationalizing your own goals. Remember the things you have seen on Shima: The cannibalism. The viciousness. The constant state of war between the different races of the species. And above all the superhuman intelligence these monsters possess.

"You think it ridiculous for me to accept money on a project I want to fail. But never in a thousand years will I have another chance to make such a fortune—and you know a thousand years is too long. It would be so terribly simple for you to fail. I'm not asking you to give up the rewards promised you. Just make an error that won't be apparent until after the rejuvenation treatments are started and you have been paid."

If nothing else, Tsumo had the gall of ten. She was obviously an idealist: that is, someone who can twist his every vice into self-righteous morality. "You're nearly as ignorant as you are impudent. S.E. won't buy a pig in a poke. I don't get a cent till my process has boosted the Shiman life span past one century." That's the hell of immortality—you can't tell until the day after forever whether you really have the goods. "This is one cat you'll have to skin yourself."

Tsumo shook her head. "I intend to get that bribe, Kekkonen. The human race is second with me. But," she looked up and her voice hardened, "I've studied these creatures. If their life span is increased beyond ten years, there won't be any Samuelson Enterprises to pay you a century from now." Ah, so self-righteous.

The discussion was interrupted as a crack of light appeared in the darkness above us. Sirbat's burred voice came faintly. "We have moved the Bible classes from this part of the building. Come out." The light above silhouetted some curves I hadn't noticed before as Tsumo crawled through the tiny trap. I followed her, groaning. I never did learn what they used that cramped box for. Maybe the reverends spied on their congregations. You could never tell about those cannibals in the back pews.

We followed Sirbat down a low, narrow corridor into a windowless room. Another Shiman stood by a table in the center of the room. He looked skinny compared to our guide.

Sirbat shut the door, and motioned us to chairs by the table. I sat, but it was hardly worth the effort. The seat was so narrow I couldn't relax my legs. Shimans are bottom heavy. They don't really sit—they just lean.

SIRBAT MADE THE INTRODUCTIONS. "THIS IS BROTHER GORST OF THE ORDER of Saint Roger. He keeps the rules at this church, by the authority of the Committee in Senkenorn. Gorst's father was probably my teacher in second school." Brother Gorst nodded shyly and the harsh light glinted starkly off his fangs. Our interpreter continued, "For this minute we are safe—from Shiman police and army forces. The Earth Police spaceship is still hanging over the water, but only Miss Tsumo can do anything about that. Gorst will help us, but we may not use these rooms for more than three days. They are needed for church purposes later this eightday. There is another time limit, too. You will not have my help after tomorrow morning. Naturally, Gorst has no knowledge of any Earth languages, so—"

I interrupted, "The devil you say! There's no such thing as half a success in this racket, Sirbat. What's the matter with you?"

The Shiman leaned across the table, his claws raking scratches in its plastic surface. "That is not your business, Worm!" he hissed into my face. Sirbat stared at me for several seconds, his jaws working spasmodically. Finally, he returned to his chair. "You will please take account of this. Things would not be so serious now if you had only given care to the Earthpol danger. If I were you I would be happy that Shima is still willing to take what you have to offer. At this time our governments take Earthpol's orders, but it is safe to say they hope by Christ's name that you are out of danger. Their attempts to get you will not be strong. The greatest danger still comes from *your* people."

The blond Earthpol agent took the cue. "We have at least forty-eight hours before Ohara locates us." She reached into a pocket. "Fortunately I am not so poorly equipped as Professor Kekkonen. This is police issue."

The pile she placed on the table had no definite form—yet was almost alive. A thousand shifting colors shone from within it. Except for its size, her *'mam'ri* seemed unremarkable. Tsumo plunged her hand into it, and the device searched slowly across the table. Brother Gorst squeaked his terror, and bolted for the exit. Sirbat spoke rapidly to him, but the skinny Shiman continued to tremble. Sirbat turned to us. "The fact is, it's harder for me to talk with Gorst than with you. His special word knowledge has to do with right and wrong, while my special knowledge is of language. The number of words we have in common is small."

I guess two years isn't much time to learn to talk, read, write and acquire a technical education.

Finally Sirbat coaxed Gorst back to the table. Tsumo continued her spiel. "Don't be alarmed. I'm only checking to see that—" and she lapsed into Japanese. Old English just isn't up to describing modern technology. "That is, I'm making sure that our . . . shield against detection is still working. It is, but even so it doesn't protect us from pre-millennium techniques. So stay away from windows and open places. Also, my *o-mamori* can't completely protect us against—" She looked at me, puzzled. "How can I explain *f'un*, Professor?"

"Hm-m-m. Sirbat, Earthpol has a weapon which could be effective against us even if we stay hidden."

"A gas?" the Shiman asked.

"No, it's quite insubstantial. Just imagine that . . . hell, that's no good. About the best I can say is that it amounts to a massive dose of bad luck. If the breaks run consistently against us, I'd guess *f'un* might be involved."

Sirbat was incredulous, but he relayed my clumsy description on to Gorst, who seemed to accept the idea immediately.

Finally Sirbat spoke in English. "What an interesting thing. With this 'fa-oon' you no longer need to be responsible for your shortcomings.

We used to have things like that, but now we poor Shimans are weighted down by reason and science."

Sarcasm yet! "Don't accuse *us* of superstition, Sirbat. You people are clever but you have a long way to catch up. In the last two centuries, mankind has achieved every material goal that someone at your level could even *state* in a logical way. And we've gone on from there. The methods—even the methodology—of Tsumo's struggle with Earthpol would be unimaginable to you, but I assure you that if she weren't protecting us, we would have been captured hours ago." I touched the police-issue 'mam'ri. In addition to being our only defense against Earthpol, it was also my only hope for finishing my biological analysis of the Shimans. Apparently, the Earthpol agent really meant to keep her part of the bargain with Samuelson *et al.* Perhaps she thought I would foul things up *for* her. Fat chance.

"Before things blew up, I was pretty close to success. Only one real problem was left. Death for a Shiman isn't the sort of metabolic collapse we see in most other races. In a way you die backwards. If I'm gonna crack this thing, I've got to observe death firsthand."

Sirbat was silent for a long moment. It was the first time I'd seen a Shiman in a reflective mood. Finally he said, "As you have knowledge, Professor, we Shimans come to birth in great groups. The fact is that those who first saw life seven hundred and nine days before now will give up living tomorrow." He turned and spoke to Brother Gorst. The other bobbed his head and buzzed a response. Sirbat translated, "There is a death place only three kilometers from here. It is necessary for people of Gorst's Order to be on hand at the time of the group deaths. Brother Gorst says that he is willing to take you there. But it will not be possible for you to get nearer than fifty or sixty meters to the place of the deaths."

"That'll be fine," I said. "Fifteen minutes is all I need."

"Then this is a very happy chance, Professor. If it was not for the group death tomorrow, you would have to take nine more days here." As he spoke, a caterwauling rose from below us. Moments later someone was pounding at our door. Gorst scuttled over and opened it a crack. There was a hysterical consultation, then the reverend slammed the door and screamed at our interpreter.

"Christ help us!" said Sirbat. "There has been a smash out at the second school two kilometers from here. A large group of young is coming this way."

Gorst came back to his chair, then bounded up and paced around the room. From the way he chewed his lip, I guessed he was unhappy about the situation. Sirbat continued, "We have to make the decision of running or not running from the young persons."

"Are there any other hideouts you could dig up in this area?" I asked.

"No. Gorst is the only living person I have knowledge of in this place."

"Hm-m-m. Then I guess we'll just have to stay put."

Sirbat came to his feet. "You have little knowledge of Shiman conditions, Professor, or you wouldn't make that decision quite so easily. It is too bad. You are probably right. Our chances are near zero, one way or the other, but . . ." He snarled something at the other Shiman. Brother Gorst replied shortly. Sirbat said, "My friend is in agreement with you. We'll be safest at the top of the building." Gorst was already out the door. Tsumo scooped her *mam'ri* off the table, and we followed. A spiral stairway climbed twenty meters to end on a flat roof no more than ten meters square. A cross towered over the open space.

It was well past midnight. Below and around us were the sounds of running feet and automobile engines being lit. The cars screeched away from their parking slots, and headed west. One by one the lights in nearby buildings went out. The traffic got steadily noisier. Then after five or ten minutes, it subsided and the neighborhood was still.

The church spire reached several stories above the nearby buildings, and from there we could see Berelesk spread many kilometers, a mosaic of rough gray rectangles. Shima's single moon had risen and its light fell silver on the city. Near the horizon bomb flashes shone through the thinning smog, and I could hear the faint *thudadub* of artillery. Berelesk wasn't on good terms with its neighbors.

Tsumo pulled at my arm. I turned. Vast, blue, the glowing Earthpol ship hung above the bay. I jerked my outfit's dark veil down across my face. It wouldn't matter how good Tsumo's equipment was if her superiors actually eye-balled us.

Gorst hustled over to the low parapet, and leaned out to look straight down. At the same time, Sirbat studied the empty streets and quiet tenements. Finally I whispered, "So where's the action, Sirbat?"

The Shiman glanced at the Earthpol ship, then sidled over to us. "Don't you see why things are so quiet, Professor? More than three thousand children are free in this part of Berelesk. And they are coming our way. Everyone with any brain has run away from here. Children will eat everything they see, and it would be death to fight them: they run together and they are very bright. In the end, they will be so full that the authorities can take care of them one by one. We are probably the only living older persons within three kilometers—and that makes us the biggest pieces of food around."

Tsumo stood behind me, close to the cross. She ignored us both as she played with her *mam'ri*. From the parapet Brother Gorst shrilled softly. "Gorst is hearing them come," Sirbat translated. I turned to look east. There were faint sounds of traffic and artillery, but nothing else.

SEVERAL BLOCKS AWAY SOMETHING BRIGHT LIT THE SIDES OF FACING BUILD-ings. There was a muffled, concussive thud. Sirbat and Gorst hissed in pain. The fire burned briefly, then gutted out: the slums of Berelesk were mostly stone—nonflammable, and much more important, inedible. Smoke rose into the sky, blocked the moonlight and laid twisting shadows on the city.

Far away, something laughed, and someone screamed. Voices growled and squabbled. Whatever they were, they seemed to be having a good time. Four blocks up the pike, a street lamp winked out, and there was the sound of breaking glass. In the moonlight the juveniles were fast-moving gray shadows that flitted from doorway to doorway. The little bastards were smart. They never exposed themselves unnecessarily and they systematically smashed every street lamp they passed. I didn't see anyone run across the street until their skirmish line was nearly even with our church. Behind those front lines more were coming. [How big was the grade school, anyway?] Their lunatic screaming was all around us now. Tsumo looked up from her work, for the first time acknowl-edging our trivial problems. "Sirbat, aren't we safe from them here? We're so far above the street."

The Shiman made a rude noise, but it was a soft rude noise. "They will smell us even up here, and don't doubt they will come this high. We're the best food left. I wouldn't be surprised if the greater part of the young people are there in the church right now eating the wood seats and giving thought to our downfall."

Feet pattered around below us, and I heard a low, bubbly chuckle. I leaned over the parapet and looked down on the church's main roof. A chorus of eager shouts greeted my appearance, and something whistled up past my face. I ducked back, but I had already seen more than enough. There was a mob of them dancing on the deck below us. They were so close I could see the white of their fangs and the drool foaming down their chins. Except that they were near naked, the juveniles looked pretty much like adult Shimans.

Was there any real difference?

Tsumo might have a point after all—but that point would be entirely academic unless we could get out of this fix in one piece.

Gorst stood a meter behind the parapet with a quarterstaff in his claws. The first head that popped up would get a massive surprise. Sirbat paced back and forth, either panicking or thoughtful, I couldn't tell which. How long did we have before the juveniles came up the wall of the steeple? It was maddening: Properly used, Tsumo's o-mamori could easily defeat this attack, but at the same time such use would certainly put Earthpol onto our location. I looked around our tiny roof. There was unidentifiable equipment in the shadows beneath the parapet. Memories of a life two centuries past were coming back, and so were some ideas. The largest object, an ellipsoidal tank, sat near the base of the cross. A slender hose led from a valve on the tank. Half crouching, I ran across to the tank and felt its surface. The tank was cool, and the valve was covered with frost.

"Sirbat," I shouted over the competition from below, "What's this gadget?" The Shiman stopped his agonized pacing and glared at me briefly, then shouted at Gorst.

"That's a vessel of liquid natural gas," he translated the reply. "They use it to heat the church, and to . . . cook."

I LOOKED AT SIRBAT AND HE LOOKED BACK AT ME. I THINK HE HAD THE IDEA the instant he knew what the tank was. He came over to the tank and looked at the valve. I turned to follow the hose that stretched along the floor to a hole in the parapet.

"Kekkonen!" Tsumo's voice was tense. "If you attract Earthpol's notice, that disguise won't hold up." Over my shoulder I could see the glowing hulk of the gunboat. "Forget it, girl. If I can't do something with this tank, we'll all be dead in five minutes." Probably less: the juveniles were much louder now. We'd have to hope that if anyone was aboard the ship, they didn't believe in old-fashioned detection methods—like photoscanning computers.

The hose was slack and flexible. Four meters from the tank it entered a small valve set in the parapet. I began cutting at it with my knife. Behind me Sirbat said, "This looks good. The vessel is nearly full and its pressure is high." There were tearing sounds. "And it will get higher now."

That hose was tougher than it looked. It took nearly a minute, but finally I hacked through the thing. As I stood up, a head full of teeth appeared over the parapet next to me. I straight-armed the juvenile. It fell backwards, taking part of my sleeve in its claws. We were down to seconds now. I looked down at the hose in my hands and discovered the big flaw in our plan. How were we going to get this thing lit? Then I glanced at Sirbat. The Shiman was frantically jamming his coat under the tank. He stepped back and pointed something at the tank. A spark fell upon the coat, and soon yellow flames slid up the underside of the container. Even as those flames spread, he turned and ran to where I stood. But then he slowed, stopped, looked down at the object in his hand. For a long moment he just stood there.

"What's the matter? The lighter dead?"

". . . No." Sirbat answered slowly. He squeezed the small metal tube and a drop of fire spurted from the end. I swore and grabbed the lighter from Sirbat's hands. I leaned over the parapet and looked down. At least thirty juveniles were coming up the wall at us. Behind me Tsumo screamed. This was followed by a meaty thud. I looked up to see the Earthpol agent swing a long broom down on the head of a second monster. I guess she had finally found something more worrisome than her superiors in the sky to the west. Gorst was busy, too. He swept back and forth along the parapet with his quarterstaff. I saw him connect at least three times. The juveniles fell screeching to the roof below. Maybe that would occupy their brothers' appetites a few more moments.

I pushed our interpreter toward the gas tank. "Turn that damn valve, Sirbat." The Shiman returned to the tank. Now the flames licked up around the curving sides, keeping the valve out of reach. He ran to the other side of the cross, picked up some kind of rod and stuck it in the valve handle.

"Turn it, turn it," I shouted. Sirbat hesitated, then gave the lever a pull. No effect. He twisted the valve again. The hose bucked in my hand, as clear liquid spewed through it and arced out into space. That hose got *cold*: I could feel my hand going numb even as I stood there. I squeezed the lighter. A tiny particle of fire spurted out, missed the stream of gas. On my next try the burning droplet did touch the stream. Nothing happened.

I wrapped the hose in the corner of my jacket but it was still colder than a harlot's smile. This was probably my last chance to ignite the damn thing. Our gas pressure would fail soon enough, even if the juveniles didn't get me first.

The liquid gas left the hose as a coherent stream, but about five meters along its arc, the fluid began to mix with the air. Hah! I shook the lighter again and aimed it further out. The burning speck dropped through the aerated part of the stream. . . . The mist didn't burn—it exploded. I almost lost my footing as a roaring ball of blue-white flame materialized in the air five meters from the end of the hose. If that fireball had been any bigger we'd have been blown right off the roof. I pointed the hose down over the parapet. The roar of the flame masked their screams, but as I swept the fire along the wall below, I could see the juveniles fall away. The concussion alone must have been lethal. As I dragged the hose along the parapet, I could feel my face blister and my hands go numb. How long did I have before we ran out of gas, or even worse, before Sirbat's little fire exploded the tank? The ball of blue flame swept across the fourth wall, till no one was left there, till the wall was cracked and blackened. The roof and street below were littered with bodies.

Then Tsumo was dragging at my arm. I turned to see five or six gray forms leap from the trapdoor in the middle of our roof. I didn't have much choice: I turned the hose inward. Hunks of masonry flew past us as the exploding gas demolished the intruders along with the trapdoor, the center of the roof, and part of the cross. The floor buckled and I fell to one knee. That hose was some tiger's tail. If I dropped it, the top of the building would probably get blown off. Finally I managed to twist it around so the steam pointed outward again.

The explosion ended almost as suddenly as it had begun. All that was left was a ringing that roared in my ears. I was abruptly aware of the sweat dripping down the side of my nose, and the taste of dust and blood in my mouth. I dropped the hose and looked down at my numb hands. Was it the moonlight, or were they really bone white?

Over by the gas tank, Sirbat was busy putting out the fire he had set. He looked O.K. except that his clothes were shredded. Tsumo stood by the parapet. Her veil and one sleeve had been ripped away. Brother Gorst lay face down beside the large hole our makeshift flamethrower had put in the roof. If anything was left alive in that hole, it was down-right unkillable.

The ringing faded from my ears, and I could hear low-pitched sirens in the far distance. But I couldn't hear a single juvenile, and the smell of barbecue floated up from the street.

SIRBAT NUDGED GORST WITH HIS FOOT. THE OTHER'S CLAWED HAND LASHED out, barely missing our interpreter. The reverend sat up and groaned. Sirbat glanced at us. "You all right?" he asked.

I grunted something affirmative, and Tsumo nodded. An ugly bruise covered her jaw and cheek, and four deep scratches ran down her arm. She followed my glance. "Never mind, I'll live." She pulled the 'mam'ri from her pocket. "You'll be pleased to know that this has survived. What do we do now?"

It was Sirbat who answered. "Same as before. We'll stay here this night. Tomorrow you'll be able to see the group death you're so interested in." He moved cautiously to the edge of the hole. The moon was overhead now, and the damage was clearly visible. The room directly below us was gutted, and its floor was partly burned through. The room below that looked pretty bad, too. "First, we have to get some way to go down through this hole."

Brother Gorst rolled onto his feet and looked briefly at the destruction below. Then he ran to a small locker near the edge of the roof. He pulled out a coil of rope and threw it to Sirbat, who tied one end about the cross. Our interpreter moved slowly, almost clumsily. I looked closely at him, but in the moonlight he seemed uninjured. Sirbat pulled at the rope, making sure it was fast. Then he tossed the other end into the hole. "If past experience is a guide," he said, "we won't have any more trouble this night. The young persons fight very hard, but they are bright and when they have knowledge that their chances are zero, they go away. Also, they fear flames more than any other thing." He turned and slowly lowered himself hand over hand into the darkness. The rest of us followed.

My hands weren't numb anymore. The rope felt like a brand on them. I slipped and fell the last meter to the floor. I stood up to see the two Shimans and Tsumo standing nearby. The Earthpol agent was fiddling with the *o-mamori*, trying to reestablish our cover.

What was left of the roof above us blocked the Earthpol ship from view. Through the jagged hole, the full moon spread an irregular patch of gray light on the wreckage around us. The floor had buckled and cracked under the explosion. Several large fragments from a marble table top rested near my feet. As my eyes became accustomed to the darkness, I could also see what was left of the juveniles who had used this route to surprise us on the roof. The room was a combination abattoir and ruin.

Gorst moved quickly to the west wall, dug into the rubble. His rummaging uncovered a ladder well: we wouldn't have to use that rope again. Brother Gorst bent over and crawled down into the hole he had uncovered. All this time Sirbat just stood looking at the floor. Gorst called to him, and he walked slowly over to the ladder.

I WAS RIGHT ABOVE TSUMO AS WE CLIMBED DOWN. HER PROGRESS WAS clumsy, slow. It was a good thing the rungs were set only fifteen centimeters apart. A single beam of moonlight found its way over my shoulder and onto those below me.

If I hadn't been looking in just the right spot, I could have missed what happened then. A screaming fury hurtled out of the darkness. Gorst, who was already on the floor below us, whirled at the sound, his claws extended. Then just before the juvenile struck, he lowered his arms, stood defenseless. Gorst paid for his stupidity as the juvenile slammed into him, knocking him flat. He was dead even before he touched ground: his throat was ripped out. Now the juvenile headed for us on the ladder.

A reflex three centuries old took over, and my knife was out of my sleeve and in my hand. I threw just before the creature reached Sirbat. One thing I knew was Shiman anatomy. Still, it was mostly luck that the knife struck the only unarmored section of its notochord. My fingers were just too ripped up for accurate throwing. The juvenile dived face first into the base of the ladder and lay still. For a long moment the rest of us were frozen, too. If more were coming, we didn't have a chance. But the seconds passed and no other creatures appeared. The three of us scrambled down to the floor. As I retrieved my knife, I noticed that the corpse's flesh was practically parboiled. The juvenile must have been too shook up by the explosion to run off with the rest of the pack.

Sirbat walked past Gorst's body without looking down at it. "Come on," he said. You'd think I had just threatened his life rather than saved it.

This was the first level where the main stairs were still intact. We followed Sirbat down them, into the darkness. I couldn't see a thing, and the stairs were littered with crap that had fallen in from the disaster area above us. Either Sirbat was a fool or he had some special reason to think we were safe. Finally, we reached a level where the electric lights were still working. Sirbat left the stairway, and we walked down a long, deserted corridor. He stopped at a half-open door, sniffed around, then stepped through the doorway and flicked on a light. "I have no doubt you'll be safe here for this night."

I looked inside. A bas relief forest had been cut in the walls and then painted green. Three wide cots were set near the middle of the room—on the only carpet I ever saw on Shima. And what did they use the place for? You got me.

But whatever its purpose, the room looked secure. A grated window was set in one wall—nothing was going to surprise us from that direction. And the door was heavy plastic with an inside lock.

Tsumo stepped into the room. "You're not staying with us?" she asked Sirbat.

"No. That would not be safe." He was already walking from the room. "Just keep memory, that you have to be up two hours before sunrise in order to get to the death place on time. Have your . . . machines ready."

The arrogant bastard! What was "safe" for us was not safe enough for him. I followed the Shiman into the hall, debating whether to shake some answers out of him. But there were two good arguments against such action: 1) he might end up shaking me, and 2) unless we wanted to turn ourselves over to Earthpol, we didn't have any choice but to play things his way. So I stepped back into the room and slammed the door. The lock fell to with a satisfying thunk.

Tsumo sat down heavily on one of the cots and pulled the 'mam'ri from its pouch. She played awkwardly with it for several seconds. In the bright blue light, her bruise was a delicate mauve. Finally she looked up. "We're still undetected. But what happened tonight is almost certainly f'un. There hasn't been a smashout from that particular school in nearly three years. If we stay here much longer, our . . . 'bad luck' is going to kill us."

I grunted. Tsumo was at her cheery best. "In that case, I'll need a good night's sleep. I don't want to have to do that job twice." I hit the light and settled down on the nearest bunk. Faint bands of gray light crossed the ceiling from the tiny window. The shadowed forest on the wall almost seemed real now.

Tomorrow was going to be tricky. I would be using unfamiliar equipment—Tsumo's 'mam'ri—out-of-doors and at a relatively great distance from the dying. Even an orgy of death would be hard to analyze under those conditions. And all the time, we'd have Earthpol breathing down our necks. Several details needed thorough thinking out, but every time I tried to concentrate on them, I'd remember those juveniles scrambling up the church steeple at us. Over the last couple of centuries I'd had contact with three nonhuman races. The best competition I'd come across were the Draelings—carnivores with creative intelligence about 0.8 the human norm. I had never seen a group whose combined viciousness and cunning approached man's. Until now: the Shimans *started* life by committing a murder. The well-picked skeletons in the alley showed the murders didn't stop with birth. The average human would have to practice hard to be as evil as a Shiman is by inclination.

Tsumo's voice came softly from across the room. She must have been reading my mind. "And they're smart, too. See how much Sirbat has picked up in less than two years. He could go on learning at that rate for another century—if only he could live that long. The average is as inventive as our best. Fifty years ago there wasn't a single steam engine on Shima. And you can be sure we in Earthgov didn't help them invent one."

In the pale light I saw her stand and cross to my bunk. Her weight settled beside me. My frostbitten hand moved automatically across her back.

"Money is no good if you are dead—and we'll all die unless you fail tomorrow." A soft hand slipped across my neck and I felt her face in front of mine.

She tried awfully hard to convince me. Toward the end, there in the darkness, I almost felt sorry for little Miss Machiavelli. She kept calling me Roger.

SOMEONE WAS SHAKING ME. I WOKE TO FIND TSUMO'S FACE HOVERING HAZily in the air above me. I squinted against the hellishly bright light, and muttered, "Whassamatter?"

"Sirbat says it's time to go to the cemetery."

"Oh." I swung my feet to the floor, and raised myself off the bunk. My hands felt like hunks of flayed meat. I don't know how I was able to sleep with them. I steadied myself against the bed and looked around. The window was a patch of unrelieved darkness in the wall. We still had a way to go before morning. Tsumo was dressed except for hood and veil, and she was pushing my costume at me.

I took the disguise. "Where the devil is Sirbat, anyway?" Then I saw him over by the door. On the floor. The Shiman was curled up in a tight ball. His bloodshot eyes roved aimlessly about, finally focused on me.

My jaw must have been resting on my chest. Sirbat croaked, "So, Professor, you have been getting knowledge of Shiman life all this time, but you did not ever take note of my condition. If it wasn't for the special substances I've been taking I would have been like this days ago." He stopped, coughed reddish foam.

O.K., I had been an idiot. The signs had all been there: Sirbat's relative plumpness, his awkward slowness the last few hours, his comments about not being with us after the morning. My only excuse is the fact that death by old age had become a very theoretical thing to me. Sure, I studied it, but I hadn't been confronted with the physical reality for more than a century.

But one oversight was enough: I could already see a mess of consequences ahead. I slipped the black dress over my head and put on the veil. "Tsumo, take Sirbat's legs. We'll have to carry him downstairs." I grabbed Sirbat's shoulders and we lifted together. The Shiman must have massed close to seventy-five kilos—about fifteen over the average adult's weight. If he had been on drugs to curb the burrowing instinct, he might die before we got him to the cemetery—and that would be fatal all the way around. Now we had a new reason for getting to that cemetery on time.

We hadn't gone down very many steps before Tsumo began straining under the load. She leaned to one side, favoring her left hand. Me, both hands felt like they were ready to fall off, so I didn't have such trouble. Sirbat hung between us, clutching tightly at his middle. His head lolled. His jaws opened with tiny whimpering sounds, and reddish drool dripped down his head onto the steps. It was obviously way past burrowing time for him.

Sirbat gasped out one word at a breath. "Left turn, first story."

Two more flights and we were on the ground. We turned left and staggered out the side door into a parking lot. No one was around this early in the morning. A sea fog had moved in and perfect halos hung around the only two street lamps left alight. It was so foggy we couldn't even see the other side of the lot. For the first time since I'd been on Shima, the air was tolerably clean.

"The red one," said Sirbat. Tsumo and I half dragged the Shiman over to a large red car with official markings. We laid Sirbat on the asphalt and tried the doors. Locked.

"Gorst's opener, in here." His clawed hand jerked upward. I retrieved the keys from his blouse, and opened the door. Somehow we managed to bundle Sirbat into the back seat.

I looked at Tsumo. "You know how to operate this contraption?"

Her eyes widened in dismay. Apparently she had never considered this flaw in our plans. "No, of course not. Do you?"

"Once upon a time, my dear," I said, urging her into the passenger seat, "once upon a time." I settled behind the wheel and slammed the door. These were the first mechanical controls I had seen in a long time, but they were grotesquely familiar. The steering wheel was less than thirty centimeters across (I soon found it was only half a turn from lock to lock). A clutch and shift assembly were mounted next to the wheel. With the help of Sirbat's advice I started the engine and backed out of the parking stall.

The car's triple headlights sent silver spears into the fog. It was difficult to see more than thirty meters into the murk. The only Shiman around was a half-eaten corpse on the sidewalk by the entrance to the parking lot. I eased the car into the street, and Sirbat directed me to the first turn.

This was almost worth the price of admission! It had been a long time since I'd driven any vehicle. The street we were on went straight to the river. I'll bet we were making a hundred kilometers per hour before three blocks were passed.

"Go, go you—" the rest was unintelligible. Sirbat paused, then managed to say, "We'll be stopped for sure if you keep driving like a sleepwalker." The buildings on either side of the narrow street zipped by too fast to count. Ahead nothing was visible but the brilliant backglow from our headlights. How could a Shiman survive even two years if he drove faster than this? I swerved as something—a truck, I think—whipped out of a side street.

I turned up the throttle. The engine tried to twist off its moorings and the view to the side became a gray blur.

Three or four minutes passed—or maybe it wasn't that long. I couldn't tell. Suddenly Sirbat was screaming, "Left turn . . . two hundred meters more." I slammed on the brakes. Thank God they'd taught him English instead of modern Japanese—which doesn't really have quantitative terms for distance. We probably would have driven right through the intersection before Sirbat would come up with a circumlocution that would tell me how far to go and where to turn. The car skidded wildly across the intersection. Either the street was wet or the Shimans made their brake linings out of old rags. We ended up with our two front wheels over the curb. I backed the car off the sidewalk and made the turn.

NOW THE GOING GOT TOUGH. WE HAD TO TURN EVERY FEW BLOCKS AND there were some kind of traffic signals I couldn't figure out. That tiny steering wheel was hell to turn. The skin on my hands felt like it was being ripped off. All the time Sirbat was telling me to go faster, faster. I tried. If he died there in the car it would be like getting trapped in a school of piranha.

The fog got thicker, but less uniform. Occasionally we broke into a clear spot where I could see nearly a block. We blasted up a sharply arched bridge, felt a brief moment of near-weightlessness at the top, and then were down on the other side. In the river that was now behind us, a boat whistled.

From the back set, Sirbat's mumbling became coherent English: "Earthman, do you have knowledge . . . how lucky you are?"

"What?" I asked. Was he getting delirious?

Ahead of me the road narrowed, got twisty. We were moving up the ridge that separated the city from the ocean. Soon we were above the murk. In the starlight the fog spread across the lands below, a placid cottony sea that drowned everything but the rocky island we were climbing. Earthpol's gunboat skulked north of us.

Finally Sirbat replied, "Being good is no trouble at all for you. You're . . . born that way. We have to work so . . . hard at it . . . like Gorst. And in the end . . . I'm still as bad . . . as hungry as I ever was. So hungry." His speech died in a liquid gurgle. I risked a look behind me. The Shiman was chewing feebly at the upholstery.

We were out of the city proper now. Far up, near the crest of the ridge, I could see the multiple fences that bounded the cemetery. Even by starlight I could see that the ground around us was barren, deeply eroded.

I pulled down my veil and turned the throttle to full. We covered the last five hundred meters to the open gates in a single burst of speed. The guards waved us through—after all, their job was to keep things from getting *out*—and I cruised into the parking area. There were lots of people around, but fortunately the street lights were dimmed. I parked at the side of the lot nearest the graveyard. We hustled Sirbat out of the car and onto the pavement. The nearest Shimans were twenty meters from us, but when they saw what we were doing they moved even further away, whispered anxiously to each other. We had a live bomb on our hands, and they wanted no part of it.

Sirbat lay on the pavement and stared into the sky. Every few seconds his face convulsed. He seemed to be whispering to himself. Delirious. Finally he said in English, "Tell him . . . I forgive him." The Shiman rolled onto his feet. He paused, quivering, then sprinted off into the darkness. His footsteps faded, and all we could hear were faint scratching sounds and the conversation of Shimans around us in the parking lot.

For a moment we stood silently in the chill, moist air. Then I whispered to Tsumo, "How long?"

"It's about two hours before dawn. I am sure Earthpol will penetrate my evasion patterns in less than three hours. If you stay until the swarming, you'll probably be caught."

I turned and looked across the rising fog bank. There were thirty billion people on this planet, I had been told. Without the crude form of birth control practiced at thousands of cemeteries like this one, there could be many more. And every one of the creatures was intelligent, murderous. If I finished my analysis, then they'd have practical immortality along with everything else, and we'd be facing them in our own space in a very short time . . . which was exactly what Samuelson wanted. In fact, it was the price he had demanded of the Shimans— that their civilization expand into space, so mankind would at last have a worthy competitor. And what if the Shiman brain was as far superior as timid souls like Tsumo claimed? *Well then, we will have to do some imitating, some catching up.* I could almost hear Samuelson's reedy voice speaking the words. Myself, I wasn't as sure: ever since we were kids back in Chicago, Samuelson had been kinda kinky about street-fighting, and about learning from the toughs he fought—me for instance.

"Give me that," I said, taking the *'mam'ri* from Tsumo's hand, and turning it to make my preliminary scan across the cemetery. Whether Samuelson and I were right or wrong, the next century was going to be damned interesting.

THE SUN'S DISK STOOD WELL CLEAR OF THE HORIZON. THE MAZES AND DEAD-falls and machine guns had taken their toll. Of the original million infants, less than a thousand had survived. They would be weeded no further.

Near the front of the pack, one of the smartest and strongest ran joyfully toward the scent of food ahead—where the first schoolmasters had set their cages. The child lashed happily at those around it, but they were wise and kept their distance. For the moment its hunger was not completely devastating and the sunlight warmed its back. It was wonderful to be alive and free and . . . innocent.

I wrote "Original Sin" around 1970. For many years, it was my favorite of all my stories. I thought I had said something about basic "human" issues. I liked the tantalizing glimpses of our future civilization ("remember spaceships?"). I deliberately wrote it without reference to any real technologies beyond 1940—the idea being that 1940 jargon should probably be as accurate as 1970 jargon in explaining the far future. The word-hacker in me was also intrigued by the Basic English vocabulary the aliens used. (It turned out to be surprisingly difficult to write in that vocabulary. Once I saw the Gettysburg address re-done in Basic English; it seemed about as eloquent as the original. I didn't realize until I was writing this story what a feat that was.)

Nevertheless, I had more trouble selling "Original Sin" than almost anything I've written. The early versions were just too cryptic. It bounced and bounced and bounced. But usually the editors liked parts of it, and often they told me what they didn't like. Between the kind advice of Harlan Ellison and Ben Bova, I eventually wrote something that could sell.

THE BLABBER

In my novel *Marooned in Realtime*, I had a brush with the Singularity. After I
finished that book, I felt a bit marooned myself. The closer my stories came to
the Singularity, the shorter the timescales and the less opportunity for the kind
of adventure stories that I grew up with. Any future history following these events
would be a short run over a cliff, into the abyss . . . with no human equivalent
aliens, no intelligible interstellar civilizations.

If I wanted to build a future-history series, it seemed that I was stuck with
honest extrapolation and a very quick end to human history—or a series that
was overtly science-fictional, but secretly a fantasy since it would be based on
the *absence* of the scientific progress that I see coming. I was stuck; the dilemma
lasted about two years.

Eventually I found a solution, one that was faithful to my ideas about progress
but which still allowed me to write fiction with human-sized characters and interstellar adventure. The solution? Basically I turned my extrapolations sideways,
as you will see in this next story. "The Blabber" was a test flight into the universe
of my Zones of Thought novels.

Some dreams take a long time in dying. Some get a last-minute
reprieve . . . and that can be even worse.

It was just over two klicks from the Elvis revival to the center of
campus. Hamid Thompson took the long way, across the Barkers' stub-
bly fields and through the Old Subdivision. Certainly the Blabber preferred that route. She raced this way and that across Ham's path, rooting
at roach holes and covertly watching the birds that swooped close on
her seductive calls. As usual, her stalking was more for fun than food.
When a bird came within striking distance, the Blab's head would flick
up, touching the bird with her nose, blasting it with a peal of human
laughter. The Blab hadn't taken this way in some time; all the birds in
her regular haunts had wised up, and were no fun anymore.

When they reached the rock bluffs behind the subdivision, there
weren't any more roach holes, and the birds had become cautious. Now
the Blab walked companionably beside him, humming in her own way:
scraps of Elvis overlaid with months-old news commentary. She went
a minute or two in silence . . . listening? Contrary to what her detractors
might say, she could be both awake and silent for hours at a time—but
even then Hamid felt an occasional buzzing in his head, or a flash of

pain. The Blab's tympana could emit across a two-hundred-kilohertz band, which meant that most of her mimicry was lost on human ears.

They were at the crest of the bluff. "Sit down, Blab. I want to catch my breath." *And look at the view. . . . And decide what in heaven's name I should do with you and with me.*

The bluffs were the highest natural viewpoints in New Michigan province. The flatlands that spread around them were pocked with ponds, laced with creeks and rivers, the best farmland on the continent. From orbit, the original colonists could find no better. Water landings would have been easier, but they wanted the best odds on long-term survival. Thirty klicks away, half hidden by gray mist, Hamid could see the glassy streaks that marked the landing zone. The history books said it took three years to bring down the people and all the salvage from the greatship. Even now the glass was faintly radioactive, one cause for the migration across the isthmus to Westland.

Except for the forest around those landing strips, and the old university town just below the bluff, most everything in this direction was farmland, unending squares of brown and black and gray. The year was well into autumn and the last of the Earth trees had given up their colored leaves. The wind blowing across the plains was chill, leaving a crispness in his nose that promised snow someday soon. Hallowe'en was next week. Hallowe'en indeed. *I wonder if in Man's thirty thousand years, there has ever been a celebration of that holiday like we'll be seeing next week.* Hamid resisted the impulse to look back at Marquette. Ordinarily it was one of his favorite places: the planetary capital, population four hundred thousand, a real city. As a child, visiting Marquette had been like a trip to some far star system. But now reality had come, and the stars were so *close.* . . . Without turning, he knew the position of every one of the Tourist barges. They floated like colored balloons above the city, yet none massed less than a thousand tonnes. And those were their *shuttles.* After the Elvis revival, Hallowe'en was the last big event on the Marquette leg of the Tour. Then they would be off to Westland, for more semi-fraudulent peeks at Americana.

Hamid crunched back in the dry moss that cushioned the rock. "Well, Blabber, what should I do? Should I sell you? We could both make it Out There if I did."

The Blabber's ears perked up. "Talk? Converse? Disgust?" She settled her forty-kilo bulk next to him, and nuzzled her head against his chest. The purring from her foretympanum sounded like some transcendental cat. The sound was pink noise, buzzing through his chest and shaking the rock they sat on. There were few things she enjoyed more than a good talk with a peer. Hamid stroked her black and white pelt. "I said, should I sell you?"

The purring stopped, and for a moment the Blab seemed to give the matter thoughtful consideration. Her head turned this way and that, bobbing—a good imitation of a certain prof at the University. She rolled her big dark eyes at him, "Don't rush me! I'm thinking. I'm thinking." She licked daintily at the sleek fur at the base of her throat. And for all Hamid knew, she really was thinking about what to say. Sometimes she really seemed to try to understand . . . and sometimes she almost made sense. Finally she shut her mouth and began talking.

"Should I sell you? Should I sell you?" The intonation was still Hamid's but she wasn't imitating his voice. When they talked like this, she typically sounded like an adult human female (and a very attractive one, Hamid thought). It hadn't always been that way. When she had been a pup and he a little boy, she'd sounded to him like another little boy. The strategy was clear: she understood the type of voice he most likely wanted to hear. Animal cunning? "Well," she continued, "*I* know what I think. Buy, don't sell. And always get the best price you can."

She often came across like that: oracular. But he had known the Blab all his life. The longer her comment, the less she understood it. In this case . . . Ham remembered his finance class. That was before he got his present apartment, and the Blab had hidden under his desk part of the semester. (It had been an exciting semester for all concerned.) "Buy, don't sell." That was a quote, wasn't it, from some nineteenth-century tycoon?

She blabbered on, each sentence having less correlation with the question. After a moment, Hamid grabbed the beast around the neck, laughing and crying at the same time. They wrestled briefly across the rocky slope, Hamid fighting at less than full strength, and the Blab carefully keeping her talons retracted. Abruptly he was on his back and the Blab was standing on his chest. She held his nose between the tips of her long jaws. "Say Uncle! Say Uncle!" she shouted.

The Blabber's teeth stopped a couple of centimeters short of the end of her snout, but the grip was powerful; Hamid surrendered immediately. The Blab jumped off him, chuckling triumph, then grabbed his sleeve to help him up. He stood up, rubbing his nose gingerly. "Okay, monster, let's get going." He waved downhill, toward Ann Arbor Town.

"Ha, ha! For sure. Let's get going!" The Blab danced down the rocks faster than he could hope to go. Yet every few seconds the creature paused an instant, checking that he was still following. Hamid shook his head, and started down. Damned if he was going to break a leg just to keep up with her. Whatever her homeworld, he guessed that winter around Marquette was the time of year most homelike for the Blab. Take her coloring: stark black and white, mixed in wide curves and swirls. He'd seen that pattern in pictures of ice-pack seals. When there was snow on the ground, she was practically invisible.

She was fifty meters ahead of him now. From this distance, the Blab could almost pass for a dog, some kind of greyhound maybe. But the paws were too large, and the neck too long. The head looked more like a seal's than a dog's. Of course, she could bark like a dog. But then, she could also sound like a thunderstorm, and make something like human conversation—all at the same time. There was only one of her kind in all Middle America. This last week, he'd come to learn that her kind were almost as rare Out There. A Tourist wanted to buy her . . . and Tourists could pay with coin what Hamid Thompson had sought for more than half his twenty years.

Hamid desperately needed some good advice. It had been five years since he'd asked his father for help; he'd be damned if he did so now. That left the University, and Lazy Larry. . . .

By Middle-American standards, Ann Arbor Town was *ancient*. There were older places: out by the landing zone, parts of Old Marquette still stood. School field trips to those ruins were brief—the pre-fab quonsets were mildly radioactive. And of course there were individual buildings in the present-day capital that went back almost to the beginning. But much of the University in Ann Arbor dated from just after those first permanent structures: the University had been a going concern for 190 years.

Something was up today, and it had nothing to do with Hamid's problems. As they walked into town, a couple of police helicopters swept in from Marquette, began circling the school. On the ground, some of Ham's favorite back ways were blocked off by University safety patrols. No doubt it was Tourist business. He might have to come in through the Main Gate, past the Math Building. *Yuck.* Even after ten years he loathed that place: his years as a supposed prodigy; his parents forcing him into math classes he just wasn't bright enough to handle; the tears and anger at home, till he finally convinced them that he was not the boy they thought.

They walked around the Quad, Hamid oblivious to the graceful buttresses, the ivy that meshed stone walls into the flute trees along the street. That was all familiar . . . what was new was all the Federal cop cars. Clusters of students stood watching the cops, but there was no riot in the air. They just seemed curious. Besides, the Feds had never interfered on campus before.

"Keep quiet, okay?" Hamid muttered.

"Sure, sure." The Blab scrunched her neck back, went into her doggie act. At one time they had been notorious on campus, but he had dropped out that summer, and people had other things on their minds today. They walked through the main gate without comment from students or cops.

The biggest surprise came when they reached Larry's slummy digs at Morale Hall. Morale wasn't old enough to be historic; it was old enough to be in decay. It had been an abortive experiment in brick construction. The clay had cracked and rotted, leaving gaps for vines and pests. By now it was more a reddish mound of rubble than a habitable structure. This was where the University Administration stuck tenured faculty in greatest disfavor: the Quad's Forgotten Quarter . . . but not today. Today the cop cars were piled two deep in the parking areas, and there were shotgun-toting guards at the entrance!

Hamid walked up the steps. He had a sick feeling that Lazy Larry might be the hardest prof in the world to see today. On the other hand, working with the Tourists meant Hamid saw some of these security people every day.

"Your business, sir?" Unfortunately, the guard was no one he recognized.

"I need to see my advisor . . . Professor Fujiyama." Larry had never been his advisor, but Hamid was looking for advice.

"Um." The cop flicked on his throat mike. Hamid couldn't hear much, but there was something about "that black and white off-planet creature." Over the last twenty-years, you'd have to have been living in a cave never to see anything about the Blabber.

A minute passed, and an older officer stepped through the doorway. "Sorry, son, Mr. Fujiyama isn't seeing any students this week. Federal business."

Somewhere a funeral dirge began playing. Hamid tapped the Blab's forepaw with his foot; the music stopped abruptly. "Ma'am, it's not school business." Inspiration struck: why not tell something like the truth? "It's about the Tourists and my Blabber."

The senior cop sighed. "That's what I was afraid you'd say. Okay, come along." As they entered the dark hallway, the Blabber was chuckling triumph. Someday the Blab would play her games with the wrong people and get the crap beat out of her, but apparently today was not that day.

They walked down two flights of stairs. The lighting got even worse, half-dead fluorescents built into the acoustic tiling. In places the wooden stairs sagged elastically under their feet. There were no queues of students squatting before any of the doors, but the cops hadn't cleared out the faculty: Hamid heard loud snoring from one of the offices. The Forgotten Quarter—Morale Hall in particular—was a strange place. The one thing the faculty here had in common was that each had been an unbearable pain in the neck to someone. That meant that both the most incompetent and the most brilliant were jammed into these tiny offices.

Larry's office was in the sub-basement, at the end of a long hall. Two more cops flanked the doorway, but otherwise it was as Hamid remembered it. There was a brass nameplate: PROFESSOR L. LAWRENCE FUJIYAMA, DEPARTMENT OF TRANSHUMAN STUDIES. Next to the nameplate, a sign boasted implausible office hours. In the center of the door was the picture of a piglet and the legend: "If a student appears to need help, then appear to give him some."

The police officer stood aside as they reached the door; Hamid was going to have to get in under his own power. Ham gave the door a couple of quick knocks. There was the sound of footsteps, and the door opened a crack. "What's the secret password?" came Larry's voice.

"Professor Fujiyama, I need to talk to—"

"That's not it!" The door was slammed loudly in Hamid's face.

The senior cop put her hand on Hamid's shoulder. "Sorry, son. He's done that to bigger guns than you."

He shrugged off her hand. Sirens sounded from the black and white creature at his feet. Ham shouted over the racket, "Wait! It's me, Hamid Thompson! From your Transhume 201."

The door came open again. Larry stepped out, glanced at the cops, then looked at the Blabber. "Well, why didn't you say so? Come on in." As Hamid and the Blab scuttled past him, Larry smiled innocently at the Federal officer. "Don't worry, Susie, this is official business."

Fujiyama's office was long and narrow, scarcely an aisle between deep equipment racks. Larry's students (those who dared these depths) doubted the man could have survived on Old Earth before electronic datastorage. There must be tonnes of junk squirreled away on those shelves. The gadgets stuck out this way and that into the aisle. The place was a museum—perhaps literally; one of Larry's specialties was archeology. Most of the machines were dead, but here and there something clicked, something glowed. Some of the gadgets were Rube Goldberg jokes, some were early colonial prototypes . . . and a few were from Out There. Steam and water pipes covered much of the ceiling. The place reminded Hamid of the inside of a submarine.

At the back was Larry's desk. The junk on the table was balanced precariously high: a display flat, a beautiful piece of night-black statuary. In Transhume 201, Larry had described his theory of artifact management: Last-In-First-Out, and every year buy a clean bed sheet, date it, and lay it over the previous layer of junk on your desk. Another of Lazy Larry's jokes, most had thought. But there really *was* a bed sheet peeking out from under the mess.

Shadows climbed sharp and deep from the lamp on Larry's desk. The cabinets around him seemed to lean inwards. The open space between them was covered with posters. Those posters were one small reason Larry was down here: ideas to offend every sensible faction of society. A pile of . . . something . . . lay on the visitor's chair. Larry slopped it onto the floor and motioned Hamid to sit.

"Sure, I remember you from Transhume. But why mention that? You own the Blabber. You're Huss Thompson's kid." He settled back in his chair.

I'm not Huss Thompson's kid! Aloud, "Sorry, that was all I could think to say. This is about my Blabber, though. I need some advice."

"Ah!" Fujiyama gave his famous polliwog smile, somehow innocent and predatory at the same time. "You came to the right place. I'm full of it. But I heard you had quit school, gone to work at the Tourist Bureau."

Hamid shrugged, tried not to seem defensive. "Yeah. But I was already a senior, and I know more American Thought and Lit than most graduates . . . and the Tourist caravan will only be here another half year. After that, how long till the next? We're showing them everything I could imagine they'd want to see. In fact, we're showing them more than there really *is* to see. It could be a hundred years before anyone comes down here again."

"Possibly, possibly."

"Anyway, I've learned a lot. I've met almost half the Tourists. But . . ." There were ten million people living on Middle America. At least a million had a romantic yearning to get Out There. At least ten thousand would give everything they owned to leave the Slow Zone, to live in a civilization that spanned thousands of worlds. For the last ten years, Middle America had known of the Caravan's coming. Hamid had spent most of those years—half his life, all the time since he got out of math—preparing himself with the skills that could buy him a ticket Out.

Thousands of others had worked just as hard. During the last decade, every department of American Thought and Literature on the planet had been jammed to the bursting point. And more had been going on behind the scenes. The government and some large corporations had had secret programs that weren't revealed till just before the Caravan arrived. Dozens of people had bet on the long shots, things that no one else thought the Outsiders might want. Some of those were fools: the world-class athletes, the chess masters. They could never be more than eighth rate in the vast populations of the Beyond. No, to get a ride you needed something that was odd . . . Out There. Besides the Old Earth angle, there weren't many possibilities—though that could be approached in surprising ways: there was Gilli Weinberg, a bright but not brilliant ATL student. When the Caravan reached orbit, she bypassed the Bureau, announced herself to the Tourists as a genuine American cheerleader and premier courtesan. It was a ploy pursued less frankly and less successfully by others of both sexes. In Gilli's case, it had won her a ticket Out. The big laugh was that her sponsor was one of the few non-humans in the Caravan, a Lothlrimarre slug who couldn't survive a second in an oxygen atmosphere.

"I'd say I'm on good terms with three of the Outsiders. But there are least five Tour Guides that can put on a better show. And you know the Tourists managed to revive four more corpsicles from the original Middle America crew. Those guys are sure to get tickets Out, if they want 'em." Men and women who had been adults on Old Earth, two thousand light years away and twenty thousand years ago. It was likely that Middle America had no more valuable export this time around. "If they'd just come a few years later, after I graduated . . . maybe made a name for myself."

Larry broke into the self-pitying silence. "You never thought of using the Blabber as your ticket Out?"

"Off and on." Hamid glanced down at the dark bulk that curled around his feet. The Blab was *awfully* quiet.

Larry noticed the look. "Don't worry. She's fooling with some ultrasound imagers I have back there." He gestured at the racks behind Hamid, where a violet glow played hopscotch between unseen gadgets.

The boy smiled. "We may have trouble getting her out of here." He had several ultrasonic squawkers around the apartment, but the Blab rarely got to play with high-resolution equipment. "Yeah, right at the beginning, I tried to interest them in the Blab. Said I was her trainer. They lost interest as soon as they saw she couldn't be native to Old Earth. . . . These guys are *freaks*, Professor! You could rain transhuman treasure on 'em, and they'd call it spit! But give 'em Elvis Presley singing Bruce Springsteen and they build you a spaceport on Selene!"

Larry just smiled, the way he did when some student was heading for academic catastrophe. Hamid quieted. "Yeah, I know. There are good reasons for some of the strangeness." Middle America had nothing that would interest anybody rational from Out There. They were stuck nine light years inside the Slow Zone: commerce was hideously slow and expensive. Middle American technology was obsolete and—considering their location—it could never amount to anything competitive. Hamid's unlucky world had only one thing going for it. It was a direct colony of Old Earth, and one of the first. Their greatship's tragic flight had lasted twenty thousand years, long enough for the Earth to become a legend for much of humankind.

In the Beyond, there were millions of solar systems known to bear human-equivalent intelligences. Most of these could be in more or less instantaneous communication with one another. In that vastness humanity was a speck—perhaps four thousand worlds. Even on those, interest in a first-generation colony within the Slow Zone was near zero. But with four thousand worlds, that was enough: here and there was a rich eccentric, an historical foundation, a religious movement—all strange enough to undertake a twenty-year mission into the Slowness. So Middle America should be glad for these rare mixed nuts. Over the last hundred years there had been occasional traders and a couple of tourist caravans. That commerce had raised the Middle American standard of living substantially. More important to many—including Hamid—it was almost their only peephole on the universe beyond the Zone. In the last century, two hundred Middle Americans had escaped to the Beyond. The early ones had been government workers, commissioned scientists. The Feds' investment had not paid off: of all those who left, only five had returned. Larry Fujiyama and Hussein Thompson were two of those five.

"Yeah, I guess I knew they'd be fanatics. But most of them aren't even much interested in accuracy. We make a big thing of representing twenty-first-century America. But we both know what that was like: heavy industry moving up to Earth orbit, five hundred million people still crammed into North America. At best, what we have here is like mid-twentieth-century America—or even earlier. I've worked very hard to get our past straight. But except for a few guys I really respect, anachronism doesn't seem to bother them. It's like just being here with us is the big thing."

Larry opened his mouth, seemed on the verge of providing some insight. Instead he smiled, shrugged. (One of his many mottos was, "If you didn't figure it out yourself, you don't understand it.")

"So after all these months, where did you dig up the interest in the Blabber?"

"It was the slug, the guy running the Tour. He just mailed me that he had a party who wanted to buy. Normally, this guy haggles. He— wait, you know him pretty well, don't you? Well, he just made a flat offer. A payoff to the Feds, transport for me to Lothlrimarre," that was the nearest civilized system in the Beyond, "and some ftl privileges beyond that."

"And you kiss your pet goodbye?"

"Yeah. I made a case for them needing a handler: me. That's not just bluff, by the way. We've grown up together. I can't imagine the Blab accepting anyone without lots of help from me. But they're not interested. Now, the slug claims no harm is intended her, but . . . do you believe him?"

"Ah, the slug's slime is generally clean. I'm sure he doesn't know of any harm planned . . . and he's straight enough to do at least a little checking. Did he say who wanted to buy?"

"Somebody—something named Ravna&Tines." He passed Larry a flimsy showing the offer. Ravna&Tines had a logo: it looked like a stylized claw. "There's no Tourist registered with that name."

Larry nodded, copied the flimsy to his display flat. "I know. Well, let's see. . . ." He puttered around for a moment. The display was a lecture model, with imaging on both sides. Hamid could see the other was searching internal Federal databases. Larry's eyebrows rose. "Hm*hm!* Ravna&Tines arrived just last week. It's not part of the Caravan at all."

"A solitary trader . . ."

"Not only that. It's been hanging out past the Jovians—at the slug's request. The Federal space net got some pictures." There was a fuzzy image of something long and wasp-waisted, typical of the Outsiders' ramscoop technology. But there were strange fins—almost like the wings on a sailplane. Larry played some algorithmic game with the display and the image sharpened. "Yeah. Look at the aspect ratio on those fins. This guy is carrying high-performance ftl gear. No good down here of course, but hot stuff across an enormous range of environment . . ." He whistled a few bars of "Nightmare Waltz." "I think we're looking at a High Trader."

Someone from the Transhuman Spaces.

Almost every university on Middle America had a Department of Transhuman Studies. Since the return of the five, it had been a popular thing to do. Yet most people considered it a joke. Transhume was generally the bastard child of Religious Studies and an Astro or Computer Science department, the dumping ground for quacks and incompetents. Lazy Larry had founded the department at Ann Arbor—and spent much class time eloquently proclaiming its fraudulence. Imagine, trying to study what lay *beyond* the Beyond! Even the Tourists avoided the topic. Transhuman Space existed—perhaps it included most of the universe—but it was a tricky, risky, ambiguous thing. Larry said that its reality drove most of the economics of the Beyond . . . but that all the theories about it were rumors at tenuous secondhand. One of his proudest claims was that he raised Transhuman Studies to the level of palm reading.

Yet now . . . apparently a trader had arrived that regularly penetrated the Transhuman Reaches. If the government hadn't sat on the news, it would have eclipsed the Caravan itself. And *this* was what wanted the Blab. Almost involuntarily, Hamid reached down to pet the creature. "Y-you don't think there could really be anybody transhuman on that ship?" An hour ago he had been agonizing about parting with the Blab; that might be nothing compared to what they really faced.

For a moment he thought Larry was going to shrug the question off. But the older man sighed. "If there's anything we've got right, it's that no transhuman can think at these depths. Even in the Beyond, they'd die or fragment or maybe cyst. I think this Ravna&Tines must be a human-equivalent intellect, but it could be a lot more dangerous than the average Outsider . . . the tricks it would know, the gadgets it would have." His voice drifted off; he stared at the forty-centimeter statue perched on his desk. It was lustrous green, apparently cut from a flawless block of jade. *Green? Wasn't it black a minute ago?*

Larry's gaze snapped up to Hamid. "Congratulations. Your problem is a lot more interesting than you thought. Why would any Outsider want the Blab, much less a High Trader?"

". . . Well, her kind must be rare. I haven't talked to any Tourist who recognized the race."

Lazy Larry just nodded. Space is deep. The Blab might be from somewhere else in the Slow Zone.

"When she was a pup, lots of people studied her. You saw the articles. She has a brain as big as a chimp's, but most of it's tied up in driving her tympana and processing what she hears. One guy said she's the ultimate in verbal orientation—all mouth and no mind."

"Ah! A student!"

Hamid ignored the Larryism. "Watch this." He patted the Blab's shoulder.

She was slow in responding; that ultrasound equipment must be fascinating. Finally she raised her head. "What's up?" The intonation was natural, the voice a young woman's.

"Some people think she's just a parrot. She can play things back better than a high-fidelity recorder. But she also picks up favorite phrases, and uses them in different voices—and almost appropriately. . . . Hey, Blab. What's that?" Hamid pointed at the electric heater that Larry had propped by his feet. The Blab stuck her head around the corner of the desk, saw the cherry glowing coils. This was not the sort of heater Hamid had in his apartment.

"What's that . . . that . . ." The Blab extended her head curiously toward the glow. She was a bit too eager; her nose bumped the heater's safety grid. *"Hot!"* She jumped back, her nose tucked into her neck fur, a foreleg extended toward the heater. "Hot! Hot!" She rolled onto her haunches, and licked tentatively at her nose. "Jeeze!" She gave Hamid a look that was both calculating and reproachful.

"Honest, Blab, I didn't think you would touch it. . . . She's going to get me for this. Her sense of humor extends only as far as ambushes, but it can be pretty intense."

"Yeah. I remember the Zoo Society's documentary on her." Fujiyama was grinning broadly. Hamid had always thought that Larry and the Blab had kindred humors. It even seemed that the animal's cackling became like the old man's after she attended a couple of his lectures.

Larry pulled the heater back and walked around the desk. He hunched down to the Blab's eye level. He was all solicitude now, and a good thing: he was looking into a mouth full of sharp teeth, and somebody was playing the "Timebomb Song." After a moment, the music stopped and she shut her mouth. "I can't believe there isn't human equivalence hiding here somewhere. Really. I've had freshmen who did worse at the start of the semester. How could you get this much verbalization without intelligence to benefit from it?" He reached out to rub her shoulders. "You got sore shoulders, Baby? Maybe little hands ready to burst out?"

The Blab cocked her head. "I like to soar."

Hamid had thought long about the Heinlein scenario; the science fiction of Old Earth was a solid part of the ATL curriculum. "If she is still a child, she'll be dead before she grows up. Her bone calcium and muscle strength have deteriorated about as much as you'd expect for a thirty-year-old human."

"Hm. Yeah. And we know she's about your age." Twenty. "I suppose she could be an ego frag. But most of those are brain-damaged transhumans, or obvious constructs." He went back behind his desk, began whistling tunelessly. Hamid twisted uneasily in his chair. He had come for advice. What he got was news that they were in totally over their heads. He shouldn't be surprised; Larry was like that. "What we need is a whole lot more information."

"Well, I suppose I could flat out demand the slug tell me more. But I don't know how I can force any of the Tourists to help me."

Larry waved breezily. "That's not what I meant. Sure, I'll ask the Lothlrimarre about it. But basically the Tourists are at the end of a nine-light-year trip to nowhere. Whatever libraries they have are like what you would take on a South Seas vacation—and out of date, to boot. . . . And of course the Federal government of Middle America doesn't know what's coming off to begin with. Heh, heh. Why else do they come to me when they're really desperate? . . . No, what we need is direct access to library resources Out There."

He said it casually, as though he were talking about getting an extra telephone, not solving Middle America's greatest problem. He smiled complacently at Hamid, but the boy refused to be drawn in. Finally, "Haven't you wondered why the campus—Morale Hall, in particular—is crawling with cops?"

"Yeah." *Or I would have, if there weren't lots else on my mind.*

"One of the more serious Tourists—Skandr Vrinimisrinithan—

brought along a genuine transhuman artifact. He's been holding back on it for months, hoping he could get what he wants other ways. The Feds—I'll give 'em this—didn't budge. Finally he brought out his secret weapon. It's in this room right now."

Ham's eyes were drawn to the stone carving (now bluish green) that sat on Larry's desk. The old man nodded. "It's an ansible."

"Surely they don't call it that!"

"No. But that's what it is."

"You mean, all these years, it's been a lie that ftl won't work in the Zone?" *You mean I've wasted my life trying to suck up to these Tourists?*

"Not really. Take a look at this thing. See the colors change. I swear its size and mass do, too. This is a real transhuman artifact: not an intellect, of course, but not some human design manufactured in Transhuman space. Skandr claims—and I believe him—that no other Tourist has one."

A transhuman artifact. Hamid's fascination was tinged with fear. This was something one heard of in the theoretical abstract, in classes run by crackpots.

"Skandr claims this gadget is 'aligned' on the Lothlrimarre commercial outlet. From there we can talk to any registered address in the Beyond."

"Instantaneously." Hamid's voice was very small.

"Near enough. It would take a while to reach the universal event horizon; there are some subtle limitations if you're moving at relativistic speeds."

"And the Catch?"

Larry laughed. "Good man. Skandr admits to a few. This thing won't work more than ten light years into the Zone. I'll bet there aren't twenty worlds in the Galaxy that could benefit from it—but we are *definitely* on one. The trick sucks enormous energy. Skandr says that running this baby will dim our sun by half a percent. Not noticeable to the guy in the street, but it could have long-term bad effects." There was a short silence; Larry often did that after a cosmic understatement. "And from your standpoint, Hamid, there's one big drawback. The mean bandwidth of this thing is just under six bits per minute."

"Huh? Ten seconds to send a single bit?"

"Yup. Skandr left three protocols at the Lothlrimarre end: ASCII, a Hamming map to a subset of English, and an AI scheme that guesses what you'd say if you used more bits. The first is Skandr's idea of a joke, and I wouldn't trust the third more than wishful thinking. But with the Hamming map, you could send a short letter—say five hundred English words—in a day. It's full-duplex, so you might get a good part of your answer in that time. Neat, huh? Anyway, it beats waiting twenty years."

Hamid guessed it would be the biggest news since first contact, one hundred years ago. "So . . . uh, why did they bring it to you, Professor?"

Larry looked around his hole of an office, smiling wider and wider. "Heh, heh. It's true, our illustrious planetary president is one of the five; he's been Out There. But I'm the only one with real friends in the Beyond. You see, the Feds are very leery of this deal. What Skandr wants in return is most of our zygote bank. The Feds banned any private sale of human zygotes. It was a big moral thing: 'No unborn child sold into slavery or worse.' Now they're thinking of doing it themselves. They really *want* this ansible. But what if it's a fake, just linked up to some fancy database on Skandr's ship? Then they've lost some genetic flexibility, and maybe they've sold some kids into hell—and got nothing but a colorful trinket for their grief.

"So. Skandr's loaned them the thing for a week, and the Feds loaned it to me—with close to *carte blanche*. I can call up old friends, exchange filthy jokes, let the sun go dim doing it. After a week, I report on whether the gadget is really talking to the Outside."

Knowing you, "I bet you have your own agenda."

"Sure. Till you showed up the main item was to check out the foundation that sponsors Skandr, see if they're as clean as he says. Now . . . well, your case isn't as important morally, but it's very interesting. There should be time for both. I'll use Skandr's credit to do some netstalking, see if I can find *anyone* who's heard of blabbers, or this Ravna&Tines."

Hamid didn't have any really close friends. Sometimes he wondered if that was another penalty of his strange upbringing, or whether he was just naturally unlikable. He had come to Fujiyama for help all right, but all he'd been expecting was a round of prickly questions that eventually brought *him* to some insight. Now he seemed to be on the receiving end of a favor of world-shaking proportions. It made him suspicious and very grateful all at once. He gabbled some words of abject gratitude.

Larry shrugged. "It's no special problem for me. I'm curious, and this week I've got the *means* to satisfy my curiosity." He patted the ansible. "There's a real favor I can do, though: so far, Middle America has been cheated occasionally, but no Outsider has used force against us. That's one good thing about the Caravan system: it's to the Tourists' advantage to keep each other straight. Ravna&Tines may be different. If this is really a High Trader, it might just make a grab for what it wants. If I were you, I'd keep close to the Blabber. . . . And I'll see if the slug will move one of the Tourist barges over the campus. If you stay in this area, not much can happen without them knowing.

"Hey, see what a help I am? I did nothing for your original question, and now you have a whole, ah, shipload of new things to worry about. . . ."

He leaned back, and his voice turned serious. "But I don't have much to say about your original question, Hamid. If Ravna&Tines turn out to be decent, you'll still have to decide for yourself about giving up the Blab. I bet every critter that thinks it thinks—even the transhumans— worry about how to do right for themselves and the ones they love. I— uh, oh damn! Why don't you ask your pop, why don't you ask Hussein about these things? The guy has been heartbroken since you left."

Ham felt his face go red. Pop had never had much good to say about Fujiyama. Who'd have guessed the two would talk about him? If Hamid had known, he'd never have come here today. He felt like standing up, screaming at this old man to mind his own business. Instead, he shook his head and said softly, "It's kind of personal."

Larry looked at him, as if wondering whether to push the matter. One word, and Ham knew that all the pain would come pouring out. But after a moment, the old man sighed. He looked around the desk to where the Blab lay, eyeing the heater. "Hey, Blabber. You take good care of this kid."

The Blab returned his gaze. "Sure, sure," she said.

HAMID'S APARTMENT WAS ON THE SOUTH SIDE OF CAMPUS. IT WAS LARGE and cheap, which might seem surprising so near the oldest university around, and just a few kilometers south of the planetary capital. The back door opened on kilometers of forested wilderness. It would be a long time before there was any land development immediately south of here. The original landing zones were just twenty klicks away. In a bad storm there might be a little hot stuff blown north. It might be only fifty percent of natural background radiation, but with a whole world to colonize, why spread towns toward the first landings?

Hamid parked the commons bicycle in the rack out front, and walked quietly around the building. Lights were on upstairs. There were the usual motorbikes of other tenants. *Something* was standing in back, at the the far end of the building. Ah. A Hallowe'en scarecrow.

He and the Blab walked back to his end. It was past twilight and neither moon was in the sky. The tips of his fingers were chilled to numbness. He stuck his hands in his pockets, and paused to look up. The starships of the Caravan were in synch orbit at this longitude. They formed a row of bright dots in the southern sky. Something dark, too regular to be a cloud hung almost straight overhead. That must be the protection Larry had promised.

"I'm hungry."

"Just a minute and we'll go in."

"Okay." The Blab leaned companionably against his leg, began humming. She looked fat now, but it was just her fur, all puffed out. These temperatures were probably the most comfortable for her. He stared across the star fields. *God, how many hours have I stood like this, wondering what all those stars mean?* The Big Square was about an hour from setting. The fifth brightest star in that constellation was Lothlrimarre's sun. At Lothlrimarre and beyond, faster than light travel was possible—even for twenty-first century Old Earth types. If Middle America were just ten more light years farther out from the galactic center, Hamid would have had all the Beyond as his world.

His gaze swept back across the sky. Most everything he could see there would be in the Slow Zone. It extended four thousand light years inward from here, if the Outsiders were to be believed. Billions of star systems, millions of civilizations—trapped. Most would never know about the outside.

Even the Outsiders had only vague information about the civilizations down here in the Slow Zone. Greatships, ramscoops, they all must be invented here again and again. Colonies spread, knowledge gained, most often lost in the long slow silence. What theories the Slow Zone civilizations must have for why nothing could move faster than light— even in the face of superluminal events seen at cosmic distances. What theories they must have to explain why human-equivalent intelligence was the highest ever found and ever created. Those ones deep inside, they might at times be the happiest of all, their theories assuring them they were at the top of creation. If Middle America were only a hundred light years farther down, Hamid would never know the truth. He would love this world, and the spreading of civilization upon it.

Hamid's eye followed the Milky Way to the eastern horizon. The glow wasn't really brighter there than above, but he knew his constellations. He was looking at the galactic center. He smiled wanly. In twentieth-century science fiction, those star clouds were imagined as the homes of "elder races," godlike intellects. . . . But the Tourists call those regions of the galaxy the Depths. The Unthinking Depths. Not only was ftl impossible there, but so was sentience. So they guessed. They couldn't know for sure. The fastest round-trip probe to the edge of the Depths took about ten thousand years. Such expeditions were rare, though some were well documented.

Hamid shivered, and looked back at the ground. Four cats sat silently just beyond the lawn, watching the Blab. "Not tonight, Blab," he said, and the two of them went indoors.

The place looked undisturbed: the usual mess. He fixed the Blab her dinner and heated some soup for himself.

"Yuck. This stuff tastes like *shit*!" The Blab rocked back on her haunches and made retching sounds. Few people have their own child-hood obnoxiousness come back to haunt them so directly as Hamid

Thompson did. He could remember using exactly those words at the dinner table. Mom should have stuffed a sock down his throat.

Hamid glanced at the chicken parts. "Best we can afford, Blab." He was running his savings down to zero to cover the year of the Tourists. Being a guide was such a plum that no one thought to pay for it.

"Yuck." But she started nibbling.

As Ham watched her eat, he realized that one of his problems was solved. If Ravna&Tines wouldn't take him as the Blab's "trainer," they could hike back to the Beyond by themselves. Furthermore, he'd want better evidence from the slug—via the ansible he could get assurances directly from Lothlrimarre—that Ravna&Tines could be held to promises. The conversation with Larry had brought home all the nightmare fears, the fears that drove some people to demand total rejection of the Caravan. Who knew what happened to those that left with Outsiders? Almost all Middle American knowledge of the Beyond came from less than thirty starships, less than a thousand strangers. Strange strangers. If it weren't for the five who came back, there would be zero corroboration. Of those five . . . well, Hussein Thompson was a mystery even to Hamid: seeming kind, inside a vicious mercenary. Lazy Larry was a mystery, too, a cheerful one who made it clear that you better think twice about what folks tell you. But one thing came clear from all of them: space is deep. There were millions of civilized worlds in the Beyond, thousands of star-spanning empires. In such vastness, there could be no single notion of law and order. Cooperation and enlightened self-interest were common, but . . . nightmares lurked.

So what if Ravna&Tines turned him down, or couldn't produce credible assurances? Hamid went into the bedroom and punched up the news, let the color and motion wash over him. Middle America was a beautiful world, still mostly empty. With the agrav plates and the room-temperature fusion electrics that the Caravan had brought, life would be more exciting here than ever before. . . . In twenty or thirty years there would likely be another caravan. If he and the Blab were still restless—well, there was plenty of time to prepare. Larry Fujiyama had been forty years old when he went Out.

Hamid sighed, happy with himself for the first time in days.

THE PHONE RANG JUST AS HE FINISHED WITH THE NEWS. THE NAME OF THE incoming caller danced in red letters across the news display: *Ravna*. No location or topic. Hamid swallowed hard. He bounced off the bed, turned the phone pickup to look at a chair in an uncluttered corner of the room, and sat down there. Then he accepted the call.

Ravna was human. And female. "Mr. Hamid Thompson, please."

"T-that's me." *Curse the stutter.*

For an instant there was no reaction. Then a quick smile crossed her face. It was not a friendly smile, more like a sneer at his nervousness. "I call to discuss the animal. The Blabber, you call it. You have heard our offer. I am prepared to improve upon it." As she spoke, the Blab walked into the room and across the phone's field of view. Her gaze did not waver. Strange. He could see that the VIDEO TRANSMIT light was on next to the screen. The Blab began to hum. A moment passed and *then* she reacted, a tiny start of surprise.

"What is your improvement?"

Again, a half-second pause. Ravna&Tines were a lot nearer than the Jovians tonight, though apparently still not at Middle America. "We possess devices that allow faster-than-light communication to a world in the . . . Beyond. Think on what this access means. With this, if you stay on Middle America, you will be the richest man on the planet. If you choose to accept passage Out, you will have the satisfaction of knowing you have moved your world a good step out of the darkness."

Hamid found himself thinking faster than he ever had outside of a Fujiyama oral exam. There were plenty of clues here. Ravna's English was more fluent than most Tourists', but her pronunciation was awful. Human but awful: her vowel stress was strange to the point of rendering her speech unintelligible, and she didn't voice things properly: "pleess" instead of "pleez," "chooss" instead of "chooz."

At the same time, he had to make sense of what she was saying and decide the correct response. Hamid thanked God he already knew about ansibles. "Miss Ravna, I agree. That is an improvement. Nevertheless, my original requirement stands. I must accompany my pet. Only I know her needs." He cocked his head. "You could do worse than have an expert on call."

As he spoke, her expression clouded. Rage? She seemed hostile toward him *personally*. But when he finished, her face was filled with an approximation of a friendly smile. "Of course, we will arrange that also. We had not realized earlier how important this is to you."

Jeeze. Even I can lie better than that! This Ravna was used to getting her own way without face-to-face lies, or else she had real emotional problems. Either way: "And since you and I are scarcely equals, we also need to work something out with the Lothlrimarre that will put a credible bond on the agreement."

Her poorly constructed mask slipped. "That is absurd." She looked at something off camera. "The Lothlrimarre knows nothing of us. . . . I will try to satisfy you. But know this, Hamid Thompson: I am the congenial, uh, *humane* member of my team. Mr. Tines is very impatient. I try to restrain him, but if he becomes desperate enough . . . things could happen that would hurt us all. Do you understand me?"

First a lie, and now chainsaw subtlety. He fought back a smile. *Careful. You might be mistaking raw insanity for bluff and bluster.* "Yes, Miss Ravna, I do understand, and your offer is generous. But . . . I need to think about this. Can you give me a bit more time?" *Enough time to complain to the Tour Director.*

"Yes. One hundred hours should be feasible."

After she rang off, Hamid sat for a long time, staring sightlessly at the dataset. What *was* Ravna? Through twenty thousand years of colonization, on worlds far stranger than Middle America, the human form had drifted far. Cross-fertility existed between most of Earth's children, though they differed more from one another than had races on the home planet. Ravna looked more like an Earth human than most of the Tourists. Assuming she was of normal height, she could almost have passed as an American of Middle East descent: sturdy, dark-skinned, black-haired. There were differences. Her eyes had epicanthic folds, and the irises were the most intense violet he had ever seen. Still, all that was trivial compared to her manner.

Why hadn't she been receiving Hamid's video? Was she blind? She didn't seem so otherwise; he remembered her looking at things around her. Perhaps she was some sort of personality simulator. That had been a standard item in American science fiction at the end of the twentieth century; the idea passed out of fashion when computer performance seemed to top out in the early twenty-first. But things like that should be possible in the Beyond, and certainly in Transhuman Space. They wouldn't work very well down here, of course. Maybe she was just a graphical front end for whatever Mr. Tines was.

Somehow, Hamid thought she was real. She certainly had a human effect on him. Sure, she had a good figure, obvious under soft white shirt and pants. And sure, Hamid had been girl-crazy the last five years. He was so horny most of the time, it felt good just to ogle femikins in downtown Marquette stores. But for all-out sexiness, Ravna wasn't *that* spectacular. She had nothing on Gilli Weinberg or Skandr Vrinimi's wife. Yet, if he had met her at school, he would have tried harder to gain her favor than he had Gilli's . . . and that was saying *a lot*.

Hamid sighed. That probably just showed that *he* was nuts.

"I wanna go out." The Blab rubbed her head against his arm. Hamid realized he was sweating even though the room was chill.

"God, not tonight, Blab." He guessed that there was a lot of bluff in Ravna&Tines. At the same time, it was clear they were the kind who might just *grab* if they could get away with it.

"I wanna go out!" Her voice came louder. The Blab spent many nights outside, mainly in the forest. That made it easier to keep her quiet when she was indoors. For the Blab, it was a chance to play with her pets:

the cats—and sometimes the dogs—in the neighborhood. There had been a war when he and the Blab first arrived here. Pecking orders had been abruptly revised, and two of the most ferocious dogs had just disappeared. What was left was very strange. The cats were fascinated by the Blab. They hung around the yard just for a glimpse of her. When she was here they didn't even fight among themselves. Nights like tonight were the best. In a couple of hours both Selene and Diana would rise, the silver moon and the gold. On nights like this, when gold and silver lay between deep shadows, Hamid had seen her pacing through the edge of the forest, followed by a dozen faithful retainers.

But, *"Not tonight, Blab!"* There followed a major argument, the Blabber blasting rock music and kiddie shows at high volume. The noise wasn't the loudest she could make. That would have been physically painful to Ham. No, this was more like a cheap music player set way high. Eventually it would bring complaints from all over the apartment building. Fortunately for Hamid, the nearest rooms were unoccupied just now.

After twenty minutes of din, Hamid twisted the fight into a "game of humans." Like many pets, the Blab thought of herself as a human being. But unlike a cat or a dog or even a parrot, she could do a passable job of imitating one. The trouble was, she couldn't always find people with the patience to play along.

They sat across from each other at the dinette table, the Blab's forelegs splayed awkwardly across its surface. Hamid would start with some question—it didn't matter the topic. The Blab would nod wisely, ponder a reply. With most abstractions, anything she had to say was nonsense, meaningful only to tea-leaf readers or wishful thinkers. Never mind that. In the game, Hamid would respond with a comment, or laugh if the Blab seemed to be in a joke-telling behavior. The pacing, the intonation—they were all perfect for real human dialog. If you didn't understand English, the game would have sounded like two friends having a good time.

"How about an imitation, Blab? Joe Ortega. President Ortega. Can you do that?"

"Heh, heh." That was Lazy Larry's cackle. "Don't rush me. I'm thinking. I'm thinking!" There were several types of imitation games. For instance, she could speak back Hamid's words instantly, but with the voice of some other human. Using that trick on a voice-only phone was probably her favorite game of all, since her audience really *believed* she was a person. What he was asking for now was almost as much fun, if the Blab would play up to it.

She rubbed her jaw with a talon. "Ah yes." She sat back pompously, almost slid onto the floor before she caught herself. "We must all work together in these exciting times." That was from a recent Ortega speech, a simple playback. But even when she got going, responding to Hamid's questions, ad-libbing things, she was still a perfect match for the President of Middle America. Hamid laughed and laughed. Ortega was one of the five who came back, not a very bright man but self-important and ambitious. It said something that even his small knowledge of the Outside was enough to propel him to the top of the world state. The five were very big fish in a very small pond—that was how Larry Fujiyama put it.

The Blab was an enormous show-off, and was quickly carried away by her own wit. She began waving her forelegs around, lost her balance and fell off the chair. "Oops!" She hopped back on the chair, looked at Hamid—and began laughing herself. The two were in stitches for almost half a minute. This had happened before; Hamid was sure the Blab could not appreciate humor above the level of pratfalls. Her laughter was imitation for the sake of congeniality, for the sake of being a person. "Oh, God!" She flopped onto the table, "choking" with mirth, her forelegs across the back of her neck as if to restrain herself.

The laughter died away to occasional snorts, and then a companionable silence. Hamid reached across to rub the bristly fur that covered the Blab's forehead tympanum. "You're a good kid, Blab."

The dark eyes opened, turned up at him. Something like a sigh escaped her, buzzing the fur under his palm. "Sure, sure," she said.

HAMID LEFT THE DRAPES PARTLY PULLED, AND A WINDOW PANE CRANKED open where the Blab could sit and look out. He lay in the darkened bedroom and watched her silhouette against the silver and gold moonlight. She had her nose pressed up to the screen. Her long neck was arched to give both her head and shoulder tympana a good line on the outside. Every so often her head would jerk a few millimeters, as if something very interesting had just happened outside.

The loudest sound in the night was faint roach racket, out by the forest. The Blab was being very quiet—in the range Hamid could hear—and he was grateful. She really was a good kid.

He sighed and pulled the covers up to his nose. It had been a long day, one where life's problems had come out ahead.

He'd be very careful the next few days; no trips away from Marquette and Ann Arbor, no leaving the Blab unattended. At least the slug's protection looked solid. *I better tell Larry about the second ansible, though.* If Ravna&Tines just went direct to the government with it . . . that might be the most dangerous move of all. For all their pious talk and restrictions on private sales, the Feds would sell their own grandmothers if they thought it would benefit the Planetary Interest. Thank God they already had an ansible—or almost had one.

Funny. After all these years and all the dreams, that it was the Blab the Outsiders were after . . .

Hamid was an adopted child. His parents had told him that as soon as he could understand the notion. And somewhere in those early years, he had guessed the truth . . . that his father had brought him in . . . from the Beyond. Somehow Huss Thompson had kept that fact secret from the public. Surely the government knew, and cooperated with him. In those early years—before they forced him into Math—it had been a happy secret for him; he thought he had all his parents' love. Knowing that he was really from Out There had merely given substance to what most well-loved kids believe anyway—that somehow they are divinely special. His secret dream had been that he was some Outsider version of an exiled prince. And when he grew up, when the next ships from the Beyond came down . . . he would be called to his destiny.

Starting college at age eight had just seemed part of that destiny. His parents had been so confident of him, even though his tests results were scarcely more than bright normal. . . . That year had been the destruction of innocence. He wasn't a genius, no matter how much his parents insisted. The fights, the tears, their insistence. In the end, Mom had left Hussein Thompson. Not till then did the man relent, let his child return to normal schools. Life at home was never the same. Mom's visits were brief, tense . . . and rare. But it wasn't for another five years that Hamid learned to hate his father. The learning had been an accident, a conversation overheard. Hussein had been *hired* to raise Hamid as he had, to push him into school, to twist and ruin him. The old man had never denied the boy's accusations. His attempts to "explain" had been vague mumbling . . . worse than lies. . . . If Hamid was a prince, he must be a very hated one indeed.

The memories had worn deep grooves, ones he often slid down on his way to sleep. . . . But tonight there was something new, something ironic to the point of magic. All these years . . . it had been the Blab who was the lost princeling . . . !

THERE WAS A HISSING SOUND. HAMID STRUGGLED TOWARD WAKEFULNESS, fear and puzzlement playing through his dreams. He rolled to the edge of the bed and forced his eyes to see. Only stars shone through the window. The Blab. She wasn't sitting at the window screen anymore. She must be having one of her nightmares. They were rare, but spectacular. One winter's night Hamid had been wakened by the sounds of a full-scale thunderstorm. This was not so explosive, but . . .

He looked across the floor at the pile of blankets that was her nest. Yes. She was there, and facing his way.

"Blab? It's okay, baby."

No reply. Only the hissing, maybe louder now. *It wasn't coming from the Blab.* For an instant his fuzzy mind hung in a kind of mouse-and-snake paralysis. Then he flicked on the lights. No one here. The sound was from the dataset; the picture flat remained dark. *This is crazy.*

"Blab?" He had never seen her like this. Her eyes were open wide, rings of white showing around the irises. Her forelegs reached beyond the blankets. The talons were extended and had slashed deep into the plastic flooring. A string of drool hung from her muzzle.

He got up, started toward her. The hissing formed a voice, and the voice spoke. "I want her. Human, I want her. And I will have her." Her, the Blab.

"How did you get access? You have no business disturbing us." Silly talk, but it broke the nightmare spell of this waking.

"My name is Tines." Hamid suddenly remembered the claw on the Ravna&Tines logo. Tines. Cute. "We have made generous offers. We have been patient. That is past. I will have her. If it means the death of all you m-meat animals, so be it. But I *will* have her."

The hissing was almost gone now, but the voice still sounded like something from a cheap synthesizer. The syntax and accent were similar to Ravna's. They were either the same person, or they had learned English from the same source. Still, Ravna had seemed angry. Tines sounded flat-out nuts. Except for the single stutter over "meat," the tone and pacing were implacable. And that voice gave away more than anything yet about why the Outsider wanted his pet. There was a *hunger* in its voice, a lust to feed or to rape.

Hamid's rage climbed on top of his fear. "Why don't you just go screw yourself, comic monster! We've got *protection*, else you wouldn't come bluffing—"

"Bluffing! *Bluffiiyowru*—" the words turned into choked gobbling sounds. Behind him, Hamid heard the Blab scream. After a moment the noises faded. "I do not bluff. Hussein Thompson has this hour learned what I do with those who cross me. You and all your people will also die unless you deliver her to me. I see a ground car parked by your . . . house. Use it to take her east fifty kilometers. Do this within one hour, or learn what Hussein Thompson learned—that *I do not bluff.*" And Mr. Tines was gone.

It has to be a bluff! If Tines has that power, why not wipe the Tourists from the sky and just grab the Blab? Yet they were so stupid about it. A few smooth lies a week ago, and they might have gotten everything without a murmur. It was as if they couldn't imagine being disobeyed—or were desperate beyond reason.

Hamid turned back to the Blab. As he reached to stroke her neck, she twisted, her needle-toothed jaws clicking shut on his pyjama sleeve. "Blab!"

She released his sleeve, and drew back into the pile of blankets. She was making whistling noises like the time she got hit by a pickup trike. Hamid's father had guessed those must be true blabber sounds, like human sobs or chattering of teeth. He went to his knees and made comforting noises. This time she let him stroke her neck. He saw that she had wet her bed. The Blab had been toilet-trained as long as he had. Bluff or not, this had thoroughly terrified her. Tines claimed he could kill everyone. Hamid remembered the ansible, a god-damned telephone that could dim the sun.

Bluff or madness?

He scrambled back to his dataset, and punched up the Tour Director's number. Pray the slug was accepting more than mail tonight. The ring pattern flashed twice, and then he was looking at a panorama of cloud tops and blue sky. It might have been an aerial view of Middle America, except that as you looked downward the clouds seemed to extend forever, more and more convoluted in the dimness. This was a picture clip from the ten-bar level over Lothlrimarre. No doubt the slug chose it to soothe human callers, and still be true to the nature of his home world—a subjovian thirty thousand kilometers across.

For five seconds they soared through the canyons of cloud. *Wake up, damn you!*

The picture cleared and he was looking at a human—Larry Fujiyama! Lazy Larry did not look surprised to see him. "You got the right number, kid. I'm up here with the slug. There have been developments."

Hamid gaped for an appropriate reply, and the other continued. "Ravna&Tines have been all over the slug since about midnight. Threats and promises, mostly threats since the Tines critter took their comm. . . . I'm sorry about your dad, Hamid. We should've thought to—"

"*What?*"

"Isn't that what you're calling about? . . . Oh. It's been on the news. Here—" The picture dissolved into a view from a news chopper flying over Eastern Michigan farmland. It took Hamid a second to recognize the hills. This was near the Thompson spread, two thousand klicks east of Marquette. It would be past sunup there. The camera panned over a familiar creek, the newsman bragging how On-Line News was ahead of the first rescue teams. They crested a range of hills and . . . where were the trees? Thousands of black lines lay below, trunks of blown-over trees, pointing inevitably inward, toward the center of the blast. The

newsman babbled on about the meteor strike and how fortunate it was
that ground zero was in a lake valley, how only one farm had been
affected. Hamid swallowed. That farm . . . was Hussein Thompson's. The
place they lived after Mom left. Ground zero itself was obscured by
rising steam—all that was left of the lake. The reporter assured his audience that the crater consumed all the land where the farm buildings
had been.

The news clip vanished. "It was no Middle American nuke, but it
wasn't natural, either," said Larry. "A lighter from Ravna&Tines put
down there two hours ago. Just before the blast, I got a real scared call
from Huss, something about 'the tines' arriving. I'll show it to you if—"

"No!" Hamid gulped. "No," he said more quietly. How he had hated
Hussein Thompson; how he had loved his father in the years before.
Now he was gone, and Hamid would never get his feelings sorted out.
"Tines just called me. He said he killed my—Hussein." Hamid played
back the call. "Anyway, I need to talk to the slug. Can he protect me?
Is Middle America really in for it if I refuse the Tines thing?"

For once Larry didn't give his "you figure it" shrug. "It's a mess," he
said. "And sluggo's waffling. He's around here somewhere. Just a sec—"
More peaceful cloud-soaring. Damn, damn, damn. Something bumped
gently into the small of his back. The Blab. The black and white neck
came around his side. The dark eyes looked up at him. "What's up?"
she said quietly.

Hamid felt like laughing and crying. She was very subdued, but at
least she recognized him now. "Are you okay, baby?" he said. The Blabber curled up around him, her head stretched out on his knee.

On the dataset, the clouds parted and they were looking at both Larry
Fujiyama and the slug. Of course, they were not in the same room; that
would have been fatal to both. The Lothlrimarre barge was a giant pressure vessel. Inside, pressure and atmosphere were just comfy for the
slug—about a thousand bars of ammonia and hydrogen. There was a
terrarium for human visitors. The current view showed the slug in the
foreground. Part of the wall behind him was transparent, a window into
the terrarium. Larry gave a little wave, and Hamid felt himself smiling.
No question who was in a zoo.

"Ah, Mr. Thompson. I'm glad you called. We have a very serious
problem." The slug's English was perfect, and though the voice was
artificial, he sounded like a perfectly normal Middle American male.
"Many problems would be solved if you could see your way clear to
give—"

"No." Hamid's voice was flat. "N-not while I'm alive, anyway. This is
no business deal. You've heard the threats, and you saw what they did
to my father." The slug had been his ultimate employer these last six

months, someone rarely spoken to, the object of awe. None of that mattered now. "You've always said the first responsibility of the Tour Director is to see that no party is abused by another. I'm asking you to live up to that."

"Um. Technically, I was referring to you Middle Americans and the Tourists in my caravan. I know I have the power to make good on my promises with them. . . . But we're just beginning to learn about Ravna&Tines. I'm not sure it's reasonable to stand up against them." He swiveled his thousand-kilo bulk toward the terrarium window. Hamid knew that under Lothlrimarre gravity the slug would have been squashed into the shape of a flatworm, with his manipulator fringe touching the ground. At one gee, he looked more like an overstuffed silk pillow, fringed with red tassles. "Larry has told me about Skandr's remarkable Slow Zone device. I've heard of such things. They are *very* difficult to obtain. A single one would have more than financed my caravan. . . . And to think that Skandr pleaded his foundation's poverty in begging passage. . . . Anyway, Larry has been using the 'ansible' to ask about what your blabber really is."

Larry nodded. "Been at it since you left, Hamid. The machine's down in my office, buzzing away. Like Skandr says, it is aligned on the commercial outlet at Lothlrimarre. From there I have access to the Known Net. Heh, heh. Skandr left a *sizable* credit bond at Lothlrimarre. I hope he and Ortega aren't too upset by the phone bill I run up testing this gadget for them. I described the Blab, and put out a depth query. There are a million subnets, all over the Beyond, searching their databases for anything like the Blab. I—" His happy enthusiasm wavered, "Sluggo thinks we've dug up a reference to the blabber's race. . . ."

"Yes, and it's frightening, Mr. Thompson." It was no surprise that none of the Tourists had heard of a blabber. The only solid lead coming back to Larry had been from halfway around the galactic rim, a nook in the Beyond that had only one occasional link with the rest of the Known Net. That far race had no direct knowledge of the blabbers. But they heard rumors. From a thousand light years below them, deep within the Slow Zone, there came stories . . . of a race matching the Blab's appearance. The race was highly intelligent, and had quickly developed the relativistic transport that was the fastest thing inside the Zone. They colonized a vast sphere, held an empire of ten thousand worlds—all without ftl. And the tines—the name seemed to fit—had not held their empire through the power of brotherly love. Races had been exterminated, planets busted with relativistic kinetic energy bombs. The tines' technology had been about as advanced and deadly as could exist in the Zone. Most of their volume was a tomb now, their story whispered through centuries of slow flight toward the Outside.

"Wait, wait. Prof Fujiyama told me the ansible's bandwidth is a tenth of a bit per second. You've had less than twelve hours to work this question. How can you possibly know all this?"

Larry looked a little embarrassed—a first as far as Hamid could remember. "We've been using the AI protocol I told you about. There's massive interpolation going on at both ends of our link to Lothlrimarre."

"I'll bet!"

"Remember, Mr. Thompson, the data compression applies only to the first link in the chain. The Known Net lies in the Beyond. Bandwidth and data integrity are very high across most of its links."

The slug sounded very convinced. But Hamid had read a lot about the Known Net; the notion was almost as fascinating as ftl travel itself. There was no way a world could have a direct link with all others—partly because of range limitations, mainly because of the *number* of planets involved. Similarly, there was no way a single "phone company" (or even ten thousand phone companies!) could run the thing. Most likely, the information coming to them from around the galaxy had passed through five or ten intermediate hops. The intermediates—not to mention the race on the far rim—were likely nonhuman. Imagine asking a question in English of someone who also speaks Spanish, and that person asking the question in Spanish of someone who understands Spanish and passes the question on in German. This was a million times worse. Next to some of the creatures Out There, the slug could pass for human!

Hamid said as much. "F-furthermore, even if this *is* what the sender meant, it could still be a lie! Look at what local historians did to Richard the Third, or Mohamet Rose."

Lazy Larry smiled his polliwog smile, and Hamid realized they must have been arguing about this already. Larry put in, "There's also this, sluggo: the nature of the identification. The tines must have something like hands. See any on Hamid's Blabber?"

The slug's scarlet fringe rippled three quick cycles. Agitation? Dismissal? "The text is still coming in. But I have a theory. You know, Larry, I've always been a great student of sex. I may be a 'he' only by courtesy, but I think sex is fascinating. It's what makes the 'world go around' for so many races." Hamid suddenly understood Gilli Weinberg's success. "So. Grant me my expertise. My guess is the tines exhibit *extreme* sexual dimorphism. The males' forepaws probably are hands. No doubt it's the males who are the killers. The females—like the Blab—are by contrast friendly, mindless creatures."

The Blab's eyes rolled back to look at Hamid. "Sure, sure," she murmured. The accident of timing was wonderful, seeming to say *Who is this clown?*

The slug didn't notice. "This may even explain the viciousness of the male. Think back to the conversation Mr. Thompson had. These creatures seem to regard their own females as property to exploit. Rather the ultimate in sexism." Hamid shivered. That *did* ring a bell. He couldn't forget the *hunger* in the tines's voice.

"Is this the long way to tell me you're not going to protect us?"

The slug was silent for almost fifteen seconds. Its scarlet fringe waved up and down the whole time. Finally: "Almost, I'm afraid. My caravan customers haven't heard this analysis, just the threats and the news broadcasts. Nevertheless, they are tourists, not explorers. They demand that I refuse to let you aboard. Some demand that we leave your planet immediately. . . . How secure is this line, Larry?"

Fujiyama said, "Underground fiberoptics, and an encrypted laser link. Take a chance, sluggo."

"Very well. Mr. Thompson, here is what you can expect from me:

"I can stay over the city, and probably defend against direct kidnapping—unless I see a planetbuster coming. I doubt very much they have that set up, but if they do—well, I don't think even you would want to keep your dignity at the price of a relativistic asteroid strike.

"I can *not* come down to pick you up. That would be visible to all, a direct violation of my customers' wishes. On the other hand," there was another pause, and his scarlet fringe whipped about even faster than before, "if you should appear, uh, up here, I would take you aboard my barge. Even if this were noticed, it would be a *fait accompli*. I could hold off my customers, and likely our worst fate would be a premature and unprofitable departure from Middle America."

"T-that's very generous." *Unbelievably so.* The slug was thought to be an honest fellow—but a very hard trader. Even Hamid had to admit that the claim on the slug's honor was tenuous here, yet he was risking a twenty-year mission for it.

"Of course, *if* we reach that extreme, I'll want a few years of your time once we reach the Outside. My bet is that hard knowledge about your Blabber might make up for the loss of everything else."

A day ago, Hamid would have quibbled about contracts and assurances. Today, well, the alternative was Ravna&Tines. . . . With Larry as witness, they settled on two years' indenture and a pay scale.

Now all he and the Blab had to do was figure how to climb five thousand meters straight up. There was one obvious way.

IT WAS DAVE LARSON'S CAR, BUT DAVEY OWED HIM. HAMID WOKE HIS NEIGHbor, explained that the Blab was sick and had to go into Marquette. Fifteen minutes later, Hamid and the Blab were driving through Ann

Arbor Town. It was a Saturday, and barely into morning twilight; he had the road to himself. He'd half expected the place to be swarming with cops and military. If Ravna&Tines ever guessed how easy it was to intimidate Joe Ortega . . . If the Feds knew exactly what was going on, they'd turn the Blab over to Tines in an instant. But apparently the government was simply confused, lying low, hoping it wouldn't be noticed till the big boys upstairs settled their arguments. The farm bombing wasn't in the headline list anymore. The Feds were keeping things quiet, thereby confining the mindless panic to the highest circles of government.

The Blab rattled around the passenger side of the car, alternately leaning on the dash and sniffing in the bag of tricks that Hamid had brought. She was still subdued, but riding in a private auto was a novelty. Electronics gear was cheap, but consumer mechanicals were still at a premium. And without a large highway system, cars would never be the rage they had been on Old Earth; most freight transport was by rail. A lot of this could change because of the Caravan. They brought one hundred thousand agrav plates—enough to revolutionize transport. Middle America would enter the Age of the Aircar—and for the first time surpass the homeworld. So saith Joe Ortega.

Past the University, there was a patch of open country. Beyond the headlights Hamid caught glimpses of open fields, a glint of frost. Hamid looked up nervously every few seconds. Selene and Diane hung pale in the west. Scattered clouds floated among the Tourist barges, vague grayness in the first light of morning. No intruders, but three of the barges were gone, presumably moved to orbit. The Lothlrimarre vessel floated just east of Marquette, over the warehouse quarter. It looked like the slug was keeping his part of the deal.

Hamid drove into downtown Marquette. Sky signs floated brightly amid the two-hundred-story towers, advertising dozens of products— some of which actually existed. Light from discos and shopping malls flooded the eight-lane streets. Of course the place was deserted; it was Saturday morning. Much of the business section was like this—a reconstruction of the original Marquette as it had been on Earth in the middle twenty-first century. That Marquette had sat on the edge of an enormous lake, called Superior. Through that century, as Superior became the splash-down point for heavy freight from space, Marquette had become one of the great port cities of Earth, the gateway to the solar system. The Tourists said it was legend, ur-mother to a thousand worlds.

Hamid turned off the broadway, down an underground ramp. The Marquette of today was for show, perhaps one percent the area of the original, with less than one percent the population. But from the air it looked good, the lights and bustle credible. For special events, the streets could be packed with a million people—everyone on the continent who could be spared from essential work. And the place wasn't really a fraud; the Tourists knew this was a reconstruction. The point was, it was an *authentic* reconstruction, as could only be created by a people one step from the original source—that was the official line. And in fact, the people of Middle America had made enormous sacrifices over almost twenty years to have this ready in time for the Caravan.

The car rental was down a fifteen-story spiral, just above the train terminal. *That* was for real, though the next arrival was a half hour away. Hamid got out, smelling the cool mustiness of the stone cavern, hearing only the echoes of his own steps. Millions of tonnes of ceramic and stone stood between them and the sky. Even an Outsider couldn't see through that . . . he hoped. One sleepy-eyed attendant watched him fill out the forms. Hamid stared at the display, sweating even in the cool; would the guy in back notice? He almost laughed at the thought. His first sally into crime was the least of his worries. If Ravna&Tines were plugged into the credit net, then in a sense they really *could* see down here—and the bogus number Larry had supplied was all that kept him invisible.

They left in a Millennium Commander, the sort of car a Tourist might use to bum around in olden times. Hamid drove north through the underground, then east, and when finally they saw open sky again, they were driving south. Ahead was the warehouse district . . . and hanging above it, the slug's barge, its spheres and cupolas green against the brightening sky. So huge. It looked near, but Hamid knew it was a good five thousand meters up.

A helicopter might be able to drop someone on its topside, or maybe land on one of the verandas—though it would be a tight fit under the overhang. But Hamid couldn't fly a chopper, and wasn't even sure how to rent one at this time of day. No, he and the Blab were going to try something a lot more straightforward, something he had done every couple of weeks since the Tourists arrived.

They were getting near the incoming lot, where Feds and Tourists held payments-to-date in escrow. Up ahead there would be cameras spotted on the roofs. He tinted all but the driver-side window, and pushed down on the Blab's shoulders with his free hand. "Play hide for a few minutes."

"Okay."

Three hundred meters more and they were at the outer gate. He saw the usual three cops out front, and a fourth in an armored box to the side. If Ortega was feeling the heat, it could all end right here.

They looked *real* nervous, but they spent most of their time scanning the sky. They knew something was up, but they thought it was out of their hands. They took a quick glance at the Millennium Commander and waved him through. The inner fence was almost as easy, though here he had to enter his Guide ID. . . . If Ravna&Tines were watching the nets, Hamid and the Blab were running on borrowed time now.

He pulled into the empty parking lot at the main warehouse, choosing a slot with just the right position relative to the guard box. "Keep quiet a little while, Blab," he said. He hopped out and walked across the gravel yard. Maybe he should move faster, as if panicked? But no, the guard had already seen him. *Okay, play it cool.* He waved, kept walking. The glow of morning was already dimming the security lamps that covered the lot. No stars shared the sky with the clouds and the barges.

It was kind of a joke that merchandise from the Beyond was socked away here. The warehouse was big, maybe two hundred meters on a side, but an old place, sheet plastic and aging wood timbers.

The armored door buzzed even before Hamid touched it. He pushed his way through. "Hi, Phil."

Luck! The other guards must be on rounds. Phil Lucas was a friendly sort, but not too bright, and not very familiar with the Blab. Lucas sat in the middle of the guard cubby, and the armored partition that separated him from the visitor trap was raised. To the left was a second door that opened into the warehouse itself. "Hi, Ham." The guard looked back at him nervously. "Awful early to see you."

"Yeah. Got a little problem. There's a Tourist out in the Commander." He waved through the armored window. "He's drunk out of his mind. I need to get him Upstairs and quietly."

Phil licked his lips. "Christ. Everything happens at once. Look, I'm sorry, Ham. We've got orders from the top at Federal Security: nothing comes down, nothing goes up. There's some kind of a ruckus going on amongst the Outsiders. If they start shooting, we want it to be at each other, not us."

"That's the point. We think this fellow is part of the problem. If we can get him back, things should cool off. You should have a note on him. It's Antris ban Reempt."

"Oh. *Him.*" Ban Reempt was the most obnoxious Tourist of all. If he'd been an ordinary Middle American, he would have racked up a century of jail time in the last six months. Fortunately, he'd never killed anyone, so his antics were just barely ignorable. Lucas pecked at his dataset. "No, we don't have anything."

"Nuts. Everything stays jammed unless we can get this guy Upstairs." Hamid paused judiciously, as if giving the matter serious thought. "Look, I'm going back to the car, see if I can call somebody to confirm this."

Lucas was dubious. "Okay, but it's gotta be from the top, Ham."

"Right."

The door buzzed open, and Hamid was jogging back across the parking lot. Things really seemed on track. Thank God he'd always been friendly with the cops running security here. The security people regarded most of the Guides as college-trained snots—and with some reason. But Hamid had had coffee with these guys more than once. He knew the system . . . he even knew the incoming phone number for security confirmations.

Halfway across the lot, Hamid suddenly realized that he didn't have the shakes anymore. The scheme, the ad-libbing: it almost seemed normal—a skill he'd never guessed he had. Maybe that's what desperation does to a fellow. . . . Somehow this was almost fun.

He pulled open the car door. "Back! Not yet." He pushed the eager Blab onto the passenger seat. "Big game, Blab." He rummaged through his satchel, retrieved the two comm sets. One was an ordinary head and throat model; the other had been modified for the Blab. He fastened the mike under the collar of his windbreaker. The earphone shouldn't be needed, but it was small; he put it on, turned the volume down. Then he strapped the other commset around the Blab's neck, turned off *its* mike, and clipped the receiver to her ear. "The game, Blab: Imitation. Imitation." He patted the commset on her shoulder. The Blab was fairly bouncing around the Commander's cab. "For sure. Sure, sure! Who, who?"

"Joe Ortega. Try it: 'We must all pull together . . .' "

The words came back from the Blab as fast as he spoke them, but changed into the voice of the Middle American President. He rolled down the driver-side window; this worked best if there was eye contact. Besides, he might need her out of the car. "Okay. Stay here. I'll go get us the sucker." She rattled his instructions back in pompous tones.

One last thing: He punched a number into the car phone, and set its timer and no video option. Then he was out of the car, jogging back to the guard box. This sort of trick had worked often enough at school. Pray that it would work now. Pray that she wouldn't ad lib.

He turned off the throat mike as Lucas buzzed him back into the visitor trap. "I got to the top. Someone—maybe even the Chief of Federal Security—will call back on the Red Line."

Phil's eyebrows went up. "That would do it." Hamid's prestige had just taken a giant step up.

Hamid made a show of impatient pacing about the visitor trap. He stopped at the outer door with his back to the guard. Now he really *was* impatient. Then the phone rang, and he heard Phil pick it up.

"Escrow One, Agent Lucas speaking, sir!"

From where he was standing, Hamid could see the Blab. She was in the driver's seat, looking curiously at the dash phone. Hamid turned on the throat mike and murmured, "Lucas, this is Joseph Stanley Ortega."

Almost simultaneously, "Lucas, this is Joseph Stanley Ortega," came from the phone behind him. The words were weighted with all the importance Hamid could wish, and something else: a furtiveness not in the public speeches. That was probably because of Hamid's original delivery, but it didn't sound too bad.

In any case, Phil Lucas was impressed. "Sir!"

"Agent Lucas, we have a problem." Hamid concentrated on his words, and tried to ignore the Ortega echo. For him, that was the hardest part of the trick, especially when he had to speak more than a brief sentence. "There could be nuclear fire, unless the Tourists cool off. I'm with the National Command Authorities in deep shelter: it's that serious." Maybe that would explain why there was no video.

Phil's voice quavered. "Yes, sir." *He* wasn't in deep shelter.

"Have you verified—" *clicket* "—my ID?" The click was in Hamid's earphone; he didn't hear it on the guard's set. A loose connection in the headpiece?

"Yes, sir. I mean . . . just one moment." Sounds of hurried keyboard tapping. There should be no problem with a voiceprint match, and Hamid needed things nailed tight to bring this off. "Yes sir, you're fine. I mean—"

"Good. Now listen carefully: the Guide, Thompson, has a Tourist with him. We need that Outsider returned, *quickly and quietly*. Get the lift ready, and keep everybody clear of these two. If Thompson fails, millions may die. Give him whatever he asks for." Out in the car, the Blab was having a high old time. Her front talons were hooked awkwardly over the steering wheel. She twisted it back and forth, "driving" and "talking" at the same time: the apotheosis of life—to be taken for a person by real people!

"Yes, sir!"

"Very well. Let's—" *clicket-click* "—get moving on this." And on that last click, the Ortega voice was gone. *God damned cheapjack commset!*

Lucas was silent a moment, respectfully waiting for his President to continue. Then, "Yes, sir. What must we do?"

Out in the Millennium Commander, the Blab was the picture of consternation. She turned toward him, eyes wide. *What do I say now?* Hamid repeated the line, as loud as he dared. No Ortega. *She can't hear anything I'm saying!* He shut off his mike.

"Sir? Are you still there?"

"Line must be dead," Hamid said casually, and gave the Blab a little wave to come running.

"Phone light says I still have a connection, Ham. . . . Mr. President, can you hear me? You were saying what we must do. Mr. President?" The Blab didn't recognize his wave. Too small. He tried again. She tapped a talon against her muzzle. *Blab! Don't ad lib!* "Well, uh," came Ortega's voice, "don't rush me. I'm thinking. I'm thinking! . . . We must all pull together or else millions may die. Don't you think? I mean, it makes sense—" which it did not, and less so by the second. Lucas was making "uh-huh" sounds, trying to fit reason on the blabber. His tone was steadily more puzzled, even suspicious.

No help for it. Hamid slammed his fist against the transp armor, and waved wildly to the Blab. *Come here!* Ortega's voice died in mid-syllable. He turned to see Lucas staring at him, surprise and uneasiness on his face. "Something's going on here, and I don't like it—" Somewhere in his mind, Phil had figured out he was being taken, yet the rest of him was carried forward by the inertia of the everyday. He leaned over the counter, to get Hamid's line of view on the lot.

The original plan was completely screwed, yet strangely he felt no panic, no doubt; there were still options: Hamid smiled—and jumped across the counter, driving the smaller man into the corner of wall and counter. Phil's hand reached wildly for the tab that would bring the partition down. Hamid just pushed him harder against the wall . . . and grabbed the guard's pistol from its holster. He jammed the barrel into the other's middle. "Quiet down, Phil."

"*Son of a bitch!*" But the other stopped struggling. Hamid heard the Blab slam into the outer door.

"Okay. Kick the outside release." The door buzzed. A moment later, the Blab was in the visitor trap, bouncing around his legs.

"Heh heh heh! That was good. That was really good!" The crackle was Lazy Larry's but the voice was still Ortega's.

"Now buzz the inner door." The other gave his head a tight shake. Hamid punched Lucas's gut with the point of the pistol. "*Now!*" For an instant, Phil seemed frozen. Then he kneed the control tab, and the inner door buzzed. Hamid pushed it ajar with his foot, then heaved Lucas away from the counter. The other bounced to his feet, his eyes staring at the muzzle of the pistol, his face very pale. *Dead men don't raise alarums.* The thought was clear on his face.

Hamid hesitated, almost as shocked by his success as Lucas was. "Don't worry, Phil." He shifted his aim and fired a burst over Lucas's shoulder . . . into the warehouse security processor. Fire and debris flashed back into the room—and now alarms sounded everywhere.

He pushed through the door, the Blab close behind. The armor clicked shut behind them; odds were, it would stay locked now that the security processor was down. Nobody in sight, but he heard shouting. Hamid ran down the aisle of upgoing goods. They kept the agrav lift at the back of the building, under the main ceiling hatch. Things were definitely not going to plan, but if the lift was there, he could still—

"There he is!"

Hamid dived down an aisle, jigged this way and that between pallets . . . and then began walking very quietly. He was in the downcoming section now, surrounded by the goods that had been delivered thus far by the Caravan. These were the items that would lift Middle America beyond Old Earth's twenty-first century. Towering ten meters above his head were stacks of room-temperature fusion electrics. With them—and the means to produce more—Middle America could trash its methanol economy and fixed fusion plants. Two aisles over were the raw agrav units. These looked more like piles of fabric than anything high tech. Yet the warehouse lifter was built around one, and with them Middle America would soon make aircars as easily as automobiles.

Hamid knew there were cameras in the ceiling above the lights. Hopefully they were as dead as the security processor. Footsteps one aisle over. Hamid eased into the dark between two pallets. Quiet, quiet. The Blab didn't feel like being quiet. She raced down the aisle ahead of him, raking the spaces between the pallets with a painfully loud imitation of his pistol. They'd see her in a second. He ran the other direction a few meters, and fired a burst into the air.

"Jesus! How many did asshole Lucas let in?" Someone very close replied, "That's still low-power stuff." Much quieter: "We'll show these guys some firepower." Hamid suddenly guessed there were only two of them. And with the guard box jammed, they might be trapped in here till the alarm brought guards from outside.

He backed away from the voices, continued toward the rear of the warehouse.

"Boo!" The Blab was on the pallets above him, talking to someone on the ground. Explosive shells smashed into the fusion electrics around her. The sounds bounced back and forth through the warehouse. Whatever it was, it was a cannon compared to his pistol. No doubt it was totally unauthorized for indoors, but that did Hamid little good. He raced forward, heedless of the destruction. "Get down!" he screamed at the pallets. A bundle of shadow and light materialized in front of him and streaked down the aisle.

A second roar of cannon fire, tearing through the space he had just been. But something else was happening now. Blue light shone from somewhere in the racks of fusion electrics, sending brightness and crisp shadows across the walls ahead. It felt as if someone had opened a furnace door behind him. He looked back. The blue was spreading, an arc-welder light that promised burns yet unfelt. He looked quickly away, afterimages dancing on his eyes, afterimages of the pallet shelves *sagging* in the heat.

The autosprinklers kicked on, an instant rainstorm. But this was a fire that water would not quench—and might even fuel. The water exploded into steam, knocking Hamid to his knees. He bounced up sprinting, falling, sprinting again. The agrav lift should be around the next row of pallets. In the back of his mind, something was analyzing the disaster. That explosive cannon fire had started things, a runaway melt in the fusion electrics. They were supposedly safer than meth engines—but they could melt down. This sort of destruction in a Middle American nuclear plant would have meant rad poisoning over a continent. But the Tourists claimed their machines melted clean—shedding low-energy photons and an enormous flood of particles that normal matter scarcely responded to. Hamid felt an urge to hysterical laughter; Slow Zone astronomers light years away might notice this someday, a wiggle on their neutrino scopes, one more datum for their flawed cosmologies.

There was lightning in the rainstorm now, flashes between the pallets and across the aisle—into the raw agrav units. The clothlike material jerked and rippled, individual units floating upwards. Magic carpets released by a genie.

Then giant hands clapped him, sound that was pain, and the rain was gone, replaced by a hot wet wind that swept around and up. Morning light shown through the steamy mist. The explosion had blasted open the roof. A rainbow arced across the ruins. Hamid was crawling now. Sticky wet ran down his face, dripped redly on the floor. The pallets bearing the fusion electrics had collapsed. Fifteen meters away, molten plastic slurried atop flowing metal.

He could see the agrav lift now, what was left of it. The lift sagged like an old candle in the flow of molten metal. So. No way up. He pulled himself back from the glare and leaned against the stacked agravs. They slid and vibrated behind him. The cloth was soft, yet it blocked the heat, and some of the noise. The pinkish blue of a dawn sky shown through the last scraps of mist. The Lothlrimarre barge hung there, four spherical pressure vessels embedded in intricate ramps and crenellations.

Jeeze. Most of the warehouse roof was just . . . gone. A huge tear showed through the far wall. *There!* The two guards. They were facing away from him, one half leaning on the other. Chasing him was very far from their minds at the moment. They were picking their way through the jumble, trying to get out of the warehouse. Unfortunately, a rivulet of silver metal crossed their path. One false step and they'd be ankle deep in stuff. But they were lucky, and in fifteen seconds passed from sight around the outside of the building.

No doubt he could get out that way, too. . . . But that wasn't why he was here. Hamid struggled to his feet, and began shouting for the Blab. The hissing, popping sounds were loud, but not like before. If she were conscious, she'd hear him. He wiped blood from his lips and limped along the row of agrav piles. *Don't die, Blab. Don't die.*

There was motion everywhere. The piles of agravs had come alive. The top ones simply lifted off, tumbled upwards, rolling and unrolling. The lower layers strained and jerked. Normal matter might not notice the flood of never-never particles from the meltdown; the agravs were clearly not normal. Auras flickered around the ones trapped at the bottom. But this was not the eye-sizzling burn of the fusion electrics. This was a soft thing, an awakening rather than an explosion. Hamid's eyes were caught on the rising. Hundreds of them just floating off, gray and russet banners in the morning light. He leaned back. Straight up, the farthest ones were tiny specks against the blue. *Maybe—*

Something banged into his legs, almost dumping him back on the floor. "Wow. So loud." The Blab had found *him*! Hamid knelt and grabbed her around the neck. She looked fine! A whole lot better than he did, anyway. Like most smaller animals, she could take a lot of bouncing around. He ran his hands down her shoulders. There were some nicks, a spattering of blood. And she looked subdued, not quite the hellion of before. "Loud. Loud," she kept saying.

"I know, Blab. But that's the worst." He looked back into the sky. At the rising agravs . . . at the Lothlrimarre barge. *It would be crazy to try . . .* but he heard sirens outside.

He patted the Blab, then stood and clambered up the nearest pile of agravs. The material, hundreds of separate units piled like blankets, gave beneath his boots like so much foam rubber. He slid back a ways after each step. He grabbed at the edges of the units above him, and pulled himself near the top. He wanted to test one that was free to rise. Hamid grabbed the top layer, already rippling in an unsensed wind. He pulled out his pocket knife and slashed at the material. It parted smoothly, with the resistance of heavy felt. He ripped off a strip of the material, stuffed it in his pocket, then grabbed again at the top layer. The unit fluttered in his hands, a four-meter square straining for the sky. It slowly tipped him backwards. His feet left the pile. It was rising as fast as the unloaded ones!

"Wait for me! Wait!" The Blab jumped desperately at his boots. Two meters up, three meters. Hamid gulped, and let go. He crashed to the concrete, lay stunned for a moment, imagining what would have happened if he'd dithered an instant longer. . . . Still. He took the scrap of agrav from his pocket, stared at it as it tugged on his fingers. There was a pattern in the reddish-gray fabric, intricate and recursive. The Tourists said it was in a different class from the fusion electrics. The electrics involved advanced technology, but were constructable within the Slow Zone. Agrav, on the other hand . . . the effect could be explained in theory, but its practical use depended on instant-by-instant restabilization at atomic levels. The Tourists claimed there were billions of protein-sized processors in the fabric. This was an import—not just from the Beyond—but from Transhuman Space. Till now, Hamid had been a skeptic. Flying was such a prosaic thing. But . . . these things had no simple logic. They were more like living creatures, or complex control systems. They seemed a lot like the "smart matter" Larry claimed was common in Transhuman technology.

Hamid cut the strip into two different-sized pieces. The cut edges were smooth, quite unlike cuts in cloth or leather. He let the fragments go. . . . They drifted slowly upwards, like leaves on a breeze. But after a few seconds, the large one took the lead, falling higher and higher above the smaller. *I could come down just by trimming the fabric!* And he remembered how the carpet had drifted sideways, in the direction of his grasp.

The sirens were louder. He looked at the pile of agravs. Funny. A week ago he had been worried about flying commercial air to Westland. "You want games, Blab? This is the biggest yet."

He climbed back up the pile. The top layer was just beginning to twitch. They had maybe thirty seconds, if it was like the others. He pulled the fabric around him, tying it under his arms. "Blab! Get your ass up here!"

She came, but not quite with the usual glee. Things had been rough this morning—or maybe she was just brighter than he was. He grabbed her, and tied the other end of the agrav under her shoulders. As the agrav twitched toward flight, the cloth seemed to shrink. He could still cut the fabric, but the knots were tight. He grabbed the Blab under her hind quarters and drew her up to his chest—just like Pop used to do when the Blab was a pup. Only now, she was big. Her forelegs stuck long over his shoulders.

The fabric came taut around his armpits. Now he was standing. Now—his feet left the pile. He looked *down* at the melted pallets, the silver metal rivers that dug deep through the warehouse floor. The Blab was making the sounds of a small boy crying.

They were through the roof. Hamid shuddered as the morning chill turned his soaked clothing icy. The sun was at the horizon, its brilliance no help against the cold. Shadows grew long and crisp from the buildings. The guts of the warehouse lay open below them; from here it looked dark, but lightning still flickered. More reddish-gray squares floated up from the ruins. In the gravel lot fronting the warehouse, there were fire trucks and armored vehicles. Men ran back and forth from the guard box. A squad was moving around the side of the building. Two guys by the armored cars pointed at him, and others just stopped to stare. A boy and his not-dog, swinging beneath a wrong-way parachute. He'd seen enough Feds 'n' Crooks to know they could shoot him down easily, any number of ways. One of the figures climbed into the armored car. If they were half as trigger-happy as the guards inside the warehouse . . .

Half a minute passed. The scene below could fit between his feet now. The Blab wasn't crying anymore, and he guessed the chill was no problem for her. The Blab's neck and head extended over his shoulder. He could feel her looking back and forth. "Wow," she said softly. "Wow."

Rockabye baby. They swung back and forth beneath the agrav. Back and forth. The swings were getting wider each time! In a sickening whirl, the sky and ground traded places. He was buried head first in agrav fabric. He struggled out of the mess. They weren't hanging below the agrav now, they were *lying* on top of it. This was crazy. How could it be stable with them on top? In a second it would dump them back under. He held tight to the Blab . . . but no more swinging. It was as if the hanging-down position had been the unstable one. More evidence that the agrav was smart matter, its processors using underlying nature to produce seemingly unnatural results.

The damn thing really was a flying carpet! Of course, with all the knots, the four-meter square of fabric was twisted and crumpled. It looked more like the Blab's nest of blankets back home than the flying carpets of fantasy.

The warehouse district was out of sight beneath the carpet. In the spaces around and above them, dozens of agravs paced him—some just a few meters away, some bare specks in the sky. Westward, they were coming even with the tops of the Marquette towers: brown and ivory walls, vast mirrors of windows reflecting back the landscape of morning. Southward, Ann Arbor was a tiny crisscross of streets, almost lost in the bristle of leafless trees. The quad was clearly visible, the interior walks, the tiny speck of red that was Morale Hall. He'd had roughly this view every time they flew back from the farm, but now . . . there was nothing around him. It was just Hamid and the Blab . . . and the air stretching away forever beneath them. Hamid gulped, and didn't look down for a while.

They were still rising. The breeze came straight down upon them—and it seemed to be getting stronger. Hamid shivered uncontrollably, teeth chattering. How high up were they? Three thousand meters? Four? He was going numb, and when he moved he could hear ice crackling in his jacket. He felt dizzy and nauseated—five thousand meters was about the highest you'd want to go without oxygen on Middle America. He *thought* he could stop the rise; if not, they were headed for space, along with the rest of the agravs.

But he had to do more than slow the rise, or descend. He looked up at the Lothlrimarre's barge. It was much nearer—and two hundred meters to the east. If he couldn't move this thing sideways, he'd need the slug's active cooperation.

It was something he had thought about—for maybe all of five seconds—back in the warehouse. If the agrav had been an ordinary lighter-than-air craft, there'd be no hope. Without props or jets, a balloon goes where the wind says; the only control comes from finding the *altitude* where the wind and you want the same thing. But when he grabbed that first carpet, it really had slid horizontally toward the side he was holding. . . .

He crept toward the edge. The agrav yielded beneath his knees, but didn't tilt more than a small boat would. Next to him, the Blab looked over the edge, straight down. Her head jerked this way and that as she scanned the landscape. "Wow," she kept saying. Could she really understand what she was seeing?

The wind shifted a little. It came a bit from the side now, not straight from above. He really did have control! Hamid smiled around chattering teeth.

The carpet rose faster and faster. The downward wind was an arctic blast. They must be going up at fifteen or twenty klicks per hour. The Lothlrimarre barge loomed huge above them . . . now almost beside them.

God, they were *above* it now! Hamid pulled out his knife, picked desperately at the blade opener with numbed fingers. It came open abruptly—and almost popped out of his shaking hand. He trimmed small pieces from the edge of the carpet. The wind from heaven stayed just as strong. Bigger pieces! He tore wildly at the cloth. One large strip, two. And the wind eased . . . stopped. Hamid bent over the edge of the carpet, and stuffed his vertigo back down his throat. *Perfect.* They were directly over the barge, and closing.

The nearest of the four pressure spheres was so close it blocked his view of the others. Hamid could see the human habitat, the conference area. They would touch down on a broad flat area next to the sphere. The aiming couldn't have been better. Hamid guessed the slug must be maneuvering too, moving the barge precisely under his visitor.

There was a flash of heat, and an invisible fist slammed into the carpet. Hamid and the Blab tumbled—now beneath the agrav, now above. He had a glimpse of the barge. A jet of yellow-white spewed from the sphere, ammonia and hydrogen at one thousand atmospheres. The top pressure sphere had been breached. The spear of superpressured gas was surrounded by pale flame where the hydrogen and atmospheric oxygen burned.

The barge fell out of view, leaving thunder and burning mists. Hamid held onto the Blab and as much of the carpet as he could wrap around them. The tumbling stopped; they were upside down in the heavy swaddling. Hamid looked out:

"Overhead" was the brown and gray of farmland in late autumn. Marquette was to his left. He bent around, peeked into the sky. There! The barge was several klicks away. The top pressure vessel was spreading fire and mist, but the lower ones looked okay. Pale violet flickered from between the spheres. Moments later, thunder echoed across the sky. The slug was fighting back!

He twisted in the jumble of cloth, trying to see the high sky. To the north . . . a single blue-glowing trail lanced southwards . . . split into five separate, jigging paths that cooled through orange to red. It was beautiful . . . but somehow like a jagged claw sketched against the sky. The claw tips dimmed to nothing, but whatever caused them still raced forward. The attackers' answering fire slagged the north-facing detail of the barge. It crumpled like trash plastic in a fire. The bottom pressure vessels still looked okay, but if the visitor's deck got zapped like that, Larry would be a dead man.

Multiple sonic booms rocked the carpet. Things swept past, too small and fast to clearly see. The barge's guns still flickered violet, but the craft was rising now—faster than he had ever seen it move.

After a moment, the carpet drifted through one more tumble, and they sat heads up. The morning had been transformed. Strange clouds were banked around and above him, some burning, some glowing, all netted with the brownish of nitrogen oxides. The stench of ammonia burned his eyes and mouth. The Blab was making noises through her mouth, true coughing and choking sounds.

The Tourists were long gone. The Lothlrimarre was a dot at the top of the sky. All the other agravs had passed by. He and the Blab were alone in the burning clouds. *Probably not for long.* Hamid began sawing at the agrav fabric—tearing off a slice, testing for an upwelling breeze, then tearing off another. They drifted through the cloud deck into a light drizzle, a strange rain that burned the skin as it wet them. He slid the carpet sideways into the sunlight, and they could breathe again. Things looked almost normal, except where the clouds cast a great bloody shadow across the farmland.

Where best to land? Hamid looked over the edge of the carpet . . . and saw the enemy waiting. It was a cylinder, tapered, with a pair of small fins at one end. It drifted through the carpet's shadow, and he realized the enemy craft was *close*. It couldn't be more than ten meters long, less than two meters across at the widest. It hung silent, pacing the carpet's slow descent. Hamid looked up, and saw the others—four more dark shapes. They circled in, like killer fish nosing at a possible lunch. One slid right over them, so slow and near he could have run his palm down its length. There were no ports, no breaks in the dull finish. But the fins—red glowed dim from within them, and Hamid felt a wave of heat as they passed.

The silent parade went on for a minute, each killer getting its look. The Blab's head followed the craft around and around. Her eyes were wide, and she was making the terrified whistling noises of the night before. The air was still, but for the faint updraft of the carpet's descent. Or was it? . . . The sound grew, a hissing sound like Tines had made during his phone call. Only now it came from all the killers, and there were overtones lurking at the edge of sensibility, tones that never could have come from an ordinary telephone.

"Blab." He reached to stroke her neck. She slashed at his hand, her needle-teeth slicing deep. Hamid gasped in pain, and rolled back from her. The Blab's pelt was puffed out as far as he had ever seen it. She looked twice normal size, a very large carnivore with death glittering in her eyes. Her long neck snapped this way and that, trying to track all the killers at once. Fore and rear talons dragged long rips through the carpet. She climbed onto the thickest folds of the carpet, and *shrieked* at the killers . . . and collapsed.

For a moment, Hamid couldn't move. His hand, the scream: razors across his hand, icepicks jammed in his ears. He struggled to his knees and crawled to the Blabber. "Blab?" No answer, no motion. He touched her flank: limp as something fresh dead.

In twenty years, Hamid Thompson had never had close friends, but he had never been alone, either. Until now. He looked up from the Blabber's body, at the circling shapes.

Alone at four thousand meters. He didn't have much choice when one of the killer fish came directly at him, when something wide and dark opened from its belly. The darkness swept around them, swallowing all.

HAMID HAD NEVER BEEN IN SPACE BEFORE. UNDER OTHER CIRCUMSTANCES, he would have reveled in the experience. The glimpse he'd had of Middle America from low orbit was like a beautiful dream. But now, all he could see through the floor of his cage was a bluish dot, nearly lost in the sun's glare. He pushed hard against the clear softness, and rolled onto his back. It was harder than a one-handed pushup to do that. He guessed the mothership was doing four or five gees . . . and had been for hours.

When they had pulled him off the attack craft, Hamid had been semiconscious. He had no idea what acceleration that shark boat reached, but it was more than he could take. He remembered that glimpse of Middle America, blue and serene. Then . . . they'd taken the Blab—or her body—away. *Who?* There had been a human, the Ravna woman. She had done something to his hand; it wasn't bleeding anymore. And . . . and there had been the Blabber, up and walking around. No, the pelt pattern had been all wrong. *That must have been Tines.* There had been the hissing voice, and some kind of argument with Ravna.

Hamid stared up at the sunlight on the ceiling and walls. His own shadow lay spread-eagled on the ceiling. In the first hazy hours, he had thought it was another prisoner. The walls were gray, seamless, but with scrape marks and stains, as though heavy equipment was used here. He thought there was a door in the ceiling, but he couldn't remember for sure. There was no sign of one now. The room was an empty cubicle, featureless, its floor showing clear to the stars: surely not an ordinary brig. There were no toilet facilities—and at five gees they wouldn't have helped. The air was thick with the stench of himself. . . . Hamid guessed the room was an airlock. The transparent floor might be nothing more than a figment of some field generator's imagination. A flick of a switch and Hamid would be swept away forever.

The Blabber gone, Pop gone, maybe Larry and the slug gone. . . . Hamid raised his good hand a few centimeters and clenched his fist. Lying here was the first time he'd ever thought about killing anyone. He thought about it a lot now. . . . It kept the fear tied down.

"Mr. Thompson." Ravna's voice. Hamid suppressed a twitch of surprise: after hours of rage, to hear the enemy. "Mr. Thompson, we are going to free fall in fifteen seconds. Do not be alarmed."

So, airline courtesy of a sudden.

The force that had squished him flat these hours, that had made it an exercise even to breathe, slowly lessened. From beyond the walls and ceiling he heard small popping noises. For a panicky instant, it seemed as though the floor had disappeared and he was falling through. He twisted. His hand hit the barrier . . . and he floated slowly across the room, toward the wall that had been the ceiling. A door had opened. He drifted through, into a hall that would have looked normal except for the intricate pattern of grooves and ledges that covered the walls.

"Thirty meters down the hall is a latrine," came Ravna's voice. "There are clean clothes that should fit you. When you are done . . . when you are done, we will talk."

Damn right. Hamid squared his shoulders and pulled himself down the hall.

SHE DIDN'T LOOK LIKE A KILLER. THERE WAS ANGER—TENSION?—ON HER face, the face of someone who has been awake a long time and has fought hard—and doesn't expect to win.

Hamid drifted slowly into the—conference room? bridge?—trying to size everything up at once. It was a large room with a low ceiling. Moving across it was easy in zero gee, slow bounces from floor to ceiling and back. The wall curved around, transparent along most of its circumference. There were stars and night dark beyond.

Ravna had been standing in a splash of light. Now she moved back a meter, into the general dimness. Somehow she slipped her foot into the floor, anchoring herself. She waved him to the other side of a table. They stood in the half crouch of zero gee, less than two meters apart. Even so, she looked taller than he had guessed from the phone call. Her mass might be close to his. The rest of her was as he remembered, though she looked very tired. Her gaze flickered across him, and away. "Hello, Mr. Thompson. The floor will hold your foot, if you tap it gently."

Hamid didn't take the advice; he held onto the table edge and jammed his feet against the floor. He would have something to brace against if the time came to move quickly. "Where is my Blabber?" His voice came out hoarse, more desperate than demanding.

"Your pet is dead."

There was a tiny hesitation before the last word. She was as bad a liar as ever. Hamid pushed back the rage: if the Blab was alive, there was something still possible beyond revenge. "Oh." He kept his face blank.

"However, we intend to return you safely to home." She gestured at the star fields around them. "The six-gee boost was to avoid unnecessary fighting with the Lothlrimarre being. We will coast outwards some further, perhaps even go into ram drive. But Mr. Tines will take you back to Middle America in one of our attack boats. There will be no problem to land you without attracting notice . . . perhaps on the western continent, somewhere out of the way." Her tone was distant. He noticed that she never looked directly at him for more than an instant. Now she was staring just to one side of his face. He remembered the phone call, how she seemed to ignore his video. Up close, she was just as attractive as before—more. Just once he would like to see her smile. *And somewhere there was unease that he could be so attracted by a murderous stranger.*

If only, "If only I could understand *why*. Why did you kill the Blab? Why did you kill my father?"

Ravna's eyes narrowed. "That cheating piece of filth? He is too tricky to kill. He was gone when we visited his farm. I'm not sure I have killed anyone on this operation. The Lothlrimarre is still functioning, I know that." She sighed. "We were all very lucky. You have no idea what Tines has been like these last days. . . . He called you last night."

Hamid nodded numbly.

"Well, he was mellow then. He tried to kill me when I took over the ship. Another day like this and he would have been dead—and most likely your planet would have been so, too."

Hamid remembered the Lothlrimarre's theory about the tines's need. And now that the creature had the Blab . . . "So now Tines is satisfied?"

Ravna nodded vaguely, missing the quaver in his voice. "He's harmless now and very confused, poor guy. Assimilation is hard. It will be a few weeks . . . but he'll stabilize, probably turn out better than he ever was."

Whatever that means.

She pushed back from the table, stopped herself with a hand on the low ceiling. Apparently their meeting was over. "Don't worry. He should be well enough to take you home quite soon. Now I will show you your—"

"Don't rush him, Rav. Why should he want to go back to Middle America?" The voice was a pleasant tenor, human-sounding but a little slurred.

Ravna bounced off the ceiling. "I thought you were going to stay out of this! Of course the boy is going back to Middle America. That's his home; that's where he fits."

"I wonder." The unseen speaker laughed. He sounded cheerfully— *joyfully*—drunk. "Your name is shit down there, Hamid, did you know that?"

"Huh?"

"Yup. You slagged the Caravan's entire shipment of fusion electrics. 'Course you had a little help from the Federal Police, but that fact is being ignored. Much worse, you destroyed most of the agrav units. *Whee.* Up, up and away. And there's no way those can be replaced short of a trip back to the Outsi—"

"Shut up!" Ravna's anger rode over the good cheer. "The agrav units were a cheap trick. Nothing that subtle can work in the Zone for long. Five years from now they would all have faded."

"Sure, sure. I know that, and you know that. But both Middle America and the Tourists figure you've trashed this Caravan, Hamid. You'd be a fool to go back."

Ravna shouted something in a language Hamid had never heard.

"English, Rav, English. I want him to understand what is happening."

"He is going back!" Ravna's voice was furious, almost desperate. "We *agreed*!"

"I know, Rav." A little of the rampant joy left the voice. It sounded truly sympathetic. "And I'm sorry. But I was different then, and I understand things better now. . . . Hey, I'll be down in a minute, okay?"

She closed her eyes. It's hard to slump in free fall, but Ravna came close, her shoulders and arms relaxing, her body drifting slowly up from the floor. "Oh, Lord," she said softly.

Out in the hall, someone was whistling a tune that had been popular in Marquette six months ago. A shadow floated down the walls, followed by . . . *the Blab?* Hamid lurched off the table, flailed wildly for a handhold. He steadied himself, got a closer look.

No. Not the Blab. It was of the same race certainly, but this one had an entirely different pattern of black and white. The great patch of black around one eye and white around the other would have been laughable . . . if you didn't know what you were looking at: at last to see Mr. Tines.

Man and alien regarded each other for a long moment. It was a little smaller than the Blab. It wore a checkered orange scarf about its neck. Its paws looked no more flexible than his Blab's . . . but he didn't doubt the intelligence that looked back from its eyes. The tines drifted to the ceiling, and anchored itself with a deft swipe of paw and talons. There were faint sounds in the air now, squeaks and twitters almost beyond hearing. If he listened close enough, Hamid guessed he would hear the hissing, too.

The tines looked at him, and laughed pleasantly—the tenor voice of a minute before. "Don't rush me! I'm not all here yet."

Hamid looked at the doorway. There were two more there, one with a jeweled collar—the leader? They glided through the air and tied down next to the first. Hamid saw more shadows floating down the hall.

"How many?" he asked.

"I'm six now." He thought it was a different tines that answered, but the voice was the same.

The three floated in the doorway. One wore no scarf or jewelry . . . and looked very familiar.

"Blab!" Hamid pushed off the table. He went into a spin that missed the door by several meters. The Blabber—it must be her—twisted around and fled the room.

"Stay away!" For an instant the tines's voice changed, held the same edge as the night before. Hamid stood on the wall next to the doorway and looked down the hall. The Blab was there, sitting on the closed door at the far end. Hamid's orientation flipped . . . the hall could just as well be a deep, bright-lit well, with the Blab trapped at the bottom of it.

"Blab?" He said softly, aware of the tines behind him.

She looked up at him. "I can't play the old games anymore, Hamid," she said in her softest femvoice. He stared for a moment, uncomprehending. Over the years, the Blab said plenty of things that—by accident or in the listeners' imagination—might seem humanly intelligent. Here, for the first time, he knew that he was hearing sense. . . . And he guessed what Ravna meant when she said the Blab was dead.

Hamid backed away from the edge of the pit. He looked at the other tines, remembered that their speech came as easily from one as the other. "You're like a hive of roaches, aren't you?"

"A little," the tenor voice came from somewhere among them.

"But telepathic," Hamid said.

The one who had been his friend answered, but in the tenor voice: "Yes, between myselves. But it's no sixth sense. You've known about it all your life. I like to talk a lot. Blabber." The squeaking and the hissing: just the edge of all they were saying to each other across their two-hundred-kilohertz bandwidth. "I'm sorry I flinched. Myselves are still confused. I don't know quite who I am."

The Blab pushed off and drifted back into the bridge. She grabbed a piece of ceiling as she came even with Hamid. She extended her head toward him, tentatively, as though he were a stranger. *I feel the same way about you*, thought Hamid. But he reached out to brush her neck with his fingers. She twitched back, glided across the room to nestle among the other tines.

Hamid stared at them staring back. He had a sudden image: a pack of long-necked rats beadily analyzing their prey. "So. Who is the real Mr. Tines? The monster who'd smash a world, or the nice guy I'm hearing now?"

Ravna answered, her voice tired, distant. "The monster tines is gone . . . or going. Don't you see? The pack was unbalanced. It was dying."

"There were five in my pack, Hamid. Not a bad number: some of the brightest packs are that small. But I was down from seven—two of myselves had been killed. The ones remaining were mismatched, and only one of them was female." Tines paused. "I know humans can go for years without contact with the opposite sex, and suffer only mild discomfort—"

Tell me about it.

"—but tines are very different. If a pack's sex ratio gets too lopsided, especially if there is a mismatch of skills, then the mind disintegrates. . . . Things can get very nasty in the process." Hamid noticed that all the time it talked, the two tines next to the one with the orange scarf had been nibbling at the scarf's knots. They moved quickly, perfectly coordinated, untying and retying the knots. *Tines doesn't need hands.* Or put another way, he already had six. Hamid was seeing the equivalent of a human playing nervously with his tie.

"Ravna lied when she said the Blab is dead. I forgive her: she wants you off our ship, with no more questions, no more hassle. But the Blabber isn't dead. She was *rescued* . . . from being an animal the rest of her life. And her rescue saved the pack. I feel so . . . happy. Better even than when I was seven. I can understand things that have been puzzles for years. Your Blab is far more language-oriented than any of my other selves. I could never talk like this without her."

Ravna had drifted toward the pack. Now she had her feet planted on the floor beneath them. Her head brushed the shoulder of one, was even with the eyes of another. "Imagine the Blabber as like the verbal hemisphere of a human brain," she said to Hamid.

"Not quite," Tines said. "A human hemisphere can almost carry on by itself. The Blab by itself could never be a person."

Hamid remembered how the Blab's greatest desire had often seemed just to *be* a real person. And listening to this creature, he heard echoes of the Blab. It would be easy to accept what they were saying. . . . Yet if you turned the words just a little, you had enslavement and rape— the slug's theory with frosting.

Hamid turned away from all the eyes and looked across the star clouds. *How much should I believe? How much should I seem to believe?* "One of the Tourists wanted to sell us a gadget, an 'ftl radio.' Did you know that we used it to ask about the tines? Do you know what we found?" He told them about the horrors Larry had found around the galactic rim.

Ravna exchanged a glance with the tines by her head. For a moment the only sound was the twittering and hissing. Then Tines spoke. "Imagine the most ghastly villains of Earth's history. Whatever they are, whatever holocausts they set, I assure you much worse has happened elsewhere. . . . Now imagine that this regime was so vast, so effectively *evil* that no honest historians survived. What stories do you suppose would be spread about the races they exterminated?"

"Okay. So—"

"Tines are not monsters. On average, we are no more bloodthirsty than you humans. But we are descended from packs of wolf-like creatures. We are deadly warriors. Given reasonable equipment and numbers, we can outfight most anything in the Slow Zone." Hamid remembered the shark pack of attack boats. With one animal in each, and radio communication . . . no team of human pilots could match their coordination. "We once were a great power in our part of the Slow Zone. We had enemies, even when there was no war. Would you trust creatures who live indefinitely, but whose personalities may drift from friendly to indifferent—even to inimical—as their components die and are replaced?"

"And you're such a peach of a guy because you've got the Blab?"

"*Yes!* Though you liked . . . I know you would have liked me when I was seven. But the Blab has a lovely outlook; she makes it fun to be alive."

Hamid looked at Ravna and the pack who surrounded her. So the tines had been great fighters. That he believed. So they were now virtually extinct, having run into something even deadlier. That he could believe, too. Beyond that . . . he'd be a fool to believe anything. He could imagine Tines as a friend, he wanted Ravna as one. But all the talk, all the seeming argument—it could just as well be manipulation. One thing was sure: if he returned to Middle America, he would never know the truth. He might live the rest of his life safe and cozy, but he wouldn't have the Blab, and he would never know what had really happened to her.

He gave Ravna a lopsided smile. "Back to square one then. I want passage to the Beyond with you."

"Out of the question. I—I made that clear from the beginning."

Hamid pushed nearer, stopped a meter in front of her. "Why won't you look at me?" he said softly. "Why do you hate me so much?"

For a full second, her eyes looked straight into his. "I *don't* hate you!" Her face clouded, as if she were about to weep. "It's just that you're such a God-*damned* disappointment!" She pushed back abruptly, knocking the tines out of her way.

He followed her slowly back to the conference table. She "stood" there, talking to herself in some unknown language. "She's swearing to her ancestors," murmured a tines that drifted close by Hamid's head. "Her kind is big on that sort of thing."

Hamid anchored himself across from her. He looked at her face. Young, no older than twenty it looked. But Outsiders had some control over aging. Besides, Ravna had spent at least the last ten years in relativistic flight. "You hired my—you hired Hussein Thompson to adopt me, didn't you?"

She nodded.

"Why?"

She looked back at him for a moment, this time not flinching away. Finally she sighed. "Okay, I will try but . . . there are many things you from the Slow Zone do not understand. Middle America is close to the Beyond, but you see out through a tiny hole. You can have even less concept of what lies beyond the Beyond, in the Transhuman reaches." She was beginning to sound like Lazy Larry.

"I'm willing to start with the version for five-year-olds."

"Okay." The faintest of smiles crossed her face. It was everything he'd guessed it would be. He wondered how he could make her do it again. " 'Once upon a time,' " the smile again, a little wider! "there was a very wise and good man, as wise and good as any mere human or human equivalent can ever be: a mathematical genius, a great general, an even greater peacemaker. He lived five hundred years' subjective, and half that time he was fighting a very great evil."

The Tines put in, "Just a part of that evil chewed up my race for breakfast."

Ravna nodded. "Eventually it chewed up our hero, too. He's been dead almost a century objective. The enemy has been very alert to keep him dead. Tines and I may be the last people trying to bring him back. . . . How much do you know about cloning, Mr. Thompson?"

Hamid couldn't answer for a moment; it was too clear where all this was going. "The Tourists claim they can build a viable zygote from almost any body cell. They say it's easy, but that what you get is no more than an identical twin of the original."

"That is about right. In fact, the clone is often *much* less than an identical twin. The uterine environment determines much of an individual's adult characteristics. Consider mathematical ability. There is a genetic component—but part of mathematical genius comes from the fetus getting just the right testosterone overdose. A little too much and you have a *dummy*.

"Tines and I have been running for a long time. Fifty years ago we reached Lothlrimarre—the back end of nowhere if there ever was one. We had a clonable cell from the great man. We did our best with the humaniform medical equipment that was available. The newborn *looked* healthy enough. . . ."

Rustle, hiss.

"But why not just raise the—child—yourself?" Hamid said. "Why hire someone to take him into the Slow Zone?"

Ravna bit her lip and looked away. It was Tines who replied: "Two reasons. The enemy wants you permanently dead. Raising you in the Slow Zone was the best way to keep you out of sight. The other reason is more subtle. We don't have records of your original memories; we can't make a perfect copy. But if we could give you an upbringing that mimicked the original's . . . then we'd have someone with the same outlook."

"Like having the original back, with a bad case of amnesia."

Tines chuckled. "Right. And things went very well at first. It was great good luck to run into Hussein Thompson at Lothlrimarre. He seemed a bright fellow, willing to work for his money. He brought the newborn in suspended animation back to Middle America, and married a woman equally bright, to be your mother.

"We had everything figured, the original's background imitated better than we had ever hoped. I even gave up one of my selves, a newborn, to be with you."

"I guess I know most of the rest," said Hamid. "Everything went fine for the first eight years—" the happy years of loving family—"till it became clear that I wasn't a math genius. Then your hired hand didn't know what to do, and your plan fell apart."

"It didn't have to!" Ravna slapped the table. The motion pulled her body up, almost free of the foot anchors. "The math ability was a big part, but there was still a chance—if Thompson hadn't welshed on us." She glared at Hamid, and then at the pack. "The original's parents died when he was ten years old. Hussein and his woman were supposed to disappear when the clone was ten, in a faked air crash. *That was the agreement!* Instead—" she swallowed. "We talked to him. He wouldn't meet in person. He was full of excuses, the clever bastard. 'I didn't see what good it would do to hurt the boy any more,' he said. 'He's no superman, just a good kid. I wanted him to be happy!' " She choked on her own indignation. "*Happy!* If he knew what we have been through, what the stakes are—"

Hamid's face felt numb, frozen. He wondered what it would be like to throw up in zero gee. "What—what about my mother?" he said in a very small voice.

Ravna gave her head a quick shake. "She tried to persuade Thompson. When that didn't work, she left you. By then it was too late; besides, that sort of abandonment is not the trauma the original experienced. But she did her part of the bargain; we paid her most of what we promised. . . . We came to Middle America expecting to find someone very wonderful, living again. Instead, we found—"

"—a piece of trash?" He couldn't get any anger into the question.

She gave a shaky sigh. ". . . no, I don't really think that. Hussein Thompson probably did raise a good person, and that's more than most can claim. But if you were the one we had hoped, you would be known all over Middle America by now, the greatest inventor, the greatest mover since the colony began. And that would be just the beginning." She seemed to be looking through him . . . remembering?

Tines made a diffident throat-clearing sound. "Not a piece of trash at all. And not just a 'good kid,' either. A part of me lived with Hamid for twenty years; the Blabber's memories are about as clear as a tines fragment's can be. Hamid is not just a failed dream to me, Rav. He's different, but I like to be around him almost as much as . . . the other one.

And when the crunch came—well, I saw him fight back. Given his background, even the original couldn't have done better. Hitching a ride on a raw agrav was the sort of daring that—"

"Okay, Tiny, the boy is daring and quick. But there's a difference between suicidal foolishness and calculated risk-taking. This late in life, there's no way he'll become more than a 'good man.' " Sarcasm lilted in the words.

"We could do worse, Rav."

"We *must* do far better, and you know it! See here. It's two years' subjective to get out of the Zone, and our suspension gear is failed. I will *not* accept seeing his face every day for two years. He goes back to Middle America." She kicked off, drifted toward the tines that hung over Hamid.

"I think not," said Tines. "If he doesn't want to go, I won't fly him back."

Anger and—strangely—panic played on Ravna's face. "This isn't how you were talking last week."

"Heh heh heh." Lazy Larry's cackle. "I've changed. Haven't you noticed?"

She grabbed a piece of ceiling and looked down at Hamid, calculating. "Boy: I don't think you understand. We're in a hurry; we won't be stopping any place like Lothlrimarre. There is one last way we might bring the original back to life—perhaps even with his own memories. You'll end up in Transhuman space if you come with us. The chances are that none of us will surv—" She stopped, and a slow smile spread across her face. Not a friendly smile. "Have you not thought what use your body might still be to us? You know nothing of what we plan. We may find ways of using you like a—like a blank data cartridge."

Hamid looked back at her, hoping no doubts showed on his face. "Maybe. But I'll have two years to prepare, won't I?"

They glared at each other for a long moment, the greatest eye contact yet. "So be it," she said at last. She drifted a little closer. "Some advice. We'll be two years cooped up here. It's a big ship. Stay out of my way." She drew back and pulled herself across the ceiling, faster and faster. She arrowed into the hallway beyond, and out of sight.

Hamid Thompson had his ticket to the Outside. Some tickets cost more than others. How much would he pay for his?

EIGHT HOURS LATER, THE SHIP WAS UNDER RAM DRIVE, OUTWARD BOUND. Hamid sat in the bridge, alone. The "windows" on one side of the room showed the view aft. Middle America's sun cast daylight across the room.

Invisible ahead of them, the interplanetary medium was being scooped in, fuel for the ram. The acceleration was barely perceptible, perhaps a fiftieth of a gee. The ram drive was for the long haul. That acceleration would continue indefinitely, eventually rising to almost half a gravity—and bringing them near light speed.

Middle America was a fleck of blue, trailing a white dot and a yellow one. It would be many hours before his world and its moons were lost from sight—and many days before they were lost to telescopic view.

Hamid had been here an hour—two?—since shortly after Tines showed him his quarters.

The inside of his head felt like an abandoned battlefield. A monster had become his good buddy. The man he hated turned out to be the father he had wanted . . . and his mother now seemed an uncaring manipulator. *And now I can never go back and ask you truly what you were, truly if you loved me.*

He felt something wet on his face. One good thing about gravity, even a fiftieth of a gee: it cleared the tears from your eyes.

He must be very careful these next two years. There was much to learn, and even more to guess at. What was lie and what was truth? There were things about the story that . . . How could one human being be as important as Ravna and Tines claimed? Next to the Transhumans, no human equivalent could count for much.

It might well be that these two believed the story they told him—*and that could be the most frightening possibility of all.* They talked about the Great Man as though he were some sort of messiah. Hamid had read of similar things in Earth history: twentieth-century Nazis longing for Hitler, the fanatics of the Afghan Jihad scheming to bring back their Imam. The story Larry got from the ansible could be true, and the Great Man might have been accomplice to the murder of a thousand worlds.

Hamid found himself laughing. *Where does that put me?* Could the clone of a monster rise above the original?

"What's funny, Hamid?" Tines had entered the bridge quietly. Now he settled himself on the table and posts around Hamid. The one that had been the Blab sat just a meter away.

"Nothing. Just thinking."

They sat for several minutes in silence, watching the sky. There was a wavering there—like hot air over a stove—the tiniest evidence of the fields that formed the ram around them. He glanced at the tines. Four of them were looking out the windows. The other two looked back at him, their eyes as dark and soft as the Blab's had ever been.

"Please don't think badly of Ravna," Tines said. "She had a real thing going with the almost-you of before. . . . They loved each other very much."

"I guessed."

The two heads turned back to the sky. These next two years he must watch this creature, try to decide. . . . But suspicions aside, the more he saw of Tines, the more he liked him. Hamid could almost imagine that he had not lost the Blab, but gained five of her siblings. And the big-mouth had finally become a real person.

The companionable silence stretched on. After a moment, the one that had been the Blab edged across the table and bumped her head against his shoulder. Hamid hesitated, then stroked her neck. They watched the sun and the fleck of blue a moment more. "You know," said Tines, but in the femvoice that was the Blab's favorite, "I will miss that place. And most of all . . . I will miss the cats and the dogs."

Though it was written first, "The Blabber" is a sequel to both *A Fire Upon the Deep* and *A Deepness in the Sky*. In this future, the centuries after the twentieth are very interesting—but discouraging and mystifying to tech optimists such as myself. Computer power increases, but somehow never produces the sentient entities we expect. In the twenty-first century, the AI gurus of the twentieth are seen as old fogies whose wild predictions never came true. Time passes. Humankind spreads through the solar system and then to the nearby stars. Some of our descendants *never* learn the truth. Others, whose slow boats and relativistic rockets take them galactic outward, eventually reach the Beyond. (Still others, on missions toward the galactic center, end in mindless destruction . . . or maybe not: the most tragic situation of all might be a colony at the *edge* of the Unthinking Depths, where even the brightest humans are retarded.)

The Beyond is an interesting place, almost like the wild interstellar playgrounds of 1930s science fiction, except that there are the Transhuman Reaches just a little further out, beckoning empires to remove themselves from human ken. Traders into those Reaches would be very strange beings . . . when they come back at all.

In particular, what about Hamid and the Blab? How did the tines race get zapped, and what about the Great Man who Hamid isn't? When I think of *other* writers' fictional universes, I imagine that they must be fully formed, and that stories simply explore an already existing place in the writer's mind. That's not the case with my writing. I do have ideas—but too many and not consistent. *A Fire Upon the Deep* was molded by "The Blabber"—but now *A Fire Upon the Deep* constrains my work to expand "The Blabber" into a full-length novel!

WIN A NOBEL PRIZE!

In 1999 and 2000 there was a remarkable market for short-short science fiction stories: *Nature*, a weekly magazine which—depending on who is talking—is the first or second most prestigious research science journal in the world. Biological sciences editor Henry Gee persuaded science fiction authors from all over the world to write 900-word stories looking forward into the next millennium. For more than a year, *Nature* printed a new story almost every week. I think every-one—writers, readers, and editors—had great fun with the stories. I know I had fun with my contribution.

   (Note: *Nature* has full color interiors. I took advantage of this, using blue ink to imply that certain words and phrases were clickable links. It was a trick that will look very old very soon, but for me it was a novel way to imply backstory! In this present "black and white" edition, I have used the tags <L> and </L> to mark the beginning and ending, respectively, of things that are supposed to be web links.)

WIN A NOBEL PRIZE!

WEALTH, CHICKS, THE SECRETS OF THE UNIVERSE— THEY CAN ALL BE YOURS

Dear Johann—
   I was sorry to learn that you have been passed over for tenure. I hope you won't give the bums on your committee another chance to abuse you.

This was going to be an ordinary letter. Then I realized that you prob-ably don't remember <L>me</L>. We took the same section of Fong's Comparative Genomics class at Berkeley, but I quit the program and drifted into the arts (see my <L>SensationXXX</L> performances). Now I work in human resources. It's a perfect fit for my technical and people skills. Johann, what I have to offer you is so extreme that I'm afraid your filters would trash my mail before you ever see it. That's why you are reading this as an advertisement in your personal copy of *Nature*: hopefully, this will show that we're serious.

In fact, writing this ad has been a lark. Yes, it's over the top . . . but it's also the absolute truth. Working with us, you can win a Nobel Prize, and that is just the beginning. So in just a few words, I have to convince you to take the next step:

I know you read outside your field, Johann. That's one reason why unimaginative drudges get tenure and you don't. Have you been following the news about MRI-with-transfection? The enabling mechanism is an HIV transfection of the subject's glial cells. The inserted genetic material expresses proteins which can be signaled by a 10-Gauss modulation of the MRI's gradient magnets. Synched with the RF pulses, they promote the production of selected neurotransmitters. If it's done right, the experimenter can trigger from an alphabet of about twenty neurotransmitters—at a spatial resolution only twice as coarse as the MRI's imaging resolution.

The neuroscience guys have fallen in love with this. And right behind them are the psych people: with whole-brain MRI/t scans, researchers could induce almost any psychopathology. In public, that possibility is just ominous speculation. In secret, at least three research labs already have whole-brain MRI/t. We have such systems ourselves, and though we haven't abused them, they are more scary than the editorials. One of the most horrifying mind-sets is something we call 'specialist fugue state.' When applied to a researcher, it creates an idiot savant, without a life beyond short-range research goals.

This is not what I'm selling you, Johann! But beware. Several labs are recruiting specialists for just this nightmare. Maybe they're getting fully-informed volunteers; more likely they are getting duped victims. Either way, the public will soon be seeing all sorts of research productivity that is secretly based on this modern form of slavery. Don't you get trapped by such a scam.

No, if you work for us, you'll be running the biotech show. Johann, you are brilliant and well-trained and . . . well, we've studied you pretty carefully. You can name your price. We have major financing from a small but wealthy nation state. If you buy in, you'll have resources that rival the CDC: a 10-Petaflops computer with a storage area network that mirrors the largest dynamic proteomics sites. All this—and the support staffs—will be fully dedicated to your personal use.

So what's our secret? Well, we've improved the MRI/t trigger mechanism to respond on millisecond time scales. We can induce direct brain I/O with the look and feel of memory and thought. For fifty years, people have been predicting mind/machine symbiosis. Now we've actually done it, Johann! You'll want to talk to Wardner. He's our first success, a perfect fit for the technique, though his specialty is strategic planning. With our MRI/t technique, Wardner is like a god.

You know how your field is these days: more breakthroughs than ever before—but it's dull, dull. A modern cell mechanics lab is like an old-time genomics site—a quietly-humming data factory. The same thing has happened in the non-bio sciences. Some theoreticians think this is heaven, but take a look at the <L>2013-01-17 editorial</L> in *Nature*: for every breakthrough, there are a thousand more hiding in the new databanks.

You can change that, Johann. Your mind will interact directly with our world-class automation. You'll solve protein dynamics problems as easily as ordinary people plan a day at the beach.

Your working conditions? They can be almost anything you want—except that you'll have to relocate. We've already built a large <L>villa</L> for you at <L>our Riviera research site</L>. You'll have complete freedom of movement. The transfection is not reversible, but it's easy to 'safe' the neuroactives when you are not actually connected. And of course, being 'connected' doesn't involve any messy electrodes. You simply enter the study that we've built in your villa. It's quite spacious, considering it's inside a four-tesla MRI system. (And we must be very careful about magnetic materials; Wardner can tell you the usual bozo stories about high-velocity jewelry.)

Well, that's my pitch, Johann. Obviously, our company must be very secretive at this stage. But please, come out and visit us. No obligation, except to sign a nondisclosure agreement. We ask that you don't tip off your colleagues about this short visit, but we want you to be absolutely comfortable about it. You have family, a cousin I believe? Feel free to let her know where you are going.

I hope you can come, Johann.

Your friend,

<signed>Helen

Helen Peerless,
Director for Human Resources, <L>Mephisto Dynamics</L>

THE BARBARIAN PRINCESS

I believe there are writers who have never been comfortable with short fiction, even when they were beginners. I had the opposite problem. For the first five or ten years of my career, it was almost impossible for me to write novel-length stories. I think I benefited from this disability. Short fiction is a wonderful medium for speculative fiction. Even though science fiction short stories normally make less money per word than novels, the SF magazines are an ideal place for the new writer: many magazines are wide open to unsolicited submissions. At the same time, most new writers collect a number of rejections before they can sell consistently. So each short story is a kind of "small experiment." A writer can get lots of feedback quickly.

Eventually, a short fiction writer can grow into writing book-length stories. In my case, this happened in especially easy steps. In 1968, Damon Knight published my novella, "Grimm's Story," in his *Orbit* series. Around that time, Damon was also editing science fiction novels for Berkley books. He told me that if I felt like writing an extension of "Grimm's Story," he could get me a book contract for the combination piece! (The preceding exclamation mark reflects my feelings about this offer. Here I had never sold a novel and now I was being solicited to write one. I thought that I had finally arrived.) I wrote the extension, and in 1969 Berkley books published the expanded story as *Grimm's World.*

Years passed. I learned that my first book sale had been unusually good luck; selling my second novel was *hard.* But by the mid 1980s, I'd had success with several novels. Jim Baen offered to reprint *Grimm's World* but with some new material. The result was *Tatja Grimm's World* (Baen Books, 1987), consisting of a new piece, "The Barbarian Princess," and a revised version of *Grimm's World.*

Returning to one of my earliest story settings was a lot of fun. I was surprised that I had new things to say—and now I had the ability to say those things well. I think "The Barbarian Princess" stands well by itself. It appeared separately in *Analog* in 1986, and made it onto the Hugo ballot.

Fair Haven at South Cape was a squalid little town. Ramshackle warehouses lined the harbor, their wooden sides unpainted and rotting. Inland, the principal cultural attractions were a couple of brothels and the barracks of the Crown garrison. Yet in one sense Fair Haven lived up to its name. No matter how scruffy things were here, you knew they would be worse further east. This was the nether end of civilization on the south coast of The Continent. Beyond South Cape lay four thousand miles of wild coast, the haunt of littoral pirates and barbarian tribes.

Rey Guille would soon sail east, but the prospect did not bother him. In fact, he rather looked forward to it. For obvious reasons, there weren't many customers along the south coast run. The Tarulle Barge would put in at two of the larger barbarian settlements, villages with a taste for some of Tarulle's kinkier publications. There was also an author living in the coastal wilderness. His production was weird and erratic—but worth an extra stop. Except for these three landfalls, the Barge would sail straight around the south coast, free of external problems. It would be thirty days before they reached the Osterlais.

Thirty days, sixty wake periods. Enough time for the translators to prepare the Osterlai and Tsanart editions, enough time for Brailly Tounse to recondition the Tarulle printers. Rey surveyed his tiny office. Thirty days. That might even be enough for him to dispose of his current backlog: manuscripts were stacked from floor to ceiling behind him. The piles on his desk blocked his view of Fair Haven harbor—and more important, the breeze that seeped in from over the water. These were all the submissions taken aboard during their passage through the Chainpearls and Crownesse. There would be some first class stories here, but most would end up as extra slush in Brailly's paper-making vats. (Thus, as Rey had once pointed out in an editorial, every submission to *Fantasie* eventually became part of the magazine.)

Rey jammed the tiny windows open, and arranged his chair so he could sit in the breeze. He was about halfway through the desk stack: the easy ones he could decide in a matter of seconds. Even for these, he made a brief note in the submission log. Two years from now the Tarulle Publishing Company would be back in the Chainpearls. He couldn't return the manuscripts, but at least he could say something appropriate to the submitters. Other stories were harder to judge: competent but flawed, or inappropriate outside the author's home islands. Over the last few days, a small pile of high priority items had accumulated beneath his desk. He would end up buying most of those. *Some* were treasures. Ivam Alecque's planet yarns were based on the latest research in spectrometry; Rey planned a companion editorial about the marvelous new science.

Alas, he must also buy stories that did not thrill him. *Fantasie* magazine lived up to its name: most of his purchases were stories of magic and mysticism. Even these were fun when the authors could be persuaded to play by internally consistent rules.

Rey grabbed the next manuscript, and scowled. Then there were the truly revolting things he must buy, things like this: another Hrala adventure. The series had started twenty years earlier, five years before he signed on with Tarulle. The first few stories weren't bad, if you liked nonstop illogical action with lots of blood and sex; old Chem Trinos wasn't a bad writer. As was Tarulle custom, Trinos had exclusive control of his series for eight years. Then Tarulle accepted Hrala stories from anyone. The fad kept growing. Otherwise decent writers began wasting their time writing new Hrala stories. Nowadays the series was popular all around the world, and practically a cult in the Llerenitos.

Hrala the Barbarian Princess: over six feet tall, fantastically built, unbelievably strong and crafty and vengeful and libidinous. Her adventures took place in the vast inland of The Continent, where empires and wars had no need to conform to the humdrum world that readers knew. She was the idol of thousands of foolish male readers and a model for thousands of female ones.

Rey paged slowly through this latest contribution to the legend. Hmph . . . for its kind, the story was well written. He'd have his assistant editor look it over, make it consistent with the background files she kept on the series. He would probably have to buy it. He tossed the manuscript under his desk and made a note in the submission log.

AN HOUR LATER, REY WAS STILL AT IT, THE IN-PILE FRACTIONALLY SMALLER. From the decks below his windows there was the continuing noise of supplies being loaded, crewmen shouting at stevedores. Occasionally he heard people working on the rigging above him. He had long since learned to tune out such. But now there was a different clatter: someone was coming along the catwalk to his office. A moment later, Coronadas Ascuasenya stuck her head in the doorway. "Boss, such a deal I got for you!"

Oh, oh. When Cor's accent thickened and her words came fast, it was a sure sign she had been swept away by some new enthusiasm. He waved her into the office. "What's that?"

"Tarulle magazines, they don't sell themselves. Other things we need to grab buyer interest."

Rey nodded. Jespen Tarulle had a small circus housed on the after decks. They put on shows at the larger ports, hyped all the Tarulle publications. Cor was fascinated by the operation; she was constantly trying to add acts representing stories and authors from *Fantasie*. She was good at it, too, a natural born publicist. Rey figured it was only a matter of time before higher-ups noticed, and he lost his assistant editor. "What have you got?"

"Who," she corrected him. She stepped back and waved at someone beyond the doorway. "I present you *Hrala*, Princess of the Interior!" She pronounced the name correctly, with a throat-tearing rasp that was painful even to hear.

The portentous intro brought no immediate action. After a moment, Cor stepped to the door and spoke coaxingly. There were at least two people out there, one of them a printsman from Brailly's crew. A second passed, and someone tall and lanky bent through the doorway.

Rey rocked back in his chair, his eyes widening. The visitor was re-markable—though not in the way Cor meant. It was a female: there was a slimness in the shoulders, and a slight broadening in the hips. And she was *tall*. The ceiling of Guille's office was six feet high; the girl's tangled red hair brushed against it. But scale her down to normal size and she might be taken for a street waif. Her face and hair were grimy. A bruise darkened her face around one eye. With her arrival the room was filled with the smell of rancid grease. He looked at her clothes and understood the source of part of the smell. She was dressed in rags. There were patches on patches on patches, yet holes still showed through. But these were not the rags of a street waif: these were of leather, thick and poorly cured. She carried a walking staff almost as tall as she was.

The circus people might have use for such a character, though scarcely as Hrala. He smiled at the girl, "What's your name?"

Her only reply was a shy smile that revealed even, healthy teeth. There was a nice face hiding under all the dirt.

Cor said, "She doesn't understand one word of Spräk, Boss." She looked out the door. "What did she call herself, Jimi?"

The printsman stuck his head into the office; there wasn't room for three visitors. "Good afternoon, Master Guille," he said to Rey. "Uh, it's hard to pronounce. The closest thing in a civilized name would be 'Tatja Grimm.' " The girl's head came up and her smile broadened.

"Hmm. Where did you find her?"

"Strangest thing, sir. We were on a wood detail for Master Tounse, a few miles south of here. Just about noon we came across her on the table land. She had that there walking stick stuck in the ground. It looked like she was praying to it or something—she had her face down near the end of the stick's shadow. We couldn't see quite what all she was doing; we were busy cutting trees. But some boys from the town came by, started hassling her. We chased them off before they could do anything."

"And she was eager to stay with you?"

"She was when she saw we were from the Barge. One of our crew speaks a little Hurdic, sir. Near as he can tell, she walked here from the center of The Continent."

Three thousand miles, through lands which—until very recently—had swallowed up every expedition. Rey cast a look of quiet incredulity at his assistant. Cor gave a little shrug, as if to say, *Hey, it will make great copy.*

The printsman missed this byplay. "We couldn't figure out quite *why* she made the trip, though. Something about finding people to talk to."

Rey chuckled. "Well, if Hurdic is her only language, she certainly came to the wrong place." He looked at the girl. During the conversation, her eyes had wandered all about the office. The smile had not left her face. Everything fascinated her: the carved wall panels, the waist-high stacks of manuscripts, Guille's telescope in the corner. Only when she looked at Rey or Cor or Jimi did her smile falter and the shyness return. *Damn.* Didn't Cor realize what she had here? Aloud he said. "This is something I should think about. Jimi, why don't you take this, ah, Tatja over to the public deck. Get her something to eat."

"Yes, sir. Tatja?" He motioned her to follow him. The girl's shoulders slumped for an instant, but she departed without protest.

Cor was silent till their footsteps had faded into the general deck clamor. Then she looked at Guille. "You're not going to hire her." It was more an accusation than a question.

"You'd find her more trouble than she's worth, Cor. I'd wager she's a local girl; who ever heard of an inlander with red hair? Watching her, I could see she understood some of what we were saying. Whatever Hurdic she speaks is probably in Jimi's imagination. The poor girl is simply retarded—probably caused by the same glandular problem that's sprouted her six feet tall before she's even reached puberty. My guess is she's barely trainable."

Cor sat on one stack of manuscripts, propped her feet on another. "Sure, she's no inlander, Boss. But she's not from Fair Haven. The Haveners don't wear leather like that. She's probably been expelled from some local tribe. And yes, she's dim brain, but who cares? No need for The Great Hrala to give big speeches in Språk. I can teach her to strut, wave a sword, make fake Hurdic war talk. Boss, they'll love her in the Llerenitos."

"Cor! She doesn't even *look* like Hrala. The red hair—"

"Wigs. We got lotsa nice black wigs."

"—and her figure. She just doesn't have, uh . . ." Guille made vague motions with his hands.

"No tits? Yes, that's a problem." The "true" Hrala danced through her adventures wearing next to nothing. "But we can fix. The vice magazine people have props. Take one of their rubber busts and wrap it in brassiere armor like Hrala wears—it'll fool an audience." She paused. "Boss.

I can make this work. Tatja may be dim, but she wants to please. She doesn't have any place else to go."

Guille knew this last was not part of the sales pitch; Ascuasenya had a soft streak undermining her pragmatism. He turned to look out at Fair Haven. A steady stream of supply lighters moved back and forth between the town's main pier and the deeper water surrounding the Barge. Tarulle was due to lift anchor tomorrow noon. It would be two years before they returned to this part of the world. Finally he said, "Your scheme could cause real problems the next time we visit this dump. Come the night wake period, go into town and look up the Crown's magistrate. Make sure we're not stealing some citizen's kid."

"Sure." Cor grinned broadly. Victory was at hand. Guille grumbled for a few more minutes: hiring an actress would mean going up the chain of command to Overeditor Ramsey, and perhaps beyond him to Jespen Tarulle. That could take days, and much debate. Guille allowed himself to be persuaded to hire the girl as an apprentice proofreader. The move had a certain piquancy: How many writers had accused him of employing illiterate nitwits as proofreaders?

Finally, he reminded his assistant editor that she still had a full-time job preparing the issues that would sell in the Osterlais. Cor nodded, her face very serious; the Hrala project would be on her own time. He almost thought he'd intimidated her—until she turned to leave and he heard a poorly suppressed laugh.

IT TOOK COR LESS THAN TWO DAYS TO UNDERSTAND WHAT A JAM SHE HAD talked herself into. The Barge was back at sea and there were no distractions from shorefolk, but now she found herself working thirty hours a day, setting up the Hrala rehearsals with publicity, looking after the Grimm girl, and—most of all—getting *Fantasie* into shape.

There were *so* many manuscripts to review. There were good stories in the slush pile, but more science-oriented ones than ever before. These were Rey Guille's special favorites, and sometimes he went overboard with them. *Fantasie* had been published for seven hundred years. A certain percentage of its stories had always claimed to be possible. But only in the last fifty years, with the rise of science, could the reader feel that there was a future where the stories might really happen. Rey Guille had been editor of *Fantasie* for fifteen years. During that time, they had published more stories of Contrivance Fiction than in all the previous years. He had Svektr Ramsey's permission to include two in every issue. More and more, he found readers whose only interest was in such stories. More and more, he found readers who were creating the science that future stories could be based on.

Cor knew that, in his heart, Rey saw these stories as agents of change in themselves. Take the spectrometry series: during the last five years, he had written a dozen editorials advertising the new science ("Spectrometry, Key to Nature's Secrets"), and soliciting stories based on the contrivance. Now he got one or two new ones at every major stop. Some of them were saleable. Some of them were mind-boggling. . . . And some were wretched.

Ascuasenya had been working on the Barge for five quarters, and as Rey Guille's assistant for nearly a year. She had read her first *Fantasie* story when she was five. It was hard not to be in awe of the magazine's editor, even if he was a crotchety old codger. (Guille was forty-one.) Cor did her best to disguise her feelings; their editorial conferences were running battles. This morning was no different. They were up in his office, putting together the first issue for the Osterlais. The slush pile had been reduced to desk height and they had plenty of room to lay out the pieces Rey had selected for the new issue. Outside Guille's office, the bright light of morning had slowly reddened. They were well into the eclipse season; once every twenty hours, Seraph blocked the sun or was itself eclipsed. Every wake period was punctuated by darkness as deep as night on the nether hemisphere. Guille had set algae glowpots on every available hook, yet he still found it hard to read fine print.

He squinted at the Ivam Alecque manuscript Cor was complaining about. "I don't understand you, Cor. This yarn is world-shaking. If we didn't put anything else in the next issue, 'Pride of Iron' could carry it all."

"But the writing, it is so wooden. The characters have no life. The plot makes me sleepy."

"By the Blue Light of Seraph, Cor! It's *ideas* that make this great. 'Pride of Iron' is based on spectro results that aren't even in print yet."

"Phooey. There have been stories with this theme before: Ti Liso's Hidden Empire series. He had houses made of iron, streets paved with copper."

"Anyone who owns jewelry could imagine a world like that. This is different. Alecque is a chemist; he uses metals in realistic ways—like in gun barrels and heavy machinery. But even that isn't the beauty of this story. Three hundred years ago, Ti Liso was writing fantasy; Ivam Alecque is talking about something that could really *be*." Rey covered the glowpots and threw open a window. Chillness oozed into the office, ocean breeze further cooled by the eclipse. The stars spread in their thousands across the sky, blocked only by the Barge's rigging, dimmed only by mists rising from the pulper rooms below decks. Even if they had been standing outside, and could look straight up, Seraph would have been nothing more than a dim reddish ring. For the next hour, the stars ruled. "Look at that, Cor. Thousands of stars, millions beyond those we can see. They're suns like ours, and—"

"—and we buy plenty of stories with that premise."

"Not like this one. Ivam Alecque knows astronomers at Krirsarque who are hanging spectro gear on telescopes. They've drawn line spectra for lots of stars. The ones with color and absolute magnitude similar to our sun show incredibly intense lines for iron and copper and the other metals. This is the first time in history anyone has had direct insight about how things must be on planets of other stars. Houses built of iron are actually possible there."

Ascuasenya was silent for a moment. The idea was neat; in fact, it was kind of scary. Finally she said, "We're all alone in being so 'metal poor'?"

"Yes! At least among the sun-like stars these guys have looked at."

"Hmm . . . It's almost like the gods, they play a big joke on us." Cor's great love was polytheistic fantasy, stories where the fate of mortals was the whim of supernatural beings. That sort of thing had been popular in *Fantasie*'s early centuries. She knew Rey considered it out of step with what the magazine should be doing now. Sometimes she brought it up just to bug him. "Okay. I see why you want the story. Too bad it's such an ugly little thing."

She saw that her point had struck home. A bit grumpily, Rey unmasked the lamps, then sat down and picked up "Pride of Iron." It really was plotless. And—on this leg of the voyage, anyway—he was the only one capable of pumping it up. . . . She could almost see the wheels going around in his head: But it would be worth rewriting! He could have the story published before these ideas were even in the scientific literature. He looked up, grinned belligerently at her. "Well, I'm going to buy it, Cor. Assume 'anonymous collaboration' makes it twice as long: what can we do for illustrations?"

It took about fifteen minutes to decide which crew-artists would work the job; the Osterlai issue would use slightly modified stock illos. Hopefully, they could commission some truly striking pictures as they passed through that island chain.

The rest of the Osterlai issue was easy to lay out; several of the stories were already in the Osterlai language. The issue would be mostly fantasy, the new art work from artists of Crownesse and the Chainpearls. The cover story was a rather nice Hrala adventure.

"Speaking of Hrala," said Rey, "how is your project coming? Will your girl be able to give a show when we start peddling this issue?"

"Sure she will. We get about an hour of rehearsal every wake period. Once she understands about stage performance, things will go just fine. So far, we work on sword and shield stuff. She can memorize things as fast as we can show her. She's awful impressive, screaming around the stage with *Death* in her hand." In the stories, the Hrala Sword was magical, edged with metal, and so heavy that an ordinary warrior could not lift it. The Tarulle version of *Death* was made of wood painted silver.

"What about her costume?" Or lack of one.

"Great. We still gotta do changes—ribbon armor is hard to fit—but she looks tremendous. Svektr Ramsey thinks so too."

"He *saw* her?" Guille looked stricken.

"Don't worry, Boss. The Overeditor was amused. He told me to congratulate you for hiring her."

"Oh . . . Well, let's hope we're all still amused when you put her on stage with other actors."

Cor gathered up the manuscripts they had chosen. She would take them, together with the production notes, over to the art deck. "No problem. You were right, she understands some Spräk. She can even speak it a little. I think she was just shy that first day. On stage she'll mainly scream gibberish—we won't need a new script for each archipelagate." Cor carried the papers to the door. "Besides, we get the chance to put it all together before we reach the Osterlais. We arrive at the Village of the Termite People in three days; I'll have things ready by then."

Guille chuckled. The Termite People were scarcely your typical fans. "Okay. I look forward to it."

Cor stepped into the darkness, shut the hatch behind her. In fact, she was at least half as confident as she sounded. Things ought to work out, if she could just find time to coach Tatja Grimm. The giant little girl was stranger than Cor had admitted. She wasn't really dumb, just totally deprived. She'd been born in some very primitive tribe. She'd been five years old before she ever saw a tree. *Everything* she saw now was novelty. Cor remembered how the girl's eyes had widened when Cor showed her a copy of *Fantasie,* and explained how spoken words could be saved with paper and ink. She had held the magazine upside down, paged back and forth through it, fascinated by both pictures and text.

Worst of all, Tatja Grimm had no concept of polemic; she must have been an outsider even in her own tribe. She simply did not accept that dramatic skits could persuade. If Grimm could be convinced of that single point, Cor was sure the Hrala campaign would be a spectacular success. If not, they might all end up with bat dreck on their faces.

THE DAY THEY WERE TO LAND AT THE VILLAGE OF THE TERMITE PEOPLE, REY took the morning off. He walked around the top editorial deck, looking for a place sheltered from the wind and passersby. This would be his first chance to play with his telescope since Fair Haven.

The marvelous weather still held. The sky was washed clean; widely spaced cumulus spread away forever. A Tarulle hydrofoil loitered about a mile ahead of the Barge, its planes raised and sails mostly reefed. Guille knew there were others out there; most of the Barge's 'foil bays were empty. The fastboats had many uses. In civilized seas, they ranged before and behind the Barge—making landfall arrangements, carrying job orders, picking up finished illustrations and manuscripts. In the wilderness east of Fair Haven, they had a different role: security. No pirates were going to sneak up on the Barge. The catapults and petroleum bombs would be ready long before any hostile vessel broke the horizon.

So far, all the traffic was friendly. Several times a day they met ships and barges coming from the east. Most were merchantmen. Only a few publishing companies had Tarulle's worldwide scope. The hydrofoils reported that the *Science* was docked at the Village of the Termite People. That ship was much smaller than the Tarulle Barge, but it published its own journal. It was sponsored by universities in the Tsanarts as a sort of mobile research station. Rey looked forward to spending a few hours on the other vessel. It would mean some sales, and would give him a chance to make contacts; these were people who appreciated the new things he was doing with *Fantasie*. Notwithstanding Cor's Hrala project, seeing the *Science* would be high point of this landfall.

Guille rolled the telescope cart into an open area at the rear of the editorial deck. Here the breeze was blocked by Old Jespen's penthouse, yet there was still a reasonable view. He clamped the cart's wheels and leveled its platform. Back in the Chainpearls—just after he bought the scope—this operation would have attracted a small crowd and begun an impromptu star- or Seraph-party. Now, passersby said hello, but few stopped for long. Rey had his toy all to himself.

He flipped the tube down and took a scan across the northern horizon. They were about fifteen miles off the coast. To the naked eye, The Continent was a dark line at the bottom of the sky. The telescope brought detail: Guille could see individual rocks on the dun cliffs. Trees growing in the lee of the hills were clearly visible. Here and there were rounded lumps he recognized as wild termite towers. The Village was hidden beyond a small cape.

Not a very impressive coast for the greatest landmass in the world. Beyond those cliffs, the land stretched more than ten thousand miles— over the north pole and part way down the other side of the planet. There was a hundred times more land there than in all the island chains put together. It was an ocean of land, and beyond its coastal fringe, mostly unknown. No wonder it had been the source of so many stories. Rey sighed. He didn't begrudge those stories. In past centuries, speculation about the Interior was a decent story base. The island civilizations weren't more than a couple of thousand years old—the human race must have originated on The Continent. It was reasonable that older, wiser civilizations lay in the Interior. Whole races of monsters and god-lings might flourish in those reaches.

But during the last thirty years, there had been serious exploration. Betrog Hedrigs had reached Continent's center. In the last ten years, three separate expeditions had trekked across the Interior. The un-known remained, but it was cut into small chunks. The myths were dead and the new reality was a dismal thing: an "ocean" of land is necessarily a very dry place. Beyond the coastal fringe the explorers found desert. In that, there was variety. There were deserts of sand and heat, deserts of rock, and—in the north—deserts of ice and cold. There was no hidden paradise. The nearest things to the "Great Lakes" of leg-end were saline ponds near Continent's Center. The explorers found that the Interior *was* inhabited, but not by an Elder Race. There were isolated tribes in the mid-latitude deserts. These folk lived naked, almost like animals. Their only tools were spears and hand axes. They seemed peaceful, too poor even for warfare. The lowest barbarians of the Fringe were high civilization compared to them. And all these years, the story writers had assumed that the Hurdic tribes were degenerate relatives of Interior races!

Yet Interior fantasies were still written. Guille saw hundreds of them a year—and worse, had to buy dozens. Ah well. It was a living, and it gave him a chance to show people more important things. Rey stepped back from the telescope, and turned its tube almost straight up. It was Seraph he really wanted to look at.

"Hel-lo?"

Rey looked up, startled. He had an audience. It was the Fair Haven waif. She stood almost behind him and about ten feet away. He had the feeling she'd been watching for several minutes. "Hello indeed. And how are you today, Mistress Grimm?"

"Well." She smiled shyly and took a step forward. She certainly looked better than when he first saw her. Her face was scrubbed clean. In place of rancid leather, she wore tripulation fatigues. If she had been five feet tall instead of six, she would have seemed a pretty pre-teener.

"Shouldn't you be rehearsing with Cor?"

"I, uh, that is la-ter."

"I see. You're off duty."

She bobbed her head, seeming to understand the term. Somehow, Rey had imagined that Cor or the publicity people would be looking after Tatja all the time. In fact, no matter how incompetent she was, there simply were not enough people to baby-sit her. The girl must have many hours to herself; no doubt she wandered all over the Barge. By the Light, the trouble she could get into!

They stared at each other for a moment. The girl seemed so attentive, almost in awe of him. He realized she wouldn't leave unless he explicitly told her to get lost. He tried to think of an appropriate dismissal, but nothing came. Damn. Finally he said, "Well, how do you like my new telescope?"

"Good. Good." The girl stepped almost close enough to touch the scope, and Rey went through the usual explanations: He showed her how the wheels could be fastened to the deck. The oil bath in the cart's base damped the sea motion and kept the optics steady. The cart itself was an old drafting rig from the art deck. Rey had removed the drawing table and substituted clamps that attached to the base of his twelve-inch scope.

Tatja Grimm didn't say much, but her enthusiasm was obvious. She leaned close to the equipment to see the details Rey pointed out. When he explained something, she would pause for an instant and then bob her head and say, "Yes. So nice."

Guille wondered if he could have been wrong about her. In some ways, she seemed a more thoughtful and enthusiastic audience than crew people he had shown the gear to. But then he noticed the uniformity of her responses. Everything seemed to impress her equally. Every explanation took the same brief moment for her to absorb. Guille had a retarded cousin, mental age around five years, physical age thirty after so much living, a retarded person learns to mimic the head movements and nonsense sounds that normal people make in conversation. Rey could imagine the blank look he would get if he asked Tatja something related to his explanations.

He didn't try such an experiment. What point was there in hurting the girl's feelings? Besides, she seemed to enjoy the conversation as much as a normal person. He aimed the scope at Seraph as he continued his spiel. The planet was in quarter phase, and the mountains of its southern continent stood in stark relief near the terminator. Wind and ship vibration jostled the image a bit. On the other hand, the line of sight was straight up, without lots of dirty air to smudge things. This was the clearest day-view he'd ever had. ". . . so my telescope makes objects seem much closer. Would you like to look?" Even a retard should be thrilled by the sight.

"Yes." She stepped forward, and he showed her how to use the eyepiece. She bent to it . . . and gave a squeal, a wonderful mixture of pleasure and surprise. Her head jerked back from the eyepiece. She stared upwards at the twin planet, as if to assure herself that it hadn't moved.

Just as quickly she took another look through the lense, and then backed off again. "So big. So *big*!" Her smile all but split her face. "How can te-le-scope—" she reached up, as if to jerk the tube's end down to eye level.

Guille caught her hands. "Oops. Be gentle. Turn it around this pivot." She wasn't listening, but she let him rotate the tube so she could look in. Her eyes went wide as she saw the expanded image of her face in the main mirror. Rey found himself explaining about "curved mirrors" and how the diagonal directed the image from the twelve-inch through the eyepiece. The girl hesitated the same fraction of a second she had after his other explanations. Then, just as before, her head bobbed with an enthusiastic imitation of total understanding. "Yes. Yes. So nice."

Abruptly, she grabbed Rey's hand. "And you think this thing? You make it?"

Tatja's grip was almost painful; her hands were slender but as outsized as the rest of her. "You mean, did I invent the telescope?" He chuckled. "No, Miss Grimm. The basic idea is two hundred years old. People don't invent telescopes just to pass the time on a dull morning. Things like this are the work of scattered geniuses. Part of an invention may exist for decades, useless, before another genius makes the idea successful."

The girl's expression collapsed. It might have been laughable if it weren't so pathetic. She had no concept of what was difficult and what was trivial, and so her attempt at bright conversation had foundered. Rey turned her gently back to the telescope and showed her how to adjust the focus. Her former enthusiasm did not completely return, but she seemed sincerely taken by the close-up view of Seraph. Rey gave her his usual spiel, pointing out the brown smudges across part of the southern continent. "Brush fires, we think. That land must be a lot like the grassy plains north of Bayfast. The religions have all sorts of visions of Seraph, but we now know it's a world much like ours." And the stories of hidden civilizations *there* might still be true. Rey had written more than one editorial about plans for detecting and communicating with Seraph's hypothetical inhabitants. One of the first steps would be to build an observatory in this part of the world, where Seraph could be observed with a minimum of atmospheric distortion.

A couple of people from Printing had stopped nearby, were watching intently. They were not the sort Rey would think attracted by skygazing; one was Brailly Tounse's bombwright. Rey glanced at her questioningly.

"Sir, we've got a line of sight into the harbor now," the bombwright waved to the north. "We were wondering if you'd take a quick look at Termite Town through your scope."

Rey hid a sigh, and gave up any hope of having the device to himself this morning. The bombwright must have noticed his irritation. She hurried on to say, "Something strange is happening with the Termite People, sir. So far the officer types ain't talking, but—take a look, will you?"

Guille eased Tatja Grimm away from the scope and tilted it toward the horizon. He made a quick adjustment with the spotter scope and then looked through the main eyepiece. "Looks about like I remember it." There were dozens of towers, from water's edge back up the hills around the harbor. The smallest ones were bigger than a house. The largest were over a hundred feet tall. The spaces between were like streets at the bottom of shadowed canyons. Even knowing the truth, one's first reaction was awe: this must be a city, the greatest one in the world. Krirsarque and Bayfast were insignificant, low-storey affairs compared to this. In fact, there were only a few thousand humans in this whole "city." They dug their burrows and staircases through the termite mounds; they poked air holes through the walls, holes that also served as windows. "Hmm. There's something different. One of the towers by the moorage . . . it looks like it was burned, or stained with soot. The dark goes as high as the windows overhanging the water."

"Yes, sir. That's what got our attention, but we couldn't see what made the stain. And there's something strange in the water, too."

Rey tilted the scope a fraction. A twisted pile of spikes and filaments stuck through the water, directly in front of the scorch-marked tower. Rey sucked in a breath. "It looks like ship's rigging, the fiberglass part."

The bombwright stepped close, and he let her take a look. She was silent for a moment, then, "Unh huh. That's where they like visitors to dock. Looks like the gooks dumped pet' bombs out those windows, right onto the moorage. The guys they ambushed didn't have a chance."

A minute before, Rey had been feeling sorry for one retarded girl. Now . . . He looked across the water. Without a telescope, the Village was a barely distinguishable skyline, the scorch unnoticeable.

The guys they ambushed . . . According to the advance reports, there had been exactly one ship tied up at the Village: the *Science*.

CREW AND PUBLISHING FOLK SPENT THE NEXT FEW HOURS SPECULATING: WHY was the *Science* ambushed? What would Tarulle do about it? The Barge stayed several miles offshore, but rumor held that fastboats were doing close recon under cover of the midday eclipse. The only word from the executive deck was that there would be no immediate landing.

Top management was not asleep—just terribly indecisive. Rey Guille bluffed his way onto the bridge shortly before eclipsend. All the Biggies were there, both from Ownership and Operations. The atmosphere was that of an incipient brawl: consensus time had not arrived.

"—and I say, sail into catapult range and burn their filthy village to the ground! Barbarians must learn that ambushing merchants is a dangerous sport." The speaker was one of Tarulle's nephews, an arrogant pip-squeak who'd be scrubbing decks if it weren't for his relatives. The little man looked angrily around the room, daring anyone to disagree. Fortunately for the Company, there were some strong personalities present:

Barge Captain Maccioso stood near the helm, facing the rest. His form was a vague, intimidating shadow in the eclipse light. Maccioso was a huge man; the bridge itself had been rebuilt to accommodate his six feet eight inch height. He was in his early fifties and only just beginning to go to fat. The first twenty years of his career had been spent in the Chainpearls Navy. The man had retired an admiral, and the greatest hero of the Loretto Bight affair. Now he crossed his ham-like arms and seemed to lean toward Tarulle's nephew. "War-like talk coming from . . ." *a wee wimp who couldn't cock a bow*, the pause seemed to say, "from those who need customers to live. It's true, I could torch the Village. It would be expensive; we wouldn't be left with much reserve. And what would we get for it? The Termite Folk are isolated, Master Craeto. There would be few to learn from the lesson. The Tarulle Company would lose one—admittedly minor—customer. The Barge has visited here four times since I've been captain. We've had less trouble than in some civilized ports. These people are not pirates. The *Science* crew did something, broke some taboo. . . ."

Maccioso turned to looked into the harbor; sunbreak was almost upon them. The land was bright with washed-out pastels. When he continued, his voice held more frustration than certainty. "Sure. We have the power to raze the place. But we could never bring off an assault landing. There's no way we can rescue the survivors and find out how to avoid such a debacle in the future."

Survivors? Someone had lived through the pet' bombing. Rey felt a surge of joy. No one else seemed moved by the news; they already knew. This must be a major point of the debate. "We can't just leave them there!" The words popped out of Guille's mouth without conscious thought.

Dead silence greeted his words. The people closest to him moved slightly away, but didn't look at him; it was as though he had made a bad smell. Maccioso turned and his gaze swept the bridge. "Master Tounse!"

"*Sir!*"

The Barge Captain pointed at Rey Guille. "Take this man out and . . ." Rey's guts went cold; there were stories about Ked Maccioso's command of the Chainpearl Armada. ". . . *brief* him."

"Yessir!"

Brailly Tounse emerged from the crowd and hustled Rey onto the open walkway beyond the bridge. The Printmaster shut the hatch and turned to face him. " 'Brief you'? The commercial life is turning Ked soft." It took a moment for Rey to realize that the other man was suppressing laughter. "Don't you understand that a rescue is what Ked is dying to do? For almost an hour, he's been trying to trick these flightless bats into backing one."

"Oh." Rey was both embarrassed and encouraged. "Maybe my, uh, little outburst will start something."

"I hope so." Brailly stopped smiling. "But even by Ked's standards, it would be risky operation pulling those *Science* people out."

He led Rey to the forward end of the walkway. All around them, twilight brightened suddenly into day as the sun came past the edge of Seraph. Swarms of daybats rose from the harbor. They swept around the towers, their cries coming clear and reedy across the water.

Brailly gestured at the bridge binoculars. "Take a look to the left of the harbor towers. That's where they're holding the survivors." It was some kind of pit, probably the root of a fallen tower. Rey saw Termite Folk camped around the edge. Tounse continued, "They're in that hole, out of sight from this angle. See how the locals have set petroleum vats along the edge? They could light and dump those in a matter of minutes . . ."

. . . incinerating the prisoners. The Tarulle people would have to sneak in a large party and overpower the guards at those vats all at once. One slip and a lot of Company people would share the fate of those in the pit. "We could offer a ransom, Brailly. It might be expensive, but the *Science* home universities would probably pay us back. . . . And there'd be lots of good publicity." The spinoffs from such an adventure could fill several issues of the Tarulle magazines.

"You don't understand: the *Science* people aren't hostages. The only reason they're still alive is that an appropriate method of execution hasn't been decided on. The local bosses tell us that no ransom will save the prisoners. They won't even tell us what 'blasphemy' the poor suckers committed. The whole matter is closed. And you know, I think the gooks actually expect to continue business as usual with the rest of us!"

"Hmm." Rey had dealt with the Village's rulers. Their interest in certain types of pulp fiction had always made them seem relatively civilized. They had not seemed religious—and now he saw that was just a sign of how damned secretive their religion must be. He stared through the binocs a moment more. Beyond the edge of that pit were some good people. "We've got to do something, Brailly."

"I know. Ked knows." The Printmaster shrugged. After a moment, the two men walked back to the command bridge. Inside, Rey saw that the tension had drained from the meeting; consensus had finally been reached. Brailly smiled sourly and whispered, "But we also know how it's going to turn out, don't we?"

Rey looked around, and with a sinking feeling he understood. The Tarulle Publishing Company had existed for seven hundred years. Few island-bound companies were that old—and yet Tarulle had been sailing the oceans of Tu all that time, contending with tempests and pirates and religionists and governments. There had been disasters; three hundred years earlier, the old Barge was burned to the waterline. Yet the Company had survived, and prospered. One doesn't last seven hundred years by rushing into everyone else's fight. The Barge and its hydrofoils were well-armed, but given a choice they simply avoided trouble. If a village or even an island chain turned to religious nuttery, they lost Tarulle's business. The years would pass, and the regime would fall—or decide that it needed trade more than its crazy convictions.

Kederichi Maccioso had done his subtle best to bring another outcome, but it was not to be: the talk now was of delivering a few threats and, if that did not help the *Science* people, weighing anchor and sailing off.

There must be some way to stop this! Then he had it: Brailly said the Termite Folk wanted business as usual. For the second time in fifteen minutes, Rey interrupted the meeting. "We can't simply take off; we have magazines to sell here, and customers who want to buy."

This outburst was greeted with the same silence as before. Only this time, it was not Ked Maccioso who responded. There was a croaking sound from somewhere behind the Tarulle in-laws. The owners looked nervously at each other, then stood aside. Out of the shadows came a very old man in a wheel chair: Jespen Tarulle himself. He rolled far enough past his relatives to get a look at Rey Guille. It was only the third time Rey had seen the man. He was wrapped in blankets, his hands clasped and shivering in his lap. Only one eye tracked and it was starred with a cataract. His voice was quavery, the delivery almost addled. "Yes. These folk haven't done us harm, and our business is to *do business*." He looked in Rey's direction. "I'm glad someone still understands this."

Maccioso didn't sound quite so enthusiastic. "It's risky, sir, not your average sales landing . . . but I could go along with it, if we can get the volunteers." Volunteers who might wangle the prisoners' freedom, or at least discover their exact situation; Rey imagined the wheels turning in the Barge Captain's head.

"Sirs. I volunteer for the landing." It was Brailly Tounse, barely hiding a smile.

"I-I volunteer." The words were coming from Rey's own mouth. He mumbled the rest, almost as a rationalization to himself: "I've handled sales landings here before."

Old Man Tarulle tilted his head at the other owners. "Are we agreed?" It was not quite a rhetorical question; the explicit recommendation of Jespen Tarulle counted for a lot, but he was not a majority stockholder. After a moment, there came mumbled acquiescence. Tarulle looked across the deck. "Operations? Are there any objections from them?"

"I have a question." It was Svektr Ramsey. He looked at Guille. "Have you finished your work on the first Osterlai issue of *Fantasie*?"

"My assistant can handle what remains, Master Ramsey." He had just finished the rewrite of "Pride of Iron."

"Ah." A smile split the gaunt Overeditor's face. "In that case, I have no objections." And if things didn't work out, there would plenty of time to put a black border around the editorial page.

THEY DIDN'T GO ASHORE UNTIL TEN HOURS LATER, IN THE NIGHT WAKE PERIOD. It had been a busy time. The landing was to look like the previous ones here. There would only be one boat, less than a dozen people. Except for Rey—who was probably known to the locals—those twelve were not the usual sorts for a commercial landing. Maccioso picked people with military and naval backgrounds. The Barge Captain had imagined many contingencies. Some involved simple gathering of information, perhaps an attempt at diplomacy; others would mean quick violence and a frantic effort to get back to sea ahead of the Termite People. From the beginning, it was agreed that no obvious weapons would be taken. Brailly Tounse produced explosive powder that could be carried in their jackets; that should pass any inspection the Termiters might make.

Though it was probably a futile contribution, Rey Guille took his telescope. It had impressed Tatja Grimm; it might have some effect on the locals. (On the other hand, such high technology might be what got the *Science* in trouble. Rey broke the scope into its components and stored them in different parts of the landing boat.)

Coronadas Ascuasenya had been furious. She wanted to take her Barbarian Princess act ashore and pretend that Tatja Grimm was *truly* Hrala. Maccioso rejected the plan—and Rey agreed with him. Ascuasenya claimed the girl had absorbed the role these last couple of days, that she was the most convincing Hrala ever produced. It really didn't matter. Rey doubted that the local rulers believed the Hrala stories. In any case, using the act to intimidate could cause the prompt massacre of both prisoners and would-be rescuers.

So Cor stayed behind, and Guille found himself on the landing boat surrounded by some very competent fighters. Except for Brailly, he knew none of them.

They were only a hundred yards from the shore. Seraph was at first quarter, and its blue light lay serene across everything. The loudest sounds were the splash of oars into water, and the occasional grunt of a rower. Beach bats and flying fish swooped low around the lighter. The smell of char and oil was stronger than the salt tang of the water. They were passing a ragged jungle of black glass—what was left of the *Science*. The bats swarmed through the twisted rigging: one creature's catastrophe is another's new home.

The termite mounds were awesome at this distance. Hundreds of airholes lined their sides. A few of the towers actually broadened with height so that they hung over the water. It was like some artist's vision of a city of the future. Even knowing what the towers really were, it was hard not to feel intimidated.

Early seafarers thought the Termite Folk were nonhuman. Alas and fortunately, this was not the work of gods. The locals were normal humans, using mounds that occurred all through this region. They brought in extra materials for the termites, then guided and pruned the structures. Basically the Termite People were Hurdic folk taking advantage of local circumstance. And strangely, they had no special pride in the towers. They seemed much prouder of the heritage they imagined having lost when they left the Interior.

Brailly Tounse kicked at the crate that was their cargo. "Still don't see why the gooks are interested in *Fantasie*."

Rey shrugged. "We don't sell them the whole thing, just stories of the Interior. My guess is, they see themselves as a great people fallen on hard times. Stories about Inner Kingdoms stoke that vision. We don't sell more than a few dozen copies per visit, but they pay several coppers for each."

Tounse whistled softly. "Gods, if only our other customers were that eager." He turned to look at the towers. On the other hand, the Barge's usual customers bought in much larger quantities . . . and didn't incinerate visitors.

The landing boat slid up to a crude pier. Some thirty guards stood along its length, their spears held in salute. The local bosses were in a group just above the landing point. As the Tarulle people climbed from the boat, low-ranking priests came down to help carry Rey's crate. So far everything seemed normal.

The tallest of the locals advanced on Rey, and gabbled something in a singsong cadence. This was the priest they usually dealt with; the guy had an excellent reading knowledge of Spräk but little chance to speak it. His vocabulary was straight out of an old-time adventure novel. After a second Rey got the avalanche of mispronounced words sorted out: "Master Guille, happy we are to see you again." The priest bowed in the direction of the magazines. "And happy we are to learn more Ancestor Truth. You and your crew are welcome in the Hall. We will examine the new truth and decide on fair payment."

Rey mumbled something appropriately pompous, and they walked toward the Village, Guille and the Termiter priests in the lead. Behind him, the landing party hung together, their tenseness obvious. This was the third time Rey had been here. He marveled that he had not been afraid before. In fact, the place had been a comic relief. *Then* when the locals spoke of "Ancestor Truth" it seemed a light turn of phrase. *Now* he had the wild impulse to run: What if there was some blasphemy in the stories? It put him in a cold sweat to think how casually he published new twists on traditional themes, or allowed small inconsistencies into story cycles. And just few days ago, he'd looked forward to testing the Hrala skit with these people!

The tall priest's tone remained friendly: "You have come at an appropriate moment, Master Guille. We have confronted blasphemers—who may be harbingers of the Final Battle. Now is a time when we must consult all sources of Truth." Another priest, an older fellow with a limp, interrupted with something abrupt. The tall guy paused, and looked faintly embarrassed; suddenly Guille knew that he was more than an interpreter, but not one of the high priests. "It will be necessary to inspect both your boat and your persons. More blasphemers may come in fair forms. . . . Don't be angered; it is but a formality. I, we recognize you from before. And if the writings you bring speak to our questions, you can expect payment even more generous than usual."

Away from the pier, the smell of burned petroleum products faded, replaced by a barnyard smell and the acrid stench of the tiny insects that built the mounds. Up close, the tower walls were not smooth sweeps. Glabrous patches were surrounded by warty growths. The "windows" were holes hacked in the irregular surface. Even Seraph's blue light could not make such things beautiful. Behind the front tier of mounds, stone corrals held a few dozen skoats—the source of the farm smell. The place really was a village, similar to backward villages the world over. Without modern science, they had no way of making strong or hard materials. Their spearheads were fire-hardened wood and obsidian. Where the termites did not build for them, their structures were simple piles of stone. It was no wonder travelers had seen no danger from these people; a squad of crossbow armed troops could take them over. No one guessed they had access to petroleum or the knowledge to produce flammables.

They walked some distance through the shadows between the towers. The Great Hall was cut into the side of one of the largest mounds. The resulting talus was pressed into steps as broad as in front of any government building in Crownesse. At the top of the steps, carved wooden barricades blocked the entrance. Rey's guide called something Hurdic and ceremonial-sounding. Spear-toting priests slid the barricades aside.

Their porters carried the crate of *Fantasies* toward the altar at the back of the Hall. The place was exactly as Rey remembered it: at least one hundred feet from entrance to altar, but with a ceiling that was nowhere more than seven feet high. It seemed more like a mine than a building. Twelve-foot-wide pillars stood in a rectangular grid across the floor. The pillars were native moundstuff, painted white. The only light came from ranks of candles that circled each of them. As the Tarulle people walked toward the altar, they saw hundreds of Termite Folk standing quietly between the farther pillars. The room couldn't be more than one hundred feet across, but the pillars seemed to go on forever. On his last visit, Rey had walked to the side of the Hall (an act of unknowing bravado, he realized now), and discovered that the pillars there were smaller, more closely spaced, and the walls were painted with the image of more pillars stretching off to a faked infinity; cleverly placed flecks of glass simulated hundreds of faraway candles. Like a lot of primitive folk, the Termiters had their own subtleties.

Rey expected the threatened body searches would come next. Instead, the Tarulle people were gestured to sit before the altar. There was a moment of near silence after Guille was asked to open the crate. Now he could hear a faint buzzing that came from all around, the sound of the real termites. They were, after all, inside an enormous hive. He pulled up the lid of the crate, and the insect sound was lost behind the Villagers' soft chanting.

The high priests lifted the top sheets from the crates. These were color illustrations that would be inside/outside covers on normally bound editions. The color didn't show well in the candlelight, but the Termiters didn't seem to mind; the best pictures from previous issues were mounted in the walls behind the altar. The priests poured over the illos, just like ordinary fans thrilled with the latest issue of their favorite magazine. Before, Rey would have smiled at their enthusiasm. Now he held his breath. At least one of those pictures showed Hrala carrying a spring-gun; could that be blasphemy?

Then the tall priest looked up, and Rey saw that he was smiling. "Wonderful, friend Guille. There is new Insight here. We will pay double." The others were lifting manuscript galleys out of the crate and solemnly laying them on velvet reading stands. There couldn't be more than a handful of locals who knew Spräk, did they *preach* from the stories? Rey let out a carefully controlled breath. It didn't matter now. The Tarulle people had passed the test and—

—outside the Hall, someone was shouting. The words were indistinct, but Hurdic. The priests straightened, listening. The shouts came louder; people were rushing up the steps to the Hall's entrance. The barricades slid aside and Seraph's light shone on the arrivals: they were spear carriers from the pier. They rushed down the aisle, still shouting. Their leader was waving something over his head. Everyone was shouting now. Rey saw that Brailly's men had slipped into a circle formation. Some of them were reaching into their jackets.

Then the newcomer reached the altar, and one of the priests—the old one with the gimp leg—gave an incredible warbling scream. In an instant, all other cries ceased. He took two objects from the guard and held them close to the candles. Strange reflections shifted across his face and the ceiling. . . . He was holding the main mirror and the diagonal bracket from Rey's telescope.

How can he know what these are, much less think them blasphemous? The thought hung for an instant in Rey's mind, and then everything went crazy. The old man threw the mirror to the floor, then turned on the Tarulle visitors and shouted in Hurdic. No translation was needed; his face was contorted with hatred. Spearmen ran forward, weapons leveled. Brailly tossed something onto the altar; there was an explosion and swirling gouts of chokesmoke. Rey dived to the floor, tried to belly crawl out from under the choke. He heard Brailly's men fighting their way toward the entrance. By the sound of it, they had some sort of weapons—strip knives probably. There were screams and ugly ripping sounds, all against a background of coughing and nausea. It sounded like all the Villagers had thrown themselves into the fight. They could never get past such a mob!

He had underestimated the Printmaster. From out of the smoke and shouting came Brailly's voice. "Down! We're gonna blast!" Rey tucked his head in his arms. A second later there was a flash of light and invisible hands crashed upon both sides of his head. He looked up. There was blue light ahead! Tounse had knocked the barricade over.

Rey came to his knees. If he could move while the locals lay stunned. . . .

His poor ears couldn't hear the rumbling; it came through his knees and palms. All around them, the hive was shaking. He saw now that the pillars near the entrance had been smashed. Avalanches of moundstuff—first small, then engulfing, spilled down from above.

With that, the tower collapsed on the Great Hall, and Rey saw no more.

————

CONSCIOUSNESS RETURNED IN PATCHES. THERE WERE UNPLEASANT DREAMS. Something was banging his head; it wasn't the knock of his alarm clock. They were dragging him feet first, and his head was bouncing off uneven ground. The dream faded to pleasant grayness, then came back in a new form: he was rolling down a hillside, the rocks cutting into his body.

Rey came to rest in foul-tasting water, and wondered if he would drown before he woke up. Strong hands pulled him from the water. Through the ringing in his ears he heard someone say, "There. A moment of sitting to catch the breath."

He coughed weakly, and looked around. No more dreams: the nightmare was reality. He was sitting by a shallow pond, near the bottom of a pit. The edge of the pit was ten yards above his head, except on one side, where it broke low and gave a view of the harbor. He was not alone. There were dozens of people here—all that remained of the *Science* crew. They clustered around the newly fallen. Looking up at their faces, Rey saw hope in some, fear and despair in others.

"You're looking bad. Can you talk?" It was the woman who had pulled him from the pond. She was in her late fifties, an Osterlai by her accent. Her clothes were neat but stained. There was a matter-of-fact friendliness in her voice. In a moment he would remember who she was.

"Y-yes," he croaked. "What happened?"

The woman gave a short laugh. "You tell us. Five minutes ago it just started raining people. Looks like the Termite Folk have found new blasphemers."

Rey swallowed. "You're right." And it was his fault.

Most of his companions were in worse shape than he. The *Science* prisoners were trying to help, but two of the Tarulle people looked freshly dead. Nowhere did he see Brailly Tounse. He glanced at the Osterlai woman and made a wan smile. "We came to rescue you." He gave his captive audience a brief account of the sales landing. "Everything was going fine. I was beginning to think they might listen to us, that we'd at least learn more about your situation. Then they found the mirror from my telescope. How could they know what it was, much less—" He noticed the look on the woman's face.

"And how do you think we got in trouble, my sir? We thought to do some observing from the peaks Inland. We had a twenty-inch mirror; the Seraph-seeing should be better here than—" She broke off in surprise. "Why, you're Rey Guille!"

Rey nodded, and she continued, "So I don't have to tell you the details; you've written enough about the idea. . . . I'm Janna Kats, Seraphist at Bergenton; we met once a couple years back." She waved a hand as recognition slowly dawned on Rey. "Anyway. We dragged that mirror ashore, gave the Termiters a look. They thought it was great stuff—till they learned what we wanted to look at." She laughed, but it was not a happy sound. "Lots of religions worship Seraph. You know: home o' the gods and such garbage. Turns out the Termiters think Seraph is something like the gods' bedroom—and mortals mustn't peep!"

So that was how they learned what the parts of a telescope look like. "It still doesn't make sense," Rey said. "In everything else, they seem to be ancestor worshippers; I've sold them dozens of Interior fantasies. How did Seraphidolatry get mixed in?"

The question brought a fit of coughing from the little man sitting beside Kats. "I can answer that." The words were broken by more rasping coughs. The fellow's face seemed shrunken, collapsed; Rey wondered that he could talk at all. "The Termite Folk are intellectual pack rats. For three hundred years they've been here, picking up a little of this, a little of that—from whoever was passing through." More coughing. "I should have seen through 'em right off. . . . I've spent my whole life studying coastal barbarians, learning Hurdic. But these folks are so secretive, I didn't understand what was driving them . . . till it was too late." A smile twisted his thin face. "I could get a nice research paper out of what we've learned here. Too bad we gotta die first."

Rey Guille had years of experience finding loopholes in impossible situations—on paper. "Maybe we don't have to die. I never thought the Termiters were killers. If their religion is such a hodgepodge, they can't take the taboos too seriously. You've been here for several days. Maybe they just want a graceful way out." It really made sense. Then he remembered Brailly's bomb, and continued more quietly, "If there's anything they'd kill for, I think it would be what my people did to the Village Hall."

"You don't understand, fellow," a third *Science* person spoke, a sharp edge in his voice. "Knocking over a termite mound is a peccadillo in their eyes—compared to invading the gods' privacy. They've kept us alive this long because they're having trouble devising a torture-death appropriate to our crime!"

"How can you know that for sure—"

"We know, Master Guille." Janna Kats's tough exterior broke for an instant, and she looked just as frightened as the others. "In the last two days they've taken three of us from the pit. W-we could hear the screams; one we could see. Each took longer to die than the last."

There was a moment of silence, and then the cougher said, "I think the Termiters are scared, too—of their Seraph gods. If they can't come up with the proper death for us, they think the gods will apply that death to *them*. The three they killed were . . . little experiments."

"But there will be no more." The toughness was back in Janna's voice.

"The next time they come, one big surprise we'll show them. We won't be skoats waiting for the slaughter."

Rey looked up, at the rim of the pit. There were Termite Folk all around. Most carried spears, but that wasn't the most deadly thing; spears kill one at a time, make a slow thing of a massacre. Much more ominous were the priests carrying torches. They stood near the three petroleum vats Brailly had spotted earlier. Each tank was mounted on a crude swivel. Should they choose, the torch bearers could drown their prisoners in flame. A few hours before, that prospect had filled him with sympathetic dread. For Janna and the others, it had come to be the only imaginable out.

THE HOURS PASSED. AT THE TOP OF THE SKY, SERAPH WIDENED TOWARD FULL, its western ocean turning dark and reddish with the start of the midnight eclipse. The Villagers marched steady patrols around the edge of the pit. Mostly they were silent. The *Science*'s anthropologist said they had long ago stopped responding to his shouted questions.

There were no more "experiments," but Rey gradually realized the pit was in itself a killing place. The only water was in the shallow pool at the bottom of the pit—and that became steadily more foul. The only food was what the Villagers threw into the pit: slabs of skoat cheese and balls of what turned out to be pressed termite larva. Rey had eaten some exotic things in his years with Tarulle, but the larva patties were half rotted. Hungry as they were, only a few of the prisoners could keep them down. Three of the Tarulle prisoners were dead, their bodies broken by the explosion. Two of the survivors had compound fractures; their moans came less frequently with each passing hour.

The prisoners were not alone in the pit. The true builders of the Village were here, too. In the silence that dragged between conversations and occasional screaming, Rey heard a *scritching* sound coming from all directions. At the corner of his vision, a pebble would move, something would scuttle from one hole to another. The termites were no bigger than a man's thumb, but there must be millions of them in the sides of the pit. They avoided the humans, but their activity was ceaseless. The sides of the pit were not ordinary earth. All the way down to the pool, this was moundstuff. It must be old, the detritus of thousands of years of towers, but it was still used by the tiny creatures. The stones in this "soil" must have washed down from the hills to the north. The coming of humans was a recent event in the hives' history.

The towers of the Village crowded around three sides of the pit, but beyond the broken southern lip, they could see the harbor. The Tarulle Barge was less than a quarter mile out. Deck piled on deck, loading cranes sticking out in all directions, masts rising slim into the reddish-blue sky—the Barge had never seemed so beautiful to Rey as now. Safety was just twelve hundred feet away; it might as well be the other side of Seraph. An hour earlier, a hydrofoil had arrived from the ocean and docked in a starboard slip. There was no other boat activity, though Rey fancied he saw motion on the bridge: another meeting? And this time, a final decision to leave?

Most of the prisoners huddled on the north slope of the depression; the corpses were carried to the other side of the pit. The prisoners were bright people. They'd had plenty of time to try to figure a way out, and no success in doing so. The arrival of Rey's group brought new hope, even though the rescue had been a failure. For an hour or two, there was renewed scheming. When it became clear that nothing had really changed, the talk gradually petered out. Many of the prisoners drifted back to inward looking silence.

There were exceptions. One thing Rey loved about scientists was *their* love for speculation. Take Tredi Bekjer, the little guy who spent the hours coughing his lungs out. Tredi was a sickly fellow who should never have been on the *Science* expedition in the first place. He was an anthropologist, and the only captive who spoke fluent Hurdic. He might be dying, but between spasms of coughing he argued about the origin and future of their captors. He predicted that, no matter what the prisoners' fate, the ambush had doomed the Termiter culture. Now, outsiders knew there was petroleum nearby. When that news got to the archipelagates, the Termiter Folk would have lots of visitors. Even if the locals were not booted off their land, they would be forced to make big changes. In thirty years, there would be a *real* city here.

There were others like Tredi, folks who could walk through the gates of death, still arguing about ideas. When the planning and the scheming was done, these few still had something to talk about. Rey found himself drawn in.

Janna Kats was the most interesting. Before specializing in Seraphy, she'd had lots of experience with other branches of astronomy. And U Bergenton had the best astronomers in the world—if you excepted the Doo'd'en fanatics on the other side of the world. Kats was just the sort of person he'd been hoping to talk to—back when he thought they'd find the *Science* in one piece. For minutes at time Rey could forget where he was and what his fate must be. Kats had had great plans for the Seraph observatory. There should be good seeing from the mountains behind the harbor. Ground resolutions better than one hundred yards would have been possible with the twenty-inch mirror. The issue of intelligent life on Seraph might finally be resolved. . . . Instead, the project had brought them all to this pit.

Rey grunted. "Other things are happening in astronomy. Things that aren't so dangerous. There have been some fantastic discoveries at Krirsarque." He described "Pride of Iron" and the spectroscopic observations it was based on. "Can you imagine! With spectroscopy, we can know what things are like on planets around other stars." He sat back, waiting for Janna's reaction to this news. It was one of the occasional pleasures of his job, to be the first person in an entire archipelagate to report a breakthrough.

Janna grinned back at him, but there was no surprise in her expression. "Ha! That's one of the results the U Tsanart people sent west with *Science*. During the last year, they've got good spectra on twenty stars in our sun's class. Every damn one of 'em is metal rich. And we have other results too. We can measure radial motions with this spectra stuff—" She laughed at the expression on his face. "You've written a lot of high-flown editorials about 'Spectroscopy, Key to the Universe.' Well, you may have understated the case. Combine the spectral shift data with proper motion studies, and it's obvious our solar system is an interloper, just passing through the local star stream."

Outcast Star. The title flashed through Rey's mind. There were writers who could run away with that idea—and surely would, if he got out of this alive. "You know, it's almost as if someone were picking on the human race," he mused. "Out of all the solar systems, that we should be the on the low metal one, the outsider." He didn't like the idea. It smacked of the theistic fantasy Cor Ascuasenya so loved: humanity as doormat to the gods.

"You've got it backward, my sir. Ever hear of the anthropic principle? Most likely, intelligent life exists on Tu *exactly because* we are different from the others. Think what an abundance of metals would mean. It's not just a matter of wealth, millions of ounces of iron available for large scale construction. My guess is such concentrations of metals would change the surface chemistry so much that life would never develop."

Janna's middle-aged features were filled with a happy smugness, but Rey did not feel put down. He was imagining deadly, treasure-house worlds. "Or life might develop, but different than here. Why, there might be—"

Janna abruptly grabbed his arm. She was looking past him, her expression intent; his speculations were suddenly of zero interest. There were scattered gasps from the prisoners. He turned and looked into the harbor. The Barge had lowered a boat to the water. It glowed with white light, a jewel in the reddening dimness. Then he realized that Tarulle had lit a flare at the focus of the bridge's signal mirror. Its light fell dazzling on the boat—which was nothing more than a freight lander painted silver and white. Before the flare guttered out, two more were lit at other mirrors. They tracked the boat as it started toward shore.

The Termiter priests were suddenly shouting. One group of spear car-riers ran to the south side of the pit, while others moved to the pet' vats and slid the covers aside. Priests dipped their torches into the vats— and the night exploded. The thunder went on and on, drowning the shouts of prisoners and Villagers alike. Flame and smoke rose from the petroleum, swirls of red and black across the mid-night eclipse. Hun-dreds of bats swarmed drunkenly in the superheated air, burning, fall-ing. The stench of pet' was everywhere. The Termiters cowered back from the pyres they had created, but Rey saw a few priests near each, setting long poles against the sides of the vats. A few good pushes, and the prison pit would be wall-to-wall fire.

Some of the prisoners collapsed, their mouths open, eyes wide. They must be screaming. Beside him, Janna Kats had caught his arm in both her hands. Her eyes were clenched shut, her face averted from the fires. Something in Rey's mind retreated and suddenly he wasn't frightened. He wasn't brave; he simply couldn't grasp the reality of his imminent torch-hood. He looked back to the harbor. The firing of the vats hadn't stopped the boat. It floated serenely toward them, still lit by the Barge's flares. He strained to see what it was carrying. The oarsmen wore black robes, their faces hidden within deep cowls. Those weren't Tarulle uni-forms, yet they were somehow familiar. There was only one other per-son on the boat. She stood at the bow, scorning all support. Her clothes were white and silver, gleaming in the faraway spotlights. Black hair cascaded around her face and shoulders.

Now Rey understood this latest rescue attempt. He damned and thanked Cor all at once for trying.

Tarulle doused the flares the instant the lighter touched shore. In the roaring red dimness, the figure on the boat was a vague thing. She did something to her robes and suddenly was near naked, and incredibly female. When she swung over the railing, red-silver glinted from her breasts and thighs. The oarsmen followed, clumsy black beetles by com-parison. They started up the hillside, and were lost to Rey's view beyond the south side of the pit . . .

. . . but not lost to the Termiters'. The spear carriers hadn't moved, but every face was turned toward the approaching party. The priests by the fire vats had dropped their poles, and stared in shock. Janna's grip loosened. She tried to ask him something, but even shouting mouth to ear, she couldn't talk over the flame-roar. Rey could only point to the rim of the pit.

A minute passed. Villagers at the southeast corner of the pit backed away . . . and the newcomers appeared. *By the Light*, what a job Cor had

done! It was strange to see—in the middle of terrible, deadly reality—
the incarnation of a hundred fantasies. This *was* Hrala, complete with a
contingent of the Sibhood Sinistre. The Sibhood followed Hrala through
most of the stories. Their motives were beyond knowing, but seemed
more evil than not. Sometimes they were Hrala's deadliest enemies,
sometimes her allies. When they were her allies, the rest of the world
better watch out. The black-cowled figures hung silently behind her,
looking a dozen times more deadly than any Termiter priests.

The fraud would have been nothing without its central character.
Tatja Grimm had come to Tarulle an outsized waif. The make-up people
had transformed her. Black hair lapped smooth down to her waist, a
perfect copy of all the illustrations. Her body was evenly tanned, though
all she wore was ribbon armor, and that only around her hips and
breasts. If he hadn't seen the girl before, Rey never would have guessed
that bosom was faked. She carried the blade named *Death*. Crafted of
"magic metal," edged with diamonds, it was a living creature and one
of Hrala's earliest conquests. Without her control, it would take up its
original mission—to corrupt the powerful and scourge The Continent.
In fact, the prop was carved from puffwood painted silver and edged
with quartz. Any sharp blow would shatter it.

Tatja Grimm walked forward, *Death's* flat resting on her shoulder as
though it weighed pounds and not ounces. Cor had coached her well.
Every motion was fluid, arrogant. She walked straight to a high point
on the pit's rim. For a long moment, she surveyed the flaming vats and
the priests. Not once did she look at the spear carriers. The Villagers
stared back, eyes wide. Rey could see the fear mounting in them.

Abruptly, Hrala's hand flashed out. She pointed at the vats and
clenched her fist. The Barbarian Princess wanted those fires *out*. The
Termiter priests scrambled to push the lids back onto the vats. Flames
burst sideways, searing the priests, but one by one the lids were forced
into place. There were scattered explosions; one of the vats trembled in
its cradle. Then a great silence replaced the violence. For a long moment,
everyone listened to the ringing in their ears.

Rey couldn't believe his eyes or ears. Did the Termiter priests actually
believe the stories? Of course, the instant the girl opened her mouth
the illusion would be broken—

The Grimm girl turned, gestured the chief Sib to stand close behind
her. The cowled figure slid forward, servile and sneaky at the same time.
That must be Coronadas Ascuasenya; she might just be close enough to
prompt the girl. There was a hissing conversation between the two,
broken off by an imperious gesture from the Princess. She looked back
at the Termiters and finally spoke. The words rattled fast, diamond hard.
They were not Spräk.

Tredi Bekjer gasped. He crawled the few feet that separated him from Rey. "That's Hurdic!"

Janna and Rey dropped to their knees beside him. "What's she saying?"

Bekjer listened a moment more. "Hard to follow. She's speaks a deep Interior dialect. . . . I've only heard it a couple times." He choked back a coughing spasm. "Says she's angry as . . . the hot pits of the earth. Termiters have no business holding her . . . property? prey? She means us, in any case. She demands reparations, replacements for the dead, and—" Tredi laughed and coughed at the same time "—and the return of the survivors."

The sharp-voiced speech ended. The Barbarian Princess stood waiting a reply. *Death* twitched in her hand, impatient to forego these diplomatic niceties.

A voice came from the priests. After a second, Rey recognized it as belonging to the tall Termiter. The words were tentative and quavery, totally lacking the menace Tatja/Hrala put into hers. Tredi continued his translation: "Local guy is explaining our blasphemy. Case you can't tell, he's practically wetting his pants. . . . If he doesn't punish us, the High Gods will torture-kill his people. And now Hrala is threatening to skewer his guts if he doesn't let us go. He's caught between two dooms."

Hrala had a reply. She swung *Death* from her shoulder and thrust it skyward. The fake metal gleamed red-silver, "diamonds" glittering. Her speech was as angry and decisive as before. Tredi's translation consisted of a single, soft-spoken, *"Wow."* Janna punched his shoulder, and the little anthropologist remembered his listeners. "Whoever she is, she's wonderful. . . . She told the Termiter to remember his place, that he's too *low* in the scheme of things to *presume* upon the High Gods' vengeance. . . . I can't translate it any better; she packed a freightload of hauteur into a couple sentences. She's telling him, if her property is offensive, then that's something between Hrala and the Gods."

Rey Guille looked from Tatja Grimm to the clustered priests. Hope was a sudden, wonderful thing. Every state religion he'd ever seen had a core of hypocrisy. That was why he'd been against bringing "Hrala" ashore—he knew the priests would never accept their theology suddenly incarnate. But Cor and the Grimm girl had taken the risk, and now, incredibly, the plan was working.

For several minutes the priests had no reply. They stood in a tight group, speaking in low voices. Around them, the spear carriers held their weapons loosely, their eyes never leaving Tatja Grimm. From beyond the rim, an anonymous voice called, "Hrala." After a moment, one of the spear carriers repeated: "Hra-la." The word was passed back and forth among the low-ranking Termiters. They pronounced the guttural "H" with a force and precision that made Rey wince. "Hra-la. Hra-la. Hra La. Hra La . . ." The chant spread around the pit, a soft drumbeat.

One of the priests shouted; the chant stumbled, guttered out. After a moment, the priest continued. His voice was placating, but without the quavering fear of before. "New guy," said Tredi. "He's talking humble, sweet as sugar. Says that for sure Hrala's claim takes precedence over theirs, but . . ." Tredi sucked in a breath. "*Bastard!* He says, in dealing with beings so deadly as the High Gods, his people need at least to go through the motions . . . of verifying Hrala's identity."

Another priest spoke up, his voice high-pitched and not nearly as confident as the first. " 'A mere formality,' the second jerk says."

"S-so what's the *formality*, Tredi!" Janna all but shook the little man.

Bekjer listened a second longer, then caught back a sob. "Nothing much. A little trial by combat."

REY'S EYES STAYED ON TATJA GRIMM ALL THROUGH THIS SPEECH. SHE DIDN'T flinch. If anything she stood taller now, her chin raised at the impudence of the "request." No amount of coaching could have taught her to do that: the girl was as gutsy as anyone he'd ever known. When the priest finished, her reply was immediate, a sharp three syllables filled with anger and arrogance.

" 'Certainly,' she says," Bekjer translated unnecessarily.

And Rey's hope fled as quickly as it had come. The girl looked down at *Death*, and for an instant he saw the gawky youngster who had come aboard Tarulle just a few days before. She wasn't afraid, just uncertain, feeling her way in a strange situation. The puffwood sword was a magnificent bluff, but they were beyond bluffs now. It couldn't cut butter, and it would shatter at the first blow.

The girl gestured imperiously at the chief Sib, the one who must be Coronadas Ascuasenya. The Sib slid forward, and spoke hissingly into Hrala's ear. The rescue party was about out of options. No doubt they were heavily armed. If they acted quickly, while the tattered bluff had some credibility, they could probably fight their way back to the landing boat—and at least save themselves.

Hrala listened to the Sib for a moment, then interrupted. The two were arguing! It was consistent with all the stories, but why now? Cor's hissing broke into full voice for an instant, and suddenly he realized this was no sham. Hrala shook her head abruptly, and handed her sword to the Sib. Cor sank beneath the pretended weight of *Death*. She didn't have much choice now. She slunk back to the other Sibs, her fear obvious but suddenly in character: she held *Death* in her hands. As a Sib

Sinistre, she could not be perverted by it (the Sibhood was already pretty perverse), but possessing *Death* and being possessed by it were very close things. It was a theme Rey had insinuated into the series himself.

Hrala turned back to the Termiter Priests. She was smiling, and the anger was gone from her words; mocking arrogance remained.

"Says she's happy to fight, but it's no . . . fun . . . wasting *Death* on such easy prey as the Termiters. She'll fight with whatever weapons her opponent chooses."

That almost started the chant again. The priests shouted it down, and after a moment one of them carried a sword-club toward Hrala/Tatja. This fellow was no fighter, just an errand boy. He laid the club on the ground ten feet from the girl, then scuttled back to safety. Hrala let him depart, then stepped from the high ground to inspect the weapon.

"If she's from deep Inland, she's never seen a sword-club," said Tredi. "Spears and pikes are all the Inlanders have. Even on the coast, it's a ceremonial weapon."

This one was clearly for special occasions; the wood was polished, unmarred. Without metals or composite materials, true swords were impossible. It looked deadly all the same. In overall shape it was something between a club and a pike. Elaborate hooks and blades, of bone or obsidian, were set along its length. There was a spike of glassy blackness at one end, and a hilt at the other. A second grip was set halfway down the pole; perhaps the thing could be used like a quarterstaff.

Hrala/Tatja picked it up, clearly as mystified as Rey. Somehow the puzzlement didn't take her out of character: she smiled her curiosity, seeming to say *how interesting, how clever*. He couldn't tell if she were acting or if this were the same frank wonderment he'd seen in her before. She swung it through a couple of clean arcs, then paused, glanced hesitantly at Cor and the others. Rey understood; this was her last chance to cut and run. Cor started toward her, but the girl turned away and shouted at the priests.

"She says she's ready."

Rey scarcely realized he was holding his breath. The girl *could win*. The spear carriers were already sold on the fraud; none of them could fight effectively. The more cynical priests weren't fooled, but they were exactly the sort that let others do their fighting. Who did that leave? Mental subnormals, too stupid to be afraid?

The crowd of priests parted and someone very broad and heavy started up the incline toward Tatja Grimm. The man's gait was slow, almost shambling. Even from here Rey could see the dullness in his features. *Thank the Light!*

Then he saw the second one.

They were nearly identical—giant, stupid . . . and armed. They carried their sword-clubs before them, both as threat and shield. Each was dressed in heavy leather. It was primitive armor, but at least real; Tatja Grimm was virtually naked, what armor she wore a gaudy fake.

Together, they outweighed her three to one.

The two separated as they approached the girl. They stopped ten feet from her, and for a moment the combatants stared at each other. Rey thought he saw traces of anxiety in the dullards' manner; you'd have to be a vegetable to ignore the mood of the Villagers and the deadly confidence that came from the enemy.

Twenty years of fantasy collided with reality tonight—and for an instant the fantasy seemed the truer vision. The scene would have made a perfect cover painting: Hrala standing straight and fearless before a pair of subhuman attackers, a city of towers spreading on and on behind her. The last blue had disappeared from Seraph's eastern ocean. The disk shaded from brighter reds to darker. The cloud of tarry smoke from the pet' vats still hung in the air, roiling Seraph's continents out of all recognition. Everything—towers, prisoners, priests, fighters—was lit with shifting reds. It was the color of blood, *Hrala's color,* the background color of her most chilling battles.

A priest shouted at the swordsmen, and the moment passed. They came in from opposite sides, their bladed clubs swinging. The girl grabbed her club at the hilt and foregrip and whirled between them. They were slow, and Tatja Grimm was terribly quick. That could only save her from quick death: she danced backwards, up the rise. She used the club like a staff, blocking. Blade fragments flew from every blow.

She bounded three great steps back, and moved both hands to the hilt of the club. She swung it in a quick sweep, her greater reach keeping the two back—till they separated again and came at her from the sides. Even so, she wasn't retreating now.

"She learns very fast," Tredi said to no one in particular.

But some lessons are learned the hard way. The bladed hooks were good for more than terror and disemboweling. One of her parries brought a crashing halt; her club had locked with the attacker's. The swordsman raised his club, swinging her slender body against him. Tatja kicked and kneed him. Even in his armor, the fellow staggered beneath the blows. The second attacker ran forward, rammed the point of his club squarely at the girl's torso. Somehow she sensed the attack, and threw herself backwards. The impaling thrust was turned into a deep slash across her chest.

She hit the ground and bounced instantly to her feet. For a moment the action stopped and the antagonists stared at each other, shocked. In the smoky red dimness, details were vague . . . yet the fake bosom still seemed to be in place. Everyone could see that the armor around her chest had been slashed open. Everyone could see the ripping wound across her breasts. Everyone could see that Hrala *did not bleed*.

The second swordsman stepped backwards and whimpered. His tiny brain finally realized that he should be terrified. He dropped his club and ran from both priests and Hrala.

The first fellow didn't seem to notice. He flipped Hrala's club over his head and advanced on her. She didn't retreat, didn't try to rush around him to the discarded clubs; she stood with knees slightly bent, hands held open. Only when the bladed club swung toward her middle did she move—and then it was too fast for Rey to follow. Somehow she caught the foregrip of the club, used it as a brace to swing her body up and ram her foot into the other's throat. The blow jarred the club loose, and the two fell in an apparently random tangle. But only one combatant rose from that fall. The other lay twitching, the point of a sword-club struck through his skull.

The girl stared at the dying man. A look that might have been horror passed across her face; her arms and shoulders were shaking. Suddenly she straightened and stepped back. When she looked at the priests, haughty pride was back in her features.

"Hrala. Hra-la. Hra La. Hra La . . ." The chant began again. This time, no priest dared shout it down.

CORONADAS ASCUASENYA HAD PLENTY OF CONTACT WITH THE RESCUED DUR-ing the next few days. Some recovered from the horror better than others. Janna Kats could laugh with good humor within ten hours of the rescue. The little anthropologist, Tredi Bekjer, was almost as cool, though it would be some time before his body recovered.

But four days out from the Village, some of the *Science* people were still starting at shadows, crying without provocation. And for every survivor, there would always be nightmares.

Cor had never considered herself especially brave, but she hadn't been trapped in that pit; she hadn't seen friends torture-murdered. Once they returned to the Barge, and the Village was irrevocably behind them, it was easy to put the terror from her mind. She could enjoy the Welcoming Back, the honor given her and Rey Guille and Brailly Tounse, the greater honor given Tatja Grimm.

It was as close to a storybook ending as could be imagined. Thirty-six from the *Science* had died, but nearly one hundred had survived the adventure and would return with the Barge (much to the surprise of their sponsoring universities, who hadn't expected to see them for two years). When Tarulle sailed into the Osterlais—and later the Tsanarts—everyone would be instant celebrities. It would be the story of the decade, and an immensely profitable affair for the Tarulle Publishing

Company. Whatever their normal job slot, every literate participant in the rescue had been ordered to write an account of the operation. There was talk of starting a whole new magazine to report such true adventures.

And management seemed to think that Cor and Rey had masterminded this publishing coup. After all, he had suggested the landing; she had produced Tatja/Hrala. Cor knew how much this bothered Rey. He had tried to convince Svektr Ramsey that he had fallen into things without the least commercial savvy. Of course, Ramsey knew that, but he wasn't about to let Rey wriggle free. So Guille was stuck with producing the centerpiece account of the rescue.

"Don't worry about it, Boss. They don't want the truth." She and the *Fantastie* editor were standing at the railing of the top editorial deck. Except for the masts and Jespen Tarulle's penthouse, this was as high as you could get on the Barge. It was one of Cor's favorite places: a third of the Barge's decks were visible from here, and the view of the horizon was not blocked by rigging and sails. It was early and the morning bustle had not begun. A cold salt wind came steadily from the east. That air was so clean—not a trace of tarry smoke. White tops showed across miles of ocean. Nowhere was there sign of land. It was hard to imagine any place farther from the Village of the Termite People.

Rey didn't answer immediately. He was watching something on the print deck. He drew his jacket close, and looked at her. "It doesn't matter. We can write the truth. They won't understand. Anyone who wasn't there, won't understand." Cor had been there. She *did* understand . . . but wished she didn't.

Rey turned back to watch the print deck, and Cor saw the object of his interest. The man wore ordinary fatigues. He wandered slowly along the outer balcony of the deck. He was either lonely, or bored—or fascinated by every detail of the railing and deck. Cor suspected the fellow wasn't bored: part of the Hrala fraud had been the demand that the Termiters replace her damaged "property" (the dead from Brailly's party and the *Science*). It seemed unwise to retract the demand completely, so five unfortunate Villagers were taken aboard.

This was one of them; he had been a Termiter priest—their spokesman/interpreter. Cor had talked to him several times since the rescue; he made very good copy. He turned out to be a real innocent, not one of the maniacs or hard core cynics. In fact, he had fallen from favor when the cynics pushed for trial by combat. He had never left the Village before; all his Spräk came from reading magazines and talking to travelers. What had first seemed a terrible punishment was now turning out to be the experience of his lifetime. "The guy's a natural scholar, Boss. We drop the others off at the first hospitable landing, but I hope he wants to stay. If he could learn about civilization, return home in a year or so . . . he could do his people a lot of good. They'll need to understand the outside world when the petroleum hunters come."

Rey wasn't paying attention. He pointed further down the deck.

It was Tatja Grimm. She was looking across the sea, her tall form slumped so her elbows rested on the railing and her hands cupped her chin. The ex-priest must have seen her at that instant. He came to an abrupt halt, and his whole body seemed to shiver.

"Does he *know*?"

Rey shook his head. "I think he does now."

In many ways the girl was different from that night at the Village. Her hair was short and red. Without the fake bust, she was a skinny pre-teener—and by her bearing, a discouraged one. But she was nearly six feet tall, and her face was something you would never forget after that night. The priest walked slowly toward her, every step a struggle. His hands grasped the railing like a lifeline.

Then the girl glanced at him, and for an instant it seemed the Termiter would run off. Instead, he bowed . . . and they talked. From up on the editorial deck, Cor couldn't hear a word. Besides, they were probably speaking Hurdic. It didn't matter. She could imagine the conversation.

They were an odd combination: the priest sometimes shaking, sometimes bowing, his life's beliefs being shot from under him; the girl, still slouched against the railing, paying more attention to the sea than to the conversation. Even during the Welcoming Back she had been like this. The praise had left her untouched; her listless replies had come from far away, punctuated by an occasional calculating look that Cor found more unsettling than the apathy.

After several minutes, the priest gave a final bow, and walked away. Only now, he didn't need the railing. Cor wondered what it must be like to suddenly learn that supernatural fears were unnecessary. For herself, the turn of belief was in the opposite direction.

Rey said, "There's a rational explanation for Tatja Grimm. For years we've been buying Contrivance Fiction about alien invaders. We were just too blind to see that it's finally happened."

"A visitor from the stars, eh?" Cor smiled weakly.

"Well, do you have a better explanation?"

". . . No." But Cor knew Tatja well enough to believe her story. She really was from the Interior. Her tribe's only weapons were spears and hand axes. Their greatest "technical" skill was sniffing out seasonal springs. She'd run away when she was eight. She moved from tribe to tribe—always toward the more advanced ones. She never found what she was looking for. "She's a very quick learner."

"Yeah. A quick learner. Tredi Bekjer said that, too. It's the key to everything. I should have caught on the minute I heard how Jimi found her 'praying' to the noontime shadow of her quarterstaff. There she had reproduced one of the great experiments of all time—and I put it down to religion! You're right; there's no way she could be from an advanced civilization. She didn't recognize my telescope. The whole idea of magnification was novel to her. . . . Yet she understood the principle as soon as she saw the mirror."

Cor looked down at the print deck, at the girl who seemed so sad and ordinary. There had been a time when Cor felt the start of friendship with the girl. It could never be. Tatja Grimm was like a hydrofoil first seen far astern. For a while she had been insignificant, struggling past obstacles Cor scarcely remembered. Then she pulled even. Cor remembered the last day of rehearsals; sympathy had chilled and turned to awe—as Cor realized just how *fast* Tatja was moving. In the future, she would sweep into a far away Coronadas Ascuasenya could never imagine. "And now she understands us, and knows we are just as dumb as all the others."

Rey nodded uncertainly. "I think so. At first she was triumphant; our toys are so much nicer than any tribe's. Then she realized they were the product of centuries of slow invention. She can search the whole world now, but she won't find anything better."

So here she must stop, and make the best of things. "I-I really do have a theory, Boss. Those old stories of fate and gods, the ones you're so down on? If they were true, she would fit right in, a godling who is just awakened. When she understands this, and sees her place in the world . . . She talked to me after the Welcoming Back. Her Spräk is good now; there was no mistaking her meaning. She thanked me for the Hrala-coaching. She thanked me for showing her the power of fraud, for showing her that people can be used as easy as any other tool."

For a long while, Rey had no response.

FAST TIMES AT FAIRMONT HIGH

The last story in this collection has not been published before. In fact, I just finished it (August 2001). "Fast Times at Fairmont High" is intended as a fairly conservative look at our near future. I hope to build it out to novel length eventually.

J uan kept the little blue pills in an unseen corner of his bedroom. They really were tiny, the custom creation of a lab that saw no need for inert fillers, or handsome packaging. And Juan was pretty sure they were blue, except that as a matter of principle he tried not to look at them, even when he was off-line. Just one pill a week gave him the edge he needed. . . .

FINAL EXAM WEEK WAS ALWAYS CHAOS AT FAIRMONT JUNIOR HIGH. THE school's motto was "Trying hard not to become obsolete"—and the kids figured that applied to the faculty more than anyone else. This semester they got through the first morning—Ms. Wilson's math exam—without a hitch, but already in the afternoon the staff was tweaking things around: Principal Alcalde scheduled a physical assembly during what should have been student prep time.

Almost all the eighth grade was piled into the creaky wooden meeting hall. Once this place had been used for horse shows. Juan thought he could still smell something of that. Tiny windows looked out on the hills surrounding the campus. Sunlight spiked down through vents and skylights. In some ways, the room was weird even without enhancement.

Principal Alcalde marched in, looking as dire and driven as ever. He gestured to his audience, requesting visual consensus. In Juan's eyes, the room lighting mellowed and the deepest shadows disappeared.

"Betcha the Alcalde is gonna call off the nakedness exam." Bertie Todd was grinning the way he did when someone else had a problem. "I hear there are parents with Big Objections."

"You got a bet," said Juan. "You know how Mr. Alcalde is about nakedness."

"Heh. True." Bertie's image slouched back in the chair next to Juan.

Principal Alcalde was into a long speech, about the fast-changing world and the need for Fairmont to revolutionize itself from semester to semester. At the same time they must never forget the central role of modern education, which was to teach the kids how to learn, how to pose questions, how to be adaptable—all without losing their moral compass.

It was very old stuff. Juan listened with a small part of his attention; mostly, he was looking around the audience. This was a physical assembly, so almost everybody except Bertie Todd was really here. Bertie was remote from Chicago, one of the few commuter students. His parents paid a lot more for virtual enrollment, but Fairmont Schools did have a good reputation. Of the truly present—well, the fresh thirteen-year-old faces were mostly real. Mr. Alcalde's consensus imagery didn't allow cosmetics or faked clothes. And yet . . . such rules could not be perfectly enforced. Juan widened his vision, allowed deviations and defacements in the view. There couldn't be too much of that or the Alcalde would have thrown a fit, but there were ghosts and graffiti floating around the room. The scaredy-cat ones flickered on-and-off in a fraction of a second, or were super-subtle perversions. But some of them—the two-headed phantom that danced behind the principal's podium—lasted gloating seconds. Mr. Alcalde could probably see some of the japery, but his rule seemed to be that as long as the students didn't *appear* to see the disrespect, then he wouldn't either.

Okay, platitudes taken care of, Mr. Alcalde got down to business: "This morning, you did the math exam. Most of you have already received your grades. Ms. Wilson tells me that she's pleased with your work; the results will make only small changes in the rest of this week's schedule. Tomorrow morning will be the vocational exam." Oh yeah. Be ready to learn something dull, but learn it very, very fast. Most kids hated that, but with the little blue pills, Juan knew he could whack it. "Soon you'll begin the two concurrent exams. You'll have the rest of finals week to work on them. I'll make the details public later in this assembly. In general terms: There will be an unlimited exam, where you may use any legally available resources—"

"All *right*!" Bertie's voice came softly in Juan's ear. All across the hall similar sentiments were expressed, a kind of communal sigh.

Mr. Alcalde's dark features creased in a rare smile. "That just means we expect something extraordinarily good from you." To pass the exam, a team had to bring in three times tuition per team member. So even though they could use any help they could recruit, most students didn't have the money to buy their way to a passing grade.

"The two concurrent exams will overlap the usual testing in visual communication, language, and unaided skills. Some of your parents have asked for more concurrency, but all the teachers feel that when you're thirteen years old, it's better to concentrate on doing a few things well. You'll have plenty of time for jumble lore in the future. Your other concurrent exam will be—Miss Washington?"

Patsy Washington came to her feet, and Juan realized that she, like Bertie, was only present as imagery. Patsy was a San Diego student so she had no business being virtual at a physical assembly. *Hmm.* "Look," she said. "Before you go on about these concurrent exams, I want to ask you about the naked skills test."

Bertie gave Juan a grin. "This should be interesting."

The Alcalde's gaze was impassive. "The 'unaided skills' test, Miss Washington. There is nothing whatsoever *naked* about it."

"It might as well be, mister." Patsy was speaking in English now, and with none of the light mocking tone that made her a minor queen in her clique. It was her image and voice, but the words and body language were very un-Patsy. Juan probed the external network traffic. There was lots of it, but mostly simple query/response stuff, like you'd expect. A few sessions had been around for dozens of seconds; Bertie's remote was one of the two oldest. The other belonged Patsy Washington—at least it was tagged with her personal certificate. Identity hijacking was a major no-no at Fairmont, but if a parent was behind it there wasn't much the school could do. And Juan had met Patsy's father. Maybe it was just as well the Alcalde didn't have to talk to him in person. Patsy's image leaned clumsily through the chair in front of her. "In fact," she continued, "it's worse than naked. All their lives, these—we—have had civilization around us. We're damned good at using that civilization. Now you theory-minded intellectuals figure it would be nice to jerk it all away and put us at risk."

"We are putting no one at risk . . . Miss Washington." Mr. Alcalde was still speaking in Spanish. In fact, Spanish was the only language their principal had ever been heard to speak; the Alcalde was kind of a bizarre guy. "We at Fairmont consider unaided skills to be the ultimate fallback protection. We're not Amish here, but we believe that every human being should be able to survive in reasonable environments—without networks, even without computers."

"Next you'll be teaching rock-chipping!" said Patsy.

The Alcalde ignored the interruption. "Our graduates must be capable of doing well in outages, even in disasters. If they can't, we have not properly educated them!" He paused, glared all around the room. "But this is no survivalist school. We're not dropping you into a jungle. Your unaided skills test will be at a safe location our faculty have chosen— perhaps an Amish town, perhaps an obsolete suburb. Either way, you'll be doing good, in a safe environment. You may be surprised at the insights you get with such complete, old-fashioned simplicity."

Patsy had crossed her arms and was glaring back at the Alcalde. "That's nonsense, but okay. There's still the question. Your school brochure brags modern skills, and these concurrent exams are supposed to demonstrate that you've delivered. So how can you call an exam concurrent, if part of the time your students are stripped of all technology? Huh?"

Mr. Alcalde stared at Patsy for a moment, his fingers tapping on the podium. Juan had the feeling that some intense discussion was going on between them. Patsy's pa—assuming that's who it was—had gone considerably beyond the limits of acceptable behavior. Finally, the principal shook his head. "You miss-take our use of the word 'concurrent.' We don't mean that all team members work at the same time all the time, but simply that they multitask the exam in the midst of their other activities—just as people do with most real-world work nowadays." He shrugged. "In any case, you are free to skip the final examinations, and take your transcript elsewhere."

Patsy's image gave a little nod and abruptly sat down, looking very embarrassed; evidently her pa had passed control back to her—now that he had used her image and made a fool of her. *Geez.*

Bertie looked faintly miffed, though Juan doubted this had anything to do with sympathy for Patsy.

After a moment, Mr. Alcalde continued, "Perhaps this is a good time to bring up the subject of body piercings and drugs." He gave a long look all around. It seemed to Juan that his gaze hung an instant in his direction. *Caray, he suspects about the pills!* "As you know, all forms of body piercings are forbidden at Fairmont Schools. When you're grown, you can decide for yourself—but while you are here, no piercings, not even ear- or eye-rings, are allowed. And internal piercings are grounds for immediate dismissal. Even if you are very frightened of the unaided skills test, do *not* try to fool us with implants or drugs."

No one raised a question about this, but Juan could see the flicker of communications lasers glinting off dust in the air, muttered conversation and private imagery being exchanged. The Alcalde ignored it all. "Let me describe the second of the concurrent exams, and then you'll be free to go. We call this exam a 'local' project: You may use your own computing resources and even a local network. However, your team members must work physically together. Remote presence is not allowed. External support—contact with the global net—is not permitted."

"Damn," said Bertie, totally dipped. "Of all the artificial, unworkable, idiotic—"

"So we can't collaborate, Bertie."

"We'll see about that!" Bertie bounced to his feet and waved for recognition.

"Ah, Mr. Todd?"

"Yes, sir." Bertie's public voice was meek and agreeable. "As you know, I'm a commuter student. I have lots of friends here, people I know as well as anyone. But of course, almost none of that is face to face since I live in Chicago. How can we handle my situation? I'd really hate to be excused from this important part of the finals just because I lack a physical presence here in San Diego. I'd be happy to accept a limited link, and do my best even with that handicap."

Mr. Alcalde nodded. "There will be no need, Mr. Todd. You are at a disadvantage, and we'll take that into account. We've negotiated a collaboration with the Andersen Academy at Saint Charles. They will—"

Andersen Academy at Saint Charles? Oh, in Illinois, a short automobile drive for Bertie. The Andersen people had long experience with team projects . . . back into prehistory in fact, the twentieth century. In principle they were far superior to Fairmont, but their academy was really more like a senior high school. Their students were seventeen, eighteen years old. Poor Bertie.

Juan picked up the thread of Mr. Alcalde's speech: "—They will be happy to accomodate you." Glimmer of a smile. "In fact, I think they are very interested in learning what our better students can do."

Bertie's face twisted into a taut smile, and his image dropped back onto the chair beside Juan. He made no additional comment, not even privately to Juan. . . .

The rest of the assembly was mostly about changes in exam content, mainly caused by the current state of outside resources—experts and technologies—that the school was importing for the nonconcurrent exams. All of it could have been done without this assembly; the Alcalde just had this thing about face-to-face meetings. Juan filed away all the announcements and changes, and concentrated on the unhappy possibility that now loomed over his week: Bertie Todd had been his best friend for almost two semesters now. Mostly he was super fun and an amazing team partner. But sometimes he'd go into a tight-lipped rage, often about things that Juan had no control over. *Like now.* If this were one of Bertie's Great Freeze Outs, he might not talk to Juan at all—for days.

The eighth-grade mob broke out of the assembly just before 4 pm, way past the end of the normal class day. The kids milled about on the lawn outside the meeting hall. It was so near the end of the semester. There was warm sunlight. Summer and the new movie-game season were just a few days off. But *caray*, there were still finals to get through and everyone knew that, too. So while they joked and gossiped and goofed around, they were also reading the exam changes and doing some heavy planning.

Juan tagged along behind Bertie Todd's image as the other moved through the crowd. Bertie was dropping hints all around about the un- limited project he was planning. The communication link from Bertie to Juan was filled with cold silence, but he was being all charming toward kids who'd never helped him a tenth as much as Juan Orozco. Juan could hear part of what was going on; the other boys weren't freezing him out. They thought Juan was part of the party. And most of them were more than pleased by Bertie's interest. For no-holds- barred collaboration, Bertram Todd was the best there was at Fairmont Junior High. Bertie was claiming high-level contacts, maybe with Intel's idea farm, maybe with software co-ops in China. He had something for everyone, and a hint that they might score far more than a good grade.

Some of them even asked Juan for details. They just assumed that he was already part of Bertie's scheme for the unlimited. Juan smiled weakly, and tried to seem knowing and secretive.

Bertie stopped at the corner of the lawn, where the junior high abut- ted the driveway and the elementary school. The eighth graders care- fully kept off the little kids' territory; you don't mess with fifth graders.

Along the driveway, cars were pulling up for students. Down by the bikestand, others were departing on bikes and unicycles. Everyone seemed to be laughing and talking and planning.

At the corner of the lawn, Juan and Bertie were all alone for a mo- ment. In fact, it was Juan all alone. For an instant, he considered turning off the consensus that made Bertie seem so visibly here. *Caray*, why not turn it all off: there. The sun was still bright and warm, the day still full of springtime. Bertie was gone, but there was still the other kids, mainly down by the bikestand. Of course, now the fancy towers of Fairmont School were the ordinary wood buildings of the old horse yard and the plascrete of the new school, all brown and gray against the tans and greens of the hills around.

But he hadn't bothered to down the audio link, and out of the thin air, there was Bertie's voice, finally acknowledging Juan's existence. "So, have you decided who you're gonna team with for the local project?"

The question shocked Juan into bringing back full imagery. Bertie had turned back to face him, and was grinning with good humor—a gaze that might have fooled anyone who didn't really know him. "Look, Bertie, I'm really sorry you can't be on a local team out here. Mr. Alcalde is a *mutha* for sticking you with the Andersen crowd. But—" Inspiration struck. "You could fly out *here* for the exam! See, you could stay at my house. We'd whack that local exam dead!" Suddenly a big problem was a great opportunity. *If I can just sell Ma on this.*

But Bertie dismissed the idea with an offhand wave. "Hey, don't worry about it. I can put up with those Andersen guys. And in the meantime, I bet I can help you with the local exam." His face took on a sly look. "You know what I got on Wilson's math exam."

"Y-yeah, an A. That's great. You got all ten questions."

Ten questions, most of them harder than the old Putnam exam problems had ever been. And in Ms. Wilson's exam, you weren't allowed to collaborate, or search beyond the classroom. Juan had gotten a C+, knocking down four of the questions. The little blue pills didn't help much with pure math, but it was kind of neat how all Ms. Wilson's talk about heuristics and symbol software finally paid off. Those problems would have stumped some of the smartest twentieth-century students, but with the right kind of practice and good software even an ordinary kid like Juan Orozco had a good chance of solving them. Two Fairmont students had cracked all ten problems.

Bertie's grin broadened, a morph that stretched his face into a cartoonish leer. Juan knew that Bertie Todd was a dud at abstract problem solving. It was in getting the right answers out of *other* people that he was a star. ". . . Oh. You slipped out of isolation." That wouldn't be hard to do, considering that Bertie was already coming in from outside.

"I would never say that, Juan my boy. But if I did, and I didn't get caught . . . wouldn't that just prove that all this 'isolated skills' stuff is academic crap?"

"I-I guess," said Juan. In some ways, Bertie had unusual notions about right and wrong. "But it would be more fun if you could just come out here to San Diego."

Bertie's smile faded a fraction; the Great Freeze Out could be reinstated in an instant.

Juan shrugged, and tried to pretend that his invitation had never been made. "Okay, but can I still be on your unlimited team?"

"Ah, let's see how things work out. We've got at least twelve hours before the unlimited team selections have to be final, right? I think it's more important that . . . you get yourself a good start on the local team exercise."

Juan should have seen it coming. Bertie was Mister Quid Pro Quo, only sometimes it took a while to figure out what he was demanding. "So who you do you think I should be matching up with?" Hopefully, someone dumb enough that they wouldn't guess Juan's special edge. "The Rackhams are good, and we have complementary skills."

Bertie looked judicious. "Don and Brad are okay, but you've read the grading spec. Part of your score in the local test depends on face-to-face cooperation with someone really different." He made as though he was looking across the campus lawn.

Juan turned to follow his gaze. There was some kind of soccer variant being played beyond the assembly hall—senior high students who wouldn't have finals for another two weeks. There were still a few clumps of junior high kids, probably planning for the locals. None of them were people Juan knew well. "Look over by the main entrance," said Bertie. "I'm thinking you should break out of narrow thinking. I'm thinking you should ask Miriam Gu."

Ay caray! "Gu?" Miss Stuckup Perfection.

"Yes, c'mon. See, she's already noticed you."

"But—" In fact, Gu and her friends were looking in their direction.

"Look, Juan, I've collaborated with all sorts—from Intel engineers in geriatric homes to full-time members of Pratchett belief circles. If I can do that, you—"

"But that's all virtual. I can't work face to face with—"

Bertie was already urging him across the lawn. "View it as a test of whether you belong on my unlimited team. Miri Gu doesn't have your, ah, quickness with interfaces," he looked significantly at Juan. "But I've been watching her. She maxed Ms. Wilson's exam and I don't think she cheated to do it. She's a whiz at languages. Yes, she's just as much of a snob as you think. Heh, even her friends don't really like her. But she has no special reason to be hostile, Juan. After all, you're no boyo. You're a 'well-socialized, career-oriented student,' just the sort she knows she should like. And see, she's walking this way."

True enough, though Gu and company were walking even more slowly than Juan. "Yeah, and she's not happy about it either. What's going on?"

"Heh. See that little video-geek behind her? She dared Miri Gu to ask you."

Juan was guessing now: "And you put her up to that, didn't you?"

"Sure. But Annette—the video-geek—doesn't know it was me. She and I collaborate a lot, but she thinks I'm some old lady in Armonk. . . . Annette likes to gossip a lot about us kids, and my 'little old lady' character plays along." Bertie's voice went high-pitched and quavery: " 'Oh, that sweet Orozco boy, I do think your friend Miriam would like him so.' "

Geez, Bertie!

They walked toward each other, step by painful step, until they were almost in arms' reach. Juan had turned off all imagery for a moment. Shed of fantasy, they were pretty ordinary-looking kids: Annette the video-geek was short and pimply-faced, with hair that hadn't seen a comb so far this month. Miriam Gu was about three inches taller than Juan. Too tall. Her skin was as dark as Juan's, but with a golden undertone. Close-cut black hair framed a wide face and very symmetrical features. She wore an expensive, Epiphany-brand blouse. The high-rate laser ports were perfectly hidden in the embroidery. Rich kids had clothes like this, usually with broad gaming stripes. This blouse had no gaming stripes; it was light and simple and probably had more computing power than all the clothes Juan owned. You had to be sharp to wear a shirt like this properly.

Just now, Miri looked as though she was tasting something bad. *You don't like what you see either, huh?* But Miri got in the first word: "Juan Orozco. People say you're a clever kid, quick with interfaces." She paused and gave a little shrug. "So, wanna collaborate on the local exam?"

Bertie pulled a monstrous face at her, and Juan realized that Bertie was sending only to him. "Okay," said Bertie, "just be nice, Juan. Say how you were thinking she and you would make a team with grade points right from the start."

The words caught in Juan's throat. Miriam Gu was just too much. "Maybe," he replied to her. "Depends on what you can bring to it. Talents? Ideas?"

Her eyes narrowed. "I have both. In particular, my project concept is a killer. It really could make Fairmont Schools 'the rose of North County.'" That was the school board's phrase. The Alcalde and the board wanted these local projects to show that Fairmont was a good neighbor, not like some of the schools in Downtown and El Cajon.

Juan shrugged. "Well, um, that's good. We'd be the kind of high-contrast team the Alcalde likes." *I really don't want to do this.* "Let's talk about it more some time."

Annette the video-geek put in: "That won't do at all! You need to team up soonest!" She flickered through various pop-culture images as she spoke, finally settled on the heroine student from Spielberg/Rowling. She grabbed the background imagery at the same time, and Fairmont Schools was transformed into a fairytale castle. It was the same set they had used at last fall's Hallowe'en pageant. Most of the parents had been enchanted, though as far as the kids were concerned, Fairmont Schools failed the fantasy test in one big way: here in real-life Southern California, the muggles ran the show.

Miriam turned to glare at her friend, now a brown-haired little English witch. "Will you shut *down*, Annette!" Then back to Juan: "But she's right, Orozco. We gotta decide tonight. How about this: You come by my place at 6 PM tonight and we talk."

Bertie was smiling with smug satisfaction.

"Well, yuh," said Juan. "But . . . in person?"

"Of course. This *is* a local project."

"Yeah, okay then. I'll come over." *There must be some way out of this.* What was Bertie up to?

She took a step forward and held out her hand. "Shake."

He reached out and shook it. The little electric shock was surely his imagination, but the sudden burst of information was not: two emphatic sentences sparkling across his vision.

Miriam Gu and her friends turned away, and walked back along the driveway. There was the sound of muffled giggling. He watched them for a moment. The video-geek was going full-tilt, picture and sound from a million old movies and news stories. Annette could retrieve and arrange video archives so easily that imaging came as naturally to her as speech. Annette was a type of genius. *Or maybe there are other flavors of little blue pills.*

Dumboso. Juan turned away from them and started toward the bikestand.

"So what did Miri Gu tell you?" *When she shook hands.* Bertie's tone was casual.

How could he answer that question without getting Bertie dipped all over again? "It's strange. She said if she and I team, she doesn't want anyone remote participating."

"Sure, it *is* a local exam. Just show me the message."

"That's the strange part. She guessed that you were still hanging around. She said, in particular, if I show you the message or let you participate, she'll find out and she'll drop the exam, even if it means getting an F." And in fact, that was the entire content of the message. It had a kind of nonnegotiable flavor that Juan envied.

They walked in silence the rest of the way to Juan's bicycle. Bertie's face was drawn down disapprovingly. Not a good sign. Juan hopped on his bike and pedaled off on New Pala, up over the ridge, and onto the long downslope toward home. Bertie's image conjured up a flying carpet, clambered aboard and ghosted along beside him. It was nicely done, the shadow following perfectly along over the gravel of the road shoulder. Of course, Bertie's faerie overlay blocked a good bit of Juan's visual field, including the most natural line of sight to see real traffic. Why couldn't he float along on Juan's other shoulder, or just be a voice? Juan shifted the image toward transparency and hoped Bertie would not guess at the change.

"C'mon, Bertie. I did what you asked. Let's talk about the unlimited exam. I'm sure I can be a help with that." *If you'll just let me on the team.*

Bertie was silent a second longer, considering. Then he nodded and gave an easy laugh. "Sure, Juan. We can use you on the unlimited team. You'll be a big help."

Suddenly the afternoon was a happy place.

They coasted down the steepening roadway. The wind that blew through Juan's hair and over his arms was something that was impossible to do artificially, at least without gaming stripes. The whole of the valley was spread out before him now, hazy in the bright sun. It was almost two miles to the next rise, the run up to Fallbrook. And he was on Bertie's unlimited team. "So what's our unlimited project going to be, Bertie?"

"Heh. How do you like my flying carpet, Juan?" He flew a lazy loop around Juan. "What really makes it possible?"

Juan squinted at him. "My contact lenses? Smart clothes?" Certainly the lense displays would be useless without a wearable computer to do the graphics.

"That's just the final output device. But how does my imaging get to you almost wherever you are?" He looked expectantly at Juan.

C'mon, Bertie! But aloud, Juan said: "Okay, that's the worldwide network."

"Yeah, you're essentially right, though the long-haul networks have been around since forever. What gives us flexibility are the network nodes that are scattered all through the environment. See, look around you!" Bertie must have pinged on the sites nearest Juan: there were suddenly dozens of virtual gleams, in the rocks by the road, in the cars as they passed closest to him, on Juan's own clothing.

Bertie gestured again, and the hills were alive with thousands of gleams, nodes that were two or three forwarding hops away. "Okay, Bertie! Yes, the local nets are important."

But Bertie was on a roll. "Darn right they are. Thumb-sized gadgets with very low power wireless, just enough to establish location—and then even lower power short-range lasers, steered exactly on to the targeted receivers. Nowadays, it's all so slick that unless you look close—or have a network sniffer—you almost can't even see that it's going on. How many free-standing nodes do you think there are in an improved part of town, Juan?"

That sort of question had a concrete answer. "Well, right now, the front lawn of Fairmont schools has . . . 247 loose ones."

"Right," said Bertie. "And what's the most expensive thing about that?"

Juan laughed. "Cleaning up the network trash, of course!" The gadgets broke, or wore out, or they didn't get enough light to keep their batteries going. They were cheap; setting out new ones was easy. But if that's all you did, after a few months you'd have metallic garbage—hard, ugly, and generally toxic—all over the place.

Juan abruptly stopped laughing "Wow, Bertie. That's the project? Bio-degradable network nodes? That's off-scale!"

"Yup! Any progress toward organic nodes would be worth an A. And we might luck out. I'm plugged into all the right groups. Kistler at MIT, he doesn't know it, but one of his graduate students is actually a committee—and I'm on the committee." The Kistler people were cutting edge in organic substitution research, but just now they were stalled. The other relevant pieces involved idea markets in India, and some Siberian guys who hardly talked to anyone.

Juan thought a moment. "Hey, Bertie, I bet that literature survey I did for you last month might really help on this!" Bertie looked blank. "You remember, all my analysis on electron transfer during organic decay." It had been just a silly puzzle Bertie proposed, but it had given Juan a low-stress way to try out his new abilities.

"Yes!" said Bertie, slapping his forehead. "Of course! It's not directly related, but it might give the other guys some ideas."

Talking over the details took them through the bottom of the valley, past the newer subdivisions and then down the offramp that led to the old casinos. Bertie and his flying carpet flickered for a second, and then the overlay vanished as his friend lost the battle to find a handoff link.

"Dunno why you have to live in an unimproved part of town," Bertie grumbled in his ear.

Juan shrugged. "The neighborhood has fixed lasers and wireless." Actually, it was kind of nice to lose the flying carpet. He let his bike's recycler boost him up the little hill and then off into Las Mesitas. "So how are we going to work the concurrency on the unlimited test?"

"Easy. I'll chat up the Siberians in a couple of hours—then shuffle that across to my other groups. I don't know how fast things will break; it may be just you and me on the Fairmont side. Synch up with me after you get done with Miri Gu tonight, and we'll see about using your 'magical memory.' "

Juan frowned and pedaled fast along white sidewalks and turn-of-the-century condos. His part of town was old enough that it looked glitzy even without virtual enhancements.

Bertie seemed to notice his lack of response. "So is there a problem?"

Yes! He didn't like Bertie's unsubtle reference to what the little blue pills did for him. But that was just Bertie's way. In fact, today was all Bertie's way, both the good and the bad of it. "It's just that I'm a little worried about the local test. I know Miri gets good grades, and you say she is smart, but does she really have any traction?" What he really wanted to ask was why Bertie had pushed him into this, but he knew that any sort of direct question along those lines might provoke a Freeze Out.

"Don't worry, Juan. She'd do good work on any team. I've been watching her."

That last was news to Juan. Aloud he said, "I know she has a stupid brother over in senior high."

"Heh! William the Goofus? He *is* a dud, but he's not really her brother, either. No, Miri Gu is smart and tough. Did you know she grew up at Asilomar?"

"In a detention camp?"

"Yup. Well, she was only a baby. But her parents knew just a bit too much."

That had happened to lots of Chinese-Americans during the war, the ones who knew the most about military technologies. But it was also ancient history. Bertie was being more shocking than informative.

"Well, okay." No point in pushing. *At least, Bertie let me on his unlimited team.*

Almost home. Juan coasted down a short street and up his driveway, ducking under the creaking garage door that was just opening for him. "I'll get over to Miri's this evening and start the local team stuff while you're in East Asia."

"Fine. Fine," said Bertie.

Juan leaned his bike against the family junk, and walked to the back of the garage. He stopped at the door to the kitchen. Bertie had gotten every single thing he had wanted. Maybe not. *I bet he still plans on messing with my local exam.* "But one thing. Miri's handshake—she was *real* definite, Bertie. She doesn't want you coming along, even passively. Okay?"

"Sure. Fine. I'm off to Asia. Ta!" Bertie's voice ended with an exaggerated *click*.

JUAN'S FATHER WAS HOME, OF COURSE. LUIS OROZCO WAS PUTTERING around the kitchen. He gave his son a vague wave as the boy came in the room. The house had a good internal network, fed from a fixed station in the roof. Juan ignored the fantasy images almost automatically. He had no special interest in knowing what Pa was seeing, or where he thought he was.

Juan eeled past his father, into the living room. Pa was okay. Luis Orozco's own father had been an illegal back in the 1980s. Grandpa had lived in North County, but in the cardboard shacks and dirt tunnels that had hid amid the canyons in those days. The Orozco grandparents had worked hard for their only son, and Luis Orozco had worked hard to learn to be a software engineer. Sometimes, when he came down to earth, Pa would laugh and say he was one of the world's greatest experts in Regna 5. *And maybe for a year or two that had been an employable skill.*

So three years of education had been spent for a couple years of income. That sort of thing had happened to a lot of people; Pa was one of those who just gave up because of it.

"Ma, can you talk?" Part of the wall and ceiling went transparent. Isabel Orozco was at work, upstairs. She looked down at him curiously.

"Hey, Juan! I thought you were going to be at finals until very late."

Juan bounced up the stairs, talking all the while. "Yes. I have a lot to do."

"Ah, so you'll be working from here."

Juan came into her work room and gave her a quick hug. "No, I was just gonna get supper and then visit the student I'm doing the local project with."

She was looking right at him now, and he could tell he had her full attention. "I just saw about the local exam; it seems like a great idea." Ma thought it was so important to get down on the real ground. When Juan was younger, she always dragged him along when she went on her field trips around the county.

"Oh, yes," said Juan. "We'll learn a lot."

Her look sharpened. "And Bertram is not in this, correct?"

"Um. No, Ma." No need to mention the unlimited exam.

"He's not here in the house, is he?"

"*Ma!* Of course not." Juan denied all snoop access to his friends when he was in the house. Mother knew that. "When he's here, you see him, just like when my other friends visit."

"Okay." She looked a little embarrassed, but at least she didn't repeat her opinion that "little Bertie is too slippery by half." Her attention drifted for a moment, and her fingers tapped a quick tattoo on the table top. He could see that she was off in Borrego Springs, shepherding some cinema people from LA.

"Anyway, I was wondering if I could take a car tonight. My teammate lives up in Fallbrook."

"Just a second." She finished the job she was working on. "Okay, who is your teammate?"

"A really good student." He showed her.

Ma grinned uncertainly, a little surprised. "Good for you. . . . Yes, she is an excellent student, strong where you are weak—and vice versa, of course." She paused, checking out the Gus. "They are a private sort of family, but that's okay."

"And it's a safe part of town."

She chuckled. "Yes, *very* safe." She respected the school rules and didn't ask about the team project. That was just as well, since Juan still had no idea what Miri Gu was planning. "But you stay out of Camp Pendleton, hear me?"

"Yes, ma'am."

"Okay, you're cleared to go as soon as you have supper. I've got some big-money customers running, so I can't take a break just now. Go on downstairs and get your father and yourself something to eat. And learn something from this local project, huh? There are many careers you can have without knowing airy-fairy nonsense."

"Yes, ma'am." He grinned and patted her shoulder. Then he was running down the stairs. After Pa's programming career had crashed, Mother had worked harder and harder at her 411 information services. By now, she knew San Diego County and its data as well as anyone in the world. Most of her jobs were just a few seconds or a few minutes long, guiding people, answering the hard questions. Some jobs—like the *Migración* historical stuff—were ongoing. Ma made a big point that her work was really hundreds of little careers, and that almost none of them depended on high-tech fads. Juan could do much worse; that was her message, both spoken and unspoken.

And looking at Pa across the kitchen table, Juan understood the alternative that his mother had in mind; Juan had understood that since he was six years old. Luis Orozco ate in the absent-minded way of a truly hard worker, but the images that floated around the room were just passive soaps. Later in the night he might spend money on active cinema, but even that would be nothing with traction. Pa was always in the past or on another world. So Ma was afraid that Juan would end up the same way. *But I won't. Whatever the best is, I'll learn it, and learn it in days, not years. And when that best is suddenly obsolete, I'll learn whatever new thing gets thrown at me.*

Ma worked hard and she was a wonderful person, but her 411 business was . . . such a *dead end.* Maybe God was kind to her that she never realized this. Certainly Juan could never break her heart by telling her such a thing. But the local world sucked. San Diego County, despite all its history and industry and universities, was just a microscopic speck compared to the world of people and ideas that swirled around them every minute. Once upon a time, Juan's father had wanted to be part of that wider world, but he hadn't been fast enough or adaptable enough. *It will be different for me.* The little blue pills would the difference. The price might be high; sometimes Juan's mind went so blank he couldn't remember his own name. It was a kind of seizure, but in a moment or two it always went away. Always. So far. With custom street drugs you could never be absolutely sure of such things.

Juan had one jaw-clenched resolve: *I will be adaptable.* He would not fail as his father had failed.

———

JUAN HAD THE CAR DROP HIM OFF A COUPLE OF BLOCKS SHORT OF THE GUS'
house. He told himself he did this so he could get a feel for the neighborhood; after all, it was not a very public place. But that wasn't the
real reason. In fact, the drive had been just too quick. He wasn't ready
to face his local teammate.

West Fallbrook wasn't super-wealthy, but it was richer and more
modern than Las Mesitas. Most of its money came from the fact that it
was right next to Camp Pendleton's east entrance. Juan walked through
the late afternoon light, looking in all directions. There were a few people out—a jogger, some little kids playing an inscrutable game.

With all enhancements turned off, the houses were low and stony-
looking, set well back from the street. Some of the yards were beautifully kept, succulents and dwarf pines arranged like large-scale bonsai.
Others were workaday neat, with shade trees and lawns that were raked
gravel or auto-mowed drygrass.

Juan turned on consensus imagery. No surprise, the street was heavily
prepped. The augmented landscape was pretty, in an understated way:
the afternoon sunlight sparkled off fountains and lush grass lawns. Now
the low, stony houses were all windows and airy patios, some places in
bright sunlight, others half-hidden in shadows. But there were no public
sensors. There was no advertising and no graffiti. The neighborhood was
so perfectly consistent, a single huge work of art. Juan felt a little shiver.
In most parts of San Diego, you could find homeowners who'd opt out of
the community image—or else demand to be included, but in some gro-
tesque contradiction of their neighbors. West Fallbrook had tighter control than even most condo communities. You had the feeling that some
single interest was watching over everything here, ready to act against intruders. In fact, that single interest went by the initials USMC.

Above him, his guide arrow had brightened. Now it turned onto a
side street and swooped to the third house on the right. *Caray.* He
wanted to slow down, maybe walk around the block. *I haven't even figured out how to talk to her parents.* Chinese-American grown-ups were an
odd lot, especially the ones who had been Detained. When they were
released, some of them had left the USA, gone to Mexico or Canada or
Europe. Most of the others just went back to their lives—even to government jobs—but with varying degrees of bitterness. And some had
helped finish the war, and made the government look very foolish in
the process.

He walked up the Gus' driveway, at the same time snooping one last
time for information on Miri's family. . . . So, if William the Goofus
wasn't really Miri's brother, who was he? William had never attracted
that much attention; there were no ready-made rumors. And Fairmont's

security on student records was pretty strong. Juan poked around, found some good public camera data. Given a few minutes he'd have William all figured out—

But now he was standing at the Gus' front door.

MIRIAM GU WAS AT THE ENTRANCE. FOR A MOMENT JUAN THOUGHT SHE WAS going to complain that he was late, but she just waved him inward.

Past the doorway, the street imagery cut off abruptly. They were standing in a narrow hallway with closed doors at both ends. Miri paused at the inner door, watching him.

There were little popping noises, and Juan felt something burn his ankle. "Hey, don't fry my gear!" He had other clothes, but the Orozco family wasn't rich enough to waste them.

Miri stared at him. "You didn't know?"

"Know what?"

"That's not *your* equipment I trashed; I was very careful. You were carrying hitchhikers." She opened the inner door and her gestures were suddenly polite and gracious. There must be grown-ups watching.

As he followed her down the hall, Juan rebooted his wearable. The walls became prettier, covered with silk hangings. He saw he had visitor privileges in the Gus' house system, but he couldn't find any other communications paths out of the building. All his equipment was working fine, including the little extras like 360 peripheral vision and good hearing. So what about those popping sounds, the heat? That was somebody *else's* equipment. Juan had been walking round like a fool with a KICK ME sign on his back. In fact, it was worse than that. He remembered assuring his mother that she would see any friends he brought to the house. Somebody had made that a lie. Fairmont had its share of unfunny jokesters, but this was gross. Who would do such a thing . . . yeah, who indeed.

Juan stepped from the hallway into a high-ceilinged living room. Standing by a real fireplace was a chunky Asian with buzzcut hair. Juan recognized the face from one of the few pictures he had of the guy. This was William Gu: Miriam's father, not the Goofus. Apparently the two had the same first name.

Miriam danced ahead of him. She was smiling now. "Bill, I'd like you to meet Juan Orozco. Juan and I are doing the local project together. Juan, this is my father."

Bill? Juan couldn't imagine addressing his own Pa by his first name. These people were strange.

"Pleased to meet you, Juan." Gu's handshake was firm, his expression mild and unreadable. "Are you enjoying the final exams so far?"

Enjoying?? "Yes, sir."

Miri had already turned away. "Alice? Do you have a minute? I'd like you to meet—"

A woman's voice: "Yes, dear. Just a moment." Not more than two seconds passed, and a lady with a pleasant round face stepped into the room. Juan recognized her, too . . . except for the clothes: this evening, Alice Gu wore the uniform of a timeshare Lieutenant Colonel in the United State Marines. As Miri made the introductions, Juan noticed Mr. Gu's fingers tapping on his belt.

"Oops. Sorry!" Alice Gu's Marine Corps uniform was abruptly replaced by a business suit. "Oh, dear." And the business suit morphed into the matronly dress that Juan remembered from the photos. When she shook his hand, she looked entirely innocent and motherly. "I hear that you and Miriam have a very interesting local project."

"I hope so." *Mainly I hope Miriam will get around to telling me what it is.* But he no longer doubted that Miriam Gu had traction.

"We'd really like to know more about it."

Miri pulled a face. "Bill! You know we're not supposed to talk about it. Besides, if it goes right we'll be all done with it tonight."

Huh?

But Mr. Gu was looking at Juan. "I know the school rules. I wouldn't dream of breaking them." Almost a smile. "But I think as parents we should at least know where you plan to be physically. If I understand the local exam, you can't do it remotely."

"Yes, sir," said Juan. "That is true. We—"

Miriam picked up smoothly where Juan had run out of words. "We're just going down to Torrey Pines Park."

Col. Gu tapped at her belt, and was quiet for a moment: "Well, that looks safe."

Mr. Gu nodded. "But you're supposed to do the local project without outside connectivity—"

"Except if an emergency comes up."

Mr. Gu just tapped his fingers thoughtfully. Juan turned off all the house imagery, and zoomed in on Miriam's pa. The guy was dressed casually, but with better clothes sense than most grown-ups had. In the house enhancement, he looked soft and sort of heavy. In the plain view, he just looked hard and solid. Come to think of it, the edge of his hand had felt calloused, just like in the movies.

Col. Gu glanced at her husband, nodded slightly at him. She turned back to Juan and Miri. "I think it will be okay," she said. "But we do ask a couple things of you."

"Nothing against the exam rules," said Miri.

"I don't think so. First, since the park has no infrastructure and doesn't allow visitors to put up camping networks, please take some of the old standalone gear we have in the basement."

"Hey, that's great, Alice! I was going to ask you about that."

Juan could hear someone coming down the stairs behind him. He looked without turning, but there was no one visible yet, and his visitor's privilege did not allow him to see through walls.

"And second," Col. Gu continued, "we think William should go along with you."

Miri's father? No . . . the Goofus. Ugh.

This time, Miri Gu did not debate. She nodded, and said softly. "Well . . . if you think that is best."

Juan spoke without thinking, "But . . ." then more diffidently: "But wouldn't that violate the exam rules?"

The voice came from behind him. "No. Read the rules, Orozco." It was William.

Juan turned to acknowledge the other. "You mean, you won't be a team member?"

"Yeah, I'd just be your escort." The Goofus had the same broad features, the same coloring as the rest of the family. He was almost as tall as Bill Gu, but scrawny. His face had a sweaty sheen like maybe—*Oh.* Suddenly Juan realized that while Bill and William *were* father and son, it was not in the order he had thought.

"It's really your call, Dad," said Mr. Gu.

William nodded. "I don't mind." He smiled. "The munchkin has been telling me how strange things are in junior high school. Now I'll get to see what she means."

Miri Gu's smile was a little weak. "Well, we'd be happy to have you come along. Juan and I want to look at Alice's gear, but we should be ready in half an hour or so."

"I'll be around." William gave a twitchy wave and left the room.

"Alice and I will let you make your plans now," Mr. Gu said. He nodded at Juan. "It was nice to meet you, Juan."

Juan mumbled appropriate niceties to Mr. and Col. Gu, and allowed Miri to maneuver him out of the room and down a steep stairway.

"Huh," he said, looking over her shoulder, "you really do have a basement." It wasn't what Juan really wanted to say; he'd get to *that* in a minute.

"Oh, yeah. All the newer homes in West Fallbrook do."

Juan noticed that this fact didn't show up in the county building permits.

There was a brightly lit room at the bottom of the stairs. The enhanced view was of warm redwood paneling with an impossibly high ceiling. Unenhanced, the walls and ceiling were gray plastic sheeting.

Either way, the room was crowded with cardboard boxes filled with old children's games, sports equipment, and unidentifiable junk. This might be one of the few basements in Southern California, but it was clearly being used the way Juan's family used the garage.

"It's great we can take the surplus sensor gear. The only problem will be the stale emrebs—" Miri was already rummaging around in the boxes.

Juan hung back at the doorway. He stood with his arms crossed and glared at the girl.

She looked at him and some of the animation left her face. "What?"

"I'll tell you *'what'*!" The words popped out, sarcastic and loud. He bit down on his anger, and messaged her point-to-point. "I'll tell you what. I came over here tonight because you were going to propose a local team project."

Miri shrugged. "Sure." She replied out loud, speaking in a normal voice. "But if we hustle, we can nail the whole project tonight! It will be one less background task—"

Still talking silently, directly: "Hey! This is supposed to be a *team* project! You're just pushing me around."

Now Miri was frowning. She jabbed a finger in his direction and continued speaking out loud, "Look. I've got a great idea for the local exam. You're ideal for the second seat on it. You and me are about as far apart in background and outlook as anybody in eighth grade. They like that in a team. But that's all I need you for, just to hold down the second seat. You won't have to do anything but tag along."

Juan didn't reply for a second. "I'm not your doormat."

"Why not? You're Bertie Todd's doormat."

"I'm gone." Juan turned for the stairs. But now the stairwell was dark. He stumbled on the first step, but then Miri Gu caught up with him, and the lights came on. "Just a minute. I shouldn't have said that. But one way or another, we both gotta get through finals week."

Yeah. And by now, most of the local teams were probably already formed. Even more, they probably were into project planning. If he couldn't make this work, Juan might have to kiss off the local test entirely. *Doormat!* "Okay," Juan said, walking back into the basement room. "But I want to know all about your 'proposed project,' and I want some say in it."

"Yes. Of course." She took a deep breath, and he got ready for still more random noise. "Let's sit down. . . . Okay. You already know I want to go down on the ground to Torrey Pines Park."

"Yeah." In fact, he had been reading up on the park ever since she mentioned it to her parents. "I've also noticed that there are no recent rumorings hanging over the place. . . . If you know something's going on there, I guess you'd have an edge."

She smiled in a way that seemed more pleased than smug. "That's what I figure, too. By the way, it's okay to talk out loud, Juan, even to argue. As long as we keep our voices down, Bill and Alice are not going to hear. Sort of a family honor thing." She saw his skeptical look, and her voice sharpened a little bit. "Hey, if they wanted to snoop, your point-to-point comm wouldn't be any protection at all. They've never said so, but I bet that inside the house, my parents could even eavesdrop on a handshake."

"Okay," Juan resumed speaking out loud. "I just want some straight answers. What is it that you've noticed at Torrey Pines?"

"Little things, but they add up. Here's the days the park rangers kept it closed this spring. Here's the weather for the same period. They've got no convincing explanation for all those closures. And see how during the closure in January, they still admitted certain tourists from Cold Spring Harbor."

Juan watched the stats and pictures play across the space between them. "Yes, yes, . . . yes. But the tourists were mainly vips attending a physicality conference at UCSD."

"But the conference itself was scheduled with less than eighteen hours lead time."

"So? 'Scientists must be adaptable in these modern times.' "

"Not like this. I've read the meeting proceedings. It's very weak stuff. In fact, that's what got me interested." She leaned forward. "Digging around, I discovered that the meeting was just a prop—paid for by Foxwarner and gameHappenings."

Juan looked at the abstracts. It would be really nice to talk to Bertie about this; he always had opinions or knew who to ask. Juan had to suppress the urge to call-out to him. "Well, I guess. I, um, I thought the UCSD people were more professional than this." He was just puffing vapor. "You figure this is all a publicity conspiracy?"

"Yup. And just in time for the summer movie season. Think how quiet the major studios have been this spring. No mysteries. No scandals. Nothing obvious started on April First. They've fully faked out the second-tier studios, but they're also driving the small players nuts, because we *know* that Foxwarner, Spielberg/Rowling, Sony—all the majors—must be going after each other even harder than last year. About a week ago, I figured out that Foxwarner has cinema fellowship agreements with Marco Feretti and Charles Voss." *Who? Oh. World-class biotech guys at Cold Spring Harbor.* Both had been at the UCSD conference. "I've been tracking them hard ever since. Once you guess what to look for, it's hard for a secret to hide."

And movie teasers were secrets that *wanted* to be found out.

"Anyway," Miri continued, "I think Foxwarner is pinning their summer season on some bioscience fantasy. And last year, gameHappenings turned most of Brazil inside out."

"Yeah, the Dinosauria sites." For almost two months, the world had haunted Brazilian towns and Brazil-oriented websites, building up the evidence for their "Invasion from the Cretaceous." The echoes of that were still floating around, a secondary reality that absorbed the creative attention of millions. Over the last twenty years, the worldwide net had come to be a midden of bogus sites and recursive fraudulence. Until the copyrights ran out, and often for years afterwards, a movie's on-line presence would grow and grow, becoming more elaborate and consistent than serious databases. Telling truth from fantasy was often the hardest thing about using the web. The standard joke was that if real "space monsters" should ever visit Earth, they would take one look at the nightmares documented on the worldwide net and flee screaming back to their home planet.

Juan looked at Miri's evidence and followed some of the major links. "You make a good case that this summer is going to be interesting, but the movie people have all cislunar space to play with. What's to think a Summer Movie will break out in San Diego County, much less at Torrey Pines Park?"

"They've actually started the initial sequence. You know, what will attract hardcore early participants. The last few weeks there have been little environment changes in the park, unusual animal movements."

The evidence was very frail. Torrey Pines Park was unimproved land. There was no local networking. But maybe that was the point. Miri had rented time on tourist viewpoints in Del Mar Heights, and then she had done a lot of analysis. So maybe she had that most unlikely and precious commodity, early warning. Or maybe she was puffing vapor. "Okay, something is going on in Torrey Pines, and you have an inside track on it. There's still only the vaguest connection with the movie people."

"There's more. Last night my theory moved from 'tenuous' to 'plausible,' maybe even 'compelling.' I learned that Foxwarner has brought an advance team to San Diego."

"But that's way out at Borrego Springs, in the desert."

"How did you know? I really had to dig for that."

"My mother, she's doing 411 work for them." *Oops.* Come to think of it, what he had seen of Ma's work this afternoon was probably privileged.

Miri was watching him with genuine interest. "She's working with them? That's great! Knowing the connection would put us way ahead. If you could ask your mother . . . ?"

"I dunno." Juan leaned back and looked at the schedule his mother had posted at home. All her desert work was under a ten-day embargo. Even that much information would not have been visible to outsiders. He checked out the privilege certificates. Juan knew his mother pretty well. He could probably guess how she had encrypted the details. *And maybe get some solid corroboration.* He really wanted to pass this exam, but . . . Juan hunched forward a little. "I'm sorry. It's under seal."

"Oh." Miri watched him speculatively. Being the first to discover a Foxwarner movie setup, a Summer Movie, would give Fairmont the inside track on story participation. It would be a sure-fire A in the exam; the size of such a win wouldn't be clear until well into the movie season, but there would be some income for at least the five years of the movie's copyright.

If this issue had come up with Bertie Todd, there'd now be intense pleadings for him to think of his future and the team and do what his ma would certainly want him to do if she only knew, namely break into her data space. But after a moment, the girl just nodded. "That's okay, Juan. It's good to have respect."

She moved back to the boxes and began rummaging again. "Let's go with what I've already got, namely that Foxwarner is running an operation in San Diego, and some of their Cinema Fellows have been fooling around in Torrey Pines Park." She pulled out a rack of . . . they looked like milk cartons, and set them on top of another box. "Emrebs," she explained opaquely. She reached deeper into the open box and retrieved a pair of massive plastic goggles. For a moment he thought this was scuba gear, but they wouldn't cover the nose or mouth. They didn't respond to info pings; he searched on their physical appearance.

"In any case," she continued, even as she pulled out two more pairs of goggles, "the background research will fit with my unlimited team's work. We're trying to scope out the movie season's big secrets. So far, we're not focusing on San Diego, but Annette reached some of the same conclusions about Foxwarner that I did. You wanna be on my unlimited, too? If this works tonight, we can combine the results."

Oh. That was really quite a generous offer. Juan didn't answer immediately. He pretended to be fully distracted by all the strange equipment. In fact, he recognized the gadgets now; there was a good match in the *2005 Jane's Sensors.* But he couldn't find a user's manual. He picked up the first pair of goggles and turned it this way and that. The surface of the plastic was a passive optical lacquer, like cheap grocery wrap in reverse; instead of reflecting bright rainbow colors, the colors flowed as he turned it, always blending with the true color of the gray plastic walls behind it. It amounted to crude camo-color, pretty useless in an environment this smart. Finally, he replied, kind of incidentally,

"I can't be on your unlimited team. I'm already on Bertie's. Maybe it doesn't matter. You know Annette's working with Bertie on the side."

"Oh *really*?" Her stare locked on him for a moment. Then, "I should have guessed; Annette is just not that bright by herself. So Bertie has been jerking all of us around."

Yeah. Juan shrugged and lowered his head. "So how do these goggles work, anyway?"

Miri seemed to stew over Annette for a few seconds more. Then she shrugged too. "Remember, this equipment is *old*." She held up her pair of goggles and showed him some slide controls in the headstrap. "There's even a physical 'on' button, right here."

"Okay." Juan slipped the goggles over his head and pulled the strap tight. The headset must have weighed two or three ounces. It was an awkward lump compared to contact lenses. Watching himself from the outside, he looked fully bizarre. The whole top of his face was a bulbous, gray-brown tumor. He could see Miriam was trying not to laugh. "Okay, let's see what it can do." He pressed the "on" button.

Nothing. His enhanced view was the same as before. But when he cleared his contact lenses and looked out with his naked eyes—"It's pitch dark from inside, can't see a thing."

"Oh!" Miri sounded a little embarrassed. "Sorry. Take off your goggles for a minute. We need an emreb." She picked up one of the heavy-looking "milk cartons."

"Meaning?"

"MRE/B." She spelled the word.

"Oh." Meal Ready to Eat, with Battery.

"Yes, one of the little pluses of military life." She twisted it in the middle, and the carton split in two. "The top half is food for the Marine, and the bottom half is power for the Marine's equipment." There were letters physically stenciled on the food container: something about chicken with gravy, and dehydrated ice cream. "I tried eating one of these once." She made a face. "Fortunately, that won't be necessary tonight."

She picked up the bottom half of the emreb, and drew out a fine wire. "This is a weak point in my planning. These batteries are way stale."

"The goggles may be dead anyway." Juan's own clothes often wore out before he outgrew them. Sometimes a few launderings was enough to zap them.

"Oh, no. They built this milspec junk to be *tough*." Miri set down the battery pack and bent Juan's goggles into a single handful. "Watch this." She wound up like a softball pitcher and threw the goggles into the wall.

The gear smashed upwards into the wall and caromed loudly off the ceiling.

Miriam ran across the room to pick up what was left.

Col. Gu's voice wafted down the stairwell. "Hey! What are you kids doing down there?"

Miri stood up and giggled behind her hand. Suddenly she looked about ten years old. "It's okay, Alice!" She shouted back. "I just, um, dropped something."

"On the ceiling?"

"Sorry! I'll be more careful."

She walked back to Juan and handed him the goggles. "See," she said. "Hardly a scratch. Now we supply power"—she plugged the wire from the battery into the goggles' headband—"and you try them again."

He slid the goggles over his eyes and pressed "on." Monochrome reds wavered for a moment, and then he was looking at a strange, grainy scene. The view was not wraparound, just slightly fisheye. In it, Miri's face loomed large, peering in at him. Her skin was the color of a hot oven, and her eyes and mouth glowed bluish-white.

"This looks like thermal infrared," except that the color scheme wasn't standard.

"Yup. That's the default startup. Notice how the optics are built right into the gear? It's kind of like camping clothes: you don't have to depend on a local network. That's going to be a win when we get to Torrey Pines. Try some other sensors; you can get help by sliding the 'on' button."

"Hey, yes!"

BAT:LOW		SENSORS		BAT2:NA
PASSIVE		ACTIVE		
VIS AMP	OK	GPR	NA	
NIR	OK	SONO	NA	
>TIR	OK	XECHO	NA	
SNIFF	NA	GATED VIS	NA	
AUDIO	NA	GATED NIR	NA	
SIG	NA			

The tiny menu floated in the corner of his right eye's view. The battery warning was blinking. He fiddled with his headband and found a pointing device. "Okay, now I'm seeing in full color, normal light. Boogers resolution, though." Juan turned around and then back to Miri. He laughed. "The menu window is fully bizarre, you know. It just hangs there at the edge of my view. How can I tag it to the wall or a fixed object?"

"You can't. I told you this gear is old. It can't orient worth zip. And even if it could, its little pea-brain isn't fast enough to do image slews."

"Huh." Juan knew about obsolete systems, but he didn't use them much. With equipment like this, there could be no faerie overlays. Even ordinary things like interior decoration would all have to be real.

There were *lots* of boxes, but no inventory data. Some of them must have belonged to the Goofus; they had handwritten labels, like "Prof. and Mrs. William Gu, Dept of English, UC Davis" and "William Gu Sr., Rainbow's End, Irvine, CA." Miri carefully moved these out of the way. "Someday William will know what do to with all this. Or maybe Grandmother will change her mind, and come visit us again."

They opened more of the USMC boxes and poked around. There were wild equipment vests, more pockets than you ever saw around school. The vests weren't documented anywhere. The pockets were for ammunition, Juan speculated. For emrebs, Miri claimed; and they might need a lot of the batteries tonight, since even the best of them tested "WARNING: LOW CHARGE." They dismembered the emrebs and loaded batteries onto two of the smallest vests. There were also belt-mount keypads for the equipment. "Hah. Before this is over, we'll be wiggling our fingers like grown-ups."

They were down to the last few boxes. Miri tore open the first. It was filled with dozens of camo-colored egg shapes. Each of them sprouted a triple of short antenna spikes. "*Feh.* Network nodes. A million times worse than what we have, and just as illegal to use in Torrey Pines Park."

Miri pushed aside several boxes that were stenciled with the same product code as the network nodes. Behind them was one last box, bigger than the others. Miri opened it . . . and stood back with exaggerated satisfaction. "*Ah so.* I was hoping Bill hadn't thrown these out." She pulled out something with a stubby barrel and a pistol grip.

"A gun!" But it didn't match anything in *Jane's Small Arms.*

"Nah, look under 'sensor systems.' " She grabbed a loose battery and snugged it under the barrel. "Even point-blank, I bet this couldn't hurt a fly. It's an all-purpose active probe. Ground penetrating radar and sonography. Surface reflection x ray. Gated laser. We couldn't get *this* at a sporting goods store. It's just too perfect for offensive snooping."

". . . It's got attachments, too."

Miri peered into the box and retrieved a metal rod with a flared end. "Yeah, that's for the radar; it fits on right here. Supposedly it's great for scoping out tunnels." She noticed Juan's eyeing this latest find and smiled teasingly. "Boys . . . ! There's another one in the box. Help yourself. Just don't try it out here. It would set off alarms big time."

In a few minutes they were both loaded down with batteries, plugged into the probe equipment, and staring at each other through their goggles. They both started laughing. "You look like a monster insect!" she said. In the infra-red, the goggles were big, black bugeyes, and the equipment vests looked like chitinous armor, glowing brightly where there was an active battery.

Juan waved his probe gun in the air. "Yeah. *Killer* insects." *Hmm.* "You know, we look so bizarre . . . I bet if we find Foxwarner down in Torrey Pines, we might end up in the show." That sort of thing happened, but most consumer participation was in the form of contributed content and plot ideas.

Miri laughed. "I told you this was a good project."

Miri called a car to take them to Torrey Pines. They clumped up the stairs and found Mr. Gu standing with William the Goofus. Mr. Gu looked like he was trying to hide a smile. "You two look charming." He glanced at William. "Are you ready to go?"

William might have been smiling, too. "Any time, Bill."

Mr. Gu walked the three of them to the front door. Miri's car was already pulling up. The sun had slipped behind a climbing wall of coastal fog, and the afternoon was cooling off.

They pulled their goggles off and walked down the lawn, Juan in front. Behind him, Miri walked hand in hand with William. Miriam Gu was respectful of her parents, but flippant too. With her grandfather it was different, though Juan couldn't tell if her look up at William was trusting or protective. It was bizarre either way.

The three of them piled into the car, William taking the back-facing seat. They drove out through East Fallbrook. The neighborhood enhancements were still pretty, though they didn't have the coordinated esthetic of the homes right by Camp Pendleton. Here and there, homeowners showed advertising.

Miri looked back at the ragged line of the coastal fog, silhouetted against the pale bright blue of the sky. " 'The fog is brazen here,' " she quoted.

" 'Reaching talons across our land,' " said Juan.

" 'Pouncing.' " she completed, and they both laughed. That was from the Hallowe'en show last year, but to the Fairmont students it had a special meaning. There was none of that twentieth century wimpiness about the fog's "little cat feet." Evening fog was common near the coast, and when it happened laser comm got whacked—and The World Changed. "Weather says that most of Torrey Pines Park will be under fog in an hour."

"Spooky."

"It'll be fun." And since the park was unimproved, it wouldn't make that much difference anyway.

The car turned down Reche Road and headed east, toward the expressway. Soon the fog was just an edge of low clouds beneath a sunny afternoon.

William hadn't said a word since they got aboard. He had accepted a pair of goggles and couple of batteries, but not an equipment vest. Instead, he carried an old canvas bag. His skin looked young and smooth, but with that sweaty sheen. William's gaze wandered around, kind of twitchy. Juan could tell that the guy had contacts and a wearable, but his twitchiness was not like a grown-up trying to input to smart clothes. It was more like he had some kind of disease.

Juan searched on the symptoms he was seeing AND'ed with gerontology. The strange-looking skin was a regeneration dressing; that was a pretty common thing. As for the tremors . . . Parkinson's? Maybe, but that was a rare disease nowadays. Alzheimer's? No, the symptoms didn't match. *Aha: "Alzheimer's Recovery Syndrome."* Ol' William must have been a regular vegetable before his treatments kicked in. Now his whole nervous system was regrowing. The result would be a pretty healthy person even if the personality was randomly different from before. The twitching was the final reconnect with the peripheral nervous system. There were about fifty thousand recovering Alzheimer's patients these days. Bertie had even collaborated with some of them. But up close and in person . . . it made Juan queasy. So okay that William went to live with his kids during his recovery. But their enrolling him at Fairmont High was gross. His major was listed as "hardcopy media—nongraded status"; at least that kept him out of people's way.

Miri had been staring out the window, though Juan had no idea what she was seeing. Suddenly she said, "You know, this is your friend Bertie Toad Vomit." She pulled an incredible face, a fungus-bedecked toad that drooled nicely realistic slime all the way to the seat between them.

"Oh, yeah? Why is that?"

"He's been on my case all semester, jerking me around, spreading rumors about me. He tricked that idiot Annette, so she'd push me into teaming with you—not that I'm complaining about *you*, Juan. This is working out pretty well." She looked a little embarrassed. "It's just that Bertie is pushy as all get out."

Juan certainly couldn't argue against that. But then he suddenly realized: "You two are alike in some ways."

"*What!*"

"Well, you're *both* as pushy as all get out."

Miri stared at him open-mouthed, and Juan waited for an explosion.

But he noticed that William was watching her with a strange smile on his face. She shut her mouth and glared at Juan. "Yeah. Well. You're right. Alice says it may be my strongest talent, if I can ever put a cork in it. In the meantime, I guess I can be pretty unpleasant." She looked away for a moment. "But besides us both being up-and-coming dictators, I don't see any similarities between me and Bertie. I'm loud. I'm a loner. Bertie Toad is sneaky and mean. He has his warty hands into everything. And no one knows what he really is."

"That's not true. I've known Bertie since sixth grade; I've known him well for almost two semesters. He's a remote student, is all. He lives in Evanston."

She hesitated, maybe looking up "Evanston." "So have you ever been to Chicago? Have you ever met Bertie in person?"

"Well, not exactly. But last Thanksgiving I visited him for almost a week." That had been right after the pills really started giving Juan results. "He showed me around the museums piggyback, like a 411 tour. I also met his parents, saw their house. Faking all that would be next to impossible. Bertie's a kid just like us." Though it was true that Bertie hadn't introduced Juan to many of his friends. Sometimes it seemed like Bertie was afraid that if his friends got together, they might cut him out of things. Bertie's great talent was making connections, but he seemed to think of those connections as property that could be stolen from him. That was sad.

Miri wasn't buying any it: "Bertie is not like us, Juan. You know about Annette. I know he's wormed into a lot of groups at school. He's everything to everyone, a regular Mr. Fixit." Her face settled into a look of brooding contemplation, and she was silent for a moment.

They were off Reche now, and on the southbound. The true view was of rolling hills covered by endless streets and houses and malls. If you accepted the roadway's free enhancements, you got placid wilderness, splashed with advertising. Here and there were subtle defacements, the largest boulders morphing into trollishness; that was probably the work of some Pratchett belief circle. Their car passed the Pala off-ramp and started up the first of several miles-long ridges that separated them from Escondido and the cut across to the coast.

"Last fall," Miri said, "Bertram Todd was just another too-smart kid in my language class. But this semester, he's caused me lots of inconvenience, lots of little humiliations. Now he has Attracted My Attention." That did not sound like a healthy thing to do. "I'm gonna figure out his secret. One slip is all it takes."

That was the old saying: Once your secret is outed anywhere, however briefly, it is outed forever. "Oh, I don't know," said Juan. "The way to cover a slip is to embellish it, hide it in all sorts of *fake* secrets."

"Hah. Maybe he *is* something weird. Maybe he's a corporate team."

Juan laughed. "Or maybe he's something really weird!" Over the next few miles, he and Miri hit on all the cinema clichés: Maybe Bertie was an artificial boy, or a superbrain stuck in a bottle under Fort Meade. Maybe Bertie was a front for alien invaders, even now taking over the worldwide net. Maybe he was an old Chinese war program, suddenly growing to sentience, or the worldwide net itself that had finally awakened with superhuman—and certainly malignant—powers.

Or maybe Bertie was a subconscious creation of Juan's imagination, and *Juan* was—all unknowing—the monster. This one was Miri's idea. In a way it was the funniest of all, though there was something a little unsettling about it, at least for Juan.

The car had turned onto Highway 56, and they were going back toward the coast. There was more real open space here, and the hills were green with a gold-edging of spring flowers. The subdivisions were gone, replaced by mile after mile of industrial parks: the automated genomics and proteomics labs spread like gray-green lithops, soaking up the last of the sunlight. *People* could live and work anywhere in the world. But some things have to happen in a single real place, close enough together that superspeed data paths can connect their parts. These low buildings drove San Diego's physical economy; inside, the genius of humans, machines, and biological nature collided to make magic.

The sun sank back behind coastal fog as they entered the lagoon area north of Torrey Pines Park. Off the expressway, they turned south along the beach. The pale cliffs of the main part of the park rose ahead of them, the hilltops shrouded by the incoming fog.

The Goofus had remained silent through all their laughter and silly talk. But when Miri got back into her speculation about how this all fit with the fact that Bertie was bothering her so much, he suddenly interrupted. "I think part of it is very simple. Why is Bertie bothering you, Miriam? It seems to me there's one possibility so fantastic that neither of you have even imagined it."

William delivered this opinion with that faintly amused tone adults sometimes use with little kids. But Miri didn't make a flip response. "Oh." She looked at William as though he were hinting at some great insight. "I'll think about this some more."

THE ROAD WOUND UPWARDS THROUGH THE FOG. MIRI HAD THE CAR DROP them off at the far side of the driveway circle at the top. "Let's scope things out as we walk toward the ranger station."

Juan stepped down onto weedy asphalt. The sun had finally, truly, set. Geez, the air was cold. He flapped his arms in discomfort. He noticed that William had worn a jacket.

"You two should think ahead a little more," said the Goofus.

Juan pulled a face. "I can stand a little evening cool." Ma was often onto him like this, too. Plan-ahead addons were cheap, but he had convinced her that they made stupid mistakes of their own. He grabbed his sensor "gun" out of the car and slid it into the long pocket in the back of his vest—and tried to ignore his shivering.

"Here, Miriam." William handed the girl an adult-sized jacket, big enough to fit over her equipment vest.

"Oh, thank you!" She snugged it on, making Juan feel even more chilly and stupid.

"One for you, too, champ." William tossed a second jacket at Juan.

It was bizarre to feel so irritated and so grateful at the same time. He took off the probe holster, and slipped on the jacket. Suddenly the evening felt a whole lot more pleasant. This would block about half his high-rate data ports, but *hey, in a few minutes we'll be back in the fog anyway.*

The car departed as they started off in the direction of the ranger station. And Juan realized that some of his park information was very out of date. There were the restrooms behind him, but the parking lot in the pictures was all gone except at the edges, where it had become this driveway circle. He groped around for more recent information.

Of course, no one was parked up here. There were no cars dropping people off, either. Late April was not the height of the physical tourist season—and for Torrey Pines Park, that was the only kind of tourist season there was.

They were just barely above the fog layer. The tops of the clouds fluffed out below them, into the west. On a clear day, there would have been a great direct view of the ocean. Now there were just misty shapes tossed up from the fog and above that, a sky of deepening twilight blue. There was still a special brightness at the horizon, where the sun had set. Venus hung above that glow, along with Sirius and the brighter stars of Orion.

Juan hesitated. "That's strange."

"What?"

"I've got mail." He set a pointer in the sky for the others to see: a ballistic FedEx package with a Cambridge return address. It was coming straight down, and from very high up.

At about a thousand feet, the mailer slowed dramatically, and a sexy voice spoke in Juan's ear. "Do you accept delivery, Mr. Orozco?"

"Yes, yes." He indicated a spot on the ground nearby.

All this time, William had been staring into the sky. Now he gave a little start and Juan guessed the guy had finally seen Juan's pointer. A second after that, the package was visible to the naked eye: a dark speck showing an occasional bluish flare, falling silently toward them.

It slowed again at ten feet, and they had a glimpse of the cause of the light: dozens of tiny landing jets around the edge of the package. Animal rights campaigners claimed the micro-turbines were painfully loud to some kinds of bats, but to humans and even dogs and cats, the whole operation was silent . . . until the very last moment: Just a foot off the ground, there was a burst of wind and a scattering of pine needles.

"Sign here, Mr. Orozco," said the voice.

Juan did so and started toward the mailer. William was already there, kneeling awkwardly. The Goofus spazzed at just the wrong instant and lurched forward, putting his knee through the mailer carton.

Miri rushed over to him. "William! Are you okay?"

William rolled back on his rear and sat there, massaging his knee. "Yes, I'm fine, Miriam. Damn." He glanced at Juan. "I'm really sorry, kid." For once, he didn't sound sarcastic.

Juan kept his mouth shut. He squatted down by the box: it was a standard twenty-ounce mailer, now with a big bend in the middle. The lid was jammed, but the material was scarcely stronger than cardboard, and he had no trouble prying it open. Inside . . . he pulled out a clear bag, held it up for the others to see.

William leaned forward, squinting. The bag was filled with dozens of small, irregular balls. "They look like rabbit droppings to me."

"Yes. Or health food," said Juan. Whatever they were, it didn't look like William's accident had done them any harm.

"Toad Vomit! What are *you* doing here?" Miriam's voice was sharp and loud.

Juan looked up and saw a familiar figure standing beside the mailer. *Bertie.* As usual, he had a perfect match on the ambient lighting; the twilight gleamed dimly off his grin. He gave Juan a little wave. "You can all thank me later. This FedEx courtesy link is only good for two minutes, so I have just enough time to clue you in." He pointed at the bag in Juan's hand. "These could be a big help once you get in the park."

Miri: "You don't have *any* time. Go away!"

Juan: "You're trashing our local exam just by being here, Bertie."

Bertie looked from from one indignant face to the other. He gave Miri a little bow, and said, "You wound me!" Then he turned to Juan: "Not at all, my dear boy. The exam proctors don't show you as embargoed. Technically, you haven't started your local exam. And I'm simply calling to check in with my loyal unlimited team member—namely you."

Juan ground his teeth. "Okay. What's the news?"

Bertie's grin broadened to slightly wider than humanly possible. "We've made great progress, Juan! I lucked out with the Siberian group—

they had just the insight Kistler was needing. We've actually built pro-totypes!" He waved again at the bag in Juan's hand. "You've got the first lot." His tone slipped into persuasion mode. "I'm not on your local team, but our unlimited exam is concurrent, now isn't it, Juan?"

"Okay." This was extreme even for Bertie. *I bet he had the prototypes ready this afternoon!*

"So we need these 'breadcrumbs' tested, and since I noticed that my loyal teammate is incidentally on a field trip through Torrey Pines Park, well, I thought . . ."

Miri glared at the intruder's image. "So what *have* you stuck us with? I've got my own plans here."

"Totally organic network nodes, good enough to be field-tested. We left out the communication laser and recharge-capability, but the wee morsels have the rest of the standard function suite: basic sensors, a router, a localizer. And they're just proteins and sugars, no heavy metals. Come the first heavy rain, they'll be fertilizer."

Miri came over to Juan and popped open the plastic bag. She sniffed. "These things stink . . . I bet they're toxic."

"Oh, no," said Bertie. "We sacrificed a lot of functionality to make them safe. You could probably *eat* the darn things, Miri." Bertie chuckled at the look on her face. "But I suggest not; they're kind of heavy on nitrogen compounds. . . ."

Juan stared at the little balls. *Nitrogen compounds?* That sounded like the summary work Juan had done earlier this semester! Juan choked on outrage, but all he could think to say was, "This—this is everything we were shooting for, Bertie."

"Yup." Bertie preened. "Even if we don't get all the standard function suite, our share of the rights will be some good money." And a sure A grade on the unlimited exam. "So. Juan. These came off the MIT organo-fab about three hours ago. In a nice clean laboratory, they work fine. Now how about if you sneak them into the park, and give them a real field test? You'll be serving your unlimited team at the same time you're working on your local project. Now, *that's* concurrency."

"Shove off, Bertie," said Miri.

He gave her a little bow. "My two minutes are almost up, anyway. I'm gone." His image vanished.

Miri frowned at the empty space where Bertie had been. "Do what you want with Bertie's dungballs, Juan. But even if they're totally or-ganic, I'll bet they're still banned by park rules."

"Yes, but that would just be a technicality, wouldn't it? These things won't leave trash."

She just gave an angry shrug.

William had picked up the half-crushed mailing carton. "What are we going to do with this?"

Juan motioned him to set it down. "Just leave it. There's a FedEx mini-hub in Jamul. The carton should have enough fuel to fly over there." Then he noticed the damage tag floating beside the box. "*Caray.* It says it's not airworthy." There were also warnings about flammable fuel dangers and a reminder that he, Juan Orozco, had signed for the package and was responsible for its proper disposal.

William flexed the carton. Empty, the thing was mostly plastic fluff, not more than two or three pounds. "I bet I could bend it back into its original shape."

"Um," Juan said.

Miri spelled things out for the Goofus: "That would probably not work, William. Also, we don't have the manual. If we broke open the fuel system . . ."

William nodded. "A good point, Miriam." He slipped the carton into his bag, then shook his head wonderingly. "It flew here all the way from Cambridge."

Yeah, yeah.

The three of them resumed their walk down to the ranger station, only now they were carrying a bit more baggage, both mental and physical. Miri grumbled, arguing mainly with herself about whether to use Bertie's gift.

Even with the fog, Bertie's "breadcrumbs" could give them a real edge in surveilling the park—if they could get them in. Juan's mind raced along that line, trying to figure what he should say at the ranger station. At the same time he was watching William. The guy had brought a flashlight. The circle of light twitched this way and that, casting tree roots and brush into sharp relief. Come to think of it, without Miri's Marine Corps gear, a flashlight would have been even more welcome than the jackets. In some ways, William was not a complete fool. In others . . .

Juan was just glad that William hadn't pushed the FedEx mailer back at him. Juan would have been stuck with carrying it around all night; the carton counted as toxic waste, and it would surely rat on him if he left it in an ordinary trash can. Ol' William had been only mildly interested in the breadcrumbs—but the package they came in, even busted, *that* fascinated the guy.

THE PARK'S ENTRANCE AREA STILL HAD FAIRLY GOOD CONNECTIVITY, BUT THE ranger station was hidden by the hillside and Juan couldn't get a view on it. Unfortunately, the State Parks web site was under construction.

Juan browsed around, but all he could find were more out-of-date pictures. The station might be uncrewed. On an off-season Monday night like this, a single 411 operator might be enough to cover all the state parks in Southern California.

As they came off the path, into direct sight of the station, they saw that it wasn't simply a rest point or even a kiosk. In fact, it was an enclosed office with bright, real lighting and a physically-present ranger—a middle-aged guy, maybe thirty-five years old.

The ranger stood and stepped out into the puddle of light. "Evening," he said to William; then he noticed the heavily bundled forms of Miriam and Juan. "Hi, kids. What can I do for you all?"

Miri glanced significantly at William. Something almost like panic came into William's eyes. He mumbled, "Sorry, Munchkin, I don't remember what you do at places like this."

"S'okay." Miri turned to the ranger. "We just want to buy a night pass, no camping. For three."

"You got it." A receipt appeared in the air between them, along with a document: a list of park regulations.

"Wait one." The ranger ducked back into his office and came out with some kind of search wand; this setup was really old-fashioned. "I shoulda done this first." He walked over to William, but was talking to all three of them, essentially hitting the high points of the park regs. "Follow the signs. No cliff climbing is allowed. If you go out on the seaside cliff face, we *will* know and you *will* be fined. Are you vision equipped?"

"Yes, sir." Miriam raised her goggles into the light. Juan opened his jacket so his equipment vest was visible.

The ranger laughed. "Wow. I haven't seen those in a while. Just don't leave the batteries lying around in the park. That's—" he turned away from William and swept his wand around Miriam and Juan "—That's very important here, folks. Leave the park as you found it. No littering, and no networking. Loose junk just piles up, and we can't clean it out like you can other places."

The wand made a faint whining sound as it passed over Juan's jacket pocket. *Boogers. It must have gotten a ping back.* Most likely Bertie's prototypes didn't have a hard off-state.

The ranger heard the noise, too. He held the wand flat against Juan's jacket and bent to listen. "Damn false alarm, I bet. What do you have in there, son?"

Juan handed him the bag of dark, brownish balls. The ranger held it up to the light. "What are these things?"

"Trail mix." William spoke before Juan could even look tongue-tied.

"Hey, really? Can I try one?" He popped the bag open as Juan watched in wide-eyed silence. "They look nice and chocolaty." He picked one out of the bag, and squeezed it appraisingly. Then the smell hit him. "Dios!" He threw the ball at the ground and stared at the brown stain that remained on his fingers. "That smells like . . . that smells awful." He jammed the bag back into Juan's hands. "I don't know, kid. You have odd tastes."

But he didn't question their story further. "Okay, folks. I think you're good to go. I'll show you the trailhead. I—" He stopped, stared vacantly for a second. "Oops. I see some people coming into Mount Cuyamaca Park, and I'm covering there tonight, too. You wanna go on ahead?" He pointed at a path that led northward from his station. "You can't miss the trailhead; even if it's down, there's a big sign." He waved them on, and then turned to talk to whoever he was seeing at the park in the mountains.

BEYOND THE TRAILHEAD, THE PARK WAS COMPLETELY UNIMPROVED, A WILderness. For a hundred feet or so, Juan had wireless connectivity but even that was fading. Miri checked in with the exam proctor service to certify that their team was going local; since the wilderness was very soon going to isolate them from the worldwide net, they might as well get official credit for the fact!

But yuk. Just knowing you can't go out in the wide world for answers was a pain. It was like having a itch you can't scratch or a sock with lump in it, only much worse. "I've cached a lot of stuff about the park, Miri . . . but some of it is kinda old." Which would have been no problem, but now he couldn't just go out and search for better information.

"Don't worry about it, Juan. Last week, I spent a little money and used a 411 service. See?" A few gigabytes flickered on laser light between them. . . . She *was* prepared. The maps and pictures looked very up-to-date.

Miri confidently picked one of several trails and got them on a gentle path that zigzagged downward toward the northwest. She even persuaded William to use the third pair of goggles instead of his flashlight. The Goofus moved awkwardly along. He seemed limber enough, but every four or five paces there was random spikey twitching.

It made Juan uncomfortable just to watch the guy. He looked away, played with his goggles' menu. "Hey, Miri. Try 'VIS AMP.' It's pretty."

They walked silently for a while. Juan had never been to Torrey Pines Park except with his parents, and that was when he was little. And in the daytime. Tonight, with VIS AMP . . . the light of Venus and Sirius and Betelguese came down through the pine boughs, casting colored shadows every which way. Most of the flowers had closed, but there were glints of yellows and reds bobbing among the manzanita and the low, pale cactus. The place was peaceful, really beautiful. And so what if the goggles' low-res pics only showed the direction you were looking at. That was part of the charm. They were getting this view without any external help, a step closer to true reality.

"Okay, Juan. Try laying out some of Bertie's dungballs."

The breadcrumbs? "Sure." Juan opened the bag and tossed one of the balls off to the side of the path. Nothing. He popped up some low-layer wireless diagnostics. Wow. "This is a quiet place."

"What do you expect?" said Miri. "No networks, remember."

Juan leaned down to inspect the breadcrumb. The park ranger had gotten a faint response with his wand, but now that Juan wanted a ping response, there was nothing. And Bertie hadn't told them an enable-protocol. *Well, maybe it doesn't matter.* Juan was a packrat; he had all the standard enablers squirreled away on his wearable. He blasted the breadcrumb with one startup call after another. Partway through the sequence, there was a burst of virtual light in his contacts. "Hah. This one's live!" He turned and caught up with Miri and William.

"Good going, Juan." For once, Miri Gu sounded pleased with him.

The path was still wide and sandy, the gnarled pines hanging fists of long needles right above his head—and right in the Goofus's face. Amid the park trivia that Juan had downloaded was the claim that this was the last place on earth these pines existed. They rooted in the steep hillsides and hung on for years and years against erosion and draught and cold ocean breezes. Juan glanced back at William's gangly form shambling along behind them. *Yeah.* Ol' William was kind of like a human "Torrey Pine."

They were in the top of the fog now. Towering and silent, pillars of haze drifted by on either side of them. Starlight dimmed and brightened.

Behind them, the node Juan had left was dimming toward a zero data rate. He picked out a second breadcrumb, gave it correct startup call, and dropped it to the side of the trail. The low-layer diagnostics showed its pale glow, and after a second it had picked up on the first node, now bright again. "They linked . . . I'm getting data forwarded from the first node." *Hah.* Normally you didn't think about details like that. The gadgets kind of reminded Juan of the toy network his father had bought him, back when Pa still had a job. Juan had been only five years old, and the toy nodes had been enormous clunkers, but laying them down around the house had engaged father and son for several happy days—and given Juan an intuition about random networks that some grown-ups still seemed to lack.

"Okay, I see them," said Miri. "We're not getting any communication from beyond the dungballs, are we? I don't want anything forwarded out to the world."

Yeah, yeah. This is a local exam. "We're isolated, unless we punch out with something really loud." He threw out five or six more breadcrumbs, enough so they could figure their relative positions accurately; in his diagnostic view, the locator gleams sharpened from misty guesstimates to diamond-sharp points of light.

Fog curled more thickly over them, and the starlight grew hazy. Ahead of him, Miri stumbled. "Watch your step. . . . You know, there's really not enough light anymore."

In patches, the fog was so thick that VIS AMP was just colorful noise.

"Yeah, I guess we should switch back to thermal IR."

They stopped and stood like idiots, fiddling with manual controls to do something that should have been entirely automatic. Near infrared was as bad as visual: for a moment he watched the threads of NIR laser light that flickered sporadically between the data ports on their clothes; in this fog, the tiny lasers were only good for about five feet.

Miri was ahead of him. "Okay, that's a lot better," she said.

Juan finally got his goggles back to their thermal infrared default. Miri's face glowed furnace-red except for the cool blackness of her goggles. Most plants were just faintly reddish. The stairstep timber by his feet had three dark holes in the top. Juan reached down and discovered that the holes felt cold and metallic. Ha, metal spikes holding the timber in place.

"C'mon," said Miri. "I want to get down near the bottom of the canyon."

The stairs were steep, with a heavy wood railing on the dropoff side. The fog was still a problem, but with TIR, you could see out at least ten yards. Dim reddish lights floated up through the dark, blobs of slightly warmer air. The bottom was way down, farther than you'd ever guess. He threw out a few more breadcrumbs and looked back up the path, at the beacons of the other nodes. What a bizarre setup. The light of the breadcrumb diagnostics was showing on his contact lenses, where he normally saw all enhancements. But it was the USMC goggles that were providing most of the augmentation. And beyond them? He stopped, turned off his wearable enhancement, and slipped the goggles up from his face for a moment. Darkness, absolute darkness, and chill wet air on his face. Talk about isolation!

He heard William coming up behind him. The guy stopped and for a second they stood silent, listening.

Miri's voice came from further down the steps. "Are you okay, William?"

"Sure, no problem."

"Okay. Would you and Juan come down by me? We wanna stay close enough to keep a good data rate between us. Are you getting any video off the dungballs, Juan?" Bertie had said they contained basic sensors.

"Nope," Juan replied. He slipped the goggles back on and walked down to her. Any breadcrumb video would have shown up on his contacts, but all he was getting was diagnostics. He started another breadcrumb and tossed it far out, into the emptiness. Its location showed in his contacts. It fell and fell and fell, until he was seeing its virtual gleam "through" solid rock.

He studied the diagnostics a moment more. "You know, I think they *are* sending low data rate video—"

"That's fine. I'll settle for wireless rate." Miri was leaning out past the railing, staring downwards.

"—but it's not a format I know." He showed her what he had. Bertie's Siberian pals must be using something really obscure. Ordinarily, Juan could have put out some queries and had the format definition in a few seconds; but down here in the dark, he was just stuck.

Miri made an angry gesture. "So Bertie gave you something that could be useful, but only if we punch out a loud call for help? No way. Bertie is not getting his warty hands on *my* project!"

Hey, Miri, you and I are supposed to be a team here. It would be so nice if she would stop treating him like dirt. But she was right about Bertie's tactics. Bertie had given them something wonderful—and was holding back all the little things that would make it useable. First it was the enable-protocol, now it was this screwball video format. Sooner or later, Bertie figured they'd come crawling to him, begging him to be a shadow member of the team. *I could call out to him.* His clothes had enough power that he could easily punch wireless as far as network nodes in Del Mar Heights, at least for a few minutes. Getting caught was a real risk; Fairmont used a good proctor service—but it was impossible for them to cover all the paths all the time. This afternoon, Bertie had as much as bragged they would cheat that way.

Damn you, Bertie, I'm not going to break isolation. Juan reviewed the mystery data from the breadcrumbs. There seemed to be real content; so given the darkness, the pictures were probably thermal infrared. *And I have lots of known video I can compare them to, everything that has been seen through my goggles during the last few minutes!* Maybe it was time for some memory magic, the edge he got from his little blue pills: If he could remember which blocks of imagery might match what the breadcrumbs could see, and pass that to his wearable, then conventional reverse engineering would be possible. . . . Juan's mind went blank for a few seconds, and there was a moment of awesome panic . . . but then he remembered himself. He fed the picture pointers back to his wearable. It began crunching out solutions almost immediately. "Try this, Miri." He showed her his best guess-image, and sharpened it over the next five seconds as his wearable found more correlation spikes.

"Yes!" The picture showed the roots of the big pine a dozen yards behind them. A few seconds passed and there was another picture, black sky and faintly glowing branches. In fact, each breadcrumb was generating a low-resolution TIR image every five seconds or so, even though they couldn't all be forwarded that fast. "What are those numbers all about?" Numbers that clustered where the picture detail was most complex.

Oops. "Those are just graphical hierarchy pointers." That was true, but exactly how Juan used them was something he didn't want pursued. He made a note to delete them from all future pics.

Miri was silent for several seconds as she watched the pictures coming in from the crumbs above them on the trail, and from the one that he'd dropped way down. Juan was on the point of asking for payback, like some straight talk about exactly what they were looking for. But then she said, "This picture format is one of those Siberian puzzles, isn't it?"

"Looks like."

Those formats were all different, created by antisocials who seemed to get a kick out of not being interoperable. "And you untangled it in fifteen seconds?"

Sometimes Juan just didn't think ahead: "Yup," he said, blissfully proud.

The uncovered part of her face flared. "You lying weasel! You're talking to the outside!"

Now Juan's face got hot too. "Don't you call me a liar! You know I'm good with interfaces."

"Not. That. Good." Her voice was deadly.

Caray. The right lie occurred to Juan a few seconds too late: He should have said he'd seen the Siberian picture format before! Now the only safe thing to do was "confess" that he was talking to Bertie. But Juan couldn't bear to tell *that* lie, even if it meant she would figure out what he had really done.

Miri stared at him for several seconds.

William's begoggled face had turned from one of them to other like a spectator at a tennis game. He spoke into the silence, and for once sounded a little surprised: "So what are you doing now, Miriam?"

Juan had already guessed: "She's watching the fog, and listening."

Miri nodded. "If Orozco is sneaking out on wireless, I'd hear it. If he's using something directional, I'd see sidescatter from the fog. I don't see anything just now."

"So maybe I'm squirting micro pulses." Juan's words came out all choked, but he was trying to sound sarcastic; any laser bright enough to get through the fog would have left an afterglow.

"Maybe. If you are, Juan Orozco, I *will* figure it out—and I'll get you kicked out of school." She turned back to look over the drop off. "Let's get going."

The steps got even steeper; eventually they reached a turn and walked on almost level ground for about sixty feet. The other side of the gorge was less than fifteen feet away.

"We must be close to the bottom," said William.

"No, William. These canyons go awfully deep and narrow." Miri motioned them to stop. "My darn battery has died." She fumbled around beneath her jacket, replacing a dead battery with one that was only half dead.

She adjusted her goggles and looked over the railing. "Huh. We have a good view from here." She waved at the depths. "You know, Orozco, this might be the place to do some active probing."

Juan pulled the probe gun from the sling on his back. He plugged it into his equipment vest. With the gun connected, most of the options were live:

BAT:LOW		SENSORS		BAT2: LOW
PASSIVE		**ACTIVE**		
VIS AMP	OK	GPR	OK	
NIR	OK	SONO	OK	
>TIR	OK	XECHO	OK	
SNIFF	NA	GATED VIS	OK	
AUDIO	NA	GATED NIR	OK	
SIG	NA			

"What do you want to try?"

"The ground penetrating radar." She pointed her own gun at the canyon wall. "Use your power, and we'll both watch."

Juan fiddled with the controls; the gun made a faint *click* as it shot a radar pulse into the rock wall. "Ah!" The USMC goggles showed the pulse's backscatter as lavender shading on top of the thermal IR. In the daylight pictures that Juan had downloaded, these rocks were white sandstone, fluted and scalloped into shapes that water or wind could not carve alone. The microwave revealed what could only be guessed at from the visible light: moisture that etched and weakened the rock from the inside.

"Aim lower."

"Okay." He fired again.

"See, way down? It looks like little tunnels cut in the rock."

Juan stared at the pattern of lavender streaks. They did look different than the ones higher up, but—"I think that's just where the rock is soaking wet."

Miri was already hurrying down the steps. "Toss out more dungballs."

DOWN AND AROUND ANOTHER THIRTY FEET, THEY CAME TO A PLACE WHERE the path was just a tumble of large boulders. The going got very slow. William stopped and pointed at the far wall. "Look, a sign."

There was a square wooden plate spiked into the sandstone. William lit his flashlight and leaned out from the path. Juan raised his goggles for a moment—and got the dubious benefit of William's light: everything beyond ten feet was hidden behind the pearly white fog. But the faded lettering on the sign was now visible: "FAT MAN'S MISERY."

William chuckled—and then almost lost his footing. "Did you ever think? Old-fashioned writing is the ultimate in context tagging. It's passive, informative, and present exactly where you need it."

"Yeah, sure. But can I point through it and find out what it thinks it means?"

William doused his flashlight. "I guess it means the gorge gets even narrower further on."

Which we already knew from Miri's maps. At the trailhead, this had looked like a valley, one hundred feet across. It had narrowed and narrowed, till now the far wall was about ten feet away. And from here . . .

"Scatter some more dungballs," said Miri. She was pointing straight down.

"Okay." They still had plenty of them. He carefully dropped six bread-crumbs where Miri indicated. They stood silently for a moment, watching the network diagnostics: the position guesstimate on one crumb was twenty-five to thirty feet further down. That was darn near the true bottom of the gorge. Juan took a breath. "So, are you ever going to tell us what precisely we're looking for, Miri?"

"I don't *precisely* know."

"But this is where you saw the UCSD people poking around?"

"Some, but they were mainly south of this valley."

"Geez, Miri. So you brought us *here* instead?"

"Look you! I'm not keeping secrets! I could see the hills above this canyon from the tourist scopes on Del Mar Heights. In the weeks after the UCSD guys left, there were small changes in the vegetation, mostly over this valley. At night, the bats and owls were at first more active and then less active than before. . . . And now tonight we've spotted some kind of tunnels in the rocks."

William sounded mystified. "That's all, Miriam?"

The girl didn't blow up when it was William asking. Instead she seemed almost abashed. "Well . . . there's context. Feretti and Voss were behind the trips to the park in January. One is into synthetic ethology; the other is a world-class proteomics geek. They both got called to San Diego all at once, just like you'd expect for a movie teaser. And I'm sure . . . almost sure . . . they're both consulting for Foxwarner."

Juan sighed. That wasn't much more than she'd said in the beginning. Maybe Miri's biggest problem wasn't that she was bossy—it was that she was too darn good at projecting certainty. Juan made a disgusted noise, "And you figure if we just poke around carefully enough, solid clues will show up?" *Whatever they may be.*

"Yes! Somebody has to be the first to catch on. Using our probe gear and—yeah—Bertie's dungballs, we're not going to miss much. My theory is Foxwarner is trying to top what Spielberg/Rowling did last year with the magma monsters. This will be something that starts small, and is overtly plausible. With Feretti and Voss as advisors, I'll bet they'll play it as an escape from a bioscience lab." *That would certainly fit the San Diego scene.*

The new breadcrumbs had located their nearest neighbors. Now the extended network showed as diamond-sharp virtual gleams scattered through the spaces both above and below. In effect, they had twenty little "eyeballs," watching from all over the canyon. The pictures were all low-resolution stuff, but taken together that was too much data to forward all at once across the breadcrumb net to their wearables. They would have to pick through the viewpoints carefully.

"Okay then," said Juan. "Let's just sit and watch for a bit."

The Goofus remained standing. He seemed to be staring upward. Juan guessed that he was having some trouble with the video Juan was forwarding to him. Things were going to get pretty dull for him. Abruptly, William said, "Do either of you smell something burning?"

"Fire?" Juan felt a flash of alarm. He sniffed carefully at the damp air. ". . . Maybe." Or it might just be something flowering in the night. Smells were a hard thing to search on and learn about.

"I smell it too, William," Miri said. "But I think things are still too wet for it to be a danger."

"Besides," said Juan, "if there was fire anywhere close, we'd see the hot air in our goggles." Maybe someone had a fire down on the beach.

William shrugged, and sniffed at the air again. *Trust the Goofus to have one superior sense—and that one useless.* After a moment, he sat down beside them, but as far as Juan could tell, he still wasn't paying attention to the pictures Juan was sending him. William reached into his bag and pulled out the FedEx mailer; the guy was still fascinated by the thing.

He flexed the carton gently, then rested the box on his knees. Despite all Miri's warnings, it looked like the Goofus wanted to knock it back into shape. He'd carefully poise one hand above the middle of the carton, as if preparing a precise poke . . . and then his hand would start shaking and he would have to start all over again.

Juan looked away from him. *Geez the ground was hard. And cold.* He wriggled back against the rock wall and cycled through the pictures he was getting from the breadcrumbs. They were pretty uninspiring. . . . But sitting here quietly, not talking . . . there were *sounds*. Things that might have been insects. And behind it all, a faint, regular throbbing. Automobile traffic? Maybe. Then he realized that it was the sound of ocean surf, muffled by fog and the zigzag walls of the canyon. It was really kind of peaceful.

There was a popping sound very nearby. Juan looked up and saw that William had done it again, smashed the mailer. Only now, it didn't look so bent—and a little green light had replaced the warning tag.

"You fixed it, William!" said Miri.

William grinned. "Hah! Every day in every way, I'm getting better and better." He was silent for a second and his shoulders slumped a little. "Well, different anyway."

Juan looked at the gap in the canyon walls above them. There should be enough room. "Just set it on the ground and it will fly away to Jamul," he said.

"No," said William. He put the carton back in his bag.

O-kay, so the box is cool. Have a ball, William.

They sat listening to the surf, cycling through the video from the breadcrumbs. There were occasional changes in the pictures, quick blurs that might have been moths. Once, they saw something bigger, a glowing snout and a blurry leg.

"I bet that was a fox," said Miri. "But the picture was from above us. Route us more pictures from the bottom of the canyon."

"Right." There was even less action down there. Maybe her movie theories were vapor, after all. He didn't pay as much attention to the movies as most people did—and just now, he couldn't do any background research. Dumb. On the way to the park, he had cached all sorts of stuff, but almost nothing about movie rumors.

"Hey, a snake," said Miri.

The latest picture was from a breadcrumb that had landed in a bush just a few inches above the true bottom of the canyon. It was a very good viewpoint, but he didn't see any snake. There was a pine cone and, beside it, a curved pattern in the dark sand. "Oh. A *dead* snake." Viewed in thermal IR, the body was a barely visible as a change in texture. "Or maybe it's just a shed skin."

"There are tracks all around it," said Miri. "I think they're mouse tracks."

Juan ran the image through some filters, and pulled up a half dozen good foot prints. He had cached pictures from nature studies. He stared at them all, transforming and correlating. "They're mouse tracks, but they aren't pocket mice or white foot. The prints are too big, and the angle of the digits is wrong."

"How can you tell?" suspicion was in her voice.

Juan was not about to repeat his recent blunder: "I downloaded nature facts earlier," he said truthfully, "and some fully cool analysis programs," which was a lie.

"Okay. So what kind of mice—"

A new picture arrived from the breadcrumb in question.

"Whoa!" "Wow!"

"What is it?" said William. "I see the snake carcass now." Apparently he was a couple of pictures behind them.

"See, William? A mouse, right below our viewpoint—"

"—staring straight up at us!"

Glowing beady eyes looked into the imager.

"I bet mice can't see in the dark!" said Juan.

"Well, Foxwarner has never been strong on realism."

Juan gave top routing priority to pics from the same breadcrumb. *C'mon, c'mon!* Meantime, he stared at the picture they had, analyzing. In thermal IR, the mouse's pelt was dim red, shading in the shorter fur to orange. Who knew what it looked like in natural light? Ah, but the shape of the head looked—

A new picture came in. Now there were *three* mice looking up at them. "Maybe they're not *seeing* the dungball. Maybe they're smelling the stink!"

"Shhh!" William whispered.

Miri leaned forward, listening. Juan pushed up his hearing and listened, too, his fists tightening. Maybe it was just his imagination: were there little scrabbling noises from below? The gleam of the breadcrumb beacon was almost thirty feet below where they were sitting.

The breadcrumb gleam moved.

Juan heard Miri's quick, indrawn breath. "I think they're shaking the bush it's on," she said softly.

And the next picture they saw seemed to be from right on the ground. There was a blur of legs, and a very good head shot.

Juan sharpened the image, and did some more comparisons. "You know what color those mice are?"

"Of course not."

"White—maybe? I mean, lab mice would be neat."

In fact, Juan had only just saved himself. He'd been about to say: "White, of course. Their head shape matches Generic 513 lab mice." The conclusion was based on applying conventional software to his cached nature information—but no normal person could have set up the comparisons as fast as he had just done.

Fortunately, Miri had some distractions: the breadcrumb's locator gleam was moving horizontally in little jerks. A new picture came up, but it was all blurred.

"They're rolling it along. Playing with it."

"Or taking it somewhere."

Both kids bounced to their feet, and then William stood up too. Miri forced her voice down to a whisper. "Yeah, lab mice would be neat. Escaped super-mice . . . This could be a re-remake of *Secret of NIMH*!"

"Those were rats in *NIMH*."

"A detail." She was already moving down the trail. "The timing would be perfect. The copyright on the second remake just lapsed. And did you see how *real* those things looked? Up till a few months ago, you couldn't make animatronics that good."

"Maybe they *are* real?" said William.

"You mean like trained mice? Maybe. At least for parts of the show."

The latest picture showed cold darkness. The imaging element must be pointing into the dirt.

They climbed down and down, trying their best not to make noise. Maybe it didn't matter; the surf sound was much louder here. In any case, the fake mice were still rolling along their stolen breadcrumb.

But while the three humans were moving mainly downward, the breadcrumb had moved horizontally almost fifteen feet. The pictures were coming less and less frequently. "*Caray.* It's getting out of range." Juan took three more breadcrumbs from his bag and threw them one at a time, as hard as he could. A few seconds passed, and the new crumbs registered with the net. One had landed on a ledge forward and above them. Another had fallen between the humans and the mice. The third—hah—its locator gleamed from beyond the mice. Now there were lots of good possibilities. Juan grabbed a picture off the farthest crumb. The view was looking back along the path, in the direction the mice would be coming from. Without any sense of scale, it looked like a picture from some fantasy Yosemite Valley.

They had finally reached the bottom, and could make some speed. From behind them, William said, "Watch your head, Munchkin."

"Oops," said Miri, and stopped short. "We got carried away there." This might be a big valley for mice, but just ahead, the walls arched to within inches of each other. She bent down. "It's wider at the bottom. I bet I could wiggle through. I know you could, Juan."

"Maybe," Juan said brusquely. He pushed past her and stepped up into the cleft. He got the active probe off his back, and held it in one hand as he slid into the gap. If he stood sideways and tilted his upper body, he could fit. He didn't even have to take off his jacket. He sidled a foot or two further, dragging the probe gun behind him. Then the passage widened enough for him to turn and walk forward.

Miri followed a moment later. She looked up. "Huh. This is almost like a cave with a hole running along the ceiling."

"I don't like this, Miriam," said William, who was left behind; no way could he squeeze through.

"Don't worry, William. We'll be careful not to get jammed." In any real emergency, they could always punch out a call to 911.

The two kids moved forward another fifteen feet, to where the passage narrowed again, even more than before.

"*Caray.* The stolen breadcrumb is off the net."

"Maybe we should have just stayed up top and watched."

It was a little late for her to be saying that! Juan surveyed the crumb net. There was not even a hazy guesstimate on the lost node. But there were several pictures from the crumb he had tossed beyond all this: every one of them showed an empty path. "Miri! I don't think the mice ever got to the next viewpoint."

"Hey, did you hear that, William? The mice have taken off down a hole somewhere."

"Okay, I'll look around back here."

Juan and Miri moved back along the passage, looking for bolt-holes. Of course there were no shadows. The fine sand of the path was almost black, the fallen pine needles scarcely brighter. On either side, the rock walls showed dark and mottled red as the sandstone cooled in the night air. "You'd think their nest would show a glow."

"So they're in deep." Miri held up her probe gun, and slipped the radar attachment back onto the barrel. "USMC to the rescue."

They traversed the chamber from one narrowness to the other. When they put the GPR snout of the guns right up to the rock, the lavender echograms were *much* more detailed than before. There really were tunnels, mouse-sized and extending back into the rock. They went through three batteries in about five minutes, but—"But we still haven't found an entrance!"

"Keep looking. We know there is one."

"*Caray*, Miri! It's just not here."

"You're right." That was William. He had crawled part way in to look at them. "Come back here. The critters jumped off the trail before it got narrow."

"What? How do you know?"

William backed out, and the kids wriggled out after him. Ol' William had been busy. He had swept the pine cones and needles away from the edges of the path. His little flashlight lay on the ground.

But they didn't need a flashlight to see what William had discovered. The edge of the path, which should have been black and cold, was a dim red, a redness that spread across the rock face like weird, upward-dripping blood.

Miri dropped flat and poked around where the heat red was brightest. "Ha. I got my finger into something! Can't find an end to it." She pulled back . . . and a plume of orange followed her hand and then drifted up, its color cooling to red as it swelled and rose above them.

There was the faint smell of burning wood.

For a moment, they just stared at each other, the big black goggle eyes a true reflection of their inner shock.

No more warm air rose from the hole. "We must have found an in-draft," William said.

Both Miri and Juan were on their knees now. They looked carefully, but the goggles didn't have the resolution to let them see the hole clearly—it was simply a spot that glowed a bit redder than anything else.

"Use the gun, Juan."

He probed the rock above the hole and on either side. The tiny passage extended two feet down from the entrance, branching several times before it reached the main network of tunnels and chambers.

"So what happened to the dungball they grabbed? It would be nice to get some pictures from in there."

Juan shrugged, and fed his probe gun still another battery. "They must have it in one of the farther chambers, behind several feet of rock. The crumb doesn't have the power to get through that."

Juan and Miri looked at each other, and laughed. "But we have lots more breadcrumbs!" Juan felt around for the entrance hole and rolled a crumb into it. It lit up about six inches down, just past the first tunnel branch.

"Try another."

Juan studied the tunnel layout for a moment. "If I throw one in just right, I bet I can carom it a couple of feet." The crumb's light disappeared for a moment . . . and then appeared as data forwarded via the first one. *Yes!*

"Still no word from the one they stole," said Miri. There were just the two locator gleams, about six inches and thirty-six inches down their respective tunnels.

Juan touched the gun here and there to the rock face. With the GPR at high power, he could probe through a lot of sandstone. How much could he figure out from what came back? "I think I can refine this even more," he said. Though that would surely make Miri suspicious. "That third fork in the tunnel. Something . . . soft . . . is blocking it." A brightly reflecting splotch, coming slowly toward them.

"It looks like a mouse."

"Yeah. And it's moving between two breadcrumbs," effectively a two-station wireless tomograph. *Maybe I can combine it all.* For a moment, Juan's whole universe was the problem of meshing the "breadcrumb tomography" with the GPR backscatter. The image showed more and more detail. He blanked out for a just a second, and for a moment after that forgot to be cautious.

It was a mouse all right. It was facing up the tunnel, toward the entrance the three humans were watching. They could even see its guts, and the harder areas that were skull and ribs and limbs. There was something stuck in its forepaw.

The whole thing looked like some cheap graphics trick. Too bad Miri didn't take it that way. "Okay! I've *had it* with you, Juan! One person could never work that fast. You *doormat!* You let Bertie and his committee—"

"Honest, Miri, I did this myself!" said Juan, defending where he should not defend.

"We're getting an F on account of you, and Bertie will own all of this!"

William had been watching with the same detachment as during Miri's earlier accusations. But this time: "I see the picture, Munchkin, but . . . I don't think he's lying. I think he did it himself."

"But—"

William turned to Juan, "You're on drugs, aren't you, kid?" he said mildly.

Once a secret is outed—

"No!" *Make the accusation look absurd.* But Juan floundered, wordless.

For an instant, Miri stared open-mouthed. And then she did something that Juan thought about a lot in the times that followed. She raised her hands, palms out, trying to silence them both.

William smiled gently. "Miriam, don't worry. I don't think Foxwarner is patching us into their summer release. I don't think anyone but us knows what we're saying here at the bottom of a canyon in thick fog."

She slowly lowered her hands. "But . . . William." She waved at the warmth that spread up the rock face. "None of this could be natural."

"But what kind of *un*natural is it, Munchkin? Look at the picture your friend Juan just made. You can see the insides of the mouse. It's not animatronic." William ran a twitchy hand through his hair. "I think somebody in the bioscience labs hereabouts really did have an accident.

Maybe these creatures aren't as smart as humans . . . but they were smart enough to escape, and fool—who was it that was poking around here in January?"

"Feretti and Voss," Miri said in a small voice.

"Yes. Maybe just hiding down here when the bottom was under water was enough to fool them. I'll bet these creatures have just a little edge over ordinary lab mice. But a little edge can be enough to change the world."

And Juan realized William wasn't talking about just the mice. "I don't want to change the world," he said in a choked voice. "I just want to have my chance in it."

William nodded. "Fair enough."

Miri looked back and forth at them. What Juan could see of her expression was very solemn.

Juan shrugged. "It's okay, Miri. I think William is right. We're all alone here."

She leaned a little toward him. "Was it Bertie who got you into this?"

"Some. My mother has our family in one of the distributed framinghams. I showed my part of it to Bertie last spring, after I flunked Adaptability. Bertie shopped it around as an anonymous challenge. He came back with a custom drug. What it does—" Juan tried to laugh, but it sounded more like a rattle. "—most people would think that what it does is a joke. See," he tapped the side of his head, "it makes my memory very very good. Everyone thinks human memory doesn't count for much anymore. People say, 'No need for eidetic memory when your clothes' data storage is a billion times bigger.' But that's not the point. Now I can remember big data blocks perfectly, and I have my wearable put hierarchial tags on all the stuff I see. So I can communicate patterns *back* to my wearable just by citing a few numbers. It gives me this incredible advantage in setting up problems."

"So Bertie is your great friend because you are his super tool?" Her voice was quiet and outraged, but the anger was no longer directed at Juan.

"*No!* I've studied the memory effect. The idea itself came from analysis of my own medical data. Even now that we have the gimmick, only one person in a thousand could be affected by it at all. There's *no way* Bertie could have known beforehand that I was special."

"Ah. Of course," she said, and was silent. Juan hated it when people did that, agreed with what you said and then waited for you to figure out why you had just made a fool of yourself. . . . *Bertie is just very good with connections.* He had connections everywhere, to research groups, idea markets, challenge boards. But maybe Bertie had figured out how to do even better: How many casual friends did Bertie have? How many did he offer to help with custom drug improvements? Most of that would turn out to be minor stuff, and maybe those friendships would remain casual. But sometimes, Bertie would hit the jackpot. *Like with me.*

"But Bertie is my best friend!" *I will not blubber.*

"You could find other friends, son," said William. He shrugged. "Back before I lost my marbles, I had a gift. I could make words sing. I would give almost anything to get that back. And you? Well, however you came by it, the talent you have now is a marvelous gift. You are beholden to no one other than yourself for it."

Miri said softly. "I—I don't know, Juan. Custom meds aren't illegal like twentieth century drugs—but they are off-limits for a reason. There's no way to do full testing on them. This stuff you're taking could—"

"I know. It could fry my mind." Juan put his hands to his face, and ran into the cold plastic of his goggles. For a moment, Juan's mind turned inward. All the old fear and shame rose up . . . and balanced against the strange surprise that out of the whole world, this old man could understand him.

But even here, even with his eyes closed, his contacts were still on, and Juan saw the virtual gleam of the breadcrumbs. He stared passively for several seconds, and then surprise began to eat through his funk. "Miri . . . they're *moving.*"

"Huh?" She had been paying even less attention than he had. "Yes! Down the tunnels, away from us."

William moved close to the mouse hole, and pressed his ear against the stone wall. "I'll bet our little friends are taking your dungballs to wherever the first one went."

"Can you get some pictures from them, Juan?"

". . . Yes. Here's one." A thermal glimpse of a glowing tunnel floor. Frothy piles of something that looked like finely shredded paper. Seconds passed, and a virtual gleam showed dimly through the rock. "There's the locator beacon of the first crumb." It was five feet deeper in the rock. "Now it has a node to forward through."

"We could lose them, too."

Juan pushed past William, and tossed two more breadcrumbs down the hole. One rolled a good three feet. The other stopped after six inches—and then began moving "on its own."

"The mice are stringing nodes *for* us!" All but the farthest locator beacon were glowing high-rate bright. Now there were lots of pictures, but the quality was poor. As the crumbs warmed in the hot air of the tunnels the images showed very little detail except for the mice themselves: paws and snouts and glowing eyes. "Hey, did you see the splinter sticking out of that poor thing's paw?"

"Yes, I think that's the one I saw before. Wait, we're getting a picture from the crumb they stole to begin with." At first, the data was a jumble. *Still another picture format?* Not exactly. "This picture is normal vision, Miri!" He finished the transformation.

"How—?" Then she gave a sharp little gasp.

There was no scale marker, but the chamber couldn't have been more than a couple of feet across. To the eye of the breadcrumb it was a wide, high-ceilinged meeting room, crowded with dozens of white-furred mice, their dark eyes glittering by the light of a . . . fire . . . in the middle of the hall.

"I think you have your 'A,' Miriam," William said softly.

Miri didn't answer.

Rank upon rank of mice, crouched around the fire. Three mice stood at the center, higher up—tending the flame? It wobbled and glowed, more like a candle than a bonfire. But the mice didn't seem to be watching the fire as much as they were the breadcrumb. Bertie's little breadcrumb was the magical arrival at their meeting.

"See!" Miri hunched forward, her elbows on her knees. "Foxwarner strikes again. A slow flame in a space like that . . . those 'mice' should all be dead of carbon monoxide poisoning."

The breadcrumbs were not sending spectral data, so who could say? Juan visualized the tunnel system. There were other passages a little higher up, and he had data on the capacity of the inlets and outlets. He thought a few seconds more and gave the problem to his wearable. "No . . . actually, there is enough ventilation to be safe."

Miri looked up at him. "Wow. You are fast."

"Your Epiphany outfit could do it in a instant."

"But it would've taken me five minutes to pose the problem to my Epiphany."

Another picture came in, firelight on a ceiling.

"The mice are rolling it closer to the fire."

"I think they're just poking at it."

Another picture. The crumb had been turned again, and now was looking outwards, to where three more mice had just come in from a large side entrance . . . rolling another breadcrumb.

But the next picture was a blur of motion, a glimpse of a mostly empty meeting chamber, in thermal colors. The fire had been doused.

"Something's stirred them up," said William, listening again at the stone wall. "I can actually hear them chittering."

"The dungballs are coming back this way!" said Miri.

"The mice are smart enough to understand the idea of poison." William's voice was soft and wondering. "Up to a point, they grabbed our gifts like small children. Then they noticed that the dungballs just kept coming . . . and someone raised an alarm."

There were still pictures, lots of them, but they were all thermal IR, chaotic blurs; the mice were hustling. The locator gleams edged closer together, some moving toward an entrance about three feet above the gully floor. The others were approaching the first hole.

Juan touched the probe gun against the wall and pulsed the rock in several places. He was getting pretty good at identifying the flesh-and-blood reflections. "Most of the mice have moved away from us. It's just a rearguard that's pushing out the breadcrumbs. There's a crowd of them behind the crumbs that are coming out by your head, William."

"William, quick! The FedEx mailer. Maybe we can trap some when they come out!"

"I . . . yes!" William stood and pulled the FedEx mailer from his bag. He tilted the open carton toward the mouse hole.

A second later there was a faint scrabbling noise, and William's arms moved with that twitchy speed of his. Juan had a glimpse of fur and flying breadcrumbs.

William slapped the container shut, and then stumbled backwards as three more mice came racing out of the lower hole. For a fleeting instant, their glowing blue eyes stared up at the humans. Miri made a dive for them, but they had already fled down the path, oceanward. She picked herself up and looked at William. "How many did you get?"

"Four! The little guys were in such a rush they just jumped out at me." He held the mailer close. Juan could hear tiny thumping noises from inside it.

"That's great," said Miri. "Physical evidence!"

William didn't reply. He just stood there, staring at the carton. Abruptly he turned and walked a little way up the trail, to where the path widened out and the brush and pines didn't cover the sky. "I'm sorry, Miriam." He tossed the mailer high into the air.

The box was almost invisible for a moment, and then its ring of jets lit up. Tiny, white-hot spikes of light traced the mailer's path as it wobbled and swooped within a foot of the rock wall. It recovered, and slowly climbed, still wobbling. Juan could imagine four very live cargo items careening around inside it. Silent to human ears, the mailer rose and rose, jets dimming in the fog. The light was a pale smudge when it drifted out of sight behind the canyon wall.

Miri stood, her arms reaching out as if pleading. "Grandfather, why?"

For a moment, William Gu's shoulders slumped. Then he looked across at Juan. "I bet you know, don't you, kid?"

Juan stared in the direction the mailer had taken. Four mice, rattling around in a half-broken mailer. He had no idea just now what security was like at the FedEx minihub, but it was at the edge of the back country, where the mail launchers didn't cause much complaint. Out beyond Jamul . . . the mice could have their chance in the world. He looked back at William and just gave a single quick nod.

THERE WAS VERY LITTLE TALK AS THEY CLIMBED BACK OUT OF THE CANYON. Near the top, the path was wide and gentle. Miri and William walked hand in hand. There were spatters of coldness on her face that might have been tears, but there was no quaver in her voice. "If the mice are real, we've done a terrible thing, William."

"Maybe. I'm sorry, Miriam."

". . . But I don't think they are real, William."

William made no reply. After a moment, Miri said, "You know why? Look at that first picture we got from the mouse meeting hall. It's just too perfectly dramatic. The chamber doesn't have furniture or wall decorations, but it clearly *is* a meeting hall. Look how all the mice are positioned, like humans at an old town meeting. And then at the center—"

Juan's eyes roamed the picture as she spoke. Yes. There in the center—almost as though they were on stage—stood three large white mice. The biggest one had reared up as it looked at the imager. It had one paw extended . . . and the paw grasped something sharp and long. They had seen things like that in other pictures and never quite figured them out. In this natural-light picture, the tool—a spear?—was unmistakable.

Miri continued on, "See, that's the tip-off, Foxwarner's little joke. A real, natural breakthrough in animal intelligence would never be such a perfect *movie poster*. So. Later tonight, Juan and I will turn in our local team report, and Foxwarner will 'fess up. By dinnertime at the latest, we'll be famous."

And my own little secret will be outed.

Miri must have understood Juan's silence. She reached out and took his hand, dragging the three of them close together. "Look," she said softly. "We don't know what—if anything—Foxwarner recorded of us. Even now, we're in thick fog. Except for the mice themselves, our gear saw no sensors. So either Foxwarner is impossibly good, or they weren't close snooping us." She gestured up the path. "Now in a few more minutes we'll be back in the wide world. Bertie and maybe Foxwarner will be wisping around. But no matter *what* you think really happened tonight—" Her voice trailed off.

And Juan finished, "—no matter what really happened, we're all best to keep our mouths shut about certain things."

She nodded.

BERTIE FOLLOWED JUAN HOME FROM MIRI'S HOUSE, ARGUING, WHEEDLING, demanding all the way. He wanted to know what Miri had been up to, what all they had done and seen. When Juan wouldn't give him more than the engineering data from the dungballs, Bertie had got fully dipped, kicked Juan off their unlimited team, and rejected all connections. It was a total Freeze Out. By the time Juan got home, he could barely put up a good front for his ma.

But strangely enough, Juan slept well that night. He woke to morning sunlight splashing across his room. Then he remembered: Bertie's total Freeze Out. *I should be frantic.* This could mean he'd fail the unlimited and lose his best friend. Instead, more than anything else, Juan felt like . . . he was free.

Juan slipped on his clothes and contacts, and wandered downstairs. Usually, he'd be all over the net about now, synching with the world, finding out what his friends had done while he was wasting time asleep. He'd get to that eventually; it would be just as much fun as ever. But just now the silence was a pleasure. There were a dozen red "please reply" lights gleaming in front of his eyes—mostly from Bertie. The message headers were random flails. This was the first time one of Bertie's Freeze Outs had not ended because Juan came groveling.

Ma looked up from her breakfast. "You're off-line," she said.

"Yeah." He slouched onto a chair and started eating cereal. His father smiled absently at him and went on eating. Pa's eyes were very far away, his posture kind of slumped.

Ma looked back and forth between them, and a shadow crossed her face. Juan straightened up a little and made sure she saw his smile. "I'm just tired out from all the hiking around." Suddenly, he remembered something. "Hey, thanks for the maps, Ma."

She looked puzzled.

"Miri used 411 for recent information on Torrey Pines."

"Oh!" Ma's face lit up. There were a number of 411 services in San Diego County, but this *was* her kind of thing. "Did the test go well?"

"Dunno yet." They ate in silence for a moment. "I expect I'll know later today." He looked across the table at her. "Hey, you're off-line, too."

She grimaced and gave him a little grin. "An unintended vacation. The movie people dropped their reservations for tour time."

". . . Oh." Just what you'd expect if the operation in East County was related to what they'd found in Torrey Pines. Miri would have seen the cancellation as significant evidence. Maybe it was. But he and Miri had turned in their project report last night, the first local exam to complete. If she were right about the mice, Foxwarner was sure to know by now that their project had been outed, and you'd think they'd have launched publicity. And yet, there were no bulletins; just Bertie and a few other students pinging away at him.

Give it till dinnertime. That's how long Miri said it might take for a major cinema organization to move into action. Real or movie, they should know by then. And his own secret? It would be outed . . . or not.

Juan had a second serving of cereal.

SINCE HE HAD A MORNING EXAM, MA LET HIM TAKE A CAR TO FAIRMONT. He made it to school with time to spare.

The vocational exam was for individuals, and you weren't allowed to search beyond the classroom. As with Ms. Wilson's math exam, the faculty had dug up some hoary piece of business that no reasonable person would ever bother with. For the vocational test, the topic would be a work specialty.

And today . . . it was Regna 5.

When Regna had been hot, back in Pa's day, tech schools had taken three years of training to turn out competent Regna practitioners.

It was a snap. Juan spent a couple of hours scanning through the manuals, integrating the skills . . . and then he was ready for the programming task, some cross-corporate integration nonsense.

He was out by noon, with an A.